THE
DEMON
TIDE

LAURIE FOREST

THE DEMON TIDE

inkyard PRESS

ISBN-13: 978-1-335-40249-3

The Demon Tide

For questions and comments about the quality of this book, please contact us at CustomerService@Harlequin.com.

Inkyard Press
22 Adelaide St. West, 41st Floor
Toronto, Ontario M5H 4E3, Canada
www.InkyardPress.com

Printed in Italy by Grafica Veneta

To my circle of writing & reading friends
because you are the best & most talented people in all the Realms.
May the purple Xishlon Moon shine down bright upon you all.

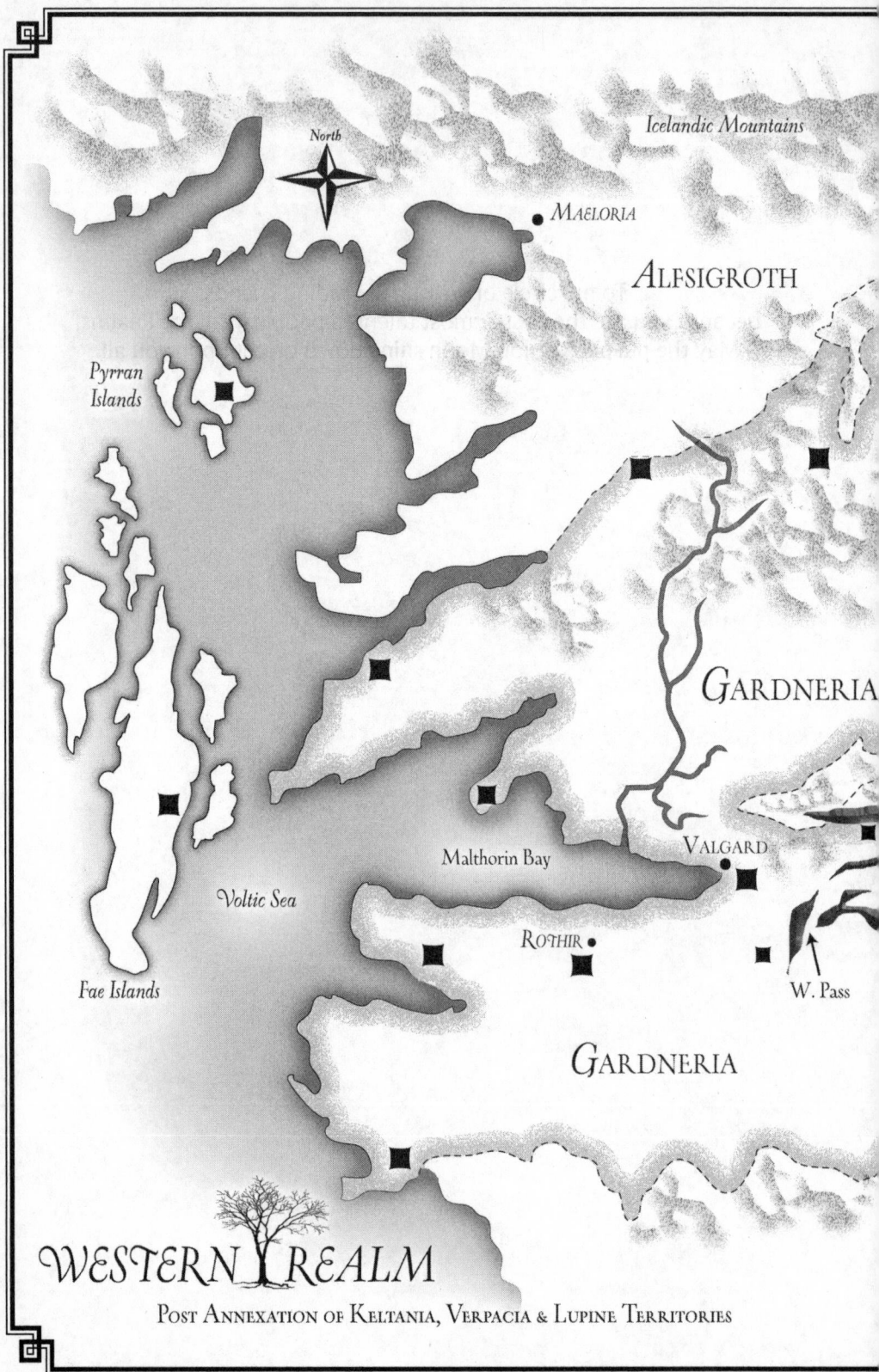

North

Icelandic Mountains

MAELORIA

ALFSIGROTH

Pyrran Islands

GARDNERIA

VALGARD

Malthorin Bay

ROTHIR

Voltic Sea

W. Pass

Fae Islands

GARDNERIA

WESTERN REALM

POST ANNEXATION OF KELTANIA, VERPACIA & LUPINE TERRITORIES

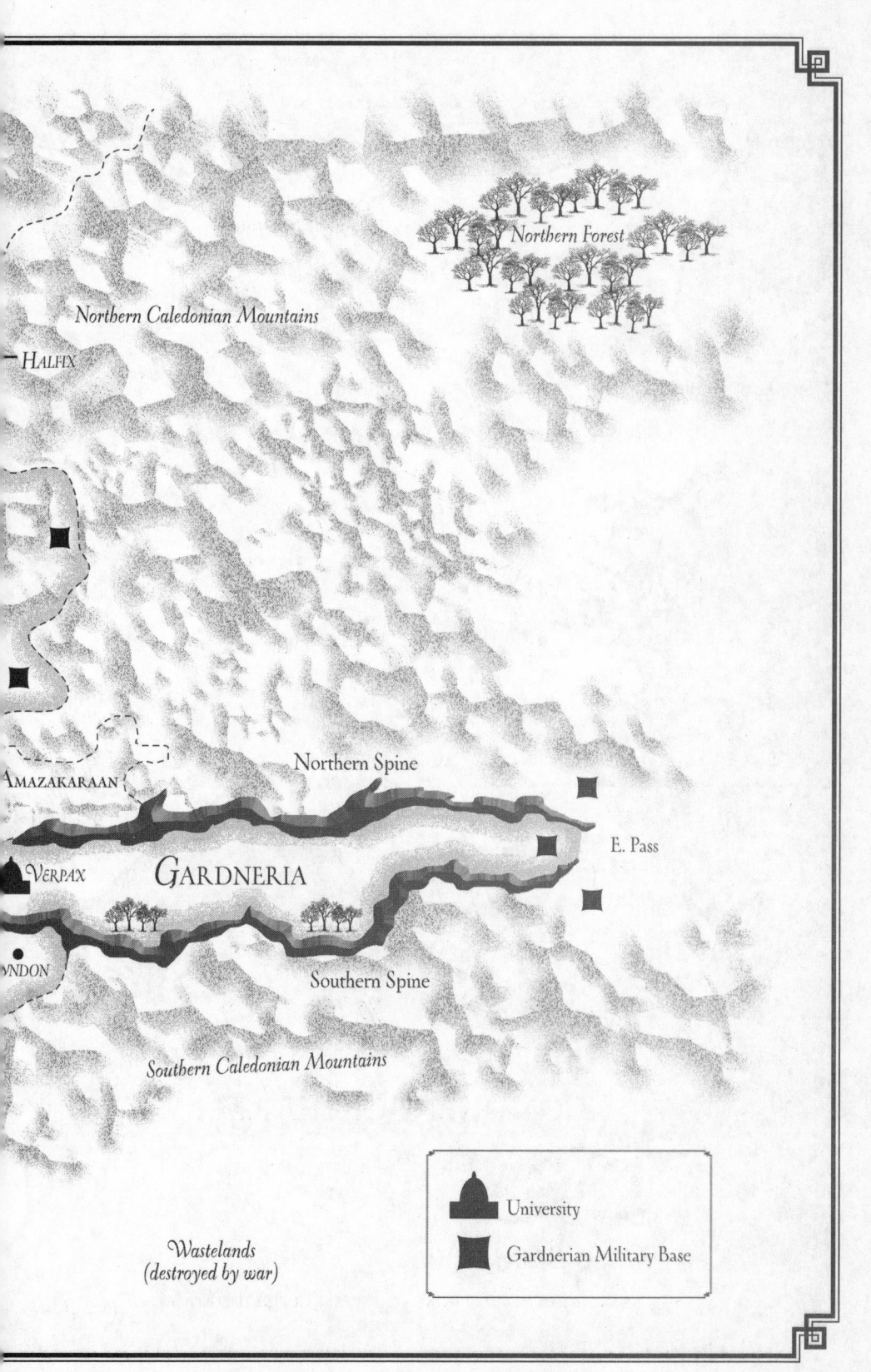

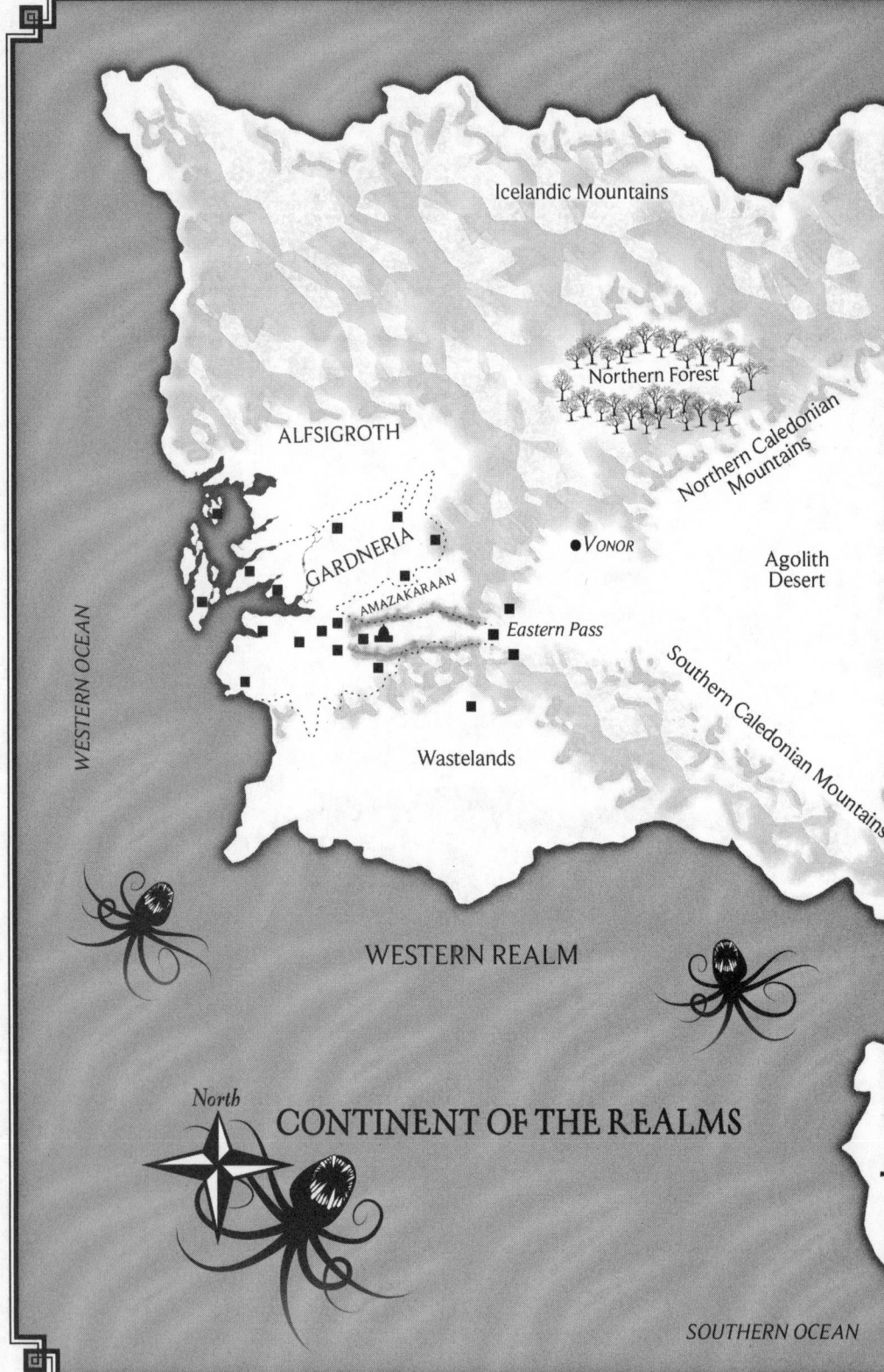

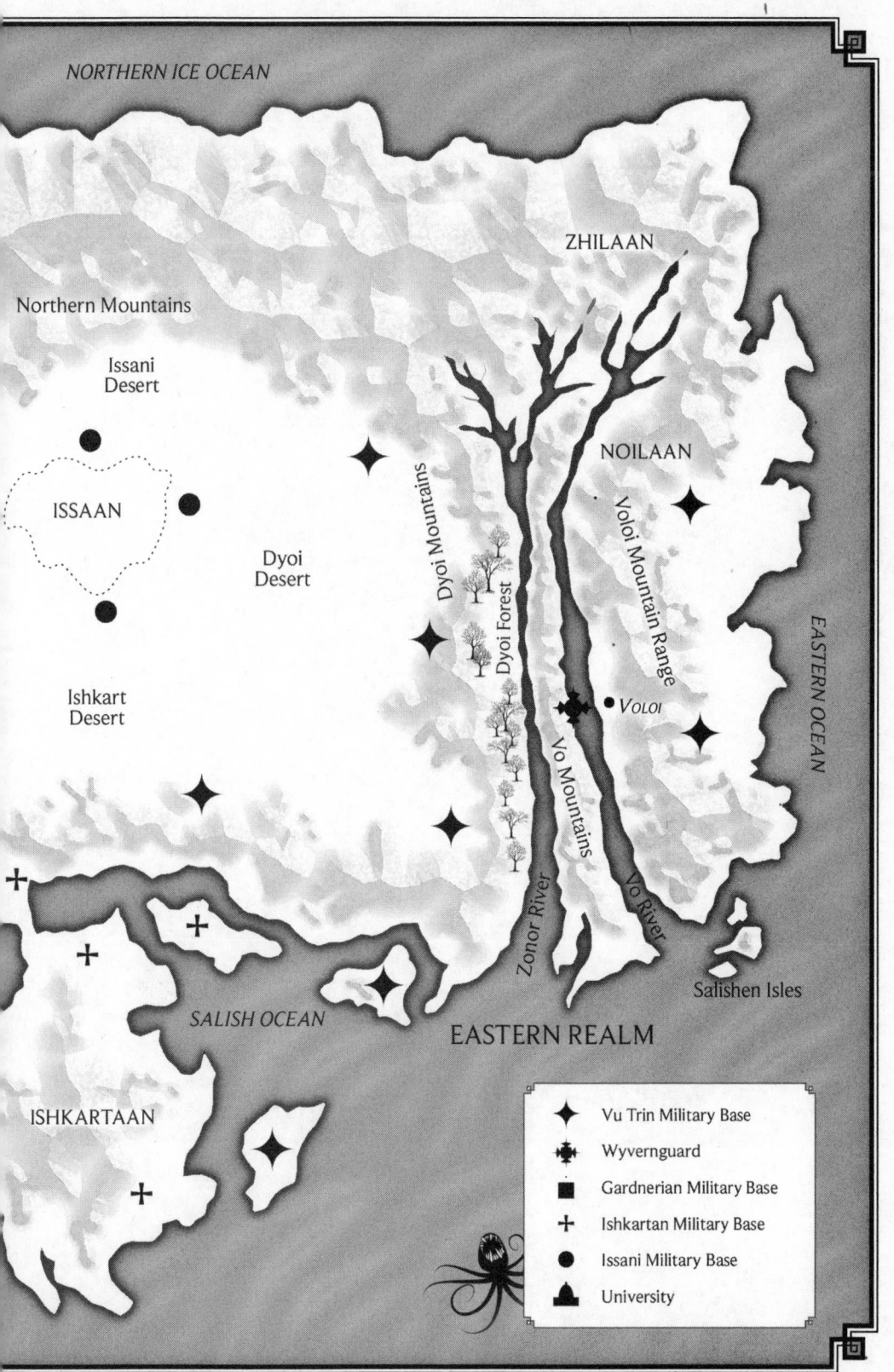

PROLOGUE

The Shadow Wand
Six years ago

**The Wand senses the touch of the ship to
Shadow
like the brush of a fly to a spider's web.**

**Its power shivers,
then it opens its Void senses...
ready to rise once more.**

THE LOST CONTINENT

Alaric Fynnes

The Western Ocean

Priest-Apprentice Alaric Fynnes grips *The Book of the Ancients* as he steps onto the *Ironflower*'s deck, an ocean breeze buffeting him. His silken priest-apprentice raiment gleams in the sunlight, the holy black garb embossed with the Ancient One's white messenger bird wrought in gleaming silver thread. The ship's sails luff and snap, the black canvas also marked with the Ancient One's bird, its talons clasping a bouquet of Ironflowers.

Alaric's seventeen-year-old heart fair bursts with joy as he takes in the sunlit sea, his mind still full of a heady disbelief that he was chosen, out of so many, to accompany his mentor, Priest Marcus Vogel, on this incredible adventure.

To seek out the Lost Continent of the West.

On the Ancient One's own sacred mission.

A smile on his lips, Alaric clasps the holy book tighter as calls of "The Lost Continent!" rise. He looks toward the Mage-mariners pointing over the whitecapped waves, an agitated excitement in the air as Alaric turns his gaze toward the inky mass hunched on the horizon, bringing to mind a menacing beast.

His heartbeat quickens. Could they finally be nearing their

quarry after weeks on the kraken- and storm-infested Western Ocean? Their crew, speeding toward the mythical Lost Continent to vanquish the Evil Ones' Wand of Power. A wand conveyed to Priest Vogel in a dream-vision, a divine leading mirrored by three church seers…and a disturbing number of heathen seers, as well. Which is why it's vital to the survival of the Magedom that Priest Vogel gets hold of the Wand first.

To destroy it.

Alaric spots his mentor near the ship's prow, peering through a runic telescope. His breath catches in his chest at the sight of the young priest's arresting features, Vogel's elegant, charismatic bearing, his shoulder-length onyx hair, a wand and an iron blade sheathed at his side.

Vogel turns and meets Alaric's gaze. His mouth twitches slightly upward and Alaric's Level Five magery breaks into an explosion of blue in the back of his mind—the sacred Ironflower-hue his light magic is blessedly oriented toward. Alaric has carefully suppressed all attraction to forbidden colors, his childhood fascination with the cursed Fae hues of purple and saffron brutally expunged from him like poison.

Alaric steps tentatively toward Vogel, who is everything he aspires to be.

Marcus Vogel was a wonder on the long, treacherous voyage, battling the Western Ocean's deadly kraken while its fabled storm band raged all around. He'll never forget watching Vogel at the prow in the dead of night, wand raised, throwing bolt after bolt of silver-bright Magefire out to kill the mammoth beasts, some hit so hard their heads exploded into bloody mist.

He'll also never forget the holy purpose he's found on this ship, the entirely male crew all Styvian Gardnerians from the strictest of Mage homes. There are no forbidden spirits hidden aboard this ship. And the whole crew is wandfasted, even the teenage cabin boys. All save Priest Vogel. And himself. Their collective piety has filled Alaric with the euphoria of being guided by the Ancient One's own hand toward the Reaping

Times, the Evil Ones soon to be cleansed from the entirety of Erthia.

Alaric comes up beside Priest Vogel's cloaked form, his heart thrumming. The dark mountaining clouds on the horizon arc outward, as if ready to enfold the ship in a dread embrace. And straight ahead, where cloud meets ocean, is the blurred form of a continent.

Vogel turns toward Alaric and the others, his piercing green eyes brimming with a zealous fire that sends a shiver through Alaric. Everyone stills.

"Blessed Mages," Vogel says, "it is time to strike at the Evil Ones' source of power."

Alaric's sense of the momentous gains ground as their ship moors inside an ancient breakwater. He grips the railing, disquiet rising as he takes in the unnatural clouds of roiling shadow above, curling into themselves like grotesque clusters of grapes, a tide of dark mist slithering toward their ship and then enveloping it, rippling over Alaric's feet.

Alaric's Level Five light affinity lines seize painfully as all the color in the world abruptly cuts out. Pulse leaping, Alaric glances at his skin to find his green hue disturbingly vanished like that of the Mages surrounding him, only a silver glimmer remaining. The Ironflowers marking the sails are now a flat gray, the previously green eyes of the crew now shades of steel.

Gripping the white bird pendant around his neck, Alaric murmurs the Ancient One's Prayer of Protection. *Purify Erthia from the stain of the Evil Ones…*

Alaric disembarks along with four cloaked Level Five soldiers, following Priest Vogel's purposeful stride. Dread rising, he takes in the dark lightning flashing in bizarre loops. He lowers his gaze to the shadows rising around them in otherworldly helices of smoke, the unnerving sense mounting that the smoke is *sentient*.

Vogel pauses, and Alaric and the soldiers pause, as well.

A forest stands before them, but it's all *wrong*. The trees are made of gray mist, their branches twisting like skeletal fingers.

Nothing green. Nothing living.

"'Lo, the wilds shall be corrupted and cast Shadows across the land,'" Vogel intones. He sets his silvered gaze on the Mages. "Take heart, brethren. The Ancient One walks with us."

Alaric's fist tightens around his wand, his courage bolstered, as they all make the five-pointed Blessing Star sign on their chests. Together, they step into the Shadow forest, the landscape unnervingly quiet, as if holding its breath.

After a time, a clearing opens up. Alaric's gaze finds its center and he startles, a lash of terror flicking through him. A pewter-hued hillock rises from its misty ground, a dark, arching entrance marking its base.

And a Death Fae demon stands before it.

The pale demon is preternaturally still and stretched to an unnatural height, its eyes solid black, no whites, its ears sharply pointed. Obsidian horns curl up from its head and countless arms ray out from its body to encircle the hillock.

Its bottomless eyes narrow as the Mages approach.

Alaric's legs threaten to give out as he reaches into his pocket and grips his compact version of *The Book of the Ancients*, murmuring prayers as they draw near Evil itself.

Vogel stops only a few handspans away and the creature straightens. What looks like vast relief spreads across the demon's face. Its horns retract into its spiked black hair, and the soulless, solid black of its eyes contracts, the whites becoming visible. The countless arms pull in, and the demon's height swiftly reduces to that of a young man standing before them.

"Dryads," the demon says, his subterranean voice resonating through Alaric with a disturbing thrum. "I sense your elemental affinity lines. Blessed be the Power of III." His gaze sweeps over their wands. "I hoped and prayed that Friends of the Balance would come for the Shadow Tool. Are there more? Do you come with a Dryad army to take hold of the Shadow Branch?"

We're Mages, not filthy Fae, Alaric expects Vogel to mercilessly correct the beast as he slays him, but Vogel remains serene.

"We come with an army," Vogel simply states and surprise darts through Alaric.

"Then come, Dryadin." The demon beckons them forward with a wave of his black-taloned hand. "The Tool is straining to rise and is luring the seers of all the lands." He pauses, a haunted look tensing his eyes. "It wants to do to your continent what it did to ours."

"We will guard against it," Vogel states reassuringly, then turns to his soldiers. "Remain here to protect our area."

And then, heart thudding, Alaric follows Marcus Vogel and the demon into the hill.

Following close behind the Fae demon and Priest Vogel, Alaric descends spiraling stairs, then journeys through a short hall into a small room. Its curving walls are lit by a suspended orb of silvery light, a circular black granite table in its middle, packed bookshelves set into the walls.

And in the table's center is a gray wand with a spiraling handle.

They pause around the table, the Death Fae's gaze riveted to the wand.

"Don't touch it," he cautions. "I'll give you cloth and a warded box to place it in."

"What did it do?" Vogel asks, indicating the world above.

The Death Fae meets Vogel's gaze and the room darkens. "The Shadow power destroyed everything. Except for me."

Suspicion bristles through Alaric. *You're a Death Fae,* he acidly muses. *What happened up there is likely your work, Evil One. That's why you're the last thing standing with the cursed Shadow Tool.*

"I fought it," the demon says, that haunted look returning. "But it proved too powerful. Take great heed, Dryadin—the more that people are divided, the more the Shadow Tool grows in power. It *feeds* on fracture. And then it destroys the Balance."

"The Balance?" Vogel inquires.

"It upends nature. Corrupts the elements. Draws power from a Void that wants to consume everything. Including us." He tightens his stare on Vogel, unflinching. "Don't let it."

The words of an Evil One, Alaric rails, even as worry pricks at him.

The Fae points one long, pale finger at the Wand. "The people of this land were fractured before the Branch gained power. They forgot the truth of the Source Tree at the center of their faiths and worshipped the fractured edges instead. They forgot their tether to the natural world." The demon's nostrils flare. "They separated themselves into factions and then—" he glances warily at Vogel "—the Keltish forces took up the Shadow Branch."

"And?" Vogel asks, his gaze locked on the Wand.

The Death Fae narrows his eyes at the Wand, as well. "The Branch doubled in power as it fed on the people's disharmony. They fought one another even more intensely as the Shadow sent its power into the natural world, poisoning the water. Corrupting the air. Strangling the trees. Bleeding color from the world and sending Shadow over everything. And while the people were fighting each other, the natural world unraveled like strings beneath their feet." The Death Fae stills, tears sheening his eyes. "And then it died."

He grows silent, and when he speaks again, his voice has a rougher, more resonant edge. "Soon, they were fighting over food. Over the remaining water. Clinging to their religions' stories of the End Times. They tried to hoard what they had and not share it. And all the while, the Shadow advanced." His gaze turns imploring, and the blazing sincerity in it upends Alaric, because, in this moment, the Death Fae doesn't look like an Evil One at all—he looks like a scared young man genuinely trying to impart a dire warning.

"Beware of its power, Dryadin," the Death Fae pleads. "Devote your lives to keeping anyone from wielding it. Or what has come to pass here will transpire over all of Erthia."

The demon looks at Alaric, and the level of stark urgency in his eyes sends another tremor of fright through the priest-apprentice. "Have you taken up the Great Wand of Myth?" he presses. "The Branch of the First Tree? It has spoken to me through dreams."

Protest rears up in Alaric to hear a Death Fae speaking of the Ancient One's Sacred Wand, but Vogel remains impressively calm in the face of such sacrilege.

"Of course," Vogel assures the demon, clearly placating the creature.

"The greening of the Branch of the First Great Tree is the last hope to bring Balance back to Erthia," the Death Fae insists. He steps toward a bookshelf and pulls what looks like a thick handwritten journal from it. "I've made records of what happened here," he says, seeming in this bizarre moment more a scholar of history than a cursed demon. "Take the story back with you," he says, pulling out one journal after another, "and tell it to all so that it doesn't happen again." He levels his dark gaze at Vogel and Alaric both. "The Shadow wants to consume all of Erthia. Don't let it. Protect the Balance." He resumes piling up journals as Vogel reaches across the table and takes the Shadow Wand in hand.

Alaric's breath pauses, his every muscle going rigid. Shadow curls up and around Vogel's arm as he looks the Wand over with calm curiosity.

The Death Fae turns and freezes.

"We are not Dryadin," Vogel says softly.

The Death Fae's face tightens in confusion. "What?"

Fast as lightning, Vogel draws his iron blade and hurls it across the table. The knife slams into the demon's chest, a look of shock passing over the young man's face as he falls to the ground, the journal thudding against stone. Horns curl up from his hair, his claws lengthening while his eyes darken and take on a look of fury as a long, black tongue darts from his mouth, flicking and lashing. Multiple arms burst from his body, scrabbling toward the knife only to bang helplessly around the iron weapon, as if stopped by an invisible shield.

Vogel resumes studying the Wand as the demon gasps and writhes, an expression of pure agony on his face.

"We are not Evil Ones," Vogel says, his voice almost gentle. "We are the Blessed First Children of the Pure and Holy Magedom. I was warned of your presence here in a vision. The blade is solid iron. You are destroyed in the name of the Ancient One on High."

The demon's horns once again draw in and the whites of his eyes return. His tongue retracts into his mouth, all arms vanishing but two.

He sets his devastated eyes on Alaric. "This is how it starts," he rasps. "You're doomed if you let him take that Wand back. You'll turn where you're going into *this*." He motions wildly toward the world above. "And the end will be *the End*..."

A dark vine-bolt collides with the Death Fae, and Alaric flinches, a gasp tearing from the Fae as the vine drives the iron blade deeper. Lateral branches of shadowy smoke burst from the blade, winding around the Fae.

Alaric whips his head toward Vogel to find him pointing the Shadow Wand at the Fae. The Death Fae gasps again, and Alaric turns in time to catch his impassioned look of warning before the Fae's eyes turn blank.

Alaric can barely move, barely breathe, as the demon's body dissolves, morphing into thick, curling black smoke that rises into the air then vanishes. Alaric hesitantly looks to Vogel, his mentor's eyes flashing like silver fire.

"It will take time to learn how to destroy this Wand," Vogel says, low and firm. "Until then, it is best to say it was obliterated."

Alaric nods shakily. Of course, they should keep it secret, this Wand that is supposedly impossible to destroy. And, of course, Vogel should be the one to take hold of it and work out how to obliterate it, as no Mage is as pure as him.

For a moment, Vogel studies Alaric and Alaric can feel that

silvered gaze straight down his spine. Then Vogel slides the Wand under his cloak, raises his hands, and calmly performs the Exorcism of the Demonic. Alaric forces himself to echo the prayer's words, but he finds that his gaze is pulled, relentlessly, toward where the Shadow Wand is now concealed.

As they sail away from the continent, color returns to their world.

The Mage crew begins to compose ballads about their journey. They sing of Vogel's defeat of the Death Fae. How he destroyed the Wand of Shadow power before the Evil Ones could take possession of it. And how they have only to find the Ancient One's Blessed Wand of Myth to complete their sacred quest.

Alaric's hands clutch the stern's railing as he looks west, his brow knotted.

The horizon stares back in an unbroken line, a brilliant, multihued sunset hanging above it. There was a sunset like this one when they set out, Alaric recalls, spilling over every color imaginable. Alaric's light magery frenzied and he struggled to beat back his reflexive joy in seeing sacred and profane hues so confusingly blended. Just like everything seems disturbingly mixed up in him right now. He watches the unsettlingly beautiful sunset, unable to shake the dread fixed in him like a stone wedged deep in his core.

"A blessed evening to you, Mage."

Alaric startles at the resonant voice as Vogel joins him, his expression serene. Excitements sparks in Alaric over finding himself alone in his mentor's charismatic, trusted presence, but is quickly dampened. He can't help it. His eyes flick warily toward the outline of the Wand sheathed under Vogel's cloak.

Struggling to suppress his unease, Alaric gives the expected, polite response. "May you be blessed by the Ancient One's Holy Light." He glances again toward the Wand, and can see, by the flick of Vogel's own gaze, that his mentor has noticed him noticing.

"What's troubling you, Mage?" Vogel asks, his pale green eyes penetrating.

"I'm concerned..." Alaric starts, striving to assemble his thoughts as Vogel patiently waits. "I'm concerned that—" his gaze flicks yet again to the Wand "—that we're making a mistake. Bringing *that* to the Continent of the Realms."

Vogel nods placidly, as if he was expecting this. "You heard the demon," he reasons. "The Wand was sending out lures to be found and taken up by heathens. It was by the Ancient One's grace that the Death Fae mistook us for Dryad demons."

Alaric nods. *A huge stroke of luck, indeed.* He scans the Wand's outline, unable to keep the seditious thoughts from rising. *Was it truly luck? Or should we run from this thing?*

"How do we know the Wand won't use us for evil?" The words rush out of Alaric, the Fae's warning something he can't shake, even though it came from an Evil One.

Vogel's lip lifts. "Because we are Mages. Filled with the Ancient One's own grace. Any Tool of Power in our hands will be transformed."

Alarm knifes through Alaric. "But...you said you were going to destroy it." His gaze darts west, and he notices that the sunset is now a dim imprint, blasts of color receded.

Swallowed by darkness.

"'Unholy is the Mage who doubts the Will of the Ancient One,'" Vogel murmurs.

Alaric's brow tenses over Vogel's ominous choice to recite this passage from the *Book*. He turns just as Vogel gently reaches for the Wand and murmurs the penitent's spell—the earth spell used to discipline priest-apprentices who stray. The spell that stings the apprentice with a small lash of power, a prod to stay on the Path of the Holy.

But Vogel is using the Shadow Wand to cast it.

Protest rises in Alaric's throat as Vogel angles the Wand at him. *"Wait—"*

Bolts of Shadow blast from the Wand's tip and roar around

him, cinching Alaric tight, the breath forced from his lungs as he's hurled into the air and thrown overboard in a stomach-lurching arc.

A wall of dark ocean flies toward his face and he collides with the waves, the cold ocean rushing over him as the Shadow power drives him down into the water's depths. Panic floods Alaric, a horrific clarity descending.

I'm being drowned. As the Shadow Wand speeds toward Gardneria.

The Shadow power recedes, and Alaric's limbs are suddenly freed. He throws his arms back and kicks toward the surface, choking on salty water.

Translucent images of silvery-white birds suddenly waver into view all around, their glowing forms illuminating the dark waters, wings outstretched as they watch him ascend. Alaric's panic turns to sheer terror as he breathes in more water and devolves into flailing instead of swimming, dark splotches forming in his vision, the surface too high to reach in time.

A large, silver seal appears in the waters before him, its blurred form rapidly morphing into a silver-haired, naked blue woman with gills on her neck.

A Selkie, Alaric registers with panicked shock. *One of the monstrous seal women.*

He's too far gone to stop her as the Selkie grabs hold of his arm, dragging him upward much faster than he could swim on his own. She glances at the luminous, suspended birds, then back at Alaric with otherworldly silver eyes, her blue lips parting to reveal pointed teeth. But the astonished look on her face…

It's human.

Not demonic or cursed at all.

Just like the Death Fae.

He desperately points upward with his last ounce of strength, his lungs screaming for air as the Selkie bolts him toward the water's surface and the world goes dark.

THE SHADOW

VOID POWER RISING

The Ironflower *Ship, headed for the Continent of the Realms*

The Shadow bides its time, as it does. Encased in the Wand gripped so righteously by the priest, a moment after the priest-apprentice was thrown overboard and thrust far below.

The Shadow senses the priest looking out over the calming waters.

And makes its move.

Slowly it sends tendrils through the priest's hand, winding around his affinity lines, waking up like a Void dragon rising.

Reveling in the fracture inside this young priest.

It slithers deep into his mind, reading him.

Repent! A woman's furious voice sounds, the priest's memory of this firmly lodged in his mind's darkest recesses. The woman is dressed all in black, her pale green eyes cruelly intent, her green-glimmering face as elegant as the priest's, her gleaming black hair pulled back into a tight, neat coil.

A white bird pendant on a slim silver chain hangs around her neck.

The woman lunges forward, and the Shadow senses the sudden pain around the priest-child's arm, her nails digging in as the room swings and he's hurled backward against one of the Ironwood trees embedded in the walls, their bare canopy of branches snaking over the ceiling.

You're evil! the woman snarls as she raises the long, dark branch in her fist, her eyes flashing with hatred. *Vow to repent!*

No, Momma…

Blows rain on the priest's face, his small shoulders as he cowers and curls into a pathetic ball, pleading in a child's voice. *Momma, stop…no! I repent! I vow to repent!*

Say it! she hisses, fisting the rod. *Say you're evil and beg the Ancient One for mercy!*

I'm evil! I'm evil! Please, Momma, no…

More blows rain down, the priest-child sobbing so hard he can barely breathe. The black-haired woman towers over him, her silks perfectly pressed, their neatness at full odds with her wild, flushed face.

Without warning, her hand clamps around the priest-child's neck and he's shoved against the tree. He goes limp, futilely gasping for air.

You will follow the Ancient One's every law perfectly, do you understand? You will bring glory to His Holy Name!

The child forces a nod against her grip. The woman's hand withdraws, and the priest-child pulls in a ragged gasp as he slumps into a devastated heap.

Say it, she insists. *I will follow the Ancient One perfectly.*

I will follow the Ancient One perfectly, the child rasps, his body trembling as his emotions splinter.

The woman stills, a prim composure taking root, like a curtain drawn. She points her branch at a small desk. *The Book of the Ancients* rests on its surface, as well as parchment, pen, and ink.

Transcribe the First Book, the woman directs, her eyes flashing with hatred as she looks the child over. *Reflect and repent. Then I will bring you food and we will pray together that the Ancient One will have mercy on your wretched soul.* With that, the woman sets the branch neatly against the wall and exits through the heavy

Ironwood door, the click of the lock splintering off another piece of the child's heart.

Desperate to please the woman, to please the Ancient One, and not be evil anymore, the boy forces his battered body up and drags his skinny form to the desk. As his shoulders convulse with silent sobs, he begins to write.

PRELUDE

Prophecy's Descent
Present day

The
Amaz Prophecy

(Foretold from Sacred Red Elm astragalomancy
by the Seers of the Goddess)

Daughters of the Goddess take heed!
A great Shadow Force rises from
the Cursed World of Men.

And amidst its darkness, a Wyvern Male
and a Black Witch shall arise and clash,
raining destruction upon the world.

Take up arms, Blessed Daughters!

The hour to save Erthia is at hand!

ZALYN'OR BINDING

Freyja Zyrr

City of Cyme, Amazakaraan
Western Realm

Queen's Guard Acting Commander Freyja Zyrr strides along the base of Cyme's translucent protective dome, searching for threats, her runic axe strapped to her back, blades sheathed all over her.

Ever primed for battle, but especially so this night.

It's balmy and quiet. Deceptive in its tranquility. Freyja peers through the dome into the dark wilds beyond. She knows the Mages are likely out there, scouting around the city. Perhaps the Alfsigr are there as well, both vile peoples wanting to consume Amazakaraan and wipe her people clear off the face of Erthia. And then there's the Prophecy, every one of their seers unnervingly certain its time is at hand. Freyja flexes her shoulders, the weight of her axe the only reassuring thing about this night.

A rustling sounds in the trees behind her. She turns, taking in the curious forms of owls suddenly perched all over the elm grove's branches, the night birds dimly lit by the dome's scarlet runes and staring at her through round, unblinking eyes. Freyja pulls a shard of golden lumenstone from her pocket, its amber light suffusing both her hazel-hued hand and the dense grove. She looks back up and scans the Goddess's night children. Three golden-eyed eagle owls, perched in a row. Two great gray owls with piercing yellow stares. Several elf owls with such ferocious expressions for their tiny size, they're almost comical.

She lowers her gaze, taking in the two white, specter-like barn owls perched on Wynter Eirllyn's shoulders, the Alfsigr Icaral standing in the shadows, as Freyja knew she would be as soon as she spotted the birds.

"May I speak with you?" Wynter shyly inquires, her dark wings pulled in snugly around her slender frame.

Freyja nods and waits as Wynter emerges into the narrow clearing that rings Cyme, the edge of the city's dome rising behind Freyja. Wynter stills before her, the dome's scarlet runes tinting Wynter's alabaster hair a soft pink.

"I seek your aid," Wynter says in a small, strained voice, the desperate gravity in her silver gaze portending a request sure to be monumental.

"What aid do you seek?" Freyja asks and waits as Wynter seems to wrestle with her plea, her lips trembling.

"I seek help for my brother Cael and his Second, Rhys Thorim," she finally blurts out. "I seek help freeing them from imprisonment in Alfsigroth." Her face tenses, as if she's fighting mightily against some internal tide that wants to keep these thoughts bound down.

Freyja narrows her eyes at the edge of the Zalyn'or necklace imprint emblazoned around Wynter's pale neck—the necklace placed on all Alfsigr when they reach twelve years. The necklace Alfsigroth demands its citizens wear that Wynter is entrapped by—that all Alfsigr are entrapped by—save for a rebellious shard of Wynter's mind that refuses to be extinguished. Freyja worries about the Zalyn'ors, and so does Queen Alkaia. And so Freyja is charged with checking in with Wynter several times a day, to guard against the possibility that Marcus Vogel has infiltrated the Zalyn'or binding and wrested control of her mind.

But it's clear that this plea of Wynter's comes from herself alone.

A plea on behalf of *men*.

"Why do you bring this to me?" Freyja inquires, glaring at Wynter with a look that reads *I know* exactly *why you're bringing this to me*.

"Because you love a man," Wynter states with the pure certainty of an empath.

Freyja curses herself for letting Wynter make contact with her hand earlier. Because Wynter now knows that Clive Soren, the head of the shattered Keltish Resistance, came to Freyja just last night.

He was standing outside the runic dome just a few paces from where they are now, his tall form washed in scarlet rune glow, obviously waiting for Freyja. His brown hair was mussed, his piercing brown eyes set on her with passionate urgency.

A ferocity of emotion ripped through Freyja at finding him there, her breath constricting, as if suddenly clenched in a vise.

"What are you doing here?" she snarled, desperately scanning the woods for Gardnerians or Alfsigr or fellow-Amaz who could render him to ash in a spli second.

A magic-free Kelt.

I'm in love with a magic-free Kelt, Freyja agonized, her heart twisting at the sight of his longed-for face.

"Go East, now!" she hissed, wanting to leap through the dome and push him so hard that he'd have to start on his way there. So he would fully realize that he was tearing her heart apart by still being here and in incredible danger when she'd thought him well on his way to Noilaan by now. "The Subland Vu Trin undercover here can portal you East, so *go*!"

"I won't go without you," Clive snarled back. "Not without you, Freyja."

"*With* me, then?" Freyja rejoined, incredulous. "You *can't* be with me. I'm on this side of this runic dome, and *this* is where I will remain." *Forever separated from you so I can protect my people. But, damn you, Clive, at least go East. Let me feel like you have a chance against the Mages when they come.*

The hard fact rose up with outstretched claws—

My people don't stand a chance against the power of the Mages.

"Get the Amaz out of here," Clive insisted. He stepped toward the shield as if it were no match for him, even though they both knew full well that the second he moved through its surface, he would burst into runic flames, the fire igniting his very core.

"And go *where*?" Freyja harshly threw back.

Clive's jaw tightened, his glare intensifying, as if he were holding back a million expletives. "*East,*" he bit out. "You're an island in the middle of a strengthening monster. Get your people *East!*"

Freyja advanced toward the dome, now only a handspan from him. "How?" she challenged, teeth gritted. "How do we go East?"

"You've Noi portal sorcerers amongst you—"

"And if we went East, how would we live there? Amongst the men? Our religion and every aspect of our culture forbids mixing with men."

Clive's expression softened with an edge of longing. "And yet, here you are. With me."

Freyja's heart twisted as she held Clive's impassioned stare and remembered the last time they were together, over a month ago. Sneaking off into the woods to the southwest. Falling into each other's arms the second they were far enough away from Amazakaraan and taking each other with an intensity that stole Freyja's breath and ignited that familiar, piercing yearning to be with Clive always. To fight the Mages with him. To never let him go.

"I've chosen my people, you know that," she told him, her tone rough with frustration. Over the impossible choice she'd been forced to make. "Clive," she said, her voice splintering around his name, "the Noi have denied us entry. As have the Ishkart."

"Then the Noi and the Ishkart can go to hell," Clive growled, drawing closer. Almost touching the dome-shield. "They've closed the door to my people, as well. So, the hell with them all. Go East anyway. Freyja, the Gardnerians are coming, with the Alfsigr on their heels. And they *will* break through this dome."

"They *can't*. Or they'd be here already."

"They took the Lupines down in a single night. They *will come*, Freyja."

Conflict whipped through her. "Queen Alkaia wants a homeland without men. Even if the Noi open their gates to us, we're not interested in being a part of Noilaan. We are Free People."

"You're not free," Clive shot back. "You're prisoners of your rigidity. Hold on to it and you'll be massacred. The Mages will kill the children, Freyja. *All* of you. They view both your people and mine as soulless heathens. They will *kill you all*."

"I have urged Queen Alkaia to bend and go East," Freyja admitted, as the urge to leap through the shield and embrace him gained ground. "I have urged the Council." A frustrated tear streaked down her face, and she swiped it away, her lips trembling up in a slight, bitter smile. "But they see me as compromised." She motioned between them. "Corrupted by this thing I never speak of."

Clive's brow furrowed, passion firing in his eyes. "Come through the shield, Freyja," he offered, his voice newly gentle, the fierce love in his expression sending a warm, stinging rush straight through her.

"No," she rasped with an emphatic shake of her head. "I stay *here*—" she pointed firmly at the ground "—on this side. *This* is where I need to be. They *need* me, Clive."

Clive's expression turned mournful as they held each other's gazes. "I know they do."

"There's a chance we'll portal to the East," she told him.

"Queen Alkaia has gathered all the Amaz under this dome, and she's having her Circle of Sorcerers construct a series of emergency portals. So…give me this one hope. That if we do portal East, I might find you there."

Clive's jaw went rigid, his fierce eyes glazing over with tears as he briefly looked away, then set his blazing brown eyes back on her. "I'll find you. There is no shield or runic wall or religion or culture that could keep me from you. I *love* you, Freyja."

Freyja pulled in a shaky breath, Clive's beloved form wavy through a veil of tears she could no longer hold back. "I love you as well, Clive Soren."

"I *will* find you," Clive vowed as he stepped back from the dome, ignoring the tears streaking down his own face. "I *will* find you in the East."

And then he turned, strode into the woods, and was gone.

"I do love a man," Freyja admits to Wynter, the words feeling explosive on the air. It feels both frightening and like a revelation to state it plainly. Honestly.

On this side of the dome.

"I know," Wynter rejoins, compassion in her eyes.

"But Wynter," Freyja ruefully adds, "we cannot save your brother and Rhys Thorim from the Alfsigr. We could not do this even if they were female. I am sorry."

Wynter winces and glances away, her frail wings tightening around her. She looks back, imploring. "Then petition the queen to get the Amaz East. And petition them to find the runic sorcerer Rivyr'el Talonir. To free the Alfsigr from our Zalyn'or bindings."

Freyja's gaze darts to the imprint around Wynter's neck. "Do you feel something in it?"

"Only the same bindings," Wynter admits tightly, as if she can barely get the words out. "Vogel has not taken control of it. Not yet."

The bottomless pain in Wynter's silver eyes lights a spark of compassion in Freyja. She steps toward her, suddenly decided, even though part of her feels as if the Goddess will fly down from the heavens to shake her in censure. "We will petition the queen together," she vows. "And when we reach the East, Wynter Eirllyn, I will help you find Rivyr'el Talonir. And we will petition the Vu Trin to help your brother and his Second."

A grateful smile lifts Wynter's alabaster lips.

The owls abruptly grow agitated, and Wynter's smile vanishes as she looks to her kindred in confusion, the owls hooting in distress before they fly away.

Freyja lowers her gaze back to Wynter only to find the Icaral's eyes widening as they lock on something over Freyja's shoulder.

Freyja unsheathes her rune axe and whips around, shock blasting through her as she takes in what's just beyond the runic dome.

Alfsigr Elves, white as moonlight. But they're bizarrely elongated, as if someone has stretched them on a rack.

And their *eyes*.

Huge and swirling with gray. Almost insectile in shape. And there are runes made of shadow marked all over their white Alfsigr garb and on the hilts of the swords in their hands.

Strange swords with spiraling blades.

A chill flashes down Freyja's spine as she does a swift count of them. *Seven Marfoir assassins.*

The Marfoir step toward the dome, their movements unnaturally coordinated.

"Get off our land," Freyja growls as she advances toward the shield.

"Don't fight them," Wynter cries. "They'll *kill* you."

Freyja's nostrils flare as she readies her weapon. "Get the Amaz Guard," she orders Wynter with a brief glance over her shoulder. "Get them *now!*"

Wynter nods, but then freezes as Freyja turns to find huge, spidery legs bursting from the Marfoir's backs, then clicking inward. Legs as salt white as the Marfoir's skin.

Freyja's chest constricts as she takes a step back.

In unison, the Marfoir grin.

Their legs click outward as one, extending then drawing inward once more toward the shield, almost touching it. Curling shadow begins to rise from the tip of each pale spider limb to flow over the dome, hugging its surface and spreading out, the Marfoir's forms darkening as the fog of Shadow advances.

The last thing Freyja sees of the outside world is the insectile eyes of the Marfoir directly before her, a terrifying smile on his bone-white lips. Horror rises, alongside the ferocious will to save her people as she swiftly weighs *attack them* versus *warn the Amaz*.

Decided, she mentally summons her forest green mare, dives into the grove to meet the beloved animal, and jumps astride. Then she prods her horse forward, yanks Wynter up behind her and urges the mare into a gallop toward the queen.

CHAPTER TWO

THE REAPING TIMES

Marcus Vogel

The Northern Spine
Overlooking the city of Cyme, Amazakaraan
Western Realm

Marcus Vogel peers down at the heathen city of Cyme. Shadow Wand in hand, he sits astride a dragon on the Northern Spine's jagged, moonlit pinnacle, snow crunching beneath the broken dragon's feet. An icy wind whips against the gauzy gray shield Vogel's thrown up around both himself and the multi-eyed raven perched on his shoulder as he watches the web of Shadow undulating over the rune-marked dome encasing the valley below.

The Amaz are trapped, he gloats. *Like insects under a cup.*

He watches, transfixed, as the fog swirls around the dome's scarlet Amaz runes. The world-altering sight of Shadow power beginning its engagement with high-level fortress runes prompts a tremor of anticipation through his firelines. He pulls in a shuddering breath.

Amazakaraan, that dogged bastion of heathen defiance, finally about to fall.

Serves them right, the blasphemous whores, Vogel seethes. *For their hostility toward the Magedom. And for harboring an Alfsigr Icaral beast in their midst.*

His righteous fury notches higher.

Never again will the Amaz defy the Holy Magedom.

The Reaping Times have come.

Over a thousand Mages on dragonback line the Spine's apex, along with a contingent of deadly Alfsigr Marfoir. And positioned just below him on an outcropping of ice-glittering stone are Fallon Bane and her brothers, Damion and Sylus, the Level Five siblings ready to advance the invasion's leading edge. With righteously brutal Commander Fallon Bane at the helm.

Fallon turns and meets Vogel's gaze, green eyes flashing. Vogel holds her stare with a nod of approval as he wonders, not for the first time, why the Ancient One charged evil-tainted Elloren Gardner Grey with Black Witch power instead of ever-righteous Fallon Bane.

"The flawed vessel can be purified."

The holy verse lights in Vogel's mind, suffusing him with a rush of hope for redemption.

Redemption for Elloren Grey.

Redemption for himself.

And for the whole of Erthia.

His grasping hope intensifies as he scans the increasingly Shadow-hazed valley. The weight of his multi-eyed raven is a centering ballast, the creature a window, when he closes his eyes and focuses through the eyes of his many-eyed ones. Vogel basks in the glow of the Ancient One's gift of this power as well as His divine fury. He can feel that fury purifying his lines, everything going according to the Ancient One's Most Holy Plan.

The Icaral of Prophecy is dead.

The Shadow Wand has been transformed by Holy Purpose.

And the Black Witch…

Vogel glances at his green-glimmering wand hand and revels in the Ancient One's unexpected leading—a leading that will place Elloren fully under his control, along with the Great Wand of Myth that the Ancient One led to her. He sighted the Great Wand's energy, granting her perfect aim when she took down his scorpios, her emergence as a warrior compelling to behold. And now, the two Wands of Power will soon be united in defense of the Magedom.

Vogel narrows his gaze back on the Amaz dome as the Shadow web slithers higher and Marfoir scuttle over it, their bone-white forms mere specks from here. With sly calculation, he considers that it will take at least three days for news of the obliteration of Amazakaraan to reach Noilaan with the time lag in even the best of the Vu Trin's hidden portals.

He smiles.

By the time Noilaan receives word of the Magedom's rune-obliterating power, it will have fallen.

And heathen Alfsigroth will soon be consumed as well through their Zalyn'or necklace bindings—including Wynter Eirllyn, the filthy winged one hiding under this dome.

Revulsion ripples through Vogel at the thought of those unnatural, feathered appendages. But then, some relief gathers, blunting his reflexive rush of hate. The Eirllyn creature is a helpless little beast, her disgusting wings ragged and incapable of flight, her fire long since doused.

She'll be easily put down.

Vogel relishes the idea of handing her over to the Elves to smite as they see fit. The Alfsigr monarch, Iolrath Talonir, insisted on taking custody of the creature, the Alfsigr religion mirroring the Gardnerian in its hatred of demon wingeds.

Let the Alfsigr have this one, blessed triumph, Vogel magnanimously considers, even as he yearns to obliterate her wings himself. *Let them gain a blessing from punishing the demon girl before we secure dominion over both them and their lands.*

The *whoosh* of broad wings sounds beside him, breaking off his thoughts. Vogel turns as an incoming Mage soldier lands his dragon. Shadow horns curl up from the glamoured pyrr-demon's Mage-black hair—horns only Vogel and his Shadow soldiers can see—the demon's eyes a glowing red under their glamoured green.

Vogel eyes the Shadow-tethered demon with barely concealed loathing. Mage dominion over Shadow power necessitates dominion over unsavory creatures—who will be disposed of after the Reaping Times.

The soldier dismounts. "A rune hawk just arrived, Your Excellency," he states, his sulfuric gaze simmering like twin coals.

"What news?" Vogel inquires.

The bottomless flame in the demon's eyes deepens to a more ominous red. "It sends word that Yvan Guryev's 'assassin,' the wandmaster Mavrik Glass, has defected to Noilaan."

A cataclysmic rush of fire sears through Vogel's lines, his sense of unimpeded triumph burned clear away as he absorbs the ramifications.

If Mavrik Glass, our most talented assassin, is a traitor…then the Icaral of Prophecy is potentially…

…still alive.

"What news has been confirmed?" Vogel asks, slow and deadly firm as an image of dark wings accosts his mind.

"We tortured a captured Vu Trin spy," the envoy replies. "She told us of Yvan Guryev's survival. His death was a ruse."

Vogel's internal fire stokes higher, violent outrage churning through him. "How can it be? The Icaral was impaled."

"He is Lasair Fae," the demon answers. "The Vu Trin said he drew on Fae healing powers to bring himself back from the brink of death."

And fooled the entire Magedom.

Silvery flames spit against Vogel's vision, but he quickly re-tethers his violent inner storm. "It is the Ancient One's will," he states, chillingly calm. "So, let the Prophecy come to completion. The Holy Magedom will soon have possession of Erthia's most dangerous weapon, and she will smite the Icaral demon without mercy."

The envoy dips his head. "Are we to step up the hunt for Elloren Grey, Excellency?"

"It is unnecessary." Vogel's lips edge up. "I know *exactly* where she is. And I have the perfect bait to draw her to me."

CHAPTER THREE

SHADOW DOME

Wynter Eirllyn

City of Cyme, Amazakaraan
Western Realm

Wynter Eirllyn stands before the huge Goddess statue in the center of Cyme's crowded plaza, dread coiling in her gut as crimson torchlight flickers over the besieged Central Plaza. The city's dome looms above, its scarlet runes casting a ruddy glow through the Shadow relentlessly churning over it.

A sea of women and girls look to Queen Alkaia, who stands, supported by her cane, on the statue's broad pedestal, her Queen's Guard—including Wynter's soldier friend, Freyja—bracketing her. A huge contingent of the Amaz military surrounds them all.

We're trapped, Wynter thinks, her fright echoed by the rose-finches perched on her shoulders.

Sensing another kindred winged, Wynter glances up and spots a lone hawk soaring down toward them, a pinprick disturbance roiling the Shadow dome where the winged must have burst through. And…the winged one is all *wrong*.

The scarlet hawk's normal blaze of ruddy coloration morphed to hues of gray, the bird's eyes unnaturally silvered. A stunned sympathy shivers through Wynter as she senses the bird's fear in the frantic motion of its wingbeats.

You're corrupting and terrifying my wingeds, she thinks of Vogel, agony mounting. And then, something Wynter is not used to feeling ignites. Something her Zalyn'or necklace usually suppresses, as it does with all Alfsigr Elfkin.

Defiance.

The spark of rebellion fuels Wynter's next thought.

Runic domes are magicked to allow wildlife passage.

The grayed hawk swoops down and lights on the Amaz fowler's outstretched arm, the message attached to the bird's rune-banded leg hastily retrieved.

The fowler's blue-hued jaw tightens, her sapphire eyes scanning the missive. "My queen," she says, looking to the Amaz monarch with outraged gravity. "It says, 'Surrender your lands to the Magedom immediately. Or face total annihilation.'"

Protests erupt as the message is conveyed across the plaza.

Queen Alkaia bears down on her cane and raises one green, rune-marked palm to her people. "Free People of Amazakaraan." Her ancient voice booms out, amplified by the scarlet rune hovering in the air just below her mouth. "The Goddess's Prophecy is *here*." She glances up at the Shadow-coated dome, her emerald eyes narrowing as if sizing it up for battle. Then she sets her fierce gaze back on her people.

"The Mages think they can terrorize us with their Shadow power. Place bonds around our throats. They falsely imagine that the Goddess's Own True Daughters can be brought to heel." She straightens, and Wynter can sense the collective will of the people rising around her as the monarch crushes the missive in her fist. "Blessed Daughters. Who here will raise weapons to journey beyond our dome and smite these invaders with the *Goddess's own fury?*"

A tremendous roar sounds as every Amaz from thirteen up

draws runic weapons and raises them in the air, the weapons' scarlet runes burning bright as those that mark the city's dome.

Wynter's throat suddenly tightens, and it's not a normal tightening.

It's a Zalyn'or tightening.

Scared that she'll lose the ability to speak if she waits a second longer, Wynter fans out her ragged wings and steps forward.

Queen Alkaia and Freyja both meet her gaze in evident surprise. The queen raises a hand for silence, and the cries of defiance settle into a thrum of gathering runic power.

"I seek to send a message!" Wynter croaks out, her wings flapping against the Zalyn'or's suffocating grip on her voice.

Queen Alkaia's gaze sharpens. "What message do you seek to send, Wynter Eirllyn?"

"I seek to send my wingeds!" Wynter rasps before she's choked off. She motions emphatically toward the Shadow-covered dome.

A subversive gleam enters Queen Alkaia's eyes. "Send your message, then, winged friend of the Amaz," she says, voice blazing with revolution. "Let the first true volley in this war be sent by a Zalyn'or-marked Icaral."

Wynter drops to one knee and lowers her head, her ragged wings fanning out to their full breadth as the Amaz step back to give her space. Burrowing into her minuscule surviving ember of Icaral power, Wynter drags in a breath, then forces her invisible sterling aura out.

The incoming rain-sound of wings beats on the air, birds closing in from all directions, some soaring through the shadowed dome: black-throated warblers, silver-crowned sparrows. Crimson tanagers. A host of hawks and owls, eagles and falcons. Flock upon flock circles down, their panicked tweets and caws overtaking the plaza as they descend toward one single target.

Wynter.

The Amaz surrounding Wynter draw back in astonishment as birds land in a thick mass around her winged form.

Foreboding swells in Wynter as she realizes that some of these birds are from the Agolith Desert, their normally vivid coloration torn away. Red desert hawks rendered to shades of gray. Cactus wrens and gilded flicker birds stripped of their gold. Sand-colored eagles with eyes that normally glow saffron, now pewter with eyes of white fire.

What's been done to you?

The birds crowd in, the ones in the forefront pressing tilted heads to Wynter. Her empathic heart tightens from their rush of love—love that she returns a thousandfold. She touches her hands to feathers and closes her eyes.

The birds' collective warning hits Wynter like a thousand bolts, her body shuddering from the onslaught.

SHADOW, SHADOW, SHADOW!

Beloved ones! Wynter counters, hurling the desperate, empathic thought out through the Zalyn'or's strangling grip.

The birds still, an almost reverent silence overtaking the plaza and Wynter draws on that silence for courage.

My loved ones, she sends out even as pain strafes her skull, her thoughts threatening to collapse into oblivion if she waits a moment longer. *Fly forth and pierce the Shadow! Find Naga the Unbroken and appeal for aid!*

The Zalyn'or clamps down and Wynter wheezes, her empathic thoughts cut off as the birds lift as one. Their wingbeats are a storm, a roar against Wynter's ears as they rise and rise then soar straight through the dome. The Shadow coating the dome briefly fragments, the Amaz battle cry rising as Wynter gapes up at what she's wrought, heart hammering.

A sudden wave of hate slashes through her mind.

She stiffens, wings shivering, swept up in the feeling that she's a butterfly caught at the end of a pointed stick. The plaza blinks out of sight, replaced by a vision of Shadow forest—undulating tree trunks and limbs of dark smoke tendriling upward from charred ground.

Thrust into panicked disorientation, Wynter glances frantically around.

Marcus Vogel strides toward her through the trees, a gray wand trailing Shadow in his hand. Wynter recoils, her trembling intensifying as Vogel fixes his pale green eyes on her.

Icaral, he says.

The Zalyn'or necklace tightens and Wynter's head arches back, a strangled cry torn from her throat. She shudders as she's swept up in a new, overpowering Zalyn'or yearning, the old yearning to be purely Alfsigr stripped away. Yes, she still wishes with everything in her for her demonic wings to be torn from her back. But there's a staggeringly fierce, new longing in her now—to have black hair, glimmering green skin, and black clothing. And to follow the one true path. Not the path of the Alfsigr faith at all, but the Mage religion.

The only path to purity and righteousness.

The only path to salvation.

Realization hits Wynter like a tide.

I'm reading him. *I'm somehow reading Vogel through the Zalyn'or.*

Galvanized, she manages a steadying breath, summons her courage and closes her eyes.

Thick smoke flows into her empathic mind as she follows her connection to Vogel, all of his Shadow power oriented toward the Wand gripped in his hand. Battling her fear, Wynter follows his tether...straight into the Wand.

Her sense of the plaza's tiles beneath her knees disappears.

Her body drops and she cries out as she plummets into a bottomless abyss, limbs flailing. Shadow eyes surround her, streaking past as she falls. Cruel, demonic eyes. Some red. Some full of roiling smoke as Wynter is assaulted by the presence of unending malice and fracture.

What have you done? she cries out to Vogel. *Do you realize what you've aligned yourself with?*

A blast of power slams against her empathic senses, and Wynter's connection to Vogel breaks. *Filthy Icaral!* screams through her as her link to him funnels away.

Wynter's consciousness is hurled back onto the red-lit Amaz

plaza, palms and knees pressed to the stone as she pants and wheezes.

"Wynter, what happened?"

She lifts her head and meets Freyja's hazel eyes. Unable to speak, she reaches up with quavering hands and yanks the collar of her tunic down so hard that the fabric tears open.

The Amaz soldiers facing her, including Freyja, draw back in horror.

Wynter looks down and sways. Dark lines of Shadow are spreading out from her Zalyn'or imprint, burrowing under her skin like a veiny sickness.

Wynter looks to Queen Alkaia, feeling like a netted sparrow as she struggles to keep the free sliver of her mind from being dragged into the Zalyn'or chasm. "Get your people East," she rasps through Vogel's choke hold. "There's no stopping him now. He's going to control all of Alfsigroth. And he can hear and see us. Through *me*."

Queen Alkaia's gaze turns lethal. "Let him hear us, then," she seethes. "Let him hear that an Icaral raises her fist to the Magedom and beats her wings against its demon tide. And let Marcus Vogel hear that we, the Free People of the Caledonian Mountains, bend the knee to no one, save our chosen Queen and the Great Goddess on High."

Wynter's sense of Vogel lights again. But he's small and sly this time. Lurking just behind her eyes as the slimmest trace of Shadow ripples over her vision and she's suddenly seeing through his eyes, looking down at Amazakaraan's shadowed dome.

Looking down with his army.

The urge to warn the queen of his intent strikes through Wynter, the words straining for release. *Get your people East, now! He's linked the Magedom to demonic power, and it's about to be unleashed!*

But, try as she might, Wynter can't speak. She draws her wings in painfully tight, struggling to scream out the vital message as a wave of nausea rises. Unable to fight it, she lurches forward, mouth forced open. Vomit bursts from her in a splatter of dark filth and spreads over the tiled plaza, sounds of alarm surging to life as Shadow rises from it.

The soldiers surrounding Wynter, save Freyja, draw weapons, arrows nocked, eyes fierce on Wynter's crumpled form. She peers helplessly up at Queen Alkaia's horrified face and struggles for breath. Struggles for her voice.

"Don't shoot!" Freyja pleads, throwing herself in front of Wynter's prone form. She casts her a fraught look. "Wynter… what did you see—?"

Freyja's words are cut off by a silver flash from the Amaz dome's crimson runes, the valley momentarily brightening.

Everyone looks up in confusion.

And then, like stars blotting out, every scarlet rune on the dome blinks out of sight.

Wynter's gut clenches. "He's here," she manages before an ear-punching blast detonates and the protective dome over Cyme explodes in a spray of Shadow.

CHAPTER FOUR

DEMON HIVE

Lukas Grey

Shadow hive cell
Location unknown

Lukas Grey roars back to consciousness, gasping for breath.

He finds himself bound by dark vines on a cavern floor in some type of prison, his cell's bars made of dark smoke, a much larger cavern just beyond. Every affinity line in his body is painfully taut, his magic stretched by overwhelming force. His gaze darts wildly around, haze spitting across his vision as he's caught up in one desperate thought.

Elloren!

There's no trace of her anywhere.

He remembers that final, agonizing glimpse of her through the portal's golden interior, screaming his name. His right fist clenches, yearning for a wand as he's seized by desperation.

Scanning the cavern, he takes in every last detail—the young Level Five guard just outside the wavering bars. The bizarre stacked catacombs rising up the sides of the colossal vaulted cavern. They seem to go on forever, like a huge wasp nest. Mage soldiers with glowing gray eyes are emerging from the waspish cells and climbing down with unnatural agility, more gray-eyed Mages striding industriously through the cavern. A few of them lead multi-eyed dragons marked with Shadow runes, the dragons' powerful bodies rendered to shades of steel.

He spots a soldier he knows, Curren Dell. He remembers Curren as a talented, idealistic Level Four soldier-apprentice back in Verpacia, well-liked and eager to defend the Magedom. Horror tightens Lukas's gut as he takes in the blank, feral look on the young man's face.

Lukas slants his eyes upward and takes in the corrupted Marfoir Elves scuttling up the walls on salt-white spider legs and the elongated, many-eyed wraith bats that hang from every outcropping. Shadow-polluted scorpios line the cavern's base, the huge insects quietly chittering, their thoraxes marked with Shadow runes. Most of the scorpios have additional eyes, and Lukas spots one with a neck and head covered in a solid mass of them.

The power in his lines fires up, hot in his chest. He scans the scene once more, gaze flickering toward the wand grasped in his guard's green-glimmering hand. Stealthily, he begins to test his Shadowy bindings and finds a slack portion just over his left hand...

As if sensing his fledgling rebellion, the guard meets Lukas's eyes with a pitiless gray stare and lifts his wand.

A bolt of Shadow hits Lukas, triggering a blast of pain that arches his spine, a rasping cry forced from his mouth as his vision blots out.

When he comes to, he's in motion, four Mages dragging him through a black stone tunnel. Torches burning with silver-spitting gray fire cast a fitful pewter light.

He grits his teeth as his back slides against the rough floor, the wounds that crisscross his skin a knife-slicing agony. He flexes his muscles, testing the tightness of his bindings. Locating the proximity of every *wand*...

His Mage guards slow, and Lukas twists his head around to find Vogel striding toward him, pale green eyes blazing. There's a white bird emblazoned on Vogel's priestly tunic, his dark cloak flowing behind him.

The Mage soldiers dump him at Vogel's feet.

Panting from the pain reverberating through his lines, Lukas forces himself to his knees. He meets Vogel's gaze dead-on and gives him a vicious smile. "Hello, Marcus. The demon-priest aesthetic suits you."

Vogel rears back and strikes Lukas across the face, white-hot rage igniting as Lukas lunges for him only to be quickly bound up in more Shadow vines by the surrounding Mage guards and pinned to the floor, arms outstretched, their four wands leveled at him.

He glares up at Vogel, teeth bared as fury pulses through him. "I'd like to see you try that without your Shadow pets to hold me back," Lukas hisses.

Even through his all-encompassing rage, he can't help but notice the flash of frustrated fury in Vogel's eyes.

"Ah," Lukas chides, ignoring the blood streaking his face and the throbbing pain in his cheek. "Have your plans gone awry?" He broadens his smile, hoping to goad Vogel, desperate for information about Elloren. "She's slipped out of your grasp, hasn't she?"

Vogel narrows his gaze and runs his fingers over his Wand, looking more composed now, though his eyes are strangely edged with silvery fire.

"You had so much potential." Vogel shakes his head. "I should have known you'd be a problem from your casual blasphemy, but I believed your loyalties to be true. Instead, you've done everything in your power to turn my Black Witch into a staen'en whore set against everything pure and good. And now, you will atone for it."

Vogel raises his Wand, and Lukas gasps as his Shadow bindings briefly turn razor-sharp, cutting into his skin like curved knives. He battles back the cry threatening to rip from his throat.

Instead, he forces a chiding laugh. "Elloren has more power than you. And she's going to *crush* you with it."

Vogel's lips lift. "Did you know the Icaral, Yvan Guryev, survived?"

A bolt of jealousy darts through Lukas's power.

Vogel's smile widens. "Oh, I felt that."

Alarm strikes. "How?" Lukas rasps, rattled by Vogel's reveal of power-empath abilities.

Vogel slides onto one knee, a calculating glint in his eyes as he lifts his Shadow Wand and presses its tip to the palm of Lukas's wand hand.

Lukas shivers as tendrils of Shadow course from the Wand to flow over his fastlines. "What are you doing?" he demands, his composure breached.

Vogel eyes him slyly, as if to say, *Ah, got you*. "Infiltrating the spell," he states. "To connect to my Black Witch."

White flashes through Lukas's vision, a growl escaping his throat as he hurls every ounce of his formidable strength against his bindings. "I'll kill you," he lashes out, mind storming. "I will *kill* you if you touch her."

Vogel's voice is low and mocking when it comes. "Does it bother you that the only reason you survived my fire is that the Icaral's taint is all over her? Because of his deep, serpentine kiss?"

Another blaze of jealousy commingled with hatred for Vogel overtakes Lukas as the reason for his survival falls into place—Elloren's Wyvernfire. From her bond to Yvan Guryev.

"Join with me," Vogel challenges, serious, his eyes flashing. "Together we can smite Yvan Guryev and raise Elloren to great power."

Lukas lunges for Vogel's Wand through a loose binding, but Vogel flinches back, viper fast. He flicks his Wand, Shadow vines flying from its tip, and Lukas grunts as his wand arm is wrenched outward. He glares murderously at Vogel as the gray cast to his vision intensifies and he stiffens, hit by what that means.

"You're going to join me by choice or by force," Vogel calmly imparts. He tilts his head, his expression turning almost sympathetic. "As will my Black Witch. She's lost her way, but I'm going to help her redeem her very soul. Elloren is going to fulfill the Prophecy, slay the Icaral demon, and cleanse the East."

A rush of protective love overtakes Lukas. Stronger than his jealousy of Yvan Guryev. Stronger than anything on Erthia, the protective surge intensifying as a horrifyingly multi-eyed raven flies down to light on Vogel's shoulder.

Find Yvan Guryev, Elloren, Lukas rages. *Find him and anyone you can with any power to ally with. Free yourself from our Sealing spell and unbind your magic.*

Then light this bastard up with the full might of your Black Witch power.

FIRE AND SHADOW

Elloren Grey

The Dyoi Forest
Eastern Realm

Elloren.

Yvan's deep voice shudders through me, quickening my pulse. The flame aura encompassing me flashes through my vision, overtaking it with chaotic gold as the hostile purple forest surrounding me cuts out of sight.

The flame aura builds, coming in from the northeast. My body shivers against its potent flow as it sweeps through my tangled affinity lines with dizzying heat. As if it's trying to burn a path across the distance between us.

I gasp, disbelieving even in the face of it. *Yvan, are you alive?*

The conflagration intensifies, and I can sense explosive yearning in its power. My mind casts about. This aura swept in so fast after the scorpio attack—after Lukas pushed me through a portal to the Eastern Realm.

Sacrificing his life for mine.

My throat clenches with choking sorrow. I can barely breathe as I remember my last glimpse of Lukas, his green eyes locked with mine as his back was hit by Vogel's dark fire.

The flame aura seems to sense my anguish, its flow intensifying around me to the point of vibration.

Sweet Ancient One.

I'm *sure* this is Yvan's flame. I've been swept up in this flow of Wyvern power before, in his bonding kiss.

A wilderness of disorientation wrests hold, hot and raw, over the world-upending possibility of Yvan, alive, and Lukas, lost to me forever. Devastated tears glaze my eyes as I remember Yvan's words—

A dragon's kiss binds him to his mate. I'll know when you're in danger. I'll sense any pain you experience.

The anguish intensifies. Could Yvan have somehow survived and be in hiding like me? On the run, my features grayed by an Elfhollen glamour...

A child's scream cleaves through the Wyvernfire's roar.

I startle, hard, and the fire rips away from my lines with such force that I'm pitched in the direction of its northeastern flow, my hands and knees slamming onto the ground. The purple landscape snaps back into view as the demon-sensing rune Sage marked on my abdomen begins to sting.

Pulse thundering, I register everything before me in one sweeping glance.

I'm in a field of swaying, violet grass, the smoking corpses of the three scorpios I just brought down splayed out to my sides, a purple forest beyond. A black-haired teenage girl with Mage features stands before me, her sickly, violet-hued, point-eared mother and young sister to her back. There's a blade in the teenage girl's hand, and their eyes are wide with horror as a *swoosh* sounds behind me, along with a rasping *hiss.*

I whip around. Four huge wraith bats, big as men, are soaring down into the clearing on leathery wings. Baring sickle-sharp fangs, they zoom toward me, the lead bat rapidly enlarging as it fills my vision, an incoming nightmare of teeth…

I roll to the side, dodging its attack, before springing up. A wing blow smacks my side and I'm hurled back to the ground, grunting from the collision, dry grass scraping my face as a visceral rush of fright streaks through me.

Lukas's voice overtakes my mind. *Suppress your fear! They feed on it!*

Teeth gritted, I pull hard on my fire power like Lukas trained me to, incinerating my emotions. I roll upright just as a clawed grip digs into my waist and hoists my body skyward, the air punched from my lungs as I'm buckled into a V. The world below swings away and I kick and flail, scrabbling for my rune blades, panic rising as the other three wraith bats fan out their wings and take flight.

The teen girl runs toward me, her heart-shaped face a mask of feral determination as she hurls her weapon, an incoming silver streak.

Her knife finds its mark above me with a dull *thwick*.

The bat lets out a furious hiss and I'm suddenly released, a wall of lavender grass flying toward my face. I reflexively bend my limbs as I crash into the ground with bone-jarring force and roll into the fall over the rough grass.

The Wand of Myth tingles against my calf and I reach for it, heart thundering, its spiraling form still sheathed in the side of my boot.

I still have perfect aim.

A vicious warrior resolve taking hold, I spring to my feet and unsheathe the two runic blades at my sides, the powerful Ash'rion blade Valasca gave me in my wand hand. Eyes narrowing, I track the bat that seized me as it lands in a snarling, jerking mass, bucking and straining as it attempts to dislodge the knife. The other three touch down behind it, their black lizard-slit eyes set on me.

Lukas, Valasca, and Chi Nam's training snaps into place and I take swift notice of the single Shadow rune marking the lower chest of each bat. *They're not deflection runes*, I coldly note as another realization strikes home in one harsh blow...

I'm at full-on war with Marcus Vogel.

A war to control my own gods-damned power.

"You can't have me," I seethe as red-hot wrath ignites, fueled by the memory of Lukas's patient hands on mine as he taught me how to use these very blades, sliding my fingers across their charged runes while murmuring the fire-amplification spell as I'm doing now.

The bats advance, their dark forms hunched, nostrils flaring as they hiss and spit and bare teeth. But I'm beyond fear now, a volcanic fury rising to singe it to ash.

"Screw your Magedom," I growl at Vogel. I draw my arms back and the Wand's guiding translucent green tracks, visible only to me, appear in the air, leading from my blades to the necks of the closest beasts—the injured bat and the one beside it.

With a harsh grunt, I hurl the knives.

The blades streak through the air and impale the two bats in their broad necks with dual *snicks*. The beasts' cavernous mouths wrench open, releasing metallic shrieks into the air, before their heads and upper torsos explode into bright balls of golden flame, the Ash'rion blade's explosion the most potent.

The other two bats launch themselves at me and I break into a dead run.

Wet snuffling noises sound behind me, and a clawed grip closes around my ankle, pitching me forward. I twist around, pressing my fingers to the weapon-retrieval runes Valasca marked on my palms, the marks hidden under my gray glamour.

My blades fly from the dead, flaming bats and hurtle to me in a blur, their hilts colliding with my palms with satisfying stings. I press my fingers to the fire runes, and stab one blade into the bat restraining me, then hurl the other at the eyes of the bat that's closing in. Both creatures' heads explode into fiery balls.

The heat rushes over me, the grip around my ankle loosening. I scuttle away, breathing hard, as the flaming bats flail and convulse, then lie still. Hoisting myself to my feet, I scan the lavender field and purple forest, every nerve on high alert. Heart thumping against my rib cage, I find no additional threats. Nothing but rustling leaves, a storm darkening sky, and the forest's aura of hostility, thick as tar.

I raise my hands and my blades rip from the beasts and fly back into my palms, their hilts scalding against my fire-resistant skin. The Wand's energy shivers against my calf as gratitude for its aid courses through me. Feeling as if liquid steel has entered my veins, I turn to face the teen girl, the Urisk woman, and the young child.

The teen's eyes are combative as they meet mine, as if she's still engaged in battle. Her mother has backed away to the forest's edge, her little girl swept behind her. The child's tear-streaked violet face peeks at me from around her mother's side and the terror on her innocent face rouses a fierce sympathy in me.

"Are you all right?" I ask.

The child startles and ducks behind her mother, who is watching me through fever-dazed eyes, shock evident on her wan face. The young teen glances at them, then me, and nods stiffly.

Forcing my bruised body into motion, I resheathe my blades and stalk to one of the smoldering bats. Through the flames, I yank the girl's knife from its tough hide. Then I turn and stride to her, ignoring the stabbing pain in my ankle. I hold the weapon out to her, hilt first.

She meets my gaze, vulnerability breaking through as she lets out a quavering breath, then nods, relief overtaking her expression as she accepts the blade.

The immensity of the situation is suddenly bearing down on me like deadweight. I'm outwardly calm, but my blood is hammering at my temples, dread unfolding in the pit of my stomach.

I'm on a collision course with Vogel and the Prophecy.

Lukas is gone. Chi Nam too. And Ancient One knows what happened to Valasca.

I rake my fingers through my tangled gray hair, a barrage of grief and longing for Lukas—for all of them—hitting me with eviscerating force. I'm splayed open by it, unmoored, my breaths coming in uneven, shuddering waves. *How can I face this alone?*

A heart-shattering memory of Lukas's voice fills my mind. *You're stronger than you think. I'm sure of it. I always have been.*

The will to fight back wrests hold, spearing up through the grief. Fueled by it.

It surprises me, how intensely and tenaciously it grips hold. *It's what he would have wanted,* I insist to myself, tightening my chest against the upswell of sorrow. *It's what they all would have wanted. They'd want me to stay sharp and persevere.*

Steadied, I stride back toward the bats, their charred heads spitting flame and dark smoke. I pause over the nearest corpse and survey the unfamiliar Shadow rune on its chest, knowing that I'm looking at my enemy.

The enemy who killed Lukas.

"Watch for movement in the trees or sky," I caution the teen over my shoulder. She nods and grips her blade tighter as I set my gaze back on the corrupted beast and lower myself to one knee before it.

Slim, almost elegant tendrils of Shadow are curling from the circular rune on its charred chest, a palpable tang of energy hovering in the air around it. Cautiously, I pass my hand through the smoke, and the tendrils flash silver as they prickle my skin with an unnatural shiver. The Wand of Myth's subtle, comforting buzz against my calf cuts out.

Like it's hiding.

Focus sharpening, I draw my hand through the tendrils, the unsettling shiver increasing, then press my palm down on the Shadow rune.

The shivering energy explodes outward, the purple world dimming. My fastlines appear from beneath my gray glamour, the dark, looping lines taking form on my hand and wrist. Alarm knifes through me as I move to wrench my hand back, only to find it fused to the rune.

A translucent image of Lukas appears, superimposed on the scene before me. He's shirtless and breathing heavily, his muscular body bound to the stony ground by some kind of Shadow vines, his wand hand splayed out and vine-webbed to a cavern's floor. Bloodred lash marks crisscross his chest, and there are bars made of Shadow behind him.

Every emotion in me surges up, hot and hard.

"Lukas!"

He meets my eyes, defiance rearing in his gaze's green depths. "Go straight to hell, Marcus," he snarls as a phantom hand clutching a dark gray wand is raised before me, seeming as if it's *my* hand, *my* vision. The wand lowers and touches Lukas's fastlines, and he groans, body stiffening in evident pain.

"Lukas!" I cry again, scrabbling to touch him, my hand passing straight through the phantom image. Energy prickles along the back of my neck, and I've the sudden, unnatural sense of an awareness provoked.

Lukas's image whisks from sight, my focus hurtling back to the wraith bat corpse before me, the Shadow rune's hold on my hand abruptly releasing.

My throat clenches. "No... Lukas...*no*."

I frantically press both hands onto the rune, but its smoke has vanished, along with the mist that was emanating from the runes on the other bats, only their gray imprints remaining. I lift my hands, a light-headed rush streaking through me as I find that my fastlines are once more hidden beneath my glamour.

As if something cut a connection.

My heart pounds harder.

Lukas is alive. He's alive.

Frantic, I struggle to find clarity. The not-fully-charged portal I went through must have had a sizable time lag, I realize, even though the journey seemed over in the blink of an eye.

My mind-bending concern intensifies. *How long has Lukas been in Vogel's grip? Why was I briefly able to see my fastlines?*

And that Shadowfire of Vogel's—how did Lukas survive it?

The answer hits me like a bolt to the heart.

The same way I survived it. Yvan's Wyvernfire bond conferred me with immunity to being burned. And I fed that Wyvernfire straight into Lukas all those times that he kissed me and drew on my power.

Which means... I must have extended Yvan's fire bond to Lukas, as well.

My mind spins. *Sweet Ancient One. Yvan's fire saved Lukas.*

But...if Lukas is alive, where is he?

My spine tightens with a flame-streaked rise of revolt, my wand hand reflexively reaching for my Ash'rion blade.

I have to return to the West and save him.

"Ny'laea!"

The teen's voice cuts through my rebellious thrall. I turn, her repeated calls of my false Elfhollen name finally registering.

"What's the date?" I demand.

She eyes me with obvious confusion. "The third week of Seventh Month, I think. I've... I've lost track of the exact days."

My mind casts about. *Over a week. Lukas has been in Vogel's grip for over a week...*

"Who were you screaming for?" she throws down, meeting me demand for demand.

I give her a level look. "Someone I need to save." Rain begins to drizzle as I rise, my gaze sweeping over the trees like I'm sighting a nocked arrow, thoughts igniting.

I need to unbind my power, and *fast*, so I can go after Lukas. Which means I need the help of people adept at complicated magic.

I need to get to the Wyvernguard.

It's where Lukas, Chi Nam, and Valasca were planning to bring me. It boasts some of the most powerful sorceresses and sorcerers in all the Realms including portal sorceresses—and if I'm going to return to the desert as quickly as possible, I'll need a portal.

And even though Chi Nam is no longer with me, I have allies there.

Trystan. I need to find my brother.

I take a quavering breath and hope against hope that my youngest brother made it to the Wyvernguard when he fled east with our older brother Rafe and other loved ones. Tierney, Sage…they were bent on joining the Wyvernguard, as well.

I glance toward the hostile forest, the immensity of the journey ahead swamping me as I visualize the map in Chi Nam's Vonor. The Vo Mountains present a formidable barrier, even without their killing storm band. And before the mountains lies the treacherous Zonor River…

"Ny'laea, what happened?" the teenager demands, green eyes blazing hotter, as if she's finally summoned enough courage to force answers from me. She points emphatically at the bats. "What are those runes?"

I meet her rattled gaze as the rain needles down. "Corrupted Mage runes," I answer, conflicted over drawing her and her family into my doomed orbit. I glance at her sickly mother and small sister. The little girl lets out a rattling cough and the incredible realization circles down—their situation is so dire that traveling with the Black Witch, hunted by a multitude of powerful forces, is likely their best shot at survival.

"I need to get to the Wyvernguard," I tell the teen.

"Why?" she asks, her heart-shaped face tensing.

Lightning forks across the sky and thunder cracks overhead. *Because I'm the Black Witch,* I almost respond in fearsome challenge. *And I want to subvert the Prophecy as spectacularly as possible.*

"My brother is in the Wyvernguard," I say instead. "He can help us." I motion toward the blade in her hand, gratitude welling. "You saved my life."

"You saved ours," she rejoins, as if that settles the matter.

"What's your name?" I ask.

She hesitates, her stance becoming confrontational. "Nym'ellia," she answers, and I immediately guess why this fierce girl feels the need to throw her name out like a challenge. Such a distinctly Urisk name. Bestowed on a girl who has the black hair, shimmering green skin and forest green eyes of a Gardnerian. Who looks completely like a Mage.

I'm unable to keep from noticing the ears that poke through Nym'ellia's stringy, unwashed hair. Jagged scars run atop edges that were obviously once pointed but were likely cropped in the West. Cruelly cut off by a mob like the one that attacked Olilly. I glance at Nym'ellia's fever-stricken mother and sister, lifting my brow in question.

Some of the girl's belligerent air draws down. "My mother's name is Emberlyyn," she offers with a worried frown, seeming to sense my line of inquiry, "and my sister is Tibryl." She eyes me levelly. "They have the Red Grippe."

"I know," I say. "I had it when I was a child." I spare another glance at Emberlyyn, who is slumped against one of the enormous purple trees, loosely embracing her child. Both are flushed with fever, spots of the Red Grippe illness cruelly fixed around their mouths.

They need Norfure tincture, and soon.

I turn back to Nym'ellia. "Your course is set for Voloi?"

She nods and draws her gold compass from her tunic's pocket. "We're less than a league from the Zonor River." She reads the compass, then jabs her finger toward a line of forest ahead. "That way."

East.

I sheathe my weapons and inhale. "Well, then, let's go." I give her a pointed look, drawing courage from the feel of warm, tingling energy rising once more from the Wand sheathed at my calf. "Let's get to Noilaan," I say. "We'll find my brother and get your mother and sister some medicine."

And pray that, over the past weeks, the Mage grandson of the Black Witch has been fully accepted and integrated into Noilaan's Wyvernguard.

PART ONE

Eastern Realm
One realm month ago

WYVERNGUARD MAGE

Trystan Gardner &
Vothendrile Xanthile

The Wyvernguard
North Wyvernguard Island, Noilaan
Eastern Realm
Sixth Month; longest month of the realm year

Vothendrile

"I hope they blast the Crow to pieces," rune sorceress Heelyn hisses from beside me as we observe the military exercise with a cluster of sapphire-uniformed soldier-apprentices. We're assembled on the obsidian river-level terrace, standing near the massive bas-relief marble dragon sculpture that wraps around the entire base of the Wyvernguard's North Island, a cool breeze gusting in from the expansive Vo River.

Heelyn's words kick up a tumultuous current through my water and wind auras as I watch Trystan Gardner assume an offensive position, his wand raised toward the six Vu Trin soldiers taking battle stances before him, his green-glimmering face a mask of determination. The black-clad sorceresses murmur a shielding spell in unison, swords and blades drawn, their gazes pinned on the Gardnerian.

The wind intensifies. I breathe in its coolness, joining it to my internal weather-based power in an attempt to smooth out my increasingly unsettled emotions over this grandson of the Black Witch I've been charged to guard. By Wyvernguard Commander Ung Li herself.

Her rationale remains unspoken, but I know I've been hand-picked as the soldier-apprentice guard most likely to drive the reviled Mage out.

Sunlight glints off the soldiers' raised rune swords, blades, and stars, the sorceresses ready to deflect Trystan's formidable Level Five magic and strike him down. A magical shield the sorceresses have thrown up adheres to their focused forms, blanketing them in an iridescent sapphire glimmer.

I glance at Heelyn, my friend since childhood and one of Noilaan's most powerful runic sorceresses. Her close-cropped black hair shines in the bright sunlight, the image of a dragon shaved into the side of it, her muscular body tense with loathing. She looks at me expectantly, obviously waiting for my affirmation of her blistering hatred of the Mage—an affirmation I would have supplied all too readily only weeks ago.

Inexplicably vexed, I turn away from Heelyn, my gaze drawn back to Trystan. The familiar storm of conflict rises.

He's truly on our side.

It's been clear from the first night he arrived, even as I fought to deny it, my Wyvern senses and power-empath abilities forcing me to confront the outrageously unexpected.

I struggle to beat back my doubts. The controversy surrounding the Gardnerian's inclusion here is explosive. How could it not be? I fought against it as well—a Crow wanting to fight for the Eastern Realm, the grandson of the Black Witch no less.

How could that be right on any level?

Impossible to accept, just as it's impossible to accept the scattering of other Mages here, the majority of the Wyvernguard wondering if High Commander Vang Troi's formidable powers of reason have come unstrung.

My thoughts fly back to before I met Trystan, when I spearheaded a petition to keep him out. *Thousands* of soldiers and apprentices signed it. And when Vang Troi refused to budge, I organized a protest that both I and my circle of friends were harshly disciplined for. Even though we had the full support of the majority of the Noi Conclave and my people's Zhilon'ile Conclave, including my entire family, as well as Commander Ung Li.

But here Trystan Gardner is, and increasingly, it cannot be denied…

He's on our side.

I can smell it on him—his fearless desire to fight with the East. And his honesty surrounding all of it.

His cursed honesty.

I've struggled to scent a lie on him, just a hint of one. Sought to detect that slight sheen of sweat that almost always accompanies untruths, to hear it in the near imperceptible increase in heartbeat. But…nothing.

My uneasy awareness has persisted throughout the past weeks as I trailed him everywhere. To weapons training, wand sparring, rune-ship navigation, meals. Never once have I sensed a lie on him, even though I searched with an intensity bordering on obsession. To justify the way he's being treated here.

The way *I'm* treating him.

Unease twists my gut, my jaw ticking with tension as I watch Trystan's green eyes go hard, watch him murmuring Roach spells to fill his wand with lethal Mage power. The same power that killed so many Noi'khin.

My family is right, I silently rage. *None of the Crows should be here. Not a one.*

Yes, some of the completely justifiable protests have devolved into abuse, but how could High Commander Vang Troi honestly believe Trystan could *ever* assimilate here, or anywhere in the East?

Still, my unease is like a ceaseless, growing tide.

Every day I've watched Trystan Gardner descend into a protective silence, and it's begun to prick at my conscience. To add to the confusion, he's increasingly shadowed by the equally silent Death Fae, who seem hells-bent on drawing him into their outcast circle.

"Vu Trin, ready your magic," Commander Ung Li calls from the sidelines, her spiked black hair gleaming in the sun, arms crossed in front of her.

Trystan focuses on the soldiers facing him, his eyes narrowing as he raises his wand a fraction higher. An invisible charge sizzles to life around him and spills into my power. Stinging threads of lightning flare over my skin.

"Fire!" Ung Li orders.

Trystan lashes his wand forward.

A blast of storming water shot through with vivid blue lightning bursts from his wand, and the incredible aura of oceanic energy coursing from it hits me like a typhoon.

The water collides with the sorceresses and throws the weapons from their hands as they're driven back, feet skidding across the terrace to its farthest railing, their weapons' runes troublingly shot through with blue lightning. The apprentices surrounding me retreat with cries of alarm as we're hit with stray forks of the Mage's stinging lightning and cyclonic side winds.

I can't help myself. I step forward, the draw of the glorious maelstrom of power impossible to resist. My horns spiral up as I inhale deeply and draw in his energy before it can dissipate. Trystan turns and meets my gaze, an invisible spark passing between us as our power connects, just as multiple bolts of sapphire light suddenly slam into the center of his chest, punching him to the ground.

I whip my head toward the soldiers as every one of them, save Commander Ung Li, throws bolt after bolt of runic power from newly drawn weapons, their expressions turned vicious. The collective emotional energy on the air becomes volatile and murderous, my shifter senses able to pick up every last shred of the rising cloud of fury.

"Die, Crow!" one of the soldiers snarls as she draws back her arm and hurls a silver rune star at Trystan.

I move to throw lightning at the star just as Trystan flicks his wand and his own blue lightning shoots from its tip, deflecting the star into the Vo River.

"Halt!" Commander Ung Li orders as she tosses a rune stone between Trystan and the soldiers. A wall of translucent blue energy blasts from the stone. Two last bolts of runic sorcery slam into the wall and ray out in compact explosions of sparking sapphire light.

Ung Li steps in front of the wall to face the soldiers. She glares at them, her battle-hardened gaze sweeping over everyone assembled. "If you *kill* him," she bites out, "we cannot learn how to subdue Level Five Mage power."

The murderous energy of the crowd is undimmed. I can taste it in the back of my throat. Trystan Gardner remains on his knees, cradling his wand hand, head down, and I can read the intense pain he's in from the way his power is chaotically flaring around his wand arm. There's a large red bruise flaring on his forehead where someone threw a bolt of runic energy directly at his face that triggers a bolt of concern straight down my spine. Concern I'm unable to beat back.

"We'll convene again tomorrow," Ung Li says to the sorceresses with a resentful glance at the Mage on his knees.

Trystan picks up his wand with a shaking hand and rises. "No," he says.

I stare at him, as does everyone else, surprise charging my power with crackling energy.

"I'm ready," Trystan tells Ung Li before setting his hardened gaze back on the sorceresses and readying his wand. "You'll be dealing with an army of Mages just like me when Vogel comes for the East. You need faster runic resonance and better counter-shielding. Because my power flew right into your runes." He looks to Ung Li, stark warning in his tone when the words come. "I threw out only a small portion of my power."

A tremor of fear flashes through the crowd, and I gape at the Gardnerian.

Ung Li frowns at Trystan. "Recalibrate your runes, Noi'khin," she orders the soldiers, not taking her eyes off him. "Prepare for Mage attack."

It's late when I escort Trystan to his Wyvernguard room.

He's silent the entire walk back, and I struggle to ignore the way he's clutching his wand arm. The guttering blue rune-fire torches that line the corridor's obsidian stone walls highlight his bruised face, his expression rigid with pain.

"What happened to you?" Sylla Vuul the Death Fae asks from the thick webs hanging above the hallway outside their rooms. I glance up to find Sylla's dark-hued and multi-eyed human face peering down at us from atop a large black spider body, concern in every one of her many eyes.

The Death Fae are somewhat recent arrivals themselves, Ung Li's housing of Trystan near one of them a blatant attempt to frighten him away.

Trystan meets Sylla's gaze briefly, as if only half seeing her through his haze of intense pain. Pain I sense lashing through his power, Trystan's wand arm in agony. I uneasily imagine that it's covered in one solid, flaming bruise.

"It's nothing," Trystan says before opening the door to his room, slipping inside, and closing it, his storming energy palpable through the door, flaring to tempestuous heights.

My throat goes dry as the backflow of Trystan's power cyclones through my own. I turn to Sylla, who has morphed back to full spider, accusation in her dark eyes. I have trouble holding that level stare. I look back toward Trystan's door.

"He fights for the East," she says, her deep tone resonating through me.

I swallow, my own power flaring into a tempest to match Trystan's as I fight against her words. Against the ramifications of those words. Everyone I'm close to here is dead set against Trystan Gardner's presence in the Realm, much less the Wyvernguard. My whole family, including my Zhilon'ile Regent father and most of the people in Zhilaan are dead set against both.

It should be an easy choice to continue to shun him.

My magic roiling, I turn back to Sylla, who has morphed fully to human save her eight eyes. The censure leaves her gaze and her expression turns deeply mournful. "Oh, Vothendrile. You fear him so."

A cornered defiance rises, my invisible aura lashing out at Sylla. Unlike most of the Wyvernguard, I don't mind the mysteriously powerful Death Fae and have formed something of an odd bond with Sylla Vuul, but sometimes her bizarre philosophizing is too much. "You think I fear him?" I snap. "My power equals his."

Sylla smirks, which is a surprisingly disconcerting expression on that multi-eyed face of hers. "You forget that I can read you," she chides, a forceful undercurrent entering her tone. "It's not his magic you fear. It is something far more powerful."

"All right, Sylla." The pent-up storm of emotion surrounding this Mage breaks loose. "Go ahead and tell me," I demand. "Tell me *exactly* what it is that I fear."

Sylla narrows every last one of her eyes with the focus of the ultimate predator, her darkness pulling in around us both and sending a chill down my spine. But still, I stand firm in the face of it.

"You fear," Sylla says, with the unflinching candor of the Death Fae, "that he's telling the truth."

Trystan

He likes men.

I realized this about my dragon-shifter guard, Vothendrile, straightaway.

It's on full display right now as I watch Vothe brazenly flirt with stunningly handsome Basyl Hollen. These observations are trivial, I realize, compared with what I'm faced with. With what the East is faced with. But still, I can't help being drawn in by these glimpses of Vothe's private life.

Vothe and the Elfhollen soldier are reclining against a gleaming stone wall only a few handspans away from where I'm seated in the Wyvernguard's black-walled dining chamber. Basyl's storm-gray fingers stroke Vothe's muscular arm, lingering a beat too long, a suggestive spark of lightning flashing in Vothe's eyes—eyes that are locked on to Basyl's arresting silver gaze.

Lightning forks chaotically through my lines, warmth blooming at the base of my neck. It's stunning to witness, their sultry flirtation so recklessly out in the open—something that would have resulted in imprisonment in Gardneria.

I try not to let my gaze linger on the way Vothendrile idly fondles a long strand of Basyl's pale slate hair. The way he *looks* at Basyl, the veins of white lightning that traverse Vothe's skin forking with heated interest. I can practically feel the crackle of magic in his Wyvern gaze, and Basyl's stare is just as thick with playful desire.

Why wouldn't it be?

Vothe is a midnight storm come to life.

My affinity lines tighten as a melancholy longing sweeps in. Why did they have to assign me such an outrageously attractive guard? He's so dauntingly beautiful, with his lightning-laced onyx skin, his silver-tipped black hair, and dark eyes with their dangerous Wyvern pupils. His perfect, angular features. His perfect, angular body.

And my power is drawn to Vothe's with the force of a blasted tide. I struggle to avert my gaze and ignore the draw of his power, but it's frustratingly impossible.

Basyl's teasing laugh sounds as his palm slides down Vothe's broad chest in a light caress, a harder spike of futile longing tightening my throat.

Vothe has no dearth of fawning admirers. All so cloyingly sympathetic that he has to guard the dangerous, reviled grandson of the Black Witch who they are intent on driving out. Even women moon over Vothe, many staring intently as he passes. Especially when he partially shifts, onyx horns spiraling up from his thick hair. And once, his black wings on full display, fanning out from his back. I momentarily lost the ability to breathe at the glorious sight.

The men who are so inclined are so open about their desire for him that it's both shocking and fascinating, every playful touch and inviting look stunning to witness. Because there's no danger in it here. No shame. Nothing in the dominant religion to condemn it.

And sometimes, I can't help but hate them all for being so uncomplicated about who they are. Hate their sense of safety and privilege as they shut me firmly out. And despise their blaring ignorance about what my whole life has been like.

I let out a long sigh and meet the world-weary, black gaze of Viger Maul, the tall, pale Death Fae sitting across from me who has surprisingly become friends with Tierney Calix. I turn and meet the inky eyes of petite Sylla, who sits by my side, a weighty understanding in her spider-shifter gaze that has been, at times, a lifeline here. The silent Death Fae are the only apprentices willing to sit with me at meals, even though they never partake of any food.

It's a quiet showing of solidarity, and it touches me deeply.

Even the poisonous black snake twining around my neck and the gentle brush of spiders' legs along my ankles are bizarrely comforting, as I can sense my Death Fae companions' intention.

Staunch acceptance, in defiance of a realm determined to mark me an outcast.

I try to remember that, outcast or no, I'm here to fight for the East alongside my family and friends, even if I can't be with them at the moment. I'm here to fight the horrors of the West so that others can have a future worth having. And if I'm not accepted here, so be it.

The snake's purple tongue flickers against my cheek as my eyes are drawn, once more, toward Vothendrile through the faint, dark mist that often swirls around the Death Fae. Basyl reaches up, threads his fingers through Vothe's silver-tipped hair, and pulls him into a sultry, farewell kiss.

Invisible lightning kicks up in my lines and crackles toward Vothe.

His eyes open and meet mine. A spark detonates, leaping between us as he breaks the kiss, and I swear I can see lightning flash in Vothe's eyes before he quickly averts his gaze. But Vothe's expression is more subdued now. Tight with tension.

You're such a mystery, I consider, feeling tangled up in this frustrating draw that has residual lightning flashing up and down my lines in a stinging rush.

And Vothe's demeanor...it's changing around me.

The change is subtle, but there. He's no longer purely hateful...more *conflicted*. I catch his looks of curiosity and scrutinize him right back.

Like I'm scrutinizing him right now.

I ponder how Vothe's sniping bursts of sarcasm aren't as frequent. How, when the stray barb does come, it's as if Vothe is defending himself against some new threat. Each time, I pare back my own acid reply, refusing to let Vothe know his biting words cut me to the quick.

Basyl departs, leaving the ever-surrounded Vothe momentarily alone. I bid Viger and Sylla farewell, angling my arm to prod Viger's serpent to slither down and return to him as the spiders scuttle off me and back to Sylla. Then I get up, step through the Death Fae mist, and approach my cursedly dazzling guard.

Vothe loses his faint smile, his neck tensing.

"It's time," I say, my words clipped as I hold up my small runic time-orb. "I've weapons training."

That increasingly familiar look of conflict flares in Vothe's gaze, his eyes briefly turning a dazzling silver that threatens to breach my composure.

"Well, then," Vothe says, his expression remote, "we'd best not keep them waiting."

Vothendrile

"We've got a surprise for the Crow."

I flinch inwardly at Heelyn's use of the slur as I stand with her on the same riverside terrace a few days later for weapons' training. It's growing increasingly infuriating, this ceaseless hurling of *Crow* and *Roach* at Trystan Gardner, my own use of the slurs having rapidly dropped away. They scrawl them on his belongings. On walls. And always, Trystan meets the abuse with his same stoic, unflappable facade. But I can sense past it. I can read in Trystan's power how much it all wounds him, and I'm increasingly troubled by this.

"I agree that he shouldn't be here," I say, "but he genuinely wants to aid the Vu Trin, so maybe everyone should stop calling him that." It's becoming exasperating, her dogged hatred. I'm exasperated with the entire Wyvernguard these days. And vexed with myself.

Heelyn seems taken aback but shakes it off, a sly, conspiratorial look sliding over her features. "We blocked his wand."

I freeze. My gaze snaps toward where Trystan is getting ready to square off against ten soldiers, my pulse kicking up. Trystan is about to be seriously injured.

"Ready your weapons!" Commander Ung Li commands.

A storm bursts to life inside my power, and I'm unable to hold my protest back.

"Wait!" I call out and step toward Ung Li, heart thudding. Not able to look at Trystan. Inwardly cursing him for what I'm about to do.

But it's not fair to give him a blocked wand. It's *absolutely unfair.*

"He's got a blocked wand," I inform Ung Li, hyperaware of Heelyn's furious glare knifing into my back.

Ung Li scowls at me as she holds out her hand toward Trystan, and I feel her ire like a spitting storm, directed at me and all the apprentices at my back. "Give me your wand, Trystan Gardner," she orders.

Outrage sweeps through my fellow apprentices. Outrage directed at *me.*

Trystan strides forward and passes over the wand. Ung Li runs her rune-marked hands over its slim surface, then grips it in both fists before closing her eyes and murmuring a spell. The runes on her hands brighten from black to sapphire, her fists raying out a flash of blue light. She opens her eyes, unmistakably infuriated. Her gaze rakes over us, and I wait as my internal power storms into chaos.

"Hand me a new wand," Ung Li directs her Vu Trin assistant, the black-clad Fir Yyo.

Fir Yyo retrieves a new weapon, gives it to Ung Li for inspection, then proffers it to Trystan, her cold, wary manner making it clear that she views him as an evil she must endure.

"Mage Gardner," Commander Ung Li says, casting a glare his way, "I'll check your weapons myself from now on."

I can read the devastation storming through Trystan's power, even though he keeps his expression carefully blank. "Yes, Commander Ung Li," he responds with a Noi salute, fist to his uniformed chest. Ung Li's formidable stare flicks over the gesture with obvious disdain.

My heart lodges in my throat. *This is wrong.*

It was wrong of Heelyn and whoever else was involved. They could have killed him.

When he's genuinely here to fight on our side.

"You helped me. Why?" Trystan asks that evening when we reach his barrack's door.

I hesitate as I struggle to suppress my power's draw toward him and can sense him doing the same. "Because I know you're telling the truth," I admit. "I know you're here to fight with us."

Trystan nods and we both grow silent, our power contained. Forcefully. Barely.

Trystan pulls in a breath, regarding me squarely. "Thank you, Vothe," he says, our eyes locked, and something about the way he says my name sends a tremor up my spine.

He closes the door, and I hesitate, feeling flustered. I can sense Sylla Vuul's eyes on me from somewhere inside the hallway's dark tunnel of webs. Not wanting to hear her annoyingly blunt Death Fae truths at this moment, I turn on my heel and stride from the hall toward the barrack's central spiraling staircase. Trystan's night guard is visible below, talking to another Noi sorceress, an odd animosity riding on the air.

"Are you a Mage lover now?" a familiar voice sounds, and I turn to find Heelyn leaning against a torchlit wall, arms crossed. Clearly lying in wait for me.

I huff out a sigh, having known this reckoning would come. Heelyn is not one to back down from a confrontation. Ever.

"No, Heelyn," I shoot back as blue torchlight flickers over us both. "I'm a lover of fairness. Trystan Gardner is here to fight on our side. You could have killed him."

Heelyn's dark gaze turns incendiary. "So, you think he should be here now?"

Traitor.

She doesn't need to voice the word. It hangs in the air between us, thrusting me into turmoil. I'm clear on where this path could lead. It could set me against all my friends and family. Against the Wyvernguard hierarchy and the majority of the Noi Conclave. I think of my uncle Sholin, cast out of Zhilaan when he befriended and then bonded to a Mage.

"I don't know what to think, Heelyn," I say, my power churning.

We glare at each other for a protracted, excruciating moment.

"Choose, Vothe," Heelyn seethes. "Choose carefully. You align with a Crow and our friendship is *over*. Align with a Crow, and every last one of us will want you gone. Even Ung Li wants him gone. And I don't think she'd shed any tears if we blast the Roach to smither—"

"Really, that's enough," I snarl as my horns spiral up.

A look of pain crosses Heelyn's features, and it cuts me to the core. "Have you forgotten that my parents were killed by Gardnerian Roaches?"

Her words are like a blow to my gut, my voice splintering when it comes. "I know they were, Heelyn."

"Then renounce him!" she growls. "Get back on the right side of things!"

"And what side would that be?" I wish I could take back the dangerously honest words as soon as they leave my mouth.

Heelyn is gaping at me now. "What's happening to you, Vothe?" She shakes her head as tears sheen her eyes. "I don't even know who you are anymore." And then she turns and strides away, leaving me alone to wrestle with the violent tempest growing inside me.

Sylla Vuul's spidery legs click against the stone floor as she rounds the hallway's corner.

I don't even turn. "Leave me be, Sylla," I snap, before making my way down the spiral stairs and out into the night.

ASRAI WAR

Tierney Calix

The Wyvernguard
South Wyvernguard Island, Noilaan
Eastern Realm
Sixth Month

Where in all the hells are you, Elloren?

Tierney stares out over the Vo River, leaning on the stone railing that edges the terrace encircling the base of the Wyvernguard's South Island, a twin to the dragon encircling the North Island. The late-afternoon sky, overcast with low-slung clouds, mirrors Tierney's brooding mood.

The Vo's water-power aura encircles Tierney, beckoning to her with joyful abandon. But her kindred river's loving embrace isn't enough to fight off the unease rippling through her. Because, even though Tierney has been assured by the Vu Trin that her powerless friend Elloren is being ushered east by a Noi military contingent, well over a month has passed since she last saw her and still…no Elloren in sight.

Tierney has sent her kelpies on covert missions to look for El-loren, but they've turned up nothing, just as they've been unable to find that trace of Shadow power Tierney so clearly sensed touching down on the Vo.

Something is *wrong*.

Tierney knows it, deep in her gut.

She fears the worst, especially after hearing the horrifying news of her friend Yvan Guriel's death—and that he was not Yvan Guriel at all, but Yvan Guryev, his true identity unknown even to those closest to him.

Tierney blinks rapidly, suppressing the tears threatening to mist her eyes.

Did you know who Yvan truly was, Elloren? And do you know that he's been slain by Vogel's forces?

Are you even alive?

A water aura whips against Tierney in a powerful lash, seizing her attention. She can sense the irritation running through the magic. Irritation that triggers her own.

"Are we interrupting your reverie, Soldier-Apprentice Calix?" A domineering male voice sounds from across the large, curving terrace.

Tierney grits her teeth and turns, sighting her young, deep-blue hued division commander, the vastly infuriating and unforgivably spectacular-looking Fyordin Lir, glowering at her from a distance away. The rest of her Wyvernguard Asrai Fae Division peers questioningly at her from where they stand spread out in a line on the terrace's broad expanse, clearly waiting for her to join the military exercises. Asra'leen Filor'ian, Tierney's rainbow-flecked, white-foam-haired lodging mate, glances from Tierney to Fyordin and back, a cautioning expression on her gentle face, which Tierney flagrantly ignores. *Diplomacy be damned.*

Tierney glares at Fyordin and blows her own invisible rush of magic into the power he's lashing at her, blasting it back, but she's unable to push it clear through him and into the Vo River. Because, to Tierney's immense frustration, the Vo has claimed both her and Fyordin as its guardians. As a result, their formidable water powers are damnably equal in strength.

"No, Division Commander Lir," Tierney replies with a caustic and pointedly exaggerated military formality. "Asrai'lir Tierney Calix, reporting for duty." She strides across the distance between them, hating how Fyordin's mesmerizingly handsome face is the same rippling deep blue as the Vo. The same hue as hers.

Sometimes, like right now, Tierney wants to tear her hair out over how drawn she is to Fyordin Lir. Because he's an arrogant ass of a Fae.

Even if he is… Tierney is loath to admit…a passably competent division commander.

Fuming and battling her exhaustion from weeks of rigorous weapons training, Tierney grabs a Noi rune stone from the outdoor weapons stand and takes her place in the line of Water Fae between Asra'leen and willowy Ra'in.

I'll be damned if I let you see how close to the breaking point you've pushed me, she privately snarls at Fyordin. Because push her he does, in every conceivable way. Seems to relish it, even, singling her out more than any other Asrai.

Fyordin stalks in front of them, his stride long and purposeful, his expression military remote. But Tierney can sense his attention on her, as it always seems to be lately, his water power lapping against hers with singular focus. Frustratingly, her own power is also drawn toward Fyordin instead of where it should be—toward the Noi rune stone in her hand.

"Asrai'kin," Fyordin booms, a gravity in his lake-blue eyes that kindles Tierney's nerves, her attention sharpening. "The Vu Trin have received intelligence from the Western Realm. The Mage forces have begun massing along the Central Desert's western border."

A ripple of tension streams through the entire division's water-power aura.

"Their push east is imminent," Fyordin states, his posture combative. "But when they advance toward our realm, we'll be there to meet them alongside the Vu Trin legions gathering along the desert's eastern edge." He stills, his eyes narrowing on them with lethal intensity. "We'll blast their dragons from the sky. We'll meet them with storm and fury." He straightens. "Asrai'kin, we deploy the day after Xishlon. Let us commence."

Fyordin strides to one side, his movements strong and fluid as Tierney's muscles tense, the will rising within her to go head-to-head with the Mage forces and send killing waves over every last legion. But then another, even stronger pull eddies conflict through her.

She glances toward the Vo River's huge expanse, a pang gripping her heart. Because as much as Tierney wants to go West and fight the Mages, she doesn't want to leave her kindred river unprotected. Increasingly, the idea of leaving the Vo feels like surrendering her heart.

"Draw on your Asrai'myyr!" Fyordin bellows, wresting Tierney's attention back to him.

Gripping her rune stone, she pulls on its sizzling flow of elemental amplification power. Then she lifts her other hand, palm out to the river, along with the entire line of Asrai, and draws on her river's power. A cool, potent current of it streams into her in a glorious, invigorating rush.

My sweet river.

She can sense Fyordin's connection in it, part of the river's power tethered to him. She stiffens, striving to wall off Fyordin's aura as she gathers the Vo's energy.

"Deploy your Asrai'myyr!" Fyordin charges.

A line of waterspouts explode into being along the river's surface, most thin and compact, Asra'leen's a slender, reverse waterfall encircled by glittering rainbows as it spouts white foam high into the sky.

Tierney hurls her gathered power toward her palm, pulse quickening in a flash of panic as she catches the backflow of Fyordin's kindred power in it. Their combined energy blasts from her hand to the Vo and forms a thick waterspout, its violently churning column of water thrusting up to collide with the low-slung clouds above. It whirls wider and wider in a strengthening typhoon, consuming all the other waterspouts in its chaotic, lashing pillar.

"Draw down your power!" Fyordin snarls as he stalks toward her.

Tierney yanks her hand down and drops the rune stone, severing her connection to the spout, the quick break feeling like the slash of a whip against the underside of her skin as Fyordin's power slingshots through her and back to him. The waterspout falls apart with a huge splash that slaps onto the terrace, drenching all of the assembled Asrai.

Soaked through and breathing hard, Tierney reluctantly turns to find Fyordin's eyes storming with fury as he stares her down. "Control your water sourcing, Asrai!"

"I didn't mean to draw on your power," Tierney growls back. "It just *happened*."

Fyordin's gaze turns cyclonic. "No. You *let it* happen. Control your power, Soldier-Apprentice Calix, as we've practiced. Or you will not deploy!"

Anger ignites in Tierney, fierce and tidal. "You're supposed to be teaching me how to control it! What we've practiced *isn't working*!"

Fyordin's magic slashes through hers as their joint aura rampages around them. A dark cloud breaks free of Tierney's control to form over her head.

She curses under her breath as Fyordin eyes the cloud with obvious aggravation. He takes another confrontational step toward her, his water-slicked face less than a handspan from hers. "It's not working because you're acting *against* my power, not with it," he seethes. "You're trying to claim the Vo River as yours and yours alone when it has claimed us *both*. Put the river before your petty territorial dispute. The Vo decides who it bonds to. *Not you*."

Tierney glares at him, thrust into emotional chaos over being river-bonded to someone as infuriating as Fyordin. Someone so intractably prejudiced against all Gardnerians, including her beloved Gardnerian friends and adoptive family who recently immigrated to Voloi. "You're the last person on Erthia I want to share the Vo with," she lashes out, crystal clear that she's crossed the line into insubordination.

"I'm well aware," he snarls back, his power a riptide. "But the fact remains—true Asrai do not work *against* their waters!"

"I'm sick of you insinuating I'm not a true Asrai!"

"Then *behave* like one!"

The cloud above Tierney's head spits out threads of lighting. "You want me to work with your power?" she fumes, moving toward him. "Fine, Fyordin."

Incensed beyond reason, Tierney grips Fyordin's muscular upper arm. Wresting hold of their joint power, she raises a palm to the sky and hurls it upward, whipping the clouds into motion.

The sky darkens to roiling slate, then darkens further as the cloud frenzy blows out fierce gusts of wind. The Vo's waves grow choppy as countless bolts of lightning scythe down over the river, the Wyvernguard, and the city of Voloi in a series of explosive, dazzling white *cracks.*

Stunned, Tierney gasps and releases Fyordin just as he reaches up to grab hold of her in turn, his grip firm around her upper arms, the anger in his eyes vanished, only a look of astonishment remaining as torrential rain breaks out over the city.

"That was extraordinary," Fyordin breathes as their powers cyclone around each other.

"Asrai Fae'kin!" a voice booms, and they turn.

A soldier is striding toward them, sharp face unforgiving. "You are both summoned to Commander Ung Li's chambers *immediately.*"

Ung Li's eyes belie her calm demeanor as their spike-haired commander stares at them from behind her indigo, dragon-marked desk in her tower chambers.

"Commander Lir and Apprentice Calix," she says. "Are you not sworn to protect Noilaan?" Her mouth is set in a tight line, as if she's restraining herself from killing them both.

"We are," Tierney answers in unison with Fyordin as their

water powers covetously eddy toward each other. Tierney yanks her power back, enraged and flustered by his damned Asrai effect on her. She shoots Fyordin a sidelong glare to find his lip giving a slight, obnoxious lift that makes her want to blast magic at his ridiculously handsome face.

"Does raining lightning down on Voloi seem like something you would do to *protect* it?" Ung Li inquires.

Remorse spears through Tierney.

"No, Nor Ung Li," both she and Fyordin answer as Tierney fights the urge to shoot him another glare.

"Commander Lir," Ung Li states, clasping her hands on the desk before her. "I'm relieving you of your position as Commander of the Asrai Division."

Tierney can feel the sudden undertow of outrage rip through Fyordin's power.

"Nor Ung Li," he says, his deep voice forcibly measured, "if I erred in pushing Apprentice Calix too hard, it's simply because she is one of the most powerful Asrai in the Vu Trin forces. Like myself, she is bound to the largest river in all of Erthia—"

"Which is why," Commander Ung Li states, "when you continue to train together, you need to *pace* yourself."

"Wait," Tierney blurts, forgetting herself. "Did you just say 'continue to train together'?"

Ung Li narrows her blade-sharp glare at Tierney. "Yes. You'll deploy west together the day after Xishlon. I'm assigning you both the new, equal rank of Fae Military Advisors. You two are the most powerful Asrai in our forces and are equally bonded to the largest river on Erthia, so it makes sense to match you in military authority. An uneven rank is proving detrimental to you both and possibly Noilaan, as well." She fixes her attention back on Fyordin. "Your initial efforts will be directed toward working with Advisor Calix as she hones her vast power." She levels another glare at Tierney. "Work *together*." She sighs, her expression losing some of its rigidity. "We need *both* of you in this fight, Asrai'kin."

Tierney looks down, humbled to be so rapidly elevated in rank and deeply cognizant that she's forgotten herself during the last few trainings. Forgotten what's important. As infuriating as it is to admit, Fyordin is right in this one thing. *I need to work with the Vo, not against it.*

And suddenly, Fyordin's power is rippling around her in a different way. Almost tentative. Almost...gently.

Tierney swallows, unsettled. She ventures a look at Fyordin to find him doggedly focused on Commander Ung Li even as his water power remains wholly fixated on Tierney.

"I'm pleased to work with Advisor Calix," Fyordin states.

Commander Ung Li eyes him. "Share your military expertise, Advisor Lir." Her gaze flashes. "But if there are any more out-of-control lightning strikes, I'll discipline you both." She fixes her attention on Tierney. "Advisor Calix, take this evening off from Asrai training to reflect on what it means to work *with* your fellow Vu Trin instead of *against* them." She holds out a formal summons, and Tierney accepts it. "For the remainder of the day, you're to report to Or'myr Syll'vir's geomancy laboratory. He's just returned from Northern Noilaan and it seems he's in need of water power. He's been informed of your elevation in rank." She stares down each of them again. "You're both dismissed."

As Tierney shoves the summons into her tunic's pocket, she doesn't look at Fyordin, finding the gentle touch of his water power in this moment to be more unnerving than the angry lash of it. She salutes Ung Li and strides out the door.

"Tierney," Fyordin calls as she stalks down the torchlit hallway. His normally dominant voice seems unsure, which whips up Tierney's unsettled emotions even further.

Ignoring him, she makes her way up several spiraling staircases toward Or'myr Syll'vir's laboratory.

Tierney barges into the purple-lit geomancy lab with the force of an incoming typhoon, her emotions a roiling mess. The tall, young rune sorcerer she finds there pauses in scribbling something down in a notebook and meets her confrontational glare.

She looks over his purple-hued, point-eared form, her attention snagging on his out-of-place deep-green eyes. They shine like beacons against the overwhelming purpleness of both him and practically everything in this laboratory, the cramped space cut right into a swath of violet stone at the pinnacle of the Wyvernguard's South Island.

His Vu Trin uniform is outrageously tinted purple, and the tables of his cluttered lab are covered with lilac crystals and stones, along with a smattering of dark stones imprinted with glowing lavender runes. There's something familiar about him. So familiar, she feels flustered by her inability to place her finger on it.

Or'myr Syll'vir holds her gaze, showing none of the unsettled intimidation Tierney is so often met with. Instead, he seems oddly arrested.

"You'd be Tierney Calix, I'm assuming," he says, a smile playing at the corner of his mouth. "I'm Or'myr Syll'vir, as you probably read on the summons. I'm to be your geomancy lab partner for a few days. I need to channel some strong water magic into weaponry—" he gestures loosely around the lab "—and, well, they tell me you're a bit gifted in that department." He extends a hand. "It's a pleasure to meet you."

The warmth in his expression triggers Tierney's defenses. She's tired of this game, played over and over, being initially met with friendliness until people find out she has her own mind— a mind that won't always obey their rigid rules.

She does not take his hand.

Instead, she crosses her arms. "Well, Or'myr," she says with open challenge in her tone, "you should know, up front, that I'm somewhat shunned here."

He cocks a brow and lowers his hand. "Are you really?"

Tierney feels herself becoming entrenched as she stares him down. "Yeah, I am. Because Trystan Gardner is my closest friend here. And Elloren Gardner is my *best* friend. I've been informed by a number of people that I'm hopelessly polluted in my alliances." Her gaze flits pointedly around his well-outfitted lab. "You seem to have some influence. So, just know that you're likely to harm your social standing if you work with me."

Or'myr lets out a short laugh, a glint of mischief in his eyes. "I'm no stranger to controversy. Seeing as I'm a grandson of the Black Witch."

Tierney's thoughts sputter. She gapes at him, everything familiar about him falling into stark place.

Elloren.

He looks just like Elloren.

A hint of challenge lights Or'myr's green gaze. "My middle surname is Gardner," he states evenly. "My mother had an affair with Edwin Gardner that she refuses to renounce. Because she was madly in love with him. So, Advisor Calix, your tendency toward forbidden affections does little to put me off."

Tierney places a hand squarely on one hip, feeling overtaken by surprise. "You'd be Elloren's cousin, then?" She blinks at him, drawn in by Elloren's own features, so disarmingly striking on a male face.

"Correct," Or'myr confirms as they stare at each other in the cluttered lab. Flustered, Tierney glances at the multitude of wands crafted from the myriad of purple woods strewn about, as well as a sizable number of charged rune stones from a plethora of cultures—including Gardnerian. He's clearly a proponent of magical mixing, this green-eyed geosorcerer, countless grimoires from all the lands haphazardly stacked throughout the laboratory.

She tilts her head. "You're a bit of your own mind, aren't you?" Delight rises at the prospect.

"And you seem like an out-and-out rebel, Asrai," Or'myr returns, his lips ticking up.

And then they're grinning at each other as Tierney is swept up in a feeling her misanthropic heart rarely encounters— instant like.

Tierney's rakish grin wavers, something deeper taking root. "I think we're going to get on quite well, Vu Trin Syll'vir."

His smile broadens. "Call me Or'myr. It's a pleasure to meet you, Advisor Calix."

"Call me Tierney," she returns, her expression taking on a more serious cast. "Or'myr...have they let you meet Trystan? Does he even know he has family here?"

He frowns. "I suspect he's heard of me by now. But no, they have not let me meet my own cousin. Even though I've petitioned Ung Li quite relentlessly." He glances out his lab's oval window, toward the Wyvernguard's North Island, a weighted tension taking hold. "If it goes on much longer, I've a mind to force the issue and just go over there."

"Have you heard what's going on?" Tierney presses, unable to suppress the outrage sparking in her tone. "How he's being called a Crow and a Roach..."

"I have, in fact," Or'myr answers. "I have some familiarity with those types of things myself." He gives her a poignant look. "Is Trystan the type who can work past it? To focus on the fight we should all be united in?"

Their gazes lock and hold, and Tierney feels her own leagues-deep pain stir. "I have trouble with that myself, sometimes," she admits, and Or'myr looks closely at her, as if surprised by her candor.

"It's hard for us all sometimes," he allows.

Tierney eyes him with some disbelief. "You're...ridiculously magnanimous."

"Not really," Or'myr counters. "I dislike most people and am generally in a bad mood."

Tierney lets out a short laugh at this. "Then you and I should get on famously." She glances around the purple-lit lab. "Shall we commence drawing water power into stones and runic weaponry?"

"So that we can drag Vogel and his forces down into a watery death?" Or'myr rejoins with a wicked smile.

Tierney grins and raises her palm, pulling in a deep breath as she forms a churning, lightning-spitting ball of water to hover just above her hand. "Yes. That. The fight we should all be united in. Let's get to work. And after that, you can repay me by being my alibi."

Or'myr lifts a sardonic brow. "So you can commit crimes?"

She bobs her head side to side. "Mmm...more like...*transgressions*. I'm going to break the rules, Or'myr. And go see Trystan. And I think you should come with me."

He gives her an arch look. "If I break the rules and go see him, I'll likely just get a stern reprimand and a demotion. *You*, on the other hand, could get yourself kicked out of here."

Tierney waves her summons at Or'myr, flashing him a sly smile. "I think not," she purrs. "We both have a great deal of power that the Vu Trin need. As does Trystan, whether they want to admit it or not."

CHAPTER THREE

SHIFTING STORM

Vothendrile Xanthile

The Wyvernguard
North Wyvernguard Island, Noilaan
Eastern Realm
Sixth Month

I realize something is up the moment I spot the kelpie peering at me from the waters of the night-dark Vo. I push away from where I'm leaning against the dragon sculpture encircling the island's base as I'm hit by auras of both water power and violet geomancy. It's coming from the river and aimed toward where Trystan stands by the lower terrace's stone railing.

Defensive power rises inside me as a young woman made of water suddenly leaps over the railing, her form glittering in the moonlight. She rapidly solidifies as she turns, extends her hand, and helps the geomancer Or'myr Syll'vir over the railing to stand beside her.

I can sense Trystan's shock as well as his close bond with this

Fae, who must be Tierney Calix. Both she and Or'myr Syll'vir look me up and down, as if taking my measure.

"Trystan," she says, voice breaking as she moves toward him. Trystan's reverberating surprise collapses into overwhelming relief as they fall into each other's arms and I stare at both Or'myr Syll'vir and Tierney in disbelief over their sheer audacity.

I know of Or'myr, this cousin of Trystan's whom he's never met. And Sylla Vuul has told me of Tierney Calix, the Asrai who fled East with Trystan. The rebellious Water Fae who refuses to disavow him and who the Wyvernguard hierarchy have lodged on the Wyvernguard's South Island to keep them apart. To isolate Trystan from his closest friend here.

Part of me can't help but be impressed. She's breaking some serious rules. Or'myr too.

I'm duty bound to turn them both in. And yet…discomfort twists inside me as I read the full force of Trystan's misery and isolation breaking free as he embraces his Asrai friend, her affection for him a touching force.

She pulls back, tears shining in her eyes as she gestures to Or'myr. "Trystan," she says, voice rough with emotion, "this is your cousin, Or'myr Syll'vir."

I feel Trystan's rush of amazement, his eyes widening as he meets Or'myr's gaze. Or'myr's invisible geomancy aura bursts to life around him in a fitful, violet glow.

"My cousin?" Trystan repeats as raw emotion pulses through his magic.

"I'm Edwin's son," Or'myr acknowledges, seeming overcome, as well. He extends his hand. "It's so good to meet you, cousin."

The pang cutting through me intensifies as tears glint down Trystan's face and he takes his cousin's hand for the first time. I know the Wyvernguard hasn't even allowed Trystan to see his Lupine brother, part of the newly established pack of the northeastern forest. They also haven't allowed Trystan to meet with any of the family he has here in the East. I stood guard behind

Trystan as Ung Li informed him of their existence, the news seeming to rock him to the core.

Trystan, Or'myr, and Tierney all cast surreptitious glances at me, then brazen ones, as if silently daring me to turn them in. I meet Trystan's defiant look.

I could get myself kicked out of the Wyvernguard for not reporting this. But I realize… I'm not going to report it. Because it's *wrong*, the way they've been isolating him. He's on our side. They're all on our side. I feel the jolt of disbelief that flashes through Trystan's power as our gazes hold and I don't budge. As I don't make a single move to turn them all in.

Tierney and Or'myr cast me reevaluating looks before they walk with Trystan to the far side of the terrace, talking in low tones, so wrapped up in their conversation they seem to forget that I have shifter senses.

Senses that have me questioning everything I thought I knew about Trystan Gardner.

And there's another thing, I breathlessly consider as I silently escort Trystan back to his room, scenting his flare of emotion. *He's attracted to me, and it's strong.*

"Thank you," Trystan says, his tone stilted as he pauses in his doorway, his power volatile at the edges as it strains toward me. "For letting me see them."

My own power kicks up into a turbulent mess in response to the level of gratitude in his eyes. I give him a tight nod, unable to formulate a response. Because there's something undeniable building here that's confusing and difficult to beat back.

So, for a brief moment, I give in. I hold Trystan's gaze and breathe in his power as the door shuts between us.

CHAPTER FOUR

RIVER BOND RISING

Tierney Calix

The Wyvernguard
South Wyvernguard Island, Noilaan
Eastern Realm
Sixth Month

The next evening, Tierney is once more down by the Vo, lean-ing against the stone railing, the moon gleaming bright, her thoughts on Trystan and the fight to come. Waves splash over the terrace's edge, lapping playfully at her feet, her boots and socks kicked off to allow the longed-for, rejuvenating connection.

The river's smooth water feeds into her Asrai veins, and she breathes in deep, reading the Vo's vast network of tributaries as easily as she can read her own Water Fae form. She stiffens, sens-ing a subtle trace of another power at the edge of that network, hovering to the west—an unnerving hint of Shadow near one of the distant streams. Poised, yet not infiltrating.

Not yet.

A flare of concern bubbles through Tierney, prompting a vow as her eyes fix on the West.

Make one move *into my river's waters, Vogel, and you'll feel the full wrath of my storm.*

But then, along with her bravado, the concern continues to swell. *Vulnerable. My river is vulnerable.*

The yearning rises to have Viger Maul here, his Death Fae stillness surrounding her as she tells him of these fears, as she's increasingly wont to do, his words always few, but his thrall often leaving her with a feeling of deep understanding. She's gotten in the habit of seeking him out, late at night, at the island's base after the evening's last call.

Her gaze slides over Noilaan's translucent protective dome and the line of storms that top the Vo Mountains, the Wyvern-fabricated storm band spitting silvery lightning and roiling with violent clouds. The storm-barrier was recently fortified, and a huge Vu Trin military force has already deployed to the east-ernmost edge of the continent's Central Desert. Another deadly barrier for Vogel to get through.

But what barrier is there to protect my river from invasion?

Troubled, she considers how the Vo will lie wholly unpro-tected when she and thousands of other soldiers deploy west to meet Vogel's forces in the desert lands.

Tierney grimaces, knowing full well that the Vu Trin will need every last shred of Fae power to help them stop the Mage-dom and Alfsigr.

But what will it matter, if Vogel manages to infiltrate the waters?

Tierney's thoughts slide to how she and Elloren used Iron-flowers to block Mage spells what seems like a full lifetime ago.

I could really use your help, Elloren, she opines. *You and I...we're quite good at puzzling things out. I bet we could puzzle out how to shield the rivers. Instead, you've disappeared without a trace. And what I'm sensing is so subtle, I doubt I could get even Fyordin to fully believe me. But...you'd listen.*

Tierney's gaze sweeps from the storm band toward the for-est and the glowing runic border. She frowns as she ponders once more...

Where are you, Elloren?

A small rush of water power ripples around her, flowing over her lines in a gentle caress.

Tierney stiffens. She knows Fyordin's connection to her same bonded river makes it difficult for him to staunch his pull toward her, the same way she has trouble keeping her power from flowing into his, but still, it's irritating. She tightens her grip on the railing, forcibly contracting her aura toward her center as she fights the urge to let her magic eddy through his.

Fyordin comes up beside her, his gaze flicking down toward the water lapping at her bare feet. "Enjoying your freedom from my reign of terror, Advisor Calix?" The amused sarcasm in his tone raises Tierney's hackles even further.

"I am." She shoots him a wry look.

Fyordin returns her sardonic look, cocking one indigo brow. "I've pushed you because you're brilliant and powerful." His domineering voice is tinged with a warmth that rattles Tierney anew. "I'm glad you've some respite this eve. You deserve it." He peers out over the Vo. "You should take time to enjoy the upcoming Xishlon festival, as well."

Xishlon.

She's surprised by his mention of the holiday. It's been a topic of conversation for weeks. The Lavender Moon festival is the biggest of Noilaan's thirteen moon holidays, most soldiers being given all or part of that day off before they deploy.

Tierney stares at the river, acutely aware of the intense way Fyordin's magic is rippling around her. He's a confusing mix of attitudes. So harsh with her during training, repeatedly pushing her until an exhaustion overtakes her that's so fierce all she wants to do is dive into the Vo and be done with the Wyvernguard. But whenever he's not snarling out commands and driving her well past her limits...his magic is so *focused* on her lately. Just like hers is on him, the draw getting stronger and stronger, like two tides determined to crash into each other.

Fyordin's water power touches hers lightly, and Tierney reflexively throws up a rippling wall of magic against it.

"We need to stop this...this trance we fall into with each other," Tierney forces out. "It's our joint bond to the Vo that's fueling it."

His jaw tenses. "I have *tried* to keep my magic in check."

"As have I," Tierney blurts out, barely able to keep hold of her composure.

"I know," he acknowledges, a mounting tension in his aura's flow. "But for me, this has moved beyond our kindred draw. As your commander I wasn't able to voice my interest in you."

Tierney's eyes widen and she blinks at him. "So..." she says, flummoxed, "you're...interested?"

Fyordin pulls his gaze from the Vo and their river-hued eyes meet. "Quite."

Tierney's cheeks flush. She shakes her head. "I never dealt with this type of attention before coming here. Honestly, I don't know how to handle it."

Fyordin's eyes tense questioningly. "You've never had anyone interested in you?"

Tierney suppresses a tingling shiver, all too aware of the masculine lines of Fyordin's body, so close to hers. She swallows, flustered. "I was glamoured from three years of age on to escape Mage attention."

"So...do you have any idea how beautiful you are?"

Tierney's flush deepens, but there's sincerity in his question. She decides to level with him. "No. It's...too big of a switch. And there's too much going on in the world to think about it."

"But you do have a mirror?"

The warmth in Tierney's cheeks spreads to her neck as she considers how she stunned herself this morning when she caught sight of her image in her washroom's mirror, her long hair such a mesmerizing, curly kaleidoscope of deep blues. Her soft, wide features undeniably arresting, her looks and newly curvaceous figure enhanced by the rippling-blue hue that perfectly matches the Vo's entrancing, changeable waters.

Tierney's gaze flicks over Fyordin's spectacular physique, highlighted by his formfitting sapphire Wyvernguard tunic. "You wouldn't understand," she rejoins. "You're used to being ridiculously. attractive."

A knowing gleam enters his gaze.

Tierney averts her eyes, irritated with herself for letting Fyordin's swoony looks fluster her. Because what she does yearn for, when she's not focused on impending war, is a connection that goes far deeper than surface attraction.

"I was glamoured as well for a time," Fyordin says, taking Tierney by surprise. "After my family fled east, we glamoured ourselves to look like Kelts to gain passage through the Central Desert. I was a young child, but I can still access a glamour." Fyordin's eyes go half-lidded, as if he's concentrating deeply. His whole form ripples and loses its blue hue as it rapidly morphs into a brown-haired, hazel-eyed Kelt.

A spectacularly attractive Kelt.

"Sweet gods," Tierney blurts out, giving up on reticence as she boldly looks him over. "No wonder you're so cocky."

Fyordin laughs, then morphs back to Asrai.

"You're quite good at glamouring," Tierney notes with a sigh. "I've no glamour abilities. If I did, I'd demonstrate *exactly* what I was trapped in to avoid wandfasting attention." She regrets the emotional tremor of her voice as soon as the words leave her lips. Her throat clenches, and she looks away from him, mortified by her flare of honesty and the way their power is now rippling around each other.

Fyordin bumps his shoulder lightly against Tierney's, the contact sending a thrilling shiver through her aura. "You might be able to glamour in time," he says, growing serious. "You don't know what you can do, Asrai'lir." He draws back and considers her closely, a warmth in his gaze that deepens Tierney's pulse. "Spend Xishlon with me."

Tierney stills, then cocks a blue brow at him. "Fyordin...our magical draw to each other aside...when you're not barking orders at me, you're debating my loyalty to the Asrai Fae because I'm close friends with Gardnerians. Now you suddenly want me to spend a purple moon holiday with you?"

"I want you to be my Xishlon'vir."

Holy hells.

Tierney blinks at him, unable to form a coherent response.

It's not an idle invitation, to be someone's Xishlon'vir—to kiss someone on the most sacred day in the Noi calendar. The night of the Sacred Lavender Vo Moon, when the Goddess Vo's manifestation of Universal Love reigns supreme. It's considered a great blessing to kiss someone on this night, and it implies the beginning of a serious courtship.

"Aren't we here to fight a war?" Tierney sputters, her thoughts scattering. "How can you swing back and forth from... *Xishlon whimsy* to preparing for the end of the world?"

Fyordin scrutinizes Tierney as if she's a puzzle he's determined to figure out. He pivots against the railing to face her fully. "We deploy soon. We'll likely be at war for a long time. But we have this one Xishlon." He's quiet for a moment, his eyes intent on hers. "I'd like to spend it with you."

Tierney blinks at him, thrown by his bizarre, forthright politeness and all too aware of her flush heating to a scald. "Are you honestly offering, Fyordin Lir?"

"Yes, Tierney Asrai'lir," he answers without hesitation. "I want to kiss you under Vo's purple moon. Or...dive with me, right now, into the depths of the Vo. And let me kiss you there."

Her pulse thudding warm, Tierney considers this. She imagines Fyordin is probably very good at kissing at the bottom of powerful rivers.

And he's right. They'll be in the thick of the fight soon. There isn't a lot of time left for purple moon festivals or kissing at the bottom of kindred rivers, and yet...

It feels empty. Enticing but empty.

Because she doesn't really know Fyordin, save what he looks like and how he barks out commands and utilizes his vast power as a weapon. And she doesn't want her first kiss to be trivial, after having waited this long.

"I... I can't. Not tonight," she says, even as her magic yearns to stream toward his.

Fyordin cocks a brow. "Perhaps another night?" he presses invitingly.

He truly wants me, Tierney considers, the idea surreal. *He's like a maelstrom ripe for the taking.* A shiver runs through her. But still, she holds back. Acutely mindful that there's one young man here who hasn't offered to be her Xishlon'vir. A young man whose offer she shouldn't want. But increasingly, she finds herself imagining what it would be like to kiss *him*.

A glimmering awareness flutters through her mind, perhaps drawn in by her thoughts of Viger Maul. *He's here*, she realizes. *He's been here all the time.*

Surprise lights over being able to sense Viger's Death Fae presence. She turns to find a spot of dark mist forming at the far side of the terrace, his tall, pale form materializing from it, his corporeal presence making her feel a bit breathless.

Fyordin follows her gaze, and Tierney can feel the spike of animosity shivering through his power. "Look at him," Fyordin jibes, as if sensing that Viger has something to do with Tierney's hesitation. "A Death Fae. So obviously besotted with you. Take care, Asrai'kin. There's no such thing as a Death Fae who is truly on the side of this realm. Or any realm."

"Are you saying that they're traitors?" Tierney asks, a defensive flare rising.

"There's a reason the Sidhe Fae courts shunned them. And a reason our religions mark them as evil—"

"Oh, you can stop right there, Fyordin." Tierney shuts him down. "I just came from a place very free with tossing around the 'Evil Ones' label, so don't even try to get me to pin it on anyone here."

Fyordin's power circles protectively around her. Which she doesn't want. She's not interested in being protected. "You're Asrai," he says, his energy taking on a covetous tension. "Just be sure you remember that."

Tierney's ire rises. "And what if I were Deathkin?" she challenges. "Or Gardnerian for that matter?"

"You're not."

"But what if I *were*, Fyordin?" she bites out, beating back her cursed water magic as it makes an attempt to surge toward his incredible power.

Fyordin's lips twitch up. "It's strong, isn't it?"

"What?" Tierney spits out.

"Your attraction to me."

Thrown by his accuracy, Tierney suddenly drops into the sensation of being pulled away from him. She glances in Viger's direction to find the pale Death Fae's focus intent on her, one black brow raised. He morphs to black smoke, disappears, then suddenly appears beside her, a visible aura of dark tendrils encircling him.

Tierney blinks at him. Viger seems almost refined at the moment. No horns or solid-black pools for eyes. His claws retracted. A pair of slim snakes curls around his shoulders and neck, purple tongues flickering.

"Good evening, Viger," Tierney wryly greets him.

Fyordin shoots Viger an unfriendly smile. "Have you pledged fealty to the Vu Trin yet, Death Fae? Recited the Eastern Realm Oath of Protection?"

Viger's eyes flick toward Fyordin. "Death aligns with no one." His tone is as even as windless water.

"See, he admits it," Fyordin says, tossing Tierney a self-satisfied smirk. "No allegiance." He turns back to Viger, resentful energy spitting through his power. "Why are you here, Viger, if you won't state your alliance?" He pointedly surveys Viger's black-tinted soldier-apprentice garb. "Wearing a Wyvernguard uniform—or some approximation of it."

Silence. Not a ripple in it, only the flickering of Viger's snakes' tongues. Tierney can't help but admire that deep-water stillness.

"War is here, Death Fae," Fyordin goads, the muscles of his neck cording. "You need to decide which side you're on."

"The side of the natural world," comes Viger's calm reply.

Fyordin barks out a mocking laugh. "Which you want to kill."

"Yes," Viger says. "In balance."

"How can you fight for something you want to kill?" Fyordin scoffs.

The very air around them darkens, Viger's night-black eyes fixed on Fyordin. "This runs deeper than you can comprehend."

"I'm Asrai, I understand the natural world, Deathkin."

"You understand but one piece of it," Viger counters, his lip curling aggressively. "You dwell in shallow waters, Fyordin Lir. Tierney Calix understands deep waters. The connections."

"I understand deep waters, Deathling," Fyordin throws down, an incensed energy whorling through his power. "I've claimed the Vo."

A hard glint enters Viger's eyes. "That doesn't mean the Vo has fully claimed you."

Shock flashes through Tierney. It's a huge insult to question the Asrai bond to their kindred waters.

Fyordin's eyes go dark as the Vo's depths. "What would you understand of water?"

"I am primordial," Viger fires back without hesitation. "We are intimately bound to the natural matrix."

Anger rushes through Fyordin's power. "Which you want to kill."

Viger's eyes black over, his horns curling up, his teeth elongating and turning black as his lips. He bares them at Fyordin, a vicious glint in his eyes that sends a chill through Tierney's water power. "We *align with Death*. That is what we do."

Fyordin steps toward Viger, and Tierney can sense his power rearing, ready to loose a cyclone straight at the Death Fae. "You seek to kill, and you won't align with the East," Fyordin snarls. "Which makes you a traitor to the natural matrix. And a traitor to Noilaan." He looks at Tierney, storming ferocity in his gaze. "Careful who you align yourself with, Asrai."

Tierney's own power cyclones up, fierce as Fyordin's.

Fiercer.

That's it. Gloves off.

"Just because I won't kiss you," she says, "doesn't make me a traitor, *Fyordin*."

Fyordin's nostrils flare, a jealous heat eddying through his power. "Tierney, you concern me. You spend your free time with Deathkin water horses and Death Fae. You were raised by a Gardnerian family and were spotted with them in Voloi wearing *Gardnerian clothing*. And you have a Gardnerian alias that you refuse to give up. Even though you have an Asrai name."

Pain slices through Tierney. *A name I haven't used since I was three years old. That makes me think of my mother screaming it every time I hear it. Or even think it.*

And there's the matter of how her newly immigrated Gardnerian family is being treated here in Voloi. Kindly by some, but cruel enough by others that Tierney is prompted to stand in blaring solidarity with them. Finding FILTHY ROACH scrawled over their dwelling's outdoor wall whipped up Tierney's defiance so high she threw on Gardnerian blacks and went to town with her adoptive kin.

One foot in the Asrai world, one foot in the Gardnerian.

Fyordin stares Tierney down, his power whipping up almost as tempestuously as hers. "And not only are you friends with Trystan Gardner, but also with his sister, Elloren Gardner. I worry, Tierney, if you've become more Gardnerian than Asrai. You look Fae, but are you a Crow deep down?"

Rage blasts through Tierney at the same time that she's overcome by a heady sense of darkness flashing through her as Viger's black smoke encircles her, his thrall pulsing to life.

"Careful," Viger warns Fyordin, calm as Death, as his poisonous snakes bare their fangs and hiss.

Fyordin doesn't take his eyes off Tierney, his mouth curling down with scorn. "So, you'll have your Death Fae smite me? Because I speak the truth?"

"He's not *my* Death Fae," Tierney snaps back as Viger's thrall engulfs her. She turns to glare at Viger.

Sweet gods, what is going on here?

Viger turns his terrifying stare on Tierney, but she's too incensed to be intimidated by either one of them.

"Get hold of your thrall, Viger," she seethes. "I fight my own battles."

Viger has the audacity to bare his teeth at her in response.

"Really?" Tierney marvels, incredulous. "Are you going to bite me, then?"

Viger's head gives a subtle flinch back, his mouth closing as the black smoke and every sense of his thrall withdraws.

"You two stay here and tear each other to shreds if you want," Tierney snaps as lightning crackles through her internal power. A storm cloud forms above her head, spitting rain as she levels a glare at Fyordin. "Fight your allies, Fyordin Lir. It's what you do best."

"Where are you going?" Fyordin demands.

She takes a confrontational step toward him, fists balled. "To the bottom of the Vo. *Alone.* And, yes, I realize the Vo has claimed you too. But tonight, the Vo is *mine.* Stay out of my waters."

Tierney turns away from them both, leaps onto the railing, dives off, and lets the cool waters of the river close around her.

When she emerges well past midnight, Viger is waiting for her.

He's sitting high up on the tail of the Vo dragon sculpture, the stars above splashed across the sky, the warm breeze a subtle caress. River and air traffic is sparse, the city's lights dampened, the rune-lit terrace deserted.

Tierney pulls herself from the water, throws the wet off herself, then crosses the terrace as Viger silently watches. There's no sense of his thrall. Just that bone-deep silence that so often surrounds him that Tierney suddenly craves.

She climbs onto the dragon sculpture and takes a seat beside him. His horns and teeth are retracted, his snakes absent. But his claws are out. She turns and meets his dark eyes, and he makes no move to pull her into his thrall.

Are you going to kiss him at the bottom of the Vo?

She can sense that Viger's thought escaped him, unbidden, from the sudden tension in his features and how the thought is whisked into oblivion, and she realizes how much fear must be wrapped around her attraction to Fyordin. Or Viger wouldn't have been able to read it in her.

Do Death Fae kiss? Tierney wonders. *Has Viger ever been kissed? And if we're mind-connected by my fears, could I follow that connection into his fears, as well?*

Do Death Fae even have fears?

Feeling reckless, Tierney inhales bracingly and opens herself to her fears—her fear of Vogel's incursion into her waters. Of losing the last of her family to war. Of never being seen for who she truly is. Of falling for Viger Maul. Wave after wave of fears come flooding in, and she senses Viger engaging with them, like a lock clicking open.

She follows the connection into him.

Where a single fear hovers, connecting them, his snake-tongue senses returning to this same fear of his over and over, his thought slipping into her mind.

I want to court you.

Tierney draws back, stunned, as a look of pain flashes across his features and she reads not just this fear, but how much physical desire is wrapped up in it.

Viger turns into dark smoke and begins to drift into the night as Tierney's emotions scrabble for purchase.

"Viger, come back," she calls to the trace of misty black.

The mist vanishes, and an inexplicable sadness wells up in Tierney as she drops from the sculpture.

"Asrai."

Tierney pivots to find Viger leaning against the dragon sculpture, his expression guarded.

"Viger," Tierney offers, feeling awkward yet firm in what she needs from him. "It may be true that...well—" she fidgets, a flush blooming "—that we have some thoughts of interest toward each other." She levels her gaze at him, ignoring her unbidden rise of feeling. "But I need you to be my friend right now. Nothing more. Can you be that for me?"

Viger moves toward her in one smooth, languid movement. He snaps his claws and the entire terrace blinks out of sight, the darkness lit only by a silver mist encasing them. He waits, silent, a slight edge to his hypnotic gaze. But Tierney can tell he's setting aside his feelings for her, and she's impressed by this.

And drawn in.

"I find you deeply alluring," Tierney says. "I'm just going to flat out admit that."

The mist blackens then abruptly silvers into suspended, ill-defined ropes encircling them both. Viger's horns arc up, a wicked gleam entering his eyes. He reaches up, and Tierney draws in a shivering breath as he traces her cheek with one claw tip, light as a feather's brush.

"I don't want to spend Xishlon kissing," Tierney says as she's swept into his thrall, feeling as if the ground is giving way as she tilts toward his dark-clad form. "I want to spend it surveying the waterways."

"I would survey them with you, Asrai," Viger offers, his deep, beckoning voice seeming to come from everywhere at once.

Tierney nods. "I'm worried, Viger. I sense a bigger battle brewing underneath the obvious one." She pauses, suddenly choked up by a swell of emotion for her river. "My bond to the Vo...it might have to come before my desire to fight with the Wyvernguard." She pauses again, scared by her subversive flare of honesty.

Viger's palm comes up and stills over her cheek, his claws a light, sharp pressure on her scalp that sends a blessedly distracting shiver down her spine. "You can tell me, Asrai," he says, voice surprisingly compassionate.

"There's something bigger at stake than dominion over the Realms," Tierney manages as the sense of being suspended in his mist deepens. She takes hold of Viger's arm to gain some sense of purchase, and he slides a hand around to the small of her back, steadying her as he floats her nearer, her body responding to his proximity with a flush of warmth, their lips so close…

What would it be like to kiss a Death Fae?

"Have we disappeared in the mist?" she asks, her breathing uneven.

"Yes, Asrai," he says in a whisper that seems to shudder straight through her.

"Can anyone hear us?"

"No, Asrai," he says, the word *Asrai* sounding delicious on his dark purple tongue.

He has a purple tongue like his snakes, Tierney distantly notes, a bit amused to be admitting her attraction to this surprising trait. *And he smells like cool, summer shadows. In the dark of night…*

"I don't think Vogel can be fought in the obvious way," she says, struggling for composure in the face of Viger's mounting thrall. "And I think the threat he brings is different from anything Erthia has faced before."

"I second this, Asrai," Viger says, his mist darkening further as Tierney takes hold of his other arm, his grip firming on her. "Vogel brings a threat to Death," Viger says, unease rippling through his power.

Tierney eyes him. "How can anything bring a 'threat to Death'?"

He's silent, their eyes locked as they float in the darkness in a loose embrace.

"I will try to show you," he finally says. "On Xishlon. Before I deploy west to call on the desert serpents in defense of the East. I will find you, and I will show you."

"I want that," Tierney concedes, feeling an unexpected pang over his upcoming departure. "Show me what you mean on Xishlon. And then help me fight the deeper battle underneath the obvious one."

The battle for the natural world, Viger thinks into her mind, reading her fear for the Vo. For all the rivers. For the natural matrix's undoing.

"Yes, Viger," she agrees as she holds his lulling, midnight stare. "The battle for the natural world."

CHAPTER FIVE

RED DESERT

Sparrow Trillium

Agolith Desert
Central Desert lands
Sixth Month

"Be careful around the Crow," Ulluwyn warns Sparrow, a grimace on the blue-hued soldier's mouth as her sapphire eyes flick
toward Thierren. "I see the way he looks at you."

Ulluwyn raises a brow at Sparrow in unspoken meaning and
Sparrow holds her earnest gaze as offense flares. It's chafing,
how Ulluwyn has taken on the unasked-for role of Sparrow's
protector during their small band's journey east across the vast,
storm-riddled desert.

When Sparrow *much* prefers Thierren's company and aid.

They've been traveling for weeks now with a Vu Trin contingent, journeying toward a hidden desert portal that will take
them to Noilaan. Gratitude rises in Sparrow every time she
considers how Thierren negotiated passage to the East for her
as well as her young charge Effrey, the small dragon Raz'zor,

and Aislinn Bane, the longed-for journey secured with the understanding that Thierren, Effrey, and Raz'zor would join the Vu Trin military, forces that Thierren has been secretly aligned with for months.

But still, much to Sparrow's dismay, Thierren's undercover work for the Vu Trin has done little to foster acceptance amongst this particular group of sorceresses.

Sparrow glances across the wide crimson-stone cavern to where Thierren is unrolling his bedding, her brow knotting as she notices, not for the first time, how careful he's being to position himself far away from everyone else. Her gaze slides to Aislinn, who, as usual, has taken a spot on the other side of Sparrow and Effrey, also positioning herself away from the Vu Trin, this soft-spoken, watchful, and deeply kind Gardnerian as unwanted as Thierren.

The maverick high commander of the Vu Trin forces, Vang Troi, gave the order allowing Thierren's and Aislinn's passage east. But, as much as the soldiers accompanying them seem to respect Vang Troi's military prowess, they are all of one intractable mind.

Mages should not be allowed in Noilaan.

Sparrow's gaze slides to the cave entrance, which frames a panoramic view of the desert landscape. The light is a luminous saffron as the sun sinks closer to the horizon, the stone walls surrounding her glittering a breathtaking gold. The goat-size ivory dragon Raz'zor sits on the cavern's ledge beside young Effrey, one of his wings fanned out against the child's back as he scans the view like a dogged sentinel, hell-bent on fulfilling a fealty-vow to Elloren Grey to keep their group safe.

The desert's expanse of crimson sand is such a gorgeous orange-red that, for a moment, Sparrow's artist mind yearns for decent drawing supplies—a sketchbook with fine parchment and colored pencils—so she can create an imprint of the ruddy stone formations that arc over the desert like great swaths of paint.

It's stunning, this edge of the continent's Central Desert, but

Sparrow is more than ready to step into that portal tomorrow and leave the West far behind. And she would have never made it this far without Thierren.

"Thierren has aided me...and Effrey too," Sparrow tries to explain to Ulluwyn as the muscular soldier lounges on her bed-roll and takes a long swig of water, eyeing Thierren with venomous dislike.

As if sensing her eyes on him, Thierren glances at Ulluwyn. His gaze slides to Sparrow, and a heated shiver runs through her that she's instantly ashamed of, especially sitting in the company of this fellow Urisk woman who spent over a year on the Fae Islands.

That familiar, piercing ache rushes through Sparrow. Her friendship with Thierren increasingly feels like one of a handful of true things in her life. Yet her growing feelings for him also seem like a betrayal of her people, illicit and unfathomable and wrong.

But...every time she thinks about leaving him behind as she starts a new, free life in the East, her heart squeezes to the point of actual pain, the bond they've forged over these past few months a source of incredible comfort...and increasingly tinged with want.

It's sparked hard, here in the desert—her growing desire to be close to him. To take his hand. To know what his black hair would feel like under her fingers. To kiss his glimmering green mouth.

His *Mage* mouth.

Her conflict rears higher.

"He's been...very kind," Sparrow tries again, endeavoring to justify this unstoppable tide to both Ulluwyn and herself. Even though she has nothing concrete to be ashamed of.

Ulluwyn spits out a sound of disgust and shoots Thierren a rancid glare. "Of course he's pretending to be kind. He wants you in his bed. But you're a rockbat to him and nothing more. Don't ever forget that."

They sting, Ulluwyn's words, dredging up Sparrow's outrage over so many humiliating cruelties endured in the Fae Island labor camps. And in continental Gardneria.

Sparrow meets Thierren's gaze once more, chagrin rising, since she can tell by the subtle tightening of his eyes that he heard Ulluwyn loud and clear. He gets up and strides outside. Effrey reaches up to touch his hand as he passes, and Thierren pauses to exchange an affectionate smile with the child and ruffle Effrey's newly short and spiked dark purple hair.

Misery floods Sparrow as Ulluwyn stoppers her flask, wipes her mouth with the back of her sleeve, and rises, as well. She sends a look of distaste toward Aislinn.

"Vang Troi is *wrong* about this," Ulluwyn insists to Sparrow, the tight coils of her short blue hair haloed by the late-day sun's wash of gold. "We shouldn't let any Mages into Noilaan. Take great care, Sparrow." The warning in her tone sets Sparrow's hackles rising. "Cut the Crow out of your life. You're about to start fresh in the East. With your talent as a seamstress, you'll find good work for good pay quickly. But you can't *ever* be Noi'khin if you've attached yourself to a Mage. You'll be hated as much as the Roaches are, and rightfully so."

Ulluwyn gives Sparrow one last significant look and strides out of the cavern, and Sparrow berates herself for her desire to leave the sheltering space as well...to find Thierren.

To simply *be* with him this eve.

She blinks back the sting of tears as she smooths down her bedding, her thoughts circling in unceasing conflict. She pulls in a wavering breath, sits down, and just *stops* for a moment, staring at the glittering wall opposite her.

"I've seen the way he looks at you too."

Sparrow turns, surprised to hear Aislinn's soft, serious voice. Aislinn hardly ever talks, hardly eats, and keeps to herself. She has a haunted look about her, and Sparrow considers, with a pang, that it's a look she's seen before, on the Fae Islands. Amongst young Urisk women after they've been preyed on by the Mages. Like Aislinn has been preyed on by perhaps the worst Mage of them all.

Sparrow witnessed Damion Bane's depravity firsthand the night he attacked Elloren Grey. She secretly cheered when Lukas Grey beat him senseless, all too aware of Damion's penchant for abuse, word passed around among the Urisk in Valgard and beyond to make themselves scarce anywhere he was ever likely to be.

And Aislinn is *fasted* to that monster.

Sparrow shudders just to think about waiflike, bookish, and exceedingly gentle Aislinn in the power of such a sadistic fiend, the only Mage willing to fast to her after she openly professed her love for a Lupine, Jarod Ulrich.

"I also see how you look at Thierren," Aislinn continues in a near whisper.

"There's nothing between us," Sparrow insists, her throat gone dry as the ache in her heart tightens. "There never can be."

Aislinn winces. They remain quiet for a protracted moment before Aislinn meets Sparrow's gaze once more, green eyes blazing. "Don't *ever* let other people tell you who you can and can't love."

The impassioned words are a dart straight through Sparrow's heart, a tremor kicking up along her mouth. She bites her lower lip to try to quell it.

Aislinn gives her a bitter, knowing look. "I let the world tell me who I could and couldn't love." Her mouth twists into a heartbreaking grimace, devastated tears glazing her eyes. "I lost the love of my life that way. And now, it's over for me. Jarod will never have me, because he's Lupine…and they mate for life. And I'm… forever sullied. But *you*—" she glances toward where Thierren left "—you could still have your love, Sparrow. Don't let that go."

A tear streaks down Sparrow's face and she shakes her head, resolution impossible and wishing for it a torment. She looks at Aislinn. "I haven't bathed in days. Do you want to go with me and clean up?"

Aislinn gives her a small, melancholy smile. "Yes…thank you. That would be nice."

★ ★ ★

Sparrow tilts her head up, eyes closed, as she revels in the hot water coursing over her.

Their Vu Trin companions have cleverly propped runic swords across a stony shelf set above an alcove around the corner from the cavern's entrance, the swords' water and heat runes magicked to create a flow of hot water pouring straight from the blades. The heat feels sensually good against the desert's rapidly cooling air, the buildup of gritty sand on Sparrow's skin flowing away.

She wonders what it would be like if Thierren suddenly rounded the corner to find her there, completely unclothed, then pulled off his own garments, got under the hot water with her, and pressed his long, muscular body against hers...

Sweet Ge'o'din. Sparrow flushes as she breaks off the scandalous thought. She busies herself cleaning off the last of the tenacious sand, briefly turning to Aislinn...

...and the reality of the world crashes down.

Aislinn's body—it's covered in bruises. Horribly so, and violent enough to linger so many days past their escape from Valgard. There are lash marks all over her form and bruising on her breasts. And bite marks...

She quickly averts her eyes, heart wrenching, and steps from the water. Deeply troubled, she grabs an indigo towel just as her exposed skin is hit by a stinging spray of red sand.

A furious, eye-battering sandstorm roars into being and Sparrow's hands fly up to shield her vision against the red, whipping haze as the desert before them rises into a granular typhoon. Alarm slashing through her, Sparrow recoils just as the sand-blurred figures of two giant gray spiders erupt from the desert floor, strange, smoking runes marked all over their thoraxes. A profusion of eyes cover the upper half of their heads, a gauzy gray mist encircling their stretched-out bodies.

Sparrow screams and lunges for the runic sword above her as a spider leaps at her, the impact forcing her to the ground, the air punched from her lungs as her towel falls away.

"Thierren!" she cries as she beats against the beast's terrifyingly nimble under-legs and their clenching grip on her bare body. The world spinning, strands of sticky silvery silk wrap around her with astonishing speed before she's lifted up tight against the spider's hard thorax.

My life cannot end like this, Sparrow rages as she growls her protest, kicking and thrashing against the beast. *My life cannot end when we're only a day away from the East!*

"Thierren!" she screams again as the creature launches into a scuttling sprint across the whipping sand.

Bolts of blue light slam into the creature, deflecting off its encircling mist in bright bursts of sapphire light, their Vu Trin protectors' fierce cries going up as Sparrow spots sand-blurred figures rushing toward her, including a furious-looking Ulluwyn, runic blade drawn.

A hard gust of wind hits the spider, blasting its shadowy shield clear away.

The world spins, the spider toppling to its side as the surrounding sandstorm dissipates. Thierren runs toward her, wand in hand, eyes like green wildfire, looking like he's ready to rip up the entire desert to get to her. The Vu Trin rush in behind him as a pale white blur streaks toward the second toppled spider and lashes vermilion fire at it, the huge insect's head exploding into a ball of red flame, its legs flailing.

Thierren growls out a spell, falls to one knee and levels his wand at Sparrow's spider.

A rush of cold hits Sparrow, a chill-sting tingling over her skin as a bolt of crystalline ice scythes from Thierren's wand and impales the spider's head, shearing it clear off in a spray of dark ichor. She drops to the ground, pummeled by wildly thrashing legs.

Thierren draws his sword and vengefully hacks off gray legs, then leans over, his strong arms coming around Sparrow to swiftly carry her away. She lets her eyes flit backward once, her gut heaving as she takes in the headless, half-legless creature twitching on its side.

Thierren lowers her to the ground and her gaze collides with his. A frisson of pure ardor blazes through her, the passionate ferocity in Thierren's eyes stunning to behold. He unsheathes a knife and begins to cut the thick, sticky webbing from her body with a single-minded drive bordering on desperation.

Sparrow cranes her head, frantically looking for Aislinn as her heart threatens to pound a hole through her chest. "Aislinn!" she calls out as she spots her friend's webbed form, her rough cry breaking off as she coughs up sand and blinks its sting from her eyes.

"She's all right," Thierren assures her, sounding rattled as he pulls away a great swath of webbing, then pauses when he finds her naked underneath. His widened eyes lift to meet hers.

"Thierren, get it *off* of me," Sparrow prods, caring more about being freed than modesty.

"Get your hands off her, Roach!" Ulluwyn's growl cuts through the air as she's suddenly there, shouldering Thierren aside, her blue eyes condemning.

Thierren moves back as he looks from Ulluwyn to Sparrow, then away, seeming dazed.

"What just happened, Crow?" Ulluwyn barks.

Thierren's head snaps to Ulluwyn as he eyes her in confusion.

She swipes her thumb toward the nearest storm spider. "The shielding only your magery could take down? The gray Crow runes *all over them*? What are you in league with?"

Thierren gapes at her. "You think I'm in league with those *things*?"

"I don't know what to think, *Mage*," Ulluwyn bites out before making quick work of the rest of the webbing with a runic blade, freeing Sparrow's limbs.

Sparrow's heart gives a hard twist at Thierren's look of devastation. Sitting up, she cranes her head to view the other Vu Trin and Raz'zor untangling Aislinn as Thierren strides to Effrey, who has broken into great, shuddering sobs, his gaze pinned with terror on Sparrow.

Thierren kneels before Effrey and brings his hand to the child's shoulder, his voice low and calm when it comes, belying none of the anguish Sparrow knows he's feeling. "She's all right. Effrey, she's all right."

Ulluwyn hands Sparrow her cloak, murmuring to her soothingly in Uriskal as she helps Sparrow to her feet. Then Ulluwyn ushers Sparrow back into the cave, her arm tight around her shoulder. She turns once to shoot Thierren an acid glare that hollows Sparrow out with frustrated rebellion.

Deeply unsettled, Sparrow seeks out Thierren that eve, her body covered in a clean, indigo Noi tunic and pants, her violet hair damp and tied back, her form washed free of the ichor and sand and web remnants.

Sparrow finds him sitting outside the cave, his gaze to the desert's crimson splash of stars.

She quietly takes a seat beside him and peers across the night-dark landscape, softly lit by a ruddy moon, this evening's events a weight bearing down on them both.

For a long while, they remain silent, but Sparrow can sense the tension brewing.

"I love you," Thierren finally says without looking at her. There's an impassioned finality to the words that steals Sparrow's breath clear away. "I know it's impossible for us to be together," he adds, gaze pinned on the storm-banded horizon, puffs of lightning flashing through it. "But I love you and always will."

Sparrow grips the edge of the stone ledge so hard that her skin strains against her bones.

I love you too, she longs to say, but can't. The words won't loosen from her throat. Not here. Not yet. Not on the edge of the Western Realm, where she's been treated as subhuman. But still, she yearns to say them. Aislinn's words light in her mind, piercing through her storm of emotion like a bright beacon.

Don't ever *let other people tell you who you can and can't love.*

The storm inside Sparrow intensifies, rivaling the churning storm band along the horizon.

Sparrow gets up and walks away from Thierren, her heart in her throat. She strides back into the dark cave lit only by a single blue-glowing rune stone. Then she curls up on her bedroll facing the cavern's wall and quietly sobs, half noticing when Aislinn gently places a hand on her shoulder and keeps it there deep into the night.

Don't ever *let other people tell you who you can and can't love.*

The words reverberate in Sparrow's mind, gaining strength as the night stretches on and Aislinn falls asleep beside her. Effrey is curled up on Sparrow's other side with Raz'zor, who is asleep as well, the edge of the dragon's ivory wing resting around Effrey's shoulder.

Sparrow sits up and turns to find Thierren, across the cavern, fast asleep. Only their sole sentinel, the young soldier Twyne Ko, is awake, standing guard near the cavern's entrance and surveying the night, her back to them all.

Sparrow gets up and pads over to where Thierren is sleeping. She lies down on the hard stone facing him, her eyes drinking in his beloved face as she watches him breathe.

I love you, she mouths before the dark of sleep claims her, as well.

Sparrow has a beautiful dream.

She's lying next to Thierren in a cave with shimmering saffron walls lit by candlelight, his forest eyes intent on her. She reaches up to caress his cheek, and his eyes widen with surprise as she slides under his blanket then wraps her arms around him. He lets out a hard exhale, then enfolds her in a loving embrace.

Sparrow sighs and sinks into him, into the gorgeous dream, his heartbeat strong against hers, their bodies pressed against each other. It feels right. *So* right.

Like finding her true home—not the East at all, but *him*.

She presses her lips to the warm nape of his neck, a thrill singing through her as Thierren shivers against her. She strokes his back, his side, his shoulder, his body responding to her brazen touch, her own body warming.

"I want you," she breathes against his neck.

"Sparrow," he whispers huskily, his breathing uneven as he moves back a fraction. "I think you're dreaming. Wake up, love."

Sparrow blinks, the haziness of the cavern solidifying, the soft, amber candlelight disappearing to be replaced by a Noi rune stone's cold blue light.

Mortification seizes hold, catapulting Sparrow out of her half-dream state as she looks at Thierren with wide-eyed remorse. "I'm sorry," she manages in a strangled voice before an exclamation sounds from across the cavern's expanse.

She turns to find Ulluwyn's furious glare knifing into her. *"Crow whore,"* the Vu Trin bites out in Uriskal.

Sparrow pulls away from Thierren and rolls onto her back, shame ripping through her. She closes her eyes to wall it all off, her hands coming up to hide her face.

"Sparrow," Thierren says, sounding as strangled by emotion as she feels, but she just can't bring herself to look at him, so great is the conflict storming inside her.

Finally, she meets his gaze. "I can't, Thierren," she agonizes. "I just can't speak of this until we're in the East. I'm so sorry I threw myself at you like that..."

He nods, eyes glazed with feeling. "Wait, then," he says, casting a sidelong glance toward Ulluwyn. "Wait until you're settled in the East to decide how you feel about me."

Sparrow nods tightly as the storm inside her churns and rages against the entire, godsforsakingly cruel world.

WYVERNGUARD

Trystan Gardner &
Vothendrile Xanthile

The Wyvernguard
North Wyvernguard Island, Noilaan
Eastern Realm
Sixth Month

Vothendrile

"Still having to trail the Crow?" Basyl teasingly asks.

I bite back my urge to protest the slur as I hold Basyl in a loose embrace, still rattled by Heelyn's reaction to my honesty a few nights back. I'm clear I could lose more than my position and friends here if I'm not careful. All I've ever wanted and worked for is to someday return to Zhilaan to uphold and protect the weather forces of the Northeast, a vital part of the broad Eastern Realm alliance.

But if I fall in with Trystan, that dream could become an impossibility.

Basyl's smile is sultry as he waits for my reply. We're reclined against a wall in one of the many hallways surrounding the labyrinthine Wyvernguard archives, the library cut into the obsidian stone beneath the base of the North Island, submerged below the Vo River.

Submerged like my frustrating draw to Trystan Gardner, I sullenly consider. I glance toward the door at the end of the hall, Trystan just past this wall somewhere, studying in the archives. As I stand guard.

Basyl's expectant look turns quizzical when I don't answer him, the hard angles of his sculpted Elfin features softened by the sapphire lantern light.

Yes, I still have to trail the Crow, and it's turning my world upside down, I yearn to confide in him.

To say the words that will have me instantly shunned, despised, unwanted.

Just like the Gardnerian.

My internal conflict rears as I consider how the rough treatment of Trystan during weapons exercises hasn't let up. But still, Trystan goes back, day after day. Stoically working with the Vu Trin as they test different runic combinations to learn how best to deflect his Mage power and deal with his surprising ability to infiltrate their runes. They attack him in ever-increasing numbers, and he endures their blows, even when soldiers purposely hurt him, to the point where Ung Li has had to step in a number of times.

It's escalated to the level where I quietly offered Trystan support a few days back when I caught sight of him checking his wand arm during a break, the bright, angry bruising down its entire length sparking a livid outrage inside me.

"I'll go with you to Ung Li's chambers to talk to her," I said as we stood apart by the terrace's stone wall. "It's not right that they treat you like this."

Trystan met my offer with a stare so blistering that it both surprised me and pierced me to the core, his usual reserve fracturing as he pointedly said nothing to me in response, which only served to agitate my tempest of emotion even more. I looked to Ung Li in that moment, noticing her taking in Trystan's injuries as he yanked down his sleeve over the bruising, my gaze darting toward the other apprentices and soldiers just in time to catch sight of one soldier's lip curling up with an expression of vengeful satisfaction.

No one moved to send him to the Wyvernguard healer, as always. And he's rebuffed my every attempt to bring him to a healer myself. Instead, he simply ignores his pain and growing collection of injuries. Ignores the soldiers' resentment over the necessity of learning to deal with Gardnerian power—power that bests theirs again and again. Power that requires advanced weaponry and large numbers of Vu Trin to force back. Because he truly wants the Vu Trin to be able to best Gardnerian magery.

Even if we kill him while learning how to do it.

"Forget the Gardnerian." Basyl's finger spirals down the center of my chest, his enticing touch taking a slim edge off my troubled thoughts.

The door at the end of the hallway abruptly opens and Trystan emerges, books tucked under his arm. His green eyes find mine, and his steps halt.

A heated charge stings through me and everything else in the world fades into the background. My lightning flashes silver against my vision as our gazes hold, my throat gone dry with a sudden, inexplicable longing.

I can sense Trystan's fierce draw to me as well, his fire power contracting and shuddering toward me with a force that sends a storming warmth through my core.

No, I urge myself as I struggle to rein in my power. *I can't feel this way about him. I can't let this take hold.*

The time to end this is now.

I draw Basyl close and feel Trystan's spark of surprise as Basyl laughs and trails kisses along the length of my neck. He presses his muscular body to mine and caresses my back, sliding his hands over my hips as he tugs me closer and I hold Trystan's gaze, our eyes locked as both my and Trystan's breathing deepens. I lean in to run my tongue just below Basyl's ear as Basyl slithers against me enticingly, everything in me wanting to drive Trystan away.

Everything in me yearning to pull Trystan in.

Trystan is mesmerized, I can feel it. Pinned in place by both desire and fascination. And suddenly, instead of wanting to keep the boundaries in place, I want to break through it all and stoke his desire. To tease him until he wants this more than he's wanted anything in his life.

Until he's on fire to be the one in my arms.

That's it, Gardnerian, I think, holding Trystan's stare as I trace my fingers down Basyl's spine and still lower. Basyl gives another throaty laugh and captures my mouth with his, our tongues finding each other, even as I keep my gaze locked with Trystan's, rich with invitation. Toying with him.

Trystan's welling power pulls in tight. He shoots me a look so scathing it could melt iron, then strides away.

A maelstrom of remorse rushes in as the sting of Trystan's reaction reverberates.

I gently push Basyl away.

He tries to pull me back in. "Come here..."

I force a wan smile. "I have to go," I say, suddenly unable to focus on Basyl's beauty and willing ways and the achingly pleasurable tightening in my groin, my friend's lighthearted desire so easy to fuel. Basyl's a distraction and nothing more, both of us caught up in a breezy flirtation. Friends who enjoy teasing each other, but nothing deeper than that running between us.

But *Trystan*.

Conflict roars to life as I sound the Mage's name in my mind.

"I'll see you tomorrow, love," I tell Basyl, kissing his cheek as he stages a pouting protest, caressing me one last time. I disentangle myself and set off at a brisk clip after Trystan.

Needing to find him as his guard, but also scared to face him.

The walls between us feeling increasingly paper-thin.

Trystan

Vothendrile's knock on my door is uncharacteristically tentative, and I fight back the jealous urge to draw my wand and throw a bolt of lightning straight through the wood. My wand hand flexed into a fist, I yank the door open, cursing the lightning that shocks through my lines when I meet Vothe's silver-flashing gaze.

Vothe's wildly conflicted gaze.

Have I made your life difficult? I want to snarl at him. *Is your own cruelty making you uncomfortable?*

Good.

"Can I speak with you?" he asks.

My internal lightning spits fire as I glare at him. Wanting to drive him away. Wanting him to get this over with, whatever *this* is.

"Just say whatever it is you have to say," I snap.

He hesitates, neck tight, like he's got a storm caught in his throat. "Not here." His gaze flits toward the hallway's exit. "Can we take a walk, perhaps? Away from everyone?"

"Will they allow that?" I ask, my voice tight with sarcasm. "Since I'm such a threat to the Realm?" I avert my gaze from Vothe's tall, magnificent form.

Why does he have to be so painfully beautiful? Why? It's like someone turned a lightning bolt into the most arresting young man imaginable. And, of course, he draws the most interesting, charismatic young men to himself. Kisses them so freely and openly. The sight never fails to send a frisson of shock through my lines. Most of the exchanges seem light and teasing, but sometimes...it's like he's feeding lightning straight into the man he's kissing.

It's even more difficult to look at Vothe now that the dreams have started.

Dreams that I don't want. Dreams of pulling Vothendrile

into my room, pinning him to the wall and showing him what lightning *really* is.

"Shouldn't you just get on with quietly guarding me?" I ask, and there's no way to keep the bitter edge from my tone.

Vothendrile gives me a long look, and it's a shock to see something new in his expression—a kind of chastened dismay. And frustration.

With *what*?

I almost go with him. I almost let him say what he has to say.

But the hurt is too raw, and I'm not interested in his blaring lack of courage. I'm not interested in feigning civility when the emotions cut too deep.

I give him another silent look that I fear reveals too much… and shut the door.

Vothendrile

The Death Fae gather around Trystan at every meal.

I watch them the next evening from the periphery, half noticing Basyl as he caresses my arm, jockeying for my attention along with several other friends. I force quick smiles, even as my attention is drawn back to Trystan in an increasingly reckless tide.

All three primordial Death Fae are seated with him, as they are at every meal—tall, powerful Viger, petite, spider-shifter Sylla, and mysterious, elegant Vesper. Every table around them has emptied, as it always does, dark mist curling around their bizarre, insular grouping.

They sit in their usual silence, poisonous scorpions and spiders and the occasional snake encircling Trystan's lean frame like a fraternal, albeit deadly, embrace. The Death Fae's presence here will be a fleeting thing, all three completing basic Vu Trin training before departing—Viger about to deploy to the Dyoi Desert to harness its huge desert serpents, Sylla soon to be stationed in the Agolith Desert to fortify the Vu Trin's ranks with deadly storm spiders. And Vesper will be stationed at a military base in Northern Noilaan, the enigmatic rune sorcerer adept at linking Death magic to Noi military runes.

Conflict whorls inside me as I find myself both relieved that Trystan has gained such staunch friends and dismayed over their imminent departure.

Because the animosity toward Trystan's presence here is growing alongside the mounting tensions between Noilaan and Gardneria. I'm becoming less a guard protecting the Wyvernguard and more a guard protecting *him*.

And the sympathy thrown my way is seriously beginning to chafe.

"So terrible that they've got you guarding the Roach!"

"Couldn't you arrange for some accident to befall him?"

"Vang Troi has lost her mind. Drive him out, Vothe. Whatever it takes."

Even letters from my family in Zhilaan show mounting confusion and censure in their refined Zhilon'ile script.

Vothe, you're the Gardnerian's guard. Why is he still here?

Vothe, WHY IS HE STILL HERE?

I'm losing patience with all of it, increasingly unable to keep from snapping back against the slurs, my large group of friends and admirers beginning to splinter away. Whispering to each other that I'm losing my way. Shifting my allegiance to the enemy. When, in fact, I'm doing exactly the opposite. And, more and more, I want to stand in open solidarity with Trystan Gardner.

But still, I remain on the sidelines, unable to take what feels like a dive off a cliff. Because the tide of hatred for Trystan is rapidly gaining strength. And I'm brutally realistic about what it would mean to get caught in its undertow, even as I'm swept up in Trystan's glimmering green tide.

My indecision intensifies as I watch him eat, a dark raven now perched on his shoulder. A current of shame ripples through me.

Because it took the Death Fae to break through all the hatred here and accept him.

★ ★ ★

It's predawn the next morning when Heelyn confronts me prior to the start of my post as Trystan's guard. She strides toward me over the Wyvernguard's mid-level terrace, a crowd of military apprentices just ahead. Heelyn's muscular frame is outlined by the overcast sky's deep gray light, her dark eyes full of zealous heat as a chilly wind rustles the parchment in her hand.

My body lights up with anticipatory tension, the angry purpose coming off Heelyn serving to drive the tension higher, my storm power jostling to life in flashes that sting the underside of my skin.

"Here," she says, thrusting the paper toward me.

"What is it?" I ask, making no move to take it.

"A chance to redeem yourself," she bites out.

I swipe it from her, knowing this longtime friend of mine can easily read the lightning flashing in my eyes. My pulse quickens as I spot Trystan's name in the paper's leading text. It's a petition to ban Trystan from wearing his Wyvernguard uniform.

Outrage strikes inside me, swift and hot, as I fist the paper in my hand. "You think you're somehow aiding the East, doing this?"

"As were you when you tried to keep him out!" she shoots back. "Have you forgotten what you used to stand for?"

I spit out a contemptuous laugh. "Please, tell me, Heelyn. What did I stand for? Condemning someone before even meeting them? Based solely on their lineage? Is that the Vothe you miss?"

I've a sudden sense of the crowd ahead stilling, their eyes on us. Their eyes on *me*.

The angry blaze in Heelyn's eyes shifts to something impassioned. "I miss the Vothe who put the Eastern Realm first. If Vang Troi needs the Gardnerian so that we can dissect his twisted magic, so be it. We use him for our military gain. Slay him in doing it, preferably. But don't put the Crow in Wyvernguard clothes. Make it clear he can *never* belong." She jabs her finger at the paper in my hand. "Get on the right side of things."

I glower at her. "It's incredible how sure you are that you're on that right side."

That light in her expression whisks away, only a teeth-gritted anger remaining. She steps toward me, fists balled. "He's an insult to all we're fighting for."

I'm unable to suppress the rise of my horns from my head. "How's that, Heelyn? How is he an insult to every last thing we're fighting for?"

Her gaze flicks over my horns, her words low and unforgiving. "That you even need to ask shows how far you've fallen." She steps back, a hard glint in her eyes. "We're going to meet with Ung Li. And mark my words, Vothe, we *will* get the Crow stripped of a uniform he should *never* have been allowed to wear. And then *we'll* be the ones to get him thrown out, since you seem so *utterly incapable* of doing it."

I'm suddenly so furious I can't stand there any longer. If I do, I might say something that will destroy any remaining shred of our friendship.

I turn my back on her as my claws extend of their own volition. Then I crumple the piece of paper, ignite it in my palm, and throw its smoking ashes to the ground.

CHAPTER SEVEN

NOI'KHIN

Trystan Gardner &
Vothendrile Xanthile

The Wyvernguard
North Wyvernguard Island, Noilaan
Eastern Realm
Sixth Month

Vothendrile

"You need to wear this from now on," Ung Li orders Trystan two nights later, her expression steely as I stand at attention by Trystan's side in her tower chamber. She pulls neatly folded black garb off a nearby shelf and my breath constricts as I realize what it is.

Gardnerian clothing.

Outrage sparks through me. You'd think the Wyvernguard was in danger of imploding and falling to the bottom of the Vo, so great is the agitation over Gardnerian features paired with Eastern Realm garb. And the strengthening protests are rendered more ludicrous still, because every shifter here is sensing the same thing from Trystan that I am, many of them admitting to me—*It seems he's really committed to fighting with the Eastern Realm.*

But they admit this only in hushed whispers where no one else can overhear, so great is the danger of sympathizing with the Gardnerian.

The hypocrisy is beginning to grate.

Trystan makes no move to accept the Gardnerian blacks. "I won't wear them," comes his icy reply.

I stiffen, my eyes flicking toward Trystan in surprise.

"You're creating havoc," Ung Li snaps.

Trystan's lips give a slight curl. "By refusing to put on clothing?"

"It's a politically charged move."

Trystan's water power rears with defiant energy, his slight smirk vanishing. "So is putting on the clothing of a group of people we're about to be at war with."

Ung Li fixes him with a narrow glare. "You're sworn to obey the Wyvernguard. If I order you to take these and you defy me, I will strip you of your apprenticeship and kick you out."

"Then kick me out," Trystan bites back in a stunning show of rebellion. "I'll still fight the Gardnerians. I'll still fight the Alfsigr. But I will not wear those clothes *ever again.*"

"I *order* you to take them."

Trystan and Ung Li face off, and it feels like two dragons going toe-to-toe as the tidal energy inside Trystan gains ground. I struggle to keep my own turbulent power from rushing toward it. But then Trystan reins it all in, consolidating the raging storm so deep in his core I can no longer sense it.

"Hoiyon, Nor Ung Li," he says as he takes the clothing, straightens and salutes our commander, fist to chest, his expression military blank. His eyes meet mine, a flash of defiance burning in them that's so explosive it sets off an answering flash of invisible lightning.

Conflict surges in me, the urge to protest this monumentally unfair thing almost impossible to suppress. I turn to Ung Li as the protest rises in my throat, but it's silenced by the look of ire she's directing at Trystan's back.

Our commander wants him gone.

There's no winning here, I realize. Not for Trystan. Not for me. Not for anyone who aligns themselves with one Mage versus all of the East. It's one thing to argue with your fellow apprentices, quite another to question your commander.

I struggle to justify my silence. *You can't keep getting emotionally involved in this and be his guard. You're continually making that error.*

Lightning crackles through me, straining toward Trystan, but I enfold it in a tight hold and force it back.

You're his guard, not his ally, I doggedly remind myself as I follow Trystan out.

Still, even as I rail against it, I know my sympathies have shifted.

"You're just making your life difficult," I warn Trystan as I follow him to the Wyvernguard's base and onto the waterside terrace. The starless sky is ink black, the river rushing by the terrace's onyx stone in a rhythmic *whoosh.*

Trystan ignores me, not slowing as he strides past a smattering of military apprentices who glare at him, then around the terrace's curve toward a deserted edge. Stopping just before the stone railing, Trystan throws the garb onto the damp stone.

Alarm sparks through me.

"You need to wear those," I caution, "and stop trying to look Noi'khin."

"I seek to be Noi'khin," Trystan throws back, green eyes blazing.

Outrage rises in me over his audacious declaration. He's deluding himself. He can never be a true citizen of the East. It's a stretch for Trystan to expect to be tolerated, let alone become an intrinsic part of this land.

I tense my brow. "Trystan, you need to accept reality. You're the grandson of the Black Witch. You can never be Noi'khin."

Trystan steps toward me, his water and fire power lashing through his lines in a surging tempest. "What am I, then?" he demands.

I step toward him in turn, my lightning forking out toward his. "A Gardnerian."

The smile that forms on Trystan's lips is dark and cutting. "So, I should just go back to the Western Realm? To be welcomed back into the fold?"

A chaotic disturbance courses out from Trystan's magic, cutting through my power. My eyes widen. Because I can feel the jagged pain in that disturbance, leagues wide.

And it dawns on me—*they hate men like us in the Western Realm.*

It's a surreal thought. Difficult to wrap my mind around. Such a bizarre thing for a religion to hate. But I've heard that there are whole passages in the Gardnerian religious book that condemn anyone who loves another of the same gender. Along with passages outlining how hatred against anyone winged or able to shift forms is absolutely demanded by the Ancient One. Hence, Marcus Vogel's obsession with slaying or breaking every Icaral in existence, as well as all of Wyvernkind.

Such a hellish, fanatically deluded place.

I realize I've never once stopped to consider what life must have been like for Trystan over there. Because the idea of such a place is just too bizarre to be believed.

I hold Trystan's tortured stare, suddenly overcome by the desire to understand.

"I know you're attracted to me." My words come in a rush, and the answering look of devastation on Trystan's face makes me feel as if I've hurled a weapon.

Trystan's lip trembles, and I'm stunned to find his impenetrable veneer of calm so effectively breached. "Everyone's attracted to you, Vothe," he shoots back, his voice edged with deep-seated bitterness.

I swallow, my own calm breached as I strive to keep my water aura from leaping straight into Trystan Gardner's. "Did you have to hide yourself there?"

Ire flashes in his stunning eyes. "What do you *think*?"

It's a blow, this rush of realization that Trystan was even more of an outcast in the Western Realm than he is here.

"They don't understand," I breathe, glancing up toward the Wyvernguard, "do they?"

Trystan's lips tighten with derision, his stare unblinkingly harsh. "And you think you do?"

I draw back from the accusation in his tone as a fuller realization washes over me. I've been so thoughtless, kissing Basyl in front of Trystan to push him away, when where Trystan's just come from, to kiss a man like that would get you hurled in prison. Or worse.

I take a step toward him. "I want to understand."

"You want to *understand*?" Trystan bites out. "Fine. I'll help you to understand. If I embraced someone over there..."

His words break off and he looks out over the river, his jaw tensing, his water power churning. "If I embraced someone there like you embrace Basyl..." He stops again and takes a deep breath, then turns back to me, eyes blazing as if he's willing me to understand from the force of his gaze alone. "If I kissed another man there, like you're able to here, they would have *arrested* us and possibly *executed* us. Our lives would be *destroyed*. Our *families'* lives would be destroyed. Unless they disowned us. My whole life I've lived like this, and you think I can just... turn it off and go back to being *Gardnerian*?"

Trystan scowls, and I can feel his vast power quivering with anger. "They tell me to wear Gardnerian clothing. That I'm a Gardnerian. But I never was." His tone takes on a vicious edge. "Who I really am is unwanted in the Western Realm. Despised. And marked an Evil One." He glances up at the Wyvernguard Island's apex, fury in his eyes, then sets his gaze back on mine as a cold half smile forms on his beautiful, green-glimmering mouth.

"I never was Gardnerian," he says with more emotion than

I've ever seen him show. "And I never will be. No matter how many times they destroy my Noi clothing. No matter what they do to drive me out. I will *never* wear Gardnerian blacks again." He takes another step toward me, gaze scorching. "And whether the people of Noilaan want me or not, I'm going to stay *right here*. And I'm going to fight with everything in me for this intolerant, tolerant land."

I'm frozen, stunned, the tear silently streaking down Trystan's angular face bringing a sting of tears to my own eyes.

"Step back, Vothe," Trystan says, his voice steely as his tear-slicked eyes take on a lethal light. His hand moves to the wand at his side.

Alarm whips up my power. "Why?"

And then Trystan draws his wand and throws a violent line of flame at the Gardnerian garb at his feet, enveloping them in a churning ball of fire.

"Min Lo." I try to reason with my childhood friend and Vu Trin soldier. "Don't arrest him. It's more complicated than you think."

"What's complicated about it?" Min Lo demands, the streaks of silver and purple in her spiked black hair glinting blue in the terrace's rune light, a line of silver stars hung diagonally across her uniform. She gestures toward Trystan, who stands motionless by the railing, the clothing smoking at his feet. She's gripping Trystan's wand in her fist as her dark gaze bores into me. "He just used Gardnerian wand magery without Wyvernguard permission. Which is enough to get him kicked straight out of not just the Wyvernguard, but the Realm itself. I thought you didn't want him here."

My lips tense with frustration. I'm about to step over a line that, once crossed, can never be traversed again. I glance toward Trystan and meet his gaze, our invisible lightning reflexively sparking toward each other.

I turn back to Min Lo. "I smell nothing but truth on him. He's honestly here to fight with the East. And, Min Lo, he likes men."

Min Lo pauses, as if she's searching for the root of what I'm getting at. She's been like this since childhood. Tough, but thoughtful and fair.

The ramifications of Trystan's situation seem to dawn in Min Lo's dark eyes. She narrows a glance back at Trystan, brow knotted, as if seeing him in a new light.

"That's illegal over there, you know that, right?" she says, gravity entering her tone as her eyes flick back to mine. "The Mages are brutal about it."

I nod, a bit dazed to be pleading leniency for the grandson of the Black Witch, but a remembrance of that tear sliding down Trystan's anguished face fills my mind and the desire to truly understand what he's been through strengthens.

"Minyl," I say, voice low, drawing on our friendship with my use of her familiar name. "Please. Make an exception. Don't turn him in."

Trystan

I wait as Vothe and the spiky-haired soldier deliberate, barely able to think through the tornado of emotion and volatile power that's wrested hold of me as I watch the Gardnerian blacks smolder, wishing with everything in me to be with family or Tierney right now. I draw in a long, shaky breath, desperate to pull myself together. Unable to pull myself together.

The soldier, Min Lo, sends me a conflicted look as she slices the air with her hands, the terrace's sapphire lantern light highlighting her razor-sharp features. Vothe and Min Lo grow quiet, regarding each other with deeply serious looks. Then they turn toward me.

I hold Min Lo's steady gaze, not able to look at Vothe. Not wanting to feel the lightning aura that ignites and fills me with excruciatingly futile want whenever our eyes meet. The concern that washes over Min Lo's features solidifies into what looks like resolve. Her jaw tightens, lips thinning as she strides toward me, my wand in her hand.

She stops before me. "I'll petition Ung Li to let you remain in your Wyvernguard uniform," she states.

Surprise bolts through me, the power in my lines whipping into a frenzy. Min Lo hands my wand back to me.

"Thank you," is all I can manage as I take it. Min Lo shoots Vothe a loaded glance. Then she strides off, her boots clicking against stone.

I stare after her, fighting the urge to meet Vothe's gaze. It's so strong, this draw. So cursedly, overwhelmingly strong. Everything in me pulsing and straining to merge with Vothe's power, I give in, turn, and meet his dark-eyed gaze.

Lightning energy streaks between us, its charge shivering through my lines straight down to the soles of my feet, and I can tell from Vothe's expression that he feels it too. His lips part, as if caught on a surprised exhale, his gaze locked tight on mine as lines of forking white lightning flash into being on his lips. His lightning-laced mouth closes then opens again, as if he desperately wants to say something, his body tensed as if brimming with the sheer force of it.

Two young female apprentices round the terrace's curve, and we turn toward them, our charged connection broken. Vothe averts his gaze and looks distractedly over the Vo, biting his lightning-glazed lips with an expression of intense frustration. The veins of light skimming his mouth rapidly blink out of sight, and a piece of my heart blinks out, as well.

He's ashamed of his attraction to me.

Despair rising, I view the young women as they draw nearer, both of them glaring at me with looks of revulsion. The taller woman, her hair done in looping black braids streaked with blue, claps Vothe on the shoulder as she passes.

"Koilu, Noi'khin," she says, meeting Vothe's eyes with a look of solidarity.

Be strong, kin of Noilaan.

Vothe's whole body stiffens. But he remains silent.

Completely silent.

The apprentices reach the other end of the terrace and pass out of sight, as my heart constricts with a vicious, shearing ache.

"I need to get back," I force out, willing myself to avoid his gaze. Not wanting to see his choice clear in it—*his choice to keep me out.*

Because I know that Vothe's rejection right now holds the power to level me.

I don't look at Vothe even once the whole way back to my room, and he initiates no conversation, his silence conveying oceans more than his words ever could as my chest grows tighter and tighter with overwhelming hurt.

We reach my room and I pause, my hand on my door's handle. I can sense Vothe pausing too, feel the storm that's gathered between us, just as I can feel Sylla's multiple eyes on me from her preferred resting spot, ensconced in the hallway's tunneling webs. I peer up and spot her dark figure in spider form near the ceiling, watching us intently, her Death Fae stillness infusing the atmosphere that surrounds us all.

"Trystan…" Vothe says, and I can hear both his struggle and capitulation to the mob in it. His unwanted apology for his cowardice. Because we both feel this thing growing between us.

"Just go," I say, wanting to throw a blaze of fire straight through Vothe's power, to drive him away for good. I keep my eyes focused on the door's handle, knowing that if I look at Vothe, my lightning will ignite something I won't be able to hold back.

He pauses for an agonizing, infuriating moment longer, so much hanging in the air between us, as I internally rage—*I don't want you! I don't want you if you can't move past all this right now when it matters!*

Vothe lets out a wavering exhale, then turns and leaves. The sound of his boots thudding against stone sends a shard straight through my heart. I don't move. I just stand there, trembling now, my hand on the door.

"I'm struggling," I admit to Sylla.

There's a rustling in the webs, like a brush over linen.

I glance up to find her still curled up near the ceiling, but morphed into her petite human form, save for eight dark eyes. She doesn't say anything, but a deeper silence descends—a Death Fae silence—and I'm filled with the sensation of tunneling down, the torchlit dimness of the hall darkening further. And I can feel it in the preternatural silence.

Her understanding.

Enveloping me like the dark mist that's now curling from the walls, and it's bolstering. Soothes my trembling and takes an edge off the ocean of anguish that's threatening to undo me.

I turn, open my bedroom door, and gasp.

Gleaming, glittering webs scallop down from the ceiling and decorate the tops of every window, looping like curtains. I'm stunned by the splendor of the designs—elaborate geometric renderings that fractal outward, more intricate than anything I've ever seen, mesmerizing in their delicate, lacey beauty.

I step into the room and absorb it all in wonder. Countless spiders hang from the designs on long, silvery strands, their attention set on me, as if in joyful anticipation.

She's orchestrated this, I realize, astonished. *She's encased my room in art.*

And in the center of one of the webs at the room's far end, she's written something in elaborate Noi calligraphy.

Noi'khin.

Tears well in my eyes, as I realize this is Sylla's radical response to the countless times I've opened my door or turned a corner to find slurs scrawled on the walls.

It's a deeply beautiful gesture.

She's made things beautiful for me.

Tears streak down my face as my sorrow breaks wide-open.

I turn to find Sylla standing in the door's frame now in partial human form, her hands neatly folded, a shy light in her eight eyes, her large, dark spider legs folded delicately around her frame, their tips demurely touching.

I take her in, fearsome and lovely all at the same time. And I realize that spiders are like that. So frightening to watch. Terrifying in what they do, how they kill. But also artists of the highest order. I glance around the room again, at the magnificent weaving that makes my heart ache from its beauty. As I realize that Sylla, too, is an artist of the highest order.

The multiple small spiders hang there, motionless, as if breathlessly waiting for my reaction to this strange and lovely showing of friendship.

"This is incredible," I tell Sylla, my voice breaking as I struggle to find the words to convey my overwhelming rush of gratitude. "What you can do is just so beautiful," I manage, the words heartfelt. "And so complex."

"Embrace the complexity," she says, tilting her head as her stillness embraces us both.

I cough out a sob, grimacing as tears fall. "I'm trying," I rasp out. "I'm trying. But I'm really struggling here."

"Embrace that too," she says, her words a low, bone-deep thrum that resonates through my core. They're prone to this, the Death Fae—cryptic, philosophical pronouncements—and right now, it feels like a lifeline.

"I feel so alone, Sylla," I admit, breaking down, unable to hold back the sobs wracking my whole frame as I shut my eyes so tight they hurt.

She makes no sound crossing the room, her spidery leg a gentle weight on my shoulder.

"Take courage, Noi'khin," she says as I sob. "And be patient with Vothendrile. He's lost, just like you."

CHAPTER EIGHT

AS'LORION

Tierney Calix

The Wyvernguard
South Wyvernguard Island, Noilaan
Eastern Realm
Sixth Month

Tierney walks to Fyordin's room. Restlessness curls in the pit of her stomach over her impulsive decision, the hour approaching midnight.

Pulling in a shaky breath, she raps on Fyordin's door, sensing the flow of his power just beyond it. The hallway is silent, its indigo walls lit by a single sapphire rune sconce. She curses under her breath, unable to control the way her water power is leaping through the door toward him with potent, turbulent force.

A flowing line of Fyordin's power connects with hers through the wooden door, his fuller power rippling to life as a slim stream of it molds itself against her tempestuous current. Heavy steps sound from inside.

The door opens, Fyordin before her.

Tierney pulls in a hard breath. He's shirtless with bare feet, nipple-piercings on full display. Thin drawstring pants ride low over sculpted hips, the masculine lines of him standing out so much more clearly than in his uniform…

But even more flustering is the look he's giving her, concern sparking to life in deep-lake eyes initially so liquid from sleep. A warrior energy gathers in that gaze as he studies her, his magic palpably ready to defend and align.

Tierney finds her ire toward him blunted by that look of Asrai'kin alliance.

"I want to swim to the bottom of the Vo with you," she blurts out.

Fyordin's water aura burgeons toward her in a potent tide, but he yanks it back with impressive strength. He gives her a searching look, a trace of rattled exasperation in it. "You are giving me a *great many* mixed signals, Advisor Calix."

"*Fyordin,*" she counters sharply, half in censure, half in urgent plea. "I need your aid."

His brow knits, a slender trace of his power breaking loose to flow through her storming aura, and she can feel him putting her obvious distress above his straining urge to let his waves crash into her magic. He opens his door wider and Tierney steps inside, not caring about propriety at this moment. Fyordin shuts the door and stills before her.

Tierney glances around the room, noticing his mussed bed, the various books and weapons strewn about, all of it lit by moonlight streaming in through arching windows overlooking the Vo.

"What aid do you seek?" he asks.

Her gaze swings to his, a jolt running through their currents as their eyes meet. "We amplify each other's power," she stiltedly begins, "and—" she swallows, her pulse quickening against the disarming caress of their magic "—so… I need to swim to the bottom of the Vo with you…and touch you."

Fyordin's blue brow goes up, a stronger current of his magic breaking toward hers.

"Not like *that!*" she blurts as a warm spark of amusement lights his eyes.

"Then how, Asrai?" he asks, warmly patient.

"I need to get a better sense of the river," Tierney attempts again, too aware of how close he is. How alone they are. How the river is *right there*. "Fyordin…" she manages as their joint powers reflexively loosen and swirl into a heated caress.

The alluring feel of it seems to catch them both off guard. Fyordin stiffens, liquid want entering his gaze as Tierney completely loses her train of thought, unable to fight the tide. Suddenly not wanting to fight the tide. She steps toward him, pulse thudding, and brings her trembling palm to his bare shoulder.

Fyordin's power breaks toward her with oceanic strength, rushing through her magic. The room's walls seem to liquefy, swirling currents of his magic tingling to life under his skin to rush through her palm.

"Oh" is all Tierney can manage, feeling swept toward him as Fyordin's eyes go half-mast, a shuddering breath escaping his lips.

"Your touch—" he rasps out "—it's better than I ever imagined…"

Their auras break loose. Tierney pulls him toward her at the same time Fyordin grabs hold of her, his magic and strong arms catching her in a swirling embrace. Tierney shudders, flooded by their joint power with such passionate urgency it steals her breath away, their magic's furious hunger swiftly rising to tempestuous levels, his body against hers a wild thrill. Fyordin's eyes are deepening pools, pupils blown wide, and his *scent*. Like the deepest depths of the Vo.

Entranced, Tierney reaches up with a trembling hand to touch his silken hair. Fyordin's breath hitches and he closes his eyes, his expression taking on a look of rapture as she threads her fingers through it, entranced by its waterfall feel. When he opens his eyes and meets her gaze once more, his eyes and power are churning with the full power of the Vo.

"I'm falling for you. *Hard*," he groans, seeming to have lost all control of his magic's surge and flow.

Another whirl of his aura spirals around her, a tingling pleasure she's never experienced before chasing its flow. "Oh," Tierney says again, eyes widening.

"Kiss me once, Asrai," Fyordin offers, leaning in decadently close, his voice pitched low. "Just once."

He's trembling, Tierney realizes, stunned by her effect on him as her own tremor of desire kicks up to dazed heights. The liquefied walls around them contract as she fights the yearning to pull him even closer and instead holds him back. "Fyordin... this is a mistake. This isn't a true draw. Most of the time we're at full odds with each other."

A bright swoosh of his power shimmers through her. "I'm not *fully* at odds with you, Asrai," he purrs, a wicked glint entering his gaze as she's even more intensely swept up in the desire to merge with him like she merges with the Vo. Fully. Nothing held back...

But...*no*. This is the river's magic at play, muddling their minds.

She takes a decided step back, breaking physical contact. Breathing hard, she meets his hungry gaze, the room's walls streaming around them. "I shouldn't have come here like this," she manages, voice shaky. "It was wrong of me—"

"Every night, since we first met," Fyordin says in a tormented voice, "I lie awake wanting to pull you to the bottom of the Vo and...join our tides." He stops himself, his jaw tensing, and Tierney senses something deeper going on—a rattled edge to this fervent desire.

"I lie awake sometimes...thinking of you, as well," she admits. "With thoughts of...drawing you down to the base of the river and..." The words trail off as her face heats.

Fyordin's eyes blaze. "Then let's go there, Asrai'lir. Right now. And fully merge our power as Asrai'lure."

Tierney's eyes widen. She knows what that means—Asrai marriage.

A forever bond of two Asrai, joining their water-bonds, joining their guardianship over those waters as one. She realizes, in that moment, just how lost Fyordin is to their feverish draw, like a stream stirred up, everything hopelessly clouded.

Tierney shakes her head to force clarity. The distance helps, dampening his watery pull as the room solidifies. She rubs the bridge of her nose as her breathing evens out. "Our Asrai pull is overriding all sense. We don't even get along."

"Asrai…"

"Fyordin," Tierney counters, "please…hear me out. I think our thoughts are drawn toward…*being* with each other at the base of the river because we don't want to leave it. Because we sense a threat."

Vulnerability crosses his expression, cutting through the desire. "You sense it too?"

"I do," she admits, her latent fear ramping up. "It's subtle, but it's been preying on me. I didn't want to come to you for help because… I was so mad at you and…" She pauses, reluctant to voice the admission. "You were right. I wanted the Vo all to myself. I didn't want your aid. But…" She pauses again, heartbeat quickening, knowing what she's about to say could get her disciplined or possibly kicked out of the Wyvernguard. "Fyordin, I don't think we should leave the waters of the East."

They both grow silent, eyes riveted on each other, gazes stark with the ramifications of such insubordination.

"Vogel's forces are to the west," Fyordin says with measured emphasis. "The Vu Trin *need* our power to fight him *there*."

"I know that," Tierney says shakily. "I struggle with that, but…you feel it, too, don't you? The unnatural power, pressing in at the edges? I think the Vo needs us. If the waters fall…life unravels. There's no winning *any* war then. It all ends."

Fyordin exhales, steps back and rakes his fingers through his hair. His fierce eyes cast about as he spits out a series of Noi epithets, then meets her gaze once more, his strong blue hands coming to his hips.

"I want you to go down to the bottom of the Vo with me, right now," Tierney says, serious. "But not to merge as Asrai'lure, because you're truly not thinking clearly. Neither am I. We're mirrors of the Vo…we're feeling the river calling to us."

"The As'lorion," Fyordin breathes, giving her a weighted look.

Tierney stills at his naming something she'd never heard of

prior to coming here—the clarion call of the Water Fae. A call that comes once in generations.

The Asrai call to protect the waters above all else.

The torment fades from his expression as he holds her intent stare, their joint power beginning to coalesce into a more unified flow.

"What are you first, Fyordin," Tierney challenges, but there's no rancor in it. "Vu Trin? Or Asrai? I think the river is asking us to decide."

Fyordin swallows, eyes riveted to hers. "Asrai, Tierney. Vu Trin as well, but Asrai first. Always." Passion swells in his gaze. "And, Tierney, my Asrai'ir, I do think I'm falling in love with you, despite our differences."

Tierney's cheeks flush as compassion rises in her for this infuriating, often thoughtless and *wrong* but unflinchingly loyal Fae'kin. "It's not me you love. It's the Vo in me. And I can't help it... I love the Vo in you, as well."

Fyordin grows quiet, their power eddying with emotion. Finally, he holds out his hand to her, tentatively, like a peace offering. Tierney takes it.

He lifts her identically blue-hued hand and eyes it thoughtfully as he caresses it with his thumb. Heat courses through Tierney's power, and Fyordin gives her a serious, knowing look. Then he raises her hand and presses his lips to the back of it, his power contained now, just a rippling stream flowing through her Asrai power in a light embrace.

"It's not just our Vo bond," he says as he lowers their hands and twines his fingers through hers. Tierney lets him, their power commingling.

"Allies, then, Fyordin?" Tierney offers. "For the Vo."

"Allies, Asrai," Fyordin agrees, his grip on her hand firming.

"Good," she says, emboldened by their joint decision to go rogue, if need be. "Then come with me, Asrai'kin. To listen to our river. Together. And see what our joint power can hear."

ZONOR STORM

Trystan Gardner &
Vothendrile Xanthile

The Wyvernguard
North Wyvernguard Island, Noilaan
Eastern Realm
Sixth Month

Vothendrile

"The problems of the Western Realm need to stay in the Western Realm!" Heelyn insists to Min Lo as she slices the air with her rune-marked hands.

I take in the dragon image of the Goddess Vo shaved on the side of Heelyn's head as I watch my two childhood friends face off. Trystan stands a short distance away, dressed in his sapphire Vu Trin apprentice uniform, my thoughts flitting to when he burned his Gardnerian garb a few nights past.

"There are *children*...families *dying* on their way to the Eastern Realm," Min Lo says to the room full of apprentices and soldiers, pointedly ignoring Heelyn's censure. "Who's willing to fly out with me tonight and help them?"

I scan the crowd assembled in the large circular weapons room, everyone awaiting Weapons Master Jyl Hin's arrival. Blue torchlight casts them in a moody glow, the armory's stone walls filled with countless runic weapons hung in neat, deadly rows.

Min Lo's dark eyes blaze, the silence she's met with only stoking her passion. "The people fleeing here have no idea what the waters of the Zonor River are like. Storms are forecast for tonight, and there's always the danger of migrating kraken. Vu Trin scouts have spotted a number of Westerners moving toward the river. They need our help."

I let out a long sigh. *Always the revolutionary, Minyl. Always taking the unpopular political side and pushing others to join you.*

"And by rescuing these Kelts and Urisk," Heelyn snaps back, "you're encouraging more to come and putting more at risk."

"You think they'll just stay put if we don't save some of them from drowning?" Minyl's question sounds calm, but I can sense her outrage rising.

"I *think*," Heelyn says, "that if we're not careful, the Eastern Realm will become the Western Realm. The Kelts and Urisk are as backward as the Gardnerians—"

"I'm quite clear on how you feel, Heelyn," Minyl throws down in an obvious attempt to shut Heelyn up.

"No women are allowed in the Keltish military," Heelyn reminds her. "Women are forbidden from bearing arms. All because their holy book tells them so. The same holy book the Crows follow minus a few pages, I might add. Is that what you want here in the Eastern Realm?"

"Have you forgotten that the Kelts were our allies in the Realm War?" Min Lo shoots back.

Heelyn spits out a sound of derision. "So were the Amaz. Who kill all men who wander into their territory. Who leave male babies in the woods to *die*."

Min Lo takes a step toward Heelyn, her fists tight around the hilts of the curved swords sheathed at her sides. "All I know, Heelyn," she counters, "is that while we stand here and debate, families are about to try and cross the Zonor with *absolutely no knowledge* of the undertow that was magicked into its center during the Realm War. Or how fast the storms and kraken can move in." Minyl glances around the room with what feels like a silent plea for compassion. "Don't you see? This could be any of us, if we were born in a place in turmoil. People are on their way here as we speak. Let's help them. Who's with me? Ung Li has granted me permission to use four rune skiffs."

I take in the uncomfortable looks being traded around the uniformly Noi apprentices and soldiers, save Trystan, and my sympathy rises for Minyl when no one volunteers.

She's fighting a losing battle. Commander Ung Li's soft spot for refugees from the Western Realm—save Gardnerians and Alfsigr—is not one of her popular stances. The tides of opinion in the Eastern Realm are turning. Before, when it was a trickle of refugees, mostly Fae who brought power to the Wyvernguard, sympathies ran high, everyone united against the Gardnerians and their allies, the Alfsigr Elves. But now, with that flow accelerating...the doors are slamming shut.

My own people are with the Noi Conclave in this, and I'm inclined to agree with them. Heelyn is right. The problems of the Western Realm need to stay in the Western Realm. The Amaz will bring their hatred of men. The Kelts their backward *Book of the Ancients*. The Urisk their class-based infighting and potentially dangerous geomancy. The Fae their revolutionary groups looking for a return to Fae supremacy over both Realms. And the Lupines...the growing Gerwulf Lupine pack bows to no one, not even the Noi Conclave. They're aligned with the East for now, but will they be forever? And now, even Mage refugees are filtering in.

The Eastern Realm is courting chaos.

"A baby drowned last week," Minyl tries again. She looks straight at me. "Vothe, you're my good friend. You've always been a person of high integrity. Come and help me."

"Minyl…" Dismay rises inside me to disappoint her so publicly. "I can't help you. You know that. I'm the son of the Zhilon'ile Regent. It would be seen as a political statement—"

"Have you forgotten what the dragon that marks your uniform stands for?" Minyl challenges, her voice thick with emotion. Her gaze sweeps the room. "The Compassionate Vo? Goddess of Mercy?"

"Goddess of the *Noi religion*," Heelyn says. "Not Goddess of the Kelts or the Urisk."

"Really, Heelyn?" Minyl counters. "Where exactly is it written in the *Teachings of the Blessed Vo* that compassion is solely for the Noi?"

"There won't be any *Teachings of the Blessed Vo*, or a Noilaan for that matter, if we let the West overrun the East!" Heelyn cries out.

"I volunteer."

Trystan Gardner's voice rings out like a hammer strike to the room.

Minyl's entire expression tightens, almost a flinch, and I can feel the apprentices and soldiers inwardly retreating from her. Heelyn sneers at Trystan, then turns to Min Lo with an unkind smile, as if to say, *See? Point proven.*

"I don't need your help," Min Lo tells Trystan as she glares at him, but as she holds his unflinching stare, I sense conflict igniting in her.

"I've just cleared flight training," Trystan says, seeming unfazed by the collective dislike in the room, and it's hard to not be impressed by his unflappable poise in this moment. "I want to help."

"None of us need your help, Crow," Heelyn growls, and I shoot her a look of censure.

"I'm a Level Five Water and Fire Mage," Trystan says to Min Lo, pointedly ignoring Heelyn's slur. "I can deal with storms and turbulent water. And I'll bet I can blast kraken clear apart."

Min Lo holds Trystan's gaze, and I can scent the softening of her resolve to keep this Mage at arm's length.

It's not easy, is it, Minyl? He's not going to make this easy for any of us, this Mage. Unsettled lightning sparks to life inside me as I take in Trystan's recklessly courageous stance. *This beautiful, determined, storming Mage.*

"What gives you the right?" Heelyn sputters at Trystan, her face a mask of fury.

Trystan meets her incensed glare. "I'm a refugee too," he says, calm as the eye of a hurricane.

"You've come here by *choice*," Heelyn seethes, her voice breaking under her fury. "But *they* are all fleeing here because *you Roaches* are destroying the entire Western Realm! And now we're supposed to let the problems of the Western Realm—problems *your kind caused*—into the Eastern Realm to destroy it too?"

I inwardly cringe in response to Heelyn's scathing words. Because I'm clear now that there's no actual choice in it for Trystan Gardner.

My inner storm whips higher, because Heelyn's question also has validity to it—validity my own people are solidly behind, the Zhilon'ile Regency in my home country of Zhilaan having recently taken a firm stand against letting any more refugees into the Eastern Realm. Pressing for the formation of several layers of storm bands past the Vo Mountain Range to keep the West firmly in the West as well as repatriating most of the refugees back to the Western Realm.

The West on one side, the East on the other. Cleanly divided. Problem solved.

"All right," Min Lo suddenly says to Trystan, her whole body tensed. "I'll accept your help, Trystan Gardner."

Sounds of surprise and censure burst through the room, and through me as well, as I scent Trystan's own surprise rolling through his water power.

Oh, Minyl, I rue as my power kicks into a storm, jostling just beneath my skin. *What have you done?*

"Be at the western dock at eighteenth hour," she orders Trystan. I stiffen as Minyl's eyes flick toward me, challenge in her gaze. "I suppose that volunteers you, too, Vothe."

Trystan

"You've needed to see this with your own eyes for some time now, Vothe," Min Lo says as she steers the rune skiff over the inky Vo River, the sapphire glow of the rune skiff's whirring runes reflected in wavering lines on the water far below.

I glance back in the direction of the Wyvernguard. We're trailed by the three other rune skiffs, piloted by some of the few apprentices sympathetic to Min Lo's cause, as well as a single soldier.

I turn and look west. The imposing Vo Mountain Range's peaks and forest are rendered a watercolor black and violet by the twilight, and a balmy wind has whipped up from the river, Vothe's silver-tipped, black hair tousled by it.

"You're unlikely to change my opinion," Vothe says. He leans against the rail, sounding a trace apologetic.

As I listen to their debate, I realize that Vothe and Min Lo must have a long history of friendship, despite their political differences.

I also know that Min Lo courts women like Vothe courts men. Out in the open. With complete acceptance here. I've seen her with her partner, the lovely, willowy soldier Ru Sol, on more than one occasion, once on the terrace, caught up in a passionate kiss, Min Lo's rune-marked hand threaded through Ru Sol's cascading black tresses. I watched them for a split second, mesmerized, feeling almost dizzy from the cultural shift. As that familiar shock sliced through me over how much better things are here in that regard, my awareness grew of how arbitrary religious rules can be. And of how much of a nightmare religious rules can become.

But there's more than one way of manufacturing nightmares for each other.

The disturbing thought rises in me as our rune skiff soars over the river's western bank and the line of Vu Trin stationed there, and then over the sapphire-glowing runic border. Every rune on the skiff briefly rays out blue light as we are waved through a military checkpoint and pass through the translucent dome encasing Noilaan.

I'm gripped by a sudden feeling of vulnerability to be traveling beyond Noilaan's sheltering dome for the first time in months. *West.*

Bracing myself, I glance down at the darkness of the refugee encampment that's sprouted up on the border's western side, the tents donated by Noi'khin sympathetic to the plight of those fleeing east, the refugees newly barred from entering. More people and tents every day.

More people than there are tents.

"There's a Red Grippe outbreak down there," Min Lo says to Vothe, her tone low with challenge as we fly toward the mountains. "They need care. Not to be housed in thin tents without enough healers to tend them all. I'm organizing physician and apothecary apprentices. We're petitioning to be allowed through the border to help them."

Vothe stays silent, his onyx brow knotted as he takes in the tents far below, the vast encampment lit only by sporadic torchlight.

"Two people were claimed by the Grippe this past week," Min Lo continues gravely. "A mother and her eight-year-old son."

As Vothe meets Min Lo's gaze, I can see the intense conflict igniting in his dark eyes.

I'm starting to realize there are two Vothes—the effortlessly powerful Vothe who charms the whole Wyvernguard and claims it as his own, and the Vothe who thoughtfully listens as Min Lo challenges him. Who refuses to shun the Death Fae and is on good terms with Sylla Vuul.

Who is capable of changing his mind, much as he seems to wrestle against this tendency.

That's the Vothe I yearn to be with. A shimmer of heat traces through my lines. *That's the Vothe I'd like to grab hold of and send lightning straight through.*

Vothe suddenly turns and catches my gaze with his slit-pupiled eyes. A frisson of lightning jumps between us, setting every nerve in my body alight.

Min Lo taps the craft's control board and our skiff swoops up toward the lightning-spitting mass of Wyvern-fabricated storms lining Vo Mountains' apex. She taps the controls and a buzzing, translucent half dome of sapphire blinks into existence around the skiff, the wind abruptly cutting out.

"Hold tight," she cautions with a glance over her shoulder as she meets my eyes. "We're flying right through those storms."

Vothendrile

A killing wind whips against our skiff as soon as we clear the Vo Range and its fabricated storm band and enter the unfabricated chaos to the west of it, the forewarned storms already here, hours before they were forecast. Our visibility is reduced to close to nil as rain hammers down and a fusillade of lightning bursts against our shield.

Our rapidly decaying shield.

Min Lo's head whips toward us, concern flashing in her dark eyes. "The storms were supposed to move in later... I don't have enough charge in the shielding runes."

My back pressed to the railing, I throw my palms backward to make contact with the shield's crackling energy, then close my eyes and let out a hard exhale as I release my water and wind magic into the shield's outer surface, thrilling at the feel of my power making contact with the larger, raging storm.

Another surge of power rushes through mine, and its sheer force steals my breath away.

I open my eyes to find Trystan's wand raised to the shield, even though he was granted sanction to use it solely for killing kraken. It's difficult to concentrate around the sensation of my power fused to Trystan's as I throw more wind into the shield, and he propels what feels like an ocean of water through it, our power a near cyclonic match.

Trystan lowers his gaze to meet mine and a backflow of our melded power flashes through us both, his lips twitching up as his eyes spark, and I fight off the sudden urge to lunge forward, pull him into a kiss, and stoke our power even higher.

A child's scream cuts through the maelstrom, breaking our thrall.

The flash of surprise in Trystan's eyes mirrors my own.

"Can you hold the shield?" I yell to him through the roar of the wind.

Trystan nods and murmurs a spell, feeding a more powerful rush of his fire and water power into it.

I throw off my tunic, close my eyes and exhale as my wings burst from my back, my horns stinging against my scalp as they arc up. Then I splay my palms against the shield and flow a final burst of water power into it and into Trystan's heady rush of magic.

I open my eyes to find Trystan's wide eyes fixed on my un-furled wings. An invigorating sting of his lightning aura crack-les over my skin as I turn and leap from the rune skiff.

The wind slams into me as soon as my body passes through the watery shield. Pulling in my wings, I dive straight toward the Zonor, as another high-pitched shriek manages to cut through the roar of the wind and thunder. I catch a glimpse of the other skiffs, mere pinpricks of fogged sapphire light against the storm's steely gray, all of them forced south. The violent, boiling sur-face of the water comes into sharper view through the sheeting rain, and my gut cinches.

Boats destroyed. People clinging to detritus.

A little blue-hued Urisk girl is struggling to stay afloat just below me, clinging to her mother on a bobbing plank of wood. As I watch, they're wrenched apart by the force of the Zonor's funneling undertow, the mother sucked into the churning vor-tex, the little girl screaming as she thrashes, then silenced as she's sucked under, as well.

There's no time to think about who should be let into the

Eastern Realm and who should be kept out. There's only the punch-to-the-gut shock of people drowning below me.

I hit the water like a crossbow's bolt, breathing it straight into my lungs as I shear through the waves, filled by the reflexive rush of pleasure that merging with water always brings, the more violent the better. I arc upward, my wings folding back tight as the hazy form of the child comes into view, skinny limbs flailing, her mother nowhere in sight. I scoop her into my arms and arrow us both up, through the choppy waves and into the raging storm.

"Mamma, Mamma!" she screams in Uriskal as she chokes out water, her hands splayed toward the river, and my heart seizes as I scan the waters, her mother nowhere to be seen. Needing to bring her to safety, I dart toward our rune skiff as the child screams hysterically and tries to pry herself from my grip, her hair tangled and knotted from the damp, her face a pale blue from the cold. She can't be older than six.

I fly through our skiff's shield and alight on its narrow deck as Min Lo hovers the craft just above the dangerous water, both the skiff and its shield stabilized, Trystan's wand now lowered, the shield holding on its own. His green eyes gain a look of urgency as he takes in the screaming child.

"I'm going to look for the mother!" I tell him as I move to hand her off to him.

"Mage!" she shrieks as she turns and catches sight of him, struggling mightily against my grip.

"Don't be afraid," Trystan attempts to reassure her as he gently touches her arm.

"No! No!" she screams, violently flinching away. "Mamma! Mamma!"

Trystan's eyes meet mine as his expression goes hard. "I'm going in."

Before I can respond, he raises his wand and murmurs a spell. A thin, watery shield courses over him, encasing his head and torso, before he jumps overboard. Min Lo gives me a determined look, and I hand her the child, then jump back in too.

The next minutes are sheer chaos. A desperate search through murky waters. The raging storm above. Children up and down the river screaming for their parents. Parents calling out for their children and each other.

I pull a Keltish woman who clearly has the Red Grippe out of the Zonor's powerful waters and help Min Lo hoist her onto our skiff, the woman slumping onto the deck and coughing fitfully while the little girl continues to scream for her mother.

I fly out and retrieve another child, a little blond Keltish boy, pale and traumatized, his teeth chattering from the cold. His father manages to swim to the skiff and is pulled up next by Min Lo. Then the boy's mother, who is screaming hysterically, "My baby! My baby!" over and over while we drag up the family's coughing and sputtering teenage son.

And then Trystan surfaces, holding an unconscious blue-hued Urisk woman. Min Lo aids me in easing her limp form over the skiff's railing and onto the dark wooden deck as Trystan descends into the water once more.

"Mamma!" the little girl screeches, and I catch hold of her before she can fling herself at the unconscious woman. Minyl drops down by the woman's side, pressing her palms into her chest in rhythmic compressions, then feels for a pulse as the child tries to claw her way out of my grip. Anguish slices through me as Minyl stops, breathing hard, her lips trembling.

No, Minyl, please no.

I release the child, who roars out her agony as she hurls herself onto her mother.

Minyl's face twists as she starts to cry, then quickly collects herself, roughly wiping away her tears. She stands and meets my gaze, sorrow lancing through us both.

The other rune skiffs have managed to soar back north and are crisscrossing the surrounding waters, their blue lights fogged by the lessening storm, but they do not land. And I realize, in another gut punch of sorrow, that anyone not pulled on board by now is likely dead.

Trystan's head breaks through the water, a blond Keltish baby in his arms that sputters and then begins to cry at the top of their lungs. I rush to the skiff's edge and take the baby, hand the child off to Min Lo, then grab firm hold of Trystan's hand, lightning crackling through our arms as I hoist him on board.

Everyone on the skiff recoils.

"Crow!" the little boy cries, scuttling back against the boat's side.

"Stay back!" the teenage boy warns, fists balled as he springs to his feet, his eyes wide with evident terror. "I'll kill you if you hurt us!"

The sick woman slumped on the skiff's floor cries out and raises her hands protectively in front of her, as if a monster has just come on board.

"Why are you working with a Crow?" the man cries to Min Lo as he pulls a knife and positions himself in front of his family, his wife hugging the baby now in her arms, fierce conflict in her gaze.

"You killed her!" the little girl screams as she clutches her dead mother, her face a mask of devastation as she levels her blue gaze at Trystan with blistering hate.

A piece of my own heart shatters for the child as I realize what's happening. How she must imagine that this storm is Mage-wrought and that Trystan's magery drowned her mother.

Trystan takes in the dead, blue-haired woman splayed out before the child and his internal power comes apart, his control breaking, a jagged blast of his lightning aura flashing through me. He steps backward near the skiff's edge, drops his wand and raises his palms.

It happens so fast, I'm unable to prevent it.

The teenage Kelt growls as he surges forward and pushes Trystan clear off the boat.

Trystan

I hit the water, and everything comes crashing down on me with the force of a thousand storm bands—the look on the refugees' faces, their justified hate, the drowned mother...the motherless child.

Crow. Roach.

Mage.

And suddenly, my magic comes untethered and I'm drowning in those words, my power churning with so much turmoil, I barely notice the river's whirling chaos as it closes around me, the funneling undertow like some distant disturbance in the face of the riptide of anguish and magic lashing through my heart and my lines.

Vothendrile

Sweet Holy Vo, I think as Trystan disappears beneath the water's surface, sucked down by the undertow.

I pull in my wings and dive after him.

Hitting the water like an arrow, I scythe down, sensing Trystan's oceanic power through the funneling energy of the river, quickly spotting his long form being dragged rapidly into its depths.

I shoot toward him and throw my arms around his torso.

Trystan glares at me and struggles mightily against my grip, his power a fractured mess as air bubbles explode everywhere around us. And I know, in that instant as I sense his completely unstrung power, that Trystan has lost his way—fighting not against me saving him, but against all the pain of the world as well as all the pain he's endured.

And I'll be damned if I'll let that pain destroy him.

You blazingly stupid idiot, I inwardly rage. *I will not let you die!*

I hold on relentlessly as our powers wage war and his lightning cracks violently against mine, visible bursts of it forking out through the water from us both.

Then, Trystan stops struggling, and there's something devastating in that too. But there's no time to feel it too deeply. I power up air behind us to propel us through the water's surface, shield us both, and soar back east.

* * *

Trystan shatters.

I can feel his power coming untethered as Ung Li questions his unsanctioned use of wand magery and I stridently make a case for him. I brace myself for his immediate dismissal from the Wyvernguard, but Ung Li simply says she must "carefully consider the facts" and we're miraculously allowed to leave without censure.

Trystan doesn't speak to me as I bring him back to his barracks, his hair and clothing sodden, a dead look in his eyes that wrenches my heart.

"What happened?" Sylla Vuul asks from the hallway's webs, concern in her voice. She quickly morphs from her giant spider form into that of a petite midnight-hued Death Fae girl and drops down from her webbing, her eight eyes pulling in to form two fully black ones.

Trystan opens his door, silently steps into his room, and shuts it.

For a moment I can't move. I can't speak. I can only stare after him.

"He scared the people we were trying to help," I finally manage, feeling close to shattering myself. "And he was pushed into the Zonor. I think, for a moment, it all got to be too much for him, and the river...it pulled him under." I'm suddenly not able to take an even breath and have to stop and fight the urge to break down myself.

I can't get the image of the little girl hugging her dead mother out of my mind, one of so many drowned this day, four more bodies, recovered from the uncaring waters.

Footsteps round the hallway and Min Lo is suddenly striding toward us with Wyn Juun, the Wyvernguard's elderly Vo priest who tends to the spiritual needs of the apprentices. Wyn Juun's sapphire priest garb is marked with embroidered dragons rendered in a multitude of colors—the many manifestations of Vo. A necklace with a pendant depicting one of Vo's sacred doves graces his neck.

The Noi priest looks at me, concern etched deep into his

wizened brown face, his snowy hair pulled back in a knot, his long beard tied into a knot as well below his chin.

"He's in here?" Wyn Juun asks, urgency in his tone as he gestures toward Trystan's door.

"I told him everything," Min Lo says to me, her clothing still soaked, her short hair sticking up in damp spikes.

"He's not part of the Vo'lon religion," I caution the priest. "He's Gardnerian."

"Is he?" Wyn Juun shoots back. He knocks on the door, his voice gentle when it comes. "Trystan Gardner. I am Wyn Juun of the Vo'lon faith. I come asking for you to speak with me."

Silence.

And then the door opens, Trystan's face wan and tearstained.

"Noi'khin Gardner," Wyn Juun says with great kindness, purposefully using the address that marks a person as firmly part of the Eastern Realm, "please allow me to come in."

Trystan's face constricts. "I tried to save her mother. I tried." His face crumples and he begins to sob. "We're doing all this. The Mages. We're forcing those people to flee. We're to blame for all of it. We're *monsters*."

"You saved a baby," Min Lo cuts in, her voice breaking with emotion.

Wyn Juun goes to Trystan and gently ushers him back so he can enter. "We will pray for her," he says, his voice low and compassionate as he places his hand on Trystan's trembling shoulder. "We will pray for all those who are fleeing to the East. And we will pray for you, as well."

Wyn Juun briefly looks to me, then Min Lo and Sylla. And then he shuts the door.

Devastation rips through me. I fall back against the cobwebbed wall, barely noticing Min Lo's and Sylla's attempts to speak with me. Barely noticing the light steps of poisonous spiders climbing all over my legs, my arms, my cheeks, as sorrow takes hold and I'm lost to it.

CHAPTER TEN

VO'KHIN

Trystan Gardner & Vothendrile Xanthile

The Wyvernguard
North Wyvernguard Island, Noilaan
Eastern Realm
Sixth Month

Vothendrile

When I come for him before dawn, Trystan emerges from his room wearing the Vo'lon prayer necklace comprised of thirteen stone prayer beads, one stone for each of the twelve image manifestations of the Goddess Vo, the ivory stone in the center symbolizing the dragon goddess in her unified form. There's a small white bird, symbolic of Vo's Ahxhil sentinels, hanging from the central ivory bead.

I catch Trystan's eye and hold his steady gaze. Neither of us speaks as my magic churns and the nightmares that woke me again and again last night crowd my mind.

The chaos of the Zonor River.

Children crying out for their parents, the parents for their children.

The dead mother.

Then the image of Trystan dropping his wand and being pushed into the churning Zonor. My arms around him as his eyes met mine under the water, blazing with a green fire that had all of his lightning crackling in it, shot through with a lifetime of pain.

"Wyn Juun has invited me to the Vo'lon service at dawn," he says.

Concern lights. I know the reaction Trystan is likely to get when apprentices and soldiers spot the sacred Vo'lon necklace around his neck.

Stop, I want to caution him. *You'll be hated even more if you go out there wearing the Vo'lon necklace.*

And I don't want you to be hated any more.

But then another image surfaces, crowding out all the others.

Trystan emerging from the waters, the baby in his arms.

I know that Wyn Juun helped Trystan in some vital, mysterious way last night. And that the Vo necklace is symbolic of it somehow. I think of my own Vo'lon necklace, pushed in the back of a drawer. Fished out for religious festivals and high holy days. The prayers said by rote with each worn-down bead. This religion has been mine all my life, and yet not mine in this powerful way. And it's of no solid help to me right now. My sleep-deprived mind struggles to understand Trystan's draw to it, my emotions a turbulent mess.

Trystan holds my gaze, as if waiting for me. Waiting for something I can't give, because I'm lost in unfamiliar waters with no solid purchase anywhere.

His eyes narrow slightly, as if seeing something in me that pains him, a disturbance rippling through the power he's keeping firmly back from me, a small frisson of lightning shuddering through it.

He looks away and starts down the hall.

★ ★ ★

We walk into the Vo temple to find about twenty soldiers and apprentices already there, Priest Wyn Juun among them. The apprentices are seated cross-legged around the central pillar-statue of Vo, the dragon goddess's ivory form twined around the column. Bas-relief starlight birds emerge from the goddess's head to fan out across the domed ceiling. The twelve manifestations of Vo mark the sectioned stone floor.

Every set of eyes snaps toward us, everyone's face taking on a look of shock, save for Wyn Juun's. The elderly priest simply greets us with a welcoming smile from where he kneels.

Minyl is there, as she told me she would be late last night with outrage crackling through her voice, her planned prayers a silent protest against a world set on walling people out.

Set on letting children drown.

Her long-tressed love, Ru Sol, sits by her side, ready to recite the verses of protection for those fleeing east. To recite the verses of mourning for those who have drowned.

Min Lo's gaze flicks toward me before fixing on Trystan, and I can read her storming emotions, can tell by the dark circles anchoring her eyes that she, too, is still on the Zonor River.

There's a ripple of disturbance in the room as Trystan and I stop on the temple's periphery, the looks of surprise rapidly turning to those of protest.

Wyn Juun's age-thinned voice resonates against the temple's circular walls as he sounds the traditional temple greeting. "Vo'nor'ysh, Vo'khin." *Blessings be upon you, Sacred Child of Vo.*

Sounds of outrage swell and the majority of the Noi'khin rise to leave, only Wyn Juun, Minyl, Ru Sol, and three dazed-looking apprentices remaining.

Trystan's lightning slashes through his lines and my own power reflexively leaps toward him, wanting to encircle him with a force that will drive everything else out. Wanting to throw my arms around him and pull him out of the uncaring waters.

Trystan's steps are measured as he walks halfway toward the

Pillar of Vo, across Vo's blue water manifestation. He takes a seat facing the pillar as the storm in him swirls, a tempest of agony and sorrow. Then he crosses his legs and places his hands on his knees, palms up.

Minyl meets my gaze, fierce sympathy in her expression. Ru Sol's long-lashed eyes dim with a troubled look as she takes in Minyl.

Minyl decidedly gets up, softly pads over to Trystan, then takes a seat beside him, touching him on the shoulder before settling into her own prayers. Then Ru Sol rises, graceful as a swan, her long, dark hair swishing behind her as she takes a seat at Trystan's other side.

I know the apprentices who have stayed. They look to me, seeming stunned, as I remain pressed against the wall, imprisoned in my role as guard. Desiring, with everything in me, to have this faith still mean something to me.

Desiring with everything in me to be the one sitting next to Trystan Gardner.

"I read this last night," Trystan says to Wyn Juun after the meditation service, holding up the book in his hand.

The Way of Vo.

The prayer text practically everyone raised in Noilaan knows by heart. As familiar to me as a children's song. Meaninglessly familiar. But I can tell that there is something new in it for Trystan.

Something revolutionary.

"Please, teach me," Trystan says to Wyn Juun.

Trystan

I never expected to find religion here. To find that religion could be so much more than I was taught. I thought it was all rigid lines. Who to hate. How to keep from being hated. Hate those with wings. Hate men who love men. Hate shifters. Hate Fae.

Hate and hate and hate.

Or be cast out as an Evil One.

But here, their holy book is not as literal. It's not full of which colors to avoid. Which clothes you have to wear. Which rigid lines you have to fit into.

The Goddess Vo is symbolic of the ineffable with Her twelve Erthia manifestations—

The elemental manifestations—Air, Water, Fire, Light, Earth.

The journey manifestations—Child, Youth, Pilgrim, Elder.

The Erthia manifestations—Life, Death.

And the central manifestation—Love.

Always, in the center of everything, Love.

As I read, something clicked in me. Something that resonates with this age-old religion, bone-deep. Something that helps me to mourn without becoming lost to it.

It was painful, when almost all the Noi'khin left Vo's temple. Excruciatingly painful to be rejected in this lifeline that's been thrown to me. But Wyn Juun welcomed me, and it was enough to dampen the storm inside me and enable me to sit down and take the prayer beads Wyn Juun gave to me in hand. To begin committing to memory the prayers associated with each manifestation of Vo.

These unfamiliar, beautiful prayers awaken something in my heart, even as a storm wreaks havoc inside me. I can feel Vo in this room, feeding strength into me, calming the storm.

Feeding love into me.

I dive into the scripture of the Eastern Realm like I'm a starving man whose soul is finally being nourished. Because there's nothing in this faith but a door flung open. And there's nothing in it that casts me out.

CHAPTER ELEVEN

NOI'KHIN GARDNER

Vothendrile Xanthile

The Wyvernguard
North Wyvernguard Island, Noilaan
Eastern Realm
Sixth Month

Trystan is changing.

He gets up before dawn to meditate with Minyl and Ru Sol. And then, after the dawn service, he spends time speaking privately with Wyn Juun, the old priest embracing Trystan paternally before he leaves and gifting him with new books on the Vo faith. Books that I groaned over having to recite as a child. Fidgeting through meditation. Eager for the service to be over to get to the gathering afterward and its profusion of food.

It fills me with an inexplicable yearning, how Trystan is finding, in my own religion, something that grounds him so powerfully. Because I feel like I'm coming unmoored.

The dreams won't go away.

Every night, I see the child, crying over her dead mother. And in the dreams, Vo's Ahxhil birds are everywhere, perched on the edges of the boat and filled with a mourning I feel straight through my heart. They look up as one and set their eyes on me.

I wake up crackling with fitful lightning and wondering how many more dead mothers there are to come. How many more motherless children.

"I'm to meet with Ung Li," Trystan informs me a few days later, his expression remote.

It's a nightmare, I want to confide in him. *What's happening just outside our borders...it shouldn't be happening. We need to help the people fleeing here. My family is wrong to want to shut them out.*

I was wrong.

Trystan, I was wrong, and I'm lost in confusion. Minyl was right. We can't wall ourselves off from the Western Realm and pretend it's not there.

But I say none of it, because I can sense that he needs to keep himself tethered firmly away from me.

So, instead, I let the lightning inside me spit and churn and consume me.

"I'm lifting your guard after Xishlon," Ung Li states succinctly from behind her Wyvernguard tower chamber's desk.

Both Trystan's power and mine ignite with surprise, my lightning aura crackling outward all over my skin.

It takes Trystan a moment to find his voice. "Does that mean..."

"I'll be granting you the same privileges as other apprentices," she says. "Privileges with the same restrictions, of course. And I'm granting you more extensive use of your wand."

Tears sting my eyes as I realize what this will mean for Trystan. I turn and take in his stunned expression.

Ung Li signs the Leave Pass before her and hands it to him. "I'm also granting you one day's leave to go to Voloi at this week's end to purchase clothing to replace all that was vandalized. I will be granting you unrestricted travel in Noilaan and to the South Wyvernguard Island beginning on Xishlon."

I can smell Trystan's heightened shock as his forking light-ning mingles in with my own.

Xishlon—the purple moon holiday only a few weeks away.

The biggest holiday in all the East. A celebration of Vo's most revered manifestation—Her manifestation of Divine Love.

"I can see my brother? My family, and Tierney?" The yearn-ing in Trystan's words tightens my heart and makes me feel like I'm yearning too.

And I know that I am—for this Mage standing beside me.

Ung Li sets down her pen and levels her gaze at Trystan, a crease forming between her brows. "You must understand why I kept you isolated, Trystan."

Trystan holds her stare, and I can sense a resentful fire spark in him, fire that he's quick to bank down. Trystan gives a slight nod, his green-glimmering mouth a tight line.

Ung Li's gaze hasn't wavered. "I heard what you did," she says, her voice lowering with import, a trace of uncharacteristic emotion in it. "I heard of the child you saved. And I've watched you endure countless painful weapons sessions to help us break through Mage magic. I was unsure at first, but I've witnessed your loyalty. You've proven yourself, Noi'khin Gardner."

Trystan straightens, rigid as a post, but I can sense the sud-den upsweep of water power in his lines. *Noi'khin*. Valued citi-zen of Noilaan.

Accepted. Arrived.

I blink back the emotion stinging my own eyes as a single tear streaks down Trystan's military-rigid face, his breathing gone slightly uneven.

"On my recommendation," Ung Li says as she threads her fingers together, "the Noi Conclave is granting you full citi-zenship here in Noilaan."

I pull in a hard breath.

Trystan slams his fist to his heart in salute, his posture ramrod stiff. "Thank you, Nor Ung Li," he says, his voice rough with emotion. "It is an honor to stand with the Noi'khin Wyvern-guard. It is an honor to stand in defense of Noilaan."

Ung Li's eyes narrow on Trystan. "I misjudged you, Noi'khin Gardner. You have more of a place here than you think, regardless of what those who do not realize how you have proven yourself say."

"I have family here, some that I've never met," Trystan says. His voice is slightly deepened by welling tears, and I fight the urge to embrace him and kiss them away.

"You do," Ung Li confirms, that always-present steel in her voice, but there's a rueful note there, as well. "We kept you from them, even as they lobbied to meet with you. We needed to see who you truly are, Noi'khin Gardner. A Vu Trin soldier's life is not for the weak. But it is time you were given leave to meet with your kin." Her mouth lifts in the touch of a smirk as she shakes her head. "Rebels, the lot of you." Her eyes soften with a rare showing of approval. "Rebels of the best kind."

Trystan gives a slight smile, and he makes no move to wipe away his tears, wearing them like a banner. And in this, too, I find him courageous. And so beautiful it makes my heart ache.

"Your apprentice pay." Ung Li slides a black wax-sealed envelope toward him, filled with the meager allowance all apprentices are granted. Funds that have been withheld from Trystan, along with everything else.

"Go," Ung Li says with a dismissive flick of her finger toward the door. She gives Trystan a shrewd look. "Replace your clothing so you have something to wear off-hours. Take a day to explore the city and see what you're defending." One black brow rises as a sardonic smile lifts her lips. "Try not to create too much havoc in Voloi."

TRANSFORMATION

Trystan Gardner &
Vothendrile Xanthile

City of Voloi, Noilaan
Eastern Realm
Sixth Month

Trystan

"I don't sell to Roaches."

The Noi man glares at me, his eyes narrowed with fury. I notice he's wearing a Vo necklace. Across the street, other merchants in Noilaan's clothing district stand, arms crossed, positioned in front of their open-air clothing shoppes as if guarding them from a hostile invasion.

Vothe stands a little to the side, his muscular arms crossed, as well. A cool breeze eases up off the river toward this Fourth Tier of the mountain city of Voloi, ruffling the silver tips of Vothe's hair as it gleams in the morning sun. He's almost too handsome to take in, even watching me with what looks like an edge of frustration. Perturbed, no doubt, over my insistence that I manage this myself without his proffered help.

Because I need to use my own voice and my own coin to become my own true self. No more hiding or sequestering who I truly want to be.

I scan the sun-drenched storefronts as white clouds scud across the vivid blue sky, violet Toi'nir birds wheeling overhead. The bustling city is a wonder, already adorned for the Xishlon holiday. Purple banners imprinted with Vo's ivory and purple dragon goddess manifestations hang from practically every storefront and snap in the wind. Tables laden with clothing and jewelry, scarves, and hair ornaments in every hue of purple spill onto the street's edges. Kiosks dotting the streets proffer rows and rows of the holiday's traditional heart-shaped wreathes of lavender flowers and pressed, purple flower cards. And interspersed amongst the stores are tattoo parlors and hairstylists advertising violet Xishlon designs, beckoning Noi'khin to begin their celebration early.

But every merchant here has turned down my coin, each refusal like a fresh blow.

"I'm looking to buy some clothing," I say to a Noi woman with a kind face. A little girl clutches her arm and peers up at me innocently. The child is hugging a lilac cloth dragon doll to her chest, both mother and child wearing tunics and pants with the same elaborate, embroidered design—bright violet irises, large as real flowers, sewn onto glistening purple silk, their hair decorated with glittering lavender gems.

The woman glances at my Wyvernguard uniform, then scrutinizes my Mage features, a trace of sympathy in her expression. But then she catches the eyes of other nearby merchants and takes in the warning in their gazes.

"I'm sorry," she tells me stiffly as she averts her eyes. "I see that you work to defend us…but it's just not possible to sell to you."

Stubbornly ignoring the sinking feeling in my gut, I continue to stop in every open-air shoppe on the thoroughfare and am turned down by merchant after merchant. Crowds stream by, and practically every person notices me. Now and then, the initial looks of bafflement morph into expressions of covert solidarity—small smiles, nods of acknowledgment. But more often than not, ire dogs my steps, along with a few slurs viciously deployed—*Crow. Roach. Filthy Mage.*

I pause, feeling stranded. Overhead, lines of glassy orbs holding luminous purple runes bob cheerily in the breeze—most of the orbs decorated with hand-painted purple roses or violet filigreed hearts—and practically every passerby is already turned out in purple Xishlon finery. There's a festive mood in the air, smiles plentiful, but they're snuffed out by confusion and discomfort when people take in my Mage face and I wonder, longingly, what it would feel like to be a true part of the upcoming Lavender Moon festival.

Vothe is quiet beside me, no doubt sensing the frustrated hurt whipping through my lines.

"What does that say?" I ask him, pointing to a sign hanging above a stall selling hair ornaments. The same sign hangs from close to half the stores and stalls—black Noi script on purple, a rendering of Vo's ivory dragon goddess next to the lettering. I've noticed the merchants of those stalls have been the most hostile toward me.

A discordant shudder passes through Vothe's water and wind power. He turns to me, his expression tensing. "It means *Noilaan for the Noi.*"

The blow connects with surprising force. For a moment, I'm back on the Zonor River. People struggling in the water, tossed around by the river's violent undertow.

Noilaan for the Noi.

I quickly get hold of myself, determination rising to battle back what feels like the leading edge of a storm. A determination not just for me, but for them.

"Trystan," Vothe says, his hand coming to my arm, "you're not going to find anyone who'll sell to you. I would help you if you'd let me." His words are tinged with frustration, but his gaze and touch are full of a solidarity that's so warm it catches me off guard and seems to catch him off guard, as well. Tension lights in the air between us and my power leaps toward his. Lightning sparks in his eyes, threads of it dancing on his lips, and my breath hitches as his eyes drop to my mouth. "We should leave," he says throatily, as if he's fallen into a daze. "Go somewhere private."

The crowds streaming around us fade away as surprise shudders through me.

He wants to kiss me.

It's new, him letting me see his desire so openly. But I sense that it's fueled by an unsettled current—an undercurrent of turmoil that seems to have taken up residence inside him ever since we came back from the Zonor. He wants to kiss me in the same way he kisses Basyl. Like he kisses two other men I've caught him ensconced with. For escape. A diversion.

And in my case, in secret.

And that's not the Vothe I yearn to kiss, because what I feel for him is beginning to run too deep, futile as it might be.

I want the impossible.

I want a Vothe who declares himself for me openly. In the middle of the city square.

"I'm not leaving until I find someone to sell to me," I say as I move back from his longed-for touch, frustrated beyond all reason. Feeling like I'm trapped in my own skin, desperate to break free.

I can't be this false version of myself anymore. It's vital that I not be *this* anymore.

This Gardnerian.

"Mage, come here!"

Surprised by a woman's jovial, arch tone, I turn and see an elderly, black-clad Zhilon'ile merchant smiling at me, her onyx face covered in swirling crimson tattoos, black horns spiraling up from her head. She's standing in front of a tattoo and clothing shoppe. Her long white hair is artfully braided, scarlet and black gems woven through it, and her skin is infused with lightning, just like Vothe's.

"Come here, Mage," she says again as lightning leaps in her eyes and her lips tilt up. "Trystan Gardner. I want to speak with you."

Vothendrile

"What do you seek?" my renegade great-aunt asks Trystan.

She holds one black-taloned hand out to him in dangerous offering, her nails filed to points and stained with tattoo ink. Bright black metallic hoops decorate her eyebrows, pointed ears, nose, and the side of her mouth. A scarlet dragon tattoo depicting Vo's warrior goddess manifestation twines down her arm.

"This is my great-aunt, Sithendrile," I tell Trystan, wishing I'd more carefully avoided my fully empathic great-aunt, having thought her visiting the Salishen Isles. I've always been close to her, but right now, I don't want her reading my feelings for Trystan or learning what's going on inside his mind. I throw a lash of water power out to her, willing her to look my way. She gives a short laugh and eyes me slyly as she effortlessly throws her own storm aura around mine and presses my magic down until it's flat on the tiled ground, a cloud of white vapor briefly forming around the three of us. She narrows her sharp gaze at me and does not lower her hand.

I cock a stubborn brow. "He should know you're empathic before he touches you," I chide her and warn Trystan at the same time, a fitful energy rising through my power.

Because I'm clear what this handshake is about.

The Wyvernguard has a sizable number of Wyvern apprentices, and it's likely that she's heard from at least one of them that an attraction has been sensed. And now she wants to read it for herself—my impossibly strong draw to this Gardnerian. This Mage whose tears I want to kiss away. Who invades my dreams and has turned my world upside down.

Trystan doesn't hesitate. He meets my great-aunt's intimidating stare, reaches out, and takes her hand.

She gives him an amused look as her taloned fingers clamp tight around it.

"I seek transformation," Trystan says, throwing the words down like a gauntlet. "I seek to be who I truly am."

My great-aunt loses her smile and inhales, her pierced brows knotting as she holds on to him, her expression morphing to one of astonishment. I pick up on her sensing the vast power that lives inside him—the constant lethal storm that abides just under his skin.

The storm I increasingly yearn to throw myself and my power into.

She closes her eyes and bows her head as she reads him, nodding a few times, sometimes with apparent surprise, sometimes as if with dawning understanding.

When my great-aunt finally opens her eyes, there's a weighted gravity there.

"You will come with me," she announces to Trystan as she releases his hand. When she beckons him to enter her shoppe with a curl of one onyx-clawed finger, he goes inside.

I move to go with them, and she holds up her palm. "No, Vothendrile. This is between Trystan, me, and Vo above. This is beyond you at the moment."

I bristle, stung. *Beyond me? The person who has been shadowing this Mage for over a month now? Who pulled him from the depths of the Zonor?*

I step back, suddenly hollowed out by a grief I don't understand.

My great-aunt's expression softens. She raises her hand and caresses my cheek, and I bite back an intense swell of inexplicable loneliness. By any measure, I shouldn't be lonely. Despite my support of Trystan, I still have a number of friends and family who are supportive of me.

But I also know that most of my family would recoil in revulsion if they knew how much I want to kiss Trystan Gardner. How I yearn for the courage to pull him into my arms like I did in the waters of the Zonor, but not to rescue him this time.

To have him rescue me.

"I see what you are feeling for each other," my aunt says softly.

Sweet Vo, she's reading it all in her touch.

I flinch away from her, ashamed by my deepest thoughts and inability to understand the difficult emotional terrain I've landed in.

"Don't leave the Zonor," my aunt says to me, her stare blisteringly intent. Her unexpected words pierce my soul. "That's where you'll find your strength," she insists. "And your transformation. Don't fear it, Vothendrile."

"Our people are wrong to want to wall off the West," I blurt out to her. To this renegade aunt of mine who is often tactlessly blunt, caustically revolutionary, and seems to regularly position herself at odds with the Zhilon'ile Regency and most of my family. Much like my friend Min Lo. "It's different," I confide in her. "Different to see it with your own eyes. People are dying trying to get here. Children. Whole families. I have nightmares about it. Every night for a week now. I can't get what's happening there out of my mind."

"Then go back," she challenges, lightning in her gaze, "and take a stand. Even if you lose everything." She squeezes my arm affectionately, over the fabric of my uniform this time, where we both know she can't read me. Then she turns and follows Trystan past the curtain, leaving me behind.

Trystan

"What would you have me do?" Sithendrile asks, her shoppe lined with neat rows of every color of tattoo ink imaginable. I pull off my tunic and sit on the long table before her.

On the wall nearest me, there's a shelf of metal jewelry of every conceivable style, larger bottles of dye just above it, and bins upon bins of cosmetics and kohl pencils to line the eyes, as is the style here for Noi men.

I think of the little girl screaming in the boat. Screaming in terror when she caught sight of my black hair. My Gardnerian features.

I reach up and fist my short, dark hair. "You can start with this," I tell her.

Vothendrile

By the time Trystan finally emerges from my great-aunt's shoppe, my emotions are a turbulent mess from hours of pacing the streets and repeatedly checking for his reemergence. The city is cast in twilight, the purple flower-and-heart decorated runic orbs strung over the streets and lit with a soft violet glow.

Trystan pauses, his eyes finding mine as I push myself off the plum tree I'm leaning against and freeze.

A complete metamorphosis has taken place.

Trystan brazenly holds my gaze as the entire world recedes around us and I pull in a shuddering breath.

His eyes are lined with kohl, the contrast changing their color from deep forest green to a blazing emerald, and the effect is so stunning that a frisson of lightning shivers through my power. There's something deeply erotic about the look, an edge to it, even though wearing kohl is all the fashion for Noi men and a common style by now.

On Trystan, it's fiercely compelling.

And his hair is a vivid blue. The black gone. Completely gone.

He's had my great-aunt pierce him. Multiple times. Black metallic hoops decorate both brows and line the entire length of his ears, and a small ring loops through one side of his lower lip. I fight back the outrageous desire to let my teeth elongate and tug on that lip piercing.

And the tattoo.

Sweet Holy Vo, the tattoo.

A sapphire dragon head covers the entire side of his neck, its serpentine body disappearing under the collar of his clothing. Blue lightning is marked all around it, forking over the entire column of Trystan's throat.

His Noi tunic and pants are a bright violet blue, a sapphire dragon embroidered down his tunic's side, a twin to the dragon on his neck.

Storming energy crackles over him as I hold his gaze, our powers sizzling toward each other with the force of twin bolts of lightning. A hint of a smile lifts Trystan's lips as his power strengthens, a force to be reckoned with.

And I get the sense, as my eyes remain locked with his devastatingly arresting gaze, that I'm staring at the real Trystan Gardner for the very first time.

Trystan notices me eyeing his tattoo all the way back to the Wyvernguard, and then again as he pauses inside his bedroom's door. Those sexy, kohl-lined eyes of his are intent as they watch my gaze slide down his neck and along the imagined path of the tattoo.

Over the imagined planes of his body.

"Does it drape over your chest?" I ask, my voice thick with a strengthening tide of desire for this beautiful, startlingly courageous, outrageous man.

Trystan doesn't answer. He simply narrows his gaze at me as the storm inside him whips up, lightning flashing. Then he steps back and throws off his tunic.

Sweet Holy Vo.

My breath catches in my throat, lightning pulsing through my veins over the sheer beauty of him. His lean chest, glittering green. The huge sapphire dragon snaking down his entire side, its tail disappearing over his hip bone...

When I lift my gaze to meet his, there's a challenge in Trystan's gaze. A dare.

I see it in his eyes, his readiness to take more than one leap into the unknown this evening. There's an unmistakable invitation in his stance, and I suddenly want him with everything in me. I want to cross his room's threshold and guard him as closely as possible.

But I don't budge. Because this won't be light and breezy. This won't be a diversion.

This would be something world-upending and true.

So, like a coward, I hesitate, letting the boundaries between us stand. I let fear of the sheer strength of this thing growing between us stand. As I violently fight a desire for him that's so tight and hard, I want to fling myself through the doorway and into his arms, and sink my teeth into the base of his neck, claiming him as my own.

But still, I don't budge.

Trystan's gaze darkens, a flash of sheer pain in it as he gives me a hard look then pushes the door closed, and I feel it snap shut, down the entire length of my spine.

Trystan

It takes everything in me to close the door on Vothe. On the unmistakable want in his eyes. Want he's clearly at war with himself over. Maybe even hates himself for.

It's ironic and surreal, how, here in the East, there's no shame in the fact that we're both men. No. There's shame in it here for an entirely different reason.

Because I'm Gardnerian.

I can sense Vothe through the door. Sense him as clearly as if I were a shifter myself.

He'll never give in to his desire for you. You'll never have him.

I stand there, cursing myself for yet again tormenting myself. Over and over. Wanting Gareth Keeler as more than a friend for years. Pining over Yvan Guriel.

And now, falling in love with the most desired young man in the Eastern Realm. A man who may be increasingly my ally, but who can never fully give in to wanting a Gardnerian.

Who will never let himself give in to wanting me.

Vothendrile

I'm falling in love with Trystan Gardner.

Vothendrile

I cannot be falling in love with Trystan Gardner.

ZONOR UNDERTOW

Trystan Gardner &
Vothendrile Xanthile

The Wyvernguard
North Wyvernguard Island, Noilaan
Eastern Realm
Sixth Month

Vothendrile

"You can't be with the grandson of the Black Witch."

I look sidelong at my elder brother, Gethindrile, my hackles rising in response to the paternal censure in his tone. A breeze from the Vo River far below flows over us as we lean against the railing of the Wyvernguard's highest walkway connecting the North and South Islands. His visit all the way from Zhilaan was unexpected, but I'm clear on the reason for it.

"Keeping track of my every attraction now?" I chide, defiance sparking. "I caution against it. You'll get little else done."

"Vothe," he says, concern in his dark eyes, "take care here."

"What if I'm done taking care, Geth?" I ask, incensed at the intrusion. "Did you know Trystan's converting to the Vo'lon faith? That he's covered in bruises from letting the Vu Trin blast magic at him in every conceivable way so they'll stand a chance against the Mages?"

"Our family will cast you out if you take him to mate," Geth counters, ever the one to calmly debate. To take Mother and Father's side. To take the Zhilon'ile Regency's side. But not unkindly, and somehow, that makes it even more infuriating. "You know they'll cast you out," he reasons. "Just as they cast out our uncle for going off with Fain Quillen. Vothe, Trystan Gardner is a *Mage*."

"Trystan saved a number of refugees, Geth," I snarl, hating the conflict that my brother is whipping up in me. A brother who has been kind to me my whole life. A brother who is trying to be kind to me now. But a brother who *truly* does not understand. "He saved a Kelt baby from drowning in the Zonor."

And now I'm drowning, I yearn to rage at him. *I'm drowning in wanting to be with Trystan Gardner.*

"That's another thing we need to speak of," Geth says, holding my gaze. I can imagine the fraught conversation that he had with our parents about me, their newly wayward son. "The Noi Conclave is in talks with ours," he says. "Vang Troi might be allowing these rescue missions for the moment, but the government is about to tighten the border." Warning darkens my brother's lightning gaze. "Vothe, no more volunteering with Minyl."

Trystan

I watch Vothe stare at the glittering city of Voloi, the tiered expanse lit up by a million purple lights in anticipation of Xishlon. He leans against the Wyvernguard's sixth-level terrace railing, illuminated by the nighttime glow of its sapphire torchlight.

"I've been forbidden from volunteering again with Minyl,"

he says. "My brother visited earlier to inform me of this. I suspect that's coming from my father."

I look at him in surprise. Vothe never confides in me about his personal life. And he's talking to me like he's been doing it all along. It feels disarmingly natural, to let this boundary between us fall. But, why not? We've been together almost every waking minute for weeks now. And he'll no longer be my guard soon.

A pang accompanies the thought, which part of me finds amusing. I remember how incensed I was to have a guard. And such a disconcertingly handsome one. How it threw me so completely off-kilter. How it still does. I lean against the railing alongside him, a single cloud drifting below. The inky river is calm tonight, a thousand stars strewn across the expansive sky.

I turn to face Vothe fully. "What are you going to do?"

He glances at me sidelong, and a spark of palpable lightning flashes between us. Vothe's gaze flicks over my tattoo. There's a frisson of want in his gaze, and his smile is subversive when it comes. Desire sparks, along with the urge to kiss him then and there and show him what subversive *really* means.

He turns to me fully as well, his power rising with striking force. "I'm going to go volunteer with Minyl," he says, power crackling. "And you and I are going to punch down the Zonor's undertow."

Vothendrile

Trystan's brow lifts in response to my declaration, surprise leaping through his power.

"All right, Vothe," he says. "Let's smooth out that river." His words are lightly conveyed, but there's nothing light about the magic flaring between us, the breeze from the Vo enveloping us in its balmy caress.

A troubling thought rises. A remembrance of Trystan being dragged into the Zonor River, overcome by his storming magic and devastation.

"Trystan..."

He seems to read my unease, his features tensing. "I'm stronger than I was," he says, power flashing between us. "And those fleeing here…they likely won't fear me now."

I still as it dawns on me in one dazed swoop why he altered his appearance so dramatically. Gardnerian yet not Gardnerian anymore. With his newly sky blue hair and piercings and tattoos which I've been told are forbidden by the Gardnerian holy book. All of this a blaring refute of the Gardnerian religion and the West.

But that's not the main reason he changed his appearance so drastically. It was never solely for himself at all. It was for a larger reason, more important to him than all the others.

To go back to the Zonor.

At training the next morning, Trystan and I link hands, our fingers threading tight as we give each other a weighted look. We stand at the edge of the riverside terrace, sunlight spearing down.

Commander Ung Li and a throng of apprentices and soldiers look on as we ready ourselves to do this revolutionary thing—seeking not to smite Trystan's vast power, but instead, to join it with mine. To test how much Mage wand magic can amplify Wyvern power.

We've informed Ung Li about our secondary motive—to still the Zonor River's unnatural killing undertow, and have earned her guarded support, along with that of most of the Asrai Fae. So we're testing our joint power first on the Vo.

I turn and take in Min Lo and Ru Sol, beaming at us amidst the multitude of glowering expressions. Gazing around, I catch the subtle uptick of Ung Li's lips, as well as scattered supportive looks from a few of the apprentices and Vu Trin. The looks of outrage on so many friends' faces pains me, but the sense of rightness to be openly aligning myself with Trystan is a wondrous thing.

A black mass on the Wyvernguard mountain's stony face snares my gaze, and I glance up to find Sylla Vuul, in spider form, clinging to the top of the bas-relief dragon's head, Tierney and Viger Maul perched beside her.

"Ready?" Trystan asks, calm as always, but I can sense the restless, excited energy sizzling through him.

I nod, and he points his wand at the water and begins to murmur spells, as I draw on my own storming energy and lift my free hand to the heavens.

"Vihlshhri, shuunir, vehlthru," I count down in Zhilon'ile. "Vheerno!"

We release our joint power, a compact tornado of wind rushing from my upraised hand toward the wispy clouds above at the same time a gusty bolt from Trystan's wand blasts down into the Vo below. Every cloud in the sky whips back to the edges of the horizon as a centrifugal tunnel shoots down through the Vo, providing a fantastical view of the river's dark silty bed. The Vo's waters slowly circle around the tunnel, then slow to a halt.

My body shudders along with Trystan's as we meet each other's eyes. Hands trembling, we keep tight hold of our joint magic running from river to sky. My wings fan out behind me, the sensation of our merged power as exhilarating as swallowing a storm, the warmth of his hand in mine sparking a rush of lightning all over my skin.

And then Trystan smiles at me and I know, in that moment, with glittering certainty, that I never want to let him go.

Trystan

Just two days later, Minyl's rune skiff is diving straight down into the maelstrom encompassing the Zonor. I catch sight of several small boats being sucked toward the river's killing whirlpool.

"Are you ready?" I ask Vothe as I lift my wand.

Vothe grins at me, teeth elongating, horns up, wings rigid behind him. We reach for each other in tandem, lightning jumping between us as our combined power forks toward both my wand hand and his upraised palm. I thrust my wand down toward the Zonor River and Vothe raises his palm skyward.

Two blasts of lightning-lit storm magic course from us in a

heated rush, one toward the Zonor's whirlpooling undertow, the other toward the angry sky above. The rain halts and the Zonor's waters even out to a sloshing froth, rapidly calming, the storm now a muffled roar against the dome of power we've sent up to encase a wide swath of river.

Minyl's gaze darts around in obvious wonder, then zeros in on the flimsy boats now gently bobbing on the calm river, the voices of the passengers ringing out clear. Three Wyvernguard rune skiffs dart toward the boats as Vothe lowers his arm and I relax my wand hand, our joint magic holding.

I marvel at the scene as lightning from the pushed-back storm crackles over our protective dome, its staccato bursts reflected in the silvery waters of the Zonor. *It's so beautiful.*

I meet Vothe's crackling gaze as we grasp tighter hold of each other's hands and Minyl pilots our skiff toward one of the boats. There's an Elfhollen family aboard it, and we aid Minyl in guiding them onto our craft—a mother and father along with their twin girls, the children's pale slate braids sodden.

Their gazes all snag on me as we help them get settled on our craft. Confusion passes over their features as they notice the wand in my hand and the green glimmer of my skin. But their flares of concern swiftly fade as they take in my blue hair and tattoo, my piercings, and Vothe's hand in mine. There's no terror this time. No fear in the children's faces. I turn to Vothe, reveling in the aura of storming power leaping through us.

We break into wide grins, and I don't think I've ever seen anything as beautiful in my life as his rain-slicked face, changeable threads of lightning coursing over his skin as our larger show of lightning flashes against our water and wind dome above.

No one drowns this day. No children lose their mothers.

And I realize, as I hold on to Vothe and a joy I've never known before sparks deep inside me, that this is why I came to the East.

No matter what happens, no matter what runic borders the countries of Erthia throw up, no matter what strictures they place around them, I'll never stop coming back to the Zonor.

CHAPTER FOURTEEN

THE CHANGE

Aislinn Bane

Eastern Lupine Territory
Northern Noi woodlands, Noilaan
Eastern Realm
Sixth Month

Aislinn takes in the purple wilds closing around her as she trails her new Vu Trin guides into the East's recently established Lupine Territory. Apprehension hovers inside her over being separated from Sparrow, Thierren, Effrey, and the dragon Raz'zor after their arduous journey across the Central Desert and through several storm-band-jumping portals, her companions set for Voloi as she continued northward.

Aislinn glances at her hands, hyperaware of her green-glowing Mage skin, its glimmer heightened by the forest's shadows, ever reminding her that she's an outsider here. Part of a horrific race who slaughtered almost everyone Jarod and his sister Diana loved. And what was done to her in the West by Damion Bane... she can't help but believe that it sullied her beyond the point of acceptance by a shifter race that will sense how damaged she is.

But still, she clings to a tether of hope that they won't cast her out on sight. And she's eager to find out, once they can speak privately, if they've gotten word from Elloren and Lukas Grey. Unfamiliar birds flit about in the twilight, a lavender crane soaring overhead as plum leaves crackle under her boot heels, the dirt path narrowing.

Bringing her ever closer to Jarod.

Tension mounts inside Aislinn, her heart in a vise as she strives to prepare herself for coming face-to-face with him. She remembers her last glimpse of Jarod in the North Tower's upstairs hallway, slumped in shock over the murder of his entire family. As she was dragged away by two Mage soldiers, kicking and screaming and snarling curses at her murderous father.

And then, fasted to Damion Bane, the monster hell-bent on breaking her.

And he did break so much of her. Save one fragile shard of will that seeks to bring him down so that he can never destroy another. But the Aislinn that she was, the pure, whole Aislinn that Jarod loved—that Aislinn has been broken beyond redemption.

Aislinn knows that seeing Jarod again, now that she can never be with him, could very well shatter her heart. But, still, she wants the Lupine Change, so she can go back and protect others.

And she wants Jarod to be the one to do it.

Boisterous conversation sounds ahead, intensifying with every step as she advances with her Vu Trin guides. Hearty voices call out to each other, and Aislinn has the sense that there's a sizable number of people gathered, a feral energy riding on the air. Her heart trips against her chest, her breath quickening. The woods open up, a tree-dotted clearing coming into view.

Aislinn observes it all in wonder. Young, amber-eyed Lupines, perhaps thirty or so from a multitude of racial backgrounds, are working together to erect a long, dome-roofed dwelling hewn from purple wood, small lean-tos encircling the clearing.

Her young soldier guides, Sorra Yil and Umbra Tir, look to

her with expressions of great import as they slow down and step back, poised at the clearing edge.

Aislinn steps forward, then freezes as she catches sight of Rafe and Diana, her heart in her throat.

As if sensing her attention, they both turn.

A dazzling, wild smile lights Diana's face. She growls out a joyful sound and breaks into a run toward Aislinn, blond hair flying as a startlingly amber-eyed Rafe grins and strides toward her, as well.

Diana catches Aislinn in a hug that's so enthusiastic she's lifted clear into the air and breathlessly swung in a circle before being set back down. Aislinn forces a smile, her lips trembling even as she searches for Jarod. The other Lupines set down tools, some morphing clawed hands to human ones, as everyone moves in to welcome her.

But then everything fades into the background as one young blond Lupine male appears at the far side of the clearing, and Aislinn stops breathing. His stride slows as obvious recognition hits, then he breaks into a run.

Aislinn's heart seizes. She's barely aware of Rafe's joyful greeting and Diana moving everyone away to give them space. Love for Jarod rushes through her in an excruciating tide as he runs toward her and the memories flood in—reading poetry with him in the university archives, late into the night, his beautiful amber eyes intent on her, always set on her, making her feel like some bright star instead of the plain thing she is; his love for the same books, the same art; his gentleness; his quiet ways and deep insight.

His kiss.

That night they kissed for the first time, Aislinn was enveloped in a bliss she never knew was possible. He seemed to know, with his Lupine senses, exactly how she wanted to be touched, how far she wanted to go, always stopping when she needed to, even though she could sense his powerful desire. With Jarod, it was always so full of love.

And she realizes, as he closes the distance between them and her eyes blur with tears, the full extent of what's been lost to her forever. She can see it in his ruddy health and powerful stride, in the feral light of his amber eyes…he's been restored here, while she's a ruined, defiled thing.

Aislinn's anguish pulls her under, a heartbroken cry escaping her throat as Jarod sweeps her into his arms.

"Aislinn," he breathes in an impassioned rasp as he kisses her temple, nuzzles her neck, and inhales her scent like it's a lifeline, his breath shuddering through his chest. Aislinn's legs buckle, a keening sob breaking free as she's swamped, fully, by the devastating loss of him.

"Aislinn," Jarod says again, alarm crossing his features as Aislinn crumples to her knees and he lowers himself to keep hold of her, his heartbreakingly beloved face wavy through her flood of agony.

"I love you so much," Aislinn cries, weeping violently now, her chest heaving. "I'm sorry, Jarod. I'm *so sorry.*"

A vast confusion overtakes Jarod's tear-streaked face. "Aislinn…why?"

"I should have left with you…when you first asked me to…" she chokes out, barely able to breathe. "They forced me…*he* forced me…"

"I know," Jarod says, pain and outrage streaking across his face. "I heard what happened, just a few days back."

"I was a *fool,*" she weeps, devastated. "I loved you then and… I should have gone with you. I'm sorry… I've destroyed everything…"

"Aislinn, wait," Jarod insists, eyes wild with emotion. "You haven't destroyed *anything.*"

She holds up her shaking hands and shows him the horrible fastlines, like a spider's web all over her hands. And wrists. A prison cage forever keeping her from him. Proof of her defilement.

"I'm ruined," Aislinn admits, low and final.

A growl rises from Jarod's throat as he tightens his hold on her. "You're *not*… Aislinn…"

She shakes her head and curls into herself, trying to pull away from the entire world, from her beloved, who *is* lost to her. It hurts to feel his strong arms around her. To smell his comforting scent, her heart breaking as she shakes her head from side to side, leans down and brings her hands over her face.

"I'm sorry, Jarod," she says again, hollowed out by grief and terrible shame.

"Aislinn." Jarod gently strokes her hair, refusing to let go. "Look at me. *Please.*"

. Aislinn swallows as the misery contracts her whole being. She looks up to find his beautiful amber eyes blazing down on her with a love so fierce Aislinn has the sensation of her whole world shifting on its axis.

"You're not ruined," Jarod insists, emphatic, his voice breaking with emotion. "Aislinn, I *love* you. I want only you. I was getting ready to go west to find you… I was finally approved to use a Vu Trin portal."

Confusion storms through Aislinn. "But…you mate for life and… I'm *used* now…and—" her face twists into a devastated grimace "—*dirtied* and…impure…"

Shock overtakes Jarod's expression. "That's not true. That's a twisted, cruel way of thinking about *anyone*. You're not *any* of those things. And I *love* you."

Her confusion intensifies, her worldview turning on its head—everything she was taught about her worth being so intimately tied to her perfect purity, her perfect submission to Mage ways. But here, under the bright illumination of Jarod's unflinching love, that worldview shrivels along the edges, revealing itself to be a weak, depraved thing. Still, it reverberates, impressed on the fabric of her soul.

"But, Jarod… I'm…"

"Mating for life," Jarod says, adamant, "means mating with the person you love with your whole heart. *Forever. That's* what it means." His lips tighten with outrage. "This belief that people can be impure and dirty...that's something the Mages believe, not us." His expression turns imploring as he cups her face with his warm hands. "Listen to me... I *love* you. You are the center of every poem I read. Every sunset I see. You are at the center of *everything* that's beautiful and good in this world to me. I love you and want you. *Only* you. *Forever.*"

Aislinn holds his impassioned gaze as it rushes through her, a tether of hope she never thought she'd find again. She latches on to it like a lifeline.

"I haven't lost you?" she says in wonderment as she blinks at him, held up by the bright thread of his unfailing love.

A smile breaks out on Jarod's beautiful face, his brow tensing with emotion as his tears give way. "Oh, Aislinn. You *found me.* You could *never* lose me."

And then he sweeps her into his arms again, and this time, Aislinn returns his embrace, a different type of tears falling as hope blooms. But then, she draws back from Jarod, her mouth trembling as the trauma wrests hold once more. She has to level with him. As awful as it will feel, she has to confide an edge of the terrible truth.

"Jarod..." She looks down and away from him, barely able to manage the jagged whisper. "He...he did terrible things." She chokes on the nightmare memories. "I don't know how long it will take... I... I can't be with you...fully...right away... I don't know when..."

"I'll wait for you," he insists, voice shot through with fierce, unconditional love. "I'd wait for you forever."

Aislinn pulls in a long breath. Then she meets his amber eyes, disbelieving and believing at the same time, his undimmed love beginning to piece together a slim fragment of her shattered body and soul.

"I almost missed your arrival," Jarod says, seeming dazed. "I was to leave tomorrow for the West. To find you—" his expression shifts, eyes glinting with ferocity "—and to kill Damion Bane."

"No," Aislinn says, firm now. "*I'll* be the one to kill him." She pauses, readying herself for the momentous request. The life-changing request. "I know it goes against your tradition, since tonight's moon is not yet full...but I can't be a Mage any longer."

She raises her hand and sets it over Jarod's strong, steady heart-beat. "Jarod, I want you to Change me."

They go deep into the purple Noi forest that night.

He brings her to a small clearing, the sliver of moon bright above, the two of them about to break with tradition with the full blessing of the pack.

"Are you ready?" Jarod asks as he takes her hand into his.

Aislinn's heart trills faster in her chest. Scared. Eager.

Certain.

"Yes," she says.

Jarod reaches up to gently push aside her tunic's collar, exposing the base of her slender throat. "I need to draw blood," he says, serious and apologetic at the same time. They both understand the subtext—there's violence in this, when she's endured far too much violence.

But Aislinn also knows that this is a very different thing, the setting down of a blood bond rather than an intended cruelty, and just the opposite in its outcome.

"It will bind you to the blood of the pack," he gently explains, "and to the Forest."

Aislinn nods with resolve even as nerves tighten her throat and speed her heart. "I understand," she says. "Do it."

Jarod steps closer, and she fights off the rush of fear as he cups her face and kisses her forehead with exquisite gentleness. His eyes blaze a brighter amber as his lips draw back and his canines elongate into wolfish points. He brings his lips to the base of her throat, kisses her once there...and sinks his teeth into her skin.

Aislinn gasps, arching against him as the rush of pain streaks through her, overwhelming in its intensity, like she's suddenly burning away. The moon above seems to enlarge and glow brighter, and even through the bright haze of pain, she's overtaken by its mesmerizing, luminous beauty, feeling, in the moment, as if her whole, burning body might float right up into it.

She grips Jarod's arms as the pain sizzles through her, but she holds steady and accepts it unflinchingly because in this fierce, moonlit moment, she's not interested in safety.

She wants transformation.

Amber light flashes across her eyes as something astonishing takes root within her. Her affinity lines diminish, then vanish, her fastlines fading to nothing as the energy of the entire Forest rises up to embrace her. The pain begins to recede as the strength of the pack floods through her, and Aislinn is filled with one single, shining thought—

No matter what comes, I will never be part of the Magedom again.

XISHLON'VIR

Trystan Gardner &
Vothendrile Xanthile

The Wyvernguard
North Wyvernguard Island, Noilaan
Eastern Realm
Sixth Month

Vothendrile

"You seem happier."

Trystan looks at me the next evening, both of us leaning against the Wyvernguard's lower terrace railing, facing west toward the Vo Mountain Range and the Zonor River beyond.

"I've carved out a small place for myself here," Trystan muses. "With Minyl and RuSolyl and Sylla and Viger..." He turns to me. "And you." A charge runs through us both, lighting up the longing in his eyes. And it's strong.

Trystan's lips part and my breath hitches, elation rushing through me.

"Be my Xishlon'vir, Trystan Gardner," I breathlessly offer.

Trystan stills. "What are you asking me?"

"A Xishlon'vir...it's the one you've chosen to kiss under the Xishlon moon. But it's more than a kiss. It's the beginning of a formal courtship. It's a great blessing to begin a courtship on Xishlon."

I wait for his answer, everything in me swept up in the yearning I feel crackling through his magic.

Trystan's lips tilt up. "You want to court me?"

My power leaps. "I do," I say, my heart bursting open. "Be my Xishlon'vir, Trystan."

Trystan pulls in a wavering breath. His brow knots, tears welling in his eyes.

"Have you ever been kissed?" I ask, teasing and deeply serious at the same time. Wanting to kiss away his tears.

Trystan lets out a short laugh. "No."

"I wish I could make you my Xislon'vir right now."

He tilts his head, bringing his pierced, green-glimmering mouth a fraction closer to mine. "I've...thought about kissing you on more than one occasion."

"Does this mean you'll say yes?"

Trystan gives me the most emotional smile I've ever seen on his face, and joy overtakes me. I can feel the yes in that smile. And in the way his magic eddies toward mine.

"Mage Gardner."

His name booms out from across the terrace and we both turn, a contingent of four soldiers striding toward us with grim, determined expressions.

Defensive lightning sparks in both Trystan and myself.

The straight-backed soldier in the lead halts directly before Trystan, her gaze locked on him, both of our smiles whisked away as I sense their urgency.

The soldier's gaze sharpens on Trystan. "You're wanted in Ung Li's chambers. *Immediately.*"

Trystan

"Your sister, Elloren Gardner, is the Black Witch."

My water power shudders then stills, suspended in my center as I stare, dumbfounded, at Commander Ung Li. Clarity avalanches in, and I understand fully, in that moment, why we're standing in Ung Li's private tower, surrounded by soldiers. Why they confiscated my wand before we entered.

And why Elloren's journey here has taken so long.

Lightning slashes across the inky sky outside, momentarily brightening the sapphire hues of the lantern-lit room. Thunder rumbles to the west.

"That can't be," I protest, desperate to strike down their horrifying misconception. Knowing what it could mean for my sister. "Elloren has no power. She's a Level One Mage—"

"She's not." Commander Ung Li's gaze is pierced with iron-hard import. "She's been wandtested by our forces."

Confusion rips through me. "I don't understand."

"Your sister was never truly wandtested. Until our forces tested her. She's more powerful than your grandmother ever was."

The certainty in Ung Li's words ignites a jolt of lightning through my internal magic. "Where is she?" I ask as the ramifications of this for Elloren shear through my mind. They've been telling me for weeks that she's en route here. Under Vu Trin protection.

There's a beat of hesitation as Ung Li's brow creases, triggering another frisson of alarm.

Because Ung Li rarely hesitates with anything.

"She's likely dead," Ung Li states, devastatingly firm.

My magic comes untethered as pain clenches my center. I double over, my hands clutching my abdomen as it tightens against the blow of her words.

"Your sister was caught in the cross fire when our Western forces attacked the Mage Council."

I lift my unfocused gaze to hers, desperate for the unsure edge to her statement to be true. "But you don't know for a fact that she's dead?"

Ung Li's dark eyes narrow. "There's a slim chance that she's still alive." Her mouth tightens. "You will see postings going up throughout the Wyvernguard and the city with your sister's likeness on them."

"Postings?" I rasp.

"If your sister has survived," Ung Li says, her tone and expression seeming to downplay the possibility, "and if she makes her way to the Eastern Realm, then she's to be brought to the Vu Trin immediately." There's a pause, a split second too long. "For her protection." Her lips lift in a slight, comforting smile that seems forced while her dark eyes remain hard as stone.

My water magic freezes as a darker nightmare descends.

They're not searching for Elloren.

They're hunting her.

Ung Li is studying me, her gaze raptor-sharp. "If your sister has survived and she comes to Noi lands," she says, her tone measured and neutral, "it is likely that she will seek out you or your brother, Rafe. If this happens, you must bring her to us without delay. Do you understand, Mage Gardner?"

Hope and fury ignite as a whoosh of my invisible water aura breaks over the room.

Elloren is alive. And you're lying to me.

I tighten my lines and wrench all my magic inward, forcing it deep into my center. Then I give Ung Li a stiff, formal salute and strike my fist firmly to my chest. "Yes, Commander," I affirm, ready to lie, as well. Ready to do whatever it takes to find Elloren and hide her from the Vu Trin. "If my sister has survived and she seeks me out, I'll bring her straight to you."

Vothendrile

"Trystan…"

He rounds on me in the cobweb-strewn hallway outside his room, his eyes fierce.

"Xishlon'vir or guard," he demands. "Choose, Vothe. You can't be with me and against my sister."

Shock and anger light. And intense remorse. Over how Ung Li's news rocked me so hard my emotions briefly shut down. Because this changes *everything*.

"Trystan," I say, "she's the *Black Witch*."

Trystan's green eyes blaze. "They're *wrong* about her."

"She's potentially a realm-destroying weapon. An Eastern Realm–leveling weapon." We don't need to delve into the subtext of his meeting with Ung Li. We're both clear that the Vu Trin aren't searching for Elloren Gardner to protect her.

Trystan faces me down, our invisible lightning forking chaotically around us both. "I know what you called me before I got here," Trystan says. "'Crow.' 'Roach.' And I know about the petition you organized to keep me out of the Wyvernguard and the East."

His words are like a knife-strike through my heart. I step toward him, overcome with fierce contrition. "I'm sorry. Trystan, I'm *sorry*—"

"I *forgive* you," he says with impassioned sincerity. "But Vothe, you called me those things because you didn't *know* me. Just like you don't know my sister. She's with us in the fight against Vogel."

"This isn't so simple, Trystan," I counter, incredulity rising. "Ask me how many people in my family were killed by your grandmother during the Realm War!" My teeth are gritted, elongating. I can feel my horns releasing from my head. "*Ask me.*"

Trystan looks straight at me, holding my gaze even though I can see the pain in his eyes and sense the agony strafing through his magic.

"*Many,*" I snarl. "And practically every household in the East lost people they loved to your grandmother's fire. So don't act like this is a clear, easy choice for me." My voice fractures, the enormity of what I feel for him breaking through. "Don't make me choose between you and the entire Eastern Realm."

"I would *never* ask you to make that choice," Trystan bites back, his expression hardening with a furious, cornered defiance. "Xishlon'vir or my guard, Vothe. *Choose*."

I can feel my heart breaking. "I want you, Trystan," I say as devastation rips through me. "But it has to be guard."

Trystan's invisible power explodes, and I feel that detonation straight through my core as he gives me a look of sheer agony, then turns, throws open his door, and steps into his room. I move to follow him as he falls back to sit on his bed, his face dropping into his hands as he clutches his blue hair.

"Stay out," he orders, and I freeze in the doorway.

The hallway's thick webs rustle and a giant spider emerges, gracefully lowering herself to the floor before scuttling toward me, her legs clicking against the stone tilework. Sylla gives me a mournful look as she enters Trystan's room.

Everything in me yearns to go to Trystan as Sylla climbs onto the bed beside him and morphs partly back into human form, save her extra sets of legs. She throws a human arm and one of her huge spider legs around Trystan.

Trystan grabs hold of the insectile leg as if grasping a lifeline.

"How did the world get to be this way?" he implores, his face hidden in his palm, his voice fractured. "How did this happen? Why are we all bent on killing each other? How does Gardneria happen? How does Vogel happen? How does one religion enthrall a whole land into hating everyone else?"

"The same way it always happens," Sylla says, a world-weary sorrow in her eight eyes as she embraces him. "By following a flawed story as if the whole of it is true."

Trystan

"Is Vothe gone?"

Sylla nods, her eyes searching mine as her dark Death Fae mist encircles us.

I face her fully, my internal magic lashing with urgency.

"Sylla, I want you to read me. I want you to read every last one of my fears."

She's quiet and still for a long moment, her gaze on me unblinking, as if she's gauging my sincerity. Then she lifts my hand, presses it to her cool, dark cheek, and closes her eyes.

The world shudders to pitch-black, only a silvery mist remaining as my terror for Elloren rises. I start to tremble.

"Your fear," she says, her otherworldly voice seeming to come from everywhere at once, "there's an ocean of it." Her voice has gone throaty, as if with sudden rapture. She slides my hand down and presses her lips to my palm.

"Follow it," I insist, trembling. "Follow every thread."

She presses her lips harder against my palm.

Her spider eyes snap into existence as she pulls back, fixated on me with a sudden, dangerous intensity. The side of her mouth lifts into a snarl.

Black Witch power could bring the End of Nature.

Her damning premonition reverberates through my mind, and it's a shock, having her thoughts sounding deep inside me as her darkness swirls around us both.

"So, you believe in the flawed story as if the whole of it is true?" I challenge.

Sylla is on me in a flash, fully morphed to spider, the room surrounding us snapping back into view, a cage of legs around my form, her jaws twitching so very close to my head.

What is it you want, Mageling? Her voice in my mind is an otherworldly vibration, but I'm beyond Death Fae intimidation at this point.

I hold her lethal, multi-eyed gaze.

"Help me find my sister," I implore her. "Before the Vu Trin do."

CHAPTER SIXTEEN

SHADOW WITCH

Fallon Bane

Amazakaraan
Seventh Month, present day

Fallon Bane soars from the Northern Spine's moonlit pinnacle on dragonback, Damion and Sylus to either side of her, spearing toward Cyme. Her black hair whips behind her, her grayed wand gripped tight in her fist.

Her wand is powerfully strengthened by Vogel's Shadow power, the magic's fabled evil transformed into Righteous Might by Mage hands. She can feel the wand's backflow of amplifying strength through her lines.

She smiles, an ecstatic shiver of grayed ice running through her as she exchanges a wickedly smug look with her brother Damion, flying to her left, then turns to meet the gleeful gaze of her brother Sylus, soaring in on her other side, a horde of Mage soldiers on broken dragons massed behind them.

Grasping tighter hold of her dragon's shoulder horn, she scowls as the Amaz battle cry rises below them like a potent tide.

We'll put an end to their bleating soon enough.

Her mother's recollections flash through her mind—memories of how the heathens oppressed the Mages for generations. How they indentured some and murdered the rest, seeking to wipe them off the face of Erthia. How, during the Realm War, her own mother was herded with other young Mage women into a livestock pen while their families were imprisoned in a nearby barn that the heathens planned to burn to the ground.

Never again. Fallon raises her wand arm higher and readies herself to take her place as Erthia's next Black Witch—that heathen's whore, Elloren Gardner, be damned. And Lukas Grey will be hers, once his hands and wrists are stripped clean of his Sealing to that staen'en bitch.

Hoarfrost spikes through her lines in a glorious chill as she murmurs a spell, wind power rushing into her wand.

"Cloak them!" Fallon calls out to her horde, signaling with an upraised hand. She swipes her arm emphatically down.

As one, Fallon and the Mages flick out their arms. Dark fog shoots forth from every wand, the fog fanning out over the valley to form a new dome of wraithlike Shadow.

"Conjure the trees!" she orders, and they all lash out their wands once more, bolts of Shadow colliding with the dome.

The dome fragments, great columns of Shadow plunging down from its curved surface, thick as buildings. Explosions sound below, reverberating through Fallon's body. She throws her head back and draws in an ecstatic breath as the columns rapidly branch out, a gigantic Shadow forest forming beneath her, the foggy dome swiftly morphing into a canopy of undulating gray limbs.

The panicked cries of civilians intensify as Fallon and her horde streak over the canopy-dome. Hunching over her dragon, Fallon gives the signal for descent. The Mages burst through the dome, the shield-safe runes on their forearms, allowing passage denied to the Amaz.

All of them trapped like penned livestock, Fallon vengefully gloats.

It's dark inside the dome, the Shadow tide Vogel cast over the valley's floor stripping Cyme of all color save the green glimmer of Mage skin, all of the Amaz heathens' precious runes stripped of their power and scarlet color by the tide.

Fallon's horde soars around the giant trees, a barrage of arrows flying toward them, the rune-stripped arrows like gnats glancing harmlessly off their gray shielding. There's a legion of ridiculously fierce Amaz soldiers massing below, rune-stripped weapons aimed at Fallon's horde as they bellow orders and women and children scatter, running toward their Queenhall.

Yes, run, Fallon crows as the children scream, reveling in the sound, remembering what her mother told her of Mage children's terror.

"Ready yourself, Mages!" she orders, lit up by the Magedom's overwhelming power advantage. She pulls back her wand, the other Mages following suit.

Ice power crackles to life throughout her body as she sounds out a spell, the surrounding air cooling as countless silver-gray spears form alongside her, ready to wreak vengeance on the terrified women and bleating children and their pathetic soldiers. *Practice,* she gloats to herself.

For what they're about to do to the Eastern Realm.

Imbued with righteous purpose, Fallon arcs back her arm and thrusts her wand forward, screaming out her order with bezerker rage.

"Fire!"

PART TWO

The Black Witch

CHAPTER ONE

EAST

Elloren Grey

The Dyoi Forest
Eastern Realm
Seventh Month, two days prior to Xishlon

Black Witch.

I scan the purple forest surrounding me with urgency as I tend to little Tibryl. She hacks out a cough, but I manage to keep the flat side of my Ash'rion blade against her neck to cool her fever, my fingers on the runic combination for ice power, the weapon stinging cold against my hand.

My temples ache, the trees pounding their ceaseless tide of hatred into me as they have throughout the day and into the encroaching twilight. But the forest be damned—I'm determined to get farther east to find my family and allies.

To find Trystan.

I tighten my fist around the Ash'rion's glacial hilt, struggling to keep my thoughts from scattering into worry for Lukas. His name sounds in the back of my mind with every beat of my heart, my nerves alight with the yearning to find him. Even as the heated echo of what felt like Yvan's Wyvernfire shimmers through my lines.

The shocking possibility that they could *both* be alive is an agonizing yet hopeful pull on my heart from opposing directions. I can't get the dual images out of my mind—the devastated look on Lukas's face as he threw me into the portal, his green eyes blazing with passion as I screamed his name. And Yvan... his eyes searing gold in the subland cavern when we said our last farewell, his hands cupping my face after he sent his Wyvernfire through me with his intense, fiery kiss.

Wait for me, he said before we were separated. But I didn't wait. I didn't question the news of his death. I Sealed to Lukas and fell in love with him with equal fervor.

An ache swells in my chest over how much it will wound Yvan—if he's truly alive—once he discovers that I've Sealed to Lukas in absolutely every way. And Lukas...how will he react to Yvan's survival?

But there's no time to resolve any of this, and it all pales in comparison to what I'm faced with.

Tibryl starts to shiver, and I move the blade away from her skin, a dart of hope rushing through me. The tips of her pointed ears seem less flushed, her eyes not as glazed. I let out a relieved breath as the forest's ceaseless tide of animosity pulses through me.

Black Witch.

Tibryl's mother, Emberlyyn, wheezes, and my trace of relief evaporates. She's slumped against Tibryl, both their backs to a violet moss-covered boulder. I spare a glance at Nym'ellia, beside me, the young teen's green-glimmering face tight with worry.

"In Voloi, sometimes the moon glows purple and everything looks like violet flowers," little Tibryl suddenly enthuses, her green and amethyst eyes glassy but alert.

I blink at her in surprise. "I remember reading something about a Lavender Moon holiday," I say, attempting an encouraging smile, even as my muscles itch with the desire to *get moving*, my eyes continually scanning the surrounding forest for more of Vogel's creatures.

"Everything's better in Noilaan," Tibryl says, seeming to cast off some of her shyness as she nods sagely in affirmation of her own statement. I imagine she's around seven years old. Her black-streaked violet hair is dirty and matted and frames her violet face in a wild mess.

"I'll have my own paints," she tells me, her fever-glazed eyes brightening, "and I'll paint the moon and *all* the flowers. There are tiny purple birds there who will sit on your finger, and the Noi children keep them as pets. And there are heart-shaped waffles flavored with violets. And everything is *so beautiful.*"

She lets out a prolonged hacking cough, and I place the cooling Ash'rion blade's side back on her neck, *shush*ing her comfortingly as her mother listlessly rubs her back and chews on the Eastern Meadowsweet leaves I've foraged for them both to lessen their fever-dazed state.

So we can hasten our dangerously slow pace.

Tibryl's spasming cough gets the better of her and she starts to whimper. I withdraw the blade again as Nym'ellia offers the child water from her flask.

I rake my fingers through my own knotted hair, acutely cognizant of Vogel's overwhelming advantage, tethered as I am to these extremely vulnerable people, my magic bound down.

"We've had a long journey from Valgard," Emberlyyn says as Tibryl drinks. "The Mages are pushing non-Mages out of the Western Realm." She glances west with tensed eyes before looking back to me, exhaustion writ hard on her face. "The desert was unforgiving." She pauses to cough into her fist.

Tibryl offers the water to her mother, and Emberlyyn takes it with a grateful nod. The child lays her head in her mother's lap and closes her eyes, Emberlyyn's hand coming down to tenderly stroke her daughter's matted hair. There's a disturbing rattle in Tibryl's lungs as she breathes. *The end stage of the Grippe.*

Nym'ellia looks at me, dread in her eyes, and I can read her fear of what will happen to her sister.

It's not safe for them to be with me, I consider guiltily as I scan the hostile wilds. *Vogel knows where I am and how I'm glamoured. But if I leave them, Nym'ellia will soon be an orphaned refugee.*

"Rest a moment longer," I offer Emberlyyn and Tibryl as I rise, then resheathe the blade and pull my tunic over it, deciding to keep my weapons hidden. "Let the Meadowsweet draw your fever down. We'll move faster once it does. I'll watch over everyone."

Emberlyyn nods, a mixture of gratitude and foreboding in her amethyst eyes—eyes that soon flutter closed. Everything is quiet save for the occasional rumble of thunder, storm-wary birdsong in the trees, insects chirring. Something brushes my thumb and I look down to find two violet spiders there, the spiders here crawling over me with disturbing frequency. So many spiders here I find myself increasingly shaking them off. At one point, a gauzy band of webbing stretched out over the forest so widely, we had to paw our way through it to keep advancing east.

I brush them off my wand hand, the purple-camouflage hues of so much of the forest wildlife here a surreal change that keeps surprising me.

"They're going to hate me in Noilaan."

Surprised, I look up and meet Nym'ellia's piercing green gaze. She's leaning against a plum-purple tree, her expression jaded— much too jaded for her young age. "They hate Roaches," she says flatly. "And I look like one."

I inwardly recoil from the slur. I don't want to believe her, but I fear there's truth to her words.

"I don't think they'll all hate you," I say, wanting to will it so. "There's always some people like that, but they won't all be that way."

Her mouth twists into a frown. "You don't understand. You don't look like a Roach."

A bitter, incredulous laugh almost escapes me. *Oh, Nym'ellia. You have no idea.*

"No one wants me anywhere." She draws herself in protectively, sparing a quick look toward her mother, both Emberlyyn and Tibryl asleep against the mossy stone.

"Well, *I* want you here," I say, meeting her tortured gaze. "And so will my family and friends."

Her brow creases. "You've friends in Noilaan?" There's a fragile trace of hope in the question.

"I do." I glance east as a rush of longing for my brothers and other loved ones washes over me anew. *And Yvan...*

Emberlyyn's eyes flutter open, breaking into the thought. She gives a start and blinks dazedly at our purple surroundings as if she's unsure how she wound up here.

"We need to go," I say, offering her my hand. She takes it while coaxing Tibryl awake with a gentle nudge, and Nym'ellia and I help them both up as the brush to either side of us rustles.

Alarm leaps through me as dark figures emerge. I move to draw my blades but freeze when the Wand sizzles warningly against my calf. My hands poised over my hidden weapons, I face down the four Vu Trin soldiers before me, their runic swords raised, charged sapphire runes marked on steel.

Holy Ancient One.

"Halt where you are," the most severe-faced soldier orders. The image of a dragon has been shorn into her close-cropped hair.

My heart slams against my rib cage as the Vu Trin draw closer, blades raised, and Tibryl clutches her mother's tunic, whimpering. My fists twitch as I ready myself to wield my weapons and that's when I notice it—the Vu Trins' eyes aren't focused on me at all, but on Nym'ellia.

"State your name, Gardnerian," the severe soldier barks in the Common Tongue and Nym'ellia flinches like she's been struck.

The terrible realization swoops down—*They think Nym'ellia is the Black Witch.*

"Please, Noi'khin, leave us be," Emberlyyn implores as Tibryl starts to cry, which seems to rouse Nym'ellia from her momentary stupor.

"Stop scaring her!" she demands.

My own outrage flares. "Nym'ellia's not Gardnerian," I insist, even as fear of discovery grips tighter hold.

"Look at her ears," Emberlyyn manages as she pulls in a wheezing breath.

The sorceress stalks forward and roughly pulls up Nym'ellia's hair. Nym'ellia recoils from her unkind touch, and I resist the urge to throttle the soldier.

"She's been cropped," another soldier pipes up in the Noi language, looking concerned. She's young and striking, her long black tresses loosely tied back. Her willowy posture slackens as she lowers her sword. "Heelyn," she says gravely to the harsh soldier, "do you understand what's been done to this girl?"

Heelyn's narrowed eyes flick over Emberlyyn and Tibryl, and I can see the situation falling into place in her mind—the girls part Gardnerian, part Urisk. She grimaces, then glares at Emberlyyn, and I can almost hear her thought. *Consorting with a Mage.*

Her gaze slides to me as my fear ramps up.

"Who are you?" she demands in Elfhollen.

"Ny'laea Shizorin," I manage, throat gone dry.

"Your destination?"

I force myself to hold her piercing stare. "East."

"Have you seen any Mages?" Heelyn glances suspiciously at Nym'ellia, as if her black hair and green glimmering skin alone make her suspect.

Ire flares. "No," I say, incensed by her treatment of Nym'ellia. "Are you looking for someone?" I regret my outburst immediately.

Heelyn's dark eyes narrow on me and a shiver of anxiety rushes down my spine. My hue has been grayed and my eyes silvered, but the shape of my Black Witch features is unchanged.

"We're searching for a Gardnerian woman," she says. "Around nineteen years old. Sharp featured. Resembles the last Black Witch."

I swallow. "I haven't seen anyone like that."

Except in the mirror.

She stares at me for an excruciatingly long moment as my stomach clenches. Then she loses the edge of her confrontational demeanor, her expression softening to what seems like jaded chagrin as she resheathes her weapon.

"Go back to where you came from," she tells us, switching to the Common Tongue. "Border's closed."

A harsh intake of breath sounds behind me as I'm rendered speechless.

"When...when did that happen?" Nym'ellia falteringly asks.

The soldier—Heelyn—shoots her an unfriendly frown and pointedly ignores her.

"Closed to everyone?" I ask, stunned.

She meets my gaze once more, a trace of sympathy lighting her eyes that is absent when she looks at Nym'ellia and her family, and I can tell I've been slotted into the right cultural category in her mind, sympathy for the Elfhollen running high in Noilaan. Sympathy for an Urisk woman and her two Mage-blooded children, not so much.

Heelyn nods stiffly. "Border's been closed for days," she tells me. "The Noi Conclave ruled it so. You should turn back. There's nothing for you here." She pauses, her brow tensing. "If you're thinking of crossing the Zonor River and Vo Mountains to get to the border, *don't*. They're dangerous. Kraken have been known to move through those waters. And in a few days, the wall of Zhilon'ile storms that lines the Vo Mountains will be extended over this entire area. Go home. It's impassable. And it's about to become even more deadly."

Home? I want to spit at her. *And where exactly would that be for Nym'ellia and Emberlyyn and Tibryl? Or for me?*

"They're sick," the long-haired soldier says to Heelyn, her dark eyes searing.

Heelyn rolls her eyes and rounds on her. "I can see that, Ru Sol," she spits out, switching back to the Noi tongue, clearly figuring that we won't understand, not counting on the glamoured translation rune behind my ear. "But that doesn't change the fact that they won't be allowed through the border. *Especially* since they have the Grippe."

"This is *wrong*," Ru Sol counters, stubbornly remaining in the Common Tongue. "They need care."

"You overstep, soldier," Heelyn snaps in Noi. "Have you forgotten what we're tasked with?"

Your cursed border is about to be struck down, I seethe. *Because Vogel can destroy Noi military runes. And you're worried about one small, desperate family getting in?*

It's a struggle to hold back the warning about Vogel's Shadow abilities that both Lukas and Valasca charged me with bringing to the Vu Trin. But I'm certain that these sorceresses would never believe me. Unless I revealed to them who I really am.

And then they *really* wouldn't believe me. They'd simply kill me.

No, I have to find my brothers and my other loved ones. And Yvan.

"I'm sorry," the soldier Ru Sol says to me, heartfelt, and I can sense the remorse balling in her throat in the way her graceful neck and jaw tense. She glances around blankly, as if she's grasping for something she can do to help. Then she reaches up and pulls off the necklace she's wearing and hands it to me.

I stare at the ivory dragon pendant hanging from the chain, realizing it depicts Vo, the Noi Goddess of Compassion and Mercy. Two small pendants hang to either side of it—Vo's messenger birds.

"Vo be with you," Ru Sol says, her voice constricted.

I meet her gaze, incredulous. "We don't need your dragon goddess," I spit out. I glance toward Emberlyyn and Tibryl, who are caught up in another round of spasmodic coughing. "We need Norfure tincture and warm beds."

And I need to prevent the imminent destruction of your entire realm!

"I'm sorry," she says again before they take their leave. Ru Sol gives me one last devastated look over her shoulder before they step into the woods and slip out of sight.

I turn to find tears streaking down Nym'ellia's face. "What do we do now?" the teen asks me, her voice tremulous.

Steel rises in me, hard and implacable. "We go east," I tell her as I fist the hilt of my Ash'rion blade. "And we get past that border."

THE ZONOR

Elloren Grey

The Zonor River
Eastern Realm
Two days prior to Xishlon

The Zonor River is a shock to the senses.

A stiff wind whips my gray hair against my face in stinging lashes as Nym'ellia, Emberlyyn, Tibryl, and I stare at its vast expanse in the twilight, its steel gray waters churning southward. It smells like cold energy. Like raw power licking the air. And I wonder what monstrous things could be lurking in its depths.

I look toward the black mountains beyond, their peaks almost as high as the Northern and Southern Spines. A lightning-charged line of storms tops its entire length. *Wyvern-crafted storms.* Deadly and impassible to all but the Noi military.

Don't think on the odds, I urge myself. *Just keep moving east.*

I turn to Nym'ellia and find the young teen eyeing the Zonor with a look of serious trepidation as she carries little Tibryl, hugging her close. Lightning forks across the darkening sky.

"Is this the spot?" I ask.

Nym'ellia tenses her brow and holds out her intricate gold compass for my perusal. All of the compass's arrows are pointing inward toward this exact spot.

"The Kelts we arranged passage with in Issaan told us to wait and the boat would come," Emberlyyn says. We turn to her. Her frail body is propped against one of the cove's purple willow trees, their cascading fronds surrounding us.

The trees have gone eerily silent, a buzz of muggy energy on the air, birdsong nonexistent as the storm to our north draws nearer.

Emberlyyn fishes a black coin from her pocket and hands it to me, a world-weary look on her face. I turn it over, its gleaming surface embossed with the image of a trout. "We paid everything we had for this passage," she admits weakly.

Risky. I palm the coin then hand it back to her. *Paying for something back in the West, trusting it to actually be here in the East.* But it's clear that this is just one more choice in a long stream of dangerous choices for this small family. It's also clear that Emberlyyn is nearing the end of her road. All the choices from here on in need to be good ones if she and her daughters are going to survive.

Please let their alliance with me be one choice they won't regret.

I tug my sleeves low and then my tunic's hem, my weapons well hidden, as Lukas and Valasca taught me. An ache tightens my heart the moment my thoughts slide to Lukas and Valasca, too, the need to find both of them like a fire burning deep in my core.

A rustling in the brush has my hands flying toward my blades. But it's not scorpios or wraith bats or Vu Trin that emerge. It's a Keltish man, ducking under the willow's purple fronds as he moves purposefully toward us. He's big and muscular with a rangy, weather-beaten look about him, his blond hair dirty and mussed.

His gaze meets mine, and my hackles go up. There's a shifty

look in his blue eyes, and I've the sense of being quickly and coldly appraised. One side of his mouth ticks up as his gaze roams quickly over me with disturbing interest. I keep my palm near the hilt of my Ash'rion blade, noticing that the Kelt has a rather large knife of his own sheathed at his waist.

No runes on it, though.

He leans down, fishes a dark rope from the dense violet brush, and gives it a tug.

A hidden craft slides from under the brambles by the shoreline's edge, the small rowboat's dark gray hue blending in seamlessly with the steely water.

"Looking for a boat?" His gaze catches on Nym'ellia and roves over her in a way that further spikes my unease.

"We've paid for passage across the river," I say as Emberlyyn steps forward and hands him the trout-coin.

The man studies the coin, then narrows his beady eyes on her. "I need two hundred more Common Trade guilders."

I balk. That's enough to buy a team of horses. And I've only 170 guilders in the purse Valasca hastily shoved into my pocket just before Lukas threw me through the portal.

"This passage is already paid for," I coldly point out.

He flicks a finger contemptuously toward Emberlyyn and Tibryl. "They're sick." He jabs his finger toward Nym'ellia, disgust in his eyes as his gaze swings damningly back to mine. "And you've got a Roach with you."

Nym'ellia is now staring at him like she's a cornered animal, devastation writ plain on her face.

I narrow my gaze on him. "That's a lot of money."

He squints at me as if taking my measure. "Then you can swim now, can't you?"

Fire rises in my lines as I realize there will be no bargaining with this man. He's obviously well practiced in taking advantage of those fleeing east.

I pull my purse of money from my pocket and hold it out. "There's a 170 here," I admit tightly.

He swipes the purse from my hand and empties it into his palm. Then he raises his gaze to look me over once more. "I think you've got yourselves passage." He gives me a chillingly suggestive smile. "You can figure out a way to make up the difference."

I glance warily toward the small boat. "All right," I venture. "Just get us across the river."

He spits out a sound of amusement at my confident tone, his face twisting with derision, as if he wants to remind me I'm in no position to give orders.

Oh, but I am in a position to give orders, I lethally consider. Because as big as this man is, he's not bigger than three scorpios and four wraith bats. And his blade is magic-free.

Yes, I can take you down, I muse, a bit stunned by the measured, predatory thought.

"You're a feisty one," he says, grinning broadly at me now. His gaze does another slow slide over my body, and I read it all in that look—he thinks he can leer openly at me and there's not a damned thing I can do about it.

"When I have to be," I say, returning his smile.

Thunder sounds with an impressively broad rumble, and we all peer anxiously at the sky.

I turn back to the vile man. "We're ready. Let's go."

He nods, all business now, and tugs the boat closer, holding it steady as I help Tibryl, Emberlyyn, and Nym'ellia get in. I pull myself on board, my power leaping as my hands make contact with the wood, its source tree flashing through my mind.

Gray Oak.

The Kelt steps into the boat, takes the oars in hand, and pushes us away from the cove's rocky bank. He pulls a flat black stone imprinted with a blue Noi rune from his pocket and presses the stone to a larger Noi rune emblazoned on the boat's gray lacquered bottom.

Six circular runes big as wagon wheels burst to life at the boat's sides, their sapphire light illuminating some of the cove's darting fish. The Kelt presses his stone onto one of the smaller runes marked on the gunnel's inner edge and the boat's runes lose their glow, shifting to the same camouflaging hue as the boat and river. He touches three more runes with the stone, and the boat gives a sudden lurch forward that has us all grasping hold of the lines affixed to its sides.

Silent and watchful, we float through the cove, willow fronds spilling over us as we pass under the trees, their ill will coursing over me.

We glide from the cove, the trees' hold on my tangled lines briefly tightening, as if they're knotting my magic down before I can flee. And then we're blessedly past the willows, their hold on my power loosening as we journey out onto the Zonor.

A tight awe grips hold.

It's one thing to view this river from the shore, quite another to be venturing over its rough waters. It stretches north to south, the obsidian mountain range edging its expanse seeming leagues away. A chill wind whips at us as the boat fitfully bobs, fighting the river's relentless draw south.

We're not the only ones trying to cross this river. There's a blond Keltish family with three young children in a boat to the north of us. And a boat beyond them holds two young Elfhollen men. I glance around and six more boats in all, most rendered tiny by the distance, all of us making our way east.

"How does your boat work?" I ask the Kelt after a time, turning to find his eyes riveted on me, noting that he seems unfazed by the incoming storm and the river's might, even though we're too far from both banks by now to swim to land.

The Kelt grins unkindly. "You're a pretty little gray thing. Come over here and I'll show you." He pats the bench beside him.

"Show me from here," I coldly reply.

"No, I'll show you from *here*," he insists, still smiling, and I sense a threat that's likely to escalate.

I imagine Lukas pulling his wand and encircling the bastard

in vines without a moment's deliberation. *Throw him overboard, Elloren*, I can almost hear Lukas's voice prodding.

I rise, crouching for balance, and move toward the Kelt. Then I take a seat beside him and meet his leering stare, my tangled power leaping toward the wood beneath my palms.

"You're a curious one, aren't you?" His hand snakes onto my thigh.

Revulsion ripples through me. "I am. So, show me how it works."

He gestures distractedly at the hull rune. "The navigation is set into that rune," he tells me, his fingers squeezing into my flesh as he leans close. "It pulls this boat east against the tide."

"So, the boat just…gets there on its own?"

"That's right," he croons. "So you'll have *plenty* of time to find a way to make up the rest of your payment. Pull off that tunic, and I'll shave five guilders off."

Now I imagine Lukas bashing his head in with an oar.

"All right," I tell him agreeably as he fondles my thigh.

I stand up and begin a slow swivel toward him as I reach under my tunic's hem, sliding my hand around the Ash'rion blade's hilt to find the air rune, my tangled wind line rippling to life. I mouth a spell, the rune quickly siphoning up a portion of my power.

"Take it off," the Kelt encourages, his voice thickening with aggressive want.

Elemental power ignites in my bound lines. In one lethal motion I unsheathe the blade and whip back my arm, the Wand's glimmering-green guidelines lighting as I hurl the blade at his shoulder.

The blade finds its mark, its fierce roar of wind catapulting the man clear over the boat's side and into the sky. Barking out a cry, he arcs over the water before plunging below the river's surface with a violent splash.

My heart hammering, I touch my retrieval rune. The blade

erupts from the river and flies back to my palm as the Kelt's head surfaces, gasping and sputtering. His eyes meet mine.

"Come near this boat and I'll kill you," I call out, leveling the blade at his head and readying the fire rune.

He throws me a hateful look and ignores my threat, starting for the boat, his uninjured arm beating out a powerful stroke as I grit my teeth and prepare to blast his damned head off.

His neck gives a sudden jerk, and he lets out a strangled cry as he's yanked underwater. I draw in a hard breath of surprise as the Wand buzzes against my calf.

Pulse spiking, I scan the water.

A large shadow flows under the river's surface. Much bigger than a man.

Fear spikes. *Holy Ancient One. No. No. No.*

"What happened to him?" Nym'ellia asks, fright in her gaze as the wind picks up, and rain starts to pelt down on us.

Our boat gives a hard tilt, as if punched from below by a great fist, and I cry out along with my companions, all of us tossed to one side as the boat nearly capsizes and water courses over us in an icy sheet. My blade falls from my hands and my feet skid out from under me, my shoulder painfully absorbing the impact as I slam into a wooden bench. I grab firm hold of Nym'ellia's arm, Emberlyyn blessedly having kept hold of both a rope and Tibryl as we all exchange looks of stark alarm.

"Kraken! Kraken!" a man's voice yells in Elfhollen from some distance away, his voice muffled by the strengthening wind and rain as additional cries of alarm go up all along the river.

"Get down," I order my companions as I retrieve my blade. "Stay low and hold tight to the side ropes."

A dark head explodes from the water, and my breath seizes in my lungs.

The distant kraken is horrific, like some unholy fusion of squid and insect, with an oily black serpentine head, massive jaws with glistening teeth, multiple limbs, and tentacles bursting up to wrap around the prow of the Kelt family's boat, the children screaming, the adults' cries unintelligible through the wind.

Nym'ellia throws herself in front of her mother and sister, her back to them as she grabs the rope handholds, her eyes bugged out. I pull back my arm, preparing to throw the Ash'rion, but the Wand's gleaming-green aim-tracks only flow out half the span, disappearing before they can reach the beast.

It's too far away, I anguish, the family screaming as their boat is yanked underwater.

More kraken heads explode from the water, triggering shouts in more than one language. The heavens open up more fully, earsplitting thunder cracking as Tibryl sobs and our boat bobs on the worsening waves, the runes at its sides sputtering out of existence.

My heart slams against my ribs as Wyvernfire abruptly rushes through me, blazing in from the northeast, my vision flashing gold. Frantic, I scan both sea and skies, praying for Yvan to suddenly descend.

Dark tentacles bolt up and I gasp, their sharp claws clicking over the boat's edge. They're larger than dragon talons, and I freeze as a kraken's gleaming head rises.

I take it in in one anguished heartbeat.

Two gigantic, membranous eyes. Huge, fetid jaws, a cavernous mouth full of gnashing teeth. Tibryl's scream cuts through my split-second reckoning as a stronger emotion wrests hold.

Pure, unadulterated wrath.

"You will *not take them!*" I cry, anger exploding through me in a wild rage. I hurl myself at the thing, leap off the boat, and thrust my knife right into one of its huge eyes, my fingers finding my blade's fire rune. I growl out a runic spell and release the blade's hilt.

Chaos descends as the kraken's head bursts into flames. It shrieks and falls back, like a fiery, toppling building, hurling me under the waves.

Another hard wall slams into me from behind, forcing the air from my lungs as I'm thrust out of the water and into the sheeting rain by the thing's massive tail. I fly through the air, gasping for breath, before hurtling back down toward the waves.

I open my eyes underwater to find a huge, wavering black shape swimming toward me. The demon-sensing rune on my abdomen begins to sting.

Panic jolting through me, I make for the surface and break through it, pulling in great gulps of air before something wraps tight around my ankle and yanks me under once more, the buzzing feel of the Wand against my calf cutting out.

Beating wildly against the water with my arms and free leg, I'm reeled in by the kraken's tentacled grip. The desperate need for air stinging my lungs, I yank at my leg as the thing draws me toward its terrifying, water-blurred head.

It's horrifically altered, with membranous, insectile eyes all over its bizarrely stretched-out kraken's head, its teeth gnashing threateningly as a sharper dread strikes me.

In the center of its massive forehead is a searching, knowing eye.

A pale green eye.

Vogel.

The ferocious will to fight sizzles through me, the Wyvernfire scorching through my firelines turning incendiary. I move to retrieve the blades strapped to my forearms, but tentacles slap around my wrists and waist and I'm thrust out of the water again, coughing and spluttering.

I gulp in air, struggling wildly, a chaos of kraken and sheeting rain and screaming people all around. Our boat is now a distance away, Nym'ellia, Emberlyyn, and Tibryl watching me with looks of pure horror. The tentacles around me tighten, the Wyvernfire blazing through my lines growing into a feverish inferno, my face held just above the water as I'm sped away from the eastern shore.

"Help!" I cry as I'm relentlessly dragged west, people screaming and boats capsizing as they're pulled under along with their hapless passengers.

The Zonor River's western shore comes into view through the battering storm, and a horrifying realization knifes through me as I take in several rune-marked scorpios massing along its edge, their predatory focus set on me.

They're bringing me to him.

Desperation breaks like a tide.

"Help!" I scream, struggling wildly against the Vogel-kraken's hold as a swarm of rune ships bursts through the clouds.

They're the size of skiffs, and incredibly...they're flying through the air like birds, illuminated in foggy haloes of blue light from the runes whirring beneath them and against their sides. They speed toward the remaining boats.

Lines of sapphire light scythe down from the rune skiffs and blow up kraken in great bursts of blue fire as the storm abruptly lessens. A horned, dark-hued winged man launches himself from one of the skiffs and takes flight, a bolt of white lightning streaking from his fists toward one of the sea beasts. The kraken's head explodes in showers of white sparking fire as thunder booms.

"Here!" I cry out to the rune skiffs in a hoarse voice. *"Help! Help me!"*

Vogel-kraken's tentacles pull me underwater and I jerk against his hold, feral in my desperation as passionate urgency shudders through the Wyvernfire blasting through my lines.

Something pale shoots through the water, like an ice spear. It slams into the kraken, impaling its body straight through, a rush of inky blood curling out from the site of impact along with a blast of cold.

The beast's hold abruptly releases and I swim frantically up and away, dodging its thrashing body. I break through the river's surface.

Sound assaults me—thunder, people screaming, kraken shrieking. I gasp and choke up river water, everything washed in blue light, gold Wyvernfire sparking in my vision.

There's a skiff before me, hovering just above the water, a dark figure silhouetted against the skiff's rune light. The young man's outline is tall and slender, a wand in his upraised hand, and I'm filled with the sense of vast water power as I struggle to see him through all the gold flashing in my sight.

A Mage. He's a Mage. But there's no time to deliberate.

"Help!" I cry. *"Please help me!"*

The young man sheathes his wand and leans over the side of his skiff.

"Take my hand!" he cries out in Elfhollen.

I'm filled with a sudden, disorienting confusion. *That voice. I recognize that voice.*

I swim closer and grab hold of the Mage's outstretched hand.

Lightning flashes and our eyes lock. Recognition explodes within me, the young man briefly illuminated as I blink against the Wyvernfire's golden sheen. He's dressed in a vivid blue Noi tunic, a white dragon emblazoned down one side, his blue hair rain-drenched into tousled strands, his green eyes lined with kohl. Black metallic hoops pierce his ears, his eyebrows, his lower lip.

My heart lurches as his eyes focus on me in equally staggered recognition and a burst of his oceanic water power rushes through me.

"Trystan!" I manage to say in a rasping, overjoyed voice as his other hand takes hold of my arm and he pulls me on board.

CHAPTER THREE

DRAGON-MARKED MAGE

Elloren Grey

Vo Mountains, Noilaan
Eastern Realm
Two days prior to Xishlon

A riptide of Trystan's magic blasts through me as he pulls me over the rune skiff's railing. Emotion blazes in his gaze as we keep tight hold of each other, time suspended as a massive knot of anguish I didn't even realize I was carrying inside me bursts open and I have to stifle the sob.

Trystan's expression morphs from shock to resolve, and I sense him forcibly reining his power in. "Get down," he orders, pointing to the skiff's floor.

I cast my gaze about, a jolt of relief bursting through me when I spot Nym'ellia, Tibryl, and Emberlyyn being helped aboard one of the blue-light-washed crafts. With urgency, I drop to the skiff's rain-slicked floor, feeling for the Wand wedged into my boot and finding it blessedly secured.

"Hide your face and pretend to be injured," Trystan says in

a tight whisper. "You're gray, but you still resemble Her. There are wanted postings of your face *all over Noilaan*."

I press my cheek to the wood, its ebony source tree's crown forming in my mind as the golden sparks of Wyvernfire abruptly clear from my vision and the last tendrils of the incoming flame aura snap away.

Yvan, I breathlessly mouth, my pulse surging, *don't lose me*.

My fire aura lashes northeast, desperate to restore the connection as a rune skiff soars up beside us. A heavily armed Vu Trin soldier stands at its helm, a Kelt family slumped down on her craft. I take her in through my fingers, anxiety tightening every muscle.

"Is everything all right?" she calls to Trystan in Noi. Her eyes narrow on me, triggering a dart of fright.

"She's badly wounded, Oura Vil," Trystan calls back, calm as a sheltered lake, but I can feel the defensive lightning spitting through his lines. "I'm bringing her to the border medic. I'll meet Vothe back here."

The soldier assesses me, seeming both conflicted and concerned. I take in her charged rune blades, praying she doesn't guess it's the Black Witch lying before her.

About to infiltrate her country.

The woman gives Trystan a succinct nod, then flies off.

I let out a breath I didn't realize I was holding as my brother moves toward a board made of linked runes that spans the skiff's prow. He rotates a rune with his wand's tip and the skiff abruptly rises into the air. I grasp hold of one of the boat's metal cleats, the river's choppy surface rapidly falling away, a rush of vertigo tightening my gut.

"Vogel can destroy Noi runes," I urgently tell Trystan the moment we're out of earshot.

His head whips toward me. "What do you mean?"

"He can destroy Noi runes with a flick of his wand. Even advanced military runes. He killed the Vu Trin's most elite portal sorceress, Chi Nam." My voice roughens around the memory, the lash of grief bitingly sharp. "There was nothing I could do to stop him, since the trees...they've bound up my power."

A jagged flash of lightning forks through my brother's affinity aura. "Keep low and I'll land somewhere hidden." He casts me a poignant look and I realize, in one dizzying swoop, why we need to hide. *He's being closely watched. Because he's my brother.*

He swerves, angling up, and as the skiff tilts I get a glimpse through the lessening haze of the river's western bank. Fright punches through me.

The knot of scorpios on the river's western bank has grown, rain-blurred shadows from this distance, but their insectile motion is unmistakable. A bolt of lightning flashes down toward them as the horned, winged man swoops in, the creatures shrieking and scattering as they're mercilessly cut down.

"Those scorpios," I say to Trystan, my voice a rasp as I shiver from the damp. "They're after me."

He throws another fraught glance my way. "The Gardnerians managed to set up a portal and sent a number of those creatures through. The Vu Trin shut it down, but we're still dealing with those things. Hold on tight." He gestures toward a wooden handhold.

I grasp hold of it as the skiff swoops up dramatically and my body skids backward, the river rapidly contracting in size as Trystan flies toward the storm band atop the Vo Mountains. The monstrous mass of clouds enlarges, lit up by streaks of lightning. Trystan taps the controls, and a translucent sapphire shield flows over us, encasing the skiff, rain driven back as Trystan swipes the chilling moisture away from our clothes with a flick of his wand.

We penetrate the storm band and the skiff begins to vibrate disturbingly, the storm a battering roar, roiling clouds pressing in. We abruptly dive downward, and my stomach lurches as Trystan points his wand skyward and murmurs a spell.

A blast of air streaks out from his wand through the shield, blowing the storm back to form a cloud-dome around us. Then Trystan arcs his wand downward, blasting out air to extend the cleared space, a landscape of jagged black peaks becoming visible below.

He guides us into a rocky depression, huge shards of pitch-dark stone rising around us as he lands. Then he points his wand straight up and draws the storm-dome down until it forms a curved ceiling of lightning-spitting chaos just above our sheltered fissure. He taps a rune on the control board, and the skiff's runic shield as well as all other light blinks out save one small rune. Bathed in dim sapphire light, Trystan sheathes his wand and turns to me.

Our eyes lock, our magical auras burgeoning as a storm of emotion gives way, my ribs feeling as if they might burst from it.

We surge toward each other, Trystan coming down onto one knee before me as we fall into a protective embrace and everything I've been holding so tightly inside fractures wide-open. I'm unable to fight back the tears, my beloved brother's back so solid and real beneath my palms.

"How did you ever find me?" I rasp into his shoulder.

"Spiders," Trystan rasps back, surprising me. "There's a Fae... she got word of incoming refugees from the spiders, only I didn't know one of them was *you*...because of the glamour..."

"I feared I'd never see you again." I can barely breathe through my relief.

"I feared I'd never see *you*."

I draw a fraction away, my brother's sapphire-lit face blurred by my tears. "Where's Rafe? Is he all right?"

Trystan nods, his voice choked. "He's fine. Everyone's fine." He cups the sides of my face, his cheeks streaked with tears. "The Vu Trin told us you were likely dead. But I didn't believe it."

My heart tightens. "Trystan, Vogel has Lukas."

His brow furrows. "Lukas Grey?"

The words come in an impassioned rush. "He's on our side. I thought he died saving me, getting me east through a portal, but I saw him through a rune. Vogel has him. I have to get my power unbound so I can go after him."

Trystan pulls in a deep breath, then takes firm hold of my hand, an expression of calm descending as his power consolidates around me. "Tell me everything that's happened."

Tripping over the words, I tell him all of it. How I was separated from Yvan and brought to the desert to train. How I created a river of fire with the candle lighting spell, and a faction of the Vu Trin turned against me and tried to kill me. How I had to flee to Gardneria and seek Lukas's protection to keep Noilaan's Vu Trin army from slaying me, and then…how Lukas revealed himself to be on the side of the Resistance and we escaped from Vogel via the only means possible—a Sealing ceremony.

And how, thinking Yvan dead, I fell in love with Lukas Grey.

I tell him how Lukas, Valasca, and Chi Nam brought me to the Agolith Desert and taught me to fight, willing to sacrifice their lives to save me and send me East.

To be a weapon for the East.

"Vogel can destroy *high-level* Noi military runes. *Easily*," I stress. "Which means he can strike down the runic domes of both Amazakaraan and Noilaan and march right into both countries."

Trystan's expression remains calm, but a torrent of lightning is crackling through his lines. "Ren, the Eastern Realm will be essentially defenseless if Vogel can dismantle Vu Trin runes. And the city would collapse. Much of Noilaan's architecture is held up by dome-supported runes. And all the rune ships here, like this one…the water ships too…they're all powered by the dome. That's why they can't stray far from the border."

I hold my brother's intense gaze. "Which is why you need to warn the Vu Trin and the Amaz. *Immediately*."

We still for one tension-fraught moment, then Trystan nods, his aura of power steadying.

"How fast can Vogel's forces get across the desert?" I ask.

Trystan draws in a breath, his jaw tensing. "A month, maybe two. So the Eastern forces might have time to gird the East against Mage attack."

"The Shadow magic in Vogel's wand... Chi Nam thought it originated from some type of primordial demonic power."

Trystan seems to consider this. "If that's the case, then Smaragdalfar varg runes might be of use against it. The Subland Elves developed those runes to fight the demons the Alfsigr use to control them."

My worry is only partially assuaged. "Could the Gardnerians have more portals they can get here through?"

Trystan shakes his head. "The scorpios tipped the Vu Trin off to the existence of that one hidden portal. They cast a searchnet over Noilaan and didn't locate anymore. The portal was stolen from the Amaz. It was incapable of sending large numbers of people or beasts across such a vast distance." He pauses and gives me a grave look. "Ren...it was the portal the Mages sent the assassin through who killed Yvan. I only just learned of it—"

"No. Yvan's alive," I emphatically counter. I tell him of the powerful Wyvernfire aura that seized hold of me when the scorpios attacked me and again when the kraken struck. "I *felt* him, Trystan. I *know* it was Yvan's fire."

"I don't understand. How?"

An ache cuts through me, chafingly raw. "Yvan kissed me and gave me his Wyvernfire. He...bound himself to me in that way. But then we were separated... I don't think the connection can be felt from far away. But when I portaled here..."

"You might be close enough," Trystan finishes, realization starting to dawn.

"What were you told about Yvan's 'death'?"

He gives me a weighted look. "Kam Vin told me that he was killed by a glamoured wandmaster sent by Marcus Vogel. Ren, Vogel sent a spy to confirm Yvan's death. Are you sure it was his fire you sensed?"

Doubt wrests hold, and I struggle to beat it back. What if Yvan was killed and I'm picking up some echo of his power that he sent out to me before he was slain? Or...what if the sensation of

Wyvernfire was some enchantment of Vogel's—something he sent through the Sealing spell to lure me?

What if Lukas and Yvan are both truly dead, and Vogel is toying with me?

"I'm not sure," I shakily admit, looking to my wand hand as I tell Trystan about the shadowy lines that briefly appeared there. "I think Vogel's infiltrated my fasting."

Trystan's eyes take on a graver cast. "He's likely found a way to send a tracking spell through it."

I blanche, gripped by the sense that I've set myself against power that can easily best and manipulate me.

"There is one bright spot," Trystan offers and I look to him in question. "If Vogel is using your wandfasting to track you, he has to keep Lukas alive and well to do it. And Ren," he says, a pointed glint entering his gaze, "tracking spells can be accessed from either end."

Realization ignites. "Which means I could track Lukas through it," I breathe out.

Trystan's lip ticks up and he nods. "You just need to get control of your power."

My mind spins over this newfound, albeit slim, advantage. I'm suddenly quivering with possibility, not just to go after Lukas, but to locate Yvan, as well.

"Yvan told me that our Wyvernbond would enable him to sense when I'm in danger. If I could connect to his Wyvernfire long enough, I might be able to find him too." My brow tenses with consternation. "I almost want to face down more kraken to trigger the connection."

Thoughts of Vogel's kraken send my hand sliding to find my Ash'rion blade.

It's in the river, I realize.

"Stand back," I caution Trystan before we both rise and I hold up my hand, pressing the glamour-hidden retrieval rune Valasca marked on my palm. After a moment, the Ash'rion hurtles through the cloud ceiling and down into our rocky crevasse, its hilt slapping against my palm. I meet my brother's look of surprise as I resheathe the blade.

He cocks a brow. "You killed some kraken down there. Didn't you."

"I killed one. And I'm going to kill Marcus Vogel."

Trystan studies me closely, as if considering me in a whole new light. "The Vu Trin might pose a bigger problem for you at the moment."

"Well, the Vu Trin tried to kill me once already, but I escaped." I let out a hard breath. "I'm a weapon the East is going to need. Whether they realize it or not. Because Vogel's Wand... I think it's the Shadow Wand talked about in all the myths." I reach down and draw the Wand of Myth from the side of my boot. It glows a soft, pearlescent green in the dim light, humming with a barely perceptible vibration against my palm.

"Is that the same wand I used in Verpacia?" Trystan asks.

"The very same," I affirm. "I think it's the mythical counterforce to Vogel's Shadow Wand. The Sacred Wand of Myth. But...if it is, we're in trouble. It's nowhere *near* as powerful as Vogel's Wand. It seems to *hide* from it."

"How did it turn green?"

"It just...did. Out in the desert. I think it's coming out of some type of dormancy."

I tell him of the Wand's gift of perfect aim and how it brings images of Watchers at unexpected times. I slide it back into my boot, a shimmering sense of rightness washing over me.

"But perfect aim isn't enough," I rue. "I need to get my Mage power unbound. And fast."

"Well, let's get it unbound, then," Trystan says, and my heart tightens with another welling of gratitude to be reunited. He draws his wand and taps the skiff's control board. The runes surrounding the skiff blink to life, beginning to rotate, as Trystan draws a shield back over us.

"Ren," he says, hesitating for a beat as the runes whir faster, whipping blue light. "We have family here. Family that was hidden from us."

Family? I'm speechless for a moment. "What do you mean?"

"We've an uncle here. And a cousin. *Nothing* is how we were told it was."

The runes speed to a blur and the skiff begins to rise. "But... how can that be?"

"Our mother's brother, Wrenfir, is alive. And Uncle Edwin has a child."

Shock flashes through me. But then I remember how Aunt Vyvian raged about Uncle Edwin having had a forbidden relationship with an Urisk woman.

"And our parents," Trystan says, growing even more serious as we ascend toward the dome holding back the storm, "they weren't killed by the Kelts."

My eyes widen. "What are you saying?"

"They were secretly fighting against the Gardnerian military. Against our own grandmother."

"Ancient One," I murmur. "Does that mean..."

Trystan nods and gives me a significant look as we're enveloped by the maelstrom, its muffled roar overtaking us. "Our parents were part of the Resistance, Ren," he says as he pilots us relentlessly forward. "And our grandmother murdered them for it."

STORMING POWER

Elloren Grey

Noilaan
Eastern Realm
Two days prior to Xishlon

Trystan blasts the rune skiff through the dense line of storms over the Vo Mountain Range's peaks, wind roaring and lightning cracking over the translucent shield. I grip tight to the handhold as we begin a rapid descent, struggling to wrap my mind around the revelation that our parents, Vale and Tessla, were Resistance fighters.

The upending thought is whisked aside as our skiff bursts through the storm band, the night sky opens up and I catch my first glimpse of the mountain city of Voloi.

It glitters blue and purple in the distance, just past the expansive Vo River, which reflects the city's light in spectacular ripples of color, the fabled purple Xishlon star of the East hanging over it all like a beacon. The city is astonishingly vertical, clinging to the sky-piercing Voloi Mountain Range in multiple staircase-like tiers that resemble streaks of sparkling paint striped horizontally across the purple and black mountains.

Trystan draws down our shield and we soar toward the city, the Vo Mountains below giving way to moonlit forest flowing down like a draped carpet. Just beyond the forest lies a sapphire glowing runic border wall hugging the Vo River's western bank, stretching as far as my eyes can see. Blips of rune skiffs dart along the rune wall's apex like industrious blue fireflies.

But none of this is what has my breath cinching tight in my throat.

Rising from the border to flow over the vast river and the mountain city is a huge, translucent dome, faint blue runes splashed over its surface.

Noilaan's dome-shield.

So large it makes the runic dome encasing the Amaz city of Cyme seem like a mere market basket tossed facedown over their valley.

Fear shivers through me as I'm struck by the image of Vogel striking down the dome over Chi Nam's Vonor with one quick swipe of his Shadow Wand.

The rune skiffs patrolling the border's apex come into sharper view, the sapphire border wall enlarging as we soar nearer. A tent city hugs its base, its darkness broken only by dots of firelight, the lack of light on this side of the border standing in stark contrast to the dazzlingly illuminated city.

I remember the words of the soldier in the purple woods—*Go back to where you came from. Border's closed.* A chill snakes down my spine. "Where are the Vu Trin bringing the survivors of the kraken attack?" I ask my brother.

Trystan angles his head toward the dark encampment in answer.

Urgency swells. "Trystan, the small family I traveled through the Dyoi Forest with…two of them are *really* sick. They need to be quarantined with physician care *immediately.*"

"Ren, a quarter of that tent city has the Grippe," Trystan

grimly counters. "It's part of the reason the Noi want to keep them walled out."

A horrified rush stings through me, my illusions about the perfect Eastern Realm crashing down. This has the feel of the Western Realm all over again. I remember Olilly's Red Grippe–encrusted mouth and reddened amethyst eyes before I snuck medicine to her in the university kitchens. The sick Smaragdalfar refugees who Professors Fyon Hawkkyn and Jules Kristian were helping to smuggle east, many of them young children. The disturbing rattle of little Tibryl's advanced cough.

"I made a promise to the three of them," I say as the border's sizzling tang of runic energy wafts over us. "I *promised* I'd help get them to safety."

"Give me their names," he offers. "I'll send someone to find them. Tonight."

I nod as we descend, only partially mollified.

What about all the other people stuck on this side of the wall?

But there's no time to dwell. The border rises in front of us, half as high as the mountain range to our backs. As its details come into sharper view, my awe of Noi runic sorcery increases. It's constructed entirely of luminous, rotating runes, stacked on top of each other and slowly revolving, like a colossal gear system.

Strands of my pale gray hair whip at my face as Trystan angles our skiff toward the border's apex, a daunting number of military rune skiffs patrolling it. They're piloted by Vu Trin soldiers, their sides marked with the same ivory dragon stamped on Noilaan's sapphire flag. The wall's apex is partitioned into segments delineated by large, floating runes, a single military rune skiff hovering inside each segment.

Trystan swerves right and makes for one of the skiffs.

As we draw near, the skiff flies toward us. A slim rod of sapphire light telescopes out and connects with our skiff's base in a flash of blue light. Multiple plate-size runes fluoresce into existence, orbiting our skiff.

"Stay low, Ren," my brother directs as he reduces our speed.

I hug the skiff's floor while we slow to a motionless hover. Pulse thudding, I dare a glance at the skiff gliding in. It's piloted by a young soldier, her short, spiky black hair streaked with silver and purple. Her sharp, dark eyes swing toward me and narrow in swift appraisal before her gaze lifts to Trystan's.

"Where have you been?" she demands, seeming relieved and troubled at the same time. "Vothe's been looking *everywhere* for you. You're not authorized to pilot that skiff without him."

Bam bam bam goes my heart.

"Minyl, she's badly injured," Trystan replies with formidable calm. He gestures toward me. "I can't worry about Vothe right now. I need to get her to Wrenfir for care."

I give a start, surprised at his mention of the uncle I've never met.

The woman frowns and leans in, lowering her voice. "Trys, you know I'm not supposed to let you through without Vothe."

"Her leg's broken in several places," Trystan cuts in severely. "You know she won't get proper care on this side of the border."

"That's a Red Level transgression."

"Does she look like the Black Witch, Minyl?" Trystan asks harshly, and my anxiety ramps up.

Minyl's lips tighten as she deliberates, her dark eyes tensing. "I'll let you through," she finally bites out, surreptitiously scanning the surrounding skies before flashing Trystan a hard look. "But *find Vothe* as soon as you can and report back."

"I will," Trystan promises as I wonder who this Vothe could possibly be.

Minyl lifts a rune-marked disc and the runes orbiting our skiff blink out of sight. Then she turns and pilots her skiff into motion, Trystan following suit, both crafts rapidly accelerating. We follow her toward the rune border, pivoting upward to soar toward her apex-segment, then clear over it. Minyl's skiff noses straight into the runic dome like it's made of water, an arc-shaped hole rippling open that we follow her through.

And then we're soaring over the Vo River toward the purple-and-blue-glimmering world of Voloi while Minyl switchbacks around, raising a hand to Trystan in quick farewell as she soars back to the border.

Relief floods me so intensely a light-headed disorientation takes hold.

Noilaan.

I'm in Noilaan.

All the preparation Lukas and Chi Nam and Valasca did to get me here is suddenly circling down, their glaring absence opening a hollow ache in my heart.

You were supposed to be here with me. All of you.

Instead, Lukas is a world away, in terrible danger, Chi Nam is dead, and Valasca—Ancient One knows where Valasca was transported by our incompletely charged portal.

My chest-tightening anguish makes a rapid slide to steel.

I'll find you, I vow to Lukas and Valasca both, as we soar toward the glimmering city, wishing with everything in me I could send the thought straight to them.

Our skiff turns due south, and a pair of island-mountains are before us, the vertical landmasses rising so high they pierce the clouds. Tiers of onyx castle-like structures spiral up their dark surfaces, their corresponding tiers connected by walkways, like the rungs of some giant's ladder. A huge bas-relief carving of an ivory dragon wraps around each of their bases, a multitude of living dragons and military air skiffs encircling them.

Ancient One. It's Noilaan's military academy.

"That's the Wyvernguard," Trystan says, giving me a tense look, and I drop closer to the floor.

We fly past, my breathing measured as I watch its highest reaches near then recede behind us, slumping with relief once we're well past it.

"Where's Rafe?" I ask Trystan, desperate to be safely surrounded by family. And desperate to see my beloved eldest brother.

"He's in the new Lupine Territory northeast of here," Trystan says, turning to meet my gaze with his kohl-rimmed eyes. "Rafe's Lupine now."

Stark relief wells. "And Diana?"

"She's with Rafe," he assures me. "And Jarod, Aislinn and Andras…they're all here. All Lupine."

"Aislinn too?"

"Jarod recently turned her. They're all part of the newly established Gerwulf pack."

I let out a hard, wavering breath, realizing that if Aislinn made it here, that means Sparrow, Effrey, and Thierren are likely here in the East, as well. "Tierney?" I ask.

"She's in the Wyvernguard. With me. She's claimed this river as her kindred." He gestures toward the staggeringly huge river below us.

An emotional laugh escapes me. "Of course she would. The largest river on all of Erthia."

Trystan shoots me a knowing grin.

"And Sage?" I ask, basking in my brother's presence despite the dire state of things.

He nods. "She joined the Wyvernguard and settled in the Eastern Sublands with her partner, Ra'Ven, and their child."

Fyn'ir. The little purple-winged Icaral child.

"Fyn'ir's under heavy Smaragdalfar guard." Trystan gives me a tense look.

"Ancient One," I breathe, remembering how Yvan kept his identity so carefully hidden in Verpacia, wings tightly glamoured down. A sudden longing for him grips my chest as I glance searchingly toward the northeast.

I know it was your fire that I felt, I think out toward Yvan. *Please, be alive.*

Trystan swerves through the thickening air traffic, rune skiffs of all shapes and sizes soaring around us. "Gareth's here," he says as he turns our course due south. "He's in the Vu Trin navy now. Stationed near the Salishen Isles. And Olilly and Fern are settled here. Jules Kristian and Lucretia. Everyone Kam Vin promised she'd bring east."

My ragged relief swells. "Oh, Trystan…"

He reaches back to take hold of my hand, and I grip his in turn as I'm hit by a strong wave of grief. "Trystan," I say, barely able to get the words out. "Uncle Edwin…"

His jaw tenses, a flare of chaotic turbulence running through his lines as he meets my eyes. "I know. Jules told me soon after he got to Voloi."

We're quiet for a moment as Trystan navigates the air traffic, glancing over his shoulder every now and then as if he's trying to spot anything that could be tailing us.

My nerves prickle with concern. "Do you think anyone will come after us?"

He tilts his head, as if equivocating. "Yes, but I'll report back before my absence raises alarms. I think our timing was…lucky."

I nod with some relief before a sudden heat sparks over my back in a static rush, every one of my muscles tensing against it. Alarmed, I turn toward its origin, my eyes widening as I peer past the skiff's stern.

A horned, winged male is flying in behind us, his eyes flashing silver. An aura of white lightning hits me, crackling straight toward us.

"Trystan," I gasp as my pulse races into a gallop. "Behind us…"

My brother turns, and recognition lights in his eyes. He pivots around and speeds up our craft, his own aura exploding in a fit of blue lightning.

"Who is that?" My gaze swings back to the winged man, who's rapidly gaining on us.

"Vothendrile," Trystan says in a tight voice. "My guard. He's a dragon-shifter and a power empath—which means he can sense magical ability. So try to pull in your magic's aura as best you can. He'll be able to read it at close range."

My alarm spikes. "What happens if he realizes who I am?"

I grip hold of my Ash'rion blade, struggling to rein in my tumultuous, tangled aura.

Trystan briefly turns. "I don't know."

I glance behind us, palm tight around my weapon. "He's getting closer."

"Oh, we won't be able to shake him." A chaotic, fiery energy shoots through Trystan's lines, further heightening my alarm.

Trystan taps his wand to the controls and we bank sharply left, following the Voloi Range's curve past the city's edge and beyond, the upper portion of the mountains dotted more sparsely with buildings, then barely at all. Trystan speeds us toward a dark purple peak, its highest, most isolated dwelling cut right into the stone. Blue runic light illuminates its windows, balconies, and broad terrace, and I swear I can make out two black dragons watching us from the surrounding stone's recesses.

"Where are you taking us?" I anxiously ask, realizing he never told me.

"Fain Quillen's estate."

The name pricks a remembrance. *Lucretia Quillen's brother in the Noi lands.*

Trystan deftly lands our skiff on the stone terrace, the craft's runes rapidly powering down and blinking out of sight.

"Stay aboard," Trystan directs, tension vibrating in his sharply contained lines. He disembarks and waits, his face to the incoming Wyvern-shifter.

I crouch in the shadows and watch as the young winged man flies in, then lands, his gaze fixed on Trystan. He draws in his black wings, and I'm hit by a wave of invisible storm magic so intense, I flinch backward.

The shifter's overwhelmingly potent lightning aura crackles out to encompass my brother, Trystan's water magery rearing violently in response, and I'm surprised when my brother makes no move to draw his wand.

The winged man strides toward Trystan, the terrace's blue light spilling over him.

He's almost otherworldly in how striking he is—tall and stunningly fit, his hue black as a starless night sky, his ears pointed, horns gleaming. His spiky onyx hair is tipped in silver, bright threads of lightning pulsing over his scandalously bare chest. But it's his eyes that I can't tear my gaze from—his irises are a mesmerizing, lightning-charged black, positively flashing with storming power.

The shifter doesn't notice me, his intensifying water and wind auras rushing so intensely toward my brother I pull in a wavering breath. He stops a few handspans from Trystan, their combined elemental auras lashing around each other like they're caught in a raging storm.

"Vothe," my brother says, a cautionary edge to his voice.

"I thought the second wave of kraken struck you down," the horned man cuts him off in Noi, his tone harsh with accusation, his deep voice strongly accented. "I flew over the mountains. Searching for you *everywhere*."

My heart thuds harder as I ready my blade.

"I'm fine," Trystan says a trace raggedly as the shifter continues to ignore me.

"Were you planning on finding me sometime this eve?" Vothe bites out.

"Eventually," Trystan hedges.

Vothe steps toward Trystan, lightning spitting through his power. "How am I supposed to guard you if you purposefully *elude me*?"

Trystan's voice is cool when it comes. "Is that what you're doing, Vothe? Guarding me? It's a bit of a ruse at this point, wouldn't you say?" Power crackles even more intensely in the air between them, and for a moment, Vothe doesn't answer.

"I thought..." Vothe breaks off as visible threads of his lightning arc around my brother. An expression of impassioned worry overtakes his expression, his voice rough when it comes. "When the second swarm of kraken came in...and I couldn't find you... I thought something *happened* to you."

Oh, Sweet Ancient One, I realize in one dizzying sweep. *Are they in love?*

My brother's power shifts, still lashing around Vothe, but its edges are forcefully straining away from me. As if willing Vothe to remain unaware of my presence.

My breath tightens in my throat.

"I'm a Level Five Mage, Vothe," Trystan remarks sharply. "I can handle a few kraken."

Now they're throwing invisible lightning toward each other so hard that white sparks through my vision while another aura of distinctive flame suddenly overtakes my lines—

Golden fire and then a streak of vermilion fire, blazing like a torch.

I gasp, Vothe's and Trystan's lightning in my sight blasted back by all the Wyvernfire streaming in, purple sparks crackling through it. My eyes widen with recognition. I know that vermilion fire as well as I know the golden blaze, even though the purple sparks are new to it.

It's *Raz'zor's*, the small dragon who pledged fealty to me.

The dual heat burns through me, blazing in from both northeast and due north in a volcanic chaos of Wyvernfire.

Holy gods, are both Yvan and Raz'zor searching for me?

Vothe's nostrils flare and his gaze swings toward me.

My heart jumps into my throat as a flash of Vothe's lightning strikes through my tangled lines, blazing through the Wyvernfire in a hot, relentless current. Trystan's power breaks free of his control to whip around me in a protective frenzy.

Wyvernfire and lightning sparking in my vision, I rise from the shadows, blade in hand.

Vothe's head tilts, his face taking on a look of confusion. "You look just like Or'myr…"

Trystan's magic gives a wildly combustive flare and Vothe's head whips toward him before his gaze swings back to me with intensifying focus. A look of shock comes over his features as the lightning forking all over his skin flashes bright.

244

"Blessed Vo," he murmurs, "this is your sister."

I take a step back as Vothe's power turns cyclonic. It crashes through me, his wings fanning powerfully out. He bares his teeth and advances.

Trystan throws himself between us and draws his wand at the same time I raise my blade, sweat breaking out all over my body.

"Vothe," Trystan pleads, even as his power doubles down, consolidating inside his wand. "*Please*. If you've ever believed me about anything..."

Vothe hisses out what sounds like a series of vehement curses in a sibilant language that my koi'lon translation rune can't decipher, his electrified eyes fixed on me.

I hold his ignited stare, ferocity suddenly rising within me to match the shifter's own. "Do you fight for the Eastern Realm?" I challenge him, fire burning through my lines.

Vothe's head flinches back. He narrows his incendiary gaze at me. "Yes, witch," he hisses. "And for the Zhilon'ile Wyvernkin and our domain."

I step decidedly down off the skiff, the force of all the elemental and Wyvern power whipping around and through me like an inferno about to overtake Noilaan.

"Ren," Trystan cautions as I shoulder past my brother and pull out of his attempt to grip my arm. I stride up to Vothe, who fans his wings farther out in a menacing display.

"You're a shifter," I bite out, "so you can sense if I'm speaking the truth. So, read me, shifter. I'm here to fight for the Eastern Realm. Tell me, do you sense a lie?"

Vothe's brow tenses tight as wild conflict churns though his aura.

"You know I speak the truth," I vehemently state, "so hear the truth. Vogel can break your runes. *All* your runes. Your rune wall, the dome over this city—" I sweep my arm in a wide arc "—the weapons of the Vu Trin army—he can destroy it *all*."

"And how would you know this?" Vothe snarls, baring elongated teeth.

"Vogel came for me in the desert. About a week ago. Because he knows I'm his enemy. And because he wants my Black Witch power for his own. He broke down the runic barrier the sorceress Chi Nam set up around her Vonor—"

"You were in Nor Chi Nam's Vonor?" He cuts me off with a look of vast confusion, a portion of his wind power breaking loose to whip around the terrace.

Grief for Chi Nam sears through my chest in a slashing ache. "She sacrificed her *life* to save me from Vogel." My voice breaks. "So, tell me, shifter—*do you sense a lie?*"

Vothe is frozen in place, his hurricane-force power crashing through mine. "Why is there dual Wyvernfire in your lines?"

An impassioned heat rises. "Because I'm bonded to the Icaral, Yvan Guryev. By his kiss. And the dragon Raz'zor has sworn fealty to me. I think they're both here somewhere...in the Eastern Realm."

Vothe exhales, his wind power kicking up into a stronger lash. "Yvan Guryev is *dead.*"

I shake my head adamantly. "No. It's his fire I'm sensing, I know it is."

Movement over the river catches my eye and my gaze flicks toward it. Three pinpricks of blue light are soaring toward us in disturbingly perfect formation—military formation.

Fear ignites, hot and hard, through my lines, the Wyvernfire blaze intensifying. "Ancient One..." I take a step backward as Vothe's and Trystan's powers rear.

Vothe locks his stormy eyes with mine for a blistering second.

"Please..." I implore him.

His lightning sparks hard against my Wyvernfire as his mouth curves into a snarl. "Get her inside," he growls at Trystan. "Or she's *dead.*"

CHAPTER FIVE

MOUNTAIN LAIR

Elloren Grey

Noilaan
Eastern Realm
Two days prior to Xishlon

Crouching low, my brother and I run across the terrace toward the mountain home's doorway under cover of Vothe's outstretched wings, while he remains behind us, facing down the incoming Vu Trin military skiffs.

Trystan pulls the door open and we rush inside. Yvan's and Raz'zor's Wyvernfire connections abruptly snap off from my affinity lines, as if I've traversed some magical threshold.

Heart in my throat, I dart to one side and drop into the shadows below one of the windows that ring the circular foyer, tightening my hold on my Ash'rion. I absently note the polished indigo floor before me, marked with a sapphire dragon stone inlay. The room is suffused in a faint indigo light emanating from two rune lights affixed to the stone walls, their frosted-glass sconces set atop coiled brass dragons.

Trystan's eyes fix on the view through the stained-glass edged windows. He straightens and draws power toward his wand hand with breathtaking oceanic force.

"I won't let them take you," he says, just as a door at the foyer's opposite end flies open. An elegantly featured Mage of about Professor Kristian's age emerges. He strides toward us with urgency, green eyes blazing.

Confusion tightens inside me like a fist.

He's dressed in conservative Gardnerian blacks, an Erthia orb necklace around his neck.

His deep-ocean aura of power rolls over me and for a moment, the whole foyer ripples as if we've all been cast underwater.

"Trystan," the Mage says, his tone one of immense relief as his vast water power encircles my brother with protective force. "Lucretia just brought word of the kraken attack. They said you didn't report to Vothe, so…" His dazzling gaze slides toward me and catches hold. "Who's this…" His eyes flick to the runic blade in my hand, then toward the outside terrace and the incoming military skiffs, then back to me as if rapidly piecing it all together.

Another wave of his ocean aura slams into me.

I gasp and recoil back, his magic inundating my lines with titanic force.

His eyes widen, and then, just like that, his power aura vanishes. I double over, catching my breath, realizing, with vast surprise, that he must be a power empath, like me.

The Mage turns toward Trystan and smiles, catlike. "Sheathe your wand, Trys," he directs as my brother's aura spits out a discordant array of invisible lightning. "You're going to go out there and report to them," he directs, smooth as satin. "I'll come with you."

"Who are you?" I rasp while Trystan slowly and carefully resheathes his wand, my brother's gaze pinned on the outside.

"Fain Quillen, my dear," the Mage says with that same exaggerated calm. "And I suggest that you stay right where you are. Or war will break out on this very terrace. And we'll all be killed. Do you understand me, love?"

I nod jerkily as Fain and Trystan exchange one piercing look, my brother's throat bobbing as he swallows before his expression goes carefully blank. Fain nods, opens the door, and they stride onto the terrace together.

I wait, feeling suspended in time, as muffled voices sound in the Noi language, dampened by the stone walls and thick windows—a woman's authoritative tone, stern and staccato; Fain's convivial response followed by Trystan's matter-of-fact one and Vothe's emphatic deep bass; Fain's amused laugh. The woman's reply, edged in sarcasm, then amusement as Fain laughs again, and then the motion of the blue rune light arcing and leaping on the walls turns even more frenetic as the roar of magically consolidated wind blasts through the stone and glass. The frenzied sapphire light shifts and slants...then rapidly fades to nothing.

Fain strides back into the foyer, and in one graceful movement eases to one knee before me with a look of piercing concern.

"Where's Trystan?" I anxiously ask.

He cuts me off by patting the air, as if attempting to assuage my worries. "Reporting in with Vothe. He's fine. It's a formality." His gaze turns a bit liquid as he peers more closely at me. "Ancient One... Elloren, you look just like your father."

The door across the foyer swings open, and Lucretia Quillen bursts into the room along with a swooshing rush of her Level Four water aura. "I saw the rune light," she says to Fain, tone shot through with urgency. "Is Trystan all right..."

Her gaze slides to me and holds there, her water power stilling as she scrutinizes my grayed features and I gape at her change in appearance. It's almost as extreme as Trystan's in how wildly she's veered away from Gardnerian. Her conservative Styvian Mage sect blacks are gone, replaced by an emerald Noi tunic over dark green pants. A large indigo dragon is embroidered down her garb's side, a wand fashioned from purple wood sheathed at her hip. A series of sapphire metallic hoops edge her ears and her long black hair is pulled back into a more Noi style of coiled braids. Her gold-rimmed spectacles the only thing left unchanged.

Her water power eddies toward me. "Elloren?" she breathes out.

"Vogel can break down runes," I blurt out to them both with no preamble. "*All* runes. He has the Shadow Wand of Myth. And its power...it's *devastating*. He knows where I am and what I am and I think he's tracking me through my fastlines. He's coming for me. He's coming for the entire Eastern Realm." My bone-deep exhaustion suddenly breaks over me and I wrestle against it. "I have what I think is the Zhilin...the Wand of Myth. And it's given me true aim. But my power...it's been bound up by the forest." My voice splinters with a wrathful frustration. "I need my magic unbound, and *quickly*. So I can fight Vogel and rescue my fastmate. He's been taken prisoner by the Mages."

Fain and Lucretia exchange a look as the remembrance of Lukas bound and beaten opens up the ground beneath me, no solid purchase anywhere.

"When did you last eat or sleep?" Fain asks.

"There's no time for it," I insist, fisting my blade's hilt, every muscle battered and bruised. "Vogel *is coming*—"

"Let him try." Fain cuts me off, voice harsh. He sweeps his hand around. "This whole lair is warded and so is the airspace around it. And we have enough Mages of power here to give him a run for his money." He gestures toward the Voloi Range's peaks. "There's also a small Vish'nile dragon horde at the top of this mountain that I'm on *excellent* terms with. Vogel, on the other hand, has forces that are currently massing on the western edge of a vast desert. They're a problem, to be sure, and perhaps a bigger one than we thought, but not an immediate one." Fain rocks back on his heels, a calculating glint in his eyes. "Vogel's army needs at least a month to cross that distance, my dear. Assuming he can strike down every last storm band with nothing but a wave of his fancy wand."

I huff out a desperate sound. "*Count* on it."

"I am," Fain says, another wave of his oceanic power rippling around me.

"Are you in the military?" I ask.

Fain smiles, as if this should be obvious. "The Vu Trin navy. With your friend Gareth Keeler." A fond look crosses his features. "I've known Gareth since he was a babe."

There's no time to wonder at how Fain Quillen knows my childhood friend, the urgency in me running too hot and chaotic. "There's no *time to waste*." I insist, growing desperate. "I don't know where Vogel has my fastmate. I have to *find* him…"

Fain reaches out to grip my shoulder and I let out a wavering exhale as his water power rushes through my tangled lines with steady, soothing force. "We're going to help you, and we'll locate your fastmate." He gently places his other hand on mine. "You're with family now, love."

I hold his steady gaze as tears glaze my eyes and a dizzying upswell of emotion overtakes me.

Fain smiles, great kindness in his expression. "Welcome home, Elloren."

CHAPTER SIX

KIN

Elloren Grey

Noilaan
Eastern Realm
Two days prior to Xishlon

"One month." An angry, male voice sounds through the closed door ahead as I follow Fain and Lucretia down a narrow hall cut into the mountain's black and purple stone. *"One month,* and the *damned Crows* will be on our doorstep."

Fain opens the door, and all conversation snuffs out as the people inside turn toward me.

I'm faced with a small library, a cobalt circular table in its center marked with a blue dragon. Two purple-hued Urisk people are seated before it—a lovely older woman in a floral, plum tunic who's about Fain's age, and a straight-backed, angular-faced man of about my age. He's garbed in a Vu Trin military uniform that's curiously tinted violet, his invisible magical aura a bright penumbra of purple. A furious-looking man stands opposite them, perhaps around Lukas's age, tension spitting through his potent aura of earth magery in spiking black vines—the same man, I'm assuming, who was railing against the "Crows" just a moment ago.

Only…he's a "Crow" himself.

And the most outrageous Mage I've ever seen, save Ariel Haven.

There's a huge raven tattoo stamped across half his green-glimmering neck, another of a black spider beside one eye, the spider's legs extending over half his forehead and his entire cheek. His guarded, angry green eyes are lined in thick, dark kohl, like Trystan's, and black metallic piercings edge his ears, eyebrows, and the bottom of his nose. He's dressed in solid-black Noi attire, his lips painted black, his midnight hair spiked, his whole aura simmeringly bleak and confrontational.

He also bears a striking resemblance to my brother Rafe.

And the purple-hued young man bears a striking resemblance to *me*.

The Urisk woman gasps, glancing toward the purple man and back to me again, a stunned look crossing her features as her graceful violet hand flies up to cover her mouth. The young Urisk man's expression has turned coolly speculative as he rocks back in his chair and looks over my glamoured form with almost amused appraisal. His sharp, forest green eyes stand out in bold contrast to his purple features, and I'm rendered spellbound.

He looks so exactly like me—if I were male, point-eared, and mostly purple-hued.

"Everyone," Fain says, slowly and with great import. "This is Elloren Gardner Grey." He glances at me. "Artfully glamoured," he amends with a slight smile.

The spider-tattooed Mage's kohl-rimmed eyes widen before he flashes me a wicked grin. "Well, isn't this an interesting turn of events." I notice there are three house cats hovering near him—two calico felines on the table, one white cat purring adoringly against his leg.

"Hello, Elloren," the purple-hued young man says in convivial greeting, his green eyes dancing. He seems remarkably at ease coming face-to-face with the Black Witch.

"Elloren," Fain says gently as he angles his head toward the purple-hued man, "this is Edwin's son, your cousin, Or'myr."

My throat tightens with shock even though Trystan told me of him. It's one thing to hear about the family I never knew I had, quite another thing to see them in person.

Slender Or'myr gets up and rises to his full impressive height, then strides around the table toward me, extending his hand. Rendered speechless, I grip it, and he gives me another faint smile, his gaze piercingly intelligent. "It's good to meet you, cousin."

Cousin. Uncle Edwin's son.

My emotions thrust into a tumult, I pick up a keener sense of Or'myr's strong core of violet fire and earth magery, his earth-lines forged from purple stone and crystal.

"We look alike," I finally manage—my resemblance to this young man I've never met before is so much stronger than my resemblance to either Rafe or Trystan.

A sardonic gleam lights his eyes. "We do. Except you are not purple."

"I'm not this either," I note as I motion toward myself.

Or'myr loses his smile. "It's good you're glamoured, cousin." His gaze slides over my grayed face. "How did you ever manage it?"

"A Smaragdalfar glamour." I cast about for the words. "One of a kind." I take in the amethyst-encrusted wand sheathed at Or'myr's side before meeting his shrewd gaze once more. He radiates a reserved calm similar to Trystan's, which loosens some of my tension. "You've wand magery, then?"

The side of Or'myr's lip twitches. "A bit." His gaze flits to Fain, and I sense from their shared, amused glance that this is a wild understatement. "I'm a Level Five Fire and Earth Mage," he clarifies. "As well as a geomancer."

I'm struck by the fact that Or'myr and I have the same predominant affinities as I note the slim chain draped diagonally across his military garb, the chain's links holding small amethysts of varying lavender hues.

Or'myr smiles. "I work with your friends Sagellyn Gaffney and Tierney Calix. We're all magical researchers at the Wyvern-guard."

Surprise snaps through me to find Sage, Tierney, and my newfound cousin connected in this way.

"And this is Or'myr's mother, Li'ra," Fain says as the willowy Urisk woman gets up and quietly approaches me. "She's Edwin's shonorin." Fain smiles warmly at both Li'ra and me. "His geo-bonded mate. Which would make her your aunt, Elloren."

An upswell of grief wrests hold as I look into the purple-lashed, amethyst gaze of the Urisk woman before me, then back toward my tall, look-alike cousin.

Here they are.

Or'myr and Li'ra.

Uncle Edwin's whole other life. Perhaps his truer life. Not with Rafe and Trystan and me at all, but here in the Eastern Realm with this woman, his secret love, and their son. A son and mate he was separated from for as long as I knew him.

And he never told us. Never breathed a word.

As if reading my conflicting emotion and the sudden sheen of tears in my eyes, Li'ra's brow furrows and she steps toward me, murmuring to me in Uriskal, her voice a gentle lilt. "El-loren, shushonin," she says as she pulls me into an embrace, tears welling in my eyes as we hug each other tightly. "I'm so glad to meet you."

When we pull away from each other, both of our faces are tear streaked, her expression mirroring my own—a mingling of grief and elation to be meeting family kept so long apart.

"And this is your uncle Wrenfir," Fain says, gesturing to the Gardnerian with the spider tattoo and profusion of cats.

Wrenfir. My mother's much younger brother.

Wrenfir extends his hand, smaller tattoos of spiders marked

all over his fingers and the back of his hand. His eyes are lit with challenge, as he's daring me to take hold of it. "Black Witch," he says, smirking.

I take his spider-marked hand, the feel of dark, subterranean roots filling me in a shuddering rush. "Hello, Uncle."

"Wren," he corrects, firm but not unkind. "You can call me Wren."

"I thought you were dead," I say, voice rough over how many lies my brothers and I were fed. "They told us you were dead."

Wren's mouth twists into a bitter frown. "Of course they did."

"They told you a lot of things, sweetling," Fain says softly, his hand coming to my shoulder. "Come." He gestures toward the table. "Sit. I'll take a look at how the forest managed to bind up your lines and see what it will take to free your power and trace your fastmate. And then we'll fill each other in on the truth of things."

THE TRUTH OF THINGS

Elloren Grey

Noilaan
Eastern Realm
Two days prior to Xishlon

"This is a complicated binding."

Fain's eyes are closed as he concentrates on my wand hand, down on one knee before me. The Wand of Myth rests on my lap, its luminous green hilt emitting a faint, comforting warmth into my hand, its starlight tree pulsing in the back of my mind. My gray, kraken-bloodstained sleeve is rolled high as Fain's water magic flows over my tangled lines in a cool, shivering rush.

"You can read affinities, can't you," I say, more an observation than a question. I'm leaden with both fatigue and a sizzling anxiety for Lukas that's difficult to think around as I cling to the Wand's ethereal tree as a grounding force. "I can read affinities, as well."

Fain's mouth quirks up as he keeps hold of me. "You get that from your mother."

I straighten. "She could do that too?"

Fain nods, then opens his eyes and meets my gaze, a melancholy look passing over his elegant features. My throat tightens as a million questions about my mother strain against my throat. Questions that will have to wait.

He releases my wand hand and looks to my cousin Or'myr. "Five tiers of elemental magic. Bound in a tight weave." He gives me a significant look. "It seems the Forest has thrown everything it has at you, my dear."

"We'll need a series of resonance runes to free her," Or'myr postulates.

I turn to my cousin. "What's that?"

Or'myr's gaze sharpens on me. "Runes that mirror every element involved in another magical system's spell."

"Almost like a translation," Fain adds, rocking back on his heels, "from Forest Elemental Magic into Realmic Rune Magic."

"First," Or'myr explains, "we'll need to assemble the resonance runes that match each portion of the Forest's binding. Then we'll have to create another series of runes to counter and strike down each one of those spell-segments."

A raw anticipation tightens my gut. "So, you think you can break the Forest's hold?"

Fain tilts his head as if cautiously equivocating. "The Forest seems...*intent* in this. It's likely to fight back against our intrusion. But yes, I think we've got a shot at it."

"You're working with some of Noilaan's most advanced magical researchers, Elloren." Or'myr gives me a savvy smile. "I imagine we're up to the task."

Fain squints at Or'myr. "Once Sagellyn links the resonance runes, how long do you think it will take to throw the Forest off of her?" He absently gives my shoulder a light, comforting squeeze as he rises and takes a seat at the table beside me.

Or'myr gives a noncommittal shrug. "One day, perhaps? Maybe two?"

Fain sends me a sly, almost feline smile. "Sagellyn is particularly adept at resonance magic. And after she sets down spells to unbind your magic, we'll connect our own tracking spell to your fastlines and locate your fastmate."

My pulse quickens. "How long will it take to track him?" I press.

"Not long," Or'myr answers. "A few hours, considering the distance. But given what you're up against, you'll need to travel west with an army. Not alone."

I rake my fingers through my knotted gray hair, feeling claustrophobic. "I'm terrified for Lukas. Waiting to act...it's torture."

"Elloren," Or'myr says gently. "No grievous harm is likely to come to him while Vogel is using him to locate you. If Vogel does harm him, he'll weaken the tracking link."

"I got a clear image of Lukas through the wraith bat's rune." I'm unable to keep the worried outrage from my tone. "His chest...it was covered with lash marks..."

"We *will* find him as quickly as we can," Fain assures me, taking my hand in his. "But we need a day or so to gather everyone in a way that won't attract the attention of the Vu Trin."

"We'll likely need Rivyr'el Talonir," Lucretia puts in.

The Alfsigr name surprises me—the same surname as the Elfin monarch, Iolrath Talonir. "Who's that?" I ask.

"A renegade Elf," Wrenfir explains. "Son of Alfsigr royalty. He joined the Resistance out West and pledged fealty to a Smaragdalfar freedom fighter, much to the horror of his illustrious family. Then he fled east with her and a group of subland refugees they rescued, most of them children. Once here, he joined the Vu Trin. He's given the Alfsigr monarchy no end of headaches."

"Yes, well, Rivyr'el gives me no end of headaches, as well," Or'myr rejoins with a long-suffering sigh. "But he's quite skilled when it comes to tracking spells and elemental siphoning." His gaze narrows on Wrenfir. "We'll need to gather some supplies from the Wyvernguard."

"Smuggle them, you mean," my uncle shoots back with a knowing smirk.

Or'myr grins. "'Gather' sounds so much nicer."

Wrenfir spits out a dismissive laugh, then looks to Fain, growing serious. "You can't keep her here for long." His kohl-rimmed gaze flicks to me. "Not with the Vu Trin keeping an eye on anyone connected to her. And the Issani and Ishkart are likely to have sent out more than a few assassins to hunt down the Black Witch."

"You should hide her in your Vonor," Fain suggests to Or'myr. "It's warded and impossible to locate."

Or'myr arches a brow at him. "Which would be ideal, except for the glaring detail that she's not intrinsically purple. So, essentially, we'd be flying her directly into a stone wall."

"She has some light magery," Fain counters, his expression turning sly.

Or'myr's brows notch upward. He turns to me, gaze sharpening as if formulating a plot.

"You have a Vonor?" I ask Or'myr, surprised that my cousin is powerful enough to have his own secret sorcerer enclave, like Chi Nam did.

Or'myr nods. "I do. And once we have Sagellyn draw out the purple in your lightlines, we'll be able to hide you there."

"Finally," Wrenfir exclaims before leveling a wry look at Or'myr, "someone will infiltrate your secret den of debauchery."

I look questioningly at my cousin as he sends Wrenfir a quick glare of derision before turning back to me. "My Vonor's glamour is linked to the purple stone at the pinnacle of this mountain range," he states reasonably. "Only someone intrinsically purple can enter, or even feel or visualize it, so I haven't had much by way of guests. You'd be the first."

"That settles things," Lucretia says to me. "We'll move you to a safer location before dawn, find a place we can bring everyone together to unbind your power and amplify the purple in your lightlines—" she looks to Or'myr "—then you can hide her in your Vonor until she gains full control of her magic."

"Then we'll press for an alliance with the Vu Trin and secure a portal west," Fain adds, giving me a reassuring look.

"Where will you take me next?" I ask, hesitant to leave their protective circle.

"Somewhere you can blend in within the city," Lucretia answers.

"We'll come for you within a day," Fain assures me. "We simply have to be smart in how we gather everyone to avoid attracting attention."

Resolve coalesces inside me, overriding my almost debilitating exhaustion. "I want the Lupines to accompany me for protection when we approach the Vu Trin," I say. "And there's a possibility of approaching them with Yvan Guryev, as well."

Surprise lights on every face in the room.

"Yvan Guryev is dead," Fain gently informs me.

I calmly refute this, telling them of my repeated, clear sensations of Yvan's fire searching for and joining with mine.

"But, how could you possibly have such a clear sense of him?" Or'myr asks, clearly flummoxed. "Power empathy doesn't extend long-distance."

I hesitate, stiffening with conflict over the impossible situation. "He's bound to me as my mate."

Wrenfir's black brows fly up. He exchanges a look of astonishment with Or'myr.

"You're the bound mate of the *Icaral of Prophecy*?" Or'myr sputters.

I nod, suddenly choked up as conflict swells over being bound to two men—two men I care for deeply and desperately want to find, even though I can't imagine how painful those reunions will be in light of my Sealing to Lukas and undimmed Wyvernbond to Yvan.

"I thought Yvan was dead," I force out to Or'myr, "and

then..." I break off, my power shuddering into a hot, storming chaos.

Sympathy lights my cousin's green eyes. "This seems complicated, to be sure. And having the people of both Realms so firmly wedded to the Prophecy surely complicates it further."

I nod, gripping hold of the Wand of Myth's spiraling hilt, drawing some comfort from Or'myr's compassion and the Wand's faint vision of its silvery tree unfurling starlight leaves.

The Eastern Realm is at stake, I remind myself. *Set all this aside and think like a warrior.*

"I'm going to need every ally I can get hold of," I tell them. "Including the dragon Raz'zor. I believe he's here in the East. I'm bound to him in a horde."

"You're in a dragon horde," Or'myr states with renewed astonishment, "with the moonskin dragon Raz'zor?"

I blink at him. "You know of Raz'zor?"

Wrenfir flashes Or'myr another wicked, black-lipped grin. "Looks like I'm no longer the biggest outlier in *this* family."

"No, I think you're the 'normal' one now," Or'myr drawls back, not taking his dazed-looking eyes off me. "Raz'zor has aligned himself with the Wyvernguard. He's stationed at a military base in Northern Noilaan."

I nod, clarity descending. "I felt his red fire coming from the north." I turn to find Fain scrutinizing me, a slight smile on his lips, as if considering me in a more expansive light.

"Do you think Yvan could be found," I ask, "through our fire bond?"

Fain hesitates. "It's unlikely. The Lazra'thil fire bond of Western Wyvernkin is intensely private magic. If you were Wyvern, you'd be able to trace Yvan Guryev, if he is, indeed, alive. But since you are not Lazra'thil, you can't locate him from your end."

"He could be tracing me as we speak," I offer.

"He *could*," Fain allows, hesitating as a grave look enters his eyes. "If it's Yvan you're truly sensing and not some echo of his power."

Echoing out after he was murdered, he means.

My hope falters for a moment, but then rebellion sparks, burning hot against the horrific thought.

"We must hope that Raz'zor is intelligent enough to not lead the Vu Trin straight to you," Fain cautions.

"The Xishlon festival will be her friend," my aunt Li'ra says, her Uriskal inflection lilting and lovely. "It will hide her well."

"I was told about the festival by the refugees I met in the Dyoi Forest," I mention.

"It's the Noi people's biggest festival," Li'ra tells me, her purple-lashed amethyst eyes sparkling. "One of Noilaan's thirteen lunar celebrations, this one honoring the Goddess Vo's love incarnation on the night of the Lavender Moon."

I recall little Tibryl's enthusiasm as she told me about Noilaan's purple moon. "Does the moon truly turn lavender?"

"It does," Li'ra answers with a smile.

"An astronomical occurrence that happens once a year," Or'myr explains. "For one night the moon and stars are aligned in such a way that they reflect the light of the purple Xishlon star. The occurrence casts a mood over Noilaan that pulls people's focus toward love of all kinds—romance, friendship, family ties. Scatters people's wits a bit if they try to think on anything else too closely. And luck would have it that the Xishlon holiday is the day after tomorrow."

"Xishlon is a ridiculous holiday," Wrenfir spits out, his spider-leg-edged mouth twisting with obvious disdain. "The Noi run around decorating everything with heart-shaped flower wreathes and runic moon orbs, professing their love and kissing each other."

Or'myr grins at this. "It's also the perfect time to evade Vu Trin notice. The soldiers who haven't deployed west yet will be caught up in the moon's thrall."

The library's black door abruptly opens.

I look toward it, along with everyone else and alarm races through my veins.

A horned man with lightning-glazed skin is standing in its frame. He's obviously another Zhilon'ile Wyvern-shifter. Like Vothe, his hue is a similar midnight black, his dark eyes silvered with lightning, his pupils vertically slit. He's attractive, his ears pointed, his horns a spiraling obsidian, and he appears to be about Fain's age, his black hair edged with a tracery of gray. My alarm draws down a fraction as I note how calm everyone is.

"Sholin'toiya," Fain enthuses, rising to greet the man, his expression lit up as his water affinity flies out to encircle the shifter, his power seamlessly met by the man's own formidable water magic.

Confusion races through me. Because the shifter is wearing Gardnerian sacred black garb, the same as Fain, a necklace with a white bird pendant gracing the shifter's neck.

"This is Sholindrile Xanthile," Fain announces with a beaming smile, "my toiyanon."

His bonded mate.

Surprise wells as Fain's hand slides around the man's waist and they lean into each other, exchanging a fond look, their magic converging in a loose caress. My shock over their Gardnerian dress is quickly subsumed as my mind reels over how startlingly different it is here in the East. No hiding in the shadows for Fain and his love.

Which means no more hiding for Trystan.

Something tight and pained buried deep inside me—something I didn't know I was holding—relaxes. The injustices of the Western Realm have been ingrained in me for so long, I could think only in terms of concealment and escape for Trystan. Never in terms of freedom from the threat of terrible cruelty.

But now, here we are, in a whole other land, this cruelty swept clear away.

And I realize, as imperfect as this new land might prove to be, there are things here that are vastly better than they are in the Western Realm. Things worth fighting to hold on to.

"Sholin'toi," Fain says, slowly and with great significance as he gestures to me, "this is Elloren Gardner Grey. Edwin and Wrenfir's niece."

My fire power shudders against Fain announcing my identity so blithely.

Sholindrile's black brow lifts, the lightning in his eyes intensifying, as Fain's gaze takes on a more serious light, likely reading my guttering magic. "Toiya, you're safe with Sholin," he assures me. "Both Sho and I are allied with my sister and Jules Kristian in all things."

I cautiously meet Sholindrile's gaze to find him studying me probingly. He has Vothendrile's same unblinking dragon stare, but his expression radiates a serenity that lessens my concern, despite his troubling attire. He acknowledges me with a formal dip of his head, his gaze weighted with import. "Welcome to our home, Daughter of the Resistance."

"Why are you wearing Gardnerian blacks?" I can't help but blurt out.

Sholindrile's mouth lifts. "I am a convert to the Gardnerian Church of the First Children and a student of many religions. I teach philosophy and theology at Noilaan's Voshir University."

My mind tilts, not understanding how this could possibly fit together. I imagine how the priests of the Western Realm would react to Fain and Sholindrile claiming the Mage faith as their own. They'd be struck down immediately.

"The Mages don't..." I pause, struggling with this concept. "They don't allow anyone but Gardnerians into the faith."

Sholindrile's look of serene calm remains unbroken. "Most faiths, when read so rigidly, have many uncrossable lines." His dark eyes take on a knowing light. "I do not read the faiths of Erthia so rigidly. This faith is important to Fain, so it is important to me." Fain and Sholindrile exchange a quick look of affection.

"I'm studying the wandfasting spell with Sagellyn," Fain tells me. "If Sage and I manage to master the spell, Sho and I are to be fasted." Fain's eyes flash with a spark of hard, intractable rebellion. *"Publicly."*

There's something so explosively seditious in Fain's expression it sparks an elated rejoicing inside of me over their sheer audacity. And I feel chastened for judging their choice of faith, difficult as it is for me to wrap my mind around. Because, truly, this is a private thing.

"What do you think, toiya?" Fain asks me with a cheeky grin. "Should we invite Marcus Vogel to our fasting and Sealing ceremonies?"

The door opens before I can respond, and Trystan strides into the room, relief lifting my heart. I move to greet him, but he gestures for me to remain seated.

"Where's Vothe?" I ask.

"Outside," Trystan answers. "Keeping watch."

"Do the Vu Trin suspect anything?" Lucretia presses.

Trystan shakes his head as his eyes lock on to mine. "I sent word to Kam Vin about Vogel's new powers via Jules Kristian, and he'll also relay your message about Valasca to Ni Vin. And I arranged help for the refugees you came here with. Bleddyn Arterra is getting them through the border and to Jules Kristian. Tonight."

Surprise bursts into being. *"Bleddyn Arterra?"* A memory of tall, muscular Bleddyn's green-hued face scowling at me fills my mind—Bleddyn, who hated me for so long in the Verpax University kitchens, our relationship wary at best.

Trystan's eyes glint. "She's joined the Vu Trin border guard. And the Eastern Realm arm of the Resistance."

"I didn't expect there to be a need for the Resistance here," I gravely note, looking to Fain and Lucretia.

Fain and his sister share a jaded look—the same look I've seen on Lucretia's and Jules's faces many times when facing down ugly truths in the West. "The Resistance network was in place from the Realm War," Fain says with a sigh. "When we smuggled Fae and others here. And now, with borders locking down and so much of the West desperately needing to get East…we've simply expanded our focus."

I consider how active Bleddyn was in the Western Realm, helping Urisk and Smaragdalfar refugees escape east. "The people I came here with…" I say, tense with worry, "their illness is advanced. They'll need medicine."

Wrenfir winces. "I'll get them Norfure tincture," he assures me, seated now with one cat in his lap, another curled around his dark-clad shoulders.

I study him, surprised by his offer. "Are you a border guard, as well?"

He shoots me a cool look. "I'm not much of a *joiner*. I work on my own. As an apothecary." He mentions this a tad confrontationally, and I've a sense that this is a loaded topic of conversation for him. "I've a stash of Norfure," he adds, softening a bit as the cat wrapped around his shoulders begins to purr and he idly strokes it. "Made from ingredients…" his eyes flick slyly toward Or'myr "…that I've 'borrowed.'"

Or'myr gives a short laugh at this, and gratitude swells inside me over the possibility of Tibryl and Emberlyyn getting hold of life-saving medicine. I nod at my spidery uncle, overtaken by the rush of bone-deep appreciation. "Wren, thank you. They're *really* sick."

What looks like pained understanding flashes through his eyes.

"Jules is sending word to everyone who can help unbind Elloren's magic and keep her safe," Trystan informs us all. "He's going to secure a location where we can gather tomorrow eve." He looks to Fain and Sholindrile. "Other Vu Trin saw me pull an 'Elfhollen woman' aboard my skiff. That might trigger some investigation. So Bleddyn's going to come for her before dawn." He turns to me once more. "You're likely safe here for the evening, Ren, but tomorrow you'll need to blend into Voloi."

CHAPTER EIGHT

DAUGHTER OF THE RESISTANCE

Elloren Grey

Noilaan
Eastern Realm
Two days prior to Xishlon

"What happened to my parents?" I ask Fain. A plate of half-consumed black bread slathered in a tangy plum paste and thin slices of smoked Vo River eel sits on the dining room table before me, my hunger assuaged by the unfamiliar food but my emotions a tumult.

Fain exhales and regards me levelly as he reclines in his chair and swirls a glass of turquoise wine, his arm draped around Sholindrile's broad shoulders. "Toward the end of the Realm War," he says, the liquid in his glass stilling as he sets it gently down, "your parents were increasingly active in the Resistance. Both your father and mother were aiding the Urisk and the Fae and later the Smaragdalfar Elves in their efforts to escape East."

"Uncle Edwin was involved in the Resistance too, Ren," Trystan softly adds, concern in his kohl-rimmed eyes. I know he understands just how mind-bendingly disorienting all this new information is. So many things we believed our whole lives turned upside down.

Fain interlaces his fingers, his aura consolidating into a dense, invisible cloud around him. "Your parents were attempting to rescue a group of Asrai Fae children before they could be shipped to the Pyrran Islands." His mouth tenses and the entire room ripples and darkens for a moment. "Your grandmother found out about it and executed them."

I look at Trystan, my throat gone dry. He's sitting beside Fain and Sholindrile, looking calm enough, but I can sense the wind and water auras coursing fitfully around him, just as my fire has kicked up into a tangled, troubled blaze.

"Your grandmother didn't want your family's illustrious name sullied," Fain continues in a bitter tone. "So she pretended they'd been killed by Kelts."

I grapple with the truth, stunned by how thoroughly this was hidden from me and my brothers. I turn to Lucretia, outrage blooming, unable to keep the accusation from my tone. "Why didn't you tell us? Why didn't Jules?" *And why didn't Uncle Edwin?*

"Elloren, we couldn't," she insists with obvious remorse, then pauses, seeming at a loss for words.

"It was too dangerous," Fain cuts in with a look of concern toward Lucretia. "*Everyone* who knew that Vale and Tessla had been involved in the Resistance was killed, with very few exceptions. Do you realize how dangerous that information is in the Western Realm? That the son of the Black Witch was a Resistance organizer?"

A memory surfaces, adding to my morass of questions.

"Aunt Vyvian told me that Jules and our mother were...*together*," I say. I'm hit by a sudden flash of unsettled water magery and turn toward its origin to find Lucretia's gaze pinned firmly on the table. Her water aura, always so tightly constrained, is sluicing through her lines with surprising intensity. I remember Diana telling me about the strong attraction she sensed between Lucretia and Jules, neither aware of the other's affections.

Fain spares a sympathetic glance toward Lucretia before setting his troubled gaze back on me. "Jules and your mother were from the same Keltish border town. Way downriver. In his youth, Jules was in love with her. But Tessla viewed him only as a close friend. There was never anything between them, and in time, Jules reconciled himself to Tessla's fasting to his closest friend, your father, Vale."

Heat pricks at my neck and my gaze flicks back to Lucretia, sorry to have poked at this private pain, even as I'm struck by the remembrance of the odd, emotional looks that would sometimes come over Professor Kristian's face when he looked at me. How he told me once that I reminded him of someone, refusing to specify who.

"So, all this time," I say to Fain, "Jules Kristian was hiding an extensive history with my own parents."

"Elloren..." Fain starts, splaying his palms toward me, as if in supplication.

"I understand," I say with a slight, halting wave. "I see why he didn't tell me." I meet Lucretia's tense gaze. "But still, I wish my brothers and I weren't left so completely in the dark." I turn to Li'ra, who is quietly sitting beside me. "How did you and Or'myr get to the Eastern Realm?"

Li'ra's lilac-hued face tenses. "During the Realm War," she says, voice low, "your grandmother found out about Edwin and me. She threatened Edwin and told him...that she'd have me killed if he didn't send me East and break off all contact." She pauses, swallowing, as if the words are difficult to voice. "Luckily, she didn't know about Or'myr, who was a baby at the time." She pulls in a shaky breath. "Or'myr and I had to leave. You don't understand what your grandmother was like. She meant it. She would have hunted me down and killed me. And she would have murdered Or'myr too. And because of me, your grandmother had the ultimate means of control over Edwin from that point on."

"My aunt told me she had only just found out about you," I say as outrage over Aunt Vyvian's cruel words scalds through my lines.

Li'ra shakes her head. "Carnissa clearly never told Vyvian about Edwin and me. If she had, your aunt would have *never* allowed Edwin to take you and your brothers in. But... Edwin and Vyvian *did* know that Vale and Tessla were murdered for treason. They both knew what your grandmother was capable of doing to hold on to power. And what the Mages, as a whole, were capable of."

"So, Uncle Edwin stayed in the Western Realm and sent you and Or'myr East to save your lives," I piece together in a constricted voice.

"And to save *yours*," Li'ra insists, growing impassioned. "Edwin cared deeply about you and your brothers. He couldn't bear the thought of leaving you alone in the West without protection." Her expression darkens. "And he feared that one of you might possess true power."

"Black Witch power," I amend, feeling distraught.

Li'ra nods, a look of great sorrow in her eyes. "Edwin knew it was a possibility. And he didn't want to see that power fall into the hands of the Gardnerians."

"He hid my power from me," I say as tears glass my eyes. "But he told me...before he died..." Grief tightens my throat and for a moment I can't speak, can barely breathe. My cousin Or'myr's long arm comes around me as a tear breaks free from Li'ra's eyes, her own face tight with sorrow. "He told me," I force out in a splintered voice, "that he was wrong to hide my power from me. He told me I should fight the Gardnerians."

"You need to understand, Elloren," Li'ra says, her own voice coarsened by tears. "The Mages thought *nothing* of killing anyone opposed to them. Edwin didn't want any more of the people he loved dying. And… I think he felt the Mages couldn't be fought. That the best one could hope for was to escape their notice."

"But he changed his mind."

Li'ra nods, seeming too overcome to say more. Trystan moves to console her, one hand coming to her arm, and she pats his hand appreciatively.

"So, you and Or'myr left the Western Realm," I finally say as tears streak down my face.

Li'ra nods again, her mouth turning down in a trembling grimace. "Edwin gave us all his money. So we could get across the desert and get settled here." Her voice fractures. "But I would have traded all that money to just have had him with us." She breaks off, quietly crying, as the realization washes over me of why we were so poor growing up and always dependent on Aunt Vyvian, the stories of my uncle squandering all his money on expensive violins a complete fabrication.

And now it's also clear why Uncle Edwin never employed Urisk servants, even when Aunt Vyvian offered to supply them, my imperious aunt often chiding my uncle for having my brothers and me do the housework, the barn work, the gardening, and the violin shopwork. I realize now why my uncle always seemed ready to break into tears when considering the Gaffneys' Urisk farmworkers' situation and how the Urisk were treated in general.

You had so much secret pain, I think, aching for him. *I wish you could have told us what was in your heart. I wish Rafe and Trystan and I could have at least tried to console you.*

"There was no other way than silence," Li'ra says, as if reading my anguished thoughts. "Truly, Elloren, there was no other way."

A rush of heat blazes over me and I look to Wrenfir across the table, Or'myr's arm still wrapped around my shoulder as Wrenfir's fire magery whips protectively around us both. "How did you get here?" I ask him.

"The Mages were killing everyone set against them," Wrenfir says, outrage flashing in his spider-edged eyes. "After they murdered my sister and Vale..." He stops, his expression tightening with what looks like a furious, grief-filled rage as he shakes his head, seeming unable to continue without setting something ablaze.

"I accompanied Wrenfir, Li'ra, and Or'myr East," Fain interjects. "I acted as their guard on the journey across the desert, a dangerous sojourn for a young woman without magic." Bitterness creeps into his expression, his water magic stirring. "It was time for me to leave the Western Realm, as well. The religious...*inflexibility* there was gaining serious ground."

"I saw the way Fain was treated," Wrenfir bites out, ferocity in his tone as he looks to Fain. "I was quite young, but I knew and understood."

And so, they all left for the East. Wrenfir must have been barely a teen at the time, I realize. This courageous family of mine. Pride swells in my chest.

"So, you crossed the entire Central Desert?" I marvel, glancing at them each in turn.

"Well, I certainly don't remember it, as I was one," Or'myr puts in with a slight smile, "but I've been told it was a dangerous trek."

Fain gives Or'myr an amused look. "Not with a Level Five Water Mage and a youth who's a Level Four Fire and Earth Mage."

Li'ra, Wrenfir, and Fain exchange the knowing looks of people with a shared history.

"So, Uncle Edwin stayed to protect us." I meet Trystan's gaze. My brother's expression is unreadable, but the tightness in his eyes and his tumultuous water magery relay his stormy feelings. I turn back to Fain. "And to protect me from falling into the hands of monsters."

"You are sitting here," Fain says, his tone weighted, "alive and on the side of the Resistance...and with a profoundly different view of things than your culture taught you to have, in large part because of Edwin Gardner."

I nod as fresh tears glass my eyes and Or'myr pulls me into a closer embrace. An embrace I'm chastened to return. Because Rafe, Trystan, and I are the reason Or'myr never had the chance to know his kind, loving, revolutionary father.

"I'm sorry you never got to know him," I tell Or'myr, meeting his gaze as our fire power breaks loose to lash around each other.

"I know," he says, voice tight but kind. "It's not your fault."

Fain pushes back his chair, picks up his wineglass, and rises, looking around at all of us. "A toast," he says with great import as he raises his glass. "To Edwin Gardner. Who I was blessed to know." His voice catches as we all raise wineglasses and tea mugs.

Fain looks to me and Or'myr, emotion filling his gaze. "Edwin would have been *so happy* to see you two together...to see all of us together. Your parents too...they would have been overjoyed and *so* gratified."

There are tears all around as we drink to Edwin, the floral taste of my tea mingling with my tears as we pay tribute to my courageous uncle. My kind uncle. And, in the end, my completely defiant uncle.

And pay tribute, as well, to my parents, Vale and Tessla Gardner.

Who died fighting for a better world.

"Uncle Edwin...he died so that we could make it here." I look to Trystan, my face damp with tears, but the press of the Wand against my calf a solid comfort.

I glance out the huge window we're leaning against, the two of us sitting alone on my bedroom's indigo window seat, the night-darkened view overlooking an impossible drop to the Vo River. My room is dark as well, all light snuffed out in case any Vu Trin fly by.

I peer down. Vothe is standing guard a story below us beside a military rune skiff on the estate's broad terrace, the black expanse of the river spread out beyond him. And beyond that, the glowing blue line of the border wall and the mammoth Vo Mountains, the storm band above it flickering with gauzy bursts of lightning.

Trystan's hand glides over mine and I grasp it tightly, the evening's revelations swirling through my mind. "Why does Wrenfir have a spider and a raven tattooed across his face and neck?" I ask, meeting my brother's steady gaze.

Trystan is silent for a moment, and I can see it flickering in his eyes—my brother's usual reluctance to speak for another about private things. "You could ask him yourself," he gently suggests.

"He doesn't seem like the most approachable person—"

"Like Ariel?" There's a hint of challenge in the words, and I feel instantly chastened as a pang of grief for Ariel twists at my heart.

"Yeah. Like Ariel."

"In the few days I've known him, I've gleaned that he's had a hard life." I wait as my brother gives me a somber look. "Wrenfir grew up in extreme poverty. As a child he was sick with the Grippe and almost died from it. Then, he was almost killed by the Kelts and the Urisk during the Realm War." Trystan pauses again, as if formulating his thoughts. "When he was about thirteen, our grandmother killed our parents, who he was *very* close to. Then he escaped the Western Realm with Fain and Li'ra and Or'myr only to come to a place that reviled him for being Gardnerian."

It pains me to learn all this, but the questions remain. "Why the tattoos, though?"

"He fell in with the only group that didn't treat him as an outcast. Death Fae refugees. The spider and the raven are among their familiars."

"Like Ariel's birds?"

Trystan nods. "Like her birds. I think the tattoos are his way of paying tribute to those Fae for their kindness."

"The kindness of Death Fae?" I don't know much about these

mysterious Fae, but from what little I've read, kindness isn't exactly what they're known for.

Trystan's lip quirks slightly. "They can be very kind. I've gotten to know two of them. But their relationship with Wren is ironic, since he's constantly working against their power."

"What do you mean?"

"He's a brilliant apothecary. Like our mother was. Like you. He spends all his time making medicines to save people's lives. Mainly from the Grippe."

Trepidation rises. "If he's working against Death Fae power... does that mean they cause the Grippe?"

Trystan shakes his head. "No. Not directly. But they're aligned with forces of nature that are...difficult."

"Like sickness?"

He pivots his head as if equivocating. "Like that. They're primordial, Ren. It's complicated, and none of us has a good understanding of their power." Trystan glances toward the blue rune border and frowns. "Wrenfir left to deliver Norfure tincture to those people you came through the Dyoi Forest with."

Profound relief rushes over me. Emberlyyn and Tibryl will be cured, just like that, by the wildly expensive medicine.

"He steals most of the ingredients," Trystan bluntly tells me. "To make medicine for those who can't afford it. Like he couldn't afford it when he was a child."

I consider this. "You shouldn't have to be rich to get medicine." Trystan nods, our powers whirling around each other decidedly even as another question rises. "Are all those cats Wrenfir's?"

Trystan nods. "He lost his childhood cat during the Realm War and he never got over it. He rescues them now."

A pang cuts through me as I think of my own cat, Isobel, who split her time between our cottage and the Gaffneys'. I hope against hope she's ensconced there now.

"When he's not rescuing cats," Trystan tells me, "Wrenfir works straight through practically every night making medicine for the people stuck on the other side of that wall. We're an odd lot, but I rather like our family."

"He'll save Tibryl's and Emberlyyn's lives, you know."

"Yes, well, Wrenfir knows what it's like to be *really* sick. And he knows what it's like to be unwanted in a new place." Trystan's gaze slides down to Vothe and catches there, his water power breaking free of his control to flow toward Vothe in a heated shudder.

Vothe abruptly looks up, the shifter's bright silver gaze meeting Trystan's, his own power flashing toward my brother in a charged current.

"You know…" I venture, "Vothe has strong feelings for you. I can sense it in his power."

Trystan turns to me, blinking with obvious, abashed surprise. "Are you Lupine now?"

I shrug, unable to suppress a faint smile. "Similar, maybe. I can sense the emotion inside people's power. Vogel triggered something in my magic when Lukas and I…" Jagged pain digs in deep, like a shard of glass. "When Lukas and I were Sealed," I tightly finish, overcome by the yearning to be back with Lukas in the imagined safety of Chi Nam's Vonor. Wrapped around each other…

Trystan's hand tightens around mine.

"I love him," I admit, heart wrenching. "I love Yvan too, but I thought him dead. And then… I fell in love with Lukas. And…it's so hard knowing that he's out there somewhere, in trouble, and I have to wait to go after him."

"You'll get to him," Trystan assures me. "Your power will be unbound in a day's time. But Ren, I think it's important that you don't act alone. Vogel's brilliant, and he's going to do everything he can to draw you in. I think all of us, working together, can help safeguard against that. Vogel's obsessed with the Prophecy, which means he'll stop at nothing to get to you and Yvan both."

I give my brother a fraught look. "I need to find Yvan too."

"I know you do."

My emotions give a hard, aching twist, tangling tighter than my lines. "But…when he finds out I'm fully Sealed to Lukas…" The ache twists harder. "It's tearing me apart to even think about it."

"Then don't, for the moment. Elloren, Yvan will get past this, and he will persevere. We all understand that there's a lot more at stake here than our own hearts."

Tears sheen my eyes, my brother's face wavy through them. "I love Yvan too," I say, my voice breaking around the admission. "I can't help it. I just do. I love them both."

A compassionate weight enters his gaze. "Life is complicated, Ren," he says. "The rigid lines don't hold. We all have to navigate that, the best we can."

I force a deep breath as I struggle to stamp all the heartache down and Trystan retreats into quiet for a moment. He glances back out the window, at Vothe, my brother's power straining toward the shifter. "What are you sensing in Vothe's power?" he asks, tentative.

I look closely at Trystan. "He's like a cyclone that wants to sweep you up." I hesitate. "He's in love with you, isn't he?"

Trystan shakes his head and swallows. "I don't know."

We're both quiet for a moment. "Are you in love with him?" I gently ask.

Trystan winces, as if his feelings are too difficult to acknowledge.

Tears are suddenly welling in my eyes, a pang forming, tight in my chest, over my brother's obvious struggle, as my heart aches for all of us.

Valasca's terrible words fill my mind, the heartache intensifying.

You will likely lose every last thing that's precious to you. But you'll lose those things so that others won't have to.

"Trystan," I say, my love for my brother making me bold. "Life is so short. And there's so much danger coming for us all. If you and Vothendrile love each other…" I pause, smiling wryly at him through tear-glassed eyes. "I suggest you give in to it before you both erupt into a massive lightning storm and take down the whole city."

Trystan's eyes widen, his magic whipping around him in a chaotic mess. "There's no way," he says, a sharp hurt seeping into his voice. "Vothe's family…they won't even countenance a friendship. His brother… He visited him to warn him away from me. I can't even enter Zhilaan, because I'm the grandson of the Black Witch. Their ruling conclave had me formally *shunned* from their lands."

I narrow my gaze at him, undaunted. "Since when does love respect diplomatic pettiness? Someone wise once told me that."

Trystan coughs out a laugh, his lip quirking. "A deeply wise brother, perhaps?"

"A *supremely* wise brother." I consider him closely, this brother who, in some ways, I feel like I'm just now getting to know. The brother who had to keep his true self hidden for so long. I lose my slight smile. "What happened, Trystan, when you came here?"

He exhales and gives me a look fraught with significance. "Oh, Ren. There's a lot to tell."

My brother fills me in on his journey East. His rocky entry into the Wyvernguard.

And he tells me about Vothendrile.

I can read in my brother's words and his magery how intensely his feelings run for this shifter. And how, despite all the prejudice against Trystan, he's finding a new life here—a place and culture and even a religion that he truly loves.

Conflicted tears well in my eyes, exhaustion fueling the rise of troubled angst.

Trystan stops speaking. "Ren, what's the matter?"

"I'm not quite sure what I'm feeling. It's just…in a way, you've found your place and you fit in here. You have Vothe, even though you think you don't. And I feel like... I don't belong anywhere."

Trystan gives me a look of appraisal. "How do you think I felt for so many years? In a place I could never fit into? A place that hated me. With a religion that hated me. And then, at university, all alone while the rest of you paired up?"

"Maybe like this?" I grudgingly offer.

"*Exactly* like this."

"I *am* glad you've found your place here, you know," I tell him, heartfelt.

Trystan coughs out an incredulous laugh. "Ren, the Wyvernguard erupted into *protest* over my inclusion."

"It's clear, though, you *have* found your place." I look him over. His kohl-rimmed eyes. The dragon tattoo snaking up his neck. His vivid blue hair and sapphire Wyvernguard uniform. And his circle of newfound family, so many of them possessing water magery just like him. "Whether you see it or not," I say, "you seem like you truly belong in the Eastern Realm."

Trystan tilts his head, as if acknowledging my point. "You do too, Ren. With me. With all of us."

A bitter sound escapes me. "Even though I'm a complete and utter freak?"

Trystan's mouth lifts. "*Especially* because you're a complete and utter freak. You say it like it's a bad thing."

I can't help but spit out a beleaguered laugh. I peer at Trystan searchingly. "Vothendrile's extremely handsome."

Trystan colors and looks away, which surprises me. Trystan isn't the blushing sort.

Then he turns back to me, actually smiling. "Despite everything," he says, "I'm so much happier here, Ren..." The words break off as tears glisten in his eyes. "It's possible to be born in the wrong place...and then suddenly find yourself in the right one."

Tears return to my own eyes as my heart swells to see my brother finally finding happiness. But then an ominous sense of vulnerability rises, the Shadow pressing in. "Trystan, I'm afraid. It's worse than they all think with Vogel."

My brother nods and grows silent, but then his expression lights with defiance. "Who needs good odds? Where would the fun be in that?"

I burst out into laughter and tears at the same time. "Someone very wise must have told you that."

Trystan smiles. "A deeply wise sister."

I lean my head onto his shoulder. "I love you, Trystan."

He leans his head down to mine and gives my hand another bolstering squeeze. "I love you too. And we'll fight Vogel, no matter what it takes. We'll fight him *together.*"

CHAPTER NINE

ALLIED

Trystan Gardner &
Vothendrile Xanthile

Noilaan
Eastern Realm
Two days prior to Xishlon

Trystan

I step out onto Fain and Sholin's rune-lit terrace, every muscle tense, feeling bound up by fierce concern for Elloren and fear over Vothe's reaction to this evening's revelations.

Vothe stills as I approach, his arresting features washed in the terrace's sapphire light, his silver-tipped hair gently buffeted by the breeze.

But there's nothing tranquil about his gaze.

It's all wild lightning—so discordant and white-flashing that it triggers a stinging rush of answering power through my lines.

I note that his horns are unfurled, spiraled up as they so often are whenever he's swept up in powerful emotion.

Cast into a more tumultuous apprehension, I glance over my shoulder, toward Elloren's bedroom. I can just make out her shadowy form in the darkened window, so small and vulnerable from this vantage point, her fate resting entirely in Vothe's hands.

I turn back to Vothe, my breath suspended, clear that what I'm asking of him is staggering in its audacity and full of a devastating level of risk.

"*Vothe,*" I implore, the word cut off by the storming look he gives me.

"I'll help you keep her safe," he bites out.

I huff out a shuddering exhale as my water power surges toward him.

Vothe's eyes flick up and down my form, clearly reading my emotional flare. His jaw ticks as some of his confrontational energy draws down to be replaced by a fraught look. "If Vogel can strike down runes," he says with a glance toward the city's translucent dome, "he'll decimate the Vu Trin."

I nod in grim assent—the Vu Trin army's weapons are just wood and steel and stone when stripped of their runic power.

"But your sister's power isn't fueled by runes," Vothe says pointedly, and for a moment, the explosive words hang in the air between us.

"No, it isn't," I affirm, just as pointed.

Vothe shakes his head and rakes a hand through his silver-tipped hair. The motion is halted by a horn, which he absently grips as he spits out a curse under his breath. He casts me another loaded look and sets his hands on his hips.

"She's telling the truth," he admits. "Just like you were, when you first arrived at the Wyvernguard. I knew you were. I *knew it*, Trystan, right from the start. But I fought against that knowing. And that could have cost the Wyvernguard a powerful ally."

His shoulders tense as he glances once more toward Elloren, as if he's fortifying himself against the ramifications of it all.

"If Vogel can truly strike down runes," he finally says, "we're going to need her power. And yours. And mine. And the Icaral she claims is not dead. We're going to need *everyone*. Former enemies and allies alike. The divisions can't stand if we're going to save the Realm."

My fire sparks to an impassioned blaze as I step toward him. "I'll fight to the death for this realm."

Vothe's gaze on me intensifies, gleaming with obvious emotion as lightning streaks through it. "I know that, toiya." His onyx lips lift. "Which is part of why I want you. So, if the Vu Trin don't cut us down for harboring your sister, will you be my Xishlon'vir?"

I bark out an astonished laugh, my eyes widening with incredulity as affection for him sweeps through me. "Are you honestly thinking about...*courting*? At a time like this?"

He turns serious. "I never stop thinking about it, toiya'lon."

Overcome, I reach up to caress the hard plane of his cheek. Vothe's breath catches as I trace the edge of his full lower lip with my thumb, delicate threads of lightning flashing to life on his mouth, every nerve inside me suddenly alight.

Vothe opens his mouth and lightly closes his teeth around my thumb's tip, eyes searing into mine.

Vothendrile

I know what this moment means as I lightly bite down on Trystan's finger, wanting to set my teeth on the piercing through his lower lip instead. And then kiss him until we engulf the entirety of Noilaan in our storm. Because I know, in this moment, that I've just stepped off the edge of the only world I've ever known to forever dwell in a new one.

Trystan shivers as I caress the tip of his thumb with my tongue then release it, holding his gaze as my power eddies toward him, the strength of its surge acknowledging the enormity of the leap of alliance we've just taken.

"I need your help," Trystan says as his power rushes out to commingle with mine.

"What do you need?" I ask, lightning singeing over my lips with a delicious, frenetic sting. Trystan's gaze flicks to my mouth with obvious desire, but I can feel him driving back that desire as resolve burgeons through his Magelines.

"Tomorrow night," he says, his green eyes locked on to mine, "we're bringing Elloren's allies together. So we can free her power and approach the Vu Trin to forge an alliance."

"You mean 'force' an alliance," I archly correct.

"No," Trystan counters. "I mean 'forge.' But we *will* fight back if they try to kill her."

"Fair enough," I concede. "But take great care, Trystan. The Vu Trin are watching everyone who might be sympathetic to her."

"Well, they're about to be distracted by a purple moon festival," he returns, a hard glint to his gaze. "And a rather odd weather disturbance. I need a weather Wyvern for that."

I cross my arms, eyeing him shrewdly as I struggle to hold the surge in my power back from him. "What did you have in mind?"

Trystan doesn't hesitate. "Something that will make it quite difficult to follow anyone."

"You want me to hide her with fog?" I postulate.

"I do," Trystan rejoins, a lethal edge entering his tone. "So she can get hold of her power, then go west with all of us. To strike down the Magedom before it can decimate Amazakaraan and advance on the East."

In answer I send out a slim line of fog and roll it around his form. Trystan shivers, his magic shimmering loose to encircle mine in rock-solid alliance.

CHAPTER TEN

WARRIOR'S RETURN

Valasca Xanthrir

City of Cyme, Amazakaraan
Two days prior to Xishlon

Valasca Xanthrir falls through the portal's golden mist and is thrust into a world at war.

A nightmare forest surrounds her, its gigantic, undulating trees made of Shadow. Ground-shuddering explosions sound and she flinches, dragons shrieking through a distance that's obscured by the strange, curling gray mist rising from the ground.

Valasca's eyes flit to the weapons in her rune-tattooed hands and a rush of alarm crackles through her. Not only has her blue skin shifted to a pewter hue, the sapphire Noi runes on the blade gripped in her left hand are stripped of their glow. Only the blade in her right hand—her most powerful, favored blade, with a wider diversity of runes—has maintained its charge, but, bizarrely, the single emerald Smaragdalfar varg rune on its hilt is feeding green into the variety of linked runes, turning the blue Noi and scarlet Amaz runes emerald.

Remembering how easily Vogel struck down Chi Nam's runic barrier, she gives a quick glance at the retrieval runes marked on her palms. Relief washes through her. *Still there.* But there's an odd coating of emerald green edging the Noi rune's lines. An odd green coating edging *all* her runic tattoos. And the small Smaragdalfar varg rune on her wrist—the ward she had the Amaz-Smaragdalfar rune sorceress, Vestylle, mark next to her weapons-amplification rune well over a year ago—its glow is unusually bright.

The ramifications of this circle through her military mind as Valasca swings around to find the portal she just flew through fading to an almost imperceptible imprint on the air.

A cyclonic roar sounds directly above. She jerks her head up, eyes widening as she takes in the funneling circle of Shadow streaking down toward her, like a giant's incoming heel.

Hurling herself sideways, she slams onto grassy ground as the funnel punches down beside her in an earsplitting *boom*. Rapidly rolling away, then springing to a crouch, she breathlessly takes in the dark column before her. Tendrils of undulating Shadow are rapidly branching from it to form another gigantic Shadow tree. Mouth agape, Valasca cranes her neck and scans the ghoulish canopy fanning out high above.

Disoriented, she rises, carefully advancing through the whirling fog. Her focus zeroes in on the screams of women and children sounding up ahead amidst ground-shaking explosions, their cries in a multitude of languages as broken dragons blast through the Shadow canopy.

The next thoughts flash through Valasca's mind in staccato jabs. *How much time has passed since Lukas Grey threw me into the partially charged portal? Where is Vogel? Where is Elloren? Where am I?*

Her thoughts cast about for purchase as she tightens her grip on her blades. "Elloren?" she calls into the tendriling fog, to no response.

More screams, one a child's at closer range.

Valasca breaks into a sprint toward the sound, darting around huge Shadow trees and down an incline. She emerges from the denser portion of Shadow forest, the fog thinning as she's met with an expansive view of the huge, Shadow-tree-riddled valley.

Her lungs seize, a light-headed *whoosh* flashing over her.

Sweet Goddess, I'm in Amazakaraan.

With a horrified sweep of her gaze, she takes in the bizarre Shadow-forest canopy hanging over the city, Amazakaraan's protective runic dome gone.

Dragons are streaming in, the Mages on their backs throwing bolt after bolt of dark, silver-spitting fire at her city, the explosions like knife-strikes to Valasca's heart. She can just make out almost uniformly grayed Amaz soldiers in the distance as they attempt to do battle with the incoming Mages, the usual glow from their runic bows and blades gone.

Valasca flinches again as a cacophony of darkened Magefire slams down from multiple attackers, all streaking toward the Central Plaza's mammoth goddess sculpture, Amazakaraan's most revered religious image. The Goddess explodes with a thunderous *bang*, the beautiful statue rendered to a smoking pile of rubble.

A vicious expletive erupts from Valasca's throat as she fists her blades tighter and makes for the plaza.

"Mum'yi!"

The little girl runs toward Valasca through the narrow street's Shadow fog, screaming in Elfhollen for her mother. Decimated buildings crackle with silvery-gray fire all around as Valasca accelerates toward the child, her heart giving a hard wrench as she recognizes her.

Inge. Sylvi's child. Not more than four years old.

A broken dragon flies through the dark canopy above, barreling toward them both. Narrowing her eyes with lethal intensity, Valasca draws back her fists, slides her fingers along the runes of her varg-rune-marked blade, then hurls both weapons forward with a guttural cry. Both slash across the sky and find their mark, one slamming into the dragon to impale its forehead, the other punching into the neck of the Mage astride the broken beast.

The Mage's neck snaps back as the dragon's head bursts into a ball of emerald flame, the dark creature's flight pattern chaotic as the Mage's wand falls from his hand.

Valasca presses her thumbs to the retrieval rune on her palm and the rune-charged blade flies back, slapping into her hand as the dragon crashes into a nearby smoking building, the Mage flying off its back and landing in a lifeless heap. Wasting no time, Valasca sheaths her blade, grabs quivering little Inge, and breaks into a run down the Shadow-fogged streets as the little girl screams *"Mum'yi! Mum'yi!"* over and over.

The child's terror is a dart straight through Valasca's emotions, even as she tries to force sympathy aside and allow her coolly vicious battle-mind to descend. But a choking feeling breaks through, rising hot in her throat as she takes in the dead women's and children's bodies strewn amidst the rubble, many of whom she knows. And the animals...beautiful horses rendered to carnage, the children's little pet Visay'un deer mangled, so many broken corpses. Bile rises in Valasca's throat as she considers what's likely become of her beloved goats, the horses she helped raise from spirited foals...

And then she spots her friend Evralyr splayed on the street amidst the rubble, her kind smile forever stilled, her normally violet face a sickly death mask of gray, her long lavender hair a black-blooded mess. Valasca struggles to keep the devastating rush of grief from completely shattering her as a more potent fury grips hold.

A young Amaz appears, running toward her through the twining gray mist—an Alfsigr girl of about thirteen. Her black Amaz facial rune marks are a stark contrast to her ivory face, her salt-white hair short and spiky, an uncharged rune blade in her fist. She sets silver eyes on Valasca just as the amorphous form of a Mage appears through the fog behind her, the glimmering green of him monstrously highlighted by the surrounding shades of gray.

"Take the child and get behind me!" Valasca snarls.

The Alfsigr teen glances once over her shoulder, then briefly turns, silver eyes wide with terror as she runs frantically to Valasca, pausing only to take hold of Inge before darting behind Valasca as Shadow dragons streak by overhead and the Mage advances.

He strides toward them almost idly, his young, handsome form solidifying as a smile curls his lips, cruel, green eyes narrowing.

Recognition explodes inside Valasca. She slows and carefully draws both her charged blade and another, concealing them behind her back. She's met this high-ranking fiend before during her diplomatic work as the head of the Queen's Guard.

Sylus Bane.

Sylus pauses in the tendriling mist, his grin widening. He raises his arm and calmly levels his wand at Valasca as she grips her favored blade and murmurs a spell, her fingers sliding over the charged blade's undimmed runes.

Gray spear-shapes blink into existence around Sylus, hovering in the air, his wand's tip emitting threads of Shadow. Quick as an asp, he thrusts his wand forward.

On reflex, Valasca crosses her blades in an X before her as the Shadow spears streak in. As soon as the blades make contact with each other, the deadened runes on the charge-stripped blade burst to magical life, the runes of both blades now flashing emerald. A puff of green light bursts into being in front of her weapons, rapidly morphing into a glassy green shield before her.

Sylus's spears slam into the shield-pane with reverberating *clangs*. The impacts send shock waves of pain through Valasca's wrists, arms, and shoulders, each strike setting off gray-fire explosions that morph into the rising forms of spiky gray trees, pitchforking toward the sky.

Valasca catches Sylus's flash of surprise.

Ah, she vengefully thinks. *You thought you rendered all of us powerless, didn't you?*

A bloodthirsty amusement rises inside *her* this time.

"Oh, you picked the wrong Amaz to come after, you absolute piece of shit," Valasca snarls as she slides her fingers over her blade's runes once more, the green-paned barrier whisked away. Before Sylus can murmur a new spell, she lunges toward him, pressing her fingers along a new runic combination on her favored blade, then hurls the knife.

Her blade slams into his throat, a flash of furious surprise crossing Sylus's expression that Valasca relishes as he rasps out a gurgling cry and falls backward.

Valasca pounces as he writhes on the ground, kicking his wand from his grasp. She lifts her rune-marked palm, and her blade tears from his bloodied neck, flying back into her grip. Then she thrusts the blade forward once more to impale Sylus's wand hand.

The blade's runes detonate in a satisfying blast of green fire, his hand instantly rendered to mangled flesh as he twitches then stills.

"Rot in hell, Mage filth," Valasca snarls as she leans over his corpse and retrieves her bloodied blade, wipes it clean on Sylus's black uniform, then rises and turns.

The Alfsigr teen emerges from the surrounding rubble a few paces away, the whimpering child grasped in her slender arms, the teen's fierce look returned.

Good, Valasca thinks as the Shadow tide curls around them both. *You're going to need that ferocity.* "What's your name?" she calls to the girl as she strides toward her.

"Sylmire." The girl throws it out like a challenge, and Valasca is doubly pleased by her confrontational response.

"Where were you running to, Sylmire? And where is everyone?" Valasca prays the answer isn't "murdered."

The teen glances in the direction of Cyme's Central Plaza. "Queenhall Cavern. The Amaz Guard told us to go there."

Understanding crystallizes inside Valasca. *The action of last resort—the emergency military portals to the East.* Portals sheltered in the subland cavern under the Queenhall, where an Amazakaraan military base is located.

Valasca's heart twists as she realizes the likely fate of any Amaz who remained in their sister villages throughout the Caledonian Mountains—villages without portals of their own.

Please, Blessed Goddess, Valasca prays, *please let the bulk of my people be safely en route to the Eastern Realm.*

A wave of devastation hits with choking intensity as she glances up at the Shadow-slathered sky, the demonic forest thickening.

It's over.

Her beloved Amazakaraan, fallen to the Mages.

Valasca grits her teeth against the pain. Because there is no time for overwhelming grief.

Not when there are Amaz to get to the East.

"Come with me," Valasca says to Sylmire, her voice shot through with warrior resolve as Inge sobs for her mother. "I'll kill any Mage or dragon that gets in our path. We're going to Noilaan."

CHAPTER ELEVEN

SURRENDER TO OBLIVION

Wynter Eirllyn

City of Cyme, Amazakaraan
Two days prior to Xishlon

Amaz soldiers bracket a kneeling Wynter Eirllyn, weapons drawn at her head. Her threadbare wings flap chaotically, stinging veins of Shadow burrowing under her skin as she struggles against the Zalyn'or's choke hold on her throat.

She sets her devastated gaze on the bottleneck of Amaz women and children waiting to enter the passage to the Queenhall's subland cavern, its Smaragdalfar rune-marked doors near the hall's central entrance thrown open, a frantic energy on the air as families rush to get to the underground military portals.

Just beyond the crowd of Amaz civilians, a thick band of Amaz soldiers surround the entire Queenhall, Queen Alkaia amongst them astride a black steed. Freyja Zyrr and the huge warrior Alcippe stand beside the monarch, axes in hand, expressions fierce. The outer ring of soldiers are down on one knee, bows in hand, arrows nocked, all of their weapons pointed toward the incoming Mage and Alfsigr Marfoir invaders.

Wynter notes that their weapons are almost uniformly stripped of power, save a smattering of glowing emerald runes that mark a few arrows, bows, and blades.

Smaragdalfar varg runes. The thought pings through Wynter's despair. *They've survived the Shadow's onslaught.*

A glassy green-tinted protective shield hangs over the archers, the civilians, and the entire Queenhall, tenuously held in place by Wynter's part-Dryad friend Alder Xanthos and the Amaz's sole Smaragdalfar rune sorceress, Vestylle Oona'rin.

The stances of the two young women brim with immovable defiance as Vestylle holds her emerald-glowing rune stylus aloft and Alder keeps her Silver Birch branch elevated, both stylus and branch pressed to the verdant shield's inner surface, the women's arms vibrating with magical tension. Vestylle's emerald-patterned skin and Alder's forest green glimmer have miraculously held on to their hues amidst the grotesquely grayed world.

Mage power is not completely invincible after all, Wynter considers.

Pressure tightens around Wynter's skull, the Zalyn'or necklace clearly wanting to blot out the rebellious thought. Which makes that rebellious, surviving shard of Wynter's free will hold on to it even tighter.

Gray slashes across Wynter's vision as she meets the frightened, silver gaze of her Alfsigr soldier-friend Ysilldir, the young Amaz warrior stripped of her weapons and down on her knees as well, ringed by soldiers, arrows aimed at her head. Like Wynter, Shadow-vomit sullies the front of her tunic, her pale skin veined with gray.

A heartbreakingly color-stripped azure finch lands on Wynter's shoulder, and she stills as the small bird sets its feathery head against her neck.

Monstrous warning fills Wynter's mind—*a woman of ice and hate on a broken dragon...*

Wynter's head jerks up just as Valasca Xanthrir rushes around a

Shadow-tree trunk halfway across Cyme's Central Plaza. Young Sylmire trails her, a sobbing gray-hued child in the Alfsigr teen's arms. There's a charged rune blade in one of Valasca's pewter-tinted hands, its hilt haloed with Smaragdalfar rune glow.

"Wynter!" Valasca calls out as she spots her, breaking into a faster sprint.

Wynter raises a frantic palm. *"Run! She's coming!"*

The giant Shadow tree beside Valasca abruptly contracts downward. Valasca skids to a halt as branches slam down around her and solidify into a cage. Smaller branches dart out, coiling and slapping around Valasca, her blades wrested away, her hands swiftly bound.

"Val!" Freyja shouts as she springs forward, seeming as if she might leap through the translucent green shield. Young Sylmire stumbles backward from the branch cage, staring at Valasca in abject horror as the little girl in her arms shrieks for her mother.

"Stay shielded!" Valasca bellows at Freyja before fixing her fierce pewter stare on Sylmire. *"Go!"* she snarls at the teen.

The teen sprints to the shield, where both she and the screaming child are hauled through by Freyja just as Fallon Bane emerges from the plaza's misty Shadow forest on the back of a broken dragon. Fog swirls around Fallon's commanding form, an army of black-clad Mages also on dragonback emerging from the mist behind her.

As Fallon closes in through the mist, the details of her military uniform sharpen—the white bird on black, five silver stripes marking her uniform's edges, one thick silver Mage Commander stripe below them.

The finch on Wynter's shoulder flies off in an explosion of terror. Wynter's horror mounts, her wings contracting as Fallon's sadistic brother Damion Bane lands his dragon beside Fallon's and several Alfsigr Marfoir Elf assassins scuttle in behind them.

The Amaz archers aim their bows at the Mages, the line of soldiers behind them hoisting axes and blades and swords.

As one, the Marfoir turn to look at Wynter through grayed, insectile eyes.

A dizzying fright stiffens her wings. Because not only is Valasca in the grip of these fiends…each Marfoir is dragging a net filled with Shadow-gagged Amaz women and children, little Pyrgo, the Icaral child Wynter has grown close to, crammed in among them.

Pyrgo's adoptive mother, the huge rose-hued warrior Alcippe, lets out a growling cry. Hoisting her axe, she lunges toward the shield, a murderous look on her rune-tattooed face. But she skids to a halt just inside its edge, and Wynter realizes that Alcippe must be rapidly assembling the same thought as Wynter's own.

The Mages don't realize they've caught an Icaral child.

Because if they did, her wings would have already been torn from her body.

A gut-clenching panic for Pyrgo grips Wynter as she notes the child is blessedly cloaked and sandwiched between two of Amazakaraan's healers, the women's arms protectively tight around her, her wings well hidden.

Wynter looks at Fallon, barely able to breathe as she forcibly pushes Pyrgo from her thoughts, terrified that Vogel might sense the child's presence through his Zalyn'or link.

Fallon sets her frigid green gaze on the queen. "I command you, Queen Alkaia, to surrender both yourself and these lands to the Holy Magedom of Gardneria."

Queen Alkaia's shrewd eyes flick over the Amaz crammed into the Shadow nets, then toward the crowd of her people bottlenecked at the Queenhall's subland entrance. Wynter's heart patters against her ribs, fast as hummingbird wings.

Queen Alkaia lifts her chin, facing Fallon down. "Unbind my people and allow them to leave for the East and I will surrender both myself and our land to you."

"No, my queen! *No!*" Valasca cries from her branch cage as a collective shock wave blasts through the assembled Amaz. Imploring, defiant calls rise in a multitude of languages from civilians and soldiers alike, including the netted Amaz.

"Blessed Mother, *no!*"

"Do not surrender to them!"

"We'll die for you!"

Fallon's lips twitch as she looks Queen Alkaia over, as if sizing up insignificant prey. The Queen's Guard soldiers surge toward their queen, weapons raised, Amaz civilians hurling out defiant curses toward the Mage and Marfoir forces.

Queen Alkaia raises a silencing palm and the vengeful cries die down, though Amaz fury burns like incandescent fire on the air. The queen surveys her people, adoration filling her eyes. "Daughters of the Goddess," she says. "My beloved ones. I command you to leave for the East. And to establish a new homeland there." She turns, her fierce grayed eyes locking on to Fallon's vicious green stare. "And to rise there, in fury and in thunder." Her head pivots toward her guard, her eyes zeroing in on Freyja. "Freyja Zyrr," she states. "I name you queen of the Amaz."

Stunned cries rise and shock ignites in Wynter, racing down her spine. She knows this is a revolutionary moment. Never has a young woman been chosen as queen of the Amaz. And everyone knows of Freyja's secret relationship with Clive Soren.

"My queen—" Freyja begins in vehement protest.

"I *command it*, Freyja." Queen Alkaia cuts her off, hard as stone.

Freyja stills, her grayed face tensing with grief. Her gaze darts toward the Mages, rage burning the silvered depths of her eyes, before she turns back to Queen Alkaia and nods.

Aided by her guard, Queen Alkaia dismounts from her horse to stand before Freyja as one of the Queen's Guard hands the monarch her wooden cane, carved into the Goddess's serpent form. Leaning heavily on her cane, Queen Alkaia removes the ivory bird pin from her tunic and holds it out to Freyja.

"Freyja Zyrr," Queen Alkaia says, an air of the momentous circling down, "lead our people into the future."

"Don't do this!" Valasca cries. "My queen! Don't surrender yourself to these beasts!"

Freyja accepts the pin, affixes it to her military tunic, then drops to her knee before the queen. She slams her fist over her heart as she grips her axe. "I will serve your people, my beloved queen. I will die for your people, my forever queen."

Devastated tears pool in Wynter's eyes as she looks toward the monster at the gates, to find Fallon's gaze suddenly pinned on *her*.

"We want the Icaral, as well," Fallon states coldly.

The world tilts as Valasca snarls out her response. "Wynter, don't take one step out of that shield!"

A rancid dizziness overtakes Wynter as she turns and takes in the crowd of families behind her. The little girls crying as they clutch toys and pets. Their loving mothers and aunts and grandmothers. Brave, beloved Freyja and Ysilldir. Alcippe and Pyrgo and Alder and so many others. These people that she has grown to love deeply in such a short period of time.

Her body trembling, her threadbare wings tight around her frail, slender frame, Wynter rises from her knees and takes a faltering step toward Fallon Bane.

"If you let the Amaz leave," Wynter says, voice tight with fear, "I will surrender myself to you."

Valasca explodes into fiercer protest. "No, Wynter, *NO!* Get to the portals and go East *now!*"

Fallon laughs and eyes Valasca with open incredulity.

"Valasca, stand down," Queen Alkaia orders, her keen gaze darting from the Mages toward her netted people and back to the Mages again.

Fallon's focus sharpens on Valasca as she shoots her a belligerent smile. "Valasca Xanthrir. I was hoping we'd meet, you heathen bitch." She loses the smile, the air taking on a more frigid chill. "You saved Elloren Gardner."

Valasca grins threateningly back at Fallon. "Oh, I did. So she can come back here and beat your arrogant ass."

Rage overtakes Fallon's expression. Lightning fast, she flicks out her wand and a streak of ice blasts toward Valasca. Valasca falls backward to the ground, a cage of ice rapidly forming around her body.

Wynter's trembling kicks up into a tight shiver as she takes in Valasca's dazed state, her head moving slightly as she groans from the blow.

"Shall I kill her, my sister?" Damion Bane asks, motioning to Valasca's prone form.

"No," Fallon firmly replies. "She's a powerful rune sorceress. Vogel will want her."

A chill knifes through Wynter as Fallon's attention settles back on her.

"My patience is wearing thin, Icaral," Fallon croons. "Surrender yourself alongside the queen, and I'll let these whores go East." Her merciless smile inches wider. "They can see if they like what they find there."

Wynter freezes.

What, exactly, is waiting for the Amaz in Noi lands?

And where is Vogel?

The horrific answer rings out in her empath mind.

Everywhere.

Wynter looks to Queen Alkaia, who nods to her in grim, mutual reckoning as renewed cries of protest go up, even Alder's forest-calm voice pleading, "No, my queen, *no*..."

Terrified, Wynter wraps her wings even more tightly around herself, legs shaking, and advances with the queen.

Amaz soldiers rush out from the shield's protection and release the netted Amaz, drawing them toward the shield's safety, while Wynter and Queen Alkaia walk through the band of Amaz soldiers, through the protective shield, and surrender themselves to true evil festooned with white birds.

CHAPTER
TWELVE

DREAM MERGE

Elloren Grey

Noilaan
Eastern Realm
Two days prior to Xishlon

From the bedroom's darkness, I watch Trystan and Vothe's military skiff soar away. Only a few sapphire-lit rune ships dot the river and sky, the night tranquil and moonlit. The Wand of Myth's spiraling hilt tingles warm against my palm.

My gaze lifts to the dome hanging over Noilaan. Sapphire runes sparsely mark the dome's translucent surface, their slowly rotating forms like benevolent presences in the sky.

Like the scarlet dome runes of Amazakaraan.

Concern rises for the Amaz—all the women I met and allied with—Queen Alkaia, Alder, Freyja…even fierce Alcippe. And Wynter and little Pyrgo, the Icarals sheltered among them. Will my warning about the runes reach them in time?

The concern knotting my chest tightens. I can feel myself compressing into an ever-constricting space between the crushing weight of my exhaustion and my fervent desire to set off to find Lukas *immediately*. His ardent green gaze fills my mind, setting off a burn in my blood. That warrior energy in his stance. His courage. His *fire*.

A choking knot of longing overtakes my throat and I struggle to pull in a breath.

Stop this, Elloren, I can almost hear Lukas snarl at me. *Gather your strength. Then fight back with everything in you.*

I force a breath. Then another as I focus on the Wand's starlight tree, branching out deep inside me, the Wand's steady energy humming against my hand.

I'm coming for you, Lukas, I mentally grit out toward the western sky. *I swear it. If I have to fight the Vu Trin to get hold of a portal west, I'll do it.*

I turn and drag my leaden, bruised body toward the bed. I'm already bathed and fully dressed in a dark purple tunic and pants with a holiday lilac moon pattern edging the collar and hems to help me blend in. Ready to flee at a moment's notice.

I slide my Wand into my right boot's side, then slump down onto the bed, overcome by the dizzying sense of melting into its absurdly indulgent softness, the feel of a mattress so foreign after weeks of sleeping on bedrolls and moss. I don't so much fall asleep as hurtle into the abyss of it, a faint sting prickling my hands before darkness draws me under.

A shot of fiery pleasure courses through my body, my spine arching against it, the sensation so heated it's nearly a shock of pain as sinuous branches twine through my lines in a rampant caress. Lips press down on mine, sending a tight shiver through me, the kiss suffused with breathless hunger. A tongue pushes into my mouth, claiming me more than kissing me. Strong hands grip my arms, a hard male body fitted to mine.

An *aroused* male body.

An emotional cry escapes my throat, the feel of his half-naked body intimately familiar against my sparsely clothed form. And that deep forest scent...

The name almost tears like a cry from my lips.

Lukas.

I open my eyes, a tremor of relief quaking through me to find myself wrapped in Lukas's arms, his lips moving against mine in an impassioned kiss.

Overtaken by a fierce rush of love, a muffled sound of joy bursts from me. I knot my fingers in his hair, grasping tight hold of his muscular arm and wrap my legs around him as I draw him into a deeper, desperate kiss.

A groan shudders through his chest, Lukas's heartbeat sounding out his longing against mine as his lips slide to the nape of my neck, his hot mouth pressing against my skin with devouring fervor.

"Elloren...gods, Elloren...my love..."

"I lost you," I raggedly say, hot tears pooling in my eyes as Lukas trails his mouth along my shoulder, my neck. "I didn't know where you were..." I manage.

"I'm *here*," he says, voice rough. "I'm right here. I *love* you."

My heart breaks open. "I love you too." I grasp at him, pulling his mouth back onto my tear-salted lips, his hands gripping my waist as his fire gives a hard surge and he begins to urgently pull at my remaining clothes. I arch up to aid him, his bedroom surrounding us, the walls shivering like water at the edges, the colors deepening.

His family's estate in Valgard...

A sensation of wrongness pricks at my mind, disorientation wresting hold as our surroundings shift to sheltering branches.

The shelter Lukas conjured...the night we fled Valgard...

Muffled thunder booms overhead as his movements gain urgency, his body pressing me into the mossy ground. But the scene is all wrong. The branches are like hazy paintings, the lantern's crimson glow strangely heightened.

The stunned realization takes hold.

Lukas is dreaming.

And I'm somehow inside it.

The scene continues to shift as Lukas kisses me, his mind forming the dream from scattered images and remembered sensations while I'm helplessly swept up in its impassioned current. A harsh sting races along my fastlines, a pained gasp tightening my throat. I look to my hand and unease shivers into being as I find my glamour gone, my fastlines visible on my green-glimmering skin.

Intuition takes root.

Vogel. This is connected to Vogel somehow.

"Lukas," I say, breaking the kiss. I grip hold of his shoulders and push.

Lukas instantly pulls back, his green eyes thick with desire and a trace of confusion, his cheeks flushed through the shimmering green, his magic grasping at my lines.

He closes in for another kiss and I wrench my head to the side, dodging his mouth. "Something is wrong. Lukas, I'm in your dream..."

Excitement flares in his eyes. "You're always in my dreams." He captures my mouth again and sends a spiraling blaze of fire through me, the intoxicating, feverish rush of his power sparking all the way down to my toes. A breath shudders through me, my thoughts scattering against his desire as I fall back into the dream, pressing the length of my body against his. And for a moment, it's all I can do not to get lost in him.

Elloren.

The almost imperceptible whisper pricks at the back of my mind as a harsher sting races along my fastlines. The haze of want clears, my gaze flicking to my wand hand, clutched around Lukas's shoulder.

Fear strikes through me.

My fastlines are emanating smoking, curling Shadow.

"Elloren," Lukas purrs, his voice throaty as he leans in to nuzzle my neck, his grip firming around my thigh. "Let me take you..."

"No, Lukas, *wake up.*" I grip his black hair and yank *hard*.

He draws back, his expression bewildered.

"I'm here! *Really here!*" I cry out, suddenly desperate to break through. "A dream connection has opened up through our fasting!"

Breathing hard, Lukas's gaze turns inward for a moment before he stares back at me, seeming dazed.

"Where are you?" I demand, noting, with mounting alarm, that the fastlines on his hands are also emanating a faint, gray mist. *"Tell me where Vogel has you!"*

The scene around us spirals away, the pressure of his body on mine lifting. We're suddenly standing in the middle of a night-darkened valley, the stars like scattered diamonds against the arc of the sky. The bone-white peaks of the Northern Spine are wrapped around our backs, the Caledonian Mountains before us.

I know exactly where we are.

The valley that contains Gardneria's Fourth Division military base, all the military buildings and structures stripped away. Only Lukas stands before me, both of us dressed in our Sealing greens and lit by moonlight.

"Elloren," he says as an Ironwood grand piano shudders into being beside him, a violin suddenly in one of my hands, its bow in the other. "Play with me," he offers, his voice suffused with emotion. "One last time, Elloren."

"No," I growl, hurling the violin and bow to the ground as I step toward him, grab hold of his shoulder, and shake him. "I'm *here*. And I'm going to rescue you. Tell me where Vogel has you!"

His eyes widen with a look of profound realization, and I know that I'm finally breaking through. "I don't know," he rasps, clearly fighting the murky dream state. "A cave."

"Where?"

He shakes his head again. "I don't know."

I press a hand over his heart. "Describe it!"

Lukas swallows and looks around with the expression of someone trying to think through the muzzy influence of strong spirits. "Dark stone," he manages. "A catacomb—like a giant hornet's nest. Shadow-corrupted Mage soldiers with gray eyes."

He closes his eyes tightly, as if willing himself alert. When he opens them once more, they blaze into mine with sudden clarity. "Elloren." He grabs my arms, his expression turning almost violent in its intensity. "Get your power *unbound*. Break the fasting spell. Get it *off* you! He's tracking you through it!"

"Where are you, Lukas?" I demand again.

"Don't come for me," he growls, impassioned. "I'm a *trap*!"

A phantom hand grabs my shoulder and shakes it. I whip my head around to find the scene fracturing at the edges, fault lines forming to crackle inward toward the bleached Spine and moonlit field, shattering.

A cry of protest rises from my throat as Lukas and I grab fiercer hold of each other, his affinity fire surging toward mine as he gives me one, last tortured look before he, too, fragments to black.

I jolt awake, desperate for Lukas and gasping for breath, my Wand's energy buzzing against my calf. A spider-tattooed man is jostling my shoulder in a night-darkened bedroom. Another man, tall and point-eared, looms, sapphire light pulsing over them both.

On instinct, I draw my Ash'rion blade and bring it to the spidery-man's throat, my fingers sliding over the hilt's runes, ready to stab him and blast off his damned head just as my dream-fog clears enough for me to realize where I am and who is before me.

My uncle Wrenfir is frozen in place, an astonished smile forming on his blackened lips as if he didn't know I had it in me to fight so viciously and is vastly pleased that I do. I swiftly draw back my knife, heart hammering, and meet Or'myr's urgent glare over Wrenfir's shoulder. I move to speak, but they both cut me off with emphatic fingers to their lips. Or'myr points toward the bedroom window.

A riot of changeable sapphire light is flashing through it, cast up from the terrace below, and alarm seizes hold of my chest.

They motion for me to get up and I catch sight of three military rune skiffs landed there as I do, four more flying in. Heavily armed Vu Trin soldiers are disembarking, Fain striding out to meet them. Firming my grip on my blade, Or'myr hastily makes my bed as Wrenfir tugs me toward the bedroom's door.

"Zhi Lo," Fain's pleasant voice chimes up from the terrace as we cross the room. "To what do I owe the pleasure?"

"This isn't a social call," a woman's voice sharply returns. "We're searching the premises."

"For what?" Fain asks, sounding convincingly confused as we exit the room.

"Set up a runic net around the entire area," the woman's voice commands as I'm led down a curving hallway at a fast clip, both Wrenfir and Or'myr pulling wands as we go.

A door slams shut a story below and I flinch as boot heels sound, running through a hall then clomping up the stairs to this floor. Or'myr pauses before the purple-veined, obsidian wall, pulls a Noi rune stone from his tunic's pocket, and presses it to the wall.

The doorway just past the hallway's bend slams open just as an archway of glowing purple runes bursts into being beneath Or'myr's stone. Or'myr pushes against the archway's interior and the stone dissolves, revealing a spiral staircase cut into the mountain.

Wrenfir urges me forward and I frantically slip onto the staircase's small landing, followed swiftly by Or'myr and Wrenfir as footsteps sound from the curving hallway's far end. Or'myr swiftly touches his wand's tip to the runic arch, murmurs a spell, and the vanished stone bursts back into being. We all still, breath suspended and cast in the blue rune light of a single hanging rune lamp as muffled boot heels thud by then rapidly fade.

Or'myr puts one finger to his lips for my continued silence and grabs the lantern. I follow them both down the stone steps, then through a long tunnel, the blue light from Or'myr's lantern swinging over us like a fitful pendulum.

We round a sharp bend in the widening tunnel and I halt

before the blue-lit military skiff waiting just ahead, a tall, muscular Vu Trin soldier aboard it.

Apprehension tightens my gut as I meet the emerald eyes of my former kitchen enemy, Bleddyn Arterra, a glowing blue rune stylus in her hand. Her craft is no larger than a rowboat and hovers a trace above the stony ground, a sapphire rune rotating beneath it.

Bleddyn's verdant hue is brightened almost to turquoise by the skiff's rune light, the multiple green-metal piercings edging her pointed ears and brow glinting. Her long green hair is styled in the same heavy coils she wore at Verpax University, but now she's garbed in Vu Trin blacks. My mind spins, our situations so wildly altered.

"You're lucky I was here early, *Ny'laea*." Bleddyn's mouth curls around my false name with unmistakable sarcasm, but her gaze is urgent as she holds her hand out to me.

"We'll come for you as soon as we can," Or'myr assures me as she pulls me aboard, then taps her stylus on the controls. Runes blink into existence on the skiff's sides and begin to whir, my uncle Wrenfir's spider tattoo eerily wavering in the brightening light.

"My fastlines," I tell them, the desire to get back to Lukas burning hot in my chest. I hold up my glamoured hand. "Vogel is running magic through them, just as we thought."

"And we'll run our own through them soon enough," Or'myr firmly counters, a glint of defiance in his forest green eyes.

"We need to *move*," Bleddyn chastises, effectively silencing us all. "Hold on to these," she orders as she hastily passes me some folded papers. I slide them into my tunic's pocket as she taps the control board again. The glow of the skiff's runes intensifies.

"Thank you," I tell Wrenfir, voice quavering as the skiff rises, "for getting medicine to Nym'ellia and her family."

Wrenfir's blackened lips twitch. "You're welcome, Ren."

"Hold tight to me," Bleddyn demands and I throw my arms around her broad waist.

The skiff abruptly darts forward like an arrow loosed and my heart leaps into my throat. I cling to Bleddyn and we zoom into the mountain's depths, switchbacking through tunnels at breathtaking speed.

Eventually, we burst through a narrow gap of stone and out over the Vo River. My lungs seize, our sudden height a shock to my senses. It was one thing to fly over the Vo on Trystan's skiff, quite another to be on this tiny skiff zooming straight off a mountaintop cliff, no railing surrounding us. The skiff swoops down toward the water with alarming velocity.

"Ancient One," I gasp, looking down at the impossible distance to the black river rushing below.

"Stop that," Bleddyn snaps over her shoulder as she swoops lower and levels the skiff out. "You're not Gardnerian anymore. You'd best remember that."

Chastened, I glance behind us toward where I imagine Fain's estate was, but it's no longer visible. We skirt closer to the river, our skiff's runic glow reflecting on the water as Bleddyn hugs another mountain curve. The two island-mountains of the Wyvernguard and the sparkling city of Voloi come into view— and what lies before them triggers a jolt of alarm.

A newly erected blue line stretches across the river's expanse, east to west, military rune skiffs patrolling it. Three gaps in its breadth appear to be heavily guarded, gluts of runic ships massed near the gaps in small queues, waiting to be allowed passage.

"What's this?" I ask Bleddyn, foreboding rippling through my gut.

"Quiet," Bleddyn grits out as she veers toward the most eastern checkpoint.

We draw up to it as a young Vu Trin soldier waves through the two ships directly before us in quick succession, her slender form backlit by the sapphire light emanating from the runic barrier. The luminous wall of runes extends down past the water's surface as far as the eye can see, eventually disappearing into a rippling, hazy glow of blue.

The heavily armed soldier is attractive, with long-lashed eyes and dark brown skin. Her full lips are painted a variety of purple hues, and violet glitter is brushed over her eyelids and cheekbones, her long black hair decorated with iridescent purple moon and filigreed heart medallions. *Xishlon festival ornamentation*, I realize, as I send up a prayer that the upcoming holiday is enough to keep this soldier distracted.

"What's this, Yu Zo?" Bleddyn congenially asks, her hand waving in a broad arc.

Yu Zo frowns, glancing west before settling her sharp gaze on Bleddyn. "Another hunt for the Black Witch. Ung Li has ordered a massive search of the city and all river traffic. *Again.*"

Bleddyn huffs out a laugh. "Good luck with that so close to Xishlon."

Yu Zo nods with an arch look of agreement. "Third search in a month's time. Papers?" She holds out her hand to me with only a cursory glance, her attention more fully set on Bleddyn.

Bleddyn gives me a tight, prodding look. Forcing calm, even breaths, I fish the papers Bleddyn gave me out of my pocket and hand them to the soldier. Yu Zo rifles through them, pausing when she gets to the third sheet, her lovely, sharp eyes seeming to snag on something.

Bleddyn leans toward her, hand propped rakishly on her hip. "Have you found the moon yet, Yulon?" she asks, her lips turning up in a dazzling smile.

Yu Zo's eyes snap to Bleddyn's, as if she's startled, and I swear I can feel a sudden spark leap between these two. The soldier's lip quirks, her brow smoothing as she moves on to the fourth sheet of my papers, her focus seeming less intent. "Have *you*?" she replies, some shy hesitation in her words.

"Of course I have," comes Bleddyn's saucy reply. She lowers her voice to a purr. "It's in my pocket. I'm holding it there for you."

Yu Zo's mouth flickers into a broader smile as she continues to rifle through my documents, but I can tell she's ceased seeing them. "You want to give me the moon?" she asks, dark eyes sparkling as she dares a look at Bleddyn, which Bleddyn meets with a wolflike grin.

"On a *silver platter*," Bleddyn drawls. "With a bouquet of Xishlon roses to go with it."

Yu Zo swallows, papers forgotten, her widened eyes fixed now on Bleddyn. "Where will you be Xishlon night?" she asks, low and covert, her gaze darting toward me with a trace of discomfort, as if I've become an unfortunate presence in their flirtatious interlude.

Bleddyn lowers her tone to a lulling whisper. "Posted at the southside dock. I'm off at twenty-first hour."

"I hear your moon burns bright," Yu Zo says a little breathlessly.

"The very brightest," Bleddyn rejoins smoothly, a seductive gleam in her emerald eyes. *"All through the night."*

A blush blooms on Yu Zo's face. She clears her throat and expeditiously hands me back the papers. "I'll find you," she says to Bleddyn, all business now as she waves us through. Bleddyn blows her a kiss, and Yu Zo cracks a smile and shakes her head, as if shaking off Bleddyn's Xishlon thrall.

Bleddyn's flirtatious smile evaporates as soon as we soar out of earshot, rapidly gaining speed. "Keep quiet when we get to the city," she brusquely orders. "And for gods' sakes, if you say the words *Ancient One* again, I swear I will clock you straight in the head."

"Fair enough," I concede, anxiety stinging through me over the size of the search for me. "Where are you taking me?" I ask as we zoom toward the glittering blue-and-purple mountain city.

Bleddyn shoots me a grin over her shoulder, her emerald eyes gleaming. "To someone who's used to dangerous company."

PART THREE

Xishlon Land

CHAPTER ONE

SMARAGDALFAR MAGIC

Mora'lee Starr'lyrion

Voloi, capital city of Noilaan
Eastern Realm

Three days ago, five days prior to Xishlon

Her ears have been cropped.

Mora'lee's gaze passes over the Urisk girl's scarred ears, outrage tightening her chest as fierce sympathy rises for the lavender-hued teen staring up at her through pale amethyst eyes. The bright, early-morning sun streams down on the girl's ear-tips where the points used to be, her short iris-hued hair chopped into a mass of irregular, floppy spikes.

They brutalized her hair too, Mora realizes, news of this type of thing going on in the Western Realm bad enough to hear about, but to actually *see* it...

In all her twenty-six years, Mora doesn't think she's ever witnessed something so heartbreaking.

She glances at Bleddyn Arterra, her newfound friend and Eastern Realm Resistance ally, struggling not to appear shocked as the breeze flowing up from the Vo River buffets their garments, puffed clouds scudding across a vivid blue sky, the bright sunlight making Mora's emerald-patterned Smaragdalfar skin sparkle. Merchant and pedestrian traffic has already picked up on Voloi's Sixth Tier thoroughfare, the main road only a few handspans away, just past her outdoor restaurant's filigreed metal railing.

Bleddyn sees that I've noticed the girl's mutilated ears, Mora'lee grimly considers as she notes Bleddyn's grave look.

"Mora," Bleddyn says in a congenial tone, her Vu Trin uniform bleached a lightened black by the bright sun, "this is Olilly. Olilly, meet Mora."

Mora smiles warmly and takes the girl's hand, used to offering friendship and shelter to refugees and Resistance workers on her Smaragdalfar-rune-powered and varg-rune-warded air ship. Olilly's handshake is uncertain, her gaze fluttering down to her feet repeatedly.

Mora's heart twists and she makes a point of not glancing again at Olilly's ears, even as a spitting anger ignites against the Mages.

Monsters. You monsters. *She can't be more than fourteen years of age.*

She remembers what Bleddyn told her about Olilly. How the two of them worked in the Verpax University kitchens together. How, on the Night of the Burning Blessing Stars, a Mage mob attacked Bleddyn and dragged Olilly into an alley and assaulted her too, slicing off her ears' points and chopping off her hair. Mora remembers her surprise over hearing that Elloren Gardner, of all people, was involved in the rescue of this girl and was also instrumental in helping Olilly and her sister flee here. But over the past few weeks, the teen's ten-year-old sister has settled into the Eastern Sublands with her new Smaragdalfar guardians, but Olilly has become increasingly withdrawn, to the point where Bleddyn decided to step in.

So now here Olilly is.

On Mora'lee's doorstep.

Or rune-ship step, would be more appropriate, Mora considers with a slight smile as they stand in an intimate little knot in her restaurant's outdoor dining area. She glances toward her ship, docked a few paces away, hovering by the cliff that edges Voloi's entire Sixth Tier.

Mora straightens and forces a broader, welcoming smile, even as her heart breaks for this girl. Because it's time for Olilly to have some light in her life.

"So, Bleddyn tells me you're a great pastry chef," Mora says with a toss of her braided green hair, her hands resting on her hips.

Olilly nods uncertainly, thin shoulders hunched.

"Would you like to learn how to make some Xishlon delicacies?" she offers.

Olilly's gaze darts up to Mora's. "For the festival?"

"Mmm-hmm," Mora says with a saucy smile. "Lavender buns stuffed with candied violets. Cave squid noodles stained purple. Subland morel pasties that glow plum. So many things I doubt you ever made or tasted in the Western Realm."

A spark lights in Olilly's eyes.

Ah, I've piqued her interest, Mora notes, pleased. *Bleddyn was right—she's got the heart of a true chef.*

"I… I'd like to learn," Olilly says. She glances at Bleddyn, as if for approval, and Bleddyn returns Olilly's look with an encouraging nod.

"Well, that's settled, then," Mora says. "If you'd like, Olilly, I'll hire you as my kitchen assistant right on the spot. Long hours soon, since Xishlon is almost upon us, but excellent pay this time of year, plus lodging and food. What do you say?"

"Pay?" Olilly looks at Bleddyn with confusion, and a new shard of pain cuts through Mora. She's heard how so many Urisk are indentured in the Western Realm. Paying off impossible-to-pay-off work contracts they've signed to get off the Fae Islands by legal or illegal means. Never actually accruing a single cent.

"Of course, you'll earn a wage," Mora says, keeping her voice bright. "And you should meet our little crew. *Ghor'li*," she calls through the open kitchen door, raising her voice in a friendly lilt.

A blue-hued point-eared Urisk child peeks out, her sapphire eyes widening as she takes in Olilly. The sketchbook Mora gifted to the little girl is tucked under one of Ghor'li's skinny arms. She's dressed in Smaragdalfar attire: an emerald tunic and pants, and Mora has done the child's hair up much like her own— braids tied back by a sparkling green cloth, and purple subland orchids decorating the child's cornflower blue locks.

Ghor'li rushes out and grabs hold of Mora's tunic, partially hiding behind her as she peeks at Olilly and Bleddyn.

Affection washes over Mora. She lovingly pats the girl's head and smiles down at her, receiving a shy returning smile. Mora's heart twists anew as she holds Ghor'li's easily frightened gaze, a gaze that has seen far too much. But Mora bats the pain away.

"This is Ghor'li," Mora says to Olilly. "Ghor'li, meet Olilly. She's going to work for me and live with us, and we'll all be good friends."

Olilly's face twists in further confusion as she peers at Ghor'li then back to Mora.

Why is this child here? Olilly's eyes seem to say.

Because she's an orphan, Mora thinks back but doesn't voice, *fished from the Zonor River with her drowned mother just a few weeks past by Vothendrile Xanthile and Trystan Gardner, of all people. And now she refuses to speak and will only draw. Mostly pictures of her flight East with her mother. The two of them in the desert. The two of them in the Dyoi Forest.*

Her mother drowning in the Zonor.

But this is not the time to answer the questions brimming in Olilly's eyes. There's been pain enough here to last ten lifetimes. It's time for the Xishlon festival's purple light.

For the Goddess Vo's loving light.

"Who would like a big bowl of nu'dul soup?" Mora asks Olilly and Ghor'li with great enthusiasm. Because if there's one thing Mora'lee believes in with all her heart, along with the idea that one should keep one's door open with a welcome mat before it, it's the power of food to bring people together and heal a piece of the world's scars. She grins at Olilly. "I'm betting you've never had Smaragdalfar soup before!"

"Were you able to get papers for Ghor'li?" Mora asks Bleddyn in low tones as they hover inside the rune ship's cramped kitchen. The room is festooned with strings of purple Xishlon runic orbs decorated with violet flowers, a big pot of broth simmering on the stove. Its side door is propped open so they can watch the girls slurping down the nu'dul soup at one of the sunlit outdoor tables.

Bleddyn cradles a cup of lavender Xishlon tea in her broad green hands, her emerald eyes glancing toward the busy main thoroughfare. "Not yet," she whispers, "but Jules Kristian is forging them." She fishes some folded parchment out of her pocket. "I have papers here for Olilly, though. She's been fully approved because she came over with the Lupines." Bleddyn shrugs, pursing her lips. "She came with the military package. Like me."

Mora frowns as she pockets the vital documents, moral outrage simmering to the surface. "A child shouldn't have to bring a military advantage with her to be allowed refuge."

"It's the way of the world, Mora," Bleddyn says with a jaded look. "Ask me how much compassion there was for Urisk children in the Western Realm."

"We should be better than that here in Noilaan," Mora insists. "We used to be better than that."

Bleddyn's mouth gives a sardonic twist. "Mora'lee, you need to accept the fact that the Noi seem hell-bent on going down the same path as the Western Realm." Bleddyn glances at the restaurant across the street, a perfectly spaced row of Noi flags hanging from its awning. There's a purple sign with black Noi lettering fastened to the restaurant's street-facing wall, a sign that

Mora has noticed cropping up more and more—NOILAAN
FOR THE NOI.

An older Noi man garbed in Xishlon purple is setting the tables. He catches their gazes and gives them an unfriendly glare.

"This is how it starts," Bleddyn says, narrowing her eyes at
the man. "First the flags go up. Then the signs. Then the touting of whatever religion is dominant as the 'One True Faith.'"
She looks at Mora. "Before you know it, children are huddled
in tents outside a runic border getting infected with the Red
Grippe. And almost no one lifts a finger to help them."

"And war is declared," Mora grimly states.

"And war is declared," Bleddyn agrees, picking up one of the
purple morel pasties piled on a lavender plate. She takes a bite
and shoots Mora a look of appreciation. But then her gaze snags
on the restaurant across the street once more, her expression regaining its grim cast. "It's all going to hell, Mora. I don't see a
happy ending to any of this." She angles her head toward Olilly
and Ghor'li. "But at least those kids can have a nice Xishlon.
And Sweet Gods, Mora, these pasties are *good*."

Mora gives a short laugh, then sighs as she looks at Olilly and
Ghor'li. "At least they get to try nu'duls before the Mages swoop
down on all our heads."

Bleddyn pats the runic blade sheathed at her hip. "We'll give
them a run for their money before they take over the world."

"Maybe Noilaan will win," Mora archly replies, but it's hard
to suppress the fear that's straining to rise up.

Bleddyn looks back at the sign on the restaurant across the
street. "Mora," she says gravely, "Noilaan is already losing."

A tall Smaragdalfar Elf man strides from the crowded street
into Mora's outdoor dining area, the sunlight filtering through
the surrounding plum trees dappling his glimmering emerald-
patterned skin with sparkling gold.

Mora's breath hitches, as it always does whenever Fyon Hawkkyn appears.

"Muth'lorithin, Mothrin," his deep voice greets Olilly and

Ghor'li in formal Smaragdalfar as he passes by, his emerald hair braided and swinging behind his back, much like Mora's, minus the glittering gems and single orchid she's slid into her own.

Mora's gaze sweeps over Fyon's lean form, drinking him in. His garb is always so stubbornly Smaragdalfar, even though he joined the Vu Trin army and has quickly become one of their most valued rune sorcerers. He's likely on midday break from military duty, but Fyon refuses to wear anything but Smaragdalfar garb.

And oh, Sweet Holy Vo, it looks good on him.

Mora grins at Fyon, her heart skipping a beat, only Fyon able to scatter her thoughts like Xishlon moon marbles.

"Muth'lorithin, Mora," he says, with a reserved dip of his head. He looks to Bleddyn. "Muth'lorithin, Bleddyn."

Mora smirks. Such a formal Smaragdalfar greeting. But that's classic reserved Fyon, who seems hells-bent on following Smaragdalfar traditions to the letter. Traditions somewhat foreign to Mora, as she grew up the adopted child of a Noi soldier and a Noi fisherwoman after she was sent East by her Smaragdalfar birth parents at the age of six. Parents who didn't make it out of the Western Realm alive. Who gave up every resource to save her.

"A good morning to you, Fyon," Bleddyn returns, good-naturedly mimicking Fyon's formal tone as she shoots Mora a mischievous sidelong glance. Mora can feel the heat rising in her cheeks and she suppresses the urge to roll her eyes at Bleddyn.

"Might you have some tea, Mora?" Fyon asks in the Smaragdalfar tongue, using the tense of the most heightened formality.

It's an odd quirk of Fyon's lately, asking her for tea in the High Tense. Before they speak of anything else. To the point that Mora always keeps a tea service ready in case he comes by.

"I have a lovely lavender tea, Fyon," Mora answers, pointedly using the Noi tongue since she knows that the rune behind Bleddyn's ear doesn't give a clear translation of formal Smaragdalfar. She wonders, not for the first time, about Fyon's insistence on speaking about something as prosaic as tea in such a formal way. As if he's not just asking for a simple cup of tea, but for an audience with the Noi Conclave.

"I am sure this tea will nourish me," Fyon says, again in High Smaragdalfar, an intense spark igniting in those dazzling silver eyes of his.

A giggle almost bubbles up, but Mora stifles it, smiling at serious, enigmatic Fyon.

"I'll leave you two to your scheming," Bleddyn says, her gaze darting knowingly between them. She raises her half-consumed pasty in a mock toast. "Have one of these, Fyon. Although I warn you, if you do, you'll want to kiss Mora's feet and pledge her undying fealty."

Fyon's silver eyes widen.

Bleddyn flashes Mora a rakish grin before leaving the kitchen. She pauses to fish a few of the traditional Xishlon candy moons wrapped in purple foil out of her tunic's pocket and hands a few to Olilly and Ghor'li before she exits through the restaurant's gate and disappears into the crowd, the proprietor of the restaurant across the street scowling after her.

The moment they're alone in the kitchen, Fyon glances through the open starboard door toward the busy thoroughfare beyond, then slips his hand into his tunic's pocket and discreetly hands a folded document to Mora, Ghor'li's name marked on it.

Mora pockets the papers. "Jules Kristian's work?"

Fyon gives her a wry look. "Good with calligraphy, that one."

"And thank goodness for it," Mora returns before pouring them both tea.

Fyon leans back against the cramped kitchen's counter, cradling the teacup in his hands as if it's a precious thing. Lavender steam rises from it, the tea's rich, floral scent wafting around them both. He glances out the open cliffside door, toward the Vo Mountains, his brow tensing.

"Mora, the Mages are threatening an imminent invasion of

Amazakaraan," he says, setting his weighted gaze back on her. "It's taken a few days for the message to get to the East. I just learned of it."

Mora pulls in a wavering breath. "Oh, Fyon…"

"They've also invaded Issan'o," he adds, naming the Issani outpost village in the western Agolith Desert. "Some of the survivors are sitting outside Noilaan's runic border. They've just arrived."

"How many?" Mora throws a worried glance toward Olilly and Ghor'li—so many people in dire straits as the nightmare of the West bears down.

"Well over two hundred Issani," he answers, his expresson grim. "Trapped behind the border. Ra'Ven Za'Nor is petition-ing the Noi Conclave to allow them passage into the sublands. But more than half the Smaragdalfar are set against this. The Noi Conclave is too."

"But…where else can they go?" Mora asks. "If the Gardneri-ans destroyed their whole village…"

He shakes his head. "There's no clear plan—just this idea that the East should stop absorbing the West's problems. And many of our own people feel that the sublands should be exclusively for the Smaragdalfar."

Mora stiffens. "The future is diverse, Fyon."

"Mora, it's complicated—"

"Is it? Should our people start hanging Smaragdalfar flags everywhere? Touting the Smaragdalfar faith as the only true religion? Pushing everyone who isn't Smaragdalfar out of the sublands?" She sweeps her hand toward the restaurant across the street. "Why not? It's what they're starting to do here. It's what they've already done in the West."

Fyon gives her a level look. "You know it's not the same for our people. Not with most of our Smaragdalfar'kin still trapped in the Western Sublands. Most come here and have freedom for the very first time in their lives, and they're ready to fight for a Smaragdalfar homeland. You can't compare that to the Noi. Or the Gardnerians."

"I know that, Fyon. I do," Mora says, growing more impassioned. "But don't you see? It's our chance to take a different path. To show that there could be *another way*. I support Ra'Ven Za'Nor in this. I believe his path is the better way forward."

Mora considers Ra'Ven Za'Nor, the young Smaragdalfar monarch. The only surviving member of the Smaragdalfar royal line. With his wildly controversial ideas about a sublands for everyone, including his Mage partner, Sagellyn.

"Ra'Ven's path could lead to chaos," Fyon cautions. "I don't see a way around that."

Mora holds his stare, unflinching. "We'll have chaos no matter what. So we might as well go down in flames loving instead of hating each other."

A sudden spark leaps between them that has Mora's heartbeat deepening.

Am I imagining it? she wonders. He's so formal and austere, Fyon. Her friend since her young teen years. Always so courageous. Willing to risk his life again and again in the West, using his runic sorcery and skills with metallurgie to smuggle their people to safety in the East. Not intimidated by anything, save, perhaps, by this thing growing between them.

We both are.

When he returned to Noilaan a few weeks ago after living for several years in the West, Mora was stunned he had survived so many missions to save the Smaragdalfar. Last she saw Fyon, he was a tall skinny teenager. Hells-bent on revolution. Hells-bent on fighting for their people, risks be damned. *Come with me, Mora*, he'd urged. Seventeen to her fifteen.

But there was no way she could leave her family and her apprenticeship with a rune-ship pilot, her rune-crafting talent firmly oriented toward the nautical, whereas Fyon's potent varg sorcery and metallurgie expertise endowed him with weapons-crafting power that was sorely needed by their people in the West.

And so she said goodbye to her brilliant, courageous friend. Her budding teenage crush.

Mora does a quick, bold scan of Fyon the man. He's so startlingly altered. Taller. Broader shouldered. The planes of his face elongated and chiseled. A powerful grace to his movements, all gangliness gone. When he suddenly showed up at her doorstep a few weeks back, he fair took her breath away. And she sensed, for the glimmer of an instant, that he felt the same. But his manner rapidly shifted to his familiar reticent demeanor. As reserved as he is courageous.

His friendship was one of the most precious things in Mora's life. She still vividly remembers that night she bade him farewell, tears streaking down her cheeks. Imagining that he would be lost to her forever. And now, miraculously, here he is. Back in her life. In her rune-ship kitchen, drinking tea. And Xishlon tea, no less.

For the love festival of Vo.

The kissing festival.

Heat lights on Mora's neck as she considers how much she wouldn't mind kissing Fyon.

No, I wouldn't mind that one bit.

But it's too strong, this thing she feels for him. So strong that as straightforward and fearless as she is, she can't move forward in this, because if she's wrong about him having feelings for her in that way, his rejection would have the power to seriously wound. *Fyon needs to make his feelings known.*

"Mora," Fyon says, suddenly seeming hesitant. "Have you considered relocating to the sublands?"

Mora's throat tightens, her pulse quickening. "Why are you asking, Fyon?"

He sips his tea, studying her, and she has the sense of him holding his thoughts back. "Because we're building something there," he finally says. "And you should be part of it." His eyes skim her emerald garb, sending a tingle through her. "You clearly seek to uphold Smaragdalfar ways."

Mora raises a brow at this. "I wear Noi clothing as well," she counters.

"You've chosen to power your air ship exclusively with Smaragdalfar runes you crafted yourself," Fyon points out, gesturing toward the green rune stylus sheathed at her hip. "And you attend Oo'na's services in the sublands every week's end."

"I love my people, it's true," Mora agrees. "And I love the teachings of Oo'na." She slides two necklaces out from under her tunic's collar. The first has a small Oo'na goddess pendant hanging from it, the Smaragdalfar deity fashioned from jade and emerald, a small white dove perched on her shoulder. The second bears an ivory dragon amulet—the Noi goddess, Vo, crafted from pearlescent shell, two small white bird pendants hanging to either side of the dragon, the sacred bird image common to both faiths. "But I also attend Vo'lon services with my mothers," Mora says. "I love the teachings of the Compassionate Vo as well as those of the Compassionate Oo'na. Do I have to choose?"

"Mora…"

They stay silent for a moment, and Mora stares over the river, feeling unsettled, before meeting Fyon's gaze once more. "Fyon… I'm not sure I fit in in the sublands. I feel like something's been lost to me, growing up as an adopted child of two women who are Noi, so removed from my birth culture. And it hurts when other Smaragdalfar call me an impostor, or laugh over my clumsy use of our language. When I'm told I'm more Noi than Smaragdalfar."

She thrusts out her arm. "But if I'm Noi, then why is my skin patterned in emeralds?" Her brow knots with consternation. "More and more, in the streets when I pass, I hear murmurs of 'Snake Elf' that make me want to don Smaragdalfar green, forsake all Noi ways, and shun everyone but the Smaragdalfar, even if I don't fit in." Mora glances over her shoulder toward the children, then sets her impassioned gaze back on Fyon. "But then…children land on my doorstep who are neither Smarag-dalfar nor Noi. Who are unwanted here and told they don't be-long. And all I want to do is forge a new path and show them that they do, in fact, belong. That we *all* do."

She pauses, knowing that what she's about to say might crush anything that's budding between them. *If* there is anything bud-ding between them. But it has to be said.

He has to know who she truly is.

"Fyon," she says, "I'm a Subland Elf who loves the sky. I don't want to live underground, beautiful as it will be. I've lived most of my life at the top of a mountain city and on rune ships soar-ing through the heavens. I'm a creature of the clouds and al-ways will be."

A slight tension tightens Fyon's brow, but only slight, his ex-pression unreadable.

Is it disappointment she's seeing? Sympathy?

As frustratingly unreadable as he is frustratingly gorgeous and wonderful.

Yearning takes hold of Mora. Trying not to fall head over heels for courageous and quietly kind Fyon Hawkkyn is like trying to stop the advance of the Xishlon moon.

Impossible. Even for the Mages.

Nothing can stop Vo's purple light.

Mora fingers the pendants of her Noi and Smaragdalfar re-ligious necklaces and smiles ruefully to herself, pulled in both directions. She's such a mishmash of beliefs, but it works. It works for her.

"Come to the sublands with me later, Mora," Fyon offers. "We'll have Smaragdalfar tea and I'll show you what we're building there."

"I will," Mora agrees, fingering her Vo pendant's curling tail. "Then come back here. We'll take my skiff into the sky, and I'll show you the stars like you've never seen them."

It's late that eve when Mora docks her skiff against her rune ship after an evening drinking tea with Fyon in the sublands before bringing him up above the clouds. After hours together, with what felt, the whole time, like a crackling attraction between them, he bade her a dauntingly chaste good-night, leaving her more confused than ever.

Mora hangs over her larger ship's railing and looks past the huge cliff drop toward the glittering tiers of the city below out over the inky expanse of the Vo, topped by a constellation of sapphire runic vessels, myriad bright white stars hanging above it all.

She frowns as an ache takes up residence in her heart. Because as strong as her feelings are for Fyon, he might feel nothing but friendship for her. Now that she's told him the truth about herself. He was quiet as they flew to the heavens, after insisting that she bring some of the Xishlon tea.

The tea of the love festival.

She felt sure, for a moment, suspended in the sky, that Fyon would kiss her. But he simply sipped the tea as the ship hovered above a lone cloud, the lights of the city twinkling far below, the storm band above the Voloi Mountains putting on a pulsing lightning show, his gaze intent on her the whole time. Unreadable.

And Mora wondered—*How can he just calmly sip tea like that, completely unmoved by the skies? How can I have fallen for a man unmoved by the skies?*

She turns and listlessly picks up the book on Smaragdalfar culture that Fyon gave to her a few nights back. She flips its embossed green leather cover open, the desire to learn more about her people rising, the Smaragdalfar such a formal people, with hundreds upon hundreds of complicated traditions, some quite subtle. And despite her heartache, Mora is suddenly intent on learning them all, especially after visiting the sublands this evening with Fyon to take in the luminous caverns, phosphorescent plant life, and fledgling farms being established there. And meeting with the Western Realm Smaragdalfar refugees whose deep-seated cultural ties and rich sense of community prompted a bittersweet yearning in Mora that she's felt throughout a life cut off from those ties.

She might be a creature of the skies, but there's a large part of Mora that privately longs to be a creature of the sublands, as well.

I'm an impossible creature, is what I am, Mora archly considers as she flips through the pages.

A chapter heading catches her eye. *Smaragdalfar Courtship Traditions.*

The pang of Fyon's aloof distance still achingly fresh, Mora skims the section, her eyes widening as her attention hooks on the last paragraph.

> *It is traditional, in Smaragdalfar society, for the man, interested in initiating a courtship, to request tea from his object of interest. No expression of interest may be allowed except for this—it is forbidden to speak of it or act on it in any way. If the woman returns his interest, she will offer him thirty cups of tea on thirty different occasions. Only after the thirty cups of tea have been offered, is he then free to express interest in courting her.*

Mora goes breathless, her heartbeat tripping into a faster rhythm as she considers Fyon's odd tea fixation ever since he got back. Ever since they laid eyes on each other again. She considers his last words to her this evening as he took a step away when she was yearning for him to lean in for a kiss. *I'll come by tomorrow for more tea.*

Mora tries to count how many cups of tea they've had. Twenty-nine? It has to be close to thirty occasions at this point. A giddy happiness bursts into being inside Mora, her heart taking flight. *Well, we'll just have to step up that tea-drinking*, Mora considers, a laugh escaping her.

"Mora'lee?"

She turns toward the unsure voice to find Olilly standing there in the moonlight.

"Hello, lovely," Mora says, beaming at the young teen and beckoning her nearer.

Olilly returns her smile with a bashful one of her own, and Mora's heart aches again at the sight of the ragged tips of Olilly's ears. At the idea of a mob holding this child down...

Hurry up, Xishlon moon, Mora prays to the Compassionate Vo and the Compassionate Oo'na, both. *We need Your healing, loving light.*

"Are you finding the room to your liking?" she asks, hopeful, having purposefully given Olilly a room on the port side overlooking the Vo River. So she can bask in the full effect when its waters are transformed into an astonishingly beautiful purple by the Xishlon moon.

"I like it very much," Olilly replies with a broader smile.

Mora remembers something from earlier. She fishes a small, purple-parchment-wrapped package out of her pocket that Bleddyn dropped off between shifts for Olilly. "This is for you," she says as she hands it to her, finding Bleddyn's maternal protectiveness toward Olilly to be touchingly kind, brash as Bleddyn can be. "It's from Bleddyn. She said to tell you that 'you're beautiful either way.' She told me it was important for you to know that."

Olilly shyly opens the package, then gasps as she views the paper box's contents. Mora pulls in a hard breath as well, immediately realizing what this is.

Ear ornaments.

The kind the Wyvern-shifters wear during Xishlon. Silver sleeves to fit over their ear points, the Xishlon ear-cuffs covered in a riot of amethyst gems.

Tears pool in Olilly's purple-lashed eyes. She wipes them away with a trembling hand. "Can you put them on me?" she asks in a rough whisper.

Mora feels the tears brimming in her own eyes as she fastens the ear-cuffs to Olilly's ears, restoring the points with a resplendent purple glimmer. "I have a mirror," Mora says. She ducks into her room and retrieves her hand mirror, then holds it up for Olilly to view.

Olilly pulls in a quavering breath, her fingers coming to the points, then down over her trembling mouth. "They helped me, you know," she finally says as the tears spill over, face tensing.

"Who did?"

"Elloren Gardner and her brothers. Along with Bleddyn and the others. That night...the night they cut my ears."

Mora considers the surprising actions of the first Black Witch's progeny. "Bleddyn told me a little about that," she says somberly. "You know, Trystan Gardner helped to rescue Ghor'li from drowning in the Zonor. I heard he almost drowned himself."

"They're not what people think," Olilly insists, growing impassioned. "But...now Elloren's in danger. I've seen the postings of her face. The Vu Trin are hunting her. But they shouldn't be. She brought me medicine for the Grippe. Then she helped me get out of the West. My sister too. I was scared of her at first, but...she's against Vogel, just like everyone here."

"Olilly, they just want her brought to the Vu Trin if she's found—"

"No," Olilly counters, emphatic. "They don't. I can tell. They're *hunting* her." Olilly's violet eyes blaze with concern. "They're hunting for her so they can kill her."

CHAPTER
TWO

EVIL WITCH

Elloren Grey

Voloi, Noilaan
Eastern Realm
One day prior to Xishlon

Bleddyn's rune skiff touches down at the city's docks just as dawn's blue glow is reaching into the still-dark sky, the desire to survive and go after Lukas thrumming hot through my core.

Maritime activity bustles all around, my breath tightening as I note the port's heavy military presence, the soldiers searching incoming vessels and standing guard along the dock's adjacent boardwalk. I'm hyperaware of both my Elfhollen glamour and the runic weapons strapped under my Xishlon garb. And the Wand pressed into the side of my boot, its bolstering starlight tree firmly ensconced in the back of my mind.

Every type of ship and skiff is either docking or embarking as far as the eye can see, some of them piloted by female crews— something not seen in Gardneria. Many are festooned with strings of Xishlon runic orbs, decorated with violet flowers or gleaming, filigreed hearts and aglow with purple light. I glance skyward and take in the vertical city rising before us like an impossibly steep staircase. Rune ships dart overhead, the soaring vessels fogged with blue runic penumbras in the predawn light.

Worry tenses my brow as I take in how rune-based the city is, most of its infrastructure dependent on huge, sapphire-glowing circular support runes on the undersides of buildings, walkways, and suspended roads—runes powered by Noilaan's dome-shield.

A chill races down my spine. *Vogel could destroy this entire city with one swipe of his Shadow Wand.*

Bleddyn finishes securing the skiff and then taps my arm, urging me to follow. We start off down the dock, all thought vaporizing as I take in the large posting nailed to a piling at its end.

> *Wanted by the Vu Trin Forces of Noilaan.*
> *Elloren Grey, formerly Elloren Gardner.*
> *Black Witch of Gardneria.*

A dazed nausea rises as my gaze lowers to the line drawing of my face, a nail hammered through my forehead. My Gardnerian features are exaggerated—harsher and more angular than they actually are. But still, if I were unglamoured, it wouldn't be much of a stretch to identify me. My light-headed rush intensifies as I glance around, wanted postings tacked to almost every piling up and down the boardwalk's length.

Bleddyn shoots me a harsh glare before grabbing my arm and pulling me back into motion. The posters fly by, one by one, some vandalized with slashing Noi script scrawled over me, my face clawed clear off another.

Bleddyn cocks an ironic brow at the faceless poster. "Rather defeats the purpose, don't you think?" Something catches her eye and she stiffens. I follow her gaze toward the heavily armed soldiers marching toward us with an air of purpose.

My pulse quickening, I angle my head down. They're clearly

on duty, scanning the pier and the ships with searching eyes. Eyes that fixate on us as we near.

The hair on the back of my neck prickles as they pass. I let out a shuddering breath, following close on Bleddyn's heels as she makes a sharp turn through a busy fish market, then into the expansive gardens that edge the city's river-level tier.

On guard against the threats that could be bearing down, my eyes dart around the lush gardens, the flowers' phosphorescent buds glowing every shade of violet against predawn's cobalt luminance. Noi Wisteria trees close in around us, their pendulous, iridescent-purple fronds cascading down. Awareness touches my tangled lines like the brush of fingers, a palpable malice shivering to life and spreading through the grove.

Black Witch!

A vision of fronds slapping around my neck from all sides accosts me, so vivid I can almost feel the phantom stings. Ire rises in my throat, thick and hot. Tensing, I exhale hard, attempting to force my fire aura toward the trees in counter-attack, but quickly discover my magic is tangled so alarmingly tight I can barely summon a trace of its invisible aura.

The trees' murderous energy fades as I follow Bleddyn out of the grove and onto a lantern-lit circular plaza. I slow, my whole body going rigid as I face what lies in its center.

A huge statue hewn from black opalescent stone stands before me. It depicts a larger-than-life Icaral who strongly resembles Yvan, wings powerfully outstretched as he throws a stream of stone-fire mercilessly toward the dead Black Witch splayed under his feet, his boot crushing her temple.

For a moment, my emotions storm, as I imagine a very different statue. A statue that defiantly rages against the cursed Prophecy images of both Realms—a tall, angular-faced Icaral and Black Witch caught up in a fire-bonding kiss.

"Look familiar?" Bleddyn asks from beside me. I glance at her, lost in an abyss of conflict, the forces bent on demonizing me feel like a multitude of walls closing in.

"Bleddyn, I need you to tell me where we're going," I say, a knot clutching my throat.

Her brow tenses as she stares at me, a surprisingly compassionate look entering her emerald gaze. She leans in close. "To the rune ship of a Resistance worker I'm friendly with. I've secured a spot for you working in her restaurant for a day or so." She lowers her voice, stressing each of her next words. "The ship is warded by Smaragdalfar varg runes." She gives me a significant look, understanding gathering inside me—it's likely that both Vogel and the Vu Trin won't be able to track me through them.

"C'mon," Bleddyn prods, motioning me forward, and we head for the plaza's far end.

I glance once over my shoulder at the statue, my heart twisting as I wonder how, if Yvan is truly alive, we'll manage to navigate a world dead set on upholding a Prophecy that casts us as mortal enemies. My thoughts slingshot to Lukas, pain lodging like a thorn in my chest over the Wyvernfire bond running hot through my lines, my heart forever cleaved in two.

But there's no time to wrestle with any of it as Bleddyn and I stride onto the First Tier's already crowded main thoroughfare, pictures of my evil face tacked onto every shoppe and lantern post and hostile tree.

Dawn breaks over the tiered Voloi Mountains, its eastern glow brightening the sky as Bleddyn and I take rune lift after rune lift toward Voloi's cloud-high Sixth Tier. We step off the final lift, and onto an amethyst-cobblestoned road, pale sunlight shafting over merchants setting out wares for tomorrow's Xishlon holiday—bunches of violet roses, heart-shaped lilac flower wreathes, lavender trinkets, moon-decorated lace and every hue of purple garb. I'm amazed by just how varied the people look here—so many hues of skin tone and hair color, but most wearing distinctively Noi-style dress.

An attractive young Noi man wearing a moon-polka-dotted plum tunic is stringing a line of violet-rose decorated runic orbs across the narrow street. He pauses, grinning as he looks toward a nearby apothecary shoppe. "Find the moon with me, Zara Ko!" he tosses out flirtatiously to the elegant teal-hued young woman in a black apron staffing the shoppe's window.

"You need to bring it to me, Mika Zir!" she flirts back with a cheeky grin as she hands a vial of deep-brown roots to another young Noi woman garbed in a dress made of overlapping metallic hearts. The two women burst into laughter as I stare at the vial, stunned.

It's Sanjire root. Vials and vials of the pregnancy-preventing root, illegal in Gardneria, but completely out in the open here.

"They sell Sanjire root," I murmur to Bleddyn in amazement. My thoughts careen to Lukas, remembering how he secured the root for us, a stab of fierce longing for him cutting through me.

"It's surprising to see it on display," Bleddyn admits. "Shocked me at first too. The Urisk don't allow it either." Her green lips twist with derision. "We're supposed to have as many babies as, well—" she gives me a jaded look "—as the Mages. Not a lot of power in the Western Realm for us women." She spits out a laugh. "Well, unless you're Amaz."

I nod in morbid solidarity as we exchange another look, the two of us seeming a trace surprised to be finding common ground as Westerners.

My attention shifts to two bedazzled Noi women striding toward us in the increasing traffic. One of the young women has spiked graphite-hued hair tipped in metallic violet. The other's looping brown braids are festooned with deep-purple clematis blossoms, her dress a riot of lilac glitter. Their skirts are scandalously short by Gardnerian standards, but no one looks at them with anything but friendly glances.

They fall into each other, laughing, as if in the midst of some private joke, and the spike-haired woman pulls the flowery woman into an embrace, kissing her deeply.

A tingling surprise sweeps through me, and I can barely keep from gaping at them.

They break the kiss, beaming at each other, as a hunched elderly flower merchant leans out from her small shoppe, a broad smile on her face as she hands them a glowing violet iris on a long spring-green stalk.

I'm swept up in an envy so strong I'm surprised by the bitter taste of it.

What would it be like to have been raised in a culture that's so free? What would it have been like for Trystan to have grown up in a land that accepted him instead of forcing him into hiding? What would it have been like for me to have freedom without the threat of wandfasting hanging over me like an ever-present shadow, with so little choice of work and study and clothing? With free access to Sanjire root?

I don't want to resent the Easterners for their vast freedom, but for a moment, I do, wondering, how could any of them possibly understand where I've come from. Or where Bleddyn's come from, her situation in the West unimaginably worse than mine. There's such mind-bending power for women and everyone else here and it's worth fighting for.

Not just for them, but for all of us fleeing here, as well.

My gaze snags on a sign hanging from a shoppe selling syrup-drenched lavender heart waffles, the same sign affixed to many of the other shoppes and outdoor restaurants. All of the signs possess the same flowing black Noi lettering stamped on purple parchment along with a depiction of the Noi people's ivory dragon goddess, Vo. I make a mental note to ask Bleddyn about the signs as the street narrows and we near a toy shoppe that does not display one.

The store's proprietor, an old Noi woman, wears a bright violet tunic embroidered with whimsical purple frogs, lilac moon-decorated lace wrapped around her white hair. She smiles broadly at us as she readies an outdoor table covered with her playful wares. A white dragon goddess pendant hangs around her neck, and ivory bird earrings grace her ears, her braided hair a cottony white and decorated with purple silken flowers.

The hand-painted figurines she's setting out catch my eye and I stop, overtaken by a surreal sense of déjà vu. I pick up a Vu Trin sorceress figurine, blue runes marked on her black uniform, curved swords at her sides, silver stars strapped across her chest. Her black hair is fashioned into artful coils, her expression heroic and determined.

These toys…they're so similar to the ones Gardnerian children play with. But completely altered in their allegiance. Instead of wicked, sneering Vu Trin with menacing poses, the sorceresses are uniformly valiant. As are the Wyvern-shifter figurines, the attractive shifters partway shifted, with horned heads and gleaming black wings. Sapphire dragons are also set out for play, their expressions strong and benevolent.

And there's an Icaral.

I pick up the figurine, my emotions tightening as my thoughts fly to Yvan and the golden thread of Wyvernfire embedded in my lines. Like Yvan in his glamoured form, the Icaral is a brown-haired Kelt, eyes a glowing gold, black feathered wings fanning out majestically.

My throat cinching, I set the figurine down.

Gardnerians and Alfsigr Elves are placed beside the Icaral figurine, their mouths twisted into sneers, violence in their eyes, their hands curled into claw-like fists around wands and bows and runic swords. The Gardnerians' skin is painted a sickly green, the pale Alfsigr abnormally stretched out and ghoul-like.

The Evil Ones. All of us uniformly, irretrievably evil.

And there, lining the shelf behind the narrow table, is the most evil toy of all.

The Black Witch.

I reach out and take one in hand, fascinated even as my stomach heaves.

My face. Only distorted, even more so than in the wanted postings, into an evil and snarling visage. A dark wand in my upraised hand.

Feeling dazed, I run my fingers along the monstrous figurine's wooden base as the unfamiliar Eastern Realm tree it's fashioned from unfolds in my mind. *Purple leaves. A dark, rough trunk. Wine-colored flowers.* Such beauty underpinning something so terrifying. My gaze slides to the small wooden mallet tied to each Black Witch figurine with pale cotton string.

"*Ny'laea,*" Bleddyn says, her tone cautionary. I look up and meet her dire look as her eyes pointedly flick from the figurine to me.

"Would you like one, toiya?" the old woman asks.

I look to her, my heart thumping. "I... I've no money," I stammer, moving to set it down.

The old woman's brown wizened hands come around mine before I can. "Take it," she says kindly. "A Xishlon gift." Her eyes briefly flick toward the shoppe across the street and flash with what looks like a spark of defiance as her smile momentarily dims.

I follow her line of sight toward this shoppe's owner, an older Noi man in a dark purple tunic stamped with an ivory dragon. He's glowering at us, and a rush of fear shoots through my lines in response to the loathing in his pale blue eyes, my tangled fire magic sparking to fitful life.

Sweet Ancient One, does he suspect what I am?

A row of Noilaan flags line his stall's roof, the white dragon on sapphire, as well as a large version of that mysterious purple sign.

"What does the sign say?" I ask Bleddyn as my apprehension mounts.

Bleddyn frowns as she and the man lock glares. "'*Noilaan for the Noi,*'" she bites out.

The grim realization courses over me. *He doesn't hate me because he knows I'm the Black Witch. He hates me simply because I'm not Noi.*

I'm both relieved and horrified at the same time.

"Ignore his horrible sign," the old woman insists, giving the man a blazing look of disgust. She gestures toward the Black

Witch toy still gripped in my fist. "Take it, toiya," she says, re-bellious support shining in her dark eyes. "You smash that witch with the mallet when the moon turns lavender." Her smile makes a faltering return as she pats my arm. "There's a prize inside her head, and it will give you good luck for the whole year. It is our tradition. You've come a long way to get here, toiya. I want to give you some luck and good wishes. I am happy you are here and safe from *Her*." She pointedly glances down at the toy.

I struggle to ignore Bleddyn's incredulous grin.

"Here, you take one too," the woman says to Bleddyn, hand-ing her another toy.

"So... I just smash her head in for luck?" Bleddyn clarifies, her grin widening. "Can I use a bigger hammer?"

The woman nods with enthusiasm. "Any hammer you like, toiya." She slices the air with her hand emphatically. "Just knock her head right off and claim your prize."

I look back at the hostile merchant and his head whips an-grily away. I notice he's selling mostly figurines of Vo, the Noi people's dragon goddess, Her purple incarnation wreathed in a spiral of white birds.

Gripping the figurine, I turn back to the old woman, who is still smiling warmly at me. I know she's trying to be kind by making a point of publicly welcoming two refugees. But as I glance at the figurine's small hammer, I can't help but think of the Gardnerian winged Yule cookies and how my people break their wings.

"Thank you," I tell her shakily. She nods and pats my arm again, perhaps taking my flustered demeanor as my being over-come with gratitude.

Bleddyn flashes one last smile at the woman, and we move to take our leave.

"Go back to where you came from!"

It startles me, the venom in the man's tone, slowing both Bleddyn's and my steps as we look at him in surprise.

"Be sure to smash the witch for luck!" the woman counters,

too loudly, and I know the comment is actually meant for the man—her way of pushing her support of us in his face. Her eyes meet ours in blaring solidarity and her defiant kindness sparks a stronger resolve in me—to get my power unbound so I can smash Vogel down before he can reach this land and this welcoming old woman selling Black Witch toys.

"There are a lot of those signs," I note as Bleddyn and I advance down the Sixth Tier thoroughfare, weaving around the thickening pedestrian and street traffic.

"A movement has sprung up," Bleddyn explains. "The Vo'nyl. They're pushing for a majority on the Noi Conclave. Their leader just won a seat using the slogan stamped on all those signs."

"Oh, Bleddyn..." Dread rippling through me as I take in sign after sign. "The Noi should be careful. Or it'll be like Verpacia all over again."

She gives me a grave look. "Oh, it could be even worse. The Vo'nyl want to shun all magic other than Noi. Forbid any religion other than Vo'lon." She frowns, her emerald eyes tightening. "They're completely reactionary, afraid all Westerners are set on polluting their magic and destroying their culture."

She quiets as we weave around a merchant's table selling purple moon pendants hanging from silver chains stamped with glowing sapphire Noi runes, then another displaying statues and jewelry and small fountains depicting the Vo'lon faith's purple Source Tree, so much like the Ironwood Source Tree present in the Gardnerian faith.

"There've been some mob attacks on refugees," Bleddyn confides.

An outraged dismay rises, sour on my tongue, as I think of the Night of the Burning Blessing Stars, assaulted by the horrific memory of Olilly in Rafe's arms, blood streaming from her mutilated ears, her hair brutally shorn, and Bleddyn, beaten bloody and crumpled in that dark alley.

"They used to hate only the Gardnerians and Alfsigr here,"

Bleddyn says as we pass a store selling countless purple finches in moon-shaped cages, "but now it's becoming a hatred of everyone fleeing the Western Realm."

I clutch the Black Witch figurine, stunned by this terrible news, barely registering the soft whir of rune ships passing above. The rich aromas of foods seasoned with unfamiliar spices wafting around us as we enter a dense restaurant district, outdoor seating areas narrowing the tree-lined central road.

"Here we are," Bleddyn announces as we slow to a stop, and my brow rises at the sight of the most fantastical restaurant I've ever seen.

It's based in a sizable rune ship tethered against the Sixth Tier cliffside, a glass-walled cockpit set above the main deck. The ship's side doors are thrown open to reveal a cramped kitchen with steaming pots set on a broad stove. There's a small seating area sided by runic-orb-decorated plum trees, the cliff's startlingly sheer drop just beyond. I recognize the flowing, deep-green script emblazoned on the ship's side to be Smaragdalfar Elfin lettering.

"What's this restaurant called?" I ask Bleddyn, not able to read the script.

"Gylloryyon," she answers. "It's a subland flower—a purple orchid that's a popular gift here at Xishlon."

A young Smaragdalfar woman strides out of the kitchen carrying a tray of steaming breakfast soup. She's striking—tall and graceful with bright silver eyes, the soft dawn light sparkling off her emerald-patterned skin. Her ears are sweepingly pointed, her long green hair done up in looping braids with a single purple orchid tucked in the coils. A purple apron imprinted with a lilac moon covers her traditional Smaragdalfar clothing of an emerald, rune-decorated tunic and matching pants. Her feet are clad in sturdy black boots, and she has a green rune stylus sheathed at her hip.

Her eyes flash like diamonds as she chats with customers, her demeanor inviting. It's obvious she's quick to laugh, her chiming amusement bright on the air.

I follow Bleddyn toward the gated entrance, sparing a glance toward the restaurant across the road, my vision assaulted by another of those awful signs—*NOILAAN FOR THE NOI.*

Noi flags hang in repeating rows above the customers, and a gray-haired Noi man in purple Xishlon garb and apron stands among them, jotting down an order. The Smaragdalfar woman, who must be Mora'lee, lets out another hearty laugh, and the man cuts a quick glare across the street, as if her happiness is an affront to the entire Eastern Realm. I'm reminded of the hostile man across the way from the elderly toy merchant.

I quickly realize how different the clientele is in the man's restaurant, only Noi customers packing the outdoor seating. Over here, diversity reigns—an elegant young Noi man dressed in sparkling violet is seated with two blue-hued Urisk women, the young women also decked out in Xishlon garb, theirs marked with embroidered lavender moons and hearts. Sitting at the table near theirs is a huge Elfhollen man with an owl perched on his shoulder, the young man engrossed in conversation with a heavily armed blonde Issani woman. Beside them sits a Smaragdalfar woman wearing a golden Ishkart scarf, a black-haired boy with her same shimmering green hue hugging her arm. A black-bearded Ishkart man sitting across from them laughs at something the woman's said, his garb a gleaming, rune-marked gold, his hand stretched across the table and entwined with hers. And seated just outside the kitchen is a little blue-hued Urisk girl with braided cornflower hair. She's dressed in emerald Smaragdalfar clothes, quietly painting.

"You should be safe here for the day," Bleddyn informs me in low tones. "Just blend in and stay in the kitchen."

"All right," I warily reply.

"There's something else you should know." Bleddyn hedges, lowering her voice further. "Olilly's here."

Alarm strikes through me. "Bleddyn," I sputter, "she'll recognize me."

"She won't turn you in."

I shoot her a look of dire concern. "How can you be so sure?"

She flashes me a slightly annoyed look. "I'm sure. Keep an eye out for Fyon Hawkkyn, though."

My mind is suddenly spinning. An image of my metallurgie professor who was secretly working for the Resistance in Verpacia fills my mind. He was fair-minded enough with me, even when he found out I'm the Black Witch, but that was when he thought me aligned with the Vu Trin. Who are currently bent on killing me.

"He's sweet on Mora," Bleddyn explains, infuriatingly blasé, "but he's on duty for the Vu Trin down at the docks, so it's unlikely you'll cross paths. But keep an eye out for him, nonetheless. He's a stickler for Vu Trin protocol, and it's likely he'd bring you in for questioning."

I narrow my eyes at her, patting the Ash'rion blade sheathed under my tunic. "He'd have to catch me first."

She shoots me a disbelieving glare. "He's a Smaragdalfar rune sorcerer well versed in varg runes and varg weaponry. Trust me, you can't best Fyon."

I consider this, deeply thrown. "Does this Mora'lee know what I am?"

Bleddyn's eyes flash. "No, and you best keep it that way."

"This is *dangerous*," I hiss in a coarse whisper.

She shoots me an annoyed look. "You *think*? Because if you have a better suggestion, I'm all ears."

A small contingent of soldiers strides into view, marching down the street in our direction, scanning each restaurant. My heartbeat accelerates to a jumping rhythm as I demurely lower my head. Bleddyn sends them a jaunty salute, which they barely acknowledge as their eyes pass over us and they're quickly swallowed up by the purple-clad crowds.

Bleddyn's green gaze bores into me as she leans in. "They're searching for you, make no mistake about it." She glances emphatically toward the wanted postings tacked onto the surrounding plum trees. "This is your best option to blend in while your allies gather."

I glare at her, furious at her for waiting until now to reveal so many important details—my fate, Lukas's fate and potentially the fate of this entire realm, resting on the whims of a young Urisk teen and the kindness of a stranger. But there's nothing to be done about it now. I grip my Black Witch figurine and follow Bleddyn into the restaurant's outdoor seating area, primed for flight.

"Go sit and I'll bring over some soup," Mora'lee jauntily calls out to us, purple teapot in hand. She flashes me a bright smile and waves us toward a table by the cliff's edge.

Bleddyn grins at me, less a true smile and more an emphatic nudge to try harder to appear normal. "Let's go sit down, then, *Ny'laea*." She hoists her Black Witch figurine. "I, for one, can't wait to smash her head and collect my prize."

I glower at her, and Bleddyn's grin widens.

We weave past deserted tables and take our seats. I'm hit by a flash of vertigo as I peer over the filigreed cliffside railing, the drop shockingly precipitous, stray clouds floating over the city's descending tiers.

"The restaurant across the street has one of those signs," I grimly note, concerned to have someone hostile to foreigners in close proximity. "And the owner keeps glaring at Mora'lee."

"Noticed old Zosh Lyyo, did you?" Bleddyn says. "So welcoming, that one."

I scrutinize Zosh Lyyo, my eyes catching on the tall teenage boy standing beside him, washrag in hand. The teen has short black hair, chiseled features, and wears a purple tunic and pants. And he's staring toward Mora's rune ship, as if searching for something.

Zosh Lyyo smacks the back of the teen's head, and the boy

flinches. He nods at the man, seeming chastened, then walks, shoulders hunched, toward their kitchen.

I turn to find Bleddyn studying me, rocked back in her chair to the point that it's pressed against the curved terrace railing, at ease lounging against what seems like a thousand-league drop. "So, let me get this straight," she says, a rakish light in her large green eyes. "You're illegally here in Noi lands needing me, of all people, to get you work in a kitchen."

I frown at her. "It's a bit more complicated than that."

"But right now, I think that's about it." She gives me a sardonic look, and I'm struck by how our situations *have* undergone a complete sea change, one realm to another.

"Relax, *Ny'laea*," she whispers, leaning in. "I won't treat you the way you treated me back in Verpacia."

Her words sting. "I'm sorry for that," I say with no small amount of remorse as I remember how I acted toward her in Verpax University's kitchen. How Lukas threatened her and everyone else in the room and I stood by and said nothing.

Her look of humor hardens. "Your head was in a vile place when I first met you."

"That's...accurate."

Her green brow lifts, her expression turning contemplative. "It is ironic, though. This twist of fate. You, the refugee needing my help."

I bristle, remembering how hostile she and Iris were. "Shall I push you into some manure?"

Bleddyn laughs. "I was a bit harsh with you back in Verpacia."

"A bit."

She lets out a long sigh. "Well, perhaps we should leave off the contest of who was the bigger ass...which would be *you*... and move on." She looks me over, her whisper almost inaudible as she leans closer, serious now. "Are you really as powerful as the Vu Trin fear?"

I set my Black Witch figurine emphatically down on the table next to hers. "Worse."

Bleddyn lets out a long, low whistle.

"Relax," I whisper bitterly. "The Forest has completely bound up my magic."

Bleddyn's eyes flick over me in cool assessment. "Well, you're turning out to be a complete disaster. Like this whole situation." She glances west, frowning. "Vogel's ordered the Amaz off their land, did you know that? We just got word."

Fear breaks like a wave, dread clutching at my throat as I think of Wynter and all the Amaz I met. "That's how it started with the Lupines," I warn, praying Kam Vin can get my warning to Amazakaraan in time.

Bleddyn gives me an intense look. "Yeah, well, the Gard-nerians and Alfsigr are intent on driving everyone who is not them out of the Western Realm." She glances toward the runic border. "That refugee camp on the other side of the border? It's *small* compared to what's coming." She huffs. "Greater Isaan and Southern Ishkartaan are also walling themselves up." She flicks her finger toward Noilaan's border. "They've built one of those monstrous runic things. Everyone's walling up, while everyone else runs for their lives or dies of the Grippe. That's what the future looks like."

"Until Vogel invades," I say.

She nods. "And everyone over here is breaking into separate groups instead of coming together to fight him." She turns and glares at Zosh Lyyo's restaurant. "Those like Zosh Lyyo can bask in their 'cultural superiority' while the Gardnerians fly in and take over every last thing." Her frown deepens. "This isn't a time for division, but we lack a unifying principle. I fear our fragmentation is going to be the Eastern Realm's downfall."

"What do you think could bring everyone together?" I ask, surprised to be finding so much common ground.

Bleddyn seems to ponder this, her green brow furrowing. "At this point, I don't know. But I think we better find that thing, and fast. 'Noilaan for the Noi' certainly won't be able to fight what's coming." She eyes me. "The East is going to have to pool the magic of every single culture, whether the Noi Conclave wants to accept that or not." She angles a finger at our Black Witch figurines and gives me a pointed look. "We're also going to need every weapon we can find. Including this little witch here. And Fae power too."

Her mention of Fae power brings a certain Fire Fae to mind. "Have you seen Iris?" I ask with some wariness. I can't risk perpetually hostile Iris happening upon me.

Bleddyn tosses me a scowl, as if reading my concerns. "She's well north of here, and won't be seeking me out anytime soon. She's become quite the Lasair zealot. She's decided the Lasair Fae are superior to everyone else, so that's put a pretty firm dent in our friendship."

I give Bleddyn a look of amazement. Their friendship seemed forged in steel.

"She hates you quite a bit," Bleddyn notes. "She will *not* be happy if she discovers you're alive and kicking."

"Well, I'd appreciate it if we could prevent that."

Bleddyn smirks, her head bobbing in a silent laugh, but then she grows somber, hesitating as if she's unsure how to say the next thing. "I'm sorry about Yvan, Elloren. It was a shock to find out the secret he was carrying. And... I know Iris wanted him...but I also know that he was in love with you."

A wave of emotional protest rises.

He's not dead. I felt his fire. He's searching for me.

I hold back the words as well as the jagged fear that they might not prove to be true.

"He was my good friend, and quite brave," Bleddyn says, her voice cracking with emotion. "It's...a great loss."

I struggle to formulate a response, but find I'm unable, as the yearning to find Yvan surges. Were those brief, Wyvernfire connections enough for him to locate me? If he's truly alive, could he be making his way toward me right now? I imagine Yvan suddenly sweeping into this restaurant and become momentarily breathless just from the idea of it. What would it be like to meet those fiery green eyes again?

My fire power knifes into a fitful, conflicted blaze as the fervid desire to go after Lukas breaks loose and blazes up alongside this heated longing to be reunited with Yvan.

But there's no way to resolve any of it.

"I have one purpose now," I whisper to Bleddyn, my voice strung tight. "To fight Vogel and his forces."

Bleddyn nods as she flashes me a look of intense solidarity. "It's what Yvan would have wanted." Both of us grow quiet for a moment. "Iris has joined a group of Fire Fae revolutionaries," she finally says, the surprising fact clearly troubling her. "They've taken over a section of Noi forest northeast of here. They say they have an ancestral claim to it."

I raise my brow at this.

"The Vu Trin are having a hard time negotiating with them, and the Zhilon'ile Wyverns have issued a warning. Like I said, we're all fragmenting. Their grievances are real. But it doesn't change the fact that we're divided."

"Infighting right now...it's not good."

"I know it." She looks toward the Noi restaurant and shakes her head. "I don't know where I fit into all this anymore. I don't align cleanly with any of the fragments. I argue with my fellow Urisk here too much to be accepted." She looks at me, green eyes flashing. "Even so, I'll fight for them. And I'll fight for everyone trying to get in here."

"Why would you have an issue with your own people?"

She blinks at me as if I've just asked something very foolish. "Have you forgotten that I'm of the Urol class? I'm on the next to lowest tier of the Urisk class system and religion. I have some *significant* issues with my own people." She huffs out a breath, her mouth forming a tight line. "I don't even know what I believe anymore. It's all so troubling. And confusing. All I know for certain is that I want no part of any culture or religion that watches *anyone's* children die of the Red Grippe on the other side of a rune wall and does *nothing* to help them." She considers the border, a seditious half smile forming on her lips. "I think *that's* my new religion. No children dying of curable things on the other side of a wall."

I raise my brow at her. "*That's* your religion? Your entire religion?"

She shrugs. "That's all I've got, Ny'laea. Seems to keep me busy enough."

My mind lights with the memory of Bleddyn caring for Smaragdalfar refugees back in Verpacia, most of them children. How gentle she was with them. And now she's here in the East, smuggling sick people like Nym'ellia's family, across the border so they can get medicine and care. It strikes me that Bleddyn, for all her confusion and harsh ways, is a deeply admirable person.

"It's a good religion," I tell her, chastened.

She laughs. "You know, I think it is. I think it's a very good religion."

"No, I mean it."

Her eyes meet mine, more serious now. She nods. "It might be the only religion worth having right now."

CHAPTER THREE

NY'LAEA SHIZORIN

Elloren Grey

Voloi, Noilaan
Eastern Realm
One day prior to Xishlon

"Welcome to Voloi," Mora'lee enthuses as she slides a steaming bowl of soup in front of me.

"Thank you for offering me work," I say, uneasily glancing at the wanted postings nailed to the hostile plum tree behind her, my own face scowling at me from over her shoulder.

She cheerfully waves away my thanks as she sets out a tea set marked with lavender moons, then pours us violet tea, a rose-scented steam curling from it. "I'm pleased to have the extra help," she confides, smiling warmly. "Especially with tomorrow's festival."

"Mora still needs to find someone to kiss," Bleddyn says with a suggestive waggle of her eyebrows as she digs into the soup. "I know of a young Smaragdalfar soldier stationed dockside who might volunteer. How many cups of tea are you two up to?"

Mora laughs, flushing, this talk of kissing dour Professor Hawkkyn, of all people, mixed with tea clearly some inside joke between them. I resist the urge to raise my brow at it.

"When's he coming by?" Bleddyn asks, and I still, realizing she's subtly scouting out the situation for me.

"Oh, not till tomorrow eve," Mora'lee responds as her mouth ticks up in a private smile, seeming a bit flustered. Visibly collecting herself, she beams at me. "You good with pastry, Ny'laea?"

I nod, feeling like the whole situation is surreal. "I'm well trained in kitchen work."

And slaying demonic scorpios, wraith bats, and kraken.

Guilt descends over the world-shattering secret that we're keeping from this kind and welcoming woman. *It's only for a day*, I justify uncomfortably.

"We'll have lots of help with the Xishlon prep," Mora says brightly, glancing toward the rune ship's partially open kitchen door. "Could you join us, Olilly?"

Tension shoots down my spine at the same moment a band of six Vu Trin emerge from the street traffic and sweep into the restaurant's outdoor seating area. And not just the usual Vu Trin.

Gray-garbed Kin Hoang. The Vu Trin's deadliest forces.

My heart leaps into my throat as I reach for the Ash'rion blade, forcing measured breaths as lavender Olilly slips out of the kitchen. I angle my gaze down and let my gray hair create a curtain around my face, keenly aware of the Black Witch figurines on the table.

Olilly pauses to brush flour from her hands as the Kin Hoang advance, a hunter's glint in the lead assassin's golden eyes, her garnet hair cut into axe-sharp angles.

I spare an anxious glance toward Olilly.

One word from her…one, single word, and your fate is sealed.

It's obvious that Olilly doesn't recognize me when she glances my way, then worriedly toward the soldiers as Bleddyn shoots me a dire look.

"We seek Mora'lee Starr'lyrion," the lead assassin states with no preamble.

Mora straightens, teapot in hand. "I am Mora'lee."

The assassin's knife-sharp gaze fixes on her. "We've received word that you're sheltering a Gardnerian."

My hand tenses around my blade's hilt as I get ready to break into a run.

Mora'lee frowns. "She's part Mage," she says with a defiant lift of her chin as confusion grips hold of me.

"We need to speak with the girl," the soldier insists.

Frowning, Mora sets down her teapot and strides to her ship's narrow wraparound walkway, stopping at the door just past the kitchen then knocking on it. "Nym'ellia?" she asks in a tone of forced calm. "Some soldiers need to speak with you."

Nym'ellia? Surprise rolls through me, Bleddyn seeming equally thrown.

The door opens, and the teen I traveled through the Dyoi Forest with steps cautiously out, her green eyes widening with alarm at the sight of the soldiers. She turns, her gaze meeting mine.

"Ny'laea," she breathes out in obvious astonishment.

My pulse skyrockets as the soldiers all briefly look at me then back toward Nym'ellia and fixate there, as I realize in a guilt-stricken flash—*They think she's me. Just like the soldiers in the Dyoi Forest.*

"Full name," the lead Kin Hoang demands.

Nym'ellia casts a fearful, unsure glance up at Mora'lee, who nods reassuringly. She swallows. "Nym'ellia Elmyllyn."

The Kin Hoang soldier scrutinizes Nym'ellia, not seeming to spare a detail as dread tightens my gut. Nym'ellia looks transformed, garbed in clean emerald Smaragdalfar clothing, her black hair neatly combed and braided. *Mora's work*, I imagine. *This kind woman I'm putting in life-threatening danger. Along with Nym'ellia.*

Feeling as if I'm about to step off a cliff, I ready myself to throw out a blast of wind with my blade and pray I can outrun these elite assassins. But then the lead sorceress seems to pause.

"What happened to your ears?" she demands of Nym'ellia, the ragged tips of the teen's ears poking up through her hair.

Nym'ellia's face tightens with a look of pained outrage.

"They were *cropped*," Mora snaps, eyes blazing.

The sorceress peers even more closely at her, then scowls and shakes her head, the dangerous tension on the air dissipating like weapons abruptly drawn down. I let out a shaky breath, remorse roiling through me over putting Nym'ellia in this situation. Again.

The sorceress turns to Mora'lee, seeming to have lost interest in Nym'ellia. "We're looking for Elloren Gardner Grey."

Mora'lee's eyes flick toward the wanted postings tacked to the furious trees. "I've seen the posters," she says shortly. "But Nym'ellia is not her. She's part Urisk, as you can plainly see."

Olilly's gaze pins on the scarred tips of Nym'ellia's ears, a look of quiet devastation in her eyes.

"You have papers for the girl?" the sorceress asks Mora'lee.

I notice that Zosh Lyyo from across the street is watching the proceedings like a hawk, his teen son wearing a look of concern.

"Of course," Mora'lee says, smooth as butter. She fishes in her pocket and draws out the identity papers.

The Kin Hoang takes a cursory look at the papers, then hands them back to Mora. "I'm sorry to have troubled you," she says, not sounding sorry at all. Sounding like someone thwarted from her true quarry. *Me.*

"A Blessed Xishlon to you," the golden-eyed sorceress curtly adds before she turns and throws out her hand in a commanding sweep, urging her fellow Kin Hoang to follow. They fall into step behind her and take their leave.

I exchange an intense look with Bleddyn, hit by a dizzying rush of relief as Nym'ellia rushes to me, the teen catching me off guard when she throws her arms around my shoulders like we're long-lost friends.

"I thought you *died*," she says as she draws back, her heart-shaped face bright with relief.

Her honest emotion sends a guilty pang through me as I angle my head down to avoid Olilly's gaze. I take Olilly in out of the corner of my eye, tension knotting my gut. Like Nym'ellia, she's a changed girl, garbed in a lovely lavender Xishlon tunic the same hue as her skin, the silk embroidered with tiny purple flowers. Her hair has grown back a bit in the past months, her short locks decorated with violet-gemmed barrettes and a single purple orchid. And her ears—their edges are adorned with be-jeweled silver tips that restore their graceful points.

Realizing I might draw more scrutiny staying quiet than answering, I launch into an attempt at normal conversation, modifying my voice by lowering and softening it. "How's your mother and sister?" I ask Nym'ellia in Uriskal.

A faltering smile forms on Nym'ellia's mouth as she indicates the rune-ship door she emerged from. "They're here too. A Mage gave them medicine when we got through the border last night. He had a spider tattooed to his face. And then…they woke up this morning, already a bit better. Tibryl can take a deep breath!"

"They're recovering from the Grippe," Mora unnecessarily tells me. "But they've been given Norfure tincture."

Gratitude for both my apothecary uncle Wrenfir and incred-ibly kind Mora'lee fair explodes in my chest. "I'm happy for you all, Nym'ellia," I tell her, briefly meeting Bleddyn's furtive look.

"What a great stroke of luck that you know each other!" Mora says to Nym'ellia and me, beaming, but then her smile dampens as she glances in the direction the Kin Hoang went. "I'm sorry our introductions happened this way." She forces a small smile, as if attempting to shake off the stress of it all. "Olilly," she says congenially, "as you've gathered, this is Ny'laea and Nym'ellia. They'll be joining our little party of castaways for a day or two." She winks at us. "Possibly more, if they'd like."

Olilly gives me a welcoming smile as my heart thumps and I doggedly keep my head lowered.

"You look all decked out for Xishlon," Bleddyn says to Olilly, overbright, in an obvious attempt to deflect her attention.

But Olilly doesn't bite. She leans down a bit to take a better look at me, a sympathetic look on her lovely face. "Welcome, Ny'laea." She extends her slender hand. "It's nice to..."

The blood drains from my head as I watch the look of shocked recognition spread across Olilly's features. I break into a cold sweat, my fate dropped into the palm of Olilly's hand.

Mora'lee gives us both a shrewd, searching look. "Do you two know each other, as well?"

Olilly nods, her gaze riveted on me. "Yes," she says as her face rearranges itself into a more neutral expression. "Do...do you remember me, Ny'laea?"

Thump, thump, thump goes my heart. "Yes, um...we were in Verpacia. I was working in the city. You were in the University kitchens, isn't that right?"

"That's right," Olilly says, nodding emphatically. "I'm... I'll be very happy to be working with you." She turns to Mora'lee and gives her a strained smile.

Mora'lee looks from me to Olilly and back to me again, one eyebrow cocked, clearly sensing the tension, but then she heaves a great sigh, her expression softening. "Well, then," she says, a trace of her smile returning as she turns to Olilly. "I trust you'll help Ny'laea get settled in while Nym and I bring some tea to her family?"

Olilly nods with forced enthusiasm. "Oh, I'd be happy to."

"Well, good," Mora'lee says, giving us all another encouraging, albeit curious, smile before departing with Nym'ellia, who throws me a brief look of immense gratitude before they slip into the kitchen. I look at Olilly, my pulse still hammering.

"Olilly," Bleddyn says in a low, beseeching tone.

Olilly reaches up and pulls the orchid from her hair. She sets the flower emphatically down in front of me, fierce gratitude blazing in her eyes. "I will *never* forget what you and Tierney did for us," she tells me in a coarse, emotional whisper. "My sister too. I will *never* forget that you helped us get out of there. *Never.*"

I reach over and grasp her hand, humbled by the intensity of her gratitude. "Thank you," I breathe out.

"Kir Lyyo!" the hateful man across the street barks, and Olilly flinches, pulling her hand from mine as she straightens. We all turn to find the teenage youth across the way staring in our direction. Staring besottedly at Olilly.

"Kirin, I'm speaking to you!" the man snaps.

Like a spell broken, the teen's head pivots to the angry man, Zosh Lyyo. Zosh Lyyo scowls at him as he waves exaggeratedly toward a table. "There are *customers*?" he growls.

Kir Lyyo nods, "Yes, Father." He sets back to work cleaning a table, but the moment his father is occupied pouring tea for a Noi couple, he looks back at Olilly, his mouth lifting into a shy smile, and I catch Olilly's returning bashful look that, unfortunately, does not escape the notice of Zosh Lyyo. He casts a scathing glare at us all just as Mora'lee and Nym'ellia emerge from the kitchen, a tea service in Mora's capable hands.

The sight of happy Mora'lee seems to set off an even fiercer conflagration of ire in Zosh Lyyo. "*Gardnerians* now?" his voice thunders from across the road.

Mora freezes in her tracks.

"Father," comes young Kir Lyyo's nervous protest.

Zosh Lyyo stalks out of his restaurant and right up to Mora's filigreed metal gate, his expression crackling with rage. "You're taking in *Roaches* now?" he demands, his pale tan eyes boring a hole into Mora'lee as outrage on Nym'ellia's behalf blasts through me.

Mora calmly sets the tea tray on a table and slips in front of Nym'ellia. She stares the man down, her silver eyes narrowing.

"Come with me," Olilly kindly offers Nym'ellia, who is frozen and looking at Zosh Lyyo with an expression of shock.

"Go," Mora says firmly to Olilly and Nym'ellia, pointing

toward the ship behind her without looking at them, her gaze pinned ferociously on Zosh Lyyo.

Olilly coaxes Nym'ellia into motion, and they disappear into the kitchen, ushering the little blue-hued Urisk girl inside with them, the child's eyes wide with fear.

Mora'lee strides up to Zosh Lyyo, and I can practically feel the sparks igniting on the air. *"Get. Away. From. My. Restaurant,"* she bites out, teeth bared, the patrons at both restaurants gone silent, even the street traffic seeming to pause.

"I'll be informing the conclave next that you're taking in Mages," Zosh Lyyo seethes at her, unfazed by Mora'lee's suddenly quite intimidating presence. "I'm sure they'll be interested in double-checking that the Crow's papers are in order."

"You do that," Mora'lee snipes back.

They turn and stomp off in opposite directions, leaving two trails of fury in their wake, and I think of the scattered signs I saw coming in here that echo the man's own—NOILAAN FOR THE NOI. I look at Bleddyn, serious concern for Nym'ellia rising.

"Pay no mind to the ass across the street," Bleddyn whispers as she cuts him a resentful glare. "Jules's identity papers are, forgive the expression, iron-proof."

A look of quiet intensity passes between us, fully acknowledging the close call I just survived. My temples tight from stress, I glance distractedly down at the food.

"Eat," Bleddyn prods. "We need you hale and hearty."

Knowing I should feign calm, I pick up one of the unfamiliar V-shaped utensils that must be the Smaragdalfar way of eating things. "Bleddyn," I say as I poke at the black, wormlike things in my bowl, glad for the diversion. "What exactly is this?"

"Nu'duls. Made from rice. They're like long bread." She points to the crab-leg-ish thing and the circular eggs floating on top of the nu'duls. "And steamed cave spider legs and eggs."

"Oh, no," I protest with a shake of my head.

Bleddyn impales an egg and pops it into her mouth. "I thought you took down a few scorpios?" she challenges in a whisper. "And a kraken? You're the Great Witch of Prophecy and you're afraid of...*food*?"

I stare at her, the immensity of my situation rushing through me anew as the trees send out their continuous buzz of noxious ire. Before I can think too closely on it, I pop a spider egg into my mouth, surprised by its rich, briny taste. "All right," I concede, digging in, "it's good."

Bleddyn's mouth slants up as she sets to eating her own food.

"How's little Fern?" I ask, forcing conversation as we settle into the disorienting but necessary ruse of a companionable Eastern Realm meal. I have wondered, many times over the past few months, how Fernyllia Hawthorne's granddaughter from the university kitchens is faring. I remember how Fernyllia charged Bleddyn and Iris with getting Fern to the East and keeping her safe.

A twinge of pain breaks through me as I also remember how heroic Fernyllia gave her life so that so many could escape to the East, including my brothers and Diana and Jarod. And how her actions, posing as the university poisoner, sheltered both me and Tierney.

"Fern's living in the Eastern Sublands," Bleddyn says, growing somber. "Sagellyn Gaffney and Ra'Ven Za'Nor have adopted her."

My brow lifts in surprise as Bleddyn sighs and picks up her tea. "She misses Fernyllia," she says, giving me a level look. "But she's happy enough. And quite a bit safer." She narrows her gaze pensively at the restaurant across the street, its countless Noi flags flapping in the stiff breeze. "Fernyllia would be glad to see Fern here," she muses, voice tight with feeling. "Problems and all." She turns back to me, tears now sheening her emerald eyes, and I remember how close Bleddyn was to Fernyllia.

"Well, I think we should toast to Fernyllia, then," I say, raising my teacup a fraction. "I think... I think that she would have liked the idea of this." I motion between us. "You and me. Sitting here..."

"Getting ready to smash Vogel to bits by any means necessary?" Bleddyn cuts in, blowing out a rough laugh, her irreverent voice shot through with emotion.

I nod and smile a bit as grief tightens my throat. "Yeah. That. Together."

Bleddyn raises her tea. "To Fernyllia, then. In tribute..." Her words break off and she shakes her head and stops herself, even though it seems as if she could say a lot more.

We clink teacups, and Bleddyn roughly wipes away a tear, then takes a swig of tea. She gives me a narrow-eyed smile and raises her mug once more. "And to you, Ny'laea." She sets down her tea, picks up her Black Witch figurine and untwines the small hammer tied to it. Then she lays the figuring on its side, and I flinch as she brings the hammer roughly down on its head. My heartbeat quickens to see my own face, in miniature, rendered to wooden shards, revealing the prize hidden inside its hollow depths.

Bleddyn picks up the tiny pearlescent white-bird pendant that is gleaming in the wood dust. She hands it to me, glancing pointedly at my Black Witch figurine. "Best crack that witch's head open, Ny'laea. You're going to need all the luck you can get."

I glance down at the evil statue, then at my glamoured fastlines. *Soon,* I remind myself as an ache for Lukas rises. *Your magic will be freed in a matter of hours. Lie in wait for now and survive.*

Then, portal west. And fight your way back to Lukas.

Grimly resolved, I pick up my Black Witch figurine and untie the hammer.

WITCH FASTING

Lukas Grey

Shadow hive
One day prior to Xishlon

Elloren.

The name pulses in the back of his mind as Lukas watches Vogel stride toward his Shadow-barred cell, the desire to break free and find her an all-consuming blaze inside him. His focus sharpens on Vogel, hackles rising, dagger sharp, as he takes in Vogel's greatly altered attire—military blacks instead of the long dark tunic of a Mage Priest.

"Did they kick you out of the priesthood?" Lukas chides as Vogel stops just outside the cell's wavering bars, his multi-eyed raven perched on his shoulder, six gray-eyed Mage soldiers falling in behind him.

Vogel's mouth gives the trace of a lift. "I stepped down from my Holy Calling this morn."

Alarm darts through Lukas, but he forces a smile, his lip swollen from the latest beating. "So…the Magedom finally realized what an unholy beast you are?"

Something lethal flashes in Vogel's pale eyes, silvery hot. "Bind him," Vogel orders.

The Mages raise their wands as one and Lukas is hit by a blast of Shadow netting that knocks him to the ground, pinning him there, arms outstretched. Breathing hard, Lukas glares piercingly at Vogel.

Vogel steps straight through the cell's Shadow bars, then gracefully lowers himself to one knee beside Lukas. He tilts his head, contemplative. "There are other callings as true as the Blessed Priestdom."

"Unbind me and give me a wand," Lukas snarls. "And I'll show you mine."

Vogel's gaze narrows. "You tainted my Black Witch." He says it lightly enough, but Lukas can sense the proprietary spite in it.

"She's *my* Black Witch," Lukas snaps, baring teeth.

"She's the *Magedom's* Black Witch," Vogel snipes back. "And you turned her against her true calling." His expression turning eerily calm, he traces his Shadow Wand's tip over the fastlines on Lukas's palm. Lukas shivers at the invasive contact, an icy, unnatural sting chasing the Wand's touch. "And so, the Ancient One has called upon me to rectify this corruption." Vogel softly begins to sound out a disturbingly unfamiliar spell, and Lukas's fastlines tint to gray.

A sharp blade of fear strikes down Lukas's spine. "What are you doing?" He curses himself for revealing his desperation, a pleased look coming over Vogel's sharp visage.

"Continuing the process," Vogel answers as he continues to trace the fastlines. "I'm going to make her pure again."

Lukas's fear for Elloren explodes, his muscles tensing as he blows out a hard exhale, blasting every ounce of his magic's aura toward Vogel's Wand. His fastlines glow red, the smoke twining from Vogel's Wand flashing crimson before it blinks out of sight.

Wrath flashes in Vogel's eyes, silver-bright. He raises his Wand and points it at Lukas's chest.

Pain strafes through Lukas's lines as he's hit by a blast of Shadow, a guttural cry escaping his throat as his body spasms. Gray flashes across his vision and his resurgent alarm spikes.

"Oh, soon I'll have your mind," Vogel croons as he sets his Wand's tip back down on Lukas's fastlines as their red glow cools to gray. "Just as I'm beginning to access hers. I know you tried to warn her in a dream. After you tried to seduce her."

"Better keep me awake," Lukas hisses. "I'll do it again."

Vogel smiles faintly. "The only one in her dreams from now on will be *me*."

Lukas's fury detonates, every muscle rage-tight. "I will *kill* you if you touch her. And if I don't, she will. You don't know what you're dealing with."

"Oh, I know *exactly* what I'm dealing with," Vogel rejoins sharply. "She's cowering right now in the Eastern Realm. Hiding from both me and the Vu Trin heathens. Unable to access any of her power. But soon, very soon, she will be unbound. She's waiting for it." He smiles coldly. "And so am I." Vogel murmurs a spell as Lukas futilely strains to free his wand hand, Shadow smoke slithering all over his fastlines. "She has plans to track you through the fasting," Vogel notes as he traces the dark lines. "Fancies herself so in love with you." His eyes flick to Lukas. "You and the Icaral both."

Lukas glares at him, refusing to rise to the taunt. It guts him, to hear of Elloren's love for Yvan. But this jealousy...it's but an ember compared to what he feels for her.

Don't come after me, Elloren, he rages through the fastline connection. *He's setting you up.*

"I will break her," Vogel serenely continues as Lukas pictures himself shoving that Shadow Wand clear down Vogel's throat. "Then I will bind her and purify her."

Vogel murmurs another spell as he touches his Wand to the center of Lukas's palm.

Lukas groans, sweat breaking out over his back as slim Shadow trees rise up from the fastlines on both his palms, the sting agonizing as their roots punch into his veins, threads of dark smoke branching out.

Elloren... Lukas breathes, feeling as if he's being rolled into an abyss. His vision sputters, tinting a darker gray.

Vogel sheathes his Wand and holds his palms above the tree forms. An enraptured smile touches his lips as the undulating canopy brushes his skin. The smoky branches twine around his hands, his smile widening as Lukas sinks further into the Void, mentally calling Elloren's name over and over as the many-eyed bird watches and waits.

CHAPTER
FIVE

NIGHTMARE

Elloren Grey

Voloi, Noilaan
Eastern Realm
The night before Xishlon

The rune ship's kitchen is a purple Xishlon world.

A string of violet-flower-decorated runic orbs wash the cramped evening space in a lavender glow as I sprinkle luminous violet sugar crystals over the traditional heart-shaped cookies for tomorrow's festival, feeling tense and restless. *Busy yourself,* I urge. *Your allies will be here for you soon enough.*

Petals of iridescent purple flowers simmer in a large copper pot beside me to make more Xishlon rose tea, its floral scent heavy on the air, the steam glowing an ethereal lilac.

I anxiously glance out the sliver of open door that affords me a view of the ship's riverside deck and scan the pitch-dark Vo River for some sign of runic flight toward me. Turning, I peer out the window of the ship's starboard side, which is closed and locked for the night, searching for friends and family coming in on foot. Purple flower-and-heart-decorated runic orbs are strung across the main thoroughfare and hung from the violet-leafed Xishlon Plum and Mountain Pear trees, casting a soft lavender glow over the steady street traffic.

The clink of porcelain sounds on the port side deck and I turn toward it. Half of Mora'lee's slender frame is visible through the slice of open door as she pours herself tea, then leans against the walkway's railing as she sips it, a green leatherbound book in her hand. She seems lost in her thoughts, glowing violet steam rising from her cup, the effect full of a melancholy beauty against the dark of night.

Rubbing my weary eyes, I move to stir the floral tea as a sharp sting slashes over my hands. My fingers flinch open, the wooden spoon dropping from my hand as a dart of alarm shocks through me. I splay my palms out, silver sparks igniting against my vision, the sting burning through my glamoured fastlines with an impaling sizzle. Panicked, I flex my hands, the sensation abruptly diminishing then vanishing. *What magic is this?*

"Hello, Fee," Mora says, and I freeze, heart racing.

A familiar, deep male voice says something to Mora in what sounds like a Smaragdalfar dialect that my glamoured koi'lon rune doesn't translate completely. I can only parse out "evening" and "tea."

Anxiety spiking, I peer through the port side door's open slit and my stomach drops through the floor. Fyon Hawkyyn, my metallurgie professor from Verpax University, stands beside Mora, tall and straight and dressed in traditional green Subland Elf clothing.

With no way to flee, I remain frozen in place as Mora hands Professor Hawkkyn a cup of tea with an expression of great import, and he accepts it with a deep level of gravitas, his silver eyes intent on hers. Seeming frozen in anticipation, she watches as he takes a sip, the sharp lines of his face illuminated by the glowing violet steam. He sets down the cup, their gazes locked.

"That would be thirty cups of tea, Fyon," Mora says, sounding breathless as she raises the green book in her hand.

Professor Hawkkyn's eyes seem to ignite as he steps toward her, his voice suddenly thick with passion. "Mora'lee Starr'lyrion, I want to court you. I can't stop thinking about you. You consume my nights."

Mora'lee's eyes widen along with mine. "Heavens, Fee."

Great Ancient One on High, I marvel, surprise cutting through my urgency. *Severe, intensely private, and stridently reserved Professor Hawkkyn...is a blazing romantic.*

"I adore you, Mora." His voice is ragged, like a man tortured by fierce love for one-too-many sleepless nights. "I'd give anything to kiss you...to hold you in my arms."

Mora pulls in a long, shaky breath, a rueful tension in her voice when it comes. "Fyon, be clear on this before you say more. You live for the sublands. I live for the skies."

"I don't wish to take you away from any of the things you love," Professor Hawkkyn declares, maintaining a respectful distance, even though it seems as if he'd scoop her into his arms and carry her off if she'd allow it.

They regard each other for a charged moment as Mora leans into the deck's metal railing, her back to the sheer drop down the mountain's side.

"Have you no feelings for me, then, Mora?" Professor Hawkkyn asks softly, as if forcefully holding back his vast tide of emotion.

Mora goes very still. "You are the bravest man I have ever met, Fyon."

He waits, but is met with stoic silence, the air seeming to grow even more heated between them.

"Mora," Professor Hawkkyn breathes, "I know who you are. I want to court you."

Mora huffs out an emotional sound and a trembling smile takes hold. "Well, that's a relief, Fee. Because I can't stop thinking about what it would be like to kiss you."

Fyon Hawkkyn's silver eyes widen, his lips parting in evident astonishment. Then a wide smile forms on his mouth and he laughs.

He's quite handsome when he smiles, I realize. In the whole time he was my professor, I rarely saw him smile, and never like this. Mora hops onto the banister, her legs dangling as she levels her own broad, dazzling smile at him, her expression turning playful.

"So, may I take you to the gardens this eve?" Professor Hawkkyn asks, as if both dazed and overcome with elated emotion.

"No, Fee," she says, a sultry edge entering her voice. "Not tonight. I need to watch over the children. But you may take me there tomorrow night on Xishlon, when a first kiss is a special Xish'nir blessing."

Professor Hawkkyn swallows. "You'll kiss me then?"

"Oh, Fee," Mora says, lowering her voice to a more intimate register. "I will kiss you many, many times."

Another low laugh bursts from Professor Hawkkyn as he stands blinking at Mora'lee, his expression full of almost disbelieving awe.

"I *would* kiss you now, Mora," he offers, a tad breathlessly.

"That would be nice, Fee," she says. "But delayed pleasure can be so gratifying. And we're just in time for Vo's Xish'nir blessing. So, kiss me in the Voling Garden Wisteria grove tomorrow eve. We've been friends for so long." She shrugs, biting her lip as if in delicious anticipation. "Tomorrow night, we'll see if we have a taste for each other."

Professor Hawkkyn holds out his hand, and Mora'lee grows serious, almost shy, as she takes it. She slides off her perch, an intensity flaring in her eyes that matches his as Professor Hawkkyn gently lifts her hand, keeping his eyes on hers, and presses his lips to the back of it.

I draw back, abashed to be witnessing this private moment between them, even as I grapple with the possibility of Professor Hawkkyn finding me.

He won't come in here, I reassure myself. *Why would he? He didn't enter this way.*

"You should go, Fyon," Mora says softly. "Because if you stand here for too much longer, there's no way I'll be able to keep from kissing you. Come for me tomorrow after we close." A smile brightens her face, her playful ebullience returning as he releases her hand and she moves toward the ship's prow. She pauses, looking to him with heated affection. "Get some sleep, Fee. I need to check on my passengers. You don't need to moon over me so. I've always been sweet on you." Then she turns and strides off.

Professor Hawkkyn watches after her like a man stunned. A man who's braved both escaping the Alfsigroth Sublands and the Western Realm, having been through Ancient One knows what to get so many others here, only to find himself suddenly landed inside his most longed for dream. He looks around, blinking at it as if momentarily disoriented. Then strides right toward me.

I jump back, reflexively drawing my Ash'rion blade as the kitchen's door swings open and we both freeze. For a moment, we just stare at each other. He narrows his eyes severely, then curses vehemently under his breath in Smaragdalfarin.

"Hello, Professor Hawkkyn," I say, leveling the blade at him.

Eyes blazing, he flashes me a scathing look and opens his varg rune-marked palm.

The blade tears from my grasp and flies straight into his. Tightening his fist around it, he takes a confrontational step toward me. "What are you doing here on Mora's ship?"

"Hiding," I rasp, feeling like the ship's floor is imploding beneath me. I hold up a beseeching palm, pulse thundering. "Professor Hawkkyn," I force out beseechingly, "I'm here to fight with the East. Vogel can destroy runes."

His face tenses with apparent surprise. *"Clarify,"* he demands, and I can sense I've secured his attention.

"Vogel has a weapon...a Shadow Wand. He'll be able to strike down Noilaan's protective dome with its magic. And render the Vu Trin's weapons useless. Varg runes, like the ones you can make, might be one of the few things that can stop him."

I watch as the blow fully connects.

"How do you know this?" he demands.

I launch into my impassioned defense, relaying Vogel's attack in the desert, my escape through Chi Nam's portal. The power of the Shadow Wand.

"Chi Nam is dead?" he says, clearly stunned.

I nod, tensing against the upsurge of distress.

He snarls out another series of Smaragdalfar epithets, then meets my gaze once more, silver eyes ablaze. "I won't turn you in, Elloren," he says. "But you *cannot* shelter here. They're looking for you."

A cornered defiance rises. *"They* meaning everyone? In the entire Western and Eastern Realms? Yeah. I'm kind of aware of that."

We stare at each other.

"You're truly the Black Witch," he marvels.

I sigh. *Well, I've certainly thrown an enormous wrench into his fantastical evening.*

"Actually, I'm worse than she ever was. Much worse. But I can't control my power. The trees have bound it. So, they're trying to figure out what to do about that."

"They?"

"The Resistance. Well, the small part of it that doesn't want me destroyed. It's a very small part. Family, mostly."

His mouth tightens. "Does Mora know who you are?"

I stiffen. "No."

Anger flashes across his angular face. "Have you gotten in touch with Jules Kristian?"

I shake my head. "Indirectly. My allies are going to come for me as soon as they can."

"We need to shelter you somewhere else," he insists. "You can't be here. Endangering Mora like this."

"Why am I in danger, Fee?"

We both flinch and turn as the door pushes open.

Mora is standing in the doorway, her gaze set on us with steely expectation, and when the question comes, the light, whimsical Mora is gone. "Tell me what's going on."

"So, I have the Black Witch on my ship." Mora's tone is hard with the full ramifications of this. With the full ramifications of *me*.

A tense silence falls over the kitchen, both doors firmly shut now. Professor Hawkkyn is leaning against a counter, his long arms crossed, his face severe. Mora sits at the prep table opposite me, her gaze on me as fierce as Professor Hawkkyn's. I'm struck by how formidable the two of them are.

"Vogel can break military runes," Mora'lee says, more a dread-laced, awful statement than a question.

I nod at her, feeling the ominous weight of this.

Professor Hawkkyn glances at Mora. "By bringing this information here, Elloren might have saved the entire Eastern Realm. They've just enough time to strengthen their runic border and weapons with varg shielding before Vogel's forces arrive."

Mora's furious glare on me hasn't budged. "Bleddyn should have told me what you are. You should have told me, as well."

My own voice is tight with remorse when it comes. "She thought it safer for you not to know—"

"*No*," she cuts me off sharply. "You both should have told me. There are children here."

I nod, chastened. "You're right. I'm sorry."

"There are children throughout this entire realm," Professor Hawkkyn gently reminds her.

She holds his stare, then turns back to me, as if caught partway between outrage and indecision. "You aided Nym'ellia's sister and her mother too. You helped get Olilly and her sister out of Verpacia. Bleddyn too."

My breathing is suspended as she carefully takes my measure. "I did," I agree.

She gives me a shrewd look. "I'll help you in turn, Elloren Gardner Grey. It seems you've proven your loyalty to our side, regardless of the prophecies being read about you."

"The prophecies are prejudiced," I insist, ire at the Forest rising. "They're all based on tree divination, and the trees hate me."

Both Mora and Professor Hawkkyn cock a brow at this.

"I'm going to find Jules," Professor Hawkkyn says to Mora. "She does need to be relocated."

"She's likely safe for the moment with that glamour," Mora points out.

"For the moment," he cautions, as if by *moment* he means *second*. Or split second.

Mora nods, then looks back at me. "Go to the bedroom I gave you and stay there. We'll come for you."

I scan the river from the bedroom's circular window, the small room softly green-lit by a single Smaragdalfar rune lamp and the varg wards marking the walls. Perched on the slim bed abutting the outer wall, I lean into the window, my cheek to its warm glass, and wait, my thoughts repeatedly circling back to Lukas then Yvan with a dual yearning that's impossible to fully suppress. Both of them out there, somewhere...

Exhaustion blurs the river's spots of rune-ship light, the emotions surrounding my feelings for the two of them impossible to navigate, capsizing me again and again. Minutes pass, bleeding into what feels like hours, my eyelids fluttering and soon closing as the conflict and longing fragment into exhaustion and I fade to sleep.

At first, everything is a dense, blessed black. But then the black gives way to an infiltrating gray mist that morphs and twists into tendrils of Shadow. I'm standing in it, fingers of gray rising to twine around my legs and weapons. Around my *Wand*.

A figure emerges from the wraithlike gloom. A hooded man,

his head tipped down and darkened by the fog. He slowly lifts his head, and Vogel's pale green eyes meet mine.

I recoil, fear knifing down my spine.

Vogel's mouth lifts in a serpentine grin and I watch, frozen in horror, as an additional eye appears on his forehead, then on his temple, then on his cheek, one eye after another, until his entire head and neck are nothing but a grotesque mass of eyes and a grinning mouth.

He opens his lips, teeth elongating, and lunges for me.

I cry out as I bolt awake and yank my cheek from the window, fire roaring through my tangled lines as my Wand vibrates urgently against my calf, my hands stinging like someone dragged a knife over my fastlines.

I glance down and fright lances through me. My fastlines are visible and no longer black. They're made of twisting smoke, twining through the glamour like steam.

I let out a strangled gasp. "No... Ancient One, help me..."

The smoke abruptly vanishes, along with the pain, but the scalding heat roaring through my lines intensifies, flashing gold against my vision and sweeping me into its blaze. I immediately recognize the unique golden quality of this burgeoning flame as I'm overtaken by a want so vast I feel as if it will burst through my ribs.

Wyvernfire.

And there's nothing vague about it. No sensation of vast distance to temper this fire. It's blasting toward me like a furnace from the direct north and as familiar to me as my own heart, my own lines. *Yvan's fire bond. Sweet Ancient One.*

A light-headed swoop rushes through me.

He's alive.

And he's found me.

CHAPTER SIX

WYVERNFIRE

Elloren Grey

Voloi, Noilaan
Eastern Realm
The night before Xishlon

I rush out of the bedroom, Wyvernfire scorching through my lines.

Yvan's fire. Close range.

He's alive, he's alive sounds out with every beat of my heart.

Hugging the ship's shadows, I round its prow, the fire aura twining around and through me like a molten lasso, stronger than anything I've ever felt from Yvan before, even during his most passionate kisses.

"Where is the Elfhollen woman?"

I skid to a halt in response to the woman's commanding voice, my gaze jerking toward the clutch of Vu Trin soldiers standing just across the street with the restauranteur Zosh Lyyo. Breathless from Yvan's all-encompassing heat, I slink toward them under the plum trees' dark cover, the trees' ire instantly ramping up.

Black Witch!

"There," Zosh Lyyo angrily jabs a finger toward Mora's rune ship. "There's a Mage girl there too—a bastard with Urisk blood. Mother whored herself out to the Crows."

"The Elfhollen woman you reported," the soldier presses, pointedly ignoring the rest, "when did she come? We've launched a citywide search for her."

My pulse jumps into a more violent rhythm, my mind racing with the implications as the fire pull from the north intensifies.

"Showed up this morning," Zosh Lyyo growls. "Brought by a Vu Trin. A green Urisk woman, not Noi." He gives the three severe-faced soldiers a knowing, vindicated look.

"Is the Elfhollen woman still there?"

He nods enthusiastically. "Been there all day. Bastard Mage girl too."

My palm instinctively reaches for my Ash'rion blade. These soldiers...they wouldn't be looking for a single Elfhollen in a city awash in Western Realm refugees if they didn't suspect *exactly* what I am.

Yvan's fire burns hotter, my vision lighting up gold as the feral will to live and fight and get to that fire seizes tighter hold. I slink over Mora's low fence, keeping to the street's darkest shadows as the Vu Trin booms out, "Halt!"

My pulse skyrockets and I break into a sprint, throwing myself into the Sixth Tier pedestrian and foot traffic, desperate not only to escape, but to lead them far away from Mora and the others aboard her ship. Swerving around pedestrians and carts loaded with purple wares, I dive toward every crowded spot, following the fire's pull north as the sorceresses' cries of "Make way!" go up.

Blazing with incoming aura-heat, I hurl myself into a crowded side street, rows of purple-glowing runic orbs strung across it like haphazardly thrown up necklaces, everything cast in their otherworldly purple glow. I launch into a faster sprint, racing down purple-rune-orb-lit street after street, dodging carts and pedestrians as hostile pear and plum trees vibrate their venom and the Vu Trin cries fade into the distance.

Every sense afire, I slow to a brisk walk as I dart around a knot of young people already turned out in Xishlon finery. They eye me curiously as I rush past, their clothing emblazoned with glowing purple moons and hearts, their faces decorated with iridescent lavender shimmer.

Catching my breath, I zigzag through narrow streets and dark alleys toward the pull of the mounting heat, sweat breaking out all over my skin from its increasing potency. Eventually, I emerge from a shadowed alley onto a broad cliffside street.

And come to an immediate halt.

A clutch of soldiers stands before me, idling near a runic roadblock. Suspended, wheel-size blue-glowing runes stretch out in a line just past them, the sorceresses' faces obscured by both the light behind them and their cloaks' dark hoods. One of the soldiers raises a piece of blue lumenstone and angles the bright shard toward me, casting us both in its glow.

Every muscle in my fire-suffused body tightens as I meet the falcon stare of Quoi Zhon—one of the soldiers I traveled with to the Agolith Desert.

One of the Vu Trin soldiers who tried to kill me.

Time warps as Quoi Zhon's piercing stare sharpens and the remembrance mushrooms into a full-blown reckoning—*If she recognizes you through the glamour, you're dead. Quietly turn and leave. Just turn and leave.*

Pulse blasting, I slowly pivot on my heels, lower my head and start a measured retreat, praying that her memory fails to connect.

"Halt!" her dominant voice booms out.

The word is an arrow shot to my back. I launch into a sprint, throwing myself into the next alley as her cry of *"Black Witch!"* goes up. Multiple boot heels give chase, my feet skidding against cobbled stone. I race forward, barely able to think around the dash of my heart against my rib cage and the intensifying firelight aura veiling my vision. Drawing on Lukas's and Valasca's training, I wrest hold of my Ash'rion blade and slide my fingers across the hilt's air runes, hastily murmuring a runic spell.

A shiver of cold hits my back. I turn and skid onto a narrow street to my left just as a whistling *whir* sounds behind me. Not slowing, I glance over my shoulder and spot countless frost-knives scything through the air behind me, along with bright streaks of silver stars.

Panic firing, I hurl myself into another alley, the stars and knives crashing and clanking against a wall to my rear as my stomach gives a nauseating twist.

The alley I've ducked into is far too long. I can't outpace them to its end.

The metallic tang of rune magic behind me powers up. I can taste it on the back of my tongue. The panicked stampede of my pulse threatens to overwhelm me as Yvan's Wyvernfire sears through my lines.

Fight them, I can almost hear Lukas and Valasca growling out at me. *You can't outrun them, so stand and fight!*

Some animal nerve deep inside me springs to life. Shoving my fear aside, I grit my teeth, whip around, and draw back my arm, the translucent green aim tracks from the Wand forming in my Wyvernfire-streaked vision. With a snarl, I hurl my arm forward and release my Ash'rion blade.

A huge gust of silver-glowing wind blasts from the blade and collides with the soldiers, scattering their raised weapons as they grunt from its force, blown against the building behind them so hard they crumple to the ground.

My breath stuttering in amazement, I curl my fingers into my palm's glamoured retrieval rune, and the Ash'rion soars through the alley, back into my hand. I pivot, ready to race away, but freeze as I take in the much larger contingent of soldiers closing in on the alley's other end.

"Stay where you are!" the lead soldier bellows.

I stumble backward as they launch themselves toward me,

unsheathing their swords with a terrifyingly uniform *screech*, the Wyvernfire in my lines surging to scorching heights. My skin slick with sweat, I fumble to read their magic and prepare a counterstrike as they fire up a multitude of elemental power.

Too much power.

As I realize, with debilitating certainty, that this is the end.

The *whoosh* of powerful wings sounds above.

My gaze snaps up, a ferocious blast of Wyvernfire aura searing down, intensely bright. Shock ignites as an Icaral swoops in and lands with his back to me, black horns arcing up from crimson hair, dark wings unfurled. He's shirtless and spectacularly muscular, his skin covered in glowing sapphire and emerald runes.

Ancient One...

Fire leaps through my vision, obscuring his form as he pushes both of his palms out to his sides and circles them in the air. A cyclonic spiral of fire flashes to life, blasting from his hands like two prone tornados of flame, smoke and wind churning around them.

He thrusts his palms out hard and the fire-tornados launch toward the Vu Trin at both alley ends, pummeling into their fire-shielded uniforms and driving them back with stunning impact. Forcing his palms out once more, he projects more flame to form two barriers of fire.

And then he turns.

Yvan's gold-blazing gaze locks on to mine as the full, dizzying rush of his fire bond grips hold of me.

"Yvan," I rasp as everything in the world but him and the fire burns away.

His eyes lighting to incandescence, he surges toward me, the heat of his fire bond turning cataclysmic as he sweeps me into his arms.

A cry escapes my throat as I'm consumed by the sensation of him—strong arms tight around me, his hot muscular back hard beneath my palms, the brush of his wings against my shoulders, his strong heartbeat against my chest, that familiar, bonfire scent of his skin.

"Grab tight hold of me!" he urges, and I thrill to the sound of Yvan's beloved voice resonating low in his chest, an ache of want scorching through me as flames leap in my vision.

He's going to fly us out, I realize through his overwhelming thrall.

I remember how hesitant I was the last time I needed him to carry me, unnerved by the scandalous, forbidden intimacy of wrapping my arms and legs around a young man I wasn't fasted to.

I show no such hesitation now.

I throw my arms around Yvan's shoulders as he slides his hot palms under my thighs, lifting me at the same time that I wrap my legs around his hips. Then he throws his wings powerfully down.

Launching us into the air.

We shoot upward with such velocity it steals my breath, the Sixth Tier falling away as the world tilts and Yvan blasts us north out of the city and over the river. We blaze through the air, his heartbeat pounding strong against mine, my cheek pressed to the hot skin of his neck, that smell of him, like a midnight fire, shearing through my heart. Tears sting my eyes as I hug him close, merging into his heat and remembering that he can scent my overwhelmed emotions.

He soars faster than a falcon's dive over the river, the mountains edging the Vo a blurred streak, the city's lights behind us now as hulking, moonlit mountains race past on either side.

Angling toward the peaks of the Voloi Mountain Range, he darts into a rocky depression, wings pivoting up. We rapidly slow, then land, his form bathed in silvery moonlight. He loosens his grip on me and my body slides down against his heated form.

Yvan's eyes flash a brighter gold as my feet touch down on stone and we stare at each other for a heated second, the air between us going taut with invisible, grasping flame.

"Elloren," he says, my name wrung from low in his throat as love for him breaks through me like a tide. He pulls me into a fervid embrace, my back connecting with the mountain's hard stone as we clutch each other close and he brings his mouth decidedly down onto mine.

Everything in me turns molten as our fires collide, the whole world alight with gold as his all-consuming Wyvernbond spirals through me, so fervently I can't think around it, his body rife with power.

I gasp and cling to him as the pure emotion in his flame sears through us both and we kiss like we'll merge straight into each other, my fingers knotting in his hair, my fire straining relentlessly toward his, the enormity of everything breaking free as we hold each other fiercely, kiss each other desperately.

A cry loosens from me as all the grief for him I've been suppressing ruptures free in one violent tide, my heart breaking clear open. Sobbing as he breaks the kiss, I grip his muscular arms, stunned anew to find him so staggeringly solid and real against me. He tucks his head against my shoulder, breathing hard, his neck hot against my cheek as I breathe in his Wyvern male scent and disbelievingly run my hands over his warm back, his taut arms and shoulders, the edges of his wings.

Alive.

I've the sense of being swept into an impossible dream, wave upon wave of grief eddying through me along with the overpowering blaze of his heightened fire.

"Elloren." His voice breaks as he breathes the word against the nape of my neck. His beautiful, deep voice. The voice I thought I'd never hear again. *"My love,"* he murmurs in ardent Lasair, breath hot on my skin. When he draws back, there are moonlight-glazed tears streaking his angular face, his fiery eyes full of emotion. He presses his full lips to my temple as he pulls in a wavering breath. *"My love,"* he says again in Lasair. "Elloren, my *love.*"

"I thought you were *dead*," I choke out as I cling to him. "They told me you were *dead*."

"Vogel almost killed me." His voice is ragged as he tenderly strokes my hair with a look of sheer wonderment, as if he can't quite believe I'm real. "He sent out an assassin who was secretly working with the Vu Trin. We let Mavrik...the assassin...attack me to the point where death seemed assured. To fool Vogel as well as both Realms. To buy me time to survive and train." He brings his forehead to mine, breathing hard, our arms looping more tightly around each other. "I healed myself," he manages. "My healing powers have grown along with my fire."

He draws back a fraction, his hands cupping the sides of my face, the enormity of this moment mirrored in the fervent blaze in his eyes.

A sob shuddering through my chest, I reach up to thread my fingers through his night-darkened scarlet hair, run my thumbs along the edges of his pointed ears. His defined cheekbones. The sides of his beloved angular face.

Yvan's voice is low and husky when it comes, his brow tightening with concern. "Elloren...what happened to your fire? It's *altered*. I can feel it when we kiss, but I can't grasp full hold of it."

I blink at him from inside our fiery daze, the world around starting to flow back in. "The trees attacked me," I manage, swallowing back the tears. "They bound up my power."

Yvan's eyes widen, the fire in them flaring. He angles his head down and presses his forehead to mine once more, the words pouring out of him. "Vang Troi told me you were likely dead. I knew it wasn't true—I would have sensed it. But... I didn't tell them." His fire surges to a whipping, torrid blaze as fury sparks in his eyes. "I could sense they'd come to see you as their enemy. And then... I started to feel your fire coming closer, but I wasn't able to *find* you. Even though I could sense you were in danger." The words continue to tumble out, torment and passion infused in them. "I sent fire out to you *constantly*. Trying to find you. And then, finally... I *felt* you."

"I have more power than the Vu Trin thought," I say as we cling to each other. "More than my grandmother had. The Vu Trin turned against me, and I had to escape."

And then... Lukas.

A hard ache rises in my throat as my feelings for Lukas crash through Yvan's fiery thrall, along with memories of everything I had to do to get here. To stay alive. To keep from being enslaved by Vogel. How Lukas gave up everything to save me.

How I bound myself to him in every way.

How I'm about to break Yvan's heart.

I'm suddenly lost in an abyss of emotion. Furious anger at the Vu Trin for lying about Yvan's death. Terrible remorse that I was with another man. Desperate, overwhelming relief to find Yvan alive. Fear of what's coming for the Eastern Realm. And the desperate yearning to find Lukas and save him.

How can I tell Yvan about Lukas? I agonize. *How will I ever let Yvan go?*

But I have to let him go.

Because even though I love him with a passion that's undimmed, I promised myself to Lukas. I *gave* myself to Lukas. And he gave himself to me. Fully.

And I love Lukas too.

"They glamoured you," Yvan marvels, caressing the side of my cheek with a gentleness that guts me, misery rising as our fire magic twines around us with an unquenchable longing that wrenches my heart anew.

I love you, Yvan. I love you so much.

But I'm bound to another.

"There are wanted postings with my face on them all over the city," I choke out, wanting to split myself in two. "And the Vu Trin aren't the only ones hunting me. Vogel is, as well. He knows I'm here. And he knows I'm glamoured."

Yvan's aura gives a violent flare. "We can't stay here." The troubled whirl of his fire mirrors my own, an expression of immense frustration tightening his jaw. "The Vu Trin will be searching for both of us." His fire stokes hotter, his eyes twin flames that quicken my pulse. "I won't let them take you, El-loren."

"We can't wage war on our allies," I counter. "I've a room on a varg-rune-warded air ship. In the center of the city's Sixth Tier. The Vu Trin…they knew I was there, but it's possible they won't check again right away."

"It might be the only place I can go without being tracked," he says. "They *will* track me down, Elloren. Quite soon."

"Do you think we can get there without being spotted?"

His glowing eyes narrow. "I do," he says. He pulls in a deep breath, his horns contracting, as his ears round and the luminous Noi runes and varg runes marking his chest fade under his partial glamour. "Hold on to me," he offers, and I nod, moving toward him.

He pulls me tight against his warm chest, a thrill coursing through my body as I'm lifted effortlessly, wrapped around his heated form once more. Carefully scanning the dark river and wall of mountains beyond, Yvan walks us to the cliff's edge. Then he throws out his wings…

And leaps off the cliff.

A queasy rush sweeps through me as we free-fall before his powerful wings beat down, lifting us into a controlled soar southward. He accelerates, keeping close to the Voloi Mountain Range's western face, the world quickly reduced to a speeding blur.

Flying under sparse cloud cover, we eventually veer up toward a broad, blue-lit rune ship then slow under its base, wrapped around each other inside the rune-encircled cavity.

The shimmering tiers of Voloi appear through gaps in the rotating runes and apprehension mounts, the city likely swarming with Vu Trin searching for us both.

The ship veers toward the Sixth Tier, and I spot Mora's rune ship, tiny from this distance, its line of green-glowing Smarag-dalfar runes unmistakable.

"There," I say, pointing.

Yvan takes off like a shot and the world blurs once more, everything a streaking tunnel around us. Our surroundings snap back into focus as Yvan lands us in the shadows of the ship's riverside walkway. My feet touch down on lacquered wood, the will to survive engulfing my fright.

We slip inside my small bedroom and I shut and lock the door behind us, douse Mora's rune lamp, and hastily draw the curtains as Yvan glamours his wings. I turn and meet his gaze in the faint emerald light emanating from the varg runes marking the walls.

A shiver rushes through me as I hold his heated gaze for a suspended moment, his powerful fire aura coursing off his body in an increasingly fervent caress. He's distinctly more muscular than he was before. The hard planes of his face starker.

Less a student, more a warrior.

Like me.

Both of us irretrievably altered by what we've been through.

A rough pain seizes hold of my heart, raw and biting, as I remember who, along with Yvan, taught me to be strong and fight back.

Lukas.

I have to tell him about Lukas.

Emotion blazing in his eyes, Yvan closes the distance between us. He reaches up to caress the side of my face like I'm some precious thing. "I wanted you every day and every night," he says, voice rough with yearning.

My gut clenches as the impassioned love in his eyes shears through my heart.

"Yvan," I say, a quaver slipping into my voice. "I had to go back to Gardneria to survive the Vu Trin. And... I had to seek out Lukas Grey's protection."

His hand lowers to my shoulder as his fire shudders around me, through me. "I thought as much. I saw the wanted postings with your new name. I imagined it was some ruse."

I swallow, my stomach clenching hard as a vise. "It wasn't a ruse. We were Sealed."

Yvan stills as his head gives an almost imperceptible tilt, nostrils flaring, and I know he's scenting my roiling, agonized emotion.

"How Sealed?" he asks.

I swallow again, feeling like I'm about to launch into a sickening free fall. "Fully."

The blaze in his eyes intensifies, his gaze narrowing. "Did he force you?"

I can't answer him for a moment, and his fire gives a sudden, hard contraction inward, as if he's reading everything in my eyes and my fire as a rancid sweep of heartache and grief and guilt sears through me with such strength I feel as if I'll tear clear apart. And when it comes, his voice has an unmistakable edge to it.

"What happened, Elloren?"

"Vogel was closing in on me in Valgard," I force out in a shredded voice. "At the same time that the Vu Trin and Ishkart assassins were moving in. Lukas and I needed a diversion to get out."

I tell him of the Sealing ceremony. And the escape. Even though it rips my heart apart to do it.

I tell him everything.

Yvan is quiet for a long moment, his hand still clutching my shoulder as if frozen there, his fire now pulled into a tight, volcanic ball in his center, but his eyes burn. Remorse hollows me out as I take in the conflagration of pain in that gaze.

"Do you love him?" he asks tightly, his gaze searing.

I nod, devastated, as tears slide down my cheeks and I struggle to breathe. "Yvan," I choke out, "I thought you were *dead*. And when I Sealed to Lukas, I made a choice. To align myself with him and survive and keep my power out of Vogel's reach. I didn't expect to grow to care for Lukas too." Agony overtakes me as Valasca's words fill my mind.

You will lose important things. You will lose and lose and lose one thing after another.

You will likely lose every last thing that's precious to you.

"Yes," I admit. "I love him."

Yvan is quiet for an excruciating moment, and then I've the sense of his fire lashing out of his control, slashing clear through me and the walls of the room with complete devastation.

"Elloren." His voice breaks around the word, his eyes molten and tensing with such fury and pain and jealousy and love that it's almost too much to bear. "I *love* you," he says. "I will always love you." His lips tremble, the fire in his eyes turning white-hot. "You made a choice to survive and keep hold of your power. That's the choice I would have wanted you to make."

Tears stream down my face as I take in his ravaged expression and incandescent eyes. "I love you too," I tell him, breaking apart.

"I know you do." His mouth tightens and he looks away, his fire aura spitting out bright flares of pain. He gives me a poignant look, his lips trembling into a slight, bitter smile. "I can scent your emotions, Elloren. I know everything you're feeling." We're quiet again as his fire escapes his control to whip around me in a chaotic storm. His hand drops from my shoulder and he steps back, wings releasing, eyes glowing as his horns spiral up from his tousled hair and his pupils contract into vertical slits, the runes marked on his chest visible once more.

"I can't hold a glamour around you right now," he rasps out. "I just can't." His mouth twists with a misery so acute that it overrides my renewed shock at once more seeing him not only horned, but with Wyvern eyes.

"This was always bigger than us," I whisper, my own voice splintering.

Yvan nods and looks at the ceiling, neck arching. He rakes his fingers through his crimson hair, his face slick with tears, his wing tips brushing the walls of the cramped room.

I take in his otherworldly beauty. The way the rune light

makes the onyx feathers of his wings gleam. The hard planes of him.

My Icaral love.

Fresh tears come to my eyes and I struggle to swallow them back. "We're two points of all the prophecies of all the lands," I force out in a quavering voice. "This was bound to break our hearts."

And Lukas's heart too.

Yvan nods again, a devastated ferocity in his luminous eyes.

"Where did the Vu Trin bring you?" I ask.

He swallows and shakes his head, as if attempting to clear his mind of overwhelming anguish so he can answer me. "At first...to a Vu Trin base far north of here. And then, after Vogel attacked...to one of their subland military bases. In the northeast, past the mountains."

"I felt your fire coming from the northeast," I say, feeling constrained around him even as my fire aura rears and manages to break loose, rushing straight to him.

A flare of his own power wrests free to arc against mine, sizzling through me. I gasp from the all-encompassing heat of it, my vision flashing gold, our bond's draw an agony to resist. I want to fling myself at him. I want to embrace him and merge our fires completely.

But, in this, I have to let him go.

"Yvan," I say, my voice and fire shot with contrition and impossible want, "I'm sorry..."

He gives me a blazingly impassioned look. And then, he's closing the distance between us, his arms coming tight around me as I grasp hold of him and cry. We cling to each other, and he reaches up to stroke my hair.

He brings his forehead to mine, but doesn't move to kiss me, even though his fire shows no such hesitation, the sear of his heat suffusing my lips and coursing over my skin in a heady rush. My palm is curved over the hot skin of his waist, my other hand wrapped over his shoulder, but I don't pull him closer. Because

I can feel it in our joint fire—we're both clear that we need to let this go.

Yvan brings his hand to my cheek, and I feel the surprising, light brush of claws, his voice throaty when it comes. "I will always be your ally."

I nod. "I know it. I know you are." *My love. My beautiful, winged love.*

"Tell me," he says, his expression gaining a determined edge that strikes me as heartbreakingly heroic, which only shatters my heart anew. "Tell me everything you know about Vogel and your power."

We talk deeper into the night, Yvan's Wyvern senses primed to detect any approaching threats, and I'm filled with the sense of falling back in with my closest friend as I tell him everything. Yvan's arms and wings stay loosely around me as we talk, the both of us having given up on restraining our fire, which refuses to obey any moral lines as we embrace each other with our power more heatedly than we should. More heatedly than we ever will physically again.

"You took down three scorpios, four wraith bats, and a kraken?" he says with no small measure of surprise, his finger tracing a light arc on my arm, his touch trailing hot sparks.

"I did." That familiar yearning for Lukas and Valasca and Chi Nam rises.

"Well done," Yvan says with a slight smile that prompts another fierce upsweep of emotion. I return his rueful smile, overcome by how beautiful he looks in this moment.

And then we're not smiling.

"Elloren…" Yvan says, low and throaty, a conflicting spark of desire racing through our joint fire, the air between us growing combustible.

His nostrils suddenly flare, his head jerking toward the door.

"What is it?" I ask, my heartbeat kicking up as I reach for my blade.

With astonishingly fast reflexes, Yvan turns, raises his hand, and bursts a bright ball of fire to life just above it, ready to be hurled at the door as its lock clicks back and it opens.

A cloaked Jules Kristian stands in the doorway's frame along with Lucretia Quillen, her purple wand in hand, along with Mora'lee and Professor Hawkkyn, who has a Smaragdalfar crossbow and quiver strapped to his back. Behind them, Commander Kam Vin stands on a small hovering rune skiff docked against our ship's walkway, her sister, Ni Vin, piloting the craft's runic controls, the sisters cloaked and garbed in their black military uniforms. Both are fully armed with runic swords and star weapons. A black scarf is knotted around Ni Vin's head under her cloak's hood.

Urgency crackles through me as Yvan pulls the ball of fire back into his hand and lowers his arm, his volcanic aura whipping protectively around me.

Mora's silver eyes have gone wide and are fixed on Yvan and his outstretched wings, horns, and fiery eyes. "Are you who I think you are?" she gasps.

"This is Yvan Guryev," comes Jules Kristian's coolly measured reply. "Blessedly alive, it would seem. And you've already met Elloren Grey." He gives both Yvan and me a warm, conspiratorial smile. "Mora, you're looking at the Prophecy."

CHAPTER SEVEN

FLIGHT

Elloren Grey

Voloi, Noilaan
Eastern Realm
The night before Xishlon

"Glamour yourself and throw this on," Jules Kristian says to Yvan from the rune ship's riverside walkway as he unfastens his woolen cloak and passes it over.

"You as well, Elloren," Kam Vin stonily insists from where she and Ni Vin stand near the controls of the hovering rune skiff. She draws off her black cloak and tosses it to me. "It seems the entire Vu Trin force is now alerted to the presence of the Prophecy descended on the Eastern Realm. Luckily for you they saw you fly off to the north and have focused the search in that direction for the moment."

"Hurry," Ni Vin urges.

"Do you have the Zhilin Wand?" Kam Vin probes as I throw on her cloak.

"I do," I assure her, its spiraling handle pressed against my calf.

She nods stiffly and levels a knifing glare at Yvan, gesturing toward the Noi runes marking his chest. "The Vu Trin will have you tracked through those iron-shielding runes within the hour if we don't get you to a more powerfully warded location. They've sent out an elite tracking dragon."

Yvan's mouth lifts into a surprisingly feral snarl. We share a loaded glance, the gold in his eyes blazing hotter.

He closes his eyes and stiffens, every one of his corded muscles going taut as he draws his wings into a tattooed impression, his horns pulling into his head. He throws on the cloak and pulls in a hard breath, morphing his hair brown and rounding his pointed ears and pupils, the runes on his chest disappearing. His eyes meet mine and a rush of heat courses through us both as we hastily exit the cramped bedroom and board the skiff along with Lucretia and Jules, Mora'lee and Professor Hawkkyn remaining behind.

I take a seat on one of the two benches siding the skiff, Yvan and I keeping our cloaked heads lowered, his warm side pressed to mine.

Ni Vin pilots the skiff into motion as Kam Vin and Lucretia scan the skies, the city's air traffic blessedly dense. I glance over my shoulder at Mora and Professor Hawkkyn, their figures already tiny as they watch us speed away.

"Do you think the Vu Trin will assume Yvan and I have fled the city?" I ask Kam Vin.

She nods. "But the tracking dragon is a serious danger. There's word he's picked up your scent from an alley you were both in. He'll be difficult to evade."

"We're too exposed," I note, the moonlit night too clear, only a smattering of clouds drifting low in the sky. My clutch of concern tightens as I spot four military rune skiffs suddenly converging on us, Yvan's fire aura powering up as he tenses beside me.

"Any moment now..." Kam Vin murmurs to herself as she scans the river's expanse, oddly unfocused on the threat bearing down.

A thick, patchy fog abruptly forms over the Vo's surface, wicking up toward us with unnatural speed. Ni Vin angles our skiff sharply down, dimming our skiff's rune lights as we soar into the gray then bank sharply right, my stomach lurching from the rapid change in direction as the incoming military skiffs are rendered to hazy streaks of blue light by the obscuring fog, rapidly disappearing in the distance.

Tension ripples through Yvan's fire aura as we exchange a wary look, the fog thickening as it consumes the world in a patchwork of moonlit clouds.

"Do you have a Zhilon'ile ally?" Yvan asks Kam Vin in a tone of amazement as we tunnel through the gray.

"Vothendrile Xanthile's work," Jules supplies, casting a shrewd look toward me. My thoughts fly to Trystan's love with no small amount of gratitude.

"Where are you taking us?" Yvan asks Jules, our dim space partly illuminated by his fiery eyes.

"To a strongly warded location in the sublands," Lucretia answers from Jules's side. "Where we can free up Elloren's magic." Her gaze sharpens on Yvan. "And buy you time so we can all plan the best way to negotiate an alliance between Elloren and the Vu Trin."

"Since there's a rather large Prophecy standing in the way of that," Jules archly notes.

Magic burns a rebellious path through the space between Yvan and me, its rush of heat sweeping through my body, and for a moment, I'm lost to it, pained memories surfacing of everything Yvan and I have been through together and what we were starting to be to each other in the West. Yvan's face colors, his fire shivering more intently around me as the fog thickens.

I look away, acutely aware of Yvan's warmth radiating through his clothes with the force of a smith's furnace, our power whipping around each other in seeking flares. A remembrance of Lukas's similarly embracing magic overtakes me and remorse unfurls, raw in my chest.

Kam Vin takes a seat by Lucretia as Ni Vin pilots us through the shifting clouds of fog, all of us silent and tense, a sliver of Lucretia's water power slipping loose to flow around Jules. I've the sense of our collective breath suspended as I fight off the powerful urge to grasp hold of Yvan's hand, the side of my finger touching the heated side of his as I'm overcome, anew, by the shock of having him so abruptly back in my life. *Alive.*

I catch Yvan's glance and know he's sensing my emotional whorl of fire.

He slides his warm hand over mine in what I can tell is an attempt at chaste support, but there's nothing restrained about the way his fire spirals up through our hands and over my skin, his heat so impassioned a flush sears through my cheeks, my pulse quickening.

He draws his hand from mine and we both look sharply away.

"Elloren," he breathes, a marked strain to his voice as his molten eyes find mine, his aura intensifying as it varnishes my skin with wanton flame. "I'm sorry," he murmurs. "I'm finding it difficult to contain the Wyvern draw. Since we're bonded—"

"Keep silent," Kam Vin whispers. "That search dragon could be within hearing range."

"I'd sense the dragon," Yvan says, nostrils flaring, and Kam Vin nods, her hand resting on the hilt of her rune sword.

The drifting clouds of fog break apart for a moment, and a lone blue speck catches my eye, skimming the river's surface then soaring up in our direction like a sky blue shooting star. It vanishes once more from sight as the patchy fog closes in around it.

Yvan grips a firmer hold of my hand before I can sound an alarm, his entire body tensing, his fire power surging as he lets out a sibilant hiss. My eyes widen at the chilling reptilian sound. He's abruptly a whole other being, his face lethally severe, his flaming eyes riveted on the fog below as it shifts and the blue speck is briefly visible once more, elongated and much nearer.

Fear seizes hold. *It's a dragon. Flying straight toward us.*

It's found us.

My heart stutters as fog obscures the blue dragon again and I reach for my rune blade.

Yvan's fire magic snaps in tight and begins to spark with a ferocity so hot and violent its radiating aura takes my breath away. He releases my hand as he, Kam Vin, and Lucretia calmly rise and Lucretia begins to murmur spells, water power swelling on the air. I rise alongside them, drawing my Ash'rion and powering up ice magic to combat Wyvern power.

The fog-clouds shift and the dragon emerges into view, and I realize with a bolt of alarm that it might be as big as Naga.

Bigger.

Yvan throws off his cloak in one smooth movement, his lips lifting in a vicious snarl as his fingers flex, his dark horns arcing up from his hair, his hands taking on a molten glow, brightest at his fingertips, dark claws forming. "He has his sights set on Elloren," he growls as the dragon begins a rapid swoop toward us, its sides marked with glowing Noi runes.

"Can you best him?" Kam Vin asks Yvan as she draws her swords with a smooth, metallic scrape.

"I can," Yvan seethes as his wings accordion out from their tattoo impression to their full breadth. "I'm going to drive him off." He brings a foot to the skiff's rail and contracts his wings inward.

Black Witch.

The words hit my mind along with a flash of vermilion fire. Realization ignites as the familiar red flame flashes brighter, purple sparking in it—this isn't a blue dragon at all, but a rune-marked white one.

Alarm punches through me.

"Stop!" I cry, lurching forward to grab hold of Yvan's arm before he can launch his lethal self at Raz'zor, my gaze flying to Kam Vin and Ni Vin and Lucretia. "Draw down your weapons! I know this dragon! He's pledged fealty to me!"

Yvan's head whips toward me, fast as a blur, astonishment strafing through his power. *"This* is the goat-size dragon?"

"It is," I say, amazed by Raz'zor's enormous size.

Raz'zor breaks through the fog, soaring up until he's flying beside us, the sight of my horde-kin kicking up a euphoria deep in my chest. He's like moonlight taken form, his huge, gleaming ivory-scaled body tinted blue from the countless Noi runes marked on his sides, a small purple rune emblazoned on the base of his neck. His powerful muscles beat broad, pale wings in a rhythmic *whoosh* as I marvel at our sudden reunion.

Death to Vogel, Raz'zor sends into my mind as red and purple fire sparks through my lines, and a heady relief sweeps through me. I move toward him, right up to the skiff's edge.

Raz'zor, I send out to him. *Are you the dragon the Vu Trin sent out to search for me?*

A lash of angry fire. *To scent and to capture. But they do not know that you have my fealty.*

Another wave of relief breaks over this blessed stroke of improbable luck.

They got the runic band off you, I marvel, the throat-band that kept him small as a lamb now absent.

Or'myr Syll'vir, friend to Dragonkin, broke my bonds, he sounds out in my mind, and I'm stunned to hear his mention of my cousin. *My fire has been fully unleashed as well, and strengthened with his purple flame. And now I will fight with you and together we will render the Gardnerians' flesh to ash and consume their bones.*

"Elloren," Yvan says, his hand coming to the small of my back. "Do you have a mind connection with this dragon?"

"I do," I reply, meeting his questioning gaze. "We're a horde."

An incredulous laugh bursts from Jules and I turn toward him. "You never cease to be full of surprises," he notes, his bespectacled gaze studying me with lively amusement.

"How ever did you manage to secure a Vish'nile dragon's fealty?" Kam Vin demands, clearly thrown. "That can take *years*."

I spare her a glance. "I think we skipped a few formalities because of some *serious* time constraints—" I break off, distracted by the reddened fire magic that's now combining with my own to whip through my lines along with Yvan's golden flame.

Yvan's fire intensifies, lashing through me and around Raz'zor's streaming fire. All the combined Wyvernfire sparks saffron and purple in my vision, and I can feel Yvan gauging Raz'zor's strength in it.

Raz'zor raises his head, sniffs the air, and narrows his slitted, red-burning eye at Yvan.

Dragonkin, he thinks to me, his eye pinned on Yvan. *Your bonded mate. He is powerful.* His crimson eye pivots to me, and I can feel the shiver of discord in his power. *He wants you, Witchling. Yet you are bound to another.*

Yvan hisses something at Raz'zor in a deeply sibilant language, and Raz'zor snarls something back. I stare at them both in amazement as they hiss out phrases, back and forth, their fires swirling around each other with the energy of sudden, fierce alliance as I realize that Yvan can speak not only Lasair but also *Dragon.*

"What are you saying?" I ask Yvan.

His golden eyes slide to mine. "I thanked him for saving your life, Elloren."

My chest tightens in response to the impassioned look he's giving me, time winding back to when Yvan first kissed me, joining us as Wyvern mates. A kiss seared into me. I remember it like it was a moment ago. The feel of his lips. That first, intimate touch of his fire…

"Do you have any other dragons under your dominion?" Kam Vin asks, breaking through my momentary thrall.

"My dominion?" I look to her, both flustered and surprised. "Like an army?"

I can feel Raz'zor's smile. *Yes, Black Witch. Like an army.*

I search my red-fire bond to Raz'zor, no other dragon's fire horded to ours. *Have you found Naga?* I press.

Raz'zor's ruddy fire flares with tight, bristling sparks. *Not as of yet*, he thinks, rebellion firing. *But Naga the Unbroken will return in glory to cast her fiery justice over all of Erthia.*

"Raz'zor and I are a horde of two," I answer Kam Vin as we speed north, so much gold and purple-sparking red fire blazing through me it's hard to think. Hard to hold any thought around Yvan's mounting thrall, his fire clearly the more explosively powerful of the two.

And Raz'zor's is powerful.

"This dragon cannot continue on with us," Kam Vin insists. "By lingering he'll eventually draw the Vu Trin straight to you."

Raz'zor's power surges resentfully and he shoots Kam Vin a ruddy glare.

"Reunite with each other after Elloren is in control of her power," Jules suggests to both Raz'zor and me with his usual calm diplomacy.

A surprisingly strong reluctance to be separated from my horde surges to life, my tangled fire giving a chaotic flare, but I press it down, mindful of the validity of Kam Vin's concern.

She's right, I think to Raz'zor. *Lead the Vu Trin away from me. I'll summon you when I've come into my power. And we'll fight Vogel together.*

Images of Gardnerian soldiers being incinerated by bolts of red Wyvernfire are suddenly flashing through my mind.

Call my name and I will come, Raz'zor snarls into my thoughts with the force of a vow. *Friend to Naga the Unbroken.*

Soon, Raz'zor, I assure him. *Soon.*

Death to Vogel, he sends out to me as he veers away from our skiff.

Death to Vogel, I return, just as emphatic.

Raz'zor sends out one final hard lash of purple-streaked vermilion fire straight through my lines, and then he's soaring away from us in a sweeping arc, speeding south in the direction of the Wyvernguard.

We're all quiet as we watch him wing away, Yvan's protective fire flickering through my lines, his gaze fixed on Raz'zor as he disappears into the fog. Yvan steps back and flexes his shoulders, draws in his wings, and retracts his horns and claws, restoring his glamour, save for his golden gaze. He flashes me a luminous look as he pulls his cloak over his muscular form. His body flexes, snagging my focus, a different type of heat sparking through our bond that I'm devastatingly unable to tamp down.

Yvan's eyes flick back to mine, a glint of recognition in them. I look away, my face heating as a rush of his fire shivers through me, conflict rearing its impossible head.

He sits back down beside me, shoulder to shoulder, and I can sense him struggling to regain hold of his fire just as intently as I am. But it's no use. Our undimmed bond is too strong to resist.

"You've become…more of a dragon," I stiltedly note, hesitant to meet his eyes as our history together courses through me in a heart-stricken tide.

A larger flare of Yvan's fire encircles me and I suppress the urge to lean into him. "I have," he stiffly agrees.

"Your hands," I say as I glance at the one he's resting on his thigh, fighting the aching desire to take hold of it. "I was…surprised when they turned bright gold. And…you've claws. And horns…" The desire to see him shift again is suddenly warming my firelines. I want to embrace him as a shifter, to run my fingers back through his crimson hair and grab tight hold of his horns, to feel those claws tracing over my skin…

I look away, thrown by the rise of such tortured longing, my chest tightening against it. "I'm sorry," I tell him as my fire aura brazenly sweeps over his skin. "Our fire draw…"

"You can't help it," he says roughly. "I can't help it either. It's our Wyvernbond. I think it's quickened along with my power." He pauses, voice strained. "I'm sorry, as well."

"You best hold on," Ni Vin directs, her voice piercing through Yvan's and my private, agonized haze as our skiff's runes light and the vessel tilts sharply down. She brings the skiff to a smooth landing on the water, the dimmed side runes churning through the river to drive us forward.

We stream into a sheltered rocky cove, then drift into a cave, its dark, glimmering walls closing in around us. Eventually, we reach a barrier made of solid-black opal, its bottom edge bridging the water streaming underneath it. Ni Vin pilots the skiff close to a prominent ledge, and Kam Vin hops onto it, striding to the opal wall. She reaches into her tunic's pocket and pulls out a rune stone marked with a single, emerald rune, then presses it to the wall.

Bright green Smaragdalfar varg runes appear all over the wall's surface in multiple, whirling circles before the opalescent wall vanishes. And there on the ledge, just past where the wall once stood, two figures stand before a heavily varg rune–lit cavern.

My heart leaps in my chest as I let out a sound of surprise.

Sagellyn Gaffney meets my gaze with an emotional look of recognition, her violet form resplendent in purple garb. She's holding a lavender wand aloft, a small orb of lilac light hovering above its tip, her arm looped through that of the tall, young Smaragdalfar man by her side.

CHAPTER EIGHT

OPAL SUBLANDS

Elloren Grey

Eastern Sublands
Eastern Realm
The night before Xishlon

"Elloren!" Sage calls from the black opal ledge. Her purple face is tense, and the expression of the man beside her—the man who I imagine is her Smaragdalfar love, Ra'Ven Za'Nor—mirrors her intensity. An awareness rises of the gray Elfhollen glamour cast over me by my Smaragdalfar runic necklace—the very same necklace once worn by Ra'Ven to glamour him Keltish so he could hide undetected in the West for years.

The turn of events is incredible.

Sage and Ra'Ven move toward our rune skiff as Ni Vin drifts it closer to the ledge. "We don't have much time to get your power unbound," Sage cautions, her words echoing off the cavern's glistening black-opal walls.

"The Vu Trin have sent search parties into the sublands," Ra'Ven warns, his words inflected with a flowing Smaragdalfar accent reminiscent of Professor Hawkyyn's. I take note of Ra'Ven's silver eyes, his Wyvern ancestry evident in his pupils, which are vertically slit like Yvan's. He holds his tall, muscular form in a similar way as well, all contained, coiled power. His attire is the traditional emerald garb of the Smaragdalfar, his ears high points, green hair cut short, a green-glowing rune stylus sheathed at his hip.

"This location is cut off from the main Eastern Sublands," Sage says as our skiff bumps against stone, inky water sloshing, "but it might not be safe for long."

Tension rises in Yvan's and my shared fire and I turn to him. His eyes flash gold as our gazes meet, a hot, upending shiver racing down my spine. His throat tightens and he looks away and rises, along with Jules and Lucretia and me, all of us aiding Kam Vin in holding the skiff flush with the rocky embankment so Ni Vin and Sage can secure it with chains of stone-fusing runes.

Ra'Ven extends his emerald-patterned hand to me and I take it, his grip strong as he hoists me onto the ledge, Yvan's heat shimmering against my back as he follows close behind.

Finding my footing, I grip Sage's shoulder in hasty greeting.

"I knew the Wand would lead you here," Sage says to me, her tone suffused with the enormity of it all. "It came to me in dreams. Do you have it still?"

I nod, angling my head toward where the Wand is sheathed in my boot's side. "I do," I assure her. "It's given me perfect aim with weaponry."

"And soon, you'll be able to wield it," she states with calm authority.

"Were you told of Vogel's ability to strike down most runes?" I ask, urgency rising. "And his incursion into my fastlines?"

"Trystan told us everything." Her gaze flits from Yvan to me as I scan her intensely violet form—her tunic covered in a kaleidoscope of glowing, linked runes from a multitude of runic systems that have all taken on a purple tint, as if demurring to the potency of her light magery. Her wand is hewn from plum-hued wood like my cousin Or'myr's, a series of slim runic styluses sheathed at her hip, along with a formidable-looking runic blade.

But her *hands*.

Piercing concern knifes through me to find Sage's broken-fasting wounds still so very much present. If anything, they look worse than they did the last time I saw her. I note the delicate chains of what I assume are pain-dampening runes draped over her hands and wrists, and wonder if she's still in constant agony but inured to it by now.

"Pull up the sleeve to your wand hand, Elloren," Sage directs as she unsheathes a glowing green rune stylus. "I need to temporarily shut down the connection between your wand hand and your bound power. Or when we send unbinding spells through you, we could inadvertently explode both you and the sublands. This rune needs to be placed *immediately*—it's going to take close to an hour to charge."

Nervous anticipation ripples through my fire power as I hold out my wand hand. Sage grips my wrist and begins to mark a bright green rune onto my palm, a slight sting chasing her stylus's movement.

"Yvan Guryev," Ra'Ven says in a poignant tone as Sage works.

A portion of Yvan's fire flares toward Ra'Ven, and I'm surprised by the rush of emotion rippling through it. "It's been a long time, my friend," Yvan says as they step toward each other and embrace.

"We will finally be able to meet as we truly are," Ra'Ven says as they pull back, gripping each other's shoulders while Sage finishes crafting the rune. "Release the glamour if you wish it," Ra'Ven offers with a significant look. "I know all too well what a burden it is."

With an intense glance at both Sagellyn and Ra'Ven, Yvan draws off his cloak and lowers his head. A hard breath escapes me as his dark wings fan out from his muscular back and I press back the tortuous urge to move into the heat of his aura. A burning flush suffuses my neck as Yvan flexes his wings, and Sage and Ra'Ven look him over, momentarily riveted.

"What a turn of events," Sage murmurs, giving us both a look of vast compassion. "The Prophecy standing before us."

Defiance shoots through Yvan's fire. "I don't believe in prophecies," he states with cutting emphasis, a ribbon of his heat flashing out to encircle me, his transient caress only stoking my flush hotter.

"Nor I," Ra'Ven staunchly agrees.

"Your Icaral child," Yvan says to Ra'Ven, "he's here in the sublands, as well?"

Ra'Ven nods. "Under heavy guard, as you can well imagine."

"It preyed on me," Yvan says, "how Vogel targeted him. Ra'Ven... I'm sorry he got caught up in this."

"We're *all* caught up in it," Ra'Ven states, immovable insistence in his silver gaze. "And the Mages' atrocities are *not* your doing." He grasps Yvan's shoulder, and Yvan nods stiffly, a tormented heat flickering through his aura that tightens my heart.

"Is Fyn'ir well?" I ask Sage, remembering the gentle, winged babe I met in Amaz lands.

"He is," she assures me. "But, as you both know, Vogel's reach extends to the Eastern Realm. And the Gardnerians aren't the only religious fanatics who want the Icarals dead."

"Which poses a problem," Professor Kristian puts in from beside us. "Seeing as how Yvan has just announced his presence here in the Eastern Realm quite dramatically." He gives Yvan a pointed look that Yvan meets unflinchingly.

"My people have claimed the Eastern Sublands as a safe haven for Icarals," Ra'Ven says. "I seek to claim them as a refuge for *everyone* fleeing the persecution of either Realm."

"You need to get Elloren and Yvan farther underground," Kam Vin cuts in, looking to Ra'Ven, "where your warding is more potent. Nilon and I will remain here and stand sentry."

Ra'Ven reaches into his tunic's pocket and tosses her a Smaragdalfar rune stone. "Contact me through this if you need to, Kamitra."

Kam Vin pockets the stone before she and Ni Vin depart.

I look to Sage. "The trees have an incredibly strong hold on me. Chi Nam, Lukas, and Valasca couldn't break it, even working together. And I think it's getting stronger."

She nods. "Which is why we're gathering allies who possess a great deal of elemental magic." She hesitates. "Even so, freeing you is a dangerous task, Elloren, there's no way around it."

"How dangerous?" Yvan interjects, protective concern rising in his fire.

Sage eyes him evenly. "*Dangerous*. Elloren's elemental power is Dryad based. It's completely linked to the trees."

I touch Yvan's arm and a spark ignites between us, his fiery eyes meeting mine. I drop my hand, my pulse thudding with renewed contrition over our effect on each other.

I turn to Sage. "I want my power back. Get me free of the Forest."

Sage gestures toward a tunnel up ahead. "Come, then." Intensity fires in her purple eyes. "We'll gather with the others and get your power unbound."

We follow Sage and Ra'Ven down a series of stony, spiraling staircases, then through a narrow tunnel that eventually spills into a shimmering cavern that widens my eyes. Black crystalline stalactites hang from the cave's low ceiling, another inky river lazily streaming beside us, everything ethereally lit green by the varg runes marked on the walls.

Relief spreads through me to find Trystan, my uncle Wrenfir, and my cousin Or'myr already waiting there.

Along with the most outlandish Alfsigr Elf I've ever seen.

The Elf leans casually against the cave wall, an irreverent smile on his ivory mouth. That alone is deeply surprising—the Alfsigr are generally such an enigmatically blank-faced people. And his sculptural, bone-white features and short, snow-hued hair are streaked with a rainbow of colors, which strikes me as revolutionary—it's written right into the Alfsigr faith that they are to wear nothing but silver and white, just as Mages are bound to our sacred blacks and permitted hues. There's an outrageous splash of rainbow glitter decorating the Elf's silver eyes, and his finely tailored ivory tunic is covered in silvery Alfsigr runes that light him up with their shimmering luminescence, his tunic edged with a riot of gems of every prismatic hue. This has to be the rune sorcerer Elf that Or'myr told me of. The Elf skilled in tracking spells who joined the Western Realm Resistance.

Rivyr'el Talonir.

The Elf who can help me find a path to Lukas.

The memory of being inside Lukas's dream rises, a flash of longing for Lukas searing through my core. I startle from the force of it. Yvan's Wyvernbond is such a potent thing, it's difficult to think or even feel anything past it when I'm near him, my emotions cast into fiery chaos.

"Yvan," Trystan breathes out as they fall into an emotional embrace while Or'myr and Wrenfir regard Yvan and me with expressions of vast surprise—the Black Witch and the Icaral of Prophecy before them, potentially the Realms' most powerful beings, quite alive and reunited as staunch allies.

The glittering Elf detaches himself from the wall and strides toward me, his lips lifting in a bemused smile, a silver stylus neatly sheathed at his side.

"Black Witch," he drawls, the words touched with an Alfsigr inflection. He extends his hand, his short nails painted with rainbow glitter. I take his hand. "Famed Destroyer of Realms," he enthuses, gaze flickering over me. "And nicely hidden under Ra'Ven's glamour at that. I'm Rivyr'el Talonir. The most dangerous and reviled of all the Alfsigr Elves. It's always nice to meet a fellow pariah."

"I think I have you bested in that," I note.

He lets out a short laugh and gently pivots my hand, scrutinizing the green rune Sage marked on my palm. "How much longer?" he asks Sage, his bemused tone whisking away.

"An hour," she answers. "Two at most."

"Are you ready to go up against the entire Forest?" I challenge him.

He flashes me a sultry smile. "Oh, tief'lin, I'm *always* ready." His eyes flick to Yvan, mischief in them. "I don't know if the Realm is prepared for you two. They can barely handle an Alfsigr Elf in the Vu Trin." He shoots me a knowing look. "Just wait till they find out how thoroughly you're thumbing your noses at their precious Prophecy."

A troubled flush heats my face as water erupts from the river near the cave's far end. My heart quickens over the eddy of water magic suddenly rippling through the air. And before I can voice my surprise, three kelpies leap onto the ledge's far side, Tierney Calix astride one of them, her deep-blue form clad in a sapphire Wyvernguard uniform.

Elation swells in my chest as Tierney grins broadly. "Elloren!" Voicing a stream of Asrai, she advances, her kelpies dissolving, her feet deftly meeting stone as she throws back both hands, whisking the water from her form as I rush to her.

I fall into her arms, only half noticing the dual auras of powerful magery flashing toward her.

Tierney draws back, gripping my upper arms as her magic circles around me, her lake-blue eyes bright with feeling. "I told you we'd meet again in the Noi lands." Her mouth tilts into a teasing grin. "Of course, I didn't imagine the bulk of the Vu Trin forces intent on slaying you."

I huff out a beleaguered laugh. "It's thrown a bit of a wrench into my settling in."

"Yes, well, we're here to throw our own wrench into the mix," she saucily returns as Yvan comes up beside me.

"Tierney," he says, his wings fanning out, prompting a shiver of want through my fire.

"The Vu Trin staged your death all too well, Lasair'kin," Tierney says with an expression of vast relief as they embrace.

"It's good to see you, Asrai'kin," he rejoins, heartfelt, as I'm swept up in the remembrance of the two of them sitting together by our bonfire in Verpacia, both glamoured and in terrible danger. A grateful ache forms in my chest to see them reunited here in the Eastern Realm, safely able to exist in their true forms.

The focused auras streaming toward Tierney intensify, snagging my attention and I turn, searching for the sources of the invisible purple lightning and warm fire. I swifly trace the impassioned lightning to Or'myr, who is studying Tierney, keeping his expression coolly analytical; then follow the fire magic to Wrenfir, my young uncle's spider-marked expression studiously devoid of emotion as his power flows toward her in a potent blaze. Even Rivyr'el seems a bit entranced.

I turn back to Tierney as it dawns on me that she's quite the stunning beauty in her true form, no longer boxed in by the unforgiving, painful glamour. I can't help but wonder if she realizes how much bedazzled attention she's inspiring, and if she does, what she must make of it all.

Distant footsteps echo and all conversation dies down, an anxious tremor passing through me as everyone turns toward the sound.

"Ren," Trystan says gently from where he's come up beside me as he touches my elbow.

I look at him, my younger brother's gaze warm with anticipation. Heart quickening, I turn back toward the terrace's dark bend as several figures emerge, striding through the shadows, their gaits powerful, their movements fluid and uniform. Runic light washes over them and my legs almost give way beneath me.

Rafe and Diana are in the lead, Jarod, Andras, and Aislinn behind them, all of them possessing the wild, amber eyes of the Southern Lupines. All of them wearing black Vu Trin uniforms.

My lungs seize as I stagger forward, then break into a breathless run just as my brother Rafe launches toward me as well, a sob tearing from my throat as he catches me up in his strong arms and hugs me tightly.

"You're Lupine," I marvel, hugging him close then drawing back to look over his tall form. Never wanting to be parted from my brother again.

Rafe laughs, tears sheening his amber eyes. "I am. And it's good, Ren."

It's an adjustment to take in his transformation, but an overwhelmingly good one, his eyes no longer the familiar Mage green but infused with amber radiance, the green glimmer of his skin suffused with a ruddy underlying glow. My elder brother has always radiated physical power, but never with the intensity he does now, his entire frame seeming bigger, stronger.

I turn to Diana, who is flashing me that dazzling Lupine smile of hers.

"Oh, Diana…" I manage, her form wavy through my tears. We pull each other into an embrace as Rafe, then Jarod and the others, embrace Yvan in turn, exclaiming their relief over finding him alive.

"My sister," Diana says as we draw back from each other and I take in her exultant grin.

I glance toward Rafe. "So, you're Lupine mates now?"

Rafe shoots Diana a rakish look. "One could say that."

"Well mated," Diana agrees, growing serious as she raises her chin, her wild eyes filling with formal import. "He is a strong and virile man. My family would have been proud of our union."

As culturally odd as it is for me to hear her speak of my brother in this way, I nod, fresh tears pooling in my eyes, my smile fading under the weight of horrific tragedy—the last time Diana and I saw each other just a day after the vicious slaughter of her entire family, her Lupine friends…almost everyone she loved. "I'm sorry," I tell her, choking up. "Your family, Diana… I'm so sorry."

She nods tightly as Rafe's arm encircles her. She leans toward him, her gaze taking on a hard, predatory glint. "We have established a pack in the Eastern Realm. A new Gerwulf pack. Over a hundred of us and growing."

I stare at them both in wonder. "So many?"

"A new branch of the Vu Trin forces," Rafe says, serious, as well. "We're building an army, Ren."

Diana's expression turns vicious. "The army Vogel feared we would build."

"Good," I say. "Because he's coming."

Diana's lip twitches. "Let him come." She flashes her teeth, and the hairs on the back of my neck prickle with an involuntary rush of intimidation. "I need to have a talk with him," she growls. *"With my teeth."*

A shiver ripples down my spine and I can sense, in the ferocity of her expression, how altered she's been by the unspeakable tragedy. There's new gravity to her, but I can also tell that she's grown fiercer for it, and I'm glad of it.

Aislinn, Andras, and Jarod step nearer, tears misting Aislinn's newly amber eyes. Aislinn and I pull each other into a close embrace and I'm overjoyed to find her slight, frail appearance so altered, her skin enhanced by a healthy glow, her form infused with a wiry muscularity.

"Your fastlines," I breathe, my eyes catching on her blank hands as Yvan embraces Diana, Rafe, and the others in turn, falling into earnest conversation with them. "They're gone."

She nods, her tear-slicked gaze hardening. "The Lupine Change took them away, along with my affinity lines." She eyes me significantly. "That's part of why we're here, Ren. Not just for your protection. If something goes awry when your magic is unbound...we can turn you."

I stop breathing, my power shivering. Yvan's fiery attention snaps to me and I meet his eyes, fire leaping between us. I'm surprised by the strength of my recoil from the idea of losing my lines. Of losing my connection to wood and earth. As well as my magical connection to both Lukas and Yvan—fire to fire.

A conflicted understanding seems to ignite in Yvan's gaze and

I know he grasps my sudden turmoil on an intimate level—what would it feel like to be stripped of fire? To be stripped of my very magical core? I turn to Rafe, conflict storming.

"If it comes down to it, Ren," my brother says, rock-solid support in his gaze, "let us Change you."

My head spins with revolt. Especially because my fastlines would be stripped away along with my power—which are my clearest path to finding Lukas. But I also know I'll do this if I have to. If it's the only way to survive, or to keep my magic from falling into Vogel's hands.

I give a quick, tight nod to my brother, unable to meet Yvan's gaze as his fire flickers through mine.

"What was it like...to Change?" I ask Aislinn, my throat tight with tension.

"There's some pain," she admits. "But...then..." An emotional gleam overtakes her gaze. "Elloren...it's glorious." Her expression dampens, her voice coarsening. "I shouldn't have waited to join them. It was a mistake to wait." She glances shyly at Jarod, and I reach out to touch his arm, overcome to be back together with all of them and looking into his kind, beloved face.

"Brother," I say, more tears pooling in my eyes, the two of us true family now.

"My sister," Jarod returns with warm emphasis.

I hug him tightly, choking up at the remembrance of my last glimpse of him, hunched over and in shock over the horrific loss of his family. When he pulls away his eyes are sheened with emotion.

"Are you two...*together* now?" I ask, looking hopefully to both him and Aislinn.

Aislinn gives a small wince and Jarod takes hold of her hand. They exchange a quick, affectionate glance.

"Not as of yet," he says, more to her than me. "In time."

I immediately regret asking, not able to imagine the trauma Aislinn endured with sadistic Damion Bane. A flash of red-hot anger scythes through my lines at the idea of my gentle friend fasted to such a monster.

Diana's laugh sounds at something Tierney is saying from a few paces away, and the unexpected sound of her throaty laughter is like a bright balm, immediately lifting my spirits as a sudden question lights my mind.

"Who's the alpha?" I ask Jarod.

Jarod's lip quirks as he glances toward Rafe and Diana. "They both are."

My eyes widen. "What? Both of them?"

He nods, an amused glint entering his amber eyes. "They couldn't best each other. They fought for almost an entire day. He's stronger than her, but she's faster and…trickier. Eventually, after many, *many* hours of them genuinely trying to dominate each other, it devolved into laughter and they went off to the woods to mate. It's…unprecedented."

"Two alphas," I marvel, astonished.

I catch Andras's eye, his tall form looming over us. "You didn't make a play for alpha?"

He laughs, deep in his broad chest, glancing toward Rafe and Diana. "Against either of *them*?" He raises one purple brow. "I saw them fight. I'm seriously outmatched."

"I'm so glad to see you, Andras," I tell him as we pull each other into a warm hug.

"Is your son well?" I remember the last time I saw Andras's son, Konnor. A sharp pain rises over the remembrance of the trauma in the small child's face that nightmarish morning. How little Konnor was found, the night before, lying under his dead adoptive parents.

"He's doing well," Andras assures me, his rune-tattooed brow tightening. "My mother cares for him much of the time. She's living with our pack."

Surprise wells. His mother, Professor Volya, had railed against the Lupines and their ways. Railed against Andras joining them and railed against him embracing his son.

"I don't think she expected to find any commonalities with Lupine culture," he tells me. "But she has. More than she ever thought possible. And she and Konnor have become strongly bonded to one another."

My heart lifts to hear this, an ember of hope lighting over what that could mean for the world at large. If Professor Volya could learn to cross cultural lines and love a grandson and embrace a culture she was taught to thoroughly despise, perhaps others might be able to embrace unity, as well.

Sage and Tierney sidle up beside me, and I can't help but notice how Tierney studiously avoids greeting Andras or even looking at him, even though I can sense her water affinity tempestuously eddying around his broad form. Andras is watching Tierney sidelong with what looks like uncomfortable concern, and I wonder what transpired between them.

Sage touches my arm, breaking into my thoughts. I let her check my rune-marked palm, a brighter green glow emanating from it. "Come," she says and motions toward another rune-lit passageway, her look of vast import sending a shiver down my spine. "That rune is almost charged."

CHAPTER NINE

AURA KISS

Elloren Grey

Smaragdalfar Sublands
Eastern Realm
The night before Xishlon

I stare at the rainbow-streaked hair of the Elf down on one knee before me, Rivyr'el's rune stylus pressed to the center of my palm. Opal stalactites hang low from the circular cavern's ceiling, glittering in the lantern light, most of our group encircling us, Or'myr's and Wrenfir's backs to the glistening walls.

Yvan stands a bit removed from me, his wings fanned out against the stone to his back.

Rivyr'el's rainbow-glitter-painted eyes meet Sage's. "Well, the trees have bound her up quite tightly." His mouth twists into an irreverent sneer. "Clever Forest."

"What's the structure of it?" Ra'Ven asks from beside Sage.

Rivyr'el lightly traces his stylus's tip along my palm in a slow oval, a prickle rushing over my skin. "The trees basically sent barrier magic over her lines," he answers, "then worked a chaos spell into it that's tangling her power inward." He lifts the stylus's tip and sweeps it toward my abdomen. "Thus, orienting her magic toward her center." He looks to Sage once more. "The Forest is using her lack of Dryad balance to pull her off-kilter. She has dominant fire and earth magic, but weaker water and air, and almost nonexistent light. We'll need to strengthen her weaker elementals before we can drive off the Forest's bindings."

Sage nods. "Then we'll feed warding power into her to shield her from another magical attack before anchoring a straightening spell to reconnect her magic to her wand hand."

"There is one issue," Rivyr'el cautions. Sage cocks a purple brow. "We'll need to veil what we're doing from the Forest until the last moment, or it could stage a counter siege. It's hooked into her power enough to do it."

"All right, then," Sage rejoins, a stubborn light in her eyes, "then we veil her. For as long as we can. And jointly drive the Forest off if it comes to that."

"Will you be able to locate my fastmate when you're finished?" I press Rivyr'el. Yvan's power contracts, my throat tensing in response to his flash of distress.

"You'll be able to locate him yourself," Rivyr'el amends, "via a tracking rune I'm going to place on you."

"How long until Elloren is freed?" Diana asks from where she stands with Rafe and the other Lupines.

"A day," he answers without hesitation. "At the most."

My breath tightens, Yvan's fire flashing through mine, perhaps reading my upending sense of destiny bearing down. *Freed.* In a day's time. With access to Black Witch power.

"I'll fly to the Vojuun base to the northeast of here," Yvan says to me. "I can send word to Vang Troi that we want an alliance." I hold his intent gaze as he fans his wings out more expansively. "I'll let her know that we won't obey the Prophecy, Elloren. We're wresting hold of it to fight Vogel. And the Vu Trin can either align with us *both* or get the hell out of our way."

A fiery riptide of love for him rushes through my power, suf-

fusing me with warmth and the desire to join with him, meld
our fires and incinerate every evil in the world.

"I'm ready to subvert the Prophecy," I agree, steely branches
rising through my core as I hold his riveting gaze.

The Noi runes marked on his chest give a bright flash.

Everyone's focus darts to the rune markings, concern sparking through everyone's magic.

"You need to leave," Ra'Ven says firmly. He gestures toward
Yvan's runes, looking to Rivyr'el. "The Vu Trin must have
charged a tracking spell. I'm surprised by their speed."

"How long until they find me?" Yvan asks.

"Not long," Sage answers, narrowing her gaze at Yvan. "They
can hook a lead into your runes in less than an hour's time."

"Elloren…" Yvan says, a conflicted flare of heat in his gaze.

"Can we have a moment?" I ask Sage and Ra'Ven, displaying the still uncharged rune on my palm.

"Be quick," Ra'Ven cautions. He gestures toward a slim corridor at the cavern's end. "Follow that upward," he says to Yvan.
"There's an opening to the sky. Send rune hawks to let us know
of Commander Vang Troi's decision." He withdraws a rune hawk
medallion from his tunic's pocket and tosses it to Yvan. "We'll
converge on the meeting place of her choice after Xishlon."

"And if she won't align with us?" I ask.

"Then we'll break with the Vu Trin," Rafe says, my brother's
amber eyes hardening with resolve, "and form our own army.
Elloren, it's important that you don't fight Vogel alone."

"Where will you take Elloren?" Yvan asks them all, his fire
whipping around me with burgeoning intensity. "Vogel's tracking her and the Vu Trin are aggressively hunting for her."

"When we unbind her," Or'myr interjects, "we're going to
orient her lightlines toward purple and glamour her that same
hue. Which will enable her to enter my Vonor in Voloi." My
cousin's tone doesn't budge from the coolly reasonable, and I
find myself admiring his unflappable calm. "It's warded and
glamoured to be accessible only to those with an intrinsic line

of purple magic. The Vu Trin and Vogel cannot reach her there. She'll be safe until she regains control of her power."

Yvan's gaze slides back to me, rebellious emotion firing in it, but I can sense a shift in him.

"I'm not the helpless girl I was in Verpacia," I assure him, patting my Ash'rion. "If Vogel comes after me, I'll do what I did to his scorpios and kraken. I'll decimate him."

Yvan's eyes burn into mine. "I'll be back for you, Elloren," he vows. "The *moment* you gain control of your power." His fire gives a hot, pained flare. "And then I'll portal west with you and help you free your fastmate."

Yvan and I step out of a sloping tunnel and into a huge black-opal cavern that spirals up to impossible heights. Its faraway pinnacle reveals a tiny patch of starlit sky. A varg rune affixed to the wall casts soft green light over us, Yvan's luminous eyes suffusing his face in a golden glow. He fans out his wings and meets my gaze, and it's like a shock of pure flame, tension charging the air between us.

"It's hard to leave you again," he says, his voice coarse with feeling. "If something happens to you when they unbind your power...it's dangerous."

"And you can do nothing to prevent that," I remind him, feeling equally engulfed by conflict over our impending separation. "*They* can."

None of his rigidity softens. "The last time we were parted, *nothing* went as planned. You were almost killed by the Vu Trin. And then you were sent back to Gardneria. *Two* assassination attempts made on your life...and then..." He rakes his fingers through his crimson hair and gives me a scorching look.

Lukas. And then Lukas, I think, agony rising.

"Safety is never a permanent state of affairs," I manage, a knot clenching hold of my throat. "I'm realizing that more and more."

He gives me a frustrated look, his jaw tensing.

"You once told me," I say, "that we had to put the safety of our loved ones above our own wants."

A short, bitter laugh escapes him.

"Your mother's here, yes?" I prod.

"She is," he answers, voice tight.

"As is close to everyone we care about. And…all of the other people here—you know as well as I do what's going to happen to them if Vogel successfully invades. He'll bring a nightmare. That we might be able to stop."

He pulls in a shuddering breath. "I know it, Elloren."

And I can feel it, our shared, revolutionary spirit rising in our fire even as we both rail against fate.

"I *will* get Vang Troi to parley with you," he bites out.

I nod, struggling to swallow back the unspoken. His fire is suddenly circling me more intensely and he steps nearer, the flow of his heat blazingly ardent.

"I can't kiss you again, Yvan," I say as opposing impulses crash through me.

"I know," he says roughly, his lips lifting even as agony slashes through his fire. "I also know that you want to."

Tears gather in my throat, making it hard to speak as I fist my wand hand, the rune still uncharged, allowing us a moment longer. "I'm sorry I hold your fire bond," I tell him, my voice splintering with fierce regret. "I wish there was a way to free you."

"Elloren…" A tremor shudders through his fire, my name wrung from him like a precious thing as he draws me into an embrace. I close my eyes and hug his hot body close as his lips come to my temple, my chest rising and falling against his, and I realize that this moment is both a solidification of our alliance and a permanent goodbye to what can never be between us.

"It's impossibly hard to leave you," he says in a ragged whisper. "Even though I know…you're his now."

Remorse ricochets through me, my heart painfully torn. "I'm the Black Witch above anything," I say roughly, drawing back from him as I blink back tears. "And there's no way of knowing what the future holds for me."

The fire in his eyes rises to an inferno. "It holds me in it as your ally," he declares, the force of his magic taking me by surprise as it burns through my lines, momentarily singeing away my tears and my grief and every terrible thing in the world, fierce love running through it.

He steps back even as his fire desperately reaches for me and mine reaches for him in turn. A hotter portion of his flame escapes his control and brushes over my lips in an impassioned kiss that he holds himself decidedly back from, sparking a powerful ache in my heart.

And then he fans out his wings, gives them a hard flap down, and lifts into the air, hovering just above me, a rhythmic flow of air whooshing down.

I'm frozen, my breath caught in my throat, his fire lingering on my lips as our eyes remain locked for one molten moment. He holds my gaze for a second more, then flies up and up toward the starlit opening high above.

A blast of his fire courses back toward me, embracing me with shimmering heat.

And then he's gone.

"Are you ready?" Ra'Ven asks, emerald rune stylus in hand, as I stand before him, partially unclothed in the circular cavern. I hold my balled-up tunic against my chest, grateful that Valasca helped me learn to manage my overwhelming Gardnerian shyness.

Everyone whose power will be needed to free my magic quietly stands in a circle around me—Sage, Rivyr'el, Or'myr, Tierney, Trystan, Lucretia, and also her brother Fain, who's just arrived. The Lupines have positioned themselves just outside the cavern's entrance to guard it.

"I'm ready," I say.

Ra'Ven brings his stylus's tip to the tattoo imprint of each of the six runic chains marked around my neck in turn, my skin prickling as each chain morphs from a flat tattoo to a three-dimensional linkage of Smaragdalfar varg runes. He gently takes hold of one of the chains and lifts it off me.

Tension releases along the top of my ears as they lose their points, a portentous feeling sizzling through me. He lifts off another chain, and a sweep of energy courses over my scalp and I glance down to find my pale gray hair morphed back to black. Another chain off, and green sparks light in my vision, the glamour lifting as the remaining chains come off one by one, and I know, as Ra'Ven straightens, that I look like the Black Witch again.

I raise my green-glimmering wand hand and take in the curling fastlines once more visible on my hands and wrists, and my heart constricts. It was so difficult to feel anything past Yvan's Wyvernbond when he was so near, but now, with him gone, the memory of finding Lukas in his dream rushes in like a tide. I clench my fists around my fastlines as if desperately grasping hold of what will soon be my path back to Lukas.

Sage and Rivyr'el take Ra'Ven's place before me as I slide my tunic back on. Lowering herself to one knee, Sage motions for me to raise my tunic's hem, then brings her purple wand's tip to the demon-sensing rune on my abdomen just as Sparrow Trillium and Thierren Stone slip into the cavern.

"You're here," I say, astonished to be reunited with my former Valgard lady's maid and Lukas's Level Five Mage ally, Thierren's uniform now that of a Vu Trin soldier. "I'm so glad you made it East," I say, swept up in the remembrance of our escape from Valgard while Sage removes a section of the rune she marked on me in Amazakaraan with a stretching sting that has me wincing.

"Aislinn sent for my aid," Thierren explains. "She said wind power was needed."

"We want to help you, Elloren," Sparrow adds, "and Lukas too. Any way we can."

I nod, grateful, as I take in the astonishingly transformed Sparrow—resplendently garbed in an opulent lilac dress embroi-

dered with irises, her pointed ears adorned with delicate looping chains festooned with glittering purple gems.

"You look so different," I marvel.

"I've found success quickly here as a seamstress and designer,"
she tells me before a startlingly painful series of jabs ripple over
the rune. I wince harder and Sparrow's gaze darts toward my
abdomen with evident concern.

"There's about to be quite a bit of power flying around this
room," Or'myr says before quietly directing Sparrow out for her
safety, Thierren remaining. The demon-sensing rune finally
gone, Sage straightens and looks to Rivyr'el.

"Are you ready?" he asks me as he lowers himself before me
and suspends his silver stylus above my abdomen, my glimmering green skin now a blank slate.

I nod, and he sweeps his stylus's tip along my stomach, fash-
ioning the outline of a large, circular silver rune before rapidly
sketching the rune's interior—a wreath of five small runes orbiting a central silver disc. He presses the tip of his stylus to the
disc and murmurs a spell.

Two of the five internal runes begin to rotate into silvery
blurs. Two others begin to spin slowly while the last internal
rune remains motionless.

Rivyr'el points his stylus at the blurred runes, looking to
Sage. "That's a measure of her fire- and earthlines." He slides
his stylus toward the two lazily rotating runes. "And here are
her weak water- and airlines." His stylus shifts to the motionless rune. "And here's her dormant light power." He gives me a
sly smile. "We're going to balance you out, Witchling, starting
with water. We'll need Fae elemental power for that. Lucky for
us you have an Asrai friend." He shoots Tierney a saucy look.
"And a quite lovely one at that."

Tierney throws him an arch look that reads, *Truly, Rivyr'el?*

He grins, undaunted. "If you're in need of a Xishlon'vir tomorrow night, my offer still stands—"

"Rivyr'el," my cousin Or'myr cuts in with a surprisingly aggravated tone. "Can you please *not* choose this particular moment to flirt with *absolutely anyone*."

Rivyr'el smirks at Or'myr, then sets about marking a ring of small shielding runes on my abdomen encircling the larger elemental rune. "You should try a little flirting now and then," he croons, glancing mischievously at Or'myr. "Unless you enjoy being the lonely sorcerer in the hidden tower." He points his stylus at one of the elemental runes, serious again. "Here, Or'myr, make yourself useful and create a pathway."

"I rather enjoy my hidden tower," Or'myr rejoins as he draws an amethyst from his pocket and presses it to the water rune, sounding out an Uriskal spell. A hot flare of his violet fire power surges through my lines, and I draw in a hard breath, gooseflesh rippling over my skin, the water rune's hue shifting from silver to lavender.

"What are you doing?" I ask him.

"Sending a siphoning spell over the rune," Or'myr explains, "to allow us to feed power into your waterlines." He looks at Tierney, Trystan, and Lucretia in turn. "Ready?"

Trystan and Lucretia unsheathe their wands while Tierney steps forward, a sense of anticipation rising in me as Or'myr continues to hold his amethyst over the slowly rotating water rune. They bunch in toward me, Tierney's body brushing against Or'myr's as she slides into place facing him.

Or'myr's fireline ignites with a potent rush of lightning, and I'm astonished by its strength, wondering, again, if Tierney has any inkling of her effect on my enigmatic cousin.

Or'myr swallows, reaching out to Tierney, his composure fraying. "So...um," he stammers, "you'll need to take my hand."

Tierney shoots him a quizzical look, then nods and slides her hand into his.

A startlingly powerful confluence of magic hits me as Or'myr's fire aura crackles out to meet Tierney's water power in an invisible, heated explosion of violet steam. Their gazes lock tight, both of their eyes widening. A shiver runs through them both, the two of them seeming shocked by their magic's heated amplification. Or'myr murmurs a spell, and they appear to get a hold of themselves as he focuses Tierney's power into a steadier stream toward the crystal he has pressed to my abdomen.

"On my mark." Sage holds her palm up as Trystan and Lucretia bring the tips of their wands close to Or'myr's stone and murmur spells. *"Go,"* Sage orders, and their wands touch down on the amethyst.

I gasp as a hard rush of Tierney's power storms into me at the same time I'm flooded with Trystan's and Lucretia's water magery. Feeling submerged in oceanic depths, everything shimmers around me and I let out a wavering breath, my waterlines strengthening until they hold as much power as my earth- and firelines.

Or'myr holds up a hand. "It's level," he says, the lavender water rune now rotating in a blur.

Trystan and Lucretia retract their wands and step back, along with Tierney, her eyes meeting Or'myr's for a brief, magic-shivering moment as his violet lightning aura forks around her, and I'm surprised to sense Tierney's Asrai power coursing out toward him in a rushing tide.

Forcibly reining in his besotted magic, Or'myr places the amethyst on the wind rune. Fain shoots me an affectionate smile as he steps forward with Thierren and they feed magic into my windlines, a tempestuous current blowing through me as my wind rune speeds to a blur.

"Your turn, Sagellyn," Or'myr announces. He moves his stone to the motionless rune.

Light.

Sage's violet eyes meet mine, a look of deep import on her face as she places her wand's tip onto Or'myr's stone, closes her eyes, and begins to sound out a series of spells.

Violet light rays from the rune as a fire strike of purple flashes through my lines.

Sage draws back her wand and Or'myr removes the stone, all five elemental runes now lit up lavender and whirring against my skin, which has glamoured to violet, my fastlines once more hidden from view. Sage's eyes flick over the runes, as if she's reading a complicated mathematical formula, my sense of the momentous building.

"What now?" I ask.

"I'm going to link them." She raises her wand and fashions small linking runes to join each of the five elemental markings, the entire wreath of runes taking on a brighter violet glow.

Awareness pricks at the back of my mind, leaves rustling.

A sizzle of fright spears through me. "Sage," I rasp out. "The trees...they know."

The cavern's opal walls suddenly punch inward and I cry out, recoiling as the stone walls bulge with the image of embossed trees, root-shapes popping up from the stone floor as everyone surrounding me blinks out of sight.

"They're here!" I cry out. "The trees are coming through the walls!"

"It's an *illusion!*" Or'myr's voice growls from the air before me as the feel of strong, invisible arms come around me from behind, grasping tight hold of my wrists.

Black-opal branches burst through the cave's walls and ceiling. I struggle against the restraining grip, desperate for my blades, the stone forest morphing into a real, storm-darkened forest, living branches now restraining me.

They wrap around my neck, my chest, my legs, smaller branches shooting from the limbs and knifing into me and through my lines with shearing pain.

I cry out in agony, wrestling against the trees' hold as my lines are hooked into and pulled in all directions, as if the Forest is attempting to rip them clear out of my body. The branches around my throat and chest tighten, the breath choked from my lungs.

"They're attacking!" I force out in a sandpaper rasp. *"Help me..."*

Violet lightning flashes through the Forest's canopy at the same time that purple flame leaps up from its ground, scorching heat mounting as the Forest rumbles in fury, limbs and leaves and roots swept up in the all-encompassing violet blaze.

"Rafe! Don't!" Sage cries as the cave snaps back into sight and the pressure around my chest, my throat, gives way, the hooks in my lines releasing so abruptly I almost retch.

I'm glazed with sweat, my elder brother's arms wrapped tight around me, his hands grasping my wrists, his teeth releasing from the base of my throat as I gasp for breath, multiple wands as well as Ra'Ven's emerald stylus all pointed toward the runes marked on my abdomen, the Lupines ringing the room.

Everyone is breathing heavily and looking spooked and wide-eyed, Sage's entire wand hand and lower arm glowing a bright, incandescent violet.

"They're gone," I rasp.

"For the moment," Or'myr growls, green eyes narrowed as if he's staring down the Forest through me. "They'll roar *right back*. We need to ward her *now*!" he urges Sage.

"I will *turn her* if they cut off her breath again," Rafe growls from behind me.

Her brow laced with sweat, Sage gives a quick nod and grinds out a spell as she presses her wand's tip to the center of the rune on my abdomen and marks a dark purple rune on its central disc.

All of the elemental runes ray out light as the forest shapes punch at the cavern's sides once more and the image of a pine-green, point-eared young man with furious eyes and branch horns shudders through the back of my vision. A cry escapes my throat as the trees scream in my head, my lines knotting with excruciating tightness as the Forest's branches attempt to dig back in, but my lines are now like slick, crystalline glass and I can sense the Forest's inability to gain purchase.

And then, in a dizzying, expansive whoosh, the Forest's magic tears away.

The stone forest imprints blink out of sight and my legs buckle.

Rafe grasps tighter hold of me as I struggle to regain my footing. "I'm all right," I gasp to him. "Rafe... I'm all right."

He loosens his grip as I draw in great gulps of air, something new taking root inside me...

Balance.

Coursing through my lines like an expansive tide.

I draw in a deep, stunned breath and the sense of perfect balance gains ground, my magic newly able to *breathe*.

A wan-looking Sage takes my wand arm in hand and meticulously draws a line of purple runes from my palm all the way to my shoulder. "These are flow runes that will reestablish your magic's link to your wand hand," she explains, gesturing toward the line of runes marked down the length of my arm. "They'll brighten as they charge from your shoulder on down. When the charge reaches your palm, your control over your power will be restored."

Rivyr'el presses a silver-rune-imprinted disc to the back of my wand hand. "And this rune I'm transferring onto you will track your fastmate." He presses his stylus to the flat disc, a quick burst of silver light raying out from its sides. He removes the disc, and my eyes widen at the intricate silver rune now marked on my hand, its outer circle encasing what look like two small, linked compasses.

A heady sense of possibility washes over me and I flex my newly purple wand hand, ready to fill it with a wand. *I'm coming for you, Lukas.*

Rivyr'el rises, still gripping my wrist. "Once your power is restored, this tracking rune will draw on your magic and take on a silver glow. When it does, you'll be able to get a measure of your fastmate's distance *here*—" he points to one of the two internal compasses "—and direction *here*."

He's explaining the finer details when Diana cuts in, nostrils flaring. "Someone's here."

Running boot heels sound and Ni Vin bursts into the cavern. "The Vu Trin have come." Her runic sword is drawn, her dark eyes fixing first on my newly purple form then snapping to Or'myr. "Get her to your Vonor, *now!*"

Or'myr grabs hold of my arm as he unsheathes his wand. We set off at a sprint, down the narrow corridor I traveled through with Yvan, Sage's voice echoing off the walls behind us.

"Or'myr, whatever you do, keep her away from the trees!"

CHAPTER TEN

SHADOW BOUND

Lukas Grey

Shadow hive
The night before Xishlon

"Elloren Grey will gain control of her magic in a few hours' time."

Vogel's words trigger a heated sear through Lukas's power. He carefully sizes up the demonic envoy looming with Vogel over his prone, bound form, four Shadow Mage soldiers with glowing gray eyes bracketing them, silver torchlight flickering over them all.

Gray flashes through Lukas's vision, the colors of the scene leeching out as his teeth clamp down around his Shadow gag, the need to throw off Vogel's power gaining fearsome strength. Vogel smirks, which only stokes Lukas's rebellious urgency higher, his heart pounding hard and hot against his ribs.

Because he knows he's in a race against the powerful advance of this corruption.

A race to Elloren.

A race for the Eastern Realm.

Vogel's smug, venomous will brushes against the edges of Lukas's mind, against the defensive shield Lukas has woven there. He can feel Vogel's presence, slick and slithering as he flexes against the Shadow bindings webbing him to his cell's floor. He's tried hurling his powerful aura against both his bindings and his cell's Shadow bars. Tried every magical and non-magical angle to slip free.

But he needs a *wand*.

Make one mistake, Marcus, Lukas seethes as he holds Vogel's infuriating stare, *and I will gut you with my magic. Make just one mistake...*

"The Black Witch has eluded us," the demon-envoy states to Vogel, voice low and resonant as his red fire-eyes flicker. "We lost her trail in Voloi."

"She's being brought to the Vonor of the sorcerer Or'myr Syll'vir," Vogel says, keeping his eyes pinned on Lukas. "He's likely warded her."

"He's powerful," the demon-envoy cautions. "And untrackable when he wants to be."

"For the *moment*," Vogel cuts back sharply, eyes flicking toward the demon before he lowers himself beside Lukas, the tip of his Wand tracing the curl of one of Lukas's fastlines. "She'll soon lay down her own track."

Lukas gives a hard recoil against the contact as a helixing Shadow rises from the lines, a painful sting shooting over the fastmarks on his hands and wrists.

"By the time Elloren regains control over her power," Vogel says, tracing the lines with an almost fond motion, his piercing eyes fixing back onto Lukas's, "she'll already be mine."

Lukas watches through his cell's dark wavering bars as his captors take their leave, Vogel idly flicking his Shadow Wand toward him.

Lukas's Shadow bindings abruptly vanish, and he grits his

teeth against the slash of pain as they rip from his skin, leaving painful welts of reddened flesh in their wake. He forces himself up and massages his aching jaw, the wheels of his furious mind turning.

He moves closer to the cell's bars, watching soldiers as they pass by, others emerging from the insectile cells affixed to the huge cavern's dark walls. His gaze sweeps toward the vast swarm of wraith bats hanging throughout the cave's vaulted upper reaches, then down toward the Shadow scorpios massed along the walls, still as statues.

Lukas focuses on the Shadow magic streaming against the tight shield he's set around his lines. The same magic that's edging up against his mind and graying his vision.

You didn't count on my superior shielding abilities, did you, Marcus? Lukas stealthily considers.

You're not the only clever one, you zealot bastard.

Forcibly slowing his breathing, Lukas closes his eyes and concentrates as he extends his shielding power out over the gray line of power Vogel has tethered to his lines.

Seconds bleed into minutes and minutes into hours.

He concentrates harder as his vision grays and his sense of time running out intensifies, sending his shielding power out further and further along Vogel's Shadow leash. A mental map of the magic Vogel has branched out over the entire hive begins to emerge, the network of power too huge and entrenched for Lukas to take down, even with a wand.

But he doesn't need the whole hive.

Drawing his shielding power back, he sends a slim thread of it out over one of Vogel's branching tethers, weaving around it silently.

To the nearest scorpio.

Lukas slinks his magic through the scorpio's head and thorax, then into its powerful forelimb. Sweat cloaking his back, his teeth gritted so hard his molars sting, Lukas exhales, rough and hard, as he forces his will into the scorpio.

Slowly, the scorpio turns its head toward Lukas, the creature's forelimb twitching, before the shield-connection snaps off and the beast goes stone-still once more.

A vengeful satisfaction rises in Lukas as he pants from the effort.

Two can wield this Shadow.

Let down your guard once, Marcus. Just once, he seethes as he readies himself to send out his shielded earth magic once more.

And I'll be waiting for you.

CHAPTER ELEVEN

XISHLON THRALL

Elloren Grey

Voloi, Noilaan
Eastern Realm
Xishlon

I hug my cousin's waist tight as we soar out of the sublands tunnel toward the Voloi Mountain Range's pinnacle, our rune skiff zooming into the cobalt predawn sky. My heart flies into my throat as I take in the number of military skiffs hovering at the base of the mountain, a more intense panic striking through me when my eyes flit down toward our skiff.

We've disappeared.

Or rather, Or'myr's camouflaging spell has us blending in with the purple stone of the mountain's rough peak so exactly it's as if we've vanished against it. Struggling to wrap my mind around the illusion of our bodies being propelled through the air with nothing beneath us, I tighten my grip around Or'myr's torso.

"Don't look down," Or'myr suggests over his shoulder. "Focus on a high point instead."

I swallow and pin my attention on the fading stars sprinkled across the sky even as worry hums through me over what will happen to everyone if they're taken into custody.

Eventually, we round a bend in the mountain range and the multitiered city of Voloi comes into view, the predawn sky rapidly brightening to azure in the East. Swooping upward, I flinch as an explosion of bright purple light flashes around us. A small two-story dwelling shivers into being just under the mountain's apex and my brow flies up at the sight of my cousin's fantastical Vonor. It's cut into the stone much like Fain's estate, its circular tower forming its top story, runes marked over its surface.

Or'myr guides the skiff to a smooth landing on his Vonor's lower terrace and we disembark and cross the terrace's violet stone, striding toward a dark plum wooden door. He grabs the lantern hung beside it and I follow him into a small foyer, then up a spiraling staircase. As we ascend, I take in the finely wrought landscapes hung on the walls: deep-violet pencil renderings of the view, most of a romantic nature—impressionistic storms, ethereal, misty mornings, moonlit nights—all marked with Or'myr's signature.

The staircase leads into a cluttered tower room, and my wand hand reflexively tightens with want. Or'myr's Vonor is a veritable indoor violet forest. Sanded deep-purple trees are set into the walls. Their branches cover the ceiling and frame the tower's semicircle of arching windows, which afford a panoramic view of the tiered city below as well as the massive Vo River beyond, the distant Wyvernguard's two walkway-linked vertical islands unnervingly in view. More branches frame stained-glass amethyst doors leading to a small stone balcony.

My gaze darts around the multitude of shelves set into the trees' nooks, holding countless books as well as a variety of scientific equipment, scores of purple-hued gems, myriad art supplies, and a variety of purple wands and runic weapons.

I ball the fist of my wand hand, my earth magic shivering as

I wrestle back the urge to press my palm to every bit of wood and send power through it.

Or'myr draws his wand and sets to lighting lanterns, lilac illumination suffusing the room as he grabs hold of a strand of crystalline purple stones and a grimoire, muttering to himself in Uriskal about "finding a good geo-amplification of Sage's spells" as he thumbs through one of the tomes.

"Let's try the zoisite stone," Or'myr murmurs as his long finger skims down the page. He sets down the grimoire and looks to me. "Hold out your arm, Elloren."

I raise my arm, and Or'myr commences wrapping the crystalline strand around its length, the plum-colored stones so dark they're almost black. He touches his wand to one of the stones. "I'm working on a hunch here," he explains, a rich violet glow lighting the stone. "This should shave a few hours off the process of unbinding your power. While we wait, we can review defensive spells and place a proper geo-shield around you...we've more than enough time, cousin, but we'll need to finish some of this before the Xishlon moon rises. It's frustratingly difficult to concentrate around its thrall—"

"Or'myr," I cut in, anxiety jabbing through both his muttering and my focus-scrambling pull toward all the wood in the room. "What happens to my brothers and everyone else if the Vu Trin take them into custody?"

Or'myr's green eyes flick up to meet mine, a somber light in them. "They'll question them and possibly hold them for a bit. No harm will come to them, Elloren. The Vu Trin aren't going to slay the alphas of the Lupine army along with their most powerful Light Mage, or any of their other formidable allies—and we simply want Vang Troi to speak with you."

"It's not that simple, Or'myr."

"I know it, cousin," he grimly rejoins.

"And then there's the Prophecy—"

"Vang Troi isn't beholden to that," he emphatically counters as he lights up another crystal. "This is the same woman who let your brother into the Wyvernguard despite multiple petitions and protests, as well as a number of other Mages and Mage-blooded soldiers, myself included. She's a maverick, but she's also the military genius responsible for keeping your grandmother out of the East during the Realm War, so she's granted quite a bit of leeway by the Noi Conclave. And don't forget, the Icaral of Prophecy himself is lobbying on your behalf."

"Still…if she denies Yvan," I press, "where does that leave you?"

He pauses, meeting my gaze. "Elloren, I'm with you."

"But you've only just met me."

He shrugs. "I've gotten to know Trystan quite well in a short span of time. And… Tierney, as well." I notice his magic kicks up when he says Tierney's name. "I tend to follow my gut on these things," he adds. "I'm with you."

I let out a long, shuddering breath. "Thank you, Or'myr."

He gives me a small smile as he finishes charging the crystals, then falls back into muttering to himself about which magicked stones are likely to provide the best geo-shield. I look around, my gaze snagging on a nearby shelf covered in small pieces of every type of wood I could imagine. My magic gives a hard lurch toward it.

I reach out to touch a few of the curving, knotty pieces—pine, cypress, cedar, ash, oak. Repeated waves of delicious rapture course through my lines as each tree unfolds in my mind, a whole forest of them. Enthralled, I pick up a gorgeous fragment of silver wood marbled with veins of bone-white. Awe shudders through me as an Alfsigr Elm tree expands in my mind. I close my eyes and breathe deep, lost to the wood's sparkling canopy.

"Can you envision trees?" Or'myr asks, cutting into my wood-trance, his tone one of complete astonishment.

I open my eyes to find him frozen, staring at me. "Can you, as well?" I ask.

He swallows, nodding. "I never thought I'd meet anyone else who could do it."

We hold each other's gaze in mutual wonderment, the whole world paused by the incredible prospect of sharing this ability with someone.

"I had a collection of wood as a child," I finally blurt out. "I hid them *everywhere*."

"I did too," he confides, suddenly just as breathless.

"Here." I tentatively slide the wood toward him. "Touch it with me."

Eyes widening another fraction, he complies, folding his hand over mine, his fingertips sliding down to meet with the wood.

The moment he makes contact with it, the tree-vision intensifies and I let out a small huff, silver-leafed branches swooping in to enfold us both as the entire elm grove forms around us. We both inhale, an enraptured shudder passing through our combined magic.

Or'myr releases the wood at the same time I do, the grove-vision dissipating as the two of us hold each other's stunned stares.

"I wonder..." I venture in an unsteady voice, "if we'd been allowed to grow up together..." my lip tics up in a rueful smile "...I wonder if we might have had a secret collection." A sudden pang knots deep in my chest, and it's clear from my cousin's tense expression that he feels it too. Because we shouldn't be discovering these things only now.

Or'myr is quiet for a moment. "I'm sorry we never got to do that, cousin."

"I had to hide this affinity over there," I falteringly tell him. "Because it's a Fae draw."

"I did too here in the East." He gives me an acerbic look. "It smacks of my Gardnerian blood." He glances around at the tree-lined space. "It's part of the reason I'd never let anyone come up here, even if they could. I can be myself here without anyone seeing the 'polluted' parts of me." The undercurrent of deep-set pain in his tone strikes hard, feeling all too familiar.

"I know all about being judged for things I have no control

over," I say as a kindred bond sets down unexpected roots between us.

Or'myr lets out a bitter laugh. "Yes, well, I'd rather judge people based on the things they *can* control, and make no mistake, cousin, that still leaves me with quite a bit to judge."

I lower my gaze toward the purple-wood flooring and notice a wine-hued violin propped in the shadows between tree trunks. My pulse deepens with emotion as I scan the entire lower portion of the circular room and take in the multitude of violins recessed between the trees, some of the instruments of an unfamiliar Noi design, black lacquered and imprinted with pearlescent dragons, some possessing extra strings.

Grief pressing in around my heart, I remember Uncle Edwin, patiently teaching me to play and sharing the craft of violin making with me. As well as Lukas's dream…how he placed the violin and bow in my hands…

"I play violin too," I tell Or'myr, my voice hitching. "I'm a luthier, as well."

"I know," he says, voice subdued. "Trystan told me."

Uncle Edwin taught me, Or'myr, I think, but am unable to say. *But he should have been able to teach you too.* Tears glistening in my eyes, I turn to the nearest violin and the haphazardly stacked pile of music next to it, taking hold of the first few pieces, absently riffling through them. My hands still as my eyes light on a familiar composition.

Winter's Dark.

"This was Uncle Edwin's favorite piece," I murmur, lips trembling, as the song's melancholy notes fill my mind. "We used to play this piece quite a bit…" A memory of Uncle Edwin, Trystan, and I playing the melody by a winter's fire in our cozy cottage in Halfix suffuses my mind, Rafe drinking hot cider as he listened.

"My mother is a musician, as well," Or'myr quietly says. "This was the song she and my father chose for their private Luth'yllion in Gardneria."

The rune behind my ear translates the Urisk word—*their binding as life mates*. Understanding rolls through me as I finally comprehend, in this moment, the mournful look that came over my uncle's face whenever he played this piece.

He was grieving when he played it. Grieving for his love, Li'ra. And for Or'myr too.

My hand flies to my mouth, and I'm barely able to hold back my tears. "He should have been able to stay with you," I manage in a forced whisper, shaking my head as I internally rail against the cursed Gardnerians. Against my cursed grandmother. "It's not right that they kept him away from you."

"I know," comes Or'myr's choked reply. Shards of violet lightning knife through his aura.

I hold my cousin's sorrowful gaze. "He would love who you are," I tell him, this certainty making the tragedy of it even more unbearable. "He would love you a great deal."

Or'myr nods stiffly and glances away, his own eyes glazed with tears, his mouth twisting into what looks like a mixture of jagged bitterness and profound grief. He sniffs, then scrubs a hand across his eyes and meets my gaze once more as he suppresses his magic's discordant flare.

He angles his wand toward the stones looped around my arm. "Let those do their work, cousin," he says, voice steadying with resolve. "We should grab an hour or two of sleep while we can. Before your power comes unbound and the whole world changes."

I wake a little over an hour later as Xishlon day fully breaks over Noilaan, sunlight streaming through the Vonor's windows. I push myself up to a sitting position on his tower room's couch as my disheveled cousin presses a steaming mug of what he informs me is "rejuvenating mushroom tea" into my hands, which strikes me as outrageously prosaic given the situation at hand.

We pore over piles of spell and rune books all morning into the afternoon, then move to magical shielding concepts, the city's rising swell of Xishlon music and celebration emanating through the tower's propped-open windows. The repeated chimes of what Or'myr tells me are "welcoming bells for Vo's love incarnation" ring bright on the air as we pause periodically for Or'myr to feed magic into the zoisite crystals wrapped around my wand arm. A palpable tension builds as we note, with a single, shared glance, that a quarter of Sage's line of runes is now lit up bright.

"Is the Xishlon moon's thrall like spirits?" I ask Or'myr as he charges the zoisite, their rich purple glow having dimmed a fraction.

He shakes his head, frowning at the stones. "No—it's not intoxicating...it's more of a shift in *focus*. Toward love. Of all kinds. And...well..." His mouth thins. "To romance." He says the word with more than a trace of disdain. "You'll see. It's exasperating. It takes more than a bit of effort to think about anyone else." Color lights on his cheeks. "I meant...about any*thing* else." He pauses, seeming annoyed with himself. "Especially for me, with all the damned purple. It's like the whole festival was set up with the sole intent to thoroughly scatter my wits."

A lavender-feathered rune hawk alights on the balcony's railing, and I look at Or'myr in surprise. We rush onto the balcony and he unfastens and unscrolls the missive, scanning its message. His eyes meet mine, a smile lifting his lips as my heartbeat accelerates.

"Is it from Yvan?"

"It is," he says with a trace of disbelief. "Vang Troi is portaling here from the Western front. Overnight. She's open to an alliance with you, Elloren. She's agreed to meet with all of us at the Wyvernguard, tomorrow morning. After Xishlon." His grin widens as he hands me the missive. "Well, cousin. It looks like we've something to celebrate this Xishlon after all."

Or'myr and I wait on his tower's balcony that evening, pausing with what seems like the entire city. A bright white full moon hangs high over the Vo Mountains, hope lit like a beacon in my center.

It's surreal, to be having this idle moment with my cousin after studying spells and shielding throughout the day at such a dedicated pace before the moon's thrall descends. It's even more surreal to consider that I might be on the brink of a true alliance with the Vu Trin forces.

"Any moment now…" Or'myr murmurs, looking toward the shining orb.

A few stars appear in the darkening sky, then a few more.

And then a luminous lavender appears around the moon's edges and flows inward, both the moon and stars morphing to a vivid, enthralling purple.

I let out a gasp as violet light washes over the Realm, wave upon wave of cheers and music exploding throughout the city, an expansive elation filling my chest as countless purple runic orbs rise from every tier and from the rune boats thickly dotting the river. Lilac fireworks burst over the river in a shimmering display as the city comes alive with joyous revelry.

I peer back up at the Xishlon moon, transfixed, its lush light washing over me in a subtle caress, the tension in my shoulders slackening of its own accord as an ardent thought rises—a vivid remembrance of the feel of Lukas's lips on mine, the two of us entwined in the forest, our matching affinities melding. My cheeks flush as longing for him swells along with the moon's strengthening glow before the memory shifts to a flush-deepening recollection of Yvan's heated embrace in the North Tower that night in my bed…

I brace myself for the stinging conflict such thoughts are bound to prompt, only to find them imbued with a softer sensation—as if the Xishlon moon itself is giving me permission to fully admit to loving and wanting them both.

And the *trees*…

All of the trees in the expansive First Tier gardens are glowing with every shade of purple. My wand hand twitches with the desire to meet with them, the garden-forest's unexpected draw almost as enticing as the moon's thrall.

Black Witch, rises on the night air, not angrily, but gently beckoning, as sinuous Xishlon music wafts up around me.

Get hold of yourself, Elloren, I harshly caution myself. *You're not some Dryad who can frolic through forest groves washed in lavender moonlight as if partaking in a lovers tryst.*

Sage's warning to Or'myr echoes through my mind—

Whatever you do, keep her away from the trees.

"Can you feel the moon's pull?" Or'myr asks.

I turn toward my cousin, not the slightest bit fooled by his unfazed tone. His aura is lit up around him like a Xishlon runic orb. "It's stronger than I thought it would be," I admit.

He lets out a long sigh. "Well, there's nothing to do now but wait Xishlon out. It would be near impossible to concentrate on anything of consequence at the moment." He gestures toward the purple tea service he's put out for us. "I'll pour you some tea, cousin."

Eager for the distraction, I accept the tea, his dark mushroom brew reminiscent of chocolate. "This is quite good, Or'myr."

His eyes glint with satisfaction. "I've a small mushroom farm here. I'm a bit of a hobbyist, you'll find." He lowers his tone to a stage whisper. "Don't tell anyone. I want them to go on picturing all manner of mystery and debauchery going on here in my glamoured tower."

We exchange bemused smiles. "I suppose mushroom farming in damp caverns might ruin your sorcerer mystique," I tease.

A short laugh escapes him. "It's not generally famed for its sexual allure."

My eyes widen, such joking not done in the Western Realm, one of so many things that serves to highlight the very different worlds we grew up in.

I lift my wand arm as the sting coursing over my upper arm slides down a notch. "I can feel Sage's magic working its way down my arm."

Or'myr nods and takes gentle hold of my wrist, his gaze roving over the line of runes, the deep-plum glow of the zoisite stones wrapped around my arm having dimmed once more.

"We've about twelve hours to go with geo-amplification," he remarks, frowning at the crystals. "I'm going to need fresh zoisite. These are only a few hours away from being depleted." His gaze slides to Rivyr'el's silvery tracking rune, the rune that will lead me to Lukas.

He looks up at me, a hesitant curiosity in his gaze. "Do you love him?" he quietly asks.

I'm silent for a moment, aware that he's likely being drawn to this focus on love by the moon's pull, the frank, personal inquiry seeming out of character for my reserved cousin. I tussle with the question, uncomfortably aware that my feelings for Yvan were on full display to Or'myr and everyone else when we convened in the sublands.

"I love Lukas a great deal," My voice catches around the words. "But… I love Yvan too. I thought Yvan was dead. And I had to align with Lukas for protection, and then…" I swallow against the sudden swell of emotion. "And then…we were Sealed. I grew to love him over a very short span of time."

We're both quiet for another moment.

"That's a difficult situation," Or'myr says, compassion in his tone.

I nod, unable to speak, his kind presence kicking up a wilderness of irreconcilable feelings. "I'm scared for Lukas. I'm trying not to think on it too deeply, because…when I do, I start to feel paralyzed…or like I want to grab hold of some wood and explode something."

"Then let it go for now," Or'myr encourages.

I nod, choked up, as I take in the lavender moon, the violet stars, the glittering purple city spread out before us. I rest my elbows on the balcony's cool, purple stone railing, feeling perilously close to baring my heart to my cousin completely. "The moon," I say instead, "it's incredibly beautiful."

"I suppose," Or'myr returns, a sardonic edge to his tone.

"Have you ever taken part in all of this?"

He raises a derisive brow. "Um...*no.* I don't partake in their festival."

I'm surprised by the exclusionary way he calls it "their" festival. Purple is Or'myr's kindred color—all his magic is oriented toward the hue. And it's clear he's romantic, given the private things I've learned about him here in his secret space. He has quite a few volumes of poetry crammed in amongst his multitude of books and grimoires.

And not just any type of poetry.

Love poetry.

I spotted something else upon arriving here, before he quickly whisked it away. A pencil sketch of Tierney rising from the Vo's waters, partially unclothed, his skill as an artist fully conveying the potency of his crush. He attempted a nonchalant air as he turned the sketch facedown, but his cheeks colored furiously.

"I thought that all of you Noi'khin were supposed to go off and find someone to kiss on Xishlon," I gently tease as glittery violet-clad crowds stream by far below.

He casts me an exasperated look. "*That* would be a completely futile quest."

I blink at him in surprise. "Why would you say that?"

He sighs, frowning. "I'm not high on anyone's Xishlon'vir list." He shakes his head, flushing as he shoots me an abashed look. "I know you saw my sketches of Tierney. Yes, I fancy her. Unrequitedly, I can assure you." His mouth tightens into an unsettled line. "I'd prefer if that could remain between us. Tierney and I have been working together for over a month now and she's become...a friend to me. I don't want to lose that."

"She's a good friend to have."

He looks back out over the spectacular view, fireworks blossoming in the sky. "She's one of the few who doesn't judge me for my lineage."

I nod at this, affection for Tierney welling, abetted by moonlight that seems to amplify love in all its forms. "Tierney's certainly of her own mind."

"Well, it's incredibly refreshing. She doesn't adhere to the rigid rules about who she's supposed to care for or be friends with. I *love* that about her." He stops, his face tensing. It's clear he's given this a lot of thought. That he's given *Tierney* a lot of thought. And that his feelings revolve more around who Tierney *is* rather than what she looks like.

"This damned moon is making me say too much," he grouses as he glares at it, then gives me a sheepish sidelong glance.

"It's okay if you say too much to me, Or'myr."

His expression softens and he nods, our eyes meeting in mutual understanding and acceptance before he looks back up at the moon. "So, you knew Tierney when she was glamoured."

"She looked quite a bit different. It was hard on her."

"She told me she was unattractive."

"It was a different world over there. For all of us." I study his profile closely—*my* profile, only male and with pointed ears. "But it's clear that the East is not without its challenges."

His lips give a bitter twist. "I had it easier here than Wrenfir, since I look Urisk except for my green eyes." He focuses them on me. "But still, most of the Urisk here view me as quite a bit 'polluted.' And, of course, many Noi'khin hate my mother for loving a Gardnerian. I'm guardedly accepted, at best, let's put it that way."

I don't press for more, sensing his angst in the way his magic is now fitfully spitting lightning. "You know," I hedge, the moonlight itself seeming to coax the words from me, "I can sense attraction."

His gaze flicks to mine with some skepticism. "Like a shapeshifter?"

I tilt my head, considering. "No, not completely. I can sense it through the flow of magic, not from smell. And..." I shrug. "I think that, perhaps, you should take a moment to find Tierney this Xishlon night."

Or'myr's eyes widen a fraction. "Why?"

I bite my lip, realizing the moon's thrall is prompting me to cross broad lines of discretion, but what does it truly matter? We're all about to go to war, and this kind cousin of mine deserves a small moment of happiness before we do. As does Tierney. I give him a knowing look.

He blinks, seeming thrown. "Did you sense something from her?"

I hesitate. "There might be a mutual pull."

Or'myr looks to the floor then to the river, as if he doesn't quite know what to do with this information. But then he gives me a level look, his cynical expression returning as violet runic orbs decorated with purple roses float up from the tier below.

"This is a frivolous conversation brought on by a frivolous moon," he insists, lightning forking through his aura. "Even if Tierney returned my interest, all it would take is one kiss to scare her away."

I blink at him, thrown. "Whyever would you say that?"

"My fireline," he spits out, giving me an incredulous look, as if I should know the answer already. "It's much too strong. Too strong for anyone to take." He lets out an exasperated sigh and leans into the railing. "There *was* a Noi woman," he grudgingly admits. "About three years ago. We attended the Wyvernguard together. And…we had *feelings* for each other. One night, in the runic lab, I professed my great love for her, and we kissed." Pain tightens the edges of his gaze. "She pushed me away with sheer terror in her eyes. And that's how I learned that it's physically painful to kiss me. Like a burn. Not a good, passionate burn. An actual *burn*. The type of burn you flinch away from and avoid from there on in."

He peers back at the city and goes stone-still, but there's nothing calm or still about the way his violet fire's crackling. Raucous cheers go up from the distant tiers as more runic fireworks explode over the river, bursting into giant lilac stars.

"You know what we'll do?" I say, flashes of purple light illuminating his angular face. "When we're done taking down Vogel and subduing the Gardnerians and Alfsigr, we'll find you a nice Lasair girl. Or maybe a Wyvern shape-shifter. Someone who isn't scared off by bolts of lightning."

Or'myr coughs out a laugh, some of the bitterness fading from his expression as he shoots me a sarcastic look. "Yes, the Fire Fae and Wyvern women are falling over themselves to kiss the grandson of the Black Witch." He shakes his head, as if resigned to fate. "No. I think Rivyr'el is correct. I'm destined to be the Lonely Old Sorcerer in the Hidden Tower."

"So tragic," I chide, the moon's loving thrall making it impossible to concede to his gloom.

"Hmm." He smirks.

One of the luminous rune orbs floats near as I bump his shoulder with mine. "I'm sorry you have such a frightening kiss, cousin."

Amusement lightens his expression. "You do realize this is a truly ridiculous conversation, faced, as we are, with the destruction of all that is good on Erthia. And I imagine your kiss is about as frightening as mine. Probably more so."

I raise my brow at this. "Are you saying that…if I kissed someone without fire power, I'd actually hurt them?"

"Undoubtedly." Or'myr narrows his gaze on me. "Clearly you haven't."

Unsettled emotions rise, even through the moon's embracing thrall.

No, just Lukas.

And Yvan.

Memories of heatedly kissing them both surface once more. As well as how Lukas shielded and protected me over and over through so many of those kisses.

"It's true, I haven't," I admit, subdued now as I struggle to tamp back the worry for Lukas threatening to rise through the moonlight like a tide. I glance at Or'myr. "Do you think it's the same for Trystan?"

"Without question," he answers, certain. "But he's found him-self a Zhilon'ile Wyvern. Perhaps the most powerful one in the Eastern Realm. Vothendrile is famous for his storm magic. Lots and lots of lightning. I doubt your brother will scare him off."

"So you know about them, then?"

He casts me a wry look. "Everyone knows about them, El-loren." He cocks his head, viewing me searchingly. "Oh…that's *right*. You're from the Western Realm where they have those horrid, fanatical views about men like Trystan and Vothe." He huffs out a derisive sound. "Vothe's entire family despises Trystan, but for reasons completely unrelated to his gender. We find other reasons to hate people here in the enlightened East-ern Realm." He sends me a look rife with cynicism.

"Vothe's family has forbidden him from seeing Trystan," I mention, outrage breaking through.

Or'myr coughs out a laugh. "Yes, that ultimatum is working out so spectacularly well. Because there's nothing at all entranc-ing about forbidden romance."

My lips quirk up at this. "I suppose Vothe's family is destined to lose that battle."

Or'myr's grin widens. "They are *completely* destined to lose that battle."

My eyes snag on a violin propped against the balcony and I gesture toward it. "So, do you play out here?"

He throws a quick look at the instrument. "I do. Tragic, heartbreaking songs of unrequited love." He grins slightly at me again, but I notice the melancholy edge that's crept in.

"I saw all your books of love poetry," I tease.

Color spots his cheeks but he smiles. "Well, that's the dan-ger of having someone invade this hallowed, private space. You know my deepest secret now. Beneath this cold, unfeeling ex-terior lies the heart of a burning romantic. Whose kiss is like a bolt of lightning. And, like I said, not in a good way. In a 'run from the bolt of lightning screaming' sort of way."

I can't help but smile in return, grateful for his humor in the face of it all. And suddenly grateful for how the moonlight is making this wait bearable. "I'm glad to have found you, cousin," I tell him, heartfelt, feeling like I've fallen right into a swift, unexpected friendship with this look-alike family member of mine. "I like you a great deal."

"I like you a great deal as well, Cousin Ren," he warmly returns as he pushes himself off from the railing. "And I need all the family and friends I can get, since I'm destined to be the Lonely Old Sorcerer in the Tower."

I laugh, but our joint amusement rapidly fades as we both glance out over the water.

Toward Gardneria.

Where Vogel's army is gathering as it gets ready to advance across the desert toward the Eastern Realm.

Even the Xishlon moon's thrall can't soften that.

"I should fetch more zoisite," Or'myr says, more serious now. "I'll be back shortly."

Protest rises in me. "Wait… Or'myr…you can't leave me here alone."

His lips quirk as he takes in the rune blades strapped all over me. "Elloren, not only are you in a well-warded, invisible Vonor, you're heavily armed with perfect aim. And I've shown you how to use the runic explosives I have stored here."

"Vogel's *tracking* me…"

"Not to *here* he isn't. And unless he can strip the color purple from the world, he can't come here. This is the safest possible place in all the Realm for you to be." A cautionary light enters his gaze. "Just don't leave."

"All right," I reluctantly concede.

"I'll only be gone for an hour or so," he says, glancing at the moon as if it's a charming nuisance. He reaches into his pocket and hands me a purple-rune-imprinted stone. "Press the center of that if you have need of me. I've got you covered, cousin."

I nod, and he turns and strides toward the terrace's open door.

"Or'myr," I call out to him, and he pauses in the door's threshold. "If the world doesn't come to an end, we'll find you your Wyvern girl."

Amusement glints in his eyes. "I'm counting on it," he shoots back before disappearing inside.

I watch, a moment later, as he boards the rune skiff docked on the lower-level terrace. The runes on the skiff's sides begin to whir and Or'myr zips off toward the docks, his hand briefly lifting in farewell. I continue to peer after him as he flies through his Vonor's translucent barrier and both he and the skiff disappear against the mountain peak's purple stone for a bit before reappearing much lower, quickly blending in with the dense Xishlon air traffic.

Cradling my magic-infused wand arm, I bask in the city's festive, purple show for a long while, my gaze sliding every so often toward the Wyvernguard island-mountains rising up from the river—the only spots untouched by purple Xishlon decorations, so many Vu Trin soldiers already deployed west of the Vo Mountains and so many more en route over the desert toward the Western Realm.

Vulnerable.

The word lingers at the back of my mind, cutting through the swoony purple light just as the tracking rune on my hand flashes silver.

My gaze flies toward the rune.

It's burning silver, its internal compasses sweeping around their circular confines, trailing light, hours before they should be.

"What?" I gasp. "How..."

The needles still, hurling me into alarm and confusion as I read Lukas's location in the tracking rune.

PART FOUR

Xishlon Moon

LIGHTNING KISS

Or'myr Syll'vir

Xishlon night, twenty-first hour

Or'myr struggles to stay sharp as the dense grove of lilac Noi Wisteria closes in around him. He quickens his pace through the expansive First Tier gardens toward his rune skiff, his tunic's pocket weighted down with more zoisite.

Vo's Holy Teeth, the damned purple.

A mind-lulling euphoria rises in his chest as the trees' glowing fronds rain down all around him, the garden path fronted by luminous violet flowers of every night-blooming variety— Xishlon roses, jasmine, creamy lilac orchids. Luminescent lavender night-lilies twine around the trees in a supple caress.

Or'myr frowns and tenses his lines in an effort to fight off the color's enchanting lure. The lavender moon's thrall certainly doesn't help. Try as he might, he can't suppress the way it prompts his heart's most loving desires to rise. Melancholy thoughts of Tierney fill his mind, his longing to be more than a friend to her near impossible to press back.

And now that he knows she might return his interest…

Or'myr huffs out a disparaging breath and glowers at the moon only to find himself swept up anew in its intoxicating mix of purple hues. His shoulders relax slightly, as if in reluctant surrender.

It's only one night. Would it kill you to let yourself be drawn in just a little?

Everything changes tomorrow. The most massive deployment of Vu Trin forces west since the Realm War. Or'myr considers how he'll likely be deploying with his Black Witch cousin and her allies, including the Icaral of Prophecy and a number of Vu Trin soldiers.

Such a stunning turn of events.

A throng of purple-garbed children jostle past Or'myr, shrieking with laughter as they trail floating strings of lavender runic orbs, drumbeats sounding from the pier boardwalk before him, music bright on the air.

The Wisteria grove opens to reveal a puppet show in progress in one of the garden's plazas, puppeteers holding a giant purple Vo'Zish dragon puppet aloft on poles above a small plum-curtained stage, purple-hued deer, lizard and frog puppets cavorting around the dragon. The puppeteers begin to weave through the audience seated on a glowing carpet of violet moss, sounds of delight rising. Nearby vendors hawk heart-shaped wreathes of purple roses and Xishlon'lure moon-necklaces sold in pairs and supposedly magicked to embolden the wearers to express the love in their hearts.

Or'myr eyes the racks of necklaces, charmed by the idea and scoffing at the same time, that familiar bitter hurt knifing through the moon's bedazzlement. He's never been offered a necklace and likely never will be, not with his lightning bolt kiss and Black Witch lineage. And there are couples kissing *everywhere*, these lower dockside gardens a notorious spot for couples to escape for secret, intimate encounters, even when this gratuitous love holiday isn't giving them even more encouragement to be so outlandishly brazen.

Jealousy wells inside Or'myr as he passes besotted couple after couple tangled around each other in the grove's shadows, some of the women so lovely...

Heat rises in his cheeks as a current of longing kicks up inside his lines.

Are you seriously pining for someone to grope against a tree? For Vo's sake, you're trying to free your cousin, the Black Witch, to stop the annihilation of the entire Eastern Realm. Not having someone to kiss is really quite minor at the moment. Get a grip on yourself.

Or'myr rounds a bend in the narrow path, his heartbeat picking up its rhythm as he catches sight of Tierney Calix. He knew she'd be on watch duty here, but still, the sight of her amidst all the purple flashes a lightning bolt around his heart.

She's standing by the stream that winds through these gardens, her graceful dark blue hand resting on the stone railing that edges the tributary, her sapphire Wyvernguard uniform standing out in bold contrast against the purple-garbed Xishlon crowds. Her head tilts up as she looks over the panoramic view visible through a break in the trees, the crowded docks just beyond.

The breeze streaming from the Vo ruffles the deep-blue curls cascading down her back in a torrent of waves, and Or'myr's pulse quickens, the lavender moon hanging above her like an enormous Xishlon rune orb whose sole, true purpose is to illuminate lovely Tierney with its soft violet tint.

But there's nothing festive about Tierney's expression, and the tension in her visage sparks both concern and beguilement in Or'myr. *Sweet gods, she's beautiful.*

A flush blooms across the back of his neck as he wrestles with his frustratingly strong attraction to her.

You can never have her, so don't even entertain the thought, he cautions himself. *Even if the attraction is mutual. If you kissed her, you'd scare her off. Like you scared Yysh Nuu. Besides, half the single people in Voloi are going to be chasing after Tierney this eve, desperate for her to be their Xishlon'vir. She's your* friend. *Your Wyvernguard research partner. Nothing more. You need to make peace with that.*

He picks up his long stride, determined to keep his wits about him. "Tierney," he hesitantly calls out by way of greeting.

Tierney turns, and the intelligence in her deep-blue eyes threatens to pull Or'myr under anew. She's so damned brilliant. And fair-minded and brave.

And her mind…it's so completely her own.

As he nears, Or'myr's gaze is drawn to the pair of Xishlon rune necklaces dangling from her hand and a pang tightens his heart. Of course she's been gifted with Xishlon'lure love necklaces. Of course she's chosen someone to be with this last eve before the fight truly begins.

He comes to a stop before her, her serious demeanor so at odds with her possession of the whimsical jewelry.

"Why are you here?" Tierney asks with that unvarnished bluntness he finds so refreshing.

Or'myr glances at the festive couples streaming by and waits for a gap in the crowds before he responds. Two laughing young women stumble close, bumping him in the arm as they pass. Wreathes made of glowing lavender moons grace their hair, multiple Xishlon'lure necklaces hanging around their necks. They're dressed head to toe in glittering purple, their arms draped around each other. As they pass, they glance over their shoulders to flash bright, joyous smiles at both Or'myr and Tierney.

"Find the moon!" they call before breaking into flirtatious laughter, and Or'myr's face warms in response to the traditional Xishlon greeting, a thinly veiled invitation to kiss…and more.

He sets his gaze back on Tierney, determined to maintain his composure. "I needed to pick up some zoisite." His voice drops to a whisper. "It's speeding the runic spells. I imagine you know that Vang Troi's agreed to meet with her?"

Tierney nods, her gaze darting around, as well. "We were detained for a bit until we got word of it. How much longer till she's freed?"

"Soon. Before morning. There's not much to do at the moment but give it time." He glances up, then gives Tierney a beleaguered smile. "And wait for this ridiculous moon to set."

Tierney smiles, nodding with obvious understanding. "It's surreal," she says with a wave of her hand. "This tiny respite. Before the coming battle." She gives him a meaningful look. "Take a moment to find your Xishlon'vir while you can, my friend."

He gestures toward the necklaces in her hand. "Are you searching for your Xishlon'vir, as well?" As soon as the teasing words leave his lips, he regrets them. He meant for them to sound lighthearted, not awkward and conveying too much of his own Xishlon longing to kiss someone.

To kiss *her*.

He resists the urge to wince.

Tierney's eyes widen, but she frowns and shakes her head, huffing out a jaded sound as she eyes the necklaces with obvious discomfort. "Thurryy Nim handed these to me as a Xishlon gift. Mostly in jest, I think."

"Likely not." He gives her an arch smile. "You're more than a bit sought-after."

"All of my loves have been unrequited, Or'myr." Tierney looks past him, scanning the lovestruck gardens like Or'myr surveys them—like someone perpetually on the outside looking in. She lifts the necklaces dismissively. "I've no interest in putting on one of these things and pursuing meaningless Xishlon kisses. Even if we weren't poised on the brink of war, I'm not interested in a love who isn't truly interested in *me*." She stops, seeming abruptly mortified. "I... I don't usually talk about such things." She shoots a discomfited glance upward. "I think it's the damned moon. None of this is important right now."

The wash of moonlight suddenly loosens Or'myr's tongue as well as he's swept up in the urge to be honest with her. "It is a strange shift of focus, it's true. But still, I could tell you of something completely requited, if that interests you."

Tierney cocks a curious brow.

The words come out in a tumble like water from a breached dam. "I'm genuinely interested in you, Tierney'lin. You're beautiful to be sure, but it's *you* I'm drawn to. And...when our powers met in the sublands...it felt like the draw might be...mutual." Shock descends over his own boldness, his heart clamping shut against the ill-guided risk he's just taken.

You just called her "Tierney'lin" he realizes with no small amount of horror—*Tierney my beloved.* And worst of all, Tierney is now frozen, staring at him in obvious bewilderment.

Well done, Or'myr, he flays himself. *You've just destroyed your friendship.*

Tierney's gaze narrows, her expression shifting to one of warm speculation. Which takes him completely off guard.

"I do find you attractive, Or'myr," she allows.

Surprise overtakes him, his heartbeat jumping into a harder rhythm. "You do?"

She nods, coloring a bit. "I never really considered it before...until our powers met in the sublands. That was...quite the sensation." She gives him a heated look before she turns and furrows her brow at the passing crowds, seeming like she's tussling with her own thoughts for a moment. "Oh, hells," she says, boldly meeting his gaze once more. "You intrigue me, Or'myr. You're so aloof...and mysterious." Her eyes glint with amusement. "Such a reclusive figure, with that secret Vonor of yours and all your unique geo-magery power that nobody completely understands but you." A spark of intense emotion lights her gaze. "And you *care*. You care what happens to the people fleeing here. You care about a lot more than just yourself and don't sort people into rigid categories."

Or'myr coughs out a laugh, cynical amusement cutting through his bedazzlement. "Well, I don't exactly fall into a rigid category myself."

"Which adds depth to your character," Tierney insists. "I really like that about you." Her gaze shifts into a different kind of intensity, warmth sparking on the air between them that sends a tingle down Or'myr's spine. "I've given fleeting thought to kissing you." An affectionate smile lifts her lips. "I imagine it would be quite nice."

Reality descends, shattering the lovely promise of the moment and Or'myr huffs out a bitter sound. "Actually, I imagine it would be pretty awful."

Tierney draws back with obvious offense.

"You misunderstand me," Or'myr clarifies, an acrid regret cutting through him. "The fact is, it's awful to kiss *me*. I've a great deal of fire power, and it's magnified by my geomancy. And…it's in my kiss." His longing intensifies, everything in him wishing he could sweep her into his arms and carry her into the grove's sweet shadows. "I've been told that my kiss feels like a bolt of lightning. It's the bane of my existence. Well, that and the threat of worldwide Gardnerian supremacy. But the damned Xishlon moon seems to render that trivial this eve."

Tierney studies Or'myr, the lavender moonlight dancing over her changeable lake-blue hue. "Is your kiss actually harmful?" she asks, a speculative glint in her eyes.

Renewed surprise washes over Or'myr as he realizes that she might still be entertaining the possibility of kissing him right here, right now, despite what he's just told her. Fire magic shivers through his lines, his mind falling into a muddled daze. "No," he manages. "It's a phantom affinity sensation."

"Here," Tierney says, and she holds out one of the violet necklaces. "If ever there was a night for purple lightning, this is it."

Or'myr looks at the necklace, a breathless, swoony feeling overtaking him. "Tierney…are you aware of the necklaces' effect? They're said to enhance the moon's draw…"

Tierney blows out an incredulous sound. "You really believe that? I think they're simply moon trinkets. But even if there's something to it, they'll give us an excuse to kiss each other and then…blame it on the necklaces."

A laugh escapes Or'myr, his heartbeat tripping in his chest as he accepts the Xishlon'lure. Runic energy tingles over his fingers as he touches the chain, and when he looks back at Tierney, he notes, in wonderment, that there's a serious light in her eyes.

And warmth.

Warmth for *him*.

"On the count of three," Tierney says with a shy smile. She raises the chain over her head and Or'myr does the same, feeling as if he's about to take a dive off a cliff. "One, two...*three*."

Or'myr slips the necklace on at the same time she does.

A rush of intense want hits him, coursing straight through his blood, the Xishlon moon's pull to loving honesty intensified a thousandfold. Words flood out of him in a passionate rush.

"I'm entranced by you, Tierney," he breathlessly enthuses, every last bit of pent-up longing unleashed. "I have been for some time. And I don't just think you're beautiful. You're *brilliant* and *clever* and *talented* and *brave*. And I want to kiss you every time we're together. I lie awake at night imagining it. Imagining how soft your lips would feel against mine..."

Or'myr wrests the necklace off at the same time Tierney does, his besotted passion immediately dampening into stunned mortification.

"I'm sorry," he says, barely able to hold her wide-eyed look of astonishment.

Those beautiful Asrai eyes. Eyes I could drown in. He pulls in a long, shuddering breath, desperate for a trace of composure as he lifts the necklace. "Looks like they...actually work."

Tierney nods slowly, a flush suffusing her blue cheeks to a deep purple. Or'myr suppresses the urge to reach up and caress her gorgeous cheek. He glances away, longing twisting his heart as he takes in the jubilant purple crowd streaming by around them.

"How long have you felt this strongly about me, Or'myr?"

His embarrassment spikes to something approaching vertigo, but what does it matter now if she knows everything? He meets her gaze. "Since that first night you came to my Wyvernguard laboratory and dared me to hate you because you're friends with Trystan Gardner."

She holds his gaze for a protracted moment. Then, to his vast confusion, she steps forward and, quietly, almost ceremoniously, holds her hand out for his Xishlon'lure necklace. Thrown, he gives it to her and watches, with immense surprise, as she slips her Xishlon necklace back around her neck and moves to place the other necklace back around his, pausing, chain outstretched, waiting for his permission.

"Tierney..." Or'myr whispers, barely able to get the word out, but the heartfelt look she's giving him stokes his courage anew. He angles his head slightly down, eyes locked on hers as she slides the Xishlon'lure back over his head.

There's a sudden deepening of the world's purple light as Or'myr's tension loosens and his suppressed affection for Tierney suffuses his entire being once more. He pulls in an unsteady breath, all the purple of the world shimmering as Tierney draws closer.

"This is actually quite nice," she says as she fingers his necklace's chain, her eyes flicking up to meet his invitingly. Then she reaches up and runs her fingertip along the base of Or'myr's neck.

He shivers.

"It is," he agrees as they shyly move to embrace each other, Tierney's hand tentatively coming to his shoulder, his palm sliding around her waist. His heartbeat deepens as he thrills to the feel of her body lightly pressed against his as the swirling, celebratory world around them fades to a dreamy, purple haze.

"All right, then, Or'myr," Tierney says, tilting her head up. "I'm ready for your lightning."

Or'myr's heart practically trips over itself as he leans his tall frame down, then touches his lips to hers, holding his firelines in check as purple affinity heat sizzles through his body.

Her lips are so warm and soft, the whole lavender world suspended by her enticing kiss, but Or'myr manages to keep his magic at bay as he deepens the kiss, ever so slightly, drawing her body toward his as she pulls him closer in turn and they kiss for a suspended, magical moment. Tierney presses her lips more firmly against his and makes an irresistible little sound of surprised pleasure, her full breasts soft against his chest, her hand coming up to caress his neck with unmistakable want.

Lightning breaks free of its magical constraints and flashes through Or'myr, through his lips and straight into hers.

Tierney cries out and jerks back, breaking the kiss. Her hand flies up to her mouth and she stumbles backward, threads of violet lightning crackling over her lips, as wave after wave of remorse swamps Or'myr.

He roughly yanks off the necklace. "I'm sorry," he says as his fire magic pounds through him. "Tierney... I'm so sorry."

"Or'myr... I'm all right," Tierney insists, contradicting herself as she massages her mouth and studies him with a look of concern bordering on pity that makes Or'myr feel even more torn up, although he'll be damned if he'll let it show.

Tierney pulls off her necklace and studies it, seeming a bit dazed. "Well...at least I can say that I've finally been kissed."

"*That* was your first kiss?" Or'myr shakes his head, another knife-strike of remorse spearing through him. "Tierney, I'm sorry. Truly." He looks away, not able to hold her pitying stare. Wanting to wrest all the gorgeous, glowing purple flowers from the ground then raise his wand and blow up the damned Xishlon moon.

Tierney reaches out to touch his arm, and he reluctantly meets her entrancing gaze. "If I was Fire Fae," she says with a slight, rueful smile, "I imagine we'd get on quite well." The suggestion in her tone only serves to make him feel ten times worse.

"It's no matter," he brusquely states, looking west toward the mountains and then up at the cursed moon. "This idiotic festival will be over soon enough, and it's a good thing too. It's making us all lose our minds, and the military here is operating on a skeleton crew."

Their eyes meet in morbid understanding, that blasted warmth sparking between them once more.

Tierney cocks her head as if considering something. "If I kiss your cheek, will it trigger more lightning?"

"I don't know," he answers, frustrated.

Tierney reaches up to touch his shoulder and Or'myr's breath hitches, another flash of lightning forking through his lines. She brings her warm lips to his cheek and gives him a gentle kiss. Then another on the edge of his jaw. Another on the very edge of his mouth, thoughtfully tracing her thumb over his lower lip.

"Happy Xishlon, sweet Or'myr."

Or'myr swallows. "After we're done decimating Vogel's forces, feel free to visit me in my geomancy lab," he offers. "Or anywhere really...for conversation...or tea...or to kiss my cheek as often as you like."

Tierney flashes him a suggestive glance. "I just might take you up on that. I rather like the look you're giving me." She slides the Xishlon'lure into her pocket, shoots him an affectionate smile, then steps away, climbing deftly over the stone railing that abuts the tributary's bank.

"Where are you going?" he asks, completely under her spell. Wishing he could spend the whole purple night with her.

Tierney frowns toward the Vo Mountains. "To the Vo Forest. My kelpies unearthed something curious there." She nods toward the Wyvernguard soldier who just arrived to take her place on the stream's other side. "My watch just ended, so I think I'll take a look. They're sending me confusing images through the water, and I don't know what to make of it."

"Images of what?"

Tierney shakes her head, as if trying to puzzle it out. "A small, stagnant pool. There's nothing out of the ordinary about this image—that's what's confusing me. The forest is full of death as well as life. It's the natural way of things."

Or'myr raises a brow. "You sound like a Death Fae."

Tierney smiles a bit at this. "I suppose I do."

"So...you're going to spend the evening investigating a stagnant pool of water?" His lip quirks in spite of how much he's pining for her. "And I thought I was going to have the least romantic Xishlon of anyone."

"No, I win," Tierney rejoins. She gives him one last rueful look. "Except for being with you for a moment, Or'myr. I like you, and I don't regret kissing you. Maybe someday we'll find a way to try that kiss again."

And then she dives straight into the stream, dissolving into the water, her sparkling blue form flowing out toward her kindred river, on her way to the forest beyond.

Or'myr watches until her shimmering outline disappears from sight, his gaze traveling toward the Vo Mountains, residual lightning crackling through his lines. He closes his eyes, struggling to gather his Xishlon-scattered wits. Then he pulls in a deep breath and resumes his trek back toward his rune skiff, wondering the whole time what Tierney's kelpies have unearthed out there.

CHAPTER TWO

VOID FOREST

Tierney Calix

Xishlon night, twenty-first hour

Tierney glances at the purple moon from where she kneels, her hand in the small forest pool, the deep plum of the trees dappled with the Xishlon moon's bright violet light.

Even though he makes no sound arriving, she can sense Viger's Death Fae presence, her skin prickling from his aura's low vibration. She wondered when he'd eventually show himself, remembering his promise to find her on Xishlon and show her how Vogel's Shadow could be a *threat to Death*.

But right now she has more immediate concerns as she concentrates on the water swirling over her hand, because it's all *wrong*. Barely perceptible tendrils of dark smoke curl up from the curiously inky puddle, everything in it dead.

Apprehension ripples through Tierney. It's the same Shadow corruption she's sensed before. But those times, the subtle trace of gray magic was both fleeting and distant. Now, here the Shadow is again. So curiously isolated. To this tiny, stagnant pool.

She can sense the river striving to wall it off. To deposit as much silt as possible to separate it from its source stream.

What are you seeding here, Vogel? Why is it scaring my river?

Tierney glances over her shoulder toward Viger, who has materialized from black mist, his pale face staring at her from just inside the forest's shadows. A small thrill runs through her magic at the sight of him, as it always does, both the sizzle of fear and her unsettling draw to him commingled. A brief spike of conflict rises to be noticing Viger this way with the sting of Or'myr's violet lightning still on her lips...

She meets Viger's dark stare, some of the conflict subsiding as she loses herself to the feel of his otherworldly draw, his gaze on her a dark, probing force. It's as if he can look right through her to pick apart her every secret corner.

And those raven eyes...

Get hold of yourself, Asrai, she chastises herself. *You're feeling the effects of that blasted moon. Are you planning on claiming all of the dangerous young men of the East as your Xishlon'virs? There are more important things to attend to this night than swooning over every young man who crosses your path.*

She meets Viger's gaze, his dark form still and motionless in the shadows. "I'm glad you've come," she says, refusing to be unnerved by his eerily seductive presence. "There's something very wrong." She pulls her hand from the pool and motions him forward, brow tight with concern. "Viger...tell me if you can sense what's been done to this water. Because this tiny puddle scared my kelpies."

Viger strides to her, lowers his long frame, then places his chalk-white hand into the water, and closes his eyes.

Tierney scrutinizes him, his severe, hard-planed face so compelling. All three of the Wyvernguard's Death Fae have his same morbid elegance—powerful Viger, spider-shifter Sylla, and mysterious, refined Vesper.

Viger opens his eyes, pulling his hand from the water. "This is not the clean death of the natural world," he states with a tight frown. "This is something twisted." He rubs the blackened water between his fingertips, dark claws forming.

A sizable bat flies out of the forest and lands on his shoulder. Not the cute dog-faced fruit-loving kind, Tierney notes. The bloodsucking kind. Viger tilts his head up, and a flock of ravens descends on the branches surrounding them, rustling the violet leaves. Closing his eyes, he whispers to the ravens in a language that seems to emanate from deep inside his throat. Tierney can feel its low vibration straight through her body. "Vialyrr," he tells them, and all the ravens and the bat take wing.

"Where are you sending them?" she asks as she rises to her feet.

"To scan the Forest," he replies as he stands and turns to face her.

Tierney pulls in a shaky breath. "I've sent my kelpies out too. To investigate all the tributaries and solitary pools."

Viger stares at her, unblinking. "This Shadow water could be the death of them."

He says this so matter-of-factly, as only a Death Fae can. Unfazed by the final passage.

"I warned my kelpies to steer clear of it if they sense it," Tierney responds tightly, upset by the idea of her kelpies meeting with harm. "They know this power could be a remnant of Vogel's brief portal-incursion here."

Viger nods, as if that's settled, and Tierney strives to shake off her flare of disquiet over how easily he speaks of death and loss. Part of her realizes that Viger's and the other Death Faes' priorities are unique. Not to avoid death, but to restore the natural balance. Quietly studying him at the Wyvernguard, Tierney has come to suspect that Viger is as close to the natural world as any Fae in his own, strange way. And she can relate to that aspect of him. She can also relate to the strong sense that he's no stranger to emotional pain.

"We need to tell the Wyvernguard about this pool," she notes. "Small as it is."

Viger tilts his head toward Tierney, as if in consideration. "Do you have a vial?"

Tierney nods, fishing out the vial from under her tunic's collar, the small flask attached to a silver necklace chain that she keeps with her in case she has to transport a kelpie.

"Draw some of the water into your vial and bring it to the Vu Trin," Viger suggests.

Tierney glances up at the purple moon and lets out a long sigh before meeting Viger's unnervingly steady gaze once more. "We are unlikely sentinels of the Realm, Viger. Two misfits out here in the forest during Xishlon. Searching for traces of the Shadow forces lapping at the edges of their peaceable world while they write each other love sonnets."

"Is that what they do?" he asks with a trace of curiosity, as if this is a subject of fascination for him.

Tierney squints at him. "They've been talking about it for weeks."

"Their festival is of no concern to me."

Tierney feels a small twinge of surprise, because she can sense it there, buried under his flat inflection.

Hurt.

Tierney points to the sky, wondering if Viger is truly immune to the moon's entrancing pull. "Do you feel its effect at all?"

He holds her stare, unblinking. "I sense it," he says, a trace of tension lighting on the air between them.

"It's supposed to be good luck, you know," she says as she presses down her disquieted feelings. "To kiss someone under the Xishlon moon. A full pairing is said to be an even greater blessing."

"Romantic nonsense," Viger scoffs, glancing down at the shadowy water. "Made up by a world that wants to deny death, destruction, and despair."

She blinks at him, unable to stifle a short laugh, his outrageously bleak attitude an unexpected balm this eve. Their eyes catch, gravity seeming to shift as Tierney stares into his midnight gaze. That sense of being drawn toward him ripples over her, everything else receding as the world darkens.

Tendrils of his dark mist shiver over her exposed skin, the odd sensation not completely without appeal. "What would it be like to kiss a Death Fae, I wonder," she muses before she can stop herself, overcome by both Viger's and the Xishlon moon's thralls.

Viger's mouth curves into a slow, feral smile that sends a shiver down Tierney's spine as dark horns spiral up from his head. "It's terrifying, I'm told," he says, and Tierney feels like her eyes are magically locking to his, a different type of danger now riding the air.

Warnings she's heard murmured at the Wyvernguard flit through her mind—kiss a Death Fae and they'll invade your nightmares. Kiss a Death Fae and be buried in the deepest dark.

Kiss a Death Fae and become one with Death itself.

Viger reaches up and pushes her hair behind her shoulder with a surprisingly silken touch, his claws skimming the base of Tierney's neck, making her shudder, his touch like shadows sliding across her skin. And his scent…it's like cool, silent places. Like secrets. A flush rises on Tierney's neck, his dark, penetrating gaze shifting to heatedly enthralling.

"Viger." She swallows as her heartbeat deepens, her water magic warming as his claw tips slowly circle the back of her neck. "I'm a Water Fae tied to the life of my river. You're a Death Fae. Do we really want to do this?"

Viger smiles, a single claw now tracing an enticing line down the length of her neck. "I think you know the answer, Asrai."

Tierney swallows, mesmerized by him, as the purple-lit forest darkens further.

"I think…maybe you should find another Death Fae to kiss on Xishlon," she suggests, attempting to sound wry as she staves off his mounting allure.

"Death Fae do not pair with other Death Fae," he croons, leaning closer, his deep voice a sensual lure. "There is no balance in it."

"You know what, Viger?" Tierney says, unable to hold herself back from his hypnotic, compelling thrall. "I'm drawn to you. I find that confusing, but…there's something about you that's beautiful."

Viger's claw tips thread through her hair. He leans in, waiting, so close…

This is *my night to kiss all the dangerous boys,* Tierney marvels as she sighs and gives in, angling her mouth toward Viger.

"Let me show you," he whispers, his dark lips brushing hers. "Let me show you what we really are."

"I want you to," Tierney whispers back.

Her lips meet his in a swirl of darkness, the purple light muting.

Tierney spirals into his embrace, into his delicious darkness. It's like she's being pulled to the ocean's deepest floor and below, down, down, down, his arms wrapped around her, hers around him, clutching tightly to each other as their kiss deepens in hunger and she finds herself pressed against his hard body and swept into the longing to merge completely with his thrall.

And then the world disappears.

Panic overtakes Tierney as she's suspended in nothingness for a long, breathless moment.

Viger is gone. Everything is gone. No color. No sensation. No sense of anything or anyone at all.

Like she's been pulled to the very center of Erthia.

And then, she has a sense of Viger's lips pulling away from hers, his grip on her loosening, and she spirals and spirals back up into the world of sights and smells and kisses and Viger and the purple forest.

Everything.

Pulsing with glorious, overwhelming, spectacular life.

Tierney grasps Viger's arms, unsteady on her feet, gasping as her gaze darts around.

Viger watches her with deeply serious eyes, his strong embrace supporting her. The purple wash of moonlight on the rustling leaves is so beautiful it's almost too much to bear. The loamy scent of the Forest. Her intrinsic sense of the network of rivers and streams all over this land, enhanced. And this beautiful, young Fae man standing before her. Waiting. Waiting for her to fully *see*. It's like she's returned to a whole new world, every sense heightened. Every glorious, living sensation flooding in. Life everywhere. Life fed by natural death.

She meets Viger's ardent gaze, stunned.

"Now, do you see?" he asks, uncharacteristically emotional.

Tierney nods, overcome. "You're the pause." She breathes out. "You're not the end. You're the beginning. The seed."

Viger's dark eyes are suddenly brimming with tears. "Now you see."

"The people here…they don't understand you at all," she says, impassioned, her senses full of the Forest, of him, of her own heartbeat pulsing in her chest, of *everything*. "You're the seed for all of it. For the entire balance of the Forest. The decay. The death. The rotted soil. It's the start of everything."

"Now go back to the pool," Viger says as he angles his head toward the shadowed puddle.

Tierney looks toward the lifeless water as trepidation swells. She kneels by the stagnant pool, pushes her hand back into the water, and closes her eyes.

Tendrils of Shadow fly though her lines, and a different sort of pull takes hold, spiraling her down, down, and down. Not into the earth. Not into a deep, dark, pause.

Into an endless void. An abyss.

The end of everything.

Tierney wrests her hand from the water and falls back onto the ground, suddenly terrified as she glares at the puddle with fresh eyes. Trees rustle all around as the flock of ravens descends once more, one perching on Viger's shoulder and pressing close to his neck. Viger stills and closes his eyes, as if listening carefully to the raven.

When he opens his eyes, there's a terrifying edge of fear in his gaze.

"It's not just one pool of Shadow death," he says. "There is water like this all over this forest."

Alarm bolts through Tierney. "He's here," she rasps out. "Somehow, Vogel's here. And he's going to destroy the natural balance."

"They think him far away across a vast desert," Viger says ominously as he eyes the dark pool like a predator eyeing a much more powerful predator. "But he is already here, somehow. And not just in the corrupted animals that have been found. His many-eyed beasts. He's entrenched in the natural world of the Eastern Realm."

"We need to ward the Vo," Tierney says, panic mounting as she rises and grasps Viger's arm, the ravens' eyes all focused on her. "I need you, Viger. I know Deathkin can conjure strong wards. Help me protect my waters and all the life of the river. And then, help me warn the Vu Trin and my Asrai'kin. We need to ward *all* of Noilaan's waterways. Xishlon needs to end *right now*."

Viger nods and Tierney's grip on him tightens as they fall into complete Fae alliance with each other. "Help me any way you can," she implores, holding his kindred stare as his eyes pool to solid black. "Or Vogel's going to destroy the natural world."

XISHLON STORM

Vothendrile Xanthile

Xishlon night, twenty-first hour

"The moon's pull…it's strong."

Trystan's words are hesitant as he gazes at the shimmering lavender orb, its reflection a dazzling spectacle on the river below.

But it's nowhere near as dazzling as Trystan, Vothe considers, captivated by the Mage sitting before him at the teahouse's outdoor table, Trystan's handsome face lifted to the moon, his hair tinted violet by its light. The piercings in his brow and lip catch sparks of the lavender light, his Xishlon tunic a dark, moody purple and embroidered with a darker purple dragon down its side. And his skin…it seems to shimmer even more brightly, with such an entrancing green that it makes Vothe want to run a finger over those glimmering lips and tug on the piercing there.

With his teeth.

Because this night has unexpectedly turned into one for celebration, with the news of Vang Troi's intention to forge an alliance with Elloren Gardner.

Yes, this is a night for the purple moon if there ever was one.

"You know, you could just give in to the moon's pull," Vothe ventures a bit breathlessly, not used to being so flustered by anyone.

Trystan's face tenses as he pulls his gaze from the moon, as if struggling to shut out its thrall. "Vogel's forces are massing at the edge of the Western Realm," he says, a hardened light in those kohl-rimmed green eyes of his. Eyes Vothe could fall into and be lost in forever. "Tomorrow, we find out if Vang Troi is truly considering aligning with my sister. And you want me to ignore all that and…give in to a purple moon?"

Vothe can feel it…the shivering warmth that's kicked up in Trystan's fireline, despite everything. He leans closer to him, a Xishlon Plum tree sheltering their cliffside space, the two of them ensconced by a railing overlooking the precipitous Sixth Tier drop. The outdoor seating area of the Sapphire Kraken teahouse is packed with purple-clad revelers, the cacophony of conversation, street music, and general celebration affording their conversation some privacy.

Vothe tries not to look at the menacing picture of Elloren Gardner Grey tacked to the tree beside them. "I know Vang Troi through my family," he says. "She's true to her word. I believe she *will* forge an alliance."

The tenuous spark of hope in Trystan's eyes sends a pang through Vothe's heart, their gazes on each other a liquid, addictive thing that threatens to completely upend his thoughts. "Your sister knew she had Black Witch power when she fled from Vogel," he adds. "She could have aligned with the Mages then. But she chose to come *here*. With vital military information. And the Icaral of Prophecy is firmly on her side. Don't think for a second that Vang Troi hasn't given all of that careful consideration." Vothe glances at the crowded streets, catching sight of a knot of Vu Trin soldiers passing by, their gazes registering Trystan and Vothe.

Keeping track of Elloren Grey's allies, no doubt.

Vothe leans even closer, dropping his voice to a whisper.

"There's nothing we can do for the moment but wait. So, perhaps giving in to Xishlon and blending in is the best thing you can do for your sister right now."

Trystan lets out a short, jaded laugh. "You want me to...*blend in*?" He raises his green-glimmering Mage hand, and Vothe can't help but notice the ever-present weapons-training bruising.

And yet, so many hostile stares followed them here. So many hostile stares emanate from the tables throughout this outdoor area as well, the hatred and fear cutting through even the Xishlon moon's enthralling light. It's dauntingly hard to ignore, anger rising inside Vothe on Trystan's behalf again and again. And Vothe can tell by the repeated storming flares of Trystan's magic—even as his expression remains remote and unaffected—that he feels this ire. Deeply.

"I'm worried, Vothe," Trystan says. "And not just about my sister. The whole Western Realm underestimated Vogel. And then he swept in and killed almost all the Lupines. Children. Babies. Diana and Jarod's whole family. Their *whole family*, Vothe..."

"And we'll be ready for him," Vothe insists. "Because of your sister."

Vothe glances up at the translucent dome, the runes marked on its surface tinted violet by the moonlight, barely perceptible. His gaze slides toward the moon as gratitude washes over him that Vogel's forces are a huge desert away, his sole portal here destroyed. There's time to prepare and strengthen all the runic power guarding the Realm. It's like the East has dodged a massive arrow at the last minute. And none of the people who are glaring at Trystan have the foggiest idea of what they've been spared.

Vothe's mind spins over the sudden shift his life has taken—not only falling for the brother of the Black Witch, but now in league with him to protect his sister.

"Take this evening," Vothe prods. "One night before the fight resumes tomorrow. You've worked ceaselessly for the East from the moment you arrived. You deserve to find the moon."

Trystan's eyes widen, and Vothe's lips lift in response. He

knows that Trystan has been here long enough to know what "find the moon" means on this night.

"It's your festival now too," Vothe insists as a raw longing for Trystan rises.

"Is it?" Trystan throws back, the words breaking with emotion as turbulent power jostles through his lines.

"Yes," Vothe answers emphatically, willing it to be so, the moon making him bold. His feelings for Trystan making him bold.

"I want to belong here," Trystan says in a rough whisper, a trace of fragile hope in the statement. Trystan's lips part as if he's about to say more, then close again as his power shudders around him in fitful arcs.

"You belong," Vothe says, knowing that if they were anywhere else, he'd pull Trystan into his arms and kiss him right now. "And this is your moon too."

"How *dare* you wear Xishlon clothes!"

Vothe and Trystan both turn, the angry, female voice like a hammer to glass as Vothe scents Heelyn's hatred, hitting them both like an incoming cyclone.

Ire sparks in Vothe and he glares incredulously at Heelyn as she strides up to their table, three of her friends behind her, all dressed in their Wyvernguard uniforms and glowering at Trystan. There's an indignant fire in Heelyn's eyes, her hawkish face twisted as she halts, one fist on the hip of her Vu Trin tunic, the other around the hilt of her curved rune sword, her fury as brittle as her close-shorn black hair.

Oh, Sweet Holy Vo, are you honestly doing this now? Vothe seethes. *Can we not have one night free of this?*

But it's increasingly inescapable. Even after Commander Ung Li publicly threw her support behind Trystan, the hatred continues to fester and grow, emboldened by the majority of the Wyvernguard doggedly wanting Trystan out.

Trystan doesn't look at Heelyn, doesn't respond. He keeps hold of his perpetual calm as he goes still as a windless lake, his gaze on the table. But Vothendrile can sense Trystan's storm-magic rising, and even the slim edge of that power dwarfs the ferocity Heelyn is attempting to intimidate him with. Heelyn waits, fist to hip, but Trystan does not apologize for his deep purple civilian tunic.

Careful, Heelyn, Vothendrile almost wants to warn her. *You've never fully appreciated what you're dealing with here. He's leagues more powerful than you are.*

"Heelyn," Vothe says, dangerously calm. "He's in Noi lands. What exactly do you expect him to wear? I challenge you to make a clothing purchase this time of year that isn't purple."

Heelyn rounds on Vothe with a stare that would intimidate most of the Wyvernguard, especially since she's got quite a bit of runic power to back it up. But she's outmatched here. Seriously outmatched.

"Was I talking to you?" she snaps, dark eyes blazing.

"You seem to be talking to every last person in the restaurant," Vothe blithely replies, keeping the anger that's rising within him firmly in check.

Heelyn sets her blistering glare back on Trystan, who continues to stare at the table with that unblinking calm of his. Jaded calm.

"Wear your own clothes from now on," she seethes. "Not ours. And not *purple*. Xishlon is off-limits to you. And you have no place in Vo's temple." She lurches forward and hooks her finger under the Vo'lon religious necklace that's visible at the edges of Trystan's collar, yanking it into full view.

Lightning spits through Vothe, silver flashing through his vision as he suppresses the urge to leap over the table and throttle Heelyn. But Trystan doesn't react. He just stubbornly keeps his eyes focused on the table before him, even as fire scythes through his lines.

"You're *Gardnerian*. Not Noi." Heelyn venomously insists. "Get back in your blacks. Your kind are *reviled* by Vo."

"You think I should wear Gardnerian clothes," Trystan says quietly. A statement, not a question. His tone is neutral, but

473

Vothe almost draws back from how intensely his waterline is now storming.

"Yes," she sneers. "Stay in your own culture."

"You think that's my culture?"

"Of course it is!"

Trystan's expression has gone very cold as he continues to stare at the table, and Vothe is momentarily overwhelmed by the sense of just how much power Trystan is holding back.

"Heelyn, leave it…" Vothe cautions.

"No, Vothe. *No.*" She swings back toward Trystan, like a torch leveled, her eyes glazed with outraged tears. "My parents were *killed* by your grandmother!"

Trystan winces. "So were mine," he says, almost inaudible.

Heelyn's mouth turns down into a trembling grimace. "I don't believe you!" she hisses. "And now your sister might be here in the Realm, as well. Where is she, Crow? Where is the Black Witch?"

Silence.

"You know, don't you," Heelyn hisses. Her hostile gaze swings to Vothe. "Do you know, as well? Have you become that much of a traitor to your own people?"

Vothe's horns spiral up from his head with a tight sting, his teeth elongating. "I stand with the Eastern Realm," he says, low and dangerous. "So does Trystan."

Heelyn leans toward Vothe. "We don't need Crows standing with the Realm." She jabs her finger toward Vothe's chest for emphasis. "And you need to start *guarding* him like the enemy that he is! Not *flirting* with him. Every shape-shifter who gets within ten feet of the two of you knows what's going on!"

"Leave. Him. Be."

Vothe turns along with everyone else, all of them collectively surprised by the deep, resonant female voice, an undercurrent of lethal threat in it.

Sylla Vuul is standing a few tables away, the petite Death Fae's dark-clad form resonating the pause before an attack, an additional six eyes sprouting around the two dark ones she has pinned on Heelyn. Elegant Death Fae Vesper is seated beside her, his gleaming black cane in hand, his eerily attractive eyes pooling to a solid black.

Heelyn attempts not to wither under Sylla's spider-shifter stare, but Vothe can sense her flash of fear. Justified fear.

A swarm of spiders flows down from the hem of Sylla's dark pants and scuttles toward Heelyn, some of the other patrons letting out sounds of alarm as they get up and move away from their tables, away from the Death Fae.

"No one wants your kind here either," Heelyn snarls at Sylla recklessly, but Vothe notices Heelyn's voice wavers as she glances at the tide of spiders closing in.

"Death is always an unwelcome visitor," Sylla states. Her multi-eyed, frightening stare is mirrored in its strange intensity by Vesper's, and Vothe can sense Heelyn's courage shriveling.

Heelyn shoots Trystan a hostile look and leaves with her silent, equally hostile uniformed companions before the spiders can reach her. Sylla and Trystan exchange a glance and Sylla nods to him, then sits back down with Vesper, her spiders scuttling back.

As Heelyn and her cohorts disappear into the Xishlon crowd, Vothe can feel some of Trystan's control over his lines fracturing, can sense how much Heelyn's hatred has affected him by the violent turbulence crashing through his lines. Trystan lifts his head and eyes Vothe with blistering resignation.

"Trys…" Vothe says.

Trystan shakes his head. "Don't," he insists, lifting his palm, his voice hard.

Vothe grows silent, realizing it's all too much at the moment, the desire mounting to leap over the table and embrace him. And show him that he belongs here.

That he belongs with me.

Instead, Vothe holds himself back, inwardly cursing all the people who are making Trystan feel like an outcast.

Which used to include you.

He inwardly winces, remembering how he fought against Trystan's inclusion, bent on hating this grandson of the last Black Witch. Now it's hard to even look at Trystan without it triggering a pang of want so fierce it threatens to undo him. Because Vothe sees the truth. Trystan Gardner is as decent and courageous and kind as he is staggeringly beautiful. And if his sister is anything like him, then the risk he's taking to help protect her is well worth it.

Trystan looks over the water, toward the mountains and the Xishlon moon hanging above it all. "I'm scared for Elloren," he admits. "If they treat *me* like this..."

Vothe doesn't have to hear the rest of the sentence.

They'll treat her far worse. Even if Vang Troi agrees to an alliance, other soldiers might band together to defy orders and kill her.

"She's with one of the most powerful sorcerers on Erthia right now," Vothe says in a whisper. "She's safe. And, like I said, there's nothing to be done at the moment but wait."

Trystan keeps his gaze focused on the moon, but Vothe can sense his effect on him in the way Trystan's water aura is now rippling through his, threads of blue lightning crackling that set Vothe's skin prickling with a heightened desire to cancel out all the hatred here.

And kiss him.

A memory slides in. That contentious night when Trystan stood in the doorway of his Wyvernguard room, his eyes newly and shockingly lined with Noi kohl, soft runic lantern light dancing over his tall, slender frame. Trystan was so stunning that Vothe felt frozen by the sight of him—his eyes blazing in contrast to the midnight kohl that transformed their deep green into a fierce shining emerald.

And the tattoo. Sweet Holy Vo.

How furious most of the military apprentices were and still are about that tattoo—that this Gardnerian dared to cast off Gardnerian ways with the rapidity of someone throwing off something that was slowly strangling him.

Vothe remembers hesitating outside Trystan's bedroom that night. He remembers the heated look Trystan gave him as he watched Vothe noticing his tattoo, watched the slow slide of his gaze.

But I didn't move.

Like a coward, Vothe rues, pained by the memory of how he let the boundaries between them stand. Let fear of what everyone else would think stand—fear of how his family would react to him aligning himself with the grandson of the last Black Witch. Would they bar him from returning home to Zhilaan, like his uncle Sholin when he fell in love with Fain Quillen?

Vothe's own storming magic rises at the thought.

I'm done with the boundaries, he inwardly growls. *Done with being a coward.*

Done with pretending I haven't fallen in love with Trystan Gardner.

"Trystan," Vothe says, and Trystan trains his fierce eyes on him. Those blazingly emerald eyes... For a moment Vothe's thoughts scatter.

Dive in, Vothe. Just dive in.

"Be my Xishlon'vir," Vothe says, leaning in, his voice pitched low, having asked before without ever receiving an answer. "Before all the hells converge. Be my Xishlon'vir, Trystan Gardner."

Trystan stills, the energy in his lines kicking up, flashing out toward Vothe.

"And not just my Xishlon'vir," Vothe says as Wyvern blood pounds through his veins. "I want to court you. A formal Zhilon'ile courting."

Trystan stops breathing, his water magic pulsing so hard, the scene momentarily liquefies around them. "With war looming?" Trystan finally manages, challenge in his tone even as his lightning forks toward Vothe.

Vothe leans toward him, growing even more impassioned. "What do you think we'll be fighting for?" He motions between them. "*This.* This is what I'll be fighting for."

"A forbidden union?"

"For *freedom*."

Trystan swallows, his magic now swirling in a torrent around Vothe. "What does…a courting entail?"

"First, a bite."

Incredulous amusement flickers in Trystan's eyes. "A *bite*?"

His confusion catches Vothe off guard, as it so often does. "Yes. The formal claim of a Wyvern."

Trystan coughs out a short laugh and narrows his gaze at Vothe. "That is not a usual offer."

Vothe's mouth quirks. "What about us is usual?"

"But your family…" Trystan says, hurt breaking through. But also concern. "You told me they'll shun you."

A defiant spark of lightning crackles through Vothe. "I don't care. I don't care what anyone makes of this. Not anymore." Vothe reaches across the table and takes Trystan's hand, a sudden, mutual flare of power coursing through them both. Trystan's breathing goes erratic as he glances around like a cornered animal and then withdraws his hand, and Vothe feels the sting of his rejection acutely.

Trystan shakes his head, as if silently refuting Vothe's thoughts, his tone strained when it comes. "You don't understand. None of you do. In Gardneria, if you and I showed any closeness in public…" His lips tighten as he looks away, his brow rigidly furrowing.

Vothe leans toward him, swept up in sudden understanding. "We are *not there*. You're not hated for this here."

Trystan coughs out a bitter laugh. "Oh, no. I'm only hated for everything else."

Emboldened, Vothe holds his hand out on the table for Trystan once more, palm up. An offering and a challenge. Trystan glances at Vothe's hand, then looks away. He swallows, his throat bobbing, and Vothe can sense a swell of heat in him that's reaching out for Vothe along with the heightened turbulence in his waterline.

"I don't want to fight this any longer," Vothe gently prods.

Trystan shakes his head, his voice fractured when it comes. "I don't either."

"Then give in to it," Vothe offers, his lips edging up. "And kiss me on this night of the Xishlon moon, since it's in unforgivably poor taste to not kiss someone on this night."

Trystan raises an ironic brow, but Vothe can feel the unsettled fire rising in him. "Vothe, think carefully about what this is going to mean for you. And…the whole world is about to descend into chaos."

"Then what's a little bit more?" Vothe takes hold of Trystan's hand, invisible sparks flying as Trystan moves to draw his hand away again, but Vothe holds on. "You're not in Gardneria," Vothe vehemently maintains. "And you need to break through this. *Tonight*. Let's walk to the center of the square." He angles his head toward the plaza beside them, a large stone statue of Vo in its center. "Kiss me there. *Right there*, Trystan. In the middle of the city. Where everyone can see us. That'll cure you of Gardneria."

Trystan coughs out a derisive sound. "You think it's so simple to cure me of Gardneria."

"No. I don't. I know I'll never truly understand. But that doesn't change the fact that you should kiss me right there. Because you *can* here, Trystan. And I know you want to kiss me as much as I want to kiss you."

Trystan holds Vothe's impassioned stare, his fire power suffusing them both, lightning sparking just under his skin. "Vothe, you're a storm Wyvern and I'm a Level Five Mage with dominant water and fire. Our affinities will fly right toward each other." The fervid heat in his gaze deepens. "We're likely to trigger true lightning."

Holy Vo.

"Well, then," Vothe says as he strokes the edge of Trystan's thumb with his own. "We'll simply have to find somewhere private, so we can keep everyone from harm's way. It *is* the sacred tradition to kiss during Xishlon. So it is very important that you do kiss me tonight, Trystan Gardner. You wouldn't want to insult the Noi people, would you?"

Trystan laughs outright, his words half in jest when they come. "My very presence seems to be an insult."

Vothe's lightning flares, a sudden seriousness taking hold. "It's *wrong* the way they treat you," he insists. "And it was wrong the way I treated you when you first came here. And...when I realized how wrong it all was, I'm sorry I remained silent for so long." His voice breaks with emotion. "You once said that you wanted to fight for this intolerant, tolerant land." Trystan gives him a jaded look, but Vothe is undaunted. "I think it's time for something different. It's time for a tolerant, tolerant land." Vothe glances poignantly at their clasped hands. "Perhaps this is a bridge to that."

Trystan's defiance seems to soften, an edge of exhausted resignation now in his gaze. "It's no matter if I'm never fully accepted. It's still so much better here."

"It's not like you're without friends."

Trystan gives him the barest trace of a smile as his gaze darts toward the Death Fae. "The outcasts, you mean?"

"Nooo," Vothe drawls with a look of mock censure. "The *interesting people* who aren't sheep. Trust me, the others grow tiresome after a time."

Vothe releases Trystan's hand, stands up, then holds his hand back out to him. "Come walk with me," *you beautiful, powerful, courageous thing*. "Let me show you that there's more to this night than righteous, bullying cowards."

Vothe walks quietly with Trystan, their fingers intertwined, as they meander through the festive crowds, attracting stares of censure along with scattered looks of kindness, nods of encouragement, a few passersby calling out to Vothe in jovial greeting. They travel down to the First Tier and walk past the edge of the city to an isolated rocky inlet, the dramatic stone cliffs rising on three sides colored deep purple by the Xishlon moon, the moonlight turning the entire Vo River violet and black.

Vothe pauses on a broad rock, water misting up from the waves pounding on the black stones all around.

Trystan stands with his face toward the water, eyes closed, head up, and breathes it all in. The water. The glorious violent energy of it.

"I come here often," Vothe tells him, pointing toward the towering, jagged bluff above them. "I fly up there and watch the tide. Feel its energy crashing through me."

Vothe reaches for Trystan and grasps his hand, abruptly filled with the sense of a building storm. Lightning sparks through them both as their fingers tighten around each other and Trystan gives Vothe a look, sudden fire in it and a rush of water strong enough to rival the crashing tide.

"Trystan..."

Vothe is unable to finish the thought. Trystan grabs hold of him, his lips coming to Vothe's. Lightning flashes through them both, sparking out in a forking explosion that sends a shock wave of heat through Vothe.

Trystan pulls back, trembling as he keeps tight hold of Vothe's arms, hesitating, his look almost pained.

Vothe grabs Trystan's tunic and yanks him roughly back, their mouths capturing each other's once more as the full force of their power collides, stealing Vothe's breath away.

Trystan's muscles are taut under Vothe's palms, his hands grasping, his hot breath cutting through the cool spray of water all around them as Vothe deepens the kiss, caressing Trystan's tongue with his own, which seems to both shock and thrill Trystan. Vothe can feel the roar of Trystan's power overtaking him, overtaking them both as they kiss and kiss. And suddenly, Vothe wants to possess Trystan fully and be possessed by him. Only him.

When they finally come up for air, Vothe's back is pressed against the cliff, Trystan's hard body pressed against his.

Trystan's lips lift into a crooked smile. "Have I honored your traditions adequately, Vothendrile?" He glances over his shoulder at the lavender moon, but underneath his intense want, Vothe scents his vulnerability, his body's slight tremor.

Vothe reaches up to caress Trystan's face, then kisses him

lightly on his cheekbone, his temple, his sharp jaw, his water magic flowing through Trystan's lines in a caressing stream. "I'm falling in love with you, toiyanon."

Trystan's whole expression tenses and he starts to silently cry.

Vothe leans close and touches the tip of his tongue to the salty tears. "Let me court you."

Trystan's mouth gives a bitter twist. "Your family will disown you—"

"To hell with all of that. Let me court you."

Trystan nods as their water power flows toward each other in a passionate, whipping stream. "Tell me again what's involved in that?" Trystan says in a quavering tone, reaching up to wipe away tears. "You mentioned a bite."

Vothe gives him a mischievous smile. "It also requires a great deal of kissing. An incredible amount of kissing. Huge amounts of kissing that are required every day of the courtship. It is a sacred part of the tradition dating back centuries and must be obeyed."

Trystan's smile broadens. "I've a sense you're making this up as you go along."

"Do you take issue with that?"

"No," he says, suddenly breathless. "Gods, no."

Vothe pulls him close and Trystan kisses him fiercely, his tongue sensually caressing Vothe's, all reserve falling away as Trystan takes complete charge. As if the lightning he's letting loose has been pent-up inside him all his life.

"It's new," Trystan finally says, his forehead pressed to Vothe's, his voice ragged as desire and love pound through them both. "To feel so…happy. It's not an emotion I've often felt."

"I want to give you my fealty," Vothe tells him, impassioned.

Trystan leans forward, his lips brushing Vothe's as their heated tide of power rises to overtake them. "And I want to kiss you until we both drown."

CHAPTER
FOUR

MATCHMAKER

Lucretia Quillen

Xishlon night, twenty-first hour

"Are you going to kiss Jules Kristian tonight?"

Lucretia almost spits out her tea. She gapes at her friend and fellow Resistance worker Soollyndrile, a smug look on the young Wyvern matchmaker's face as she reclines against the embroidered plum-velvet cushions of the Painted Dragon Patisserie's cliffside seating. Soo sips her purple Xishlon tea, her unblinking, vertically slit-pupiled stare fixed on a flustered Lucretia.

"Of course not," Lucretia protests. "We're good friends, nothing more."

Soo laughs and takes another sip of the glowing rose-scented tea, the two of them allies for years—two points of a network stretching from West to East, aiding Fae youth, amongst others, fleeing East.

Soo's onyx lips, eyelids, and horns are decorated with violet Xishlon glitter, the Wyvern-shifter's garb a shimmering riot of purple gems, her long black hair streaked with violet. Her partially dragon-shifted body is covered in ebony scales and Soo's rare ability to hold a partial-shift is drawing more than a few stares. As is Lucretia's green-glimmering Mage skin, but Lucretia is too shocked by Soo's question to give much notice to any of it.

"Toiya," Soo says, her wide, scaled nose crinkling up in apparent disbelief over Lucretia's naivete. "Jules Kristian is *not* just your friend. You two need to mate. Immediately."

Lucretia blinks at her, rendered speechless.

Soo chuckles. "Claim him as your Xishlon'vir, Lu. Claim him tonight."

Lucretia can feel the flush blooming on her face. "You do realize I'm Gardnerian," she sputters. "We...we don't just claim a—" she glances around, feeling scandalous to even voice the word "—a *mate*. Are you quite sure he...feels that way for me?"

Soo's glittering purple lips lift into a sly smile. "I am a Wyvern-shifter, toiya. A matchmaker by trade. Of course, I am sure. He wants to devour you whole."

A shocked laugh bursts from Lucretia.

It can't be. There's no way calm, tea-sipping, reserved Jules wants to...devour her whole? Lucretia's water magic spirals into an excited churn, her usually unflappable nerves completely and thoroughly lit up.

Soo turns serious as she reaches out to take Lucretia's hand, the points of her plum-painted talons resting featherlight on Lucretia's skin. "I love you, Lu," Soo says with that warm, velvet voice of hers. "And I know how many Fae youth are here in the East because of you." She glances around the seating area, easily finding narrow-eyed disapproval focused on Lucretia.

Soollyndrile frowns. "I also see how you are shunned because of the Mage green of your skin." Her expression softens. "Lulu, take your moment of happiness on this Xishlon. Jules Kristian returns your passion. Go claim your mate."

Tears are suddenly brimming in Lucretia's eyes. *Can it be true? After so many years of secretly working together for the Resistance, breaking the laws of every Realm together, risking our lives together...*

"I told you. I'm Gardnerian," Lucretia says, an attempt to

be wry, but her voice hitches around the words. "I don't know how to…claim a mate."

"But you seek to devour him, as well," Soo puts in, silver eyes sparkling.

Lucretia shrinks down, feeling as if she's a diary read aloud to the whole patisserie.

Soo's smile broadens, her sharpened teeth on display. "Break with Mage ways in this. You already have in everything else. Go find your mate and bring him the moon."

Lucretia glances up at the Xishlon orb, the luminous purple moon lightning up the Vo River in a dazzling display of rippling violet, the world transformed into a purple garden, ripe with romantic possibility. And suddenly, Lucretia's very skin is lit up by the draw of this moon, the way it coaxes a heart's hidden affections to life and pushes away life's shadows.

"Listen to me, Lu," Soo says, leaning farther in, emphatic now. "War is coming to this land. Who knows how much time any of us has. And this festival, it might seem like a frivolous thing, but none of it is trivial. *This*, toiya—" she motions loosely around at the scattered Noi couples kissing at tables, under plum trees "—*this* is the reason to work for a better world." She laughs, squeezing Lucretia's hand. "It's all about the love."

Lucretia finds herself unexpectedly moved beyond words, a tear sliding down her cheek. And she realizes, in that moment, that fellow Resistance worker Soo, with all her dramatic, Wyvern flair, her outrageous outfits and ribald sense of humor, might have the most important job in all the Realms—revealing people's love for each other.

Because there's so much of it.

Everywhere.

"Go find Jules," Soo insists, her glittering purple lips turning up in a playful, suggestive smile. "Embrace the moon and go claim your mate."

"It's the night of the Xishlon moon," Lucretia says as she enters Jules's cramped First Tier apartment. This crowded, port-level section of Voloi is home to many of the Realm's recent immigrants. She glances toward the window beside him that looks over the river, its curtains shut, as always.

Jules doesn't look up from where he's carefully forging residency documents, calligraphy pen to parchment, but his lip quirks. "Ah, yes. Their lavender love moon. Its thrall is...interesting."

"It's truly lavender."

Jules glances up and gives her another reserved smile, his gaze not once straying to her gleaming, formfitting lavender-lace dress Soo gifted Lucretia, with purple Xishlon roses embroidered all over it. Lucretia's resolve wavers. She knows that she looks like a resplendent garden, come to offer herself to Jules in a dazzling bouquet, ripe for the taking, her black hair streaked with purple glitter, her lips gleaming with Soo's purple-glimmer lipstick.

"I hear it's quite lovely," Jules says warmly, still not noticing.

"Have you seen it, though?" Lucretia presses.

"No. I'm trying to finish these..." His tiny apartment is littered with maps. Maps tacked to the walls and spread out on the table. Official maps of the Eastern Realm as well as secret maps of the sublands. And stacks of forged identity papers to send back to the Western Realm. To help desperate refugees get to Noi lands.

Away from Vogel's reach.

"Come see the moon," Lucretia insists.

Jules tilts his head and views her searchingly. "Lucretia, we'll be advocating for the Black Witch this time tomorrow. These need to be done—"

"And they will be," she insists, emotion rising in her tone. "I'll help you finish them. But we need to stop every now and then and remember why we're doing any of this. It's...because of Lavender Moon festivals and children dressed in lilac running around trailing strings of runic orbs...young people searching for someone to kiss. This is what we're doing all this for.

So that everyone can have lovely things like this. *Everyone*. No exceptions."

Jules stills and looks closely at her. "All right, Lucretia," he says. "Show me the moon."

Lucretia strides to the window and pulls the curtains open, the riverside room instantly suffused with purple light, the Vo River shimmering violet below, mountains just beyond.

The Xishlon moon suspended above it all.

Jules sets down his pen and silently takes in the moon, then meets Lucretia's gaze, serious. "It's beautiful. What's troubling you, Lucretia?"

Lucretia forces a deep, wavering breath, every nerve alight. "I spoke to Soo. She…she told me that you're attracted to me. She said…it's one of the strongest attractions she's ever sensed." Lucretia can barely get the words out, can barely breathe evenly.

Jules's gaze changes, something powerful flashing in his eyes that she's never seen before. He looks away, his jaw ticking. "I'm sorry. I've always tried to keep that to myself. But I can't change how I feel about you." The words are tight with contrition, rigidly contained.

And Lucretia realizes, in that moment, how tightly contained she's kept her own feelings. Is it any wonder they've misread each other for so many years? She takes in his beloved face, washed in lavender. His mussed brown hair, rumpled clothing and tarnished spectacles.

"Well, you see," Lucretia stammers, "the thing is… I feel exactly the same for you."

Jules's eyes widen as they meet hers.

"I've been in love with you for years," Lucretia admits in an impassioned rush.

Jules pulls in a sharp breath and swallows. "Lucretia," he says, his voice rougher than she's ever heard it sound, "every time I see you…" He breaks off, as if the emotion is too intense to be voiced. Too long held inside, carefully guarded.

"Why didn't you ever tell me?" she asks.

He gives her a rueful look. "Because I never once imagined that you could possibly feel for me what I was feeling for you."

"Why?" Lucretia asks, stunned. "Because I was constantly feigning interest in one cursed Gardnerian suitor after another? To escape fasting?"

"No." He shakes his head. "You just never gave any indication."

Lucretia loosens a sigh. "If we could read affinities like Lupines and Wyverns, this would have been a lot easier."

"What would I have read in you, Lucretia?"

"That I have loved you ever since I first laid eyes on you," she says, her voice breaking. "You would have been swept under by an overwhelming tide." With a trembling hand, Lucretia reaches into her tunic pocket, draws out a small vial of herbs, and sets it decidedly down on the table between them.

Jules stills, his eyes on the vial, his gaze lifting to Lucretia's in question.

"Sanjire root," she says as heat spreads up her neck, her voice stilted with nerves. "I'd like to stay the night. With you. Be my Xishlon'vir, Jules Kristian."

Jules swallows as he focuses on the herbs. Unmoving. "I have nothing to offer you, Lucretia," he says, voice low and taut with feeling. "I'm a powerless history professor in a world about to descend into chaos."

"You could become Lupine if you want power."

His head bobs in silent amusement. He shoots her a knowing glance. "I prefer to be the alpha of my own life. It's a trade-off."

Lucretia lets out a short laugh. "Yes. I can't picture you deferring to anything but your own mind."

He returns her affectionate smile. "And you're quite the same. Only with Level Four magery."

"So, I'll protect you."

Jules grins as they consider each other for a moment.

"You could have your pick of men," he says, growing serious again. "Men with more normal lives."

"Oh, really," Lucretia returns. "I've spent almost my entire life dressed like a Styvian Gardnerian. And for much of the past year, I've sported one of those wretched Vogel armbands. What type of men do you think *that* attracted?"

Jules's lips quirk. "Not quite the pick of the litter?"

"Not really."

"You're not in the West anymore." He lets his gaze roam over her, a sudden, unguarded glint in his eyes as he takes in her formfitting, rose-festooned Xishlon dress, following the curves of her body. "And you certainly don't look like a Styvian anymore." He smiles suggestively at her. "See what happens? You give me a glimmer of permission and now I'm ogling you without reservation."

"How long have you noticed me?" she asks, delight in her tone.

"A *very* long time," he softly admits, then grows quiet, his whole self constrained, but the obvious desire in his gaze sends a stream of heat rippling through Lucretia's water power.

"Lucretia," he finally says, his tone grave. "I've set myself against the full might of the Gardnerians. And the Alfsigr Elves. How do you think that's going to play out?"

Lucretia considers this with a tilt of her head. "Not well. But since I won't stop helping refugees flee East *and* am about to be deployed West, I'd say my future looks about as predictable as yours."

"I'm bringing chaos to the tranquil Eastern Realm."

"Chaos is coming for the tranquil Eastern Realm," Lucretia throws down. "You're bringing their only chance for a future. They're too divided and dependent on a monolithic magical system. If that falls and the Gardnerians invade, their main line of protection will be the Smaragdalfar and all those Fae youth in the Vu Trin forces—and they're all here because of you."

"Not just me."

More quiet.

"I love you, Jules," she says, her eyes glassing over. "I have for years, and now you know."

Jules holds her intense gaze. "I love you too, Lucretia."

She smiles crookedly, joy bursting into being. "Well, at least that's out in the open now. Our sordid secret."

Jules laughs and sits back, regarding her with open warmth.

"There's a tradition to this festival," she says, feeling giddy and lit up. "You're supposed to kiss someone you love under the lavender moon. It brings good luck for the entire year and a blessing from Vo."

He arches his brow. "Are you asking me to kiss you, Lucretia?" His eyes flick toward the vial of Sanjire root.

"Yes, Jules," Lucretia breathlessly agrees. "And I'm asking you to kiss me whenever you want to from here on in."

He gives her a narrow look of amusement. "You wouldn't get anything done."

Lucretia can't suppress her besotted smile. "Well, then… I want you to kiss me as much as you want *tonight*. We can go back to devoting our lives to trying to get ourselves arrested or killed tomorrow."

His expression turns ardent. "I've held myself back for so long, so careful not to openly pine for you."

"So have I."

He smiles at her, then gets up, moves to his small rune stove, then places his worn, copper kettle on it.

"Would you like some tea?" he offers. He points back idly at the vial of herbs on the table, a spark of mischief lighting his eyes. "To go with the Sanjire root?"

Heat shoots up Lucretia's spine, warm water from her affinity lines curling around it, speechless for a moment as Jules's lips form a fuller smile.

"Yes, Jules," she finally says, unable to suppress her own grin. "I'd love some tea."

CHAPTER FIVE

LUPINE

Aislinn

Xishlon night, twenty-first hour

Aislinn can sense Jarod's silent approach with every fiber of her Lupine self, his affection enveloping her like the caress of the forest, his warm summer scent prompting a tingling anticipation that quickens her breath.

She grips the Wyvernguard banister, waiting for him as she looks over the Vo River. Everything is bathed in the Xishlon moon's luxuriant purple glow, its gentle thrall making it easy to set aside the incoming threat of Vogel for just this one night. Just this one pause before Elloren's power is unbound, an alliance is forged, and they all deploy west.

Together.

Aislinn waits as Jarod strides nearer, the two of them so breathtakingly high up on this highest of the crisscrossing walkways that connect the two Wyvernguard island-mountains like a series of ladder rungs. A few small, purple-tinted clouds lazily drift below.

Aislinn considers that she'll never grow fully used to the sheer beauty of the Wyvernguard's expansive views of the Vo River.

She grips the railing harder as Jarod draws up beside her, also garbed in a Vu Trin uniform, blond hair tousled by the wind. His arm brushes hers lightly and she looks into those beautiful, amber eyes, a small smile on his lips.

"I have something for you," he says, holding out a rectangular present wrapped in purple parchment and secured with violet twine, a small Xishlon rose slid through the binding.

Aislinn's nostrils flare as she accepts the gift, her enhanced Lupine senses drawing in the purple rose's intoxicating floral scent as well as that dry parchment smell that always thrills her archivist mind. She shyly forms a sharp claw on her index finger, easily snaps the twine, then morphs her claw back to a tapered fingernail and folds back the parchment.

A black tome marked with a lavender Xishlon moon is nestled inside, purple flowers painted on its spine and Noi lettering in silver foil embossed on the cover. Just below the book is a curious square of flat glass, framed by small Noi runes.

Aislinn's pulse quickens as she realizes what this is. She places the glass over the book's title and the Noi lettering instantly transforms into the Common Tongue.

Lavender Garden of My Heart.

Aislinn knows of this text—one of Noilaan's classic collections of love poetry, read throughout Noilaan on Xishlon night.

"Oh, Jarod," she breathes, meeting his loving gaze. "Thank you."

Hugging the gift to her chest, she reaches up to take hold of his sinewy upper arm, stands on her tiptoes and kisses him, their lips lingering past a simple thank-you as Jarod's arms wrap around her waist. Aislinn's heartbeat deepens in her chest as that familiar spark of desire ignites in them both.

She wants to pull him into the purple forest and kiss him for hours. She wants to press her body closer to him, as close as she can...

Aislinn hesitates as Jarod draws back, looking at her search-ingly as her familiar trepidation wrests hold, cutting into the lovely moment like a tight binding. She knows Jarod can read her growing desire as clearly as she can read his. But she also knows that Jarod is keenly aware that her strengthening physi-cal draw to him is mixed up with so much trauma and anger over what Damion did to her that she fears it might keep them physically apart forever.

Aislinn's breath shudders through her like the breeze coming off the Vo as Jarod releases her, now touching her only lightly on her arm.

Her brow tightens as she peers over the river, unable to meet Jarod's gaze for a moment as glowing Xishlon runic orbs are released from a crowded ship in the near distance.

She wants Jarod more than she's ever wanted him before, her desire further heightened by the ominous fact that war is clos-ing in. And she desperately wants to be Jarod's full mate be-fore it does.

But every time she comes close to taking him, flashes of Da-mion Bane assault her mind. Aislinn winces as she struggles to beat back the dark memories that threaten to accost her even now. How Damion forced and humiliated her. The unspeak-able, painful things he did. His cruelty. His bottomless cruelty.

And yet, both Jarod's unflinching love and the love of the Forest have been like a constant, caressing balm this past month, gradually dulling the edges of what Damion Bane took from her like persistent water coursing over jagged stone. And creat-ing a safe space for her to gain strength and heal.

And there's so much loving desire in him. Aislinn can sense it coursing through him as she takes in the lines of violet rip-pling over the Vo. It started out as intimidating, this new Lu-pine ability to read his overpowering want for her so vividly. Troubling at times, so clear that he wants more than to just kiss and hold her.

But her sense of his desire has since morphed into its own

kind of comfort because Jarod's intense passion is stripped of any cruelty. Even though his touch on her arm in this moment is featherlight, she can feel the warm echo of his strong arms around her, night after night, like a bolstering imprint. Loath to ever be separated again, the two of them have fallen asleep beside each other every evening since their reunion, even though, at first, she awakened crying out in terror from the persistent nightmares, and even though Jarod sometimes had trouble sleeping as his desire for her burned through his body.

She's seen him unclothed both before and after a Change—and once she even saw his desire for her in shockingly vivid terms. And yet, he's always holding back and careful to tread gently around her spikes of fear, her flashes of revulsion and outrage. Waiting.

I'll wait for you forever, he's told her more than once as he cradled her in his arms.

And so, night after night, Aislinn has fallen asleep to Jarod embracing her in the darkness, every Lupine sense heightened as she breathed in the intoxicating male scent of him, as he stroked her arm, kissed her forehead, her lips. So gentle, when the desire in him was anything but.

And slowly, she's felt herself beginning to heal. To the point where, these past days, things have turned a corner, her love and desire for Jarod starting to feel stronger than the trauma.

Aislinn turns her gaze from the river and looks at Jarod, warmth coursing over her as their eyes meet. She swallows, her mouth and throat suddenly thirsty with want for him, her nerves alight with what she's about to offer.

"Take me to mate."

Jarod pulls in a hard breath, and Aislinn can feel the hot flare of his desire, every part of him controlled but straining to move toward her.

Jarod nods slowly, a slightly stunned look on his face. There's no need to ask if she's sure. Aislinn knows he can scent her feelings and desire as clearly as she can his. He knows that she's also keeping herself back from him, in this moment, with as much force as she can summon. Scared, yet not scared. And ready to make him her own.

"I can't announce this to a group," she tells him shakily and with real remorse, the emotional storm inside her kicking up. "I know it's the Lupine way, but… I just can't."

They broached this a few nights ago, well past midnight as she lay awake, caught up in wanting him while being afraid of opening the door to the nightmare memories and dangerous vulnerability. Jarod roused alongside her, perhaps sensing her tossing emotions and seeming to read the war going on inside her. They talked through the night, and she finally told him, raging and storming as she sobbed into his hard shoulder, exactly what was done to her.

"That was violence," Jarod said, holding her tight as rage on her behalf coursed through him. "That wasn't mating."

Aislinn's thoughts sweep back from the memory to the present as tears glass her eyes and Jarod's fingers gently touch her arm, light as gossamer, as if he knows how fragile this moment is. He coaxes her around to face him, then reaches up to caress the side of her face.

"There are no rules in this for us," he says, voice low and unfailingly kind.

Grief kicks up in Aislinn. "But… I know it's important for you. To…honor the Lupine ways." Aislinn can't say more. She can feel the flare of grief in him, as well. His people, dead. His parents, his younger sister, murdered. And, in light of all of his terrible trauma, it pains her to have to say no to this most basic of Lupine traditions—the announcement, to the entire pack, of a couple's desire to take each other to mate.

Tears glisten in Aislinn's eyes. He's being so kind, but she's asking too much of him. She's always asking far too much of him.

Jarod embraces her loosely, his amber gaze on her searching

as a tear slides down her cheek. "Aislinn," he says, "sometimes tradition needs to yield to something greater."

She manages a faltering smile. "Like true love?"

Jarod returns her smile. "Yes. Like love. It always needs to yield to love."

And that's when Aislinn begins to cry in earnest, her sense of safety enlarging.

"I love you," she says, her heart opening wide even as fear tries to close it back up. His strong arms wrap around her and she can feel his smile against her hair, and then his kiss on it as she clings to him.

"I love you too," he says, adamant.

"I'm ready, Jarod." She pulls away to look up at him, more decided than she's ever been in her whole life. "Let's leave."

"Where do you want to go?" he asks, a bit breathless, as he glances in the direction of the soldier barracks. "To our room here?"

"No," Aislinn says, the word coming out harsh, rebellion streaking through her. "Not in an enclosed room like a Gardnerian. I want to take each other like Lupines. In the arms of the Forest."

Jarod holds her hand gently in his like it's the most delicate thing in the world, even though Aislinn can clearly read that what he wants is to pull her close and kiss her deeply. He gives her a significant look. "There's that patch of wilds we both love. Just north of Voloi."

Aislinn brings her other hand over their clasped ones, caressing him in turn as she looks up at him. This beautiful, patient, overwhelmingly kind love of hers. Her forever love.

"Take me there," she says.

FIND THE MOON

Sparrow Trillium

Xishlon night, twenty-first hour

Sparrow stands before the full-length mirror in Mii Vun's famed dress shoppe, stunned by the Xishlon transformation reflected in it.

The Xishlon transformation in *her.*

Gone is the drab servant garb and makeup-free face of the Western Realm. Because she's no longer trapped in a world where her beauty puts her in extreme danger. But still, she knows her makeup is gloriously bold for her first Xishlon celebration—an intricate violet orchid drawn in a sweep along the entire edge of her face, her lips colored a deeper purple than their natural shade and dusted with violet glitter. And her lilac hair adorned with iridescent-purple Xishlon flowers.

But the biggest rebellion of all is the dress it took Sparrow over a week to craft, its design a celebration of the famous Noi book of love poems, *Lavender Garden of My Heart*, each poem steeped in the lore surrounding Xishlon's thirteen iconic purple flowers. Her entire dress is constructed from silk roses, hyacinths, pansies, cosmos, and the rest of the fabled purple-moon festival blooms, its skirt long in the back, short in the front, her legs on display from midthigh down—which would have been both shocking and forbidden in Gardneria. Violet orchids twine up the length of her silk stockings and her delicate, plum-velvet shoes are decorated with hand-painted purple crocuses.

Sparrow's nerves are alight to dare to be this brazen, but she refuses to be cowed by her past. Because here, in the Eastern Realm, women can wear whatever they want, their safety vigorously and mercilessly enforced by the mostly female Vu Trin. And she's further emboldened by the rune blade strapped to her side, women bearing arms a common sight here.

Let the Gardnerians try to come here and enslave me again, Sparrow thinks as she takes in the blade's reflection as well as her decadently rebellious appearance. *I'll go down fighting and take quite a few of them with me.*

"Ah, Little Bird, you are a complete *vision.*"

Mii Vun, the shoppe's proprietress and Sparrow's sponsor here, edges into the mirror's reflection. The kind Noi woman's white hair is styled in looping braids, violets woven through them, embroidered violets dotting her lavender silken tunic and pants.

"Everyone's talking about you, Sparrow!" young Fyya Lo gushes as she shoulders into the reflection's other side. The young apprentice seamstress rests her pointed chin on Sparrow's shoulder, an impish grin on her pretty face. "Those clothing sketches you put together...you've become a star overnight!"

Gratitude sweeps through Sparrow as she moves to the side to better take in Fyya Lo's beautiful reflection, her Xishlon garb a resplendent vision that Sparrow helped fashion, Fyya Lo's dark hair festooned with glass orbs filled with violet rune light, her velvet dress such a lush, dark violet it's almost black. A bright lavender moon is embroidered over the young seamstress's torso, the Vo river and its rippling purple reflection embroidered down the dress's slim skirt.

"I have something rather delicious to tell you," Fyya Lo croons, taking Sparrow's hands in hers. Her vivacious tone turns confiding. "Syr Vho wants to see you tonight."

Sparrow remembers him well. The Noi architect. One of the city's other young rising stars, who she met at the banquet Mii Vun held to support Noilaan's most talented and up-and-coming designers.

"He's clearly besotted," Fyya Lo enthuses, unable to repress her grin. "I think he's more than eager to give you your first Xishlon kiss."

Defiance rears up in Sparrow. She knows full well what Fyya Lo is up to. She also realizes her response will be the equivalent of setting off a runic explosive in the middle of the elegant, floral-decorated shoppe.

"That's a lovely compliment," Sparrow says, forcing an even tone. "But I've decided to spend Xishlon night with Thierren Stone."

Fyya Lo's impish grin vanishes as Mii Vun's dark eyes take on a grave light that cinches Sparrow's heart with concern. They both know of her friendship with Thierren, but to spend Xishlon night with someone here in the East...

Sparrow knows that's a whole other thing.

Her concern notches higher as Mii Vun lets out a shaky sigh and averts her eyes as if in careful deliberation. The elderly seamstress has been incredibly kind ever since Sparrow set foot in this huge, bustling city only a few weeks ago, taking Sparrow under her wing after seeing just a few samples of her embroidery and sketches of her designs. And the pay here, it's created a sea change in Sparrow's life. She'll never forget the feel of that first coin purse Mii Vun placed into her palm. Enough to afford a small one-room apartment in Voloi's First Tier artists' district with a balcony overlooking the river. Enough money for good food and art and sewing supplies—silken thread of every color, fabric, a sewing machine, and some canvases along with a watercolor set and brushes.

But the Eastern Realm has meant more to Sparrow than just the blessing of a fair wage for hard work.

It's meant freedom.

Freedom that Sparrow has no intention of ceding ever again. And that includes freedom to love who she loves.

Fyya Lo's purple-glittering mouth has turned down in a tight, judgmental frown. "You're going to spend Xishlon night with a *Gardnerian*," she flatly states.

"Yes, Fyya Lo," Sparrow evenly replies. "I'm spending it with a Gardnerian. And I'm going to ask him to be my Xishlon'vir."

Mii Vun pulls in a tight breath as Fyya Lo narrows her amethyst-glittering gaze on Sparrow, her tone biting when it comes. "You will not attract a single benefactor if you are connected to a Crow and I cannot, in good conscience, remain your friend."

Steel rises in Sparrow. She straightens and glares at Fyya Lo, no longer needing to pretend to be timid and demure. Not here. Sparrow has no intention of feigning intimidation ever again. "Don't call him a Crow," she firmly throws down.

"I agree," Mii Vun says, and Sparrow's head whips toward the elderly seamstress, astonished to find her giving Fyya Lo a look of censure.

"They shouldn't be here!" Fyya Lo insists to them both as purple-clad Xishlon revelers stream past the shoppe's open doors. "It's a mistake to let them in."

"Let who in?" Sparrow challenges, growing ever more incensed. "The refugees from the Western Realm? Like Effrey? Like *me*?"

"Heavens, no," Fyya Lo cries, seeming honestly bewildered. "*You* belong here. And Effrey too. But the Gardnerians and the Alfsigr are our *enemies*. They're not like us! And you make yourself an enemy too by falling in with them!"

Sparrow catches sight of Thierren and Effrey striding through the festive crowds toward the shoppe's entrance, Thierren's black Vu Trin naval uniform standing out in bold relief against the sea of purple garb, the emerald shimmer of his skin blaringly pronounced. Effrey stands in bright contrast beside him, looking like a Xishlon beacon in his purple garb, a soft violet geomancy glow surrounding him.

Thierren's green eyes find Sparrow's, a palpable charge passing between them that feels enhanced by the Xishlon moonlight. She drinks him in, an excited flutter in her belly. Because everything has shifted here, and her feelings for him are shifting, as well.

From staunch friendship...to the admission of something much stronger.

"Thierren, my love," Mii Vun enthuses as she steps forward, and Sparrow's throat tightens with vast, grateful relief. The seamstress warmly kisses him on both cheeks as Fyya Lo glowers at Thierren, arms tightly crossed against the Xishlon moon on her torso.

"I'm thrilled to see you both," Mii Vun gushes as she pats Effrey's head, purple moon rings sparkling on the seamstress's artistic brown fingers. "A joyous Xishlon to you."

Thierren dips his head, a weighty gratitude in his eyes. "To you as well, Nor Mii Vun."

Fyya Lo knifes a glare at Thierren in response to his respectful Noi greeting. She spits out a sound of disgust, then turns on her pretty, moon-decorated heels and disappears into the shoppe's back rooms, shutting the door behind her with an emphatic slam.

Outrage kindles in Sparrow, fast and hot. Rattled, she meets Effrey's bespectacled amethyst gaze, some of her ire drawing down as she takes in how transformed he is here after such a short time—his magic taking off like a shooting star to the point that he's surrounded by the color aura that eventually manifests around all strafelings—the most powerful class of Urisk geomancers. Apprenticed with Or'myr Syll'vir to hone his magic, his purple hair cut short, his large, pointed ears sweeping up through it. And tonight, he's all decked out for Xishlon, whimsical violet-glowing lizards embroidered up the side of his purple tunic.

Effrey motions worriedly for Sparrow to lean in, placing his hand on her shoulder to draw her close. "Some Noi'khin called Thierren names on the way here," he confides in a troubled whisper. "They spat at him when he passed. Cursed at him and told him he doesn't belong. Like they did to us in the West."

"I know," Sparrow grimly whispers back. "It's hard to hear."

Effrey's brow knots with concern. "Or'myr's half Gardnerian, and he doesn't get treated like that. And he's the grandson of the Black Witch herself."

"That's true," Sparrow concedes. "But it's different with Or'myr, you know that."

And it is, most Noi'khin seeming to concentrate on Or'myr's blaringly obvious Urisk half and selectively ignoring his Gardnerian green eyes and the echo of the Black Witch's visage on his face. But Sparrow also knows that many of her fellow Urisk hold Or'myr suspect, reviling his mother, Li'ra, for consorting with a Mage.

"Thierren's my friend," Effrey states, the declaration full of defiance.

Sparrow nods, emotion welling. She glances at Thierren and their gazes catch, a flush warming her cheeks from the intensity that crackles on the air whenever she and Thierren get within a few feet of each other.

As Mii Vun and Thierren exchange pleasantries, Sparrow takes note of the expressions of the Noi entering the shoppe, their eyes snagging on the Gardnerian in their midst before many quickly exit, their angry epithets trailing back to Sparrow with a biting sting. It's so unfair—Thierren's getting ready to deploy west to fight the Gardnerians. And she's seen the bruising on his wand arm from sparring with fellow soldiers so they can learn how to subdue Mage power.

She moves toward Thierren and watches as his eyes fix on her tight Xishlon dress, heat kindling in his gaze. Sparrow basks in his reaction, unable to suppress a slight smile.

Thierren leans close to her ear, his hand gently touching her arm as he ignites a deeper warmth within her with that low voice of his. "You're almost too beautiful to take in."

"Does that mean you won't take me?" Sparrow whispers back.

Thierren exhales a shocked sound. She knew this would catch him by surprise, this new Xishlon-Sparrow. Emboldened by the moon's draw that shifts one's focus to matters of the heart. And the difficult, unavoidable fact that Thierren deploys tomorrow.

Thierren looks Sparrow over more boldly, his gaze going a bit liquid. "It's hard to...think around how beautiful you are..." He gives her a significant look.

"Go, you two," Mii Vun says, breaking into their sudden thrall, a knowing smile on the seamstress's lips. "Effrey is going to spend the evening with me."

"I am?" Effrey's head whips toward Mii Vun, his eyes widening with possibility.

Sparrow smiles. Mii Vun is a delight with children, patient and full of good humor. And she's extraordinarily well connected, which holds the promise of a Xishlon evening full of beautiful sights and every kind of child's purple delight.

"Unless you're not interested in seeing the Xishlon lizard exhibition," Mii Vun teases Effrey. "Or in picking a violet-checkered salamander for your very own. And eating steamed crab buns in the gardens. Oh, and there might be a string of rune orbs involved in all of this as well as a trip to the port side gem markets." She winks at Sparrow and Thierren.

The breath catches in Sparrow's throat as it dawns on her what Mii Vun is doing and Thierren looks just as surprised.

Alone. With Thierren. All evening.

"Go in the back room and see what you find," Mii Vun prods Effrey. "There might be a piece of purple moon agate for you there." Effrey's violet eyes light up like a beacon and he sets off at a sprint into the shoppe's recesses.

Mii Vun leans toward Sparrow after Effrey is out of earshot. "I had a bottle of fine Xishlon wine sent to your apartment." She winks again at them both. "Go. Seize the moon. This night is for young lovers." She peers up at the lavender Xishlon moon, seeming wistful. "I remember my first Xishlon with my love. Feng Loi. She was…so beautiful. It was the night I told her I wanted to spend my life with her. To take her as my toiyanon." Her dark eyes glitter with feeling. "And she said yes."

Sparrow is moved by this rare showing of Mii Vun's private heart. "Is she the soldier in the painting?" Sparrow asks tentatively, remembering the portrait Mii Vun keeps by her favorite sewing machine.

Mii Vun's wistful smile disappears, replaced by an uncomfortable, pained look as she glances at Thierren. She blinks, as if clearing away tears before they can form, before meeting Sparrow's gaze. "She was a Vu Trin soldier. She died in the Realm War."

Killed by the Gardnerians.

The information cuts deep.

Thierren's face has constricted, his angular jaw gone rigid. He looks away, his brow tensing with obvious remorse.

Mii Vun approaches him. "Thierren," she says gently.

"I'm sorry." He shakes his head, seeming unable to meet her eyes. "I'm sorry that happened to her."

"It's not your fault," Mii Vun adamantly states. "And you'll find your place here. You *will.*" Thierren's mouth flexes as he finally looks at her, his gaze tortured.

Mii Vun reaches up to remove the Vo dragon goddess pendant around her neck, small white bird pendants surrounding that central Vo charm. "Bend down," she coaxes him, holding up the necklace.

Thierren pulls in a shaky breath and relents, and Mii Vun slips the necklace over his head. "I want you here," she says as he straightens, placing her hand on his shoulder. "And there are others who do too. I'm grateful for what you're doing."

Thierren gives a tight nod. "Thank you, Hoiyon Nor."

She smiles, as if pleased by his use of the respectful title. "This is not a night for grim thoughts," she insists. "Tomorrow you deploy west, but tonight you bask in Vo's love. Go, Zish hoi'enin'lianon." *Go, find your moon.*

Mii Vun pulls Thierren into an emotional embrace, then hugs Sparrow warmly.

"Thank you for everything," Sparrow says as she wipes away a stray tear.

Mii Vun waves off the thanks, tears in her own eyes as she walks toward the shoppe's back rooms. "I love you two," she calls over her shoulder as she opens the back door, her voice thick with emotion as she gives them a sly, prodding smile. "Go. And drink that wine."

Sparrow boldly offers Thierren her hand, ignoring the subtle and not-so-subtle looks of censure from passersby. Thierren's fingers thread through hers, a stunned look on his face as he takes in their clasped hands. They've always shied away from initiating physical closeness, save falling asleep near each other that one time in the desert.

"Sparrow..." he starts. "What does this mean?"

"It means," Sparrow purrs, tracing his finger with her thumb, thrilled to be giving in to her desire to touch him, "that I want to ask you..." Nerves alight once more, as vulnerability cracks open. "To be my Xishlon'vir."

Thierren's green eyes widen. He exhales and goes very still. "I would be honored," he finally says in Uriskal, "to be your Xishlon'vir, Sparrow Trillium." Her name slides off his tongue, infused with longing.

"But before we go anywhere else," Sparrow says, flushing at the idea of going back to her apartment, "I'm taking you to the Vuulish Tavern." She has it all planned—the famed, floral-themed cocktail bar that overlooks the Vo River the perfect place to share a Xishlon kiss.

Their first kiss.

Sparrow flushes over her bold scheming as Thierren's gaze slides over her silken dress, an ardent warmth lighting in his eyes. "You belong somewhere like that this evening," he manages throatily. "Somewhere beautiful and covered in flowers, like you. And even with a Crow on your arm, they won't be able to resist letting you in."

Sparrow cradles her fragrant violet cordial, Thierren beside her at their corner table on the tavern's open-air balcony, the Vo River's warm breeze caressing them both. A wooden trellis supporting vines covered in lavender blossoms surrounds them, the Xishlon moon's purple light filtering through.

Reclining back in her luxurious floral dress, Sparrow feels like an intrinsic part of the surrounding explosion of blossoms. And the moon's beckoning pull makes it easier to cast off the shadows of the world for just this one evening, but still, Sparrow's gaze is ever drawn toward the storm-limned mountains in the distance.

Toward the West.

Where a nightmare is gathering. Threatening this miracle of a realm.

The East has time to strengthen their defenses, Sparrow comforts herself. And both Elloren and Yvan Guryev are aligned with them, the entirety of the Prophecy on their side.

Sparrow looks to Thierren, a warm swell of emotion blooming. "Not long ago," she says, "you and I were huddled together in the desert, fending off storm spiders and wraith bats. Not knowing which day might be our last. And now…here we are."

A deeper warmth ignites, fed by their shared history and the way the cherished angles of his glimmering green face are highlighted by the moon's purple glow.

Thierren takes her hand, a spark of affection firing in their locked eyes as they both attempt to ignore the glares Sparrow can feel boring into them, unfriendly murmurs rising up from the packed tables. Thierren glances out over the river, his gaze sliding up the mountains and fixing there, his mouth turning down in a troubled frown, and Sparrow can tell he's having similar thoughts about what's coming for the East.

"We should fight with them," Thierren says as he stares west.

"You're about to," Sparrow says, confused by his pronounce-ment.

He turns to her. "I mean the Dryad Fae. There are never any of them among the refugees who are streaming in. Have you noticed that?" He peers northwest. "But they're out there. In the Northern Forest, most likely. The Gardnerians seemed sure of it. They'll go after them, if they haven't already." Thierren's gaze turns haunted, and Sparrow can tell he's thinking of the massacre he witnessed in the farthest northeastern reaches of Gardneria, not one Fae left alive.

Sparrow's grip on his hand tightens, this thing between them so much more than their physical attraction. She loves the trau-matized thing inside Thierren that has solidified into rebellion.

Because that same thing lives inside of her.

A kinship was forged the night she first laid eyes on Thi-erren, so many months ago. The night she and Effrey fled by boat from the Fae Islands to the continent, braving the stormy ocean and kraken, and hid in Thierren's family's deserted horse stables in Gardneria. Thierren had stumbled in, strung-out on nilantyr and spirits.

Sparrow recklessly stopped him from incinerating himself with Magefire that night. Convinced him that there was an-other path. Another way to channel the guilt and despair that was eating him alive.

Rebellion.

Full-blown rebellion.

"Convince the Vu Trin to find the Dryad Fae," she urges as tears sting her eyes. "Then fight with them."

Thierren's eyes gleam with his own tears as he meets her gaze and nods.

"But give me tonight," Sparrow insists, able to absorb his in-tensity because she understands his darkness. Understands the tortured side of him that's seen too much. "And kiss me," Spar-row says. "Right here. In full view of the city."

Thierren's eyes widen a trace. "Are you sure?" he asks. "You'll harm your place here if we're that open about this."

Defiance sparks in Sparrow's eyes. "I had to hide my true self for far too long in the West. No more. The Eastern Realm needs to come to terms with me, not the other way around."

An ardent warmth lights his gaze. "I love you, Sparrow."

"I love you too, ish'sholuun." Sparrow reaches up to caress his cheek, and Thierren's breath hitches. "This is *exactly* what the Gardnerians and the Alfsigr and even some here want to destroy. *Love.* The kind that breaks down their boundaries and defies their rules. So kiss me and then come back to my lodging with me. We'll drink Mii Vun's wine and fight the Western Realm without weapons tonight."

"Ish'uuldur imorz ish'sholuun," Thierren murmurs ardently, the Uriskal words for *I love you* fluent on his tongue. And then he leans in, brings his lips to hers, and Sparrow falls into his loving, passionate kiss, the murmurs of disapproval all around them floating away on the lavender Xishlon moonlight.

CHAPTER SEVEN

XISHLON GARDEN

Mora'lee Starr'lyrion

Xishlon night, twenty-first hour

Mora'lee watches Fyon come to her, her eyes lit with loving amusement, as he strides toward her through the violet-washed garden where Mora waits for him beneath her favorite tree in all of Voloi—the large Wisteria ensconced in the garden's outer edge.

Her restaurant, normally only open for breakfast and lunch, has just closed for the evening after a wildly successful Xishlon. Every last pastry and morsel was sold, and Mora's spirits are buoyant from the enjoyment Olilly, Nym'ellia, and even painfully shy Ghor'li seemed to draw from all the delicious food as well as the moon's lovely embrace.

And her heart is more buoyant still, with the promise of Fyon's kiss.

She can barely keep her soles on the ground.

Fyon's silver eyes blaze as he catches sight of her and deftly sweeps aside the tree's veil of floral tresses, his gaze sliding over her short, tight-fitting Xishlon dress patterned with a blooming

Wisteria tree embroidered on deep-purple velvet in gleaming, phosphorescent thread.

Mora runs her own gaze over Fyon, who is garbed in a dark green formal Smaragdalfar tunic, the design worn solely during a formal courting.

Now that we've had those millions of cups of tea, Mora laughs to herself, delight bubbling up that's impossible to contain. Leaning back against the Wisteria, Mora sighs and gives in to the moon's pull toward matters of the heart, grateful for its aid in drawing her focus away from war as she forces back the hard reality of Fyon's imminent deployment. But the looming truth can't be fully erased—she's all too clear that this might be the last chance for her and Fee and everyone else in the Eastern Realm to embrace each other before the coming fight.

"Mora, tia'lin," Fyon breathes out as he draws near, *Mora, my beloved.* "You're the most beautiful thing in this garden."

Mora smiles and reaches up to trace a fingertip lightly down his silken tunic. A warm knot of emotion forms in her throat as she thrills to the feel of him so solidly *here* before her.

"I meant what I said on my ship," she tells him, pushing aside the nervous reticence fluttering inside her. "Kiss me all you like."

The intensity of Fyon's gaze deepens, his voice rough and emphatic when it comes, as if he can't quite wrest hold of his emotions. "I've wanted you for so long, Mora…"

Mora grins, lit up. "Then take me," she playfully eggs him on.

"Mora," he says, serious. "I don't think you understand. Not just to touch and hold."

The look in his eyes is so passionate, tears spring into Mora's eyes. "I know that, Fee. But the fact of the matter is that I've been yours for quite a while now and it will be nice to stop imagining kissing you and actually kiss you instead."

Fee swallows, hesitating, as if his want is too great for him to handle. He briefly looks to the West, at the lavender moon hung over the skyline, his elegant face tensing. He turns back to her, his gaze weighted with feeling. "To be pulled apart from you now, of all times…"

"I know," Mora agrees, part of her railing against him going west again when they've finally found each other in this new way, but also knowing he has to go.

Fyon reaches up to gently touch Mora's cheek, as if he's touching something precious and fleeting. "Tia'lin…" His voice catches on the Smaragdalfar endearment. His fingertips slide down and brush along the base of her glitter-dusted neck, so lightly it's barely a touch, and a delightful shiver courses through her.

And then Fyon cups her cheek, leans down, and brings his lips to hers.

The moment their mouths touch is suspended in bright magic as warmth slides through Mora's body, and Fyon's hands—those elegant sorcerer *hands* of his—slide around her waist and up through her braided hair, his honeyed kiss deepening as Mora traces her fingers down the long column of his neck, over the straight line of his back, thrilled to finally touch this friend she's pined for, for so long. Who she's dreamed of so many nights. Mora traces her hand over Fyon's lean, muscular chest, reveling in the masculine feel of his body as they kiss each other under the Wisteria, rapidly losing all track of time.

Mora pulls him closer, caught up in wanting more of him as she parts her lips and dares to kiss him with her tongue, as well.

Fyon lets out a surprised groan, his hands tightening on her, his kiss losing its softness, his newfound urgency setting off a pleasurable tightness low inside Mora as he grasps her so deliriously close.

"What do you think, Fee?" she asks, breathless from wanting him and feeling like a decadent confection. "Do you like the taste of me?"

Fyon smiles, his eyes molten silver. "Yes, Mora. Can't you tell?"

Mora grins enticingly and grasps hold of the sides of Fyon's tunic, drawing him even closer. *Yes, Fee, I can tell*, she thinks. *It's a bit startling how much I can tell.*

"I've an inkling," she says instead, and he gives a low laugh.

"Come back to my ship with me," she huskily invites. "I've Sanjire root…"

Fyon draws back, his green brow tensing. "So fast, Mora? Are you sure? You might not be thinking clearly with the lull of the Xishlon moon on the air. This thing between us…it isn't some fleeting Noi holiday for me. We should wait…"

"For what, Fyon?"

He blinks at her. "The twenty days of tia'linel. All of the courting rituals. The presentation of my intentions."

Mora gives him a suggestive look, her eyes sliding down his long frame. "Oh, I think you've presented them well enough."

He purses his lips at this. "Mora…"

"Fee," she rejoins, suddenly serious. "You know I'm a Subland Elf who loves the sky. Raised by a Vu Trin soldier and a Noi fisherwoman. Do you honestly think I'm going to stand on Smaragdalfar convention in this?"

Fyon arches a brow. "There is some romance to the twenty days."

Mora lets out a small laugh, affection for him welling. *Ah, Fee. You're such a true romantic.* She sighs as an unwelcome shadow passes over her thoughts. "There is romance in it," she agrees. "But who knows what the future holds?" She glances worriedly toward the West, then back at him, the man she knows is destined to be her great love. "Tomorrow, you deploy. Who knows when we'll see each other again."

Or if.

Mora presses that wrenching thought away even as it twists at her heart. "I want one night with you. I don't want to regret waiting."

Fyon gently presses his forehead to hers, his palms tenderly cupping the sides of her face in the Smaragdalfar gesture of affection. "Tief'lia'lin, I love you with all my heart. I always have. And I always will."

"I know that, Fyon," she says, her eyes suddenly blurring with tears as she smiles brazenly at him, his love making her bold. "Now love me with the rest of you."

CHAPTER EIGHT

HOPE

Olilly Emmylian

Xishlon night, twenty-first hour

Olilly leans against the rune ship's balcony and gazes at the stunningly violet Vo River, filled with an unexpected elation from the joyful bustle of cooking and serving food with welcoming Mora all day and into the eve. The purple Xishlon moon is high in the sky, little Ghor'li settled into sleep with Nym'ellia's family.

A muffled whimper sounds through Olilly's bedroom door behind her.

It's Nym'ellia, she realizes with concern. Turning her back on the gorgeous evening, she knocks on the door. "Nym'ellia?" she hesitantly calls. "Can I come in?" Getting no answer and growing more concerned by Nym's sustained crying, she tentatively opens the door.

Nym'ellia is curled up in a ball on Olilly's narrow bed, hugging a blanket close, an angry bruise on her temple.

Instantly filled with distress, Olilly goes to her and gently presses her slender hand to the girl's heaving shoulder. "What happened?"

"I...t-tried to go outside," Nym'ellia forces out. "To...to see all the puppets. But...they called me a Roach and a Crow. Told me to go back to Gardneria. And then...one of them threw a rock at me and it *hurt*." Nym'ellia's whole face convulses at the memory, her shut eyes tightening as she sobs.

Tears sting Olilly's eyes as her heart gives a wrenching twist. In just one day, she's seen how Nym'ellia is treated here, and it's much worse than what other Westerners endure. At least most of the people have been welcoming to Olilly, some overtly so. But Nym'ellia—she's hated by so many because she looks Gardnerian, especially with the points of her ears shorn off.

A bold idea overtakes Olilly, springing from her heart with such strength she's unable to hold it back. Heart thrumming, she reaches up and removes the jeweled and pointed ear-cuffs from her ears, her fingers brushing the scarred arcs of her ears' mutilated edges.

"I have a present for you," Olilly says, holding out the ornaments in the palm of her hand.

Her face slick with tears, Nym'ellia gazes at the ear-cuffs. She pulls in a hard breath and shakes her head. "I couldn't."

Olilly pushes her offering slightly closer to the girl. "Please. I want you to have them. It's a gift. For Xishlon."

"But..." Nym'ellia's lip trembles as fresh tears fall from her eyes. "They *cropped* you."

"Yes, I know," Olilly says, trauma clawing at the edges of her, but she beats it back. Because this moment feels stronger than all of it. "Just like they cropped you. But everyone knows I'm Urisk. Because I'm purple."

Nym'ellia sits up and lets Olilly hand her the ear decorations. She stares at the silvery points for a long moment, then looks at Olilly searchingly, but Olilly doesn't budge in her offer.

"If I wear them," Nym'ellia says, her expression hardening with pain, "people will yell at me even more. They'll rip them from my ears and tell me I have no right to wear them. Just like they tell me I have no right to wear Noi clothes."

Olilly is undaunted. "Then wear them when you're by your-self. To remember who you are. And to remember that *you* get to decide that. Not them."

Nym'ellia begins to sob again as she balls the jeweled ear points in her fist and clutches them to her heart.

Overcome as a lightness blooms inside her, Olilly throws her arms around Nym'ellia and envelopes her in a hug that's warmly returned. Then she sits back and smiles falteringly at Nym'ellia. "Go ahead, put them on," she prods.

Nym'ellia hesitates, then fumbles with the ear-cuffs. Olilly reaches up to help her, feeling a bit breathless, knowing the moment is fraught with an importance that runs much deeper than most things.

Olilly reaches toward the side table and lifts a small handheld mirror. She holds it up to Nym'ellia, who stills, as if mesmer-ized by the point-eared girl staring back at her.

"You're beautiful," Olilly breathes and is rewarded by Nym'ellia's lovely, trembling smile. "I'll go down to the pier," Olilly offers, returning her smile. "And I'll bring back Xishlon necklaces for both of us."

Nym'ellia nods, roughly wiping away her tears. "Olilly," she says, heartfelt, as she runs her finger over one of the sparkling silver ear-cuffs. "I'm glad you're my friend."

"Forever," Olilly vows, holding out her free hand.

Nym'ellia grasps it, their fingers interlacing. "Forever," Nym'ellia vows in turn, matching Olilly's wide, beaming smile.

Olilly closes the door to Nym'ellia's room, and the beauty of the Xishlon night hits her anew, every shade of purple cascad-ing over the Vo River's surface in rippling designs.

Beautiful.

She pauses, leaning over the balcony, entranced as she kicks up her feet in a small dance, unable to suppress the happiness that's sparking along the edges of her ever-present grief and trauma and fear. The echo of the Western Realm's cruelty is so strong, it has the power to overtake everything else. To scar a person's heart and never let go.

But not tonight.

She reaches up to touch her scarred ears and waits for the familiar misery to overtake her, but only a trace of it jabs in. And oddly, in this moment, Olilly feels more Urisk than she ever has before. Regardless of the lack of points on her ears. A wide smile overtakes her face as she finds herself suddenly exhilarated to be in this new place, so full of possibility.

"Olilly."

The shy male voice rides out to her from the far end of the ship's walkway.

Olilly straightens with the speed of a startled bird, her heart picking up into a swifter rhythm as she turns.

Handsome Kir Lyyo from the restaurant across the street steps toward her, then stops, seeming unsure. He blinks at her in that quietly intent way of his. She watched him throughout the entire day, their eyes shyly meeting multiple times as they cleared tables, brought out food, both restaurants having just closed for the evening, their covert glances and shared smiles growing slightly more bold as the purple moonlight shimmered to life.

Olilly steps away from the metal balcony to face him, over-aware of herself. He's holding a phosphorescent river lily in his hand, a puff of violet light emanating from the graceful flower.

"This…this is for you," he says, holding the flower out to her, a besotted look on his face, the purple moonlight gleaming off his spiky black hair.

Olilly's heart is now pattering fast as a hummingbird's. She takes the lovely flower, their fingers brushing as she does so, and Olilly feels that brief touch straight to her toes.

"I've… I've seen you from across the street," he says, the words tumbling out in a breathless rush. "You're…very beautiful, and… I wanted to wish you a joyous Xishlon."

Suddenly, Olilly is feeling equally breathless. She glances

away, emotions fluttering, then dares a glance back at those riveting kohl-lined eyes of his.

"I'm Kir Lyyo, but you can call me Kirin," he encourages, and Olilly is touched by his offer to let her use the familiar form of his Noi name.

"I know," she says shyly, her mind awhirl. *He's given me a flower.*

Kirin's brow tenses. "Your ears," he says, motioning to his own ear, "the points are gone."

The Western Realm abruptly intrudes, knotting Olilly's throat, bringing the pain that always prowls around the edges of any happiness that tries to get a tentative start in her heart. An image of Kirin's angry father accosts her mind. The sign on their restaurant. *Noilaan for the Noi.* And the Noi flags. The religious banners. Olilly knows *exactly* what those flags and banners are meant to convey, and it isn't his father's love for the Vo religion or the Eastern Realm.

Olilly looks Kirin right in the eye. "A mob in the Western Realm cut the points off my ears. They were chanting 'Erthia for Gardnerians' while they did it."

She catches his flinch, as if he's been physically struck by the horrible truth.

Kirin swallows, looking stunned. "I'm sorry," he says, almost a whisper.

"I gave my jeweled points to Nym'ellia," she tells him evenly. "Because they cut off her ears' points too. She's Urisk, like me."

More shock, and she can see the wheels of his mind turning.

"I'm sorry that happened to you both," he finally says, obviously rattled but unmoving. Still here. Stubbornly still here.

"Your father wouldn't want you talking to me," Olilly says in challenge as tears mist her eyes, the grim reality of the world intruding. The never-ending exclusion of her life. *He'll leave.*

But Kirin's gaze solidifies on hers, his obviously rattled nerves giving way to something that looks like rebellion. "I know he wouldn't," he admits.

Hurt bubbles up inside Olilly. Hurt she's been keeping down for far too long. "Your father," she says. "He has that sign. The same kind of sign they had in the West."

Kirin nods, remorse now flooding his gaze. "I don't believe any of that," he says stridently. "I'm glad you're here."

"Lots of people aren't. They call us names."

"Well, *I* don't. And I never will. And I'm not the only one here who feels that way."

There. All of it, out in the open.

A sudden lightness softens Olilly's heart. And a sense of possibility, like a window being thrown open deep inside her, something entirely new streaming in.

"Would you walk with me to the pier?" he asks, seeming suddenly lit up as well, his mouth tilting into the edge of a smile. "You're the color of the festival. You should be part of it."

Olilly smiles demurely, happiness welling inside her in response to his earnestness, and yet, an edge of the pain remains. Her smile falters. "It's not my festival…"

"Yes, it is," he cuts in, emphatic. "You're part of the Eastern Realm now. It belongs to you too."

"It's a kissing festival," she says shyly and boldly all at the same time, a flush overtaking her, not quite believing she just said such a thing. Feeling like she's just shown him her recent imaginings of what it would be like to hold his hand, to kiss him. How she's noticed Kir Lyyo's intelligent eyes watching her from the restaurant across the street as she watched him back, liking his quiet way.

Kirin raises an eyebrow, as if stunned by her voicing what, perhaps, he's all too aware of, and Olilly is newly charmed by the way his hair sticks out at odd angles and wonders if it would be soft to the touch. He's so lovely. And she imagines kissing Kirin would be lovely too.

"We could walk through the Voling Garden Plaza," he offers, tripping over the words. "There are dancers and puppeteers and all sorts of food."

Olilly's brow knots. "But...your father."

Kirin holds out his hand, serious now. "He's wrong. About all of it. And we should go see the festival."

Olilly stares at lovely, rebellious Kirin's hand, his palm up in invitation as something deeply knotted inside her loosens for the first time ever. And there it is, suddenly singing inside her, like a bird too long caged, taking wing.

Hope.

Hope for the future.

Olilly steps forward, a bright smile now on her face as she looks into Kirin's beautiful dark eyes and takes his hand into hers.

CHAPTER NINE

SHADOW LINES

Elloren Grey

Xishlon night, twenty-first hour

Xishlon music and revelry waft up from the tiers below as I stare at the tracking rune on the back of my hand, frozen in disbelief.

The rune reads that Lukas is right *here*.

But...how can that be?

I draw my Ash'rion blade, frantically scanning the cascade of purple-glittering tiers, as if I could fight my way to Lukas through the city's drum-pulsing chaos led by fierce desire alone.

A stinging swoosh of magic crackles down my wand arm.

I wince, gripping my arm as the Ash'rion slips from my grasp and hits the terrace with a clatter, energy sizzling through me. My eyes widen. The last runes Sage marked on my forearm have brightened, the whole line charged to rotating, luminescent life.

A second rush of power surges up from my feet, through my lines, forcing a gasp from my throat, the power arrowing straight toward my wand arm. The surge passes like a wave, my elemental magic consolidating into a compressed force, and

I watch, stunned, as my purple glamour fizzles away and my fastlines emerge, only a slim band of purple coloration around my wrist remaining. I flex my fist, a sense of destiny descending as my magic begins to stream toward my wand hand like a river's unimpeded flow.

I'm the Black Witch, I realize in a sweep of reckoning as points of tickling energy spring to life on my wand hand. My gaze snaps to my palm, my attention seized by lines of gray splotching into being there and rapidly linking to form delicate lines encased in a circle.

Dread clenches my stomach. *A rune...*

I raise my other hand, ready to press my fingers to the summoning rune stone Or'myr gave me, only to find its purple rune dimmed to dull gray. Before my alarm-fettered mind can fully register what's happening, a wave of power slams into me from the West.

The full body-blow of it shatters all thought. I grunt, driven back a step, a dark tree blasting to life in my mind, its Shadow energy spreading out from the rune to snake through my affinity power in an undulating rush.

I yank my wand hand back into view and all the blood drains from my head.

My fastlines are slithering across my hand, morphed from black to Shadow gray, save for a few stationary Sealing loops around my wrist, the gray lines twining around the dark rune.

"No," I rasp as I frantically scrape at the rune, nails drawing blood. *"No, no, no..."*

The protest is torn from my throat as the dark tree punches into my vision once more. I stagger back, disorientated, ropes of gray smoke streaming from my wand hand. They begin to whip around and over me in a terrace-encompassing orb-net, the ropes looping into a swirling mimicry of my fastlines' design. A battle-rage overtakes me, and I reach down and draw my Wand.

"Elloren!"

I whirl around, leveling the Wand, and shock explodes, the

ground threatening to give way as pent-up emotion rushes through my chest in a hot tide.

Standing at the far end of the terrace, encased in the swirling orb emanating from both my hands and his, is Lukas, his form oddly translucent, his green eyes aglow with streaks of slivery-gray, his chest bare and covered in bloody lash marks, a wand gripped in his fist.

"Lukas!" I cry, lurching toward him, a wave of yearning overtaking me that's so immense it feels like vertigo.

Lukas's grayed eyes ignite with feeling as he steps toward me. But his movements...they're all wrong, just that one step sliding him instantly close, the distance retracting like I'm in some warping dream. I reach out to grasp his arm, but my fingers close around nothing, his limb as insubstantial as smoke.

"*Ancient One,*" I rasp as I scrabble to take hold of him to no avail.

"Elloren," Lukas cuts in, his gaze shot through with such intense longing it brings me right back to the Agolith. Right back into his passionate embrace. "Listen to me," he insists, voice rough.

"Why can't I touch you? Ancient One... I'm dreaming..."

"You're *not* dreaming," he says, emphatic, as our fastlines whirl around us both. "But I'm not really here."

"Then where are you?" I cry. "I have a tracking rune." I thrust my wrist toward him. "It says you're *right here.*"

"Because of the fasting link."

"Lukas...your *eyes*..."

A tortuous look overtakes him, his mouth twitching with what seems like barely contained agony. "Vogel's turning me into one of his drones. And it's a good thing you can't touch me yet. But that's going to change."

My mind storms with desperation. "I don't understand..."

"*Listen* to me," Lukas insists, his foggy image solidifying. "I think I'm somewhere near Amazakaraan. Vogel's been coming and going from there. Amazakaraan has fallen."

The devastating reality slams down, my thoughts whirling to Wynter.

"Vogel has been feeding Shadow power into our fasting," he grits out, every muscle straining toward me, as if he'd hurl himself to me through our fasting link if he could. "The only thing holding him back from complete control over you was the Forest's grip on your lines." His mouth tightens with fury. "He's seeking to take hold of us both."

I shake my head emphatically, my resolve bursting into a firestorm. "I'm coming for you before he can." I raise my Wand, my power churning through my lines. "I'm coming for you *to-night*," I insist, fierce love for him breaking like a wave, "and *nothing* can stop me. I'm going to fly to the Wyvernguard and take control of a portal…"

"There's no time," Lukas counters harshly. "Elloren, *look* at my eyes. Vogel's going to absorb me into his hive."

"His hive?"

"I'll try to show you. I can merge you to me through Vogel's Shadow tether."

Confusion rattles me. "How?"

"Through my shielding magic. It's stronger than Vogel's, and I can trace his magical bindings through it." He holds up the wand in his fist. "That's how I got hold of this."

I remember the strength of Lukas's shields as he wove them into me, again and again, during our escape from Valgard.

"Show me," I press.

Lukas closes his eyes and inhales, neck cording. The ropes of Shadow around us draw sharply in, Lukas's earth power branching around both me and the Shadow. All the energy in my lines suddenly warps toward Lukas's power, my body arching toward him as I'm swept into the bizarre sensation of my very essence pulling out of my body and into his.

Lukas's translucent form slips over mine, the terrace snapping out of sight.

I blink uncomprehendingly at what now lies before us—a cavern's shadowy alcove, a larger cave just beyond. A knot of multi-eyed, grotesquely stretched-out scorpios scuttle past without taking notice of us. Another Shadow-corrupted scorpio stands stock-still before us, as if on guard, its powerful forelimbs coated in blood. Lukas turns his head, and we take in the dead Mage soldier lying crumpled in the shadows, his body mutilated, as if slashed clear through before being dragged to the back of the cave and stuffed into its darkest recess.

I remember this space—the prison Lukas was in when I connected to him via the dead wraith bat's Shadow rune. A fragile hope lights. Somehow, he's gotten hold of a wand and struck down the prison's Shadow bars...

Lukas moves forward, and the motion pulls me with him. We peer into a gigantic cave opening just beyond our alcove...and fear grips hold. It's mammoth, expanding seemingly forever, the height of the vaulted ceiling rising to obscurity. Affixed all over the cave's obsidian walls is an organic growth resembling combs of a wasp's nest—if wasps were as large as humans.

Soldiers are emerging from the nest's wall of hexagonal cells, their eyes glowing gray as they drop to the stony ground. And not just Mage soldiers, Alfsigr too, their ivory bodies elongated, their eyes an enlarged, insectile gray.

Lukas sweeps our gaze over the scene, and I take in the Marfoir scuttling across the cavern's higher reaches, bone-white spider legs sprouted from their stretched-out forms. Multi-eyed dragons are lined up in formation, corrupted wraith bats hang from outcroppings of stone, and scorpios hunch in neat rows along the cavern's base, a nightmare army ready to be unleashed.

The scene breaks off and I almost lose my footing as I'm hurled back into my own body on the Vonor balcony, Lukas's translucent image once more before me.

"My cousin, Or'myr," I force out as I steady myself, determination reigniting, "he'll be back any moment. He's a powerful Mage and geomancer. We'll get hold of a portal and travel West *tonight*. Once there, we'll track you—"

"There's no more *time*," Lukas snarls. "I can't hold off Vogel's control much longer. And once he has complete hold of me, he'll be able to take full hold of *you*." Agony slashes across Lukas's livid features, his eyes taking on a look of such tortured love it scares me. "Elloren, our fasting link has to be destroyed."

"It can't be removed!"

His gaze burns into me. "No. It can't. But there *is* a way to break the link between us."

My mind reels. As a female, my fastlines are forever. But the *link* between us...

Understanding crashes home.

He means breaking it with his death.

"No, Lukas, *no*," I cry, my protest feral in its intensity, fire blasting through my lines.

"*Stop*," he commands. "As soon as this spell quickens to the point that I can touch you, I need to draw on as much of your power as I can. I'm going to buy you and the Eastern Realm time." That fierce, pained love enters his gaze once more. "Elloren, you were right all along. There are bigger things to fight for than just power. Bigger things to die for." His expression shifts, turning dagger-hard. "I'm going to kill Marcus Vogel and take out as much of this hive as I can. And then you'll be free to finish what I started."

The terrible reality crushes me like a vise. I can barely breathe against it. He's already set the wheels in motion by breaking free of Vogel's imprisonment. Which means he has to stage his attack on Vogel *now*, before he's discovered.

Sick panic knifes through my heart. "Lukas..."

"That green wand..." His eyes flick toward the spiraling weapon in my hand. "Vogel wants it. It must have more power than we know. Elloren, keep it away from him—"

Lukas's warning cuts off as I'm hit by a sudden pulse of power so strong it rattles my teeth. Vogel's dark tree shivers to life in my mind, luminous gray magic seeping through my lines in a twining stream. Lukas forcibly tenses, and the whorling fastline power around us contracts, pulling my essence into his misty body and the cavern once more.

"He's coming," Lukas murmurs, his mouth moving against the essence of mine as we peer into the massive cave. "Can you feel him?"

And I can, the gray power's incoming flow directional. Lukas looks toward its source, and a tighter dread shudders through me as I spot Marcus Vogel emerging from the sea of soldiers. His priest attire is inexplicably gone, his black garb that of a soldier. He's gripping his Shadow Wand, his form bracketed by the same demonic Mage envoys that were with him in the Agolith Desert, their eyes smoldering red, spiral horns made of smoke rising from their heads.

Vogel raises his Wand, and the sea of gray-eyed soldiers turns to him and stills.

Horror sears through me as Lukas flexes his power against mine. I rasp out a breath as I'm blasted back onto Or'myr's balcony, the shadowy fastline-ropes once more streaming around us. Heart thundering, I meet Lukas's gaze.

"Elloren," he says, a look of brutal finality overtaking his expression. "Align yourself with Yvan Guryev. Align yourself with *anyone* powerful enough to help you fight Vogel's forces."

Confusion ignites over his mention of Yvan. "Lukas…"

"I *saw* you with him."

Pain spears through me, straight through my center. "What do you mean?"

"Vogel can mindlink to you off and on," Lukas says, voice strained. "He forced the images of you and Yvan on me, trying to turn me against you."

Remorse drives into me with ravaging strength, like a bolt through my chest. I can tell from the tension on Lukas's face that he saw Yvan kissing me. That he saw it all. "I'm sorry," I choke out, stripped raw.

He shakes his head, his mouth tightening into a harder line. "Don't be." And then a heat enters his gaze that's so saturated in love for me, my heart can barely hold it. "Elloren," he says, "I know you chose me." As if forgetting himself, he reaches for me and...

...his hand closes around my arm, his grip real and firm, his form no longer translucent.

We both freeze, the entire world suspended in this one moment of terrifying realization. And then Lukas's look of dawning horror is subsumed into something fierce as his gaze rises to meet mine.

"I love you," he says, voice guttural. "I'll love you forever."

And then he grabs hold of me, pulls me close and brings his mouth passionately down onto mine.

Sparks strike to an inferno, fast and hot, my whole body shuddering in response to his sudden, rampant pull on my power, a radiant surge of love for him shearing through my heart. My lines contract toward his with such force I feel as if I'm turning to molten steel, welding to his body, a dizzying rush overtaking me as my inferno of fire, storming rush of wind and water, and one bright violet shard of light flow into Lukas with catastrophic force, his lines lighting up like an invisible torch from the force of his power and mine commingling as I'm drawn into the cave and his form once more.

Lukas lifts his wand arm, my arm inside it, his deep voice vibrating through me as he murmurs the Fire Strike spell, filling his wand with a devastating level of power. Then he lunges out of the cave's alcove and draws his wand arm back just as Vogel's pale eyes meet ours. Lukas thrusts the wand forward with a growl, our combined magic roaring into it with Erthia-shattering force.

Our power slams into his wand's tip, then ricochets backward.

Our vision ignites, a harsh groan wrenching from our throats as our magic's backflow stretches our lines with unbearable force, the pain like the torching of every vein. We fall, our backs colliding with the stone ground, stars splashing across our vision.

Vogel smiles and levels his Wand at ours as we convulse,

hot agony strafing through our bodies, the wand in our hands crackling with sizzling energy before it's rendered to ash. Vogel murmurs another spell and we grunt as dark vines lash out in a blur to bind us in tight coils, our arms rigidly outstretched, a vine wrapping around our mouths in a tight gag.

Vogel steps forward to loom over us as Lukas and I furiously struggle against the vines, his red-eyed envoys closing in to bracket his sides. Lukas knifes a murderous glare at him, but I can feel the stark desperation sizzling through his power.

Vogel meets Lukas's gaze with venomous calm. "Did you really think I knew nothing of your incursion into my magic?" He tilts his head, pale eyes glinting. "Did you really think I'd give your guard an unblocked wand?" His gaze sharpens on Lukas, a vicious light in it. "Don't think for a *second* that I don't feel her inside you." He motions to his demonic envoys with a slight flick of his Wand. "Consume him."

"*NO!*" I cry against Lukas as the envoy-demons rush forward, morphing into their true, fiery forms. Teeth of flame sear into our shoulders and our backs spasm, the impaling pain like multiple knife-strikes. A growl chokes from our throats as claws of white-hot fire dig into our sides, the ripping pain unendurable as our vision fractures and the world goes black.

SHADOW FASTING

Elloren Grey

Xishlon night, twenty-first hour

When the world springs back into focus I'm encased in a new body. Lukas is lying at my feet, blood streaming from fiery gashes on his neck, shoulders, and sides, his expression blank, his eyes full of gray fire.

My emotions spin into chaos, roiled by a love so fierce it bucks my hold. *Lukas!* I yearn to scream, but I can't move, my devastation whiplashing into a violent confusion.

I'm paralyzed, Vogel's Shadow surging over my affinity lines in a writhing violation, his dead tree branching through my mind. I look down and find myself in Mage soldier garb, the white bird on silken black marking my flat, masculine chest, a silver Erthia orb pinned near my shoulder.

The mark of Gardneria's High Mage.

Rage spasms through me.

I'm going to kill you! I lash out from where I'm trapped inside of Vogel as his gray tree winds around my lines in a viselike tether. And then we're moving, Vogel's vicious triumph infusing my frenzied thoughts as he forces me to survey his endless lines of soldiers and dragons and Shadow creatures. He doesn't slow as he drags me past them, their heads pivoting toward him with terrifying synchronicity. Then he turns, and we advance through a narrow, dark stone tunnel, its far end suffused with violet light that intensifies as the tunnel opens onto a small, flat terrace.

Vogel strides onto the windswept ledge, a precipitous drop before us, a cool breeze whipping at our hair, a dark mountain range spread out to either side.

And a luminous purple moon hanging overhead.

The horrific realization hits with ravaging strength, like a dagger-strike to my soul, the breath seizing in my lungs as I take in the vast river before us, dotted with countless boats sparkling with violet light, the glowing blue borderline and dark tent city just before it. And the tiered mountain city rising from the river's distant bank, every tier bathed in festive purple light, Noilaan's protective dome arcing above it all.

Vogel's here, I think as shock breaks through me. *He's been right here all this time.*

Building an army inside the Vo Mountain Range.

Vogel slides our eyes over the river toward the apex of the distant Voloi Mountains, his gaze zeroing in on the exact spot where I imagine Or'myr's glamoured Vonor to be.

Horror claws through me with unraveling power as the thought sears into being—

You're a warrior, Elloren. Fight him.

Lukas's words blaze through my mind and I choke against them, grappling with my terror, but the words hold firm.

He'd want you to rise up.

He'd want you to fight.

A vicious calm descends as love for Lukas burns through me, charring my fear to ash as the will to fight gains bright, gleaming claws. Incandescent with mounting fury, I tense every affinity line to the breaking point, draw on every last ungrayed shred of my fire power, then blast my aura outward in a violent torrent.

Straight through Vogel's branching tree.

The tree explodes with dark lightning, Vogel's fury scything through me as I fling his Shadow off my lines and the scene blinks out of sight.

In a heartbeat I'm back on Or'myr's balcony, palms to its stone floor, pulling in great gulps of air, the Wand of Myth and my Ash'rion blade strewn on the floor beside me. Shadow flashes across my vision and a sting races through my hands. Pushing myself onto my knees, I splay my palms out and dread clutches hold.

My fastlines are still overtaken by Shadow, tendrils of smoke curling up.

Pulse surging, I grab my Wand and hoist myself to my feet, peering over the purple Xishlon world toward the dark Vo Mountain Range.

Toward Vogel and his nightmare army.

Vogel's Shadow power knifes over the fasting and my lines, the invisible branch points stabbing into me, and a pained cry scrapes from my throat. Gripping the railing and Wand, I grit my teeth and hurl my wind power out with repelling force, the air torn from my lungs along with it as I thrust Vogel's magic firmly back once more.

I see you, Elloren.

I freeze, Vogel's voice resonating inside my head as a buzz of energy rises along the Wand of Myth's hilt, warming my palm.

My gaze flies to the Wand just as all the runes Sage marked down my wand arm burst into an explosion of green light. I flinch, the runes' energy sizzling toward the Wand, their light dimming as the Wand's verdant glow intensifies.

Hope igniting, I tighten my grip around the Wand's spiraling hilt. An emotional huff of gratitude bursts from my throat, tears stinging my eyes.

Finally.

The Wand has finally come into its power when I need it most.

Ready to save us all.

A sparking burn sears through my wand hand, green light raying from it. I cry out in pain and confusion, my fingers flying open, and the Wand falls from my hand and rolls over the edge of the balcony.

Horror explodes and I throw myself against the railing, scrambling to catch it only to find it hurtling down toward a distant crevasse.

No. No. No!

An indigo kestrel darts in, catches the Wand in its talons, then speeds northeast, both the bird and the Wand quickly disappearing from sight.

My heart thunders in my chest, my eyes widened in sick astonishment as I stare after it.

It's gone. The Wand of Myth is gone.

I grip hold of the railing as the Shadow fastlines slither over my hands, my vision tinting more heavily gray while the terrible understanding descends.

It left me.

Because it knows I'm about to become a Shadow thing.

Vogel's Black Witch.

Carved open by horror, I look toward the Vo Mountain Range.

The Prophecy is right, I realize, my pulse in my throat. *Vogel is going to consume me, just like he's consumed Lukas. And turn me into the Prophecy's hellish Black Witch.*

The last soft piece of me breaks off.

My mouth curls into a snarl as the memory of Lukas's defiance rises up inside of me, burning bright.

Fine, I throw out toward the Wand as my mounting rebellion sparks into a firestorm.

I'll fight Vogel without you.

I know I'll likely have just this one chance before Vogel takes complete hold of both my magic and my mind.

And I'm going to take it.

Defiance blazing, I sprint into Or'myr's dwelling, straight to his circular sorcery workroom, and scoop up every last wand in the room, the world shuddering gray as Vogel's power begins to press down on my lines once more. Head arching back from the sudden pressure, I catch my own gaze in an amethyst-framed wall mirror, another flash of shock lancing through me.

Glowing silver encircles my irises.

Clear that my whole world has contracted into this one, blazing chance to wage war, grab hold of Lukas, and strike Vogel down, I race back out onto the balcony. Eyes fixing on the Vo Mountains, I pull my power's aura into a tight ball then push the full, violent force of it behind one word, thrown into the air, out over the entire Eastern Realm.

Raz'zor!

PART FIVE

Void Moon

CHAPTER ONE

SHADOW INVASION

Vothendrile Xanthile

Xishlon night, twenty-second hour

"We're sparking," Vothe teases as he presses his lips to the base of Trystan's neck, the Vo's purple-lit waves crashing against the rocks around them.

Trystan pulls Vothe into another deep kiss, his hand cupping the back of Vothe's head, fingers woven insistently through Vothe's hair as he throws a line of bright lightning through him that Vothe feels straight down his spine.

Vothe groans and shudders against Trystan, every muscle in his body rock-hard, a shower of visible sparks flying out from them both. "Holy Vo, you can kiss," he manages, breathing heavily as his mouth curves into a smile, wanting this Mage more than he's ever wanted anyone in his entire life.

Trystan's shimmering green lips turn up, his forest eyes deep pools of pent-up desire. "You made it clear that a great deal of kissing is required of this courtship," he murmurs, his voice hitching with a trace of nervous heat.

Vothe nods, completely under his spell. "It is...and tradition must be obeyed—"

Trystan cuts off Vothe's words with another storming kiss, fire and lightning exploding through them both as Vothe surrenders himself to beautiful, intoxicating Trystan Gardner.

The air around them splits with an ear-shattering *boom*.

Vothe flinches against Trystan and they break the kiss, shock racing through Vothe in response to the image he's met with over Trystan's shoulder. Trystan's head whips around to witness what Vothe has already gained a full, horrifying view of.

The side of the Vo Mountains has exploded outward, leaving a huge, linear gash, a line of impossibly huge, gray-glowing runes marking its top, the mountain's peak still intact. A flood of black smoke is pouring from the gash like a demonic tide, foggy gray mist rising from its maw toward the purple-mooned sky.

They grip tighter hold of each other as cries rise from the city and the shadowy tide rapidly inks down the mountain range, rushing toward the Vo River. Vu Trin alarm horns blare and dragons launch from the distant Wyvernguard, rune ships fleeing toward Voloi as the moon's edge tints a dull, ashen gray.

Vothe exchanges a horror-filled glance with Trystan.

"He's here," Trystan says, his voice full of a terrible certainty. "Vogel is *here*."

Vothe throws off his tunic, lightning flashing in his vision and over his skin as he sends his horns spiraling up from his head and his wings spring free from his back. He meets Trystan's gaze, his power crackling with controlled ferocity. "I'm Changing," he says, his Wyvern tail lashing behind him.

"Good," Trystan replies as he unsheathes his wand. "Because we're going to fly to our battalion, link our power to the Vu Trin and drive the godsforsaken Mages from our lands."

IMPENDING DEATH

Tierney Calix

Xishlon night, twenty-second hour

An earsplitting explosion blasts from the mountains above. Tierney ducks toward the forest stream's bank as Viger launches his dark form at her.

His hard body collides with hers, forcing her sideways to the forest floor just as a huge piece of the mountain crashes through the trees and lands with a concussive thud where she was standing, smaller pieces of mountain raining down.

Viger's smooth forehead presses against Tierney's, his strong hands holding tight to her arms, his chest rising and falling against hers as she clutches him, as well. She can feel his sharp claws biting through her tunic's fabric.

Get hold of yourself, Tierney urges herself, her flash of panic reverberating. Wresting the fear aside, she forces herself up as Viger rolls off, alarm horns blaring from the direction of the runic border. Cautiously, they both rise to their feet.

"How did you know where we'd be safe?" Tierney asks,

stunned and breathless as she eyes the huge pieces of stone cratered into the forest floor.

Viger's black eyes glint in the debris-ashed light. "I can sense impending death."

A strange hissing sound rises from above and they peer up through the canopy's boulder-smashed breaks. A line of huge gray runes glows just above a gash near the range's peaks and Tierney watches, horror-struck, as a tide of dark mist bubbles from the gash and waterfalls downward, barreling straight toward them.

They step backward, their hands finding each other while a thinner, gauzy fog rises from the gash toward the heavens.

And then the Xishlon moon's purple light cuts out.

A fuller darkness descends, and Tierney moves closer to Viger at the same time that he pulls her into a half embrace. Pulse racing, she yanks a rune light from her pocket and flicks it on.

The Noi rune inside the glass vial casts the stark planes of Viger's face in an otherworldly sapphire glow as a tide of undulating, thigh-deep fog advances through the trees. Tierney's throat tightens as they take another step backward, the Shadow twining around trunks and brush, streaming relentlessly in.

Viger snarls as they're engulfed in it, both Tierney's blue hue and the vial of sapphire rune light tinting to shades of gray. Fright rearing, Tierney holds up the grayed vial and her alarmingly color-stripped hand.

Demonic Shadow, Viger says into her mind, his deep voice vibrating through her. His fully blackened gaze intensifies. "Vogel is in the mountains."

Tierney's internal power bursts into storming chaos. Her thoughts fly to the combined magic she and Viger sent toward the Vo and Zonor Rivers to ward-protect them.

"Do you think our warding of the waters will hold?" she asks.

Viger's beat of hesitation ratchets up Tierney's protective fright as a helix of Shadow curls around her rune light. The light blinks out of existence, thrusting them into complete darkness.

Tierney swallows, gripping her now useless light. "It's just like Elloren warned," she rasps. "Vogel's Shadow destroys runes."

She can feel Viger's gaze sharpen on her. *Elloren Grey is here?*

Tierney freezes, realizing she's just revealed Elloren's presence to a Death Fae whose true allegiance is unknown. "Viger, you don't understand this," she forces out. "You've only read my fears…"

Viger's hand clamps around her arm. "The Black Witch is in the Eastern Realm?"

"She's our *ally*," Tierney entreats as the chilling Shadow courses around them.

A low, undulating language rises from Viger's throat and resonates through Tierney. He grows silent as a chorus of earsplitting screeches breaks out overhead.

Ice flashes through Tierney's power.

Broken dragons.

A nearby *whoosh* of wings sounds through the darkness as something huge flies in, the branches above Tierney jostled by the incoming beast. Fear exploding, she struggles to pull away from Viger as her panicked mind whirls. *Did he summon a broken dragon here? Are the Death Fae in league with Vogel? Was Fyordin right about them all this time?*

The beast moves toward them, cracking branches and brush.

"Viger," Tierney pleads with him in the darkness. "Please, gods, tell me you're on my side."

Points of soft, silvery light appear inside the Shadow tide and plume to life around them, scuttling up Viger's legs, the whirling smoke that engulfs Viger's lower body now eerily lit up by the wraithlike glow. In a flash, Tierney realizes the glowing, scuttling things are phosphorescent millipedes.

Her gaze lifts to the crashing beast, her heart catching in her throat.

It isn't a dragon at all, but a huge, horse-size raven, its dark feathers illuminated by the millipedes' glow.

Viger releases Tierney's arm and croons to the bird in his

strange, resonating language as she gapes at the beast of myth, stunned. The raven cocks its head, as if listening intently to this fellow creature of the night, then lowers its body, and Viger deftly climbs onto its back, the millipedes still swarming all over him as long fingers of smoke rise from the ground.

"I'm on your side," he says, his voice a deep thrum as he extends a hand to her. "Come, Asrai. We will strengthen our warding of the rivers and find your Black Witch."

CHAPTER THREE

PREDATOR

Aislinn Ulrich

Xishlon night, twenty-second hour

Aislinn clings to Jarod, a soft bed of leaves under them both, the purple moonlight mottling the night-darkened canopy above. She draws in a deep, sultry breath. The rich scent of the forest mingles with the clean masculine smell of Jarod's skin, along with the deeper musky note of their pairing, both of them slick with sweat as they curl around each other in the Xishlon moonlight.

Joy bubbles up inside Aislinn, the feral pleasure of mating with Jarod still pulsing warm through her body, the caress of the Forest secure around them both. Jarod's face is flushed, his breathing deepened, a kind of stunned amazement lighting his amber eyes as his lips curve into an adoring smile. "I love you so much," he says as he brushes his fingers down the length of Aislinn's bare back, sending a shiver through her that he deftly reads, a knowing heat in his eyes.

Being with him was more than she could ever have expected. A revelation.

His Lupine senses were able to read her desire and emotions so clearly, to scent the things that heightened her want and draw away from the things that stirred up conflict to the point that they quickly fell into an irresistible rhythm that spoke of the full joining to come. Aislinn's fear fell away, layer by layer, as blazing delight rushed in. And she could read him too.

Read how much he loved to finally feel the length of her unclothed body against his, to nuzzle her neck and inhale her scent as he ran his mouth along her skin. To kiss her lingeringly, holding back. Always holding back, until he felt her fear and conflict drop away, and then seamlessly pushed into her. She pulled in a shocked breath at the surprising pleasure of it as he grew still, waiting for her desire to rush back in like a tide to match his own, her body arching against his as they fell into a new, deeper rhythm with each other.

Aislinn can't suppress her own wide returning smile as tears come to her eyes. She caresses the spot on the base of her neck where Jarod bit her that night under the moon, transforming her into a Lupine and stripping away both her fastlines and affinity lines. Turning her into a creature of the Forest. A creature of new sensations and strength and awareness of the natural world. A creature with the heightened desire to pair with her true love.

"I love you too," she says, overcome. Feeling like a new being.

An explosion suddenly rocks the forest floor beneath them.

Their hold on each other tightens. Military horns blare from the direction of the Wyvernguard as they exchange a look of wordless shock. They spring to their feet, break into a run, Lupine fast, to a small clearing just before a precipitous drop affording a clear view of the city.

Aislinn gasps and grips Jarod's arm. A great waterfall of Shadow is flowing down out of the entire length of the gouged-out Vo Mountain Range, a misty shadow veil rising from the gash's top toward the Xishlon moon, a huge line of gray runes above the exploded section.

They watch, frozen, as the moon's purple light snuffs out, Aislinn's every muscle tensing as the moon's lovely thrall is stripped from the world. The unnatural shrieks of broken dragons rend the air, the dreadful sound emanating from the mountain gash, and Aislinn's and Jarod's eyes meet in mutual, horrified understanding.

"Vogel," Jarod rasps in a stunned voice as the swarm of broken dragons—mere specks from this distance—launch themselves from the mountaintop's gaping maw.

Aislinn feels an entirely new sensation of heightened strength rushing into her from the forest floor. She narrows her eyes at the incoming invasion as a predator-calm overtakes her.

"If Damion Bane is on one of those dragons," she says, low and deadly as Lupine claws flick into being where her nails once were and coarse black fur spreads over her arms, "I'm going to tear him limb from limb." She turns to Jarod, aware of how sleekly lethal her body is now, even in human form. Aware that she can likely rip the head clear off one of those dragons.

"We need to join with our pack," Jarod growls, and Aislinn can sense the strength of the Forest rising in him, as well.

"I'm ready," she affirms as the wild force of the pack-bond thrums inside her. She bares her canines and looks to Jarod. "I'm ready to fight."

CHAPTER FOUR

BOOKS AND WANDS

Lucretia Quillen

Xishlon night, twenty-second hour

Lucretia finishes her tea, the bittersweet taste of the Sanjire root lingering on her tongue like a bright, reckless note of promise.

A match lit.

Her eyes lock on to Jules where he stands, leaning against his kitchenette's counter, heatedly watching her, the Xishlon moon's jeweled-purple light washing over them both.

Strains of music filter in from outside, the erotic rhythm quickening Lucretia's desire for her longtime secret love. She glances out his open window at the countless rune-orb-decorated boats crowding the docks, a mix of laughter and festive conversation bright on the air.

Everything is so lush this eve, Lucretia considers, reveling in it. Even Jules's cramped dwelling is lush in its own way. With books. She affectionately marvels at how Jules collects books so rapidly, two shelves already overfull. It charms her. It always has.

It's as if they love him and swarm to him, swept up in a draw to match Lucretia's own.

Brimming with love, she sets her teacup on Jules's scuffed, secondhand wooden table, the sound a final thing, and she can see the brazenness of her decision reflected in the glaze of steady want in his eyes.

She holds his gaze for a long, delicious moment, and she can feel it—the amorous pull of Xishlon's glorious moon. Coaxing all her affection and love for Jules Kristian with its dreamy purple light, the words she's never voiced falling easily from her tongue.

"I love that your glasses are always splotched and you only half notice it." Her mouth tilts into a besotted smile as she gives in to Xishlon. "And I love how your clothes are always wrinkled because you're so busy aiding people fleeing east that you have no time to iron them."

Jules's head bobs in a subtle, silent laugh as he returns her ardent look.

Her smile fades, a more serious passion rising. "I love that you have bad eyesight from staying up much too late for years now, painstakingly forging documents to help so many. And I love how you always smell of walnut ink and parchment and strong tea."

Jules's subtle smile turns serious as he steps forward, closing the distance between them. Lucretia's pulse quickens at having him suddenly so near, after they've been so careful, for so many years, to maintain a polite distance. She takes an unsteady breath as he reaches up to trace a fingertip along the edge of her tunic's neat collar, a current of warmth trailing his careful touch.

"You're always such a contrast to me," he teases. "Always so well pressed and tidy."

Lucretia gives him an inviting look. "I think it's high time you mussed me up."

A husky laugh escapes Jules's throat, and Lucretia's flush deepens over her sudden boldness, unable to suppress a delighted smile as Jules's gaze slides over her in a new way—as if she's a

Xishlon sweet he wants to devour. And when he raises his brown eyes to meet hers once more, there's a molten light in them that shimmers her water power into a tingling rush.

Jules's voice is pitched lower when it comes. "I've let my mind stray to the idea of mussing you up on more occasions than I'd care to admit." The moon's purple light glints off his glasses as Lucretia thrills to the suggestion in his tone.

His gaze drifts down as he gently fingers the white bird pendant hanging from the glittering silver chain around Lucretia's neck. "You kept this," he says, a question in his tone as his eyes flick back up to meet hers. "Through everything."

Lucretia shrugs, heatedly aware of him touching her necklace, her collar, so freely. Taking his time. As if savoring the open invitation she's laid out this evening. "I've cast so much of my religion away," she says, "but...I still believe in this." She gives him a meaningful look. "And in you."

Tentatively, she places her palm on the center of his chest and slides it up over his soft, worn shirt. She can feel the heat of him through it, his strong heartbeat, his deepening breaths. It's surprisingly soft to the touch, his deep-brown woolen shirt. A shirt she's seen on him countless times over the years, his clothing as familiar to her as her own. But what lies beneath the clothes and what he would feel like in the throes of passion is a mystery she's pondered more than the mysteries of religion.

Her own breathing unsteady, she traces a line over his shirt and fondles his top button, the polished mahogany wood of it sensuously smooth beneath the pads of her fingertips as she flicks it open. She meets Jules's eyes, her pulse quickening as she thrills to the deep, shuddering breath Jules takes in response to her touch.

"Lucretia," he says, a ragged edge to his tone. He cups his palm around her waist, then slides it up to caress her back, coaxing her closer, as he leans down and brings his lips to hers.

Lucretia's water power surges toward him as she presses her mouth to Jules's warm lips, the clean taste of bergamot on his breath. Heat blooms in her center and her magic eddies toward him, a small, eager sound of pleasure escaping her lips.

Jules's mouth ticks up in response, his kiss slow and lingering, and Lucretia lets herself go pliant beneath it, immersed in their desire for each other laid bare. His lips skim over her mouth to kiss her cheek, his hand caressing the edge of her jaw, careful and deliberate.

His lips still on her temple. "Have you ever been with anyone, Lu?"

Lucretia smirks at Jules's question, warmed by the sense of the desire that rides just under his careful touch, yearning to give way. "I'm a good and pure Gardnerian maiden."

Jules lets out a sultry laugh at this. "Well, it's high time we put an end to that."

Lucretia returns his heated look. "Agreed."

An affectionate gleam lights his eyes. "I'm teasing you, you know." He reaches up, his fingertips gently skimming the edge of her jaw, his expression warmly serious. "It's an honor to be your first."

"And *only,*" Lucretia adamantly states, the events of the world clamoring at the edges of their happy Xishlon moment.

A shadow passes over Jules's features, his caress of her cheek stilling as his expression grows ardent. "That would be my fondest wish."

Lucretia returns his passionate look, then glances at Jules's messy, unmade bed, suddenly nervous. Yet ready to cross this threshold after so many years of wanting him.

Clearly noticing her hesitancy and where her gaze is drawn, Jules pulls her into a closer embrace and kisses her temple as he rubs a deft line down her spine. "I'll treat you with care, Lu."

The threats bearing down on the Realm are suddenly rearing up inside her. "Don't," she counters, moving back a fraction to meet his gaze, acutely aware of what a bright, shining, and possibly tenuous thing this moment is. "I'm not fragile," she insists.

"And Vogel's coming for all of us. So, don't hold back. I want to know *exactly* how much you've wanted me all these years."

Jules studies her, his brow creasing. "Are you sure?"

Lucretia nods as heat blooms all along her skin, eddying through her lines. "Show me what you've imagined during all those late nights together."

Jules lets out a short laugh, looking at her now with a speculative heat. There's a stronger hunger in his eyes, like a curtain has been brushed away, and it sends a swift current of desire straight to her toes.

Ah, Lucretia thinks. *I always imagined there was more to you than the private, contained Jules.* She's seen hints of it, this passion in him. Fleeting looks through the curling steam of the tea that sent quick flares of heat through her—looks always so quickly composed she'd find herself wondering if she'd imagined them.

She glances at his bed again. At the pile of books on the bed table beside it and the two strewn on the covers—two books she recently gifted him. Military histories of the Realms, one written by a Zhilon'ile Wyvern, one by a Noi sorceress.

A warmer current runs through her.

How she loves his *mind*. His delicious mind, the two of them having been on such an intimate level with each other intellectually for years now. Staying up all night sometimes, over steaming pots of tea, lost in heated discussions about history, philosophy, religion. But always keeping that careful distance.

Lucretia moves closer to Jules. "What is it you want?"

Jules reaches up and begins to slowly undo the buttons down the front of her lavender floral Xishlon tunic. The sound of their deepened breathing against the backdrop of sinuous, muffled drumbeats stokes a feverish, anticipatory heat in Lucretia.

Jules coaxes her tunic open, his brown eyes meeting hers for a brief, searing moment, before his gaze slides back to her thin, lavender camisole edged with embroidered violets. Jules stills as he takes in the curves of her breasts, visible through the slightly translucent fabric. He lets out a shuddering breath, his gaze becoming blurred with longing.

Their eyes meet and heat ignites to fire.

Lucretia pulls Jules in at the same time he grabs hold of her, his lips claiming hers with such urgency, warmth shoots straight through her lines. She clutches his worn, woolen shirt as he deepens the kiss, his tongue brushing hers in such a surprisingly seductive way her knees threaten to buckle as she realizes that quiet, intellectual Jules is fiendishly skilled with his tongue. Ocean waves of want break through her lines, his hands all over her now, frantically unbuttoning her camisole as she unbuttons his shirt with trembling fingers.

A huge explosion rattles the walls. They break the kiss, their eyes widening at each other.

Together they rush to the window...to find war has come to the Eastern Realm.

Lucretia blinks at the nightmarish scene, her throat clenching as Wyvernguard alarm horns blare and she takes in the gash along the top of the Vo Mountain Range, the line of gray runes above it, the tide of darkness flowing down.

"Oh, gods," Lucretia murmurs, horrified as the moon's purple light begins to fade. "I thought we had time."

"Vogel was in the mountains all along," Jules says flatly. Their eyes meet with a look of grim, mutual reckoning.

A chorus of shrieks sound from the mountain as broken dragons pour from the exploded peak, the crowds outside beginning a panicked flight away from the harbor.

A veil of cold purpose descends over Lucretia, water magic rising as her shock gives way to that familiar, hardened rebellion. Rapidly rebuttoning her clothing, she turns, picks up her wand, and holds out her free hand to Jules as a distinctive Vu Trin alarm sounds.

"That's my battalion's call," she says. "Come with me. I've more than enough water magery to kill dragons."

Jules grins as his gaze takes on a fierce light. "Well, it's a good thing, Lucretia, since I can't do much but throw a book at them."

Lucretia returns his smirk, amazed they can be joking at a time like this, the two of them always having possessed an odd talent to default to extreme calm in the midst of the most horrible situations.

"You won't need that book," Lucretia says. "I'll protect you. I'm going to help the Vu Trin blast those dragons clear out of the sky. You can deflower me after we're done."

"That's my girl," Jules says, a sly look in his eyes to match her own. "Let's go fight Marcus Vogel."

SHADOW MAGE

Sparrow Trillium and Thierren Stone

Xishlon night, twenty-second hour

"What do you want to do?" Sparrow asks Thierren, both of them so shy to be truly alone on her First Tier apartment's small balcony, the moon's lulling purple light cast over the world.

She leans back against the balcony's metal railing, gripping its edge, *hard*.

Raucous crowds stream by below, the sky above the dome steeped in a wash of violet stars. Music rises on the air, the ragged beats and sultry chords filling Sparrow with a sweet, almost painful anticipation. Thierren watches her, his breath seeming suspended, as she opens the vial of Sanjire root and places a small tendril of the bitter root in her mouth, a spot of color rising high on his cheeks.

He gives her a secretive smile, his voice a murmur when he finally answers her. "I want to do *all* the forbidden things."

A thrill rushes through Sparrow even as her mouth quirks

upward in amusement. "Everything's forbidden in Gardneria, Thierren. That covers quite a bit of ground."

He breathes a short, silent laugh at this and they exchange a deeply knowing look. Because in so many ways, the two of them have more in common as Westerners than they do with these startlingly brazen Easterners and their lovely, outrageous purple moon celebration of love. Even the purple hue itself is a forbidden thing in Gardneria, one of a long list of "heathen" colors forbidden by the Mage *Book of the Ancients*. And the gem-hued Xishlon wine Mii Vun left for them...forbidden, as well.

And *Sanjire root*? Sparrow grows breathless over just the thought of it. That's in a whole other category of forbidden in both Thierren's former world and hers.

Sparrow's possession of the pregnancy-preventing root was awkwardly acknowledged by them both when she signaled its presence. She can barely believe she summoned the courage to purchase it, feeling, the whole time, like she was engaged in a sordid activity that would bring not just the authorities but the vengeance of the Ge'o deities down on her head. She hesitated in the shadows at first, watching young Noi women chat and joke with the elderly apothecary as they purchased their own Sanjire root without a whit of shame, some exchanging ribald Xishlon sayings and tales. Completely open about all of it.

It was a stunning revelation, a raw resentment pricking at Sparrow as the subversive thought rose—why shouldn't *all* women have this freedom and power? Western and Eastern alike?

"Perhaps let's start with some forbidden wine," Thierren gently suggests, coaxing her from her thoughts, the sudden softness to his deep voice belying some understanding of her tumultuous culture shock. His mouth tics up. "And after that, I'll kiss the forbidden purple glitter off your beautiful lips."

Sparrow's eyes widen. Thierren grins warmly at her even as he flushes, seeming pleased by his own brazen statement. Her heart swells with affection as she realizes they're both doing the same thing—harnessing the moon's Xishlon light to experiment with being bold. To experiment with showing and telling each other the truth of their desires, both of them in a state of active rebellion against the West.

Because, Sparrow realizes, she has the *right* to ribald jokes and Sanjire root and welcoming this man she loves into both her heart and her body if she so chooses. Just like Thierren has the right to not just desire someone, but to love them deeply. *Anyone* he chooses.

The West be fully damned.

"Well, then, pour me some wine, Thierren Stone." Her bravado has her own blush flaring hotter. "And then I'll cover every inch of you in forbidden purple glitter."

Completely lovestruck, Thierren pours wine into the long-stemmed glasses Mii Vun left for them on the balcony's small table, their violet crystal decorated with lavender moons.

"Oh, Thierren," Sparrow enthuses, seeming entranced by the glowing beauty of the rose-flavored spirits. "It's like you're pouring pure moonlight."

Thierren smiles, charmed by her observation as he hands her a glass of the iridescent purple liquid. Sparrow's fingers brush against his, and it sends a tingle straight through him as their eyes meet, that ever-present desire firing between them.

Sparrow pulls in a wavering breath, then settles back against the banister, sipping the wine, and he follows her bashful gaze out over Voloi. A myriad of jewel-bright purple rune orbs drip from every eave and from the branches of the pear trees that line the street and surround their balcony.

"The West seems so far away, doesn't it?" Sparrow closes her eyes and breathes in deep, the air perfumed with the delicate scents of rose mingled with jasmine incense and sweet pears, one of the pear trees so close Thierren could reach out and pluck the ripe, lilac fruit.

Just like Thierren wants to reach out and pluck Sparrow. They've been on a collision course with each other for some time now, he considers, his feelings for her running much too strong to ever be denied again.

Sparrow's eyes warm with affection as she looks at him, the purple glitter on her eyes and mouth sparkling in a way that deepens his pulse and heats his lines. "It's *interesting...*" she says, glancing at the violet orb above. "The moon's draw toward focusing on love." She casts him a knowing smile. "I think being here in the East...where it's so free...it's making us both ridiculously bold."

"I don't need a moon or a change in place to be drawn to you," he huskily states, then sets down his glass and gives in fully to the Xishlon moon, taking her into his arms, both of them laughing as they pull each other inside.

Thierren pushes the balcony doors shut, the pulsing outdoor music only amplifying this combustive moment between them. Sparrow reaches up to caress his cheek, and Thierren's desire for her ignites like wildfire. They draw each other into an embrace, their lips hungrily claiming each other with none of the politeness of their tavern kiss, the two of them lit by the lavender glow of a single Xishlon lamp covered in moon and star cutouts, a violet-bright constellation cast over them both.

"Il'nyylia iv'riel fhir'lion nur..." Thierren murmurs in Uriskal as he presses a breathless kiss to the nape of Sparrow's neck. *My precious lavender flower. My love. My whole heart...*

Sparrow's eyes sheen with tears in response to Thierren's heartfelt stream of words—words made so much more powerful by his use of her own language.

"Il'nyylia ar'gyn zu'lia, fhir'lion nur..." she returns, voice hitching as she finishes the quote from the famous Uriskal love poem, a poem reserved for one's great love. *My shining gem. My forever love...*

My whole heart.

An explosion rocks the world.

Sparrow flinches against Thierren, the lovely moment shattering as the floor beneath them shudders, Sparrow's meager kitchenware clinking in the cupboards. They draw back from each other, eyes wide, as the rhythm of the music cuts out and muffled shouts go up, Vu Trin alarm horns beginning to bray.

Thierren grabs his wand from Sparrow's bedside table and rushes to the balcony's doors, Sparrow following close behind. He pushes the doors open and steps out, and Sparrow slips out after him, her gut clenching as they find the city enveloped in chaos. Panic-stricken revelers are streaming away from the docks in a purple tide, children crying and trailing strings of purple runic orbs as they're swiftly dragged away.

Sparrow lifts her gaze toward the Vo Mountains and her heart seizes.

A waterfall of dark gray smoke is billowing down from a huge crater near the range's top, a lighter curtain of mist rising skyward as Vu Trin soldiers yell orders and race down the street below against the flow of the crowd. It's clear, from the line of huge gray runes topping the crater, that this was no natural occurrence.

"Thierren," Sparrow manages as the purple moonlight grays, "do you think the Mages are invading?" Her eyes swing to meet his, the feel of a shared nightmare clear in that one, rattled look. "Effrey and Mii Vun," she rasps, wild desperation singeing to life. "They're in the Voling Gardens."

Distant shrieks split the air, and Sparrow watches in sick astonishment as black specks launch themselves from the mountains' Shadow-spewing gash.

Broken dragons.

And just like that, she's thrust back onto the Fae Islands, hellbent on getting Effrey to safety, no matter what she has to fight through to do it. She draws her rune blade, a reckless, trauma-forged courage rising.

Thierren takes hold of her arm, his expression gone raptorhard. "Sparrow, listen to me. We'll find Effrey *together*, but you need to stay close to me. If Vogel cuts out the runic dome—"

his eyes flick to her blade "—that rune blade will be useless. And the city will turn into a weapon against itself when every runic support gives way."

A deeper desperation unfolds in the pit of Sparrow's stomach as the Xishlon moon's loving purple light vanishes. Bordering on full-blown panic, she vaults over the balcony's railing onto the fire escape's black metal ladder, her heart galloping in her chest as she scrambles down the rickety structure.

Thierren drops to the street behind her and catches her as she's nearly knocked over by a fleeing Noi woman covered in purple glitter.

"Stay close," he insists. "Every rune is about to lose power, but my wand *won't*. Stay *right by my side*."

Sparrow nods, and they set off at a sprint toward the pier, Thierren's hand tight around hers, running against the crowd's flow as broken dragons screech in overhead and screams rise, the dragons' hue a bizarre steely gray. Sparrow and Thierren skid to a halt as one of the dragons sets course directly for them, rears back its serpentine head then whips it forward.

A blaze of dark fire erupts from the dragon's mouth just as Thierren yanks Sparrow against his chest and growls out a spell, a translucent blue shield flowing over them before the fire slams into a building behind them. The ground beneath them shakes, debris pummeling their shield before they turn to find Sparrow's apartment building exploding into silvery black flames.

Thierren's heart clenches as he pulls Sparrow back into a run, her hard-won home, gone in the blink of an eye. And any people inside…

Another dragon zooms in, dark fire streaking from its shrieking jaws to slam into the building across the street. Thierren hurls both himself and Sparrow sideways as another huge explosion sounds, debris colliding with their shield in a repelling punch that comes close to knocking them both off their feet.

His heart pounding against Sparrow's back, Thierren holds

tight to her as the smoke partially clears, people screaming all around. Horror sears through him as he spots an entire family ablaze just across the street. A toddler with hair on fire, shrieking with pain and terror as her mother frantically pats her hair to put out the flames. A screaming little boy wails nearby, his string of runic orbs aflame, his father struggling to pry it from his fists.

Before Thierren can react, the street heaves and buckles as the unnaturally burrowing fire streaks through the very ground and the surrounding buildings begin to collapse.

Thierren growls out a spell, pulls back his arm and slashes a wide arc of water over the flaming people, dousing the steely fire before he and Sparrow launch back into a run and the panic of the crowds devolves into chaotic terror. Thierren meets Sparrow's horrified gaze once before they swerve right, breaking into a faster run as they launch themselves onto a path through the Voling Gardens.

They burst onto the Voling Plaza just as the Icaral and Black Witch statue in its center explodes into a ball of dark flame. Sparrow flinches, dragons shrieking and soaring across the sky while battles break out between the Vu Trin and the Mages on the ground and in the air, sapphire and silver-black explosions detonating.

"Sparrow!" a child's familiar voice cries out.

Relief blazes into being as Sparrow spots Effrey by the plaza's edge. He's huddled with Mii Vun under a translucent violet shield he's clearly conjured, a glowing amethyst shard in Effrey's raised hand, the base of the shield cleverly tethered to amethyst Xishlon jewelry that Effrey must have requisitioned from a nearby up-ended jewelry cart.

Mii Vun is embracing three terrified-looking children under the luminous shield, all of them pressed against the stone fencing at the garden's edge.

"Effrey! Stay there!" Thierren calls out. "Hold your shield!"

A gray dragon zooms in low, skimming the tops of the purple Wisteria trees. Thierren yanks Sparrow against his chest and raises his wand at the same time the gray-eyed Mage on the dragon's back lifts his wand, horror leaping in Sparrow as she takes in the incoming dragon's four eyes.

Thierren throws out his arm, and a blast of air whooshes from his wand, spearing toward the Mage and dragon and punching them back in a spray of silver sparks. The dragon rights itself, and Shadow Mage and dragon surge forward once more as the Mage flicks out his wand and a bolt of dark fire streaks toward them.

Thierren spells out another blast of wind, diverting the fire to explode the Wisteria grove beside them in a silver-sparking inferno as the dragon lands before Sparrow and Thierren with a concussive thud.

Sparrow is suddenly thrust to the side by Thierren's insistent shove. "Go! Get under Effrey's shield!" he growls.

She hesitates for a split second, then sprints toward Effrey and Mii Vun as more broken dragons stream in. Another blast of dark fire to her left sends Sparrow darting sideways and almost losing her footing in her shoes' slim heels. A thick tide of smoke rolls through the trees, Sparrow's eyes widening as it morphs the Wisterias' purple coloration to gray and quickly overtakes the plaza as three more broken dragons zoom down from above. They land around Sparrow, their repeated impacts reverberating through her as the chest-high gray fog envelopes her body.

Her eyes meet those of the nearest Mage, his gray-glowing eyes burning into her through the thickening mist. Horror grips Sparrow's chest as a chilling grin spreads over his mouth—

Tilor!

Her young tormentor from the Fae Islands—one of the main reasons Sparrow and Effrey risked death by kraken to escape to the continent.

Terror spiking, Sparrow scuttles backward.

"I found you!" Tilor sneers as he dismounts with otherworldly speed, his gaze raking lasciviously over Sparrow's tight dress. "Look at you now, you little whore."

Outrage rips through Sparrow and she lifts her blade only to find its runes blinked out, her hue shockingly grayed.

Tilor raises his wand arm, thrusts it forward, teeth gleaming. A tendriling whip made of Shadow snaps from his wand's tip and lashes around her wrist, wresting the blade from her hand. Sparrow cries out as another whiplike binding lashes around her ankles and she topples, yanked to the plaza's stone.

All sight cuts out as she hits the tile and the Shadow fog closes over her.

"Thierren!" she cries as the bindings encircle her body and she's wrenched upward like a netted animal.

Tilor's cruel face comes into view as she's lifted from the fog tide with inhuman strength then thrown over the back of Tilor's dragon. Her stomach collides with scaled, gray hide and Tilor swiftly tethers her there, belly down, Shadow rising all around.

"Thierren!" Sparrow shrieks against the multitude of explosions as she fights against her bindings, unable to see past the few, murky feet surrounding her.

Her head is wrenched up by her hair and Sparrow gasps, Tilor's glowing gray eyes before her, his Mage face gloating.

"He spoiled you, didn't he?" he sneers. "But I get you next. Vogel's going to use you to draw Thierren Stone right to him. Like a beautiful little lure. Oh, Vogel knows *all* about what you and Thierren did in Valgard. He wants every last staen'en traitor—Thierren Stone, Mavrik Glass, the Gardner brothers, Gareth Keeler—to punish them. And I get to punish *you*. You should have waited for me, Sparrow. Vogel's granted me so much power. You should have come to me on the Islands."

"Thierren!" Sparrow screams again through the cacophony of explosions and battle chaos as Tilor reaches over her to run his grasping hand over her body. Rage firing, Sparrow growls at him, violently wrestling against her bindings as Tilor laughs, swings himself astride the dragon and takes its dark reins in hand.

The dragon fans out gray wings and throws them down, the

plaza's ground falling away beneath Sparrow as her stomach lurches from vertigo and desperate fright.

A cyclonic blast of air from the plaza's direction suddenly forces the Shadow fog away, the scene below Sparrow now visible, the plaza and gardens stripped of color, the surrounding trees alight with silvery Shadowfire.

Thierren is standing with three dead dragons surrounding him, several slain Mages splayed out on the plaza's emptying center, Effrey and the others gone. Thierren's head lifts to the skies, and his eyes meet Sparrow's in mutual horror.

"It's a trap!" Sparrow screams as he raises his wand and runs toward her, before the dark fog closes over him and he's swallowed, once more, by the Shadow tide.

SMARAGDALFAR BATTLESHIP

Mora'lee Starr'lyrion

Xishlon night, twenty-second hour

A huge explosion jostles Mora's rune ship. She startles against Fyon's chest, their arms wrapped around each other under the soft blankets of Mora's narrow bed.

"Holy Vo," she exclaims, drawing back to meet Fyon's silver eyes, his skin flushed from their fevered coupling, emerald lips swollen from so much passionate kissing.

He throws back the blanket and jumps from the bed, yanking her circular window's curtain aside as Mora grabs her Wisteria dress and wrestles it on, her alarm doubling as Vu Trin alarm horns begin to bray.

"Mora," Fyon says, turning to her, the moment so fraught with unbearable tension his verdant nudity only half registers. "Are all of the children on board?"

"I think so," Mora says, the words strained as she rushes to the window and takes in the gash across the mutilated mountains, the dark smoke pouring from it, pale fog rising up.

She looks to Fyon, horrified.

The purple moonlight glinting on his emerald-patterned face darkens, the chiseled edges of his features cast in ashen shadows. They look back out the circular window to find the Xishlon moon turned into a Shadow moon and an avalanche of darkness barreling down the rune-marked Vo Mountains toward the tent city just past its base.

"Vogel's invading." Fyon's jaw ticks as he points toward the second line of misty runes forming in the storm band above the mountain's apex, a strange, dark lightning now coursing through it. He sets his piercing gaze back on Mora. "He's taken hold of the storm band. To keep our forces trapped west of the Vo Range."

The pieces assemble themselves into terrible clarity inside Mora's mind. How the Mage forces appeared to be gathering at the Central Desert's western edge to draw Noilaan's forces west to meet with them, the East now essentially unprotected and caught up in Xishlon...

"Holy gods, Fyon..."

"We need to get the children and anyone else we can fit onto this ship," he says. "Then we need to take them to the sublands." He jabs his finger toward the borderline. "Then we'll fly out there and help get everyone trapped behind the border to the sublands, as well."

Mora nods, her resolve gaining a steeliness to match Fyon's as they swing into action.

He throws on his emerald pants and tunic, then rapidly fastens his Smaragdalfar rune blade and stylus onto himself before grabbing his crossbow and quiver. Mora yanks open a side-table drawer and pulls out her rune stylus and dagger, the varg runes imprinted on her blade casting her in a green glow as she fastens her belt sheath around her waist and secures her weapons.

Fyon reaches out to grip her arm as she moves toward the door. "Mora, listen to me. We'll need to get to the fyyl'vor'in subland entrance, since it's warded with varg runes. Get the ship ready to launch and I'll connect a stronger varg ward to its power. Those runes are the only runes in this city likely to survive."

"Which means we'll be the only ship left in the skies," Mora warns. "So we'll have a giant target on our backs."

Fyon narrows his gaze, emanating lethal calm. "We'll deal with it."

Mora nods, no time left to deliberate the odds as Fyon throws open the door and they rush onto the starboard deck.

Nym'ellia and Ghor'li are gripping the ship's railing, along with Nym'ellia's blanket-wrapped mother, Emberlyyn, and her little sister, Tibryl, their eyes stark with fear as they watch the incoming Shadow tide.

Cold panic ices Mora's spine. "Where's Olilly?"

Thumping footsteps sound, and relief flashes through Mora as Olilly and the teen from across the street, Kir Lyyo, race around the ship's stern, hand in hand. A wreath of glowing purple flowers adorns Olilly's lilac tresses, a few petals scattered in Kir Lyyo's short black hair.

"Nym'ellia," Mora says with measured calm as she meets the black-haired teen's stunned gaze, noticing that the metal points Bleddyn gave to Olilly are now on Nym'ellia's ears instead. "We're evacuating to the sublands. Go untie the ship from our moorings." Nym'ellia nods and runs off as Mora looks to the teen's mother. "Emberlyyn, please bring Ghor'li and Tibryl inside and keep them there."

Emberllyn nods and gently ushers the two whimpering children away.

"Olilly," Fyon says to the obviously fear-struck teen, Ollily's amethyst eyes wide as Xishlon moons, "I need you to bring all the copper and aluminum kitchenware to the ship's stern. And I'll need two of Mora's large ceramic pots and a mixing spoon."

"We'll get them to you," Mora affirms as Fyon briefly meets her gaze then makes for the ship's stern, crossbow in hand.

A chorus of terrible shrieks rend the air. Everyone's heads snap toward the mountains as Mora takes in the broken dragon horde that's launched itself from the faraway crevasse, her throat momentarily clogging with fear. She shakes it off, setting her gaze back on Olilly. "You need to be strong, Olilly. Can you do that for me?"

Olilly jerkily nods her assent.

"Then *go*," Mora urges.

Olilly and Kir Lyyo exchange an urgent look before Olilly bolts toward the kitchens.

"My father…" Kir Lyyo manages in a ragged voice as a battle breaks out over the Wyvernguard, explosions flashing.

"Go get him and as many other people as you can on my ship," Mora orders. *"Right. Now."*

Kir Lyyo shakes his head. "My father won't get on a Smaragdalfar ship…and he's against the sublands…"

"Then he's going to *die*." Mora bites out as a deeper gray washes over the world, the moon darkening to the color of slate.

Kir Lyyo's expression hardens to flint. "I'll get him," he says. "Even if I have to drag him on board."

"Do it," Mora urges, and Kir Lyyo breaks into a sprint toward his family's restaurant while Mora makes for the ladder leading to her ship's glass-walled control room. She scrambles up it, glancing through the glass toward Nym'ellia, who is swiftly untying their rope moorings.

Good girl, Mora thinks, grateful for Nym'ellia's calm under pressure. Then Mora unsheathes her glowing green rune stylus and powers up the control board, taking in the panoramic view in one sweeping glance. A sizable dragon horde is zooming straight toward Voloi, Mora's ship smack-dab inside that target.

With mounting urgency, Mora calibrates the ship's control runes as the first dragons reach the shoreline. Her neck tightens as screams rise, dragons throwing bolts of dark fire onto the First Tier. Forcing an even breath, Mora keeps Nym'ellia in her sights as scattered civilians stream onto her ship and the Shadow tide reaches Voloi, rapidly coursing over the pier, and Mora notes, with horrified astonishment, that it's cutting out all color in its wake. She glances over her shoulder and spots Olilly dragging aluminum and copper cookware to Fyon while Kir Lyyo and his hateful father run onto Mora's ship along with a few more civilians just as Nym'ellia releases the rune ship's final tether.

"Unmoored!" Nym'ellia calls up as the ship bobs away from the cliffside.

"Get everyone inside," Mora calls to Nym'ellia, then taps a series of control runes. Six huge varg runes blink to life around her ship, three on each side, all of them beginning to rotate.

She turns once more and takes in the deft sweep of Fyon's arm as he finishes fabricating an additional emerald varg rune just above the ship's stern. He taps the floating rune, and a translucent green shield flows out from it over the entire ship. Then he turns and meets Mora's eyes, a look of blazing gravity in his silver gaze.

Ferociously determined, Mora gives the acceleration rune a hard spin, and her ship shoots forward. She glances toward the Vo Mountains at the exact moment that the blue borderline flashes silver then explodes into gray with a low *boom* that reverberates through her very bones. What looks like a spiderweb of Shadow courses up from the newly gray border and ripples over Noilaan's dome.

The dome's runes blink out of sight, the whole city cast in a sudden darkness that jolts fear down Mora's spine.

Screams rise as the blackened forms of every ship in the sky hurtle toward the ground, walkways and buildings collapsing toward the tiers below. A series of explosions sound, and Mora gasps in horror as the rune-supported restaurants all along the Sixth Tier's cliffside crack off from the street to hurtle downward.

Tears stinging her eyes, Mora guides her ship into a hard swerve northwest. She glances through the glass wall behind her and takes in a distant knot of dragons that have broken off from the main dragon horde, six of the Shadow beasts fly straight toward her ship.

CHAPTER SEVEN

SHADOW DRAGONS

Olilly Emmylian

Xishlon night, twenty-second hour

"Throw all the copper kitchenware into this pot," Fyon Hawk-kyn directs as their rune ship soars forward.

He lifts his emerald stylus, crouched with Olilly, Nym'ellia and Kirin at the ship's stern as he fabricates two plate-size Smaragdalfar runes above the two ceramic pots before him, his silver eyes flicking toward the dragons closing in. Keeping his stylus's tip on one of the runes, he gestures toward the other pot. "Toss the aluminum into this one."

Heart thumping in a wild rhythm, Olilly sets to work with Nym'ellia and Kirin, hastily filling the pots.

"Can they get through our shield?" Kirin asks Fyon, a slight tremor in his voice.

"Perhaps," Fyon answers as he feeds energy into the runes hovering above the pots. "But they'd need to get quite close. And we're going to keep them from doing that."

Olilly struggles to keep her breathing even as Fyon deftly

magicks the runes into a slow rotation, green magic sparking in the air. She absently notes that his emerald-patterned feet are bare and his tunic is buttoned wrong, but she doesn't have time to wonder at it.

"All right, get back," Fyon directs as the lead dragon lets out a malefic shriek and the Mage on its back comes into sharper view. Fyon gestures toward one of the ceramic pots. "The copper in here is about to get quite hot."

The runes flash verdant light and Olilly is hit by a blast of heat as the copperware is suddenly transformed to black ash and the aluminum is shredded into minuscule filings.

Fyon rapidly fabricates another rune over the copper ash and sets it whirring, an ice-cold cloud puffing out from it. "To cool the reaction," he calmly explains. "So we don't blow up the ship." He waves his stylus over the runes, and they vanish. Then he hoists one of the ceramic pots and pours the copper ash into the pot filled with aluminum filings as the lead dragon soars closer. "All right, Olilly," he says, raising his silver eyes to her, "I need you to mix this."

Olilly nods and sets to work, barely able to breathe as Fyon empties his quiver into the space between them and the dragons let out another chorus of shrieks, Fyon's metal-tipped runic arrows rattling onto the ship's planks.

"We need to fill the arrows with the metal mixture, and *quickly*," Fyon urges.

"What will it do?" Nym'ellia asks as they unscrew the conical arrowheads and fill them with the mixture before screwing the arrows back together.

"These are magnesium arrow tips," Fyon says as he hastily works. "The runes imprinted on their sides will burst into fire upon impact, which will trigger a copper thermite reaction."

"Which will do what?" Nym'ellia presses as Fyon nocks a filled arrow in his crossbow and pivots on his knees toward the incoming dragons.

"This." He levels the crossbow and fires.

The arrow punches into the nearest dragon's head, and the beast veers east then explodes with a crackling *boom* into a churning ball of green flame.

Olilly gapes at the sight as a draft of heat slams into them.

"Holy gods," Nym'ellia breathes out as two more dragons advance and Fyon nocks another arrow. "I'm glad you're a metal sorcerer."

"It comes in handy," Fyon agrees, raptor-focused as he fires again and hits the second dragon, triggering another fiery explosion that has Olilly gaping anew. "Get inside, all of you," he sternly directs, but Olilly remains frozen.

A hand wraps tightly around her arm and she jerks up her head to meet Kirin's stare. "Let's go," he says, urgent and encouraging at the same time, decidedly taking her hand in his.

Emboldened, she sets off at a sprint with him and Nym'ellia toward the ship's prow as another explosion sounds behind them. They rush inside her bedroom, and Olilly freezes again as her eyes light on Kirin's hateful father, Zosh Lyyo, slumped on her bed, holding a cloth to his bleeding head.

He meets Olilly's gaze, and she recoils at the sight of the awful man. He seems dazed, blinking at Olilly's and Kirin's linked hands with a look of pure cognitive dissonance. Little Ghor'li has somehow found her way in here as well and is huddled in a corner, her sapphire eyes wide with terror as she sobs, and Olilly's heart twists at the sight.

She lets go of Kirin's hand and moves toward the child just as the ship pitches and she falls sideways against the room's circular window, Nym'ellia and Kirin slamming against it to either side of her. Ghor'li screams and scuttles to Olilly, clutching at her tunic. Olilly pulls her into a protective embrace, the entire ship jostling and vibrating, as she's suddenly so overwhelmed with fear and outrage she can barely pull in a breath.

The ship levels off, and she rounds on Zosh Lyyo, remembering the slurs he hurled at them. How he told them they should get out of the Eastern Realm.

Noilaan for the Noi.

"Now do you see?" Olilly lashes out at him. "Do you *finally* understand what we were running from? Why we had *no choice* but to come here?" Her eyes sting with tears as the pent-up outrage breaks through. "Why did you have to call us names for it? *Why?*"

Zosh Lyyo meets Olilly's gaze, his whole face tensing, and Olilly can't tell if it's with anger or remorse.

The ship drops, and Olilly lets out an involuntary cry as the floor drops beneath them, her stomach flying up as both Kirin's and Nym'ellia's hands reach out to steady her. And then the ship's free fall gives way to an abrupt, cushioned rise as the craft thrusts forward then tilts upward, the dark Vo Mountains visible in the distance. A Shadow moon hangs above the menacing landscape, the undulating sea of Shadow coursing over the entire span of the Vo River as dragons continue to pour out of the mountain range.

A sense of surreality sweeps through Olilly, her legs turning watery. Her eyes light on a plate of Xishlon heart cookies upended on the floor, frosted violet flowers scattered around the sweets.

A scream of protest rises in her throat, threatening to loosen.

The beautiful festival. Purple everywhere. Sweet Kirin washed in lavender moonlight as he leaned in to press his lips gently to hers in that lovely first kiss for the both of them. His besotted, flustered smile afterward as their fingers laced together even more tightly in unspoken joy and hope for a better future.

Destroyed.

All of it destroyed.

Olilly presses her face to the glass of the circular window and takes in the gray world, her friends' hands bracingly on her back as the ship pivots and the city of Voloi momentarily comes back into view. Explosions of silvery-gray fire are erupting on every tier as columns of smoke rise. And the Wyvernguard…

Olilly pulls in a sharp breath.

Its South Island is gone, only a smoking char remaining, a battle raging around the North Island, which is encased in some kind of cottony webbing.

"I can't live under the Mages again," Olilly rasps, desperate to shut out this new reality. Desperate to go back a few hours to her lovely Xishlon world.

Nym'ellia grabs her hand as Kirin's arm comes around her shoulders.

"We'll fight them," Nym'ellia vows, holding tight to Olilly.

Olilly shakes her head. "They'll kill us all. We're nothing but evil creatures to them." Panic mounting, she reaches up to touch her mutilated ear, all of it rushing back. The mob of Mages yelling vicious taunts as they held her down and cut the tips from her ears.

Rockbat! Urisk whore!

Mage land for the Mages!

Olilly's whole body trembles as she clings to her ear and watches the city erupt with explosions of dark flame.

A large, pale dragon flashes past, white as the Noi goddess Vo, flying due south toward the chaos.

Olilly gives an inward start as she watches the dragon expeditiously take out broken dragons with blast after blast of vermilion flame as it soars over the river at incredible speed, dodging streaks of Shadowfire. Olilly's brow creases as she finds herself desperately wishing that dragon had a powerful Noi soldier on its back.

A question bursts into her mind.

"Where is she?" Olilly thinks aloud as the pale dragon speeds toward Voloi in a white, curving blur.

"Where is *who*?" Nym'ellia asks.

Olilly turns to her, the words feeling explosive on her tongue. "The Black Witch."

Nym'ellia's green-glimmering face tenses. "What do you mean, the Black Witch?"

"She's here," Olilly replies, pulse accelerating. "In Noi lands."

CHAPTER
EIGHT

WAR

Elloren Grey

Xishlon night, twenty-second hour

Raz'zor lands on Or'myr's balcony with a resounding thud, his
churning red-and-purple Wyvernfire aura blasting through my
lines, the violet rune Or'myr placed on his neck's base glowing bright.

He sets his red fire-eyes on me as explosions detonate across
the collapsing city, nausea filling me over the horror of it.
Raz'zor's gaze swings to the wands bunched in my fist and the
Shadow smoke rising from my fastlines, then swiftly toward my
glowing gray eyes. The turbulent flow of my fire intensifies,
Vogel's branching power tightening around my lines.

Grimly cognizant of my ever-closing window of free will,
I grasp Raz'zor's powerful, ivory-scaled forearm and open my
mind to him. For a stretched-out second Raz'zor stills, horned-
head lowering, lava-red eyes unblinking on mine as his empathic mind reads it all—the demonic power ensnaring my lines.
Lukas's possession.

How the Wand left me.

And how my sole chance to fight back and save Lukas and the East with Black Witch power is before me.

A blast of Yvan's Wyvernfire abruptly sears through my lines, so much stronger than Raz'zor's, and my heart tightens against the idea of Yvan sensing my peril and flying to my aid.

Will you fight with me? I ask Raz'zor as I force back the anguish and embrace the terrible power that was my destiny all along.

Scarlet fire intensifies in Raz'zor's eyes and he sends one overpowering thought to me with murderous force.

Death to Vogel.

With that one thought and the hatred oceaning around it, Raz'zor flattens himself against the terrace's floor and fans out his wings in silent invitation.

I'm going to blow up the mountain, rescue Lukas, and destroy Vogel's forces, I warn him, gray fire lashing through my vision. *There's a risk I'll blow us up along with them.*

Raz'zor throws out the next thought with such vehemence that I'm almost propelled backward by the heat in it.

Death. To. Vogel.

"All right," I say, our joint ferocity blooming hot in my breast. "We kill him. But… Raz'zor…" Our joint flame ratchets up, as if he can sense what I'm about to say, my heart knotting against it. "If he fully turns me, you need to kill me."

A scorchingly pained look, and then a blast of fervid affirmation heats our fire.

Fealty, Raz'zor sends out, my graying eyes locked with his molten ones, unshakable respect streaming between us. Time warps in that agonizing second as I take in everything about his eyes—their striations of shimmering crimson and tracings of purple against the hotter scarlet glow. His vertically slitted pupils that gleam like rain-slicked stone in the depths of night.

Pain cuts through my chest. These may be some of the last images of my life.

But I'm ready to die fighting for Erthia.

On fire with determination, I slide the bunched wands into

my tunic's pocket and pull myself astride Raz'zor, grasping hold of his ivory shoulder horns. He rises in one powerful motion, our joint fire rising along with us, just as the balcony's door slams open.

"Elloren!" Or'myr's voice rings out as I'm hit by his fierce lightning aura. Raz'zor and I whip our heads back to stare at his frozen figure, Or'myr's horrified green eyes pinned on me.

"Cousin," he says, his voice tight and careful. "What happened to you?"

I tell him, then lift my wands. "Raz'zor and I are going to fly to the Vo Mountains to rescue my fastmate, kill Marcus Vogel, and blow up his army."

Shock blasts through Or'myr's gaze. He rushes toward me and draws his purple, gem-encrusted wand, his violet lightning aura crackling around me. *"Stop,"* he commands, taking firm hold of my arm. "You're not acting alone."

Anger lights, swiftly whipping into fury as I glance at his hand, the gray in my vision intensifying while Vogel's power slithers over my lines. "Take your hand off me, Or'myr."

"Elloren." His tone is low and measured, and he doesn't loosen his grip. "Your eyes are glowing gray. That is *not* a good sign, my cousin."

"I know *exactly* where Vogel is." I jab my finger toward the center of the desecrated mountain range. "I have this one small chance to destroy him, and I'm going to take it."

Explosions rock the city as my cousin's face hardens. "I'm coming with you."

"It's *too dangerous*—"

"Which is why you *need* help," he counters with some asperity. "You haven't the foggiest idea how to shield a dragon properly. You'll be struck down before you're even halfway across the river. And...even if you are about to become the most evil Black Witch the world has ever known...you're *family*. And family sticks together."

I blink at him, stunned and touched by his bizarre, over-reaching sense of family loyalty. "I'm going to level the entire mountain with Mage- and Wyvernfire," I caution.

Or'myr's eyes flick toward the wands. He draws in another breath, then nods, as if coming to full acceptance. "I'll shield myself, if it comes to that. Or maybe I'll get blown up too. But, regardless, I'm coming with you."

"On one condition," I insist, the wrathful power inside me burgeoning. "If Vogel fully turns me...you and Raz'zor need to kill me."

His expression conveys fresh horror, but then he gives me another quick, curt nod. Then he looks to Raz'zor, who nods once then flattens to ease Or'myr's leap onto his back. My cousin's arms come around my waist and he takes hold of one of Raz'zor's ivory shoulder horns, his purple hand closing around it above mine. The fingers of his free wand hand slide over the crystals affixed to his wand as he sounds a spell.

An aqueous violet sheath flows from his wand and courses around us, sending a prickling tingle over my skin. Or'myr flicks his wand, and tendriling violet vines fly from its tip to curl around our legs, securing us to Raz'zor's back.

"I'm going to try to hold back my power until I get near Vogel," I tell him as Vogel's barely repelled Shadow claws around my power. "I don't want to destroy Voloi or the tent city beyond the border. But if I touch you, I'll likely amplify your magic."

"Take hold of me then, cousin," Or'myr rejoins, defiance in his tone. "We'll evade that demon tide and light it up a nice shade of purple."

Raz'zor flexes his powerful wings in an emphatic snap, and I grab the hand Or'myr has wrapped around Raz'zor's shoulder horn. I've a sense of both Raz'zor's red, purple-sparking Wyvernfire and Yvan's passion-imbued golden flame ramping up inside us all.

"All right, Black Witch," Or'myr says against my cheek as the multicolored fire churns volcano-hot. "Let's go to war."

PART SIX

Demon Tide

The Gardnerian Prophecy

*(Divined from Ironwood cleromancy
by the Priest Seers of the First Children)*

**A Great Winged One will soon arise and cast
his fearsome shadow upon the land.**

**And just as Night slays Day
and Day slays Night,**

**so also shall another Black Witch
rise to meet him,
her powers vast beyond imagining.**

**And as their powers clash upon the field of
battle, the heavens shall open, the mountains
tremble, and the waters run crimson.**

**And their fates shall determine
the future of all Erthia.**

BATTLE MAGE

Elloren Grey

Voloi, Noilaan

Raz'zor launches himself toward the Vo Mountain Range like a bolt shot from a crossbow. Nothing prepares me for the speed at which we fly, Or'myr and I leaning low to cut the wind battering the geo-shield prickling over our forms. Power surges through me like a storm ready to burst from my skin as I grip my cousin's wrist to enhance his power with mine.

Raz'zor swoops down over Voloi's besieged tiers so abruptly my stomach heaves as we speed around pillars of smoke toward the Vo River and Vogel's incoming horde.

Or'myr spits out a curse as a Mage on dragonback veers toward us, gray eyes glowing bright. The Mage lifts his wand, and I'm assaulted by an aura of dark trees aflame with gray fire.

"He's an Earth and Fire Mage," I snarl over my shoulder.

Or'myr murmurs a spell, his purple aura contracting inward with lethal force. He flicks his wand out the same moment the Shadow Mage does, a gust of iridescent violet wind blasting from

Or'myr's wand as a silver-dark blaze of fire flies from the Mage's. Or'myr's gust slams against the Shadowfire, driving it back in a spray of violet sparks. The Mage's dragon splays out gray wings as Or'myr thrusts his wand arm out again, hurling a bolt of purple lightning that forks all over the Mage's silver-flashing shield.

The corrupted dragon screeches as Or'myr's lightning pierces its shield. Raz'zor swings us sideways to avoid a collision just as the Mage and his dragon erupt in an explosion of purple flame.

The blast ringing in my ears, we level off, soaring over the Shadow-tide-enveloped First Tier, then zooming over the Vo River. Shadow dragons streak through the sky as they swarm Voloi and battle Noilaan's sparse forces, explosions detonating, the Wyvernguard Islands' ladder of connecting walkways collapsed and hanging like broken branches from its surviving North Island.

A fresh rush of Yvan's Wyvernfire floods my lines, flashing gold through my graying vision, my heartbeat quickening with urgency. Two more Shadow Mages close in from the left and right, alarm sparking through my nerves as I realize they're zooming in too quickly for us to prepare a counterstrike. They level their wands, dark lines of earth magery whizzing toward us.

Raz'zor retracts his wings and drops into free fall.

I jerk my head up just as the Mages' vine spears collide, their dragons shrieking as their magic punches into each other. Raz'zor splays his wings out, halting our rapid descent and narrowly avoids contact with the color-muting Shadow tide.

Heart thundering, I glance over my shoulder to find the two Mages and their dragons tangled in vine-netting and pinwheeling toward the Shadow-coated river.

A cyclonic fog aura suffuses my mind and I whip my head around to find another Shadow Mage closing in, his foggy magic shot through with dark lightning.

"He's got air and fire…" I manage just before the Mage swirls his wand and draws up a portion of the Shadow tide to envelop us in a dark haze. Or'myr's diaphanous amethyst shield spits purple lightning then vanishes, a slithering rush of Shadow coursing over my skin.

"Elloren," Or'myr gasps as he holds up his wand hand, tendrils of the Shadow smoke snaking over it.

Alarm tightens my throat. Or'myr's purple coloration is gone, as is the purple of his geo-wand, no color remaining on him save the Gardnerian green of his gaze.

Which means Or'myr's purple-oriented power is shut down.

Or'myr curses as his bindings tying us to Raz'zor begin to give way and Raz'zor arcs straight up out of the Shadow tide. I fall back against Or'myr's chest as we blast through it, the breath whisked from my lungs as another Mage zeroes in, his aura of cold icing through me.

"Ice!" I cry, and Raz'zor pitches left as a dark spear lances through the air beside us in a frigid whoosh, barely missing Raz'zor's wing. Another Shadow-ice spear zips past our right and Raz'zor tilts to evade it, the spear just missing Or'myr's head.

Raz'zor swoops upward, the river's surface to my back, the ghoulish Void moon directly above like a giant, all-knowing Vogel-eye.

We level off and I look at the crater-slashed mountain before us, dragons spilling out of its gaping maw. A bloodred conflagration ignites within Raz'zor as he accelerates toward the incoming horde, his scaled hide growing feverishly warm.

He opens his jaws, whips his head to one side then lashes it forward, spraying a line of red fire in a punishing arc, the incoming dragons exploding into balls of ruddy flame.

Death to Gardneria, Raz'zor snarls into my mind and I draw in a hard breath, Yvan's magic crackling hotter under my skin as we zoom forward, more than halfway across the river now as Raz'zor begins to restore his depleted flame. Vogel's Void tree shudders into the back of my mind, silvery-black fire crackling all around its gnarled form.

Oh, you sense me, do you? I seethe.

Rage firing through me, I reach into my grayed tunic's pocket and grab my wands. A cataclysmic wave of power rushes toward my wand hand and I ready the Fire Strike spell, my quivering hand fusing to the wood as the wands take on a red-hot glow.

We zoom over the grayed borderline and Raz'zor darts through a gap in the Shadow-net dome rising from it. My emotions tighten as I take in the pillars of Shadow smoke coursing up from the decimated tent city, but then a spot of relief lights—I can make out mist-obscured people rushing toward several varg-rune-encircled holes leading directly into the earth, a green-hued Vu Trin soldier who I'm certain is Bleddyn ushering people into one of them, Smaragdalfar aiding people into the others. *Subland escape routes.*

We soar up over the Vo Forest and I narrow my gaze in Vogel's direction as another swarm of Mages on dragonback pour out of the mountain's gash, zooming toward us. My pulse quickens as I sense Raz'zor struggling to restore his still-depleted power while Or'myr draws in gasping breaths, frantically pulling on the purple-hued magic trapped in his center.

My heart in my throat, I raise my wands, readying my attack and praying Lukas survives it…as the mammoth horde zooms past us, soaring toward Voloi.

Astonishment lashes through me as I'm flooded by wave upon wave of the Mages' corrupted Shadow affinities as they soar past, dazed by their powerful auras of dark fog, dead branches, writhing vines, and grayed ice and fire.

My Black Witch.

My affinity lines give a violent jostle forward, a rasp torn from my lungs as I've the bloodcurdling sensation of Vogel fisting hold of my lines and wrenching them toward the Vo Mountains.

And then I spot him.

A tiny figure, garbed in Mage black, stands in the center of a stony ledge at the base of the mountaintop's long crater. Mages on dragons stream out to either side of him, along with the Shadow tide and rising Shadow veil, Vogel poised in the center of it all, as if he's cleared a space for us. As if he's cleared a space for *me*.

Elloren.

My fist tightens around my wands in response to his smooth voice in my head. Raz'zor accelerates toward him, my power surging as my mind empties itself of all but one bright lethal thought—*Bring Vogel down*. Gritting my teeth, I arc back my wand hand—then pause midspell, a surge of horror igniting as not only Lukas's bound form is dragged onto the ledge by two Shadow Mages…but Sparrow Trillium's, as well.

My chest constricts with emotion as I take in Sparrow's struggling, grayed form, my pulse slamming with a painful intensity, clear that Lukas would survive my inferno, but it would incinerate Sparrow. As if sensing my panicked indecision, Raz'zor frantically throws his wings out as the world blips out of sight, replaced by a dark, murky haze.

Raz'zor struggles to slow us, wings flapping in the dark while I blink against the haze's sudden sting in my eyes, desperate to locate Lukas and Sparrow as I cough against the vapor's acrid taste. Raz'zor angles his flight pattern straight up, perhaps in an attempt to burst through the top of the blinding Shadow, but there's seemingly no end to it.

Bindings lash around my body, the breath forced from my lungs as my wands are wrenched from my hand and I'm yanked away from Or'myr and Raz'zor with a force so violent I'm thrown into the churning mist at terrifying speed. Hurtling downward, my imprisoning bindings cinch tight as I accelerate into free fall.

A hard upward jerk on my bindings forces a cry from my throat as I'm yanked skyward, suddenly bobbing in the Shadow like a pendulum as the smoke dissipates. My gaze darting frantically around, I take in the nightmarish situation. I'm hanging in a net of Shadow, tethered to a gray dragon above me. Pulse thundering, I search through the lingering fingers of smoke and spot Raz'zor and Or'myr also caught in Shadow nets, Or'myr's captured form dangling from another dragon, Raz'zor's huge pale form tethered to four.

All of us being flown straight toward Marcus Vogel, his Shadow Wand clasped in his upraised hand.

CHAPTER TWO

BLACK WITCH RISING

Elloren Grey

Vo Mountains

Like a sack of grain, I'm dumped onto the rocky mountaintop ledge near Vogel's booted feet, my vine-bound body slamming onto stone.

Gold sears across my grayed vision, Wyvernfire scorching through me as I sense Yvan drawing ever nearer. I blink the gold away to find Sparrow's bound form before me, the fear in her eyes so stark I'm hit by a fresh jolt of panic. Frantic, I turn toward Lukas and meet his gray-glowing eyes.

"Lukas!" I cry, my heart blazed through with the yearning to break through to him, but his gaze remains chillingly blank.

For a moment, my emotions splinter around the horror of seeing him so cruelly altered. I can barely think past it. But then a shock wave of animalistic rage surges through me.

Tensing every muscle against my Shadow bindings, I draw power into my lines, ready to blast my full aura against Vogel's

Shadow tether. But before I can move against Vogel, his magic clenches in and I wheeze out a huff, his power a suffocating coil.

Vogel slices his Wand through the air above me, and vines dart from his Wand's tip, webbing me to the stone like a captured insect. A portion of the bindings slither upward, gagging me and pinning my head to the floor, another portion whipping around my blades and emptying them onto the ledge, where they're hastily retrieved by surrounding soldiers.

I strain to look past Lukas and Sparrow as I mentally hurl out—*Raz'zor!*

An answering blaze of crimson fire scalds my lines. I tilt my head backward, Or'myr and Raz'zor just behind me near the ledge's edge, also webbed to stone. Raz'zor is snarling against the cords muzzling his jaw shut, his eyes two enraged coals, as Or'myr glares murderously at Vogel, his wand gone.

Yvan's incoming fire surges hotter and desperation strikes through my gut.

Yvan! NO!

Vogel steps nearer, his tall form eerily backlit by Shadowfire torches placed just inside the mountain's cavernous maw, several Shadow Mages striding close to bracket him. I meet his intent gaze, quivering with rage. Excitement flickers in his eyes' pale green depths and I want to spring free and claw them out, barely able to think past my aura's violent flare.

Naga the Unbroken! Raz'zor's snarling, defiant call sounds in my mind, his aura spitting crimson and purple sparks. *I summon thee, Defender of Dragonkin! Friend of the Bound Wingeds!*

"What shall we do with the dragon, Excellency?" one of the Shadow Mages inquires.

"They're especially cursed, the white ones," Vogel evenly replies, keeping his eyes pinned on me. "Break him. Then use him as bait for training the larger creatures."

"No!" I growl against my bindings as Raz'zor attempts to snap his teeth against his gag.

Naga the Unbroken! he blares at the heavens.

Vogel steps toward Raz'zor's bound muzzle and presses the tip of his boot over it, bearing down, Raz'zor's enormous chest puffing in and out. Fury explodes in me as waves of Raz'zor's crimson fire aura lash through my lines and a multitude of soldiers surround him.

Naga the Destroyer! Raz'zor sends out as one of the soldiers raises his wand and hurls a bolt of dark earth magic toward his head.

I recoil against the blow, Raz'zor's fire extinguishing as he's knocked senseless, our horde connection blocked as the Mage sends a second tether of Shadow vine around him. Dazed by the blow's reverberation through my mind, I watch, unable to stop the soldiers as they grip my horde-kin's Shadow netting and drag him into the mountain with unnatural strength.

I become vicious, biting and hurling every ounce of my strength against my bindings to no avail as Vogel strides to Or'myr. He lowers himself onto one knee beside my gagged cousin, Or'myr's green eyes blazing back at him with a feral look of rage. Vogel takes hold of Or'myr's face, his nails digging into my cousin's temples. Then he lifts Or'myr's head with bizarre ease, effortlessly stretching his Shadow binding, before slamming the back of his skull against the stone so hard I flinch at the sickening smack.

Vogel withdraws his hand, a trickle of dark blood now flowing from Or'myr's temple. My cousin's ferocious green stare is undimmed, lethally focused as if he's trying to impale Vogel with it.

"Break his mind," Vogel orders his soldiers as he rises. "Then absorb him into the lesser hive with the other heathens."

"Your Excellency," the Shadow Mage beside Sparrow says, a wicked smile on his mouth as he motions toward her. "You said she could be mine."

Vogel turns toward the young Mage as Sparrow's grayed eyes find mine with furious desperation. "Do what you will with her, Tilor," Vogel says, eyes flicking toward Sparrow with clear distaste. "But keep her alive and bring her West. She'll draw Thierren Stone to her soon enough."

Pain slashes through Sparrow's eyes, and I fist my wand hand so hard, my nails bite into my skin, everything in me desperate for wood as another hard rush of Yvan's heat flashes through me. Panic tightens my throat. *Don't come here, Yvan!*

My cousin and Sparrow are dragged into the cavern as Vogel draws near and glides down onto one knee beside me, viper calm. He gestures to the soldiers beside him with a flick of his hand, and they drag Lukas closer. My heart tightens with agony when Lukas has no reaction to our proximity save his lips lifting into a snarl, my insides cleaved through with longing.

"Lukas!" I cry against my gag, wild with desperation to break through to him. *It's me, Lukas! Come back to me! I love you!*

Vogel closes his eyes and murmurs a spell.

My emotions spin into violent chaos as he touches the Wand's tip to Lukas's hand, then mine, then his own. Multiple thin tendrils of Shadow twine up and wrap around all three of our wand hands in a complicated, undulating net. Then Vogel murmurs another spell, and the net cinches tight, confusion ripping through me as our hands pull together.

I watch, my confusion giving way to shocked horror as Lukas's fastlines turn gray...

...then transfer to Vogel's skin.

Only the dark Sealing lines around Lukas's wrists remain, his smoking fastlines now marking Vogel's hands.

"My fastmate," Vogel croons as he slides one slender finger over my identical fastlines. "Elloren Vogel."

An obliterating rage shoots red through my mind, the feral urge to tear the finger clear off Vogel's hand ripping through me as my power lashes out in vengeful chaos, pummeling against Vogel's hold on my lines. Vogel gives a slight shudder, his gaze on me narrowing tight, as if sensing my mutiny. He flicks a finger, and two Mages move forward and grab hold of Lukas's bindings, dragging him away from me.

"Leave him be!" I cry against the gag, scoured out by the ravaging desire to go after him, furious tears scalding my vision.

"Silence," Vogel bites out as he brings his Wand's tip to my neck and murmurs another spell.

Pain shoots through my fastlines as Vogel's power strikes through my lines with merciless force, my teeth chattering against the cord in my mouth.

Yvan's Wyvernfire ramps up, as if he senses my agony, and Vogel's eyes flash silver. "His Wyvernbond...it's *all over you*." His face twists with a look of almost jealous betrayal before he grasps my hair, his nails biting against my scalp. "Did he force his Icaral kiss on you?" he seethes. "Push his serpentine tongue into your mouth?" He murmurs another spell, and my gag bindings disappear so fast my teeth clamp down on my tongue.

I level an acid glare at Vogel. "Yvan Guryev didn't force me," I snarl, baring my teeth, tasting blood on them. "I *wanted* his Icaral kiss."

Vogel's eyes spit silver fire. He draws back a hand and slaps me across the face so hard a breath is forced from my mouth. Outrage spasms through me.

"We're fasted now," Vogel states, chillingly calm as he stares me down. "You'll speak no more of your staen'en taint. And soon, you will be fully Sealed to me."

Shock seizes hold at the implications. "You're a *priest*."

Vogel's piercing gaze remains unnervingly intent. "I relinquished my priestly role before I took hold of this fasting, as is allowed by the Blessed *Book*." His look shifts to one of alarming intimacy. "Elloren, the Ancient One has made it clear to me. We are each other's destiny."

I can barely breathe, so great is my astonished horror.

"We're tainted, you and I," he rues as I gape at him in confusion. "You'll understand in time," he obscurely adds. "But together, the Ancient One will restore us to purity. We'll atone for our sins by fulfilling the Prophecy. And then join our magic through our Blessed Sealing, for the Glory of the Ancient One."

My shock turns volcanic. "You're going to have to bind me a lot tighter than this, *Marcus*," I seethe. "I will *never* Seal to you willingly."

Vogel's eyes flash that odd silver fire as Yvan's incoming aura ramps up into a hotter blaze. His gaze sharpens. "Do you feel him coming for you, Elloren?" he croons, his branching magic biting into my lines.

Yvan! Stay away!

"Let him come," he says bitingly. "Because you're about to destroy him."

He jabs his Wand's tip into my neck and I scream, the shock of pain unbearable as dark branches impale my lines and the world blinks out of sight, my nails scrabbling against the stone ledge beneath me as Vogel's power fully punctures mine, gray completely overtaking my vision.

Then a fiery silver.

I spiral up out of the dark, pain searing through me as my magic inverts to Shadow, my fire turning gray as steel.

"You're mine, Black Witch," Vogel says, voice deep and certain. "The will of the Ancient One cannot be defeated." He touches his Wand to my forehead, like a solemn benediction, and my Shadow bindings fall away.

I move to lunge at him, seize his Wand and strike him down, but find I'm unable. Instead, I slowly push myself up from the stone, panic mounting as I'm unable to stop myself. Bucking and writhing against the prison of my own body, I still before Vogel.

Vogel reaches up to gently stroke my cheek, an intense look in his pale eyes. I inwardly howl out my protest, wanting to drive his Shadow Wand straight through his eye as he slides his palm around my neck, leans down, and slants his mouth against mine.

Everything in me roars against the contact as he grips the back of my head, his Shadowfire cataclysmic as it spirals through every inch of my body, claiming me like a Wyvern would, Yvan's golden-fire connection snapping off.

I realize, in a rush of shock, that Vogel has not only stolen my fasting to Lukas…he's wresting hold of Yvan's Wyvernbond. Turning me into his fire-bonded mate.

It's horrifyingly *wrong*, this corrupted Wyvern binding. Full of a desperate, controlling *want* as Vogel clenches tighter hold of me and forces his fire into my mouth, his flame sizzling through me in a devouring array.

He draws back, breathing hard, his eyes gleaming with off-kilter excitement as his steel-hued fire streams through me in a revolting caress. "My fastmate," he breathes, nostrils flaring.

An explosion of golden fire breaks out in the distant sky, bolts of flame spearing over the river to knock a wide swath of Vogel's legions clear out of the heavens, blasting them into a bright conflagration. My world implodes as Vogel forces me to take in the winged figure advancing toward me in a blur of golden fire.

Yvan!

We're no longer fire-bonded, but I can sense Yvan's incoming furious blaze of power.

"Hand my fastmate a wand," Vogel orders, not taking his penetrating gaze from mine.

A Shadow Mage strides forward and hands me a pale Snow Oak wand. My gut clenches tight as I recall that Snow Oak is a power-enhancing wood, the tree necklace Lukas gave me back at university spinning into my mind as my alarm skyrockets.

Fight back! I can almost hear Lukas snarl. *Drive the bastard out of you!*

I tense, straining to hurl my power's aura out against Vogel's hold, but this time his grip on me doesn't budge and I'm magically forced to reach out, my fingers clasping the wand's hard handle. My corrupted power surges toward the wand with apocalyptic force, my fingers fusing to the weapon as my wand hand takes on a silvery glow.

Another Shadow soldier advances, leading a multi-eyed dragon forward as an army of Mages on dragonback stream onto the huge ledge, followed by a swarm of wraith bats.

Vogel glances at his corrupted army and swings his intent

gaze back to me as Yvan battles back line after line of Shadow Mages. "You're going to bring on the Reaping Times, my fast-mate," he smoothly intones. "Destroy the Icaral, Black Witch. And take the East for the Magedom."

And then my feet are in motion and I'm forced astride a Shadow dragon, the army of Mages astride dragons falling into formation around me. Vogel touches his Wand to my dragon's flank and sends out Shadow bindings to secure me to its back, then spells a translucent gray shield around me that sends a slithering chill over my skin.

A soldier holding the white-bird flag of Gardneria secures its pole to my dragon as I internally scream my revolt.

"Rise, my Black Witch," he triumphantly prods, beaming at me as both he and the soldier step back. "Rise for the Holy Magedom."

Tightening my lines to the near-breaking point, I struggle to draw my power back from Vogel as my dragon advances toward the ledge's cliff. Dread racing through my veins, the dragons fan out shard-scaled wings, accelerate across the ledge and leap off it, vertigo assaulting me as the horde takes to the sky along with a swarm of wraith bats. Wings slam down in a unified, powerful *whoosh* as I'm launched forward out toward the Shadow-covered dome and river, everything within me screaming—

Take me down, Yvan!

CHAPTER THREE

NOI'KHIN STORM

Trystan Gardner

Voloi, Noilaan

I lean over Vothe's scaled back as he soars down toward the Vu Trin massed across the First Tier's Voling Plaza, keeping tight hold of one of his shoulder spikes as lightning scythes through us both. Outrage sizzling through me, I take in the tide of Shadow rolling across the plaza, all color cut out save my blaringly Mage green skin.

The plaza rising beneath us is a temporary oasis, tenuously controlled by Vu Trin forces. Wyvern Vu Trin are positioned around it, two of them casting a lightning spitting shield over its expanse.

Vothe and I easily penetrate the shield, our joint magic briefly pushing back the dense lightning. I take in the heaps of Mage and Shadow dragon corpses. But the Mages keep coming in seemingly endless waves, and even though Vothe and I took out scores of them as we flew in, it's clear we're disastrously outnumbered.

Columns of smoke billow from the city's tiers, blue lightning spitting in my vision as I take in the decimation, broken dragons lording over the skies, battling the sparse Vu Trin forces stationed on this side of the Vo Mountains.

Vothe lands and I leap off his back while he shifts to human, drawing black-scaled armor over his still winged and horned form. Our battalion's captain, Heelyn, meets my gaze, a rune-stripped sword gripped in her fist, a slash of blood across her hawkish face. We rush toward her through the Shadow smoke.

Heelyn raises her palm in a halting gesture as the Vu Trin surrounding her nock arrows and ready blades and stars in lethal unison, all their rune-stripped weapons aimed at me.

I skid to a stop.

"Heelyn, there's no time for this!" Vothe thunders, lightning crackling through his power.

"Don't make a move for that wand, Crow!" she orders me, ignoring him.

"No, Hee Muur," I emphatically return, careful to use her formal name. "I really *should* make a move toward this wand!"

"Hear him out!" Vothe insists before she can spit out a protest. She knifes a murderous look at him.

"During our weapons training," I call out over the surrounding din, paying no heed to the weapons aimed at my chest, "do you remember how my magic knocked the sorcery out of your weapons and filled them with my power?"

The hate in her eyes intensifies. "So, you're looking to overtake us with your magery? Is that it, Crow? Was that the plan all along?"

"*No,*" I level back at her, just as vehement, "but it should be the plan now!"

Confusion twists Hee Muur's features as Vothe steps toward her. "Heelyn, let him link his power to yours and charge it so you can set up a runic barrier!"

Her eyes swing toward his. "Are you *mad*?"

Jules Kristian and Lucretia Quillen shoulder through the surrounding Vu Trin, the two of them surprisingly holding hands, but there's no time to wonder at the sight.

"There's historical precedent," Jules calls out to Heelyn, holding up a text. "Accounts of Dryad power being linked to a variety of magics during the Elfin wars to form barriers against demonic power. And Trystan's power is, essentially, Dryad power."

Heelyn meets this with an outraged look at Jules's hand, linked with green-glimmering Lucretia's.

Lucretia calmly meets Heelyn's glare. "Trystan has enough of a storm in him to draw everyone's power into any framework of a barrier you can create," she offers.

"And any Smaragdalfar varg power you get hold of," Jules adds.

"Help me wall off the city!" I press Heelyn, emboldened by the support.

Heelyn's acid glare swings back to Vothe. "He's *lying!*" she snarls. "They all are!"

"Have you completely forgotten that I'm a power empath?" Vothe snarls back in glaring disbelief. "They're *not* lying!"

"Trystan!"

I turn toward the familiar rugged voice, relief swooping through me to find my blood-streaked brother, Rafe, jogging toward us, his tunic thrown off.

We grip each other's arms as he looks to Hee Muur, the Shadow tide unable to strip the amber color from his eyes, the green glimmer to his skin as undimmed as mine. "We can't keep holding them off," Rafe tells her. "We keep killing them, and they keep coming. There are simply too many."

A sapphire Vu Trin dragon lands beside us. "Nor Hee Muur," the young Vu Trin sorceress on its back says, military stiff. "The Death Fae, Sylla Vuul, has encased the Wyvernguard's North Island with a web barrier, but the Mages have begun to break it down. The Vu Trin Mages Fain Quillen and Wrenfir Harrow and the Wyvern Sholindrile Xanthile have secured part of the Third Tier with a horde of Vish'nile dragons, but send word that they can't hold off Vogel's forces for long. Hundreds of civilians are trapped on that level."

An Asrai Fae, Fyordin Lir, is suddenly running toward us, his fierce, lake-blue eyes fixing on me. "Where's Tierney?" he demands, and I can read his hostility, but also the intense worry in his gaze.

I shake my head. "I don't know."

He looks to Heelyn. "Tierney Calix has warded the Vo River. The wards are Deathkin wards, but the power running through them…it's *all hers*. Vogel's Shadow magic can't get through those wards, but we can't either. Which means we can't draw on its power."

"Then let us siphon your magic into the barrier Hee Muur and I are going to create," I challenge him.

Heelyn rounds on me. "I never said I'd work with you!"

"If we don't wall off the Mages," the Vu Trin scout insists, "they're going to level the city."

Dragons shriek overhead, catching Heelyn's eye, a large portion of the Shadow beasts arrowing straight toward the Third Tier.

"Please, Noi'khin Hee Muur," I plead. "I can't fight them alone! Neither can you. *None* of us can. We need to pool our magic!"

Heelyn looks at me, *really* looks at me, her fury shifting to an expression of tortured indecision just as a bright flash of golden fire streaks over the river from the north. We all turn, shock lighting as I make out the luminous figure in the distance, wings outstretched as he hurls a bolt of flame at a knot of incoming Mages and huge swaths of them explode in golden conflagrations.

"So much power," Vothe breathes out. "That can only be Yvan Guryev…"

Heelyn breathes out a hard huff of relief. "The Icaral has

come." She narrows a glare at me. "It looks like we won't be needing your magic after all, Trystan *Gardner.*"

Vothe's whole body gives a sudden, violent shudder. Concerned, I look to him, his eyes clamping tightly shut as every one of his muscles tense, his skin flashing silver lightning like it's been hit by a wave of power that's much stronger than his internal storm.

His eyes snap back open, raw horror in them. "Get that barrier up, Heelyn!" he snarls, lightning crackling over his skin. "The time for division is *over*! Get the barrier up *right now*!"

I reach for my wand. "Vothe...*what*..."

His gaze swings to mine, stark pain flashing through it that both silences me and sends a chill down my spine. "Trystan," he says, "the Prophecy...it's here. Vogel's taken control of your sister."

ICARAL OF PROPHECY

Elloren Vogel

Over the Vo River

Yvan, no! I mentally scream as he fights his way toward me over the river, blasting through Mages and their dragons, his body trailing Wyvernfire through the ghoulish night.

Horror mounting, I soar toward Yvan with Vogel's horde, a chill wind whipping against my shielded form as heavily outnumbered Vu Trin do battle against the Mage forces and are mercilessly cut down from the sky in explosions of silver-gray light.

Bucking and writhing against Vogel's hold over my body, I watch as Yvan advances, hurling fireball after fireball. His gold-glowing eyes come into view and my desperation intensifies, his gaze two fiery stars, set tight on me. Vogel's malefic excitement shivers through me, the poisonous thought darting through my mind—

Come closer, Beast.

It's a trap! I try in vain to scream to Yvan, my wand hand sizzling hot with a catastrophic level of power.

Yvan throws out a great arc of Wyvernfire, lighting up the grayed night as Mages are incinerated. But still, Vogel stays my wand hand, the feel of his presence inside me enlarging, my lungs hot and tight as he gathers my power.

Three huge Noi runes suddenly burst into being above Voloi's riverbank, shot through with blue lightning. A churning wall of storm roars out of the runes, and I startle as a great stormwall forms along Voloi's coast, Yvan's flash of mutual surprise hitting me from clear across the expanse between us.

The stormwall surges skyward, the magic at play so powerful I can feel its bright-energy tang from clear across the river, as well as a distinctive Mage energy suffusing it.

Trystan's.

Fear strikes with the force of a hammer to anvil. Because I know, beyond any doubt, that this power building inside me dwarfs any stormwall my brother and his allies can conjure.

Vogel's brutal delight surges. Sending a command through his Shadow tether, he forces both me and his Shadow horde to slow until we're hovering in midair as one.

Yvan launches himself toward me with renewed force, everything about the scene taking on a horrifying vividness as he blasts his way forward. Vogel lifts my wand arm ever so slightly and begins to murmur a spell through my mind, his focus sharpening on Yvan's wings.

Get back, Yvan! I yearn to scream. *He's luring you!*

And then Vogel thrusts my wand arm violently forward.

A gale-force blast jets through my arm, billowing painfully just under my skin. It blasts through and out of my wand toward Yvan in a dark, churning stream, my gut heaving as this small portion of my magic slams into his chest and he's blown backward, his wings forced into furious backbeats, shock crackling through his fire aura.

He rapidly rights himself, and even though our bond has been broken I can sense his passionate determination redoubling in the flow of his fire. Gold-glowing hands slashing, he rapidly takes out three more Shadow dragons with bright, sonic booms, then renews his surge toward me.

Vogel's seismic hate detonates. *Winged demon!*

The horde parts before me as I'm flown toward Yvan, Vogel once more drawing up only a fraction of the power I'm capable of, even as he patiently gathers an annihilating ball of magic in my center. The rancid certainty swells in my breast—*Yvan's love for me will be his undoing.*

Because Vogel will have me strike at him again and again, whereas Yvan won't strike at me even once.

My heart sheared through, Vogel forces my wand arm toward Yvan.

A huge bolt of blade-sharp vine streaks from my wand's tip, but Yvan dodges it in a fiery blur, slashing out flame to singe the bolt to ash. He arcs around, his scorching eyes meeting mine, and a feral panic overtakes me as Vogel gathers my fuller power, my body trembling.

"Elloren!" Yvan snarls as he blasts a path forward, eyeing my shielded form. "Can you speak through his hold?"

Slowed to a hover, I level my wand at his chest.

Yvan fans out his wings, halting his momentum as his eyes lock on to mine with burning intensity. Snarling, he throws his palms out to the sides.

Fire blasts from his hands, my dragon bucking beneath me as Yvan's flame lashes around us to form a great, shielding orb, the advancing Mages and Shadow world cut from sight.

"Drop the wand, Elloren," he commands, teeth gritted. "Hook into my fire power, force Vogel back, and *drop the wand.*"

My mouth is forced into a cruel, mocking sneer as the Void presence inside me burgeons. *"Beast,"* Vogel wrenches from my lips, everything within me violently rebelling against the word. *"Filthy. Winged. Beast!"*

Yvan's look of shock lasts for one unbearable second, swiftly replaced by one of lethally intent purpose, his eyes narrowing to two furious embers.

He lunges for me, and it all happens at once.

Vogel thrusts my wand hand upward, and power erupts from my wand in a silvery, bolting torrent. A roar explodes through my ears, the magic rushing out of my body in a shock wave of pain. Both Yvan and the fire-sphere surrounding us are blasted back by the burst of magic, my stomach heaving as he's hurled across the sky along with the scattering of Vu Trin forces on this side of Trystan's stormwall, Vogel's Mage horde now positioned disturbingly low just over the rippling Shadow tide.

My bolt of power hits Noilaan's shadowed dome and fans out over its expanse.

The dome breaks apart in a crackle of thunder, its Shadow rolling into silvery orbs of Shadowfire suspended all over the gray sky. The orbs solidify and luminesce, like hundreds upon hundreds of explosive moons.

Vogel's surge of righteousness ripples through me as I read the zealous punishment he's about to rain down upon this land. To punish the Noi for their Vo Goddess love festival. To make a deadly mockery of their adoration of Xishlon's purple moon.

Yvan begins to wing his way back toward me from across the sky, eyes scorching, and I can feel Vogel's smile as he pulls on my Shadow-corrupted earth power.

My stomach quails as Vogel hisses a spell and forces my arm down, pointing my wand toward the river below.

Power explodes through me with seismic force, my silent scream ripping through my lines with the brutal wave of magic, a dark branch spearing from my wand to violently impale the river below.

The branch slams down through the water and triggers the manifestation of a great column of Shadow. It surges upward through the Shadow tide, straight toward me, large as a Wyvern-guard Island, colossal branches bursting from it as it rises.

Yvan is forced backward, dodging branches as the column's pinnacle slams into my dragon, the impact forcing my breath from my lungs as I'm pushed skyward and the great Shadow tree takes form. Its branches crash into Trystan's stormwall, an explosion of blue lightning detonating as the wall collapses in a mist-clouding *boom*, my Shadow tree's branches multiplying and thickening to form a new dome encasing the whole of Noilaan.

The skies split with shrieks as another wave of dragons pours from the Vo Mountains, the Shadow dragons massed above the river surging forward toward Voloi, the city once more heart-breakingly vulnerable.

Vogel forces me to flick my wand toward Yvan, my emotions rioting as my tree's Shadow branches blast out to bind him. Panic curls under my ribs as Vogel drags him forward until he's suspended before me, his arms and wings forced outward, hands bound into tight fists, his eyes a furious blaze as they meet mine.

A more devastating horror carves through me as I realize what Vogel has done. Yvan can't cast fire and free himself with his hands fisted so tightly.

The Prophecy has come.

Vogel's triumph surges through me with heart-shattering force as explosions break out over Voloi, Vogel's hatred for Yvan's wings reaching a fever pitch as the sadistic words are forced from my mouth.

"I rip these wings from your body, Foul Beast, in the name of the Ancient One on High!"

A strangled scream rips through me as my Shadow branches punch through Yvan's wings. His eyes blow wide-open and he arches his back in agony, my heart torn from me by the sight. I lose all emotional control, a shattering rage blasting white against my vision.

LET HIM GO! I rail against Vogel, violently straining against his hold. *I'll KILL you!*

His will clamps down on mine, his writhing Shadow enlarging within me as he forces me to read his full horrific intent. He's going to force me to rip Yvan's wings off. He's going to compel me to impale hundreds upon hundreds of Noi'khin with Shadow branches. And he's going to let the silver-fire moons fall and scorch through the entirety of Voloi, turning it into a fiery terror for everyone trapped there as he renders it to ash.

Then he's going to unleash the much larger nightmare army he's assembled in the Vo Mountains and send it out over the entire East and Central Desert, taking the rest of Erthia for the Magedom.

An annihilating panic tears through my core. I strain against Vogel's hold, struggling to regain control of my wand hand, desperate to turn the wand on myself and strike myself off the face of Erthia before I can commit mass murder.

Before I can kill everyone and everything that I love.

Vogel's will clamps down tighter around my consciousness, his hold on me intensifying. I meet Yvan's agonized stare, his image blurring as I slip toward the Shadow abyss and Vogel's will begins to crush my mind, my focus beginning to waveringly collapse.

Yvan narrows his gaze at me with dangerous intensity, his molten heat igniting on the air. His muscles tighten, wrists and body straining against his branch bonds with such force blood starts to flow from the wounds.

And then his blood catches fire, igniting the branches restraining his hands.

Without warning, he blasts fire through his bonds and leaps toward me, breaking free, the branches tearing through his wings in a spray of fiery blood. Fast as a lightning strike, he extends dark claws and slashes through the shadow vines binding me to the dragon, drags me off its back and onto the Shadow tree's pinnacle, wrests my wand from my hand and impales the corrupted beast through the neck with it. The dragon growls and Yvan punches it clear off the tree trunk's apex.

Shock rips through me as Yvan throws one arm up and blasts his shielding fire-orb back to life around us, then pulls me against him and brings his lips to mine.

I gasp against his hot mouth, sparks striking to a burn, fast and bright, as Yvan's power floods into me and flexes *hard* against

Vogel's. Yvan's body shudders against mine as Vogel blasts his horde's full might against Yvan's shield, rage spitting through Vogel's power as he growls a vicious cry of alarm through my mind and is burned back.

My own will snaps back into being, Yvan's mouth pure heat on mine. Wyvernfire roars though me, blazing against Vogel's hold, my blood turning to wildfire as Yvan kisses me so intensely, I feel as if my very bones will meld into his fierce embrace.

Seeming emboldened, Yvan tightens his hold and sends his fire into me with renewed vigor. My own power surges as my heart takes on a frenzied beat, scalding heat racing through my wrists' Sealing lines.

A vision of Lukas lights in my mind, overlayed across the scene before me, his muscular form bound against dark stone, his Sealing lines lit up gold. Lukas's eyes fly open and shock sears through me.

They're no longer gray, but *green*.

Golden Wyvernfire lights the edges of Lukas's irises as our Sealing bond burns hot against my wrists and the Shadow net pinning him to the wall sparks gold. I can sense Yvan's slash of surprise and his sudden awareness of Lukas as he draws back, arm quivering as he holds his shield in place.

A molten look passes between us. One look that conveys everything better than any words ever could—our complete and utter surrender to the greater good, the three of us aligning in one unified force.

Yvan's mouth claims mine once more, forcing a stream of power into me that drives Vogel's hold on me back a fraction further. I gasp against his lips, my limbs suddenly under my own control, ferocity rising as I grasp tight hold of Yvan, fisting his hair, drawing both his fire and mine through me with staggering force, straight through the Sealing bond and out toward Lukas. I can feel Yvan's shock over my newly regained volition through the leaping flash of his fire. He draws me closer and we fully join our fires, blasting our combined power into my Sealing lines.

Into Lukas.

Lukas's Shadow netting catches fire. Wasting no time, he bursts through it and explodes into action, punching down his guard before kicking him viciously in the face and grabbing his wand. Countless soldiers start toward him, wands raised, Vogel striding in amongst them, his eyes spitting silver fire as he raises his Shadow Wand.

Lukas's form is bright in my mind as he lifts his wand and blasts a fire-shield over himself while Yvan and I flood fire power into us all.

Magic slams into both Yvan's shield and Lukas's, pummeling against them in silvery flashes. Lukas closes his eyes, pulls in a deep breath, and draws both Yvan's Wyvernfire and my Black Witch–fire into his lines while Shadow power rages and batters against Yvan's fire-dome and Lukas's shield. A stream of fear enters my heart as I realize that both shields are about to give way.

In my mind's eye, Lukas's eyes lock with mine, blazing with passion as Yvan and I roar as much magic into him as we can, the three of us melded into one conduit of burning revolution. And I can read it in our joint will as I sense the outer branches of the great Shadow tree beginning to waver and fracture—we're all ready to sacrifice our lives to bring Vogel down.

And then, Lukas's eyes shift hue once more, and my heartbeat stutters.

His eyes are burning gold.

Wyvernfire gold.

He smiles at me through our Sealing connection and mouths, *I love you.*

I can feel his fierce triumph in his devastatingly impassioned smile, my love for him flaring straight through our fire. Then Lukas lifts his wand and murmurs a spell, his luminous, golden gaze remaining locked on to mine as my eyes widen with the terrible realization of what he's about to do.

Lukas, NO!

A world-breaking explosion detonates, shattering our fire-trance, searing pain ripping through my Sealing lines as both Yvan's fire and mine are wrenched from our bodies. I gasp for breath, Yvan and I breaking the kiss, my vision of Lukas vanishing along with Yvan's fire-shield as gold flashes over us. The top third of the Vo Mountain Range erupts in an ear-shattering *boom* and I shudder, the explosion reverberating through my body as the range implodes in on itself along with its corrupted storm band.

Wild grief punches through my chest.

"LUKAS!" The cry tears from my throat as my wrists' Sealing lines disappear, my knees buckling as I realize that not only Lukas, but Or'myr, Raz'zor, and Sparrow are likely destroyed.

Yvan's embrace loosens, his depleted aura guttering into chaos. My wild, grief-bludgeoned focus shifts to him, his eyes alarmingly cooled to green, a dazed, wan look on his face. I catch a glimpse over his shoulders of the Shadow tree surrounding us beginning to fragment, its branches juddering into smoke. Fear strikes through my gut and I lurch toward him, time seeming to slow. Yvan's mouth opens, his eyes fluttering closed as the portion of solid Shadow beneath his feet morphs into smoke.

He falls backward, my hold on him tearing away.

"YVAN!" I cry as the world speeds back up with horrific clarity and I scrabble to regain my grip on him, unable to stop gravity's vicious pull. My lungs strangle, the small portion of trunk beneath my feet shriveling inward.

"Yvan, no!" I cry again while he whirls away from me, plummeting toward the Shadow-coated river far below, his torn wings fluttering like shredded fringe.

A blast of golden heat hits me from above, and I gasp at the elemental rush, a hot spasm streaking through my lines. I jerk my devastated gaze upward just as the silver-fire moons explode into balls of churning yellow fire, countless black dragons suddenly bursting through the gold-burning moons.

Surprise knifes through my grief-ravaged mind. Because they're not broken dragons.

They're Western Wyverns, one dragon in the lead, bigger than all the others. One of her ears is gone, her eyes lit bright with golden fire, a Mage Council *M* branded on her side.

Naga the Unbroken!

The horde's fiery power focuses in on me with violent intensity.

Reflexive terror cinches my gut as the dragons soar toward me and thrust their heads forward, jaws open wide, just as the remaining Shadow tree gives way to smoke and I fall.

I cry out, heart flying into my throat, while the dragons blast countless bolts of Wyvernfire toward me and I hurtle downward, limbs flailing, my world reduced to the blazing singularity of one, excruciating thought.

This is the moment I die.

My emotions splintering, I half feel the gray magic seeping back into my fastlines while I plummet toward then crash through the river's demon tide. Shadowy magic slithers around my lines and the fearsome thought connects—*Sweet Ancient One. Vogel survived.*

The vicious urge to fight sparks, spiraling through me as I'm enveloped in the Shadow tide's gray smoke. Gold blasts to life through the darkness above as the Wyvernfire reaches the tide's surface and courses toward me.

"*No!*" I cry out in futile protest, clear I'll never survive the fiery blow.

Strong arms slap around my body from behind and I startle, a muscular chest slamming against my back. The abrupt halt to my descent clamps my jaw shut so hard pain shards through my teeth, a powerful aura of golden Wyvernfire rushing through me as I'm yanked sideways with blurring speed.

Yvan!

But…how?

Bolts of Wyvernfire slam into the space I just occupied, the gold fire obscured by the churning smoke as I'm raced away through the Shadow tide. I struggle to catch my breath while Yvan's grip tightens around me, the heat of his fire aura sweeping through me as we fly like an arrow loosed and I'm thunderstruck by astonishment.

How did he survive?

Pivoting upward, we burst through the surface of the Shadow, and I catch a glimpse of the battle raging, Naga's Wyverns and surviving Vu Trin slashing through Vogel's forces throughout the Shadow-riddled sky.

A harsh, scuffing wind blasts over the battle scene, clearing the air. Breathless and grief-dazed, I spot Trystan on the back of a lightning-covered dragon, wand raised, the two of them taking out Mage after Mage with bolts of blue and silver lightning. A white streak speeds past him from the direction of the decimated mountains, and I pray that it's Raz'zor with Or'myr and Sparrow on his back.

And then Naga sweeps into view, flying up from the Shadow tide, a young, red-haired Icaral male gripped in her talons, his body hanging limp, his wings shredded to dark ribbons.

Yvan!

My mind reels, fright blasting to life as I'm sped away from the chaos. Away from Yvan.

Because if that's Yvan…then who's holding me?

I twist in the stranger's muscular grip, straining to see.

"Hold still, Black Witch!" a startlingly familiar voice snarls. The grip around me tightens, a small raven closing in beside us as I force my head around as far as I can.

Shock explodes. "Ariel!" I rasp out.

Ariel Haven.

Her glossy black wings beating down on the air.

Ariel.

Not dead at all.

But powerfully alive.

CHAPTER FIVE

WYVERN WINGS

Elloren Vogel

Vo Forest

"Ariel!" I choke out as she zooms away from the chaos, the raging war behind us rapidly reduced to muffled booms and puffs of bright light. Gray slashes across my vision as the images of Lukas blasting into gold and Yvan falling away from me replay in my mind, carving my heart open even as I realize, with mounting devastation, that Vogel's hold on me is once more gaining ground.

Ariel soars over the grayed runic border, toward the night-darkened forest beyond, my panic cresting as Vogel's power digs into me. Cast into internal war, I painfully contract my lines, desperate to flee from him and barely able to register Ariel angling us toward a clearing and descending. The trees' dark canopy rises to meet us, the Forest's hatred bearing down with suffocating weight as we land in a clearing and Ariel releases me.

I stagger, thrown off-balance, then wheel around to face her in the dark as tendrils of Shadow ripple back over my lines. The gut-wrenching reckoning strikes home—the only one who can drive Vogel from me with his Wyvernfire kiss has been decimated by my own hand—Yvan, lost to me, possibly slain.

And Lukas…

I can barely finish the thought, barely wrap my mind around the finality of it.

Gone forever.

Brutal, eviscerating despair grips hold and it's hard to breathe around it, my emotions gutted as I struggle not to come unmoored.

A sudden burst of silvery-gold light illuminates the clearing and I flinch, a churning ball of flame hovering just above Ariel's upturned palm, her raven kindred perched on her shoulder.

A dart of shock punctures my agony and for a split second, all I can do is gape at her.

She's a marvel—strong, glistening wings fanning out from her back, her eyes burning gold with Wyvernfire. She's filled out and more muscular now, her jaw seeming squarer, her black hair spiked, her fingers tipped with black talons. She has the same defiant gaze, but her eyes are no longer manic. Solid and strong, she positively radiates power, and I can sense the flame that's coursing through her unimpeded.

A fire that burns with incredible heat.

Her fiery eyes give me the once-over, fierce concern in them. "You don't look so good, Black Witch."

I lurch toward her. "Ariel, kill me," I rasp. "Vogel's taking over my power and my mind." I hold up a Shadow-fasted hand and blanch, undulating loops of smoke slithering over it.

"What did he do?" Ariel growls.

A more vicious rush of Vogel's power blasts into me, slicing over my affinity lines in a razing tide. I cry out and fall to the forest floor.

As soon as my Shadow-fasted palms make contact with the ground, Ariel and the Wyvernfire-lit forest snap out of sight. Alarm shocks through me as a new scene flashes into view. I'm staring through another's eyes, glancing at familiar Shadow fast-lines looping over a masculine, green-glimmering hand.

Havoc barrels through me.

Vogel.

I scream out my rage against his mind but he pays me no heed, dragging my will inside him and walking briskly through a downward-slanting tunnel of stone, the sounds of warfare fading behind us. A portal appears ahead, its frame made of Shadow runes, its interior filled with quivering smoke. Four military envoys with horns and glowing red eyes bracket it.

Raving out my protest, I'm dragged by Vogel into the portal's smoking center…and out into another scene.

An impossibly huge alabaster cavern. Much bigger than the hollowed-out Vo Mountain Range. Its pale walls seem to rise forever, covered with hives as far as the eye can see, the cells filled with countless Shadow soldiers. Marfoir Elves scuttle over the cave's expanse, their ivory forms blending with the stone, countless multi-eyed creatures amongst them.

Where are we? I growl against Vogel's hold on my mind.

Silence, Elloren.

A slash of Vogel's wrath constricts my lines, his desire for retribution flowing hot through his power as he makes a sharp turn, strides up to the pale, rocky wall before us, and touches his Wand to it. The stone dissolves and he steps through, forcing me into a pale corridor, a knot of Level Five Mage soldiers with Gardnerian-green eyes coming into view, the young men saluting Vogel as he passes and walks to the corridor's end and out into the night.

Stars glisten overhead, torchlit military structures formed from Ironwood spread out over the forest-surrounded clearing ahead, dark branches tangling over their roofs.

"Your Excellency, we've gotten hold of her."

Vogel turns toward the horribly familiar voice, a smiling Damion Bane coming up beside us, an imperious-looking Fallon Bane flanking him. The siblings wear the silver-banded cloaks of Mage Commanders. Damion flicks his wand and a tightly vine-bound prisoner slides over the dark earth, coming to rest on the ground before their feet.

Valasca Xanthrir's blue eyes glare murderously up at us.

My pulse climbs into my throat, my horror at finding her here notching even higher as I take in the Northern Spine rising up behind the scene, its jagged white peaks gleaming in the moonlight, these landmasses dwarfing all other mountain ranges in sheer size and length. I realize, in a sickening flash, that what Vogel built in the Eastern Realm's Vo Mountains is but a small, experimental taste of what's coming.

Vogel's spite ripples through me as I'm filled with the will-siphoning, fury-inducing sensation of his power intimately caressing my lines.

My fastmate, he croons as he runs our eyes over the mammoth Northern Spine. *Did you truly imagine you could run from the Ancient One's Holy Will? This is your destiny, Elloren. Your army.*

His focus on me sharpens, like a spike-strike straight between my eyes.

I know where you are.

CHAPTER SIX

DOWNFALL

Elloren Vogel

Vo Forest

Vogel abruptly releases his thrall over me and I snap back into myself.

I pant for air, down on my hands and knees, my grayed vision intensified, everything taking on a lurid, steely glow. Ariel is on one knee beside me, clasping my arm, her conjured ball of fire hovering above her shoulder as she jostles me, saying my name over and over.

Vogel's attention inside me makes a raptor-hard turn toward every dead branch.

My wand hand flexes of its own accord and I wrench it toward my chest, stark terror snapping through me. I grasp hold of Ariel. "Kill me now! And warn Naga and the Vu Trin... Vogel's filling the Spine, the *entire Spine*, with his Shadow hive army!"

"I know!" Ariel growls back, glancing toward the flock of ravens massed in the trees surrounding us, all of their gleaming midnight eyes set on me. "Wynter's kindreds from the West told me. We need to go west to fight him and find Wynter!"

Before I can stage a protest, Vogel's clawing branches impale me once more, a gasp torn through my throat by the explosive agony as Shadow floods my lines. A dazed hunger swirls through me as my gray-lit gaze sweeps over the clearing. Branches everywhere.

Wands everywhere.

Just one touch, Elloren, Vogel intones in my mind, as his power suffuses my lines with silvery heat, so potent it makes me shudder. *Noi Birch. Plum Cedar,* he gently whispers. *One touch and you'll sense the* whole tree...

I clamp my teeth hard, staggering backward as I constrict my lines in an attempt to throw off his thrall. Because if I pick up any one of those branches, it will be *over.*

"He's in my head, Ariel," I say, a tremor kicking up all over my body. "He's infiltrated my fasting and he's *in* me. Don't let me touch wood..."

Vogel's presence rams through me. My eyes roll back in my head as I lose control over my body. He darts me forward with a rough growl, leaping toward a branch as I rage against his invasion. My fingers close around wood.

Ariel slams me to the ground and whips me onto my back, her elbow coming painfully down on my arm. She wrests the wood away and hurls it aside, then pins my hands against my chest, straddling me, her eyes scorching as Vogel forces me to struggle against her. I snap my teeth at her in a feral attempt to tear into her flesh. To bite those wings of hers clear off her back.

"Icaral demon," my mouth seethes, my voice deepened into Vogel's chilling, male tones as she keeps me pinned to the ground. *"I see you."*

Ariel grins, baring teeth, her eyes widening with wicked delight. "Oh, you see me, do you?" She flicks her wings out to their full, powerful span and leans in close. "Well, take a good, long look, *Marcus.*" Her smile sharpens, her eyes two lethal embers. "Go straight to hell, you rotted piece of Mage filth. You made a mistake when you failed to break me."

Vogel laughs in the back of my mind, and a swell of violent outrage rises within me. I painfully wrench in my lines, regaining a sliver of agency.

"He's laughing at you," I rasp against Vogel's grip as Ariel keeps my arms pinned with her knee and expeditiously rips a strip of dark fabric from the bottom edge of her tunic.

"Oh, go ahead and laugh, priest," Ariel snipes, flashing him a belligerent grin as she yanks my wrists together and binds my hands tight. "I still won't let you take her."

Vogel roars back into me, shooting agony through my lines and wresting hold of my lips. I bare my teeth at her. "I'll rip your wings off," I hiss with a vicious smile. "And feed them to you, *demon spawn*. Then I'll shove nilantyr down your throat until you beg for more."

Horror flickers through Ariel's eyes at the mention of the powerful drug, a growl rising from her throat as I rage against Vogel's cruelty and tense my lines against his unbearable hold, wresting tenuous control over my voice and body once more.

"Ariel," I roughly force out. "I can't hold him back."

"Then we'll find a way to break his hold on you," Ariel viciously counters, the golden conflagration in her eyes rising.

"Destroy me and get to safety," I insist. "Get back to Naga. He's coming for me."

"No," Ariel snarls, and I'm stunned by her foolish tenacity. "I'm going to bring you back to my horde. Naga can burn him out of you."

Vile winged thing!

Hot tears glaze my eyes, Vogel's dead tree pulsing against my vision. "I can't risk him getting full hold of me again," I vehemently press. "I almost killed everyone in Voloi. The Prophecy is right, Ariel. My magic...it's *evil*. And if by some miracle Yvan survived, I need to be struck down so that he can be the one to prevail and fight."

Vogel's rage explodes inside me.

"I don't believe in prophecies!" Ariel lashes back with blistering defiance.

"It doesn't matter whether you believe in it or not!" I cry out. "It's *real!*"

Ariel's look is a scorch of lightning. "Then *subvert it!*"

The whoosh of powerful wings beats down from above, and Ariel and I jerk our heads toward the sound. Ariel springs to her feet as three Shadow dragons fly into our clearing, glowing-gray-eyed Mages on their backs.

Dread strikes through me as Ariel darts forward, pulls her wings in tight and lifts her taloned hands. Her fingers ignite to gold, the glow of the Mages' corrupted eyes burning bright as they lift their wands in unison.

With a growl, Ariel throws her hands forward, a stream of fire coursing from her palms just as the Mages blast streaming bolts of Shadow forward to collide with her flame, yellow sparks exploding sideways as she halts the bolts midair. Dark branches tendril out from the relentless streams of gray magic to form a tangling wall, and Ariel's fire rises against it to form a counter-wall of golden flame as they push mightily against each other's power. Ariel skids backward, arms extended, leaning into her blazing power as the Shadow wall ignites with steely fire.

The gray-fire wall crackles unnaturally downward, burrowing into the forest floor. The ground beneath Ariel's feet begins to buckle as the Shadow advances against her fire, a crevasse filled with dark flame forming just behind her.

Ariel looks at me over her shoulder as she's pushed toward it. "Run," she says.

Heart slamming against my ribs, I set off at a sprint into the forest, hands bound and straining against Vogel's press of power. I'm devastated to be leaving her, but horrifically clear that all is lost if those Mages get hold of me. The trees' hatred and fear pour down on me from all sides as I speed over branches and brush, the dark Forest increasingly illuminated by my eerily silvered vision.

Black Witch. Black Witch. Black Witch, the Forest pulses at me as I run, the crackling roar of the battle behind me spurring me on.

My foot slams into a huge root, lodging under it, and I pitch forward, a cry escaping me, my trapped ankle twisting so hard I can hear the bone crack. I fall facedown on the loamy ground, pain lancing through my leg. Pulse thundering, I jerk my head toward the direction of the Mages, knowing that there's only one way out now.

Gritting my teeth, I thrust my bound hands against the broad trunk before me, a huge Noilaan Spruce.

The Forest's hatred turns seismic.

Tangle my lines, I plead. *Tangle them, and I'll send a spell through them that will double back and destroy me.*

A collective pause. As if every tree in the world has suddenly set its focus directly on me.

Please, I beg the Forest as Vogel's power bears down on mine.

Vast elemental power surges toward me from all directions, all of it converging on a single target—the Black Witch.

Agony explodes through me with the pain of a thousand spears. I clench my teeth against the scream, my nails digging into the bark as the Forest seizes hold of my corrupted lines and strains to force them into a knot in my center.

Vogel's power rears up, slashing Shadow against the trees' power, and I gasp for air, my body spasming as I grip the spruce and the battle rages inside me with unbearable ferocity, my knotting lines about to give way to Vogel's superior force. Knowing it's now or never, I ready the elemental strike spell that will kill me.

Shimmering white light blasts over me from above, suffusing the woods with a starlight glow. Startled, I glance up.

Watchers. Looking down at me from the trees with serene focus.

And that's all it takes, that split second of distraction.

Vogel wrenches my lines away from the Forest, brutally un-knots them and links them back to my wand hand. A burning line of agony shoots straight through my arm and I cry out, his Shadow power knifing through me with heightened force. I glance down at my bound hands in disbelieving horror—Shadow seeps from the fastlines beneath my bindings, thicker than before.

A sense of devastating surrealness wends through my chest in an ever-tightening spiral. I lift my gaze toward the Watchers. "What do you want?" I croak at them, loss crushing me, my shoulders bowing under the weight of it. *Lukas. Yvan. So many innocents in Voloi...*

Outrage sparks, rising up in a fiery riptide. "Do you know what you've just done?" I hurl out.

They don't budge. They simply sit there, being their unfor-givably pristine, otherworldly selves.

"Why are you here?!" I rage. "To keep me linked to my power? *Why?* So Vogel can destroy everything?"

Nothing. No movement. No reaction. They remain still as fixed stars.

"What good are you?" I cry. "The Gardnerians are going to *win*! Everyone I love is going to die! One of the best men I've ever known just sacrificed his *life to* save mine, to try to save us *all*, while you sit there watching and watching while evil takes over and you do absolutely *nothing*!" I try to rise, but my broken ankle buckles with pain. "Vogel's going to destroy the world," I lash out at them, my voice coarsening with tears. "And he's going to do it with your image plastered all over everything. Because your *image* is stronger than you are!"

And then the Watchers blink out of sight and the darkness rushes in, which only stokes my despair higher.

"Go ahead!" I rage after them. "Disappear! It's what you do best!"

"Elloren!"

Shock surges through me and I whip my head in the direction of Ariel's voice, blinking away tears as I squint into the darkness. Her bootsteps sound, rustling through the brush, and the sheer impossibility of the situation strikes me.

She's survived. And now, after everything she's been through…after everything I put her through in Verpacia…she's doggedly coming back to help me.

The desperate thought lights—*Maybe she's right*. Maybe prophecies should be fought and subverted rather than numbly accepted. No matter the odds. Lukas never stopped fighting. Neither did Yvan. And then there's Ariel, who, in spite of everything, rises again and again.

"Ariel!" I cry out to her. "I'm here!"

More rustling in the woods. And then…an unnaturally large amount of rustling, coming not only from Ariel's direction, but from both sides of her, as well.

Ariel snarls. Ravens caw. The sounds of struggle crackle in the brush, and a loud *thump* reverberates before ravens explode from the trees in panicked flight. Then silence.

Fear jolts through me. "Ariel?" I call, my voice high-pitched with fear.

More rustling sounds from behind me, and I turn just as a hard blow connects with my head. A shower of stars lights my vision before the world goes dark.

PART SEVEN

The Forest

The
Dryad Prophecy

*(Read directly from images and
emotion sent out by the trees)*

**An Icaral rises!
Fire! Smoke! Burning!
And the Black Witch returns!**

FIRE! FIRE! FIRE!

**A Shadow Branch of Ruination
Gray power seeping into the Forest
!!!!!!!!!!!!!!!!!!!!!!!!!!!!!!!!!!!!!!**

CHAPTER ONE

DRYADIN

Elloren Vogel

The Forest

The first thing I become aware of is the rhythmic swinging motion of my netted body. Hard twine digs into the entire length of me. My hands are tightly bound behind my back, my legs lashed together, my broken ankle throbbing.

And Shadow ripples through me, steady as a tide.

It's so much stronger now, its slithering grayness invading every line to the point that I can't connect with a single wispy remnant of ungrayed power. My vision aglow with silver gray, I sink deeper and deeper into my corrupted state. I've the inescapable sense of Vogel lurking in my mind, his thoughts filled with images of his Shadow host winging toward me...

Black Witch.

The words knife into me from the Forest, and I open my eyes, roused from my stupor. I wince, my head throbbing where the blow that knocked me out connected.

My gaze darts around the nighttime scene, frantically searching for Ariel, my glowing vision allowing some gray sight into the dark. The shadowy forest passes by through the gaps in my net, the nearest trees illuminated by flickering light as I'm carried through the wilderness like a captured animal.

Carried by a group of green-glimmering Fae.

Soldiers, garbed in armor formed from leaves and bark, their verdant hue able to cut right through my Shadow-tinted vision. *Dryads.*

The stunning revelation grips hold as I remember the pictures in Aislinn's books at university—pen and ink depictions of the Forest Fae. Supposedly wiped out during the Realm War...

My heartbeat kicks up into a harder rhythm as I look at the huge young man carrying the front of my net, his armor formed from dark plates of bark. Branch antlers grow from his head, his long green hair tied up, his ears rising in sharp points. A green-glowing staff is strapped to his back and a massive black bear lumbers beside him.

A petite young woman walks on his other side, a flowering plant covering this soldier's head where hair would usually be, blossoming vines encircling her slender arms. Her movements are graceful as a dancer and she holds a branch aloft, a puff of emerald light floating above it. A branch bow and a quiver are strapped to her back, and even in my wretched state, when she turns to glance at me with a look of wary concern, her fantastical beauty momentarily captivates me.

My demonic gaze is forced back to her branch bow, Vogel's cruel attention tightening on it and my wand hand flexes of its own accord beneath my bindings.

My pulse quickens further.

Footsteps sound to my left and I turn my head a fraction as a rangy young Dryad strides into view. He radiates intensity, like hot oil crackling in a pan. He doesn't look at me. His harsh, masculine face is set straight ahead with an expression of fervent purpose. His forest green skin is coated with a patina of deep-green glimmer, his pine-bough hair gathered behind his back, compact branch horns growing from his scalp. His bark-plate armor is fashioned from thick, pressed leaves that seem melted together. A crossbow hewn from irregular wood hangs from his back and a variety of branches are sheathed at his waist, each imbued with a deep-green glow. His severe demeanor and potent aura of elemental power sends a chill down my spine.

Vogel's entrenched power digs deeper, gouging painfully into my lines, a rasping cough forced from my throat. The Shadow... it's so strong. Coursing through me as if it were never driven out. As if Lukas, Yvan, and I had never fought back against him at all.

The memory of the triumphant look on Lukas's face before he blew up the mountain and himself to save the realm grips hold of my mind, grief seizing my throat with choking force as the terrible thought breaks through—

Everyone's sacrifices will be meaningless if Vogel regains hold of me.

Devastation crushes my chest, the nightmare of Vogel forcing me to impale Yvan's wings accosting me. How I mercilessly pinioned him, the fire stripped from his eyes as he plummeted toward the Shadow tide, his shredded wings fanning out like ripped cloth.

Carved open by a gutting anguish, I slide further into Vogel's abyss, realizing it's only a matter of time before he regains full control. I know Lukas and Yvan would urge me to fight to the end, but I'm certain there's only one way to prevail now.

My power must be destroyed. *I* must be destroyed.

And I need these captors of mine to do it.

I look at the rangy young soldier as Vogel's fierce hatred of him crackles through me like a jolt of lightning. Perhaps sensing my attention, the branch-horned Dryad turns and sets his furious gaze on me.

Black Witch, the trees pulse damningly, their condemnation echoed in his livid stare.

"Vogel's about to control me," I rasp out to him, and I've a sense, through the static rush through his power, of his blistering outrage at hearing me speak.

A hard blow to the back of my head sets stars flashing in my eyes. I cry out, a voice behind me growling something vicious in a language that's dry and crackling, like autumn leaves scraping against each other. A language that could camouflage itself inside the sounds of the forest. I wrench my head to look over my shoulder, straining to see who leveled the blow.

Another Dryad soldier is glaring at me—a young woman with an athletic build and long green hair woven into buns, oak branches dotted with acorns emerging from them, a deep-brown wolverine stalking next to her. She bares her teeth and lifts a River Oak staff marked by a spiraling, green glow, looking like she's getting ready to rain another blow upon my head. She barks something at the rangy young man, and he snaps back.

"Did you hear me?" I cry out at them both.

My outburst seems to startle them. They collectively slow to a stop, studying me with deep wariness as I hang suspended.

"The Gardnerian leader, Marcus Vogel, is *inside me*!" I warn. "He has a Shadow Wand and he's taken control of my power. He wants to kill everyone who isn't a Mage and take over all the Realms. So, *don't let me get near wood*!"

The rangy soldier lunges toward me, grabs the net, and yanks my head up. *"Be quiet,"* he demands in heavily accented Common Tongue. "You will be *quiet*, Black Witch."

I gape at him, startled by his use of my language. His other fist tightens around his crossbow's strap, and I dizzily wonder if he plans to use the weapon on me.

He releases the net, and my head falls against the twine. Then he steps back, still glaring at me as thoughts of Ariel rise.

"The Icaral who was coming for me," I demand of him, "what did you do to her?"

He glares at me, incensed. "She was freed."

A trace of relief shivers through my breath, only to be rapidly overtaken by my hellish reality. "You need to kill me before Vogel comes," I insist. "He's tracking me again. He'll track me *right here*—"

Another violent blow to my ribs silences me as the oak-branch-festooned soldier draws back her staff and barks out something in the Fae tongue.

Black Witch! A torrent of the Forest's fury lashes out alongside her belligerent words and I realize that it was likely the trees that led these Dryads to me.

"Have done with it and destroy me!" I cry at the woods and the Dryads both as Vogel's Shadow tightens around my power. "Vogel's forces are *coming!*"

The angry woman pummels my side again and yells something harsh.

I force my head toward her, not caring when the rough net scrapes at my face. "You think I *asked* for this?" I yank my head back toward the fierce-eyed young man, unable to hold back my devastation. "You think I want to be this *evil power?!*" I rage, spittle flying from my mouth as Shadow power spasms through me. "I *don't!* And I tried to fight them!"

Indecision flickers in the rangy soldier's eyes, but then the gray glow to my vision intensifies as Vogel forces my mouth into a chilling snarl. The Dryad's eyes widen with horror, his livid expression returning. He waves everyone forward and, once again, we move through the Forest.

"Where are you taking me?" I eventually ask him, my voice constricted by the descent of a terrified resignation.

He glares at me, his face tightening with a look of brutal resolve. "To *die.*"

We journey deeper into the woods, and I catch glimpses of constellations shimmering overhead as I struggle to brace myself to meet my end.

Northwest, I grief-strickenly consider. *We're moving northwest.*

A new Dryad has moved into view, talking in low tones with the flower-haired soldier with the branch light, who I've named Flora for her graceful ways and surprisingly gentle expression.

The new Dryad doesn't seem gentle at all. She's streamlined

and muscular, her hue a pale mint, fanning iridescent mushrooms for hair. Green-glowing zigzags mark the sides of the soldier's face like verdant lightning. She wears pale birch bark armor, two branch-staff weapons strapped to her back, and like the others, she has the imprint of a tree on the palm of her right hand. Her bearing is all compact energy, her expression predatory, a silvery panther slinking beside her. When she glances at me, there is no mercy in her eyes, and I name her Lightning.

Who will be the one to kill me? I dully wonder, bracing myself against the inevitability of my fate. *Lightning? Or maybe Pine*, which is the name I've given to the rangy man with pine-bough hair who seems to be in charge. Or maybe it will be the large, silent, branch-antlered Dryad before me with the bear companion, carrying the front of the net. I've named this soldier Sithoy for the huge trees of the West's Sithoy Forest. And then there's the brooding Dryad who carries my net's other end.

This Dryad is like a chill at my back.

I've managed a single glimpse of him, but that one look is branded into my mind. He's a slender, wiry young man with a chiseled, triangular face, his lime-green visage shadowed by the hood of his cloak of dark leaves.

But his eyes.

They're anchored with dark circles and narrowed with easy malice. And the shadows under his eyes don't make him look wan and sickly.

No.

They make him look like he swallowed the night whole, and he practically radiates the potential for violence. Wooden blades are strapped all over his black-clad body, and I've named him Darkness. Perhaps he'll be the one to kill me, I consider. Or maybe it will be the acorn-decorated, furious young woman with the staff who can't seem to stop striking me. I've named her Vicious.

I'm sure Flora won't be the one to kill me. Not her. She glances at me, her gaze riddled with conflict. And then, sorrow ripples over her expression. It undoes me, breaking my tightly held grief apart as I murmur the names of the loved ones I'll never see again—

Rafe. Trystan. Lukas. Yvan. Tierney. Diana. Aislinn. Or'myr…

My captors slow to a stop.

Two huge Black Oak trees stand before us, the branches of their crowns entwined.

Pine stalks forward. He grabs one of the branches sheathed at his waist, murmurs a windswept line of their language, and swipes the branch between the two trees in a circular motion. Wind begins to swirl, leaves and dead brush caught up in the gust's circular flow, faster and faster, until there's a blurred but perfectly formed oval between the trees.

The scene in the center of the oval wavers, then mists over, and I'm swamped by a caustic sense of Vogel's surprise. *A portal*, I realize. A sense of staggering finality drops down through my soul. Because I know that wherever it leads is where I'll meet my end.

Pine glares at me over his shoulder, then motions everyone forward as the Forest's ire pulses like an executioner's drumbeat. *Black Witch. Black Witch. Black Witch.*

I steel myself as I'm carried through the swirling wind and the portal closes around me.

CHAPTER TWO

III

Elloren Vogel

Northern Forest

The Dryad soldiers carry me through the portal into a predawn forest, the surrounding leaves shifting from steely black to a paler gray in my Shadow vision. Despite their altered color, the enormous trees have the distinctive crenelated bark I'd recognize anywhere.

Ironwood.

They loom over me, their hulking forms struck by furious recognition—*Black Witch!*

Loathing bears down with suffocating weight as their elemental force rushes in around my corrupted affinity lines.

Vogel's venom unfolds. My lines tense of their own accord and I shudder, my Shadowfire aura blasting out at the Forest so violently, its catapulted force has me gasping. The energy of the mammoth trees gives a collective recoil, a frisson of horror rippling through them that's so potent the air seems to waver from it.

The Fae steal an alarmed glance at the Forest canopy before their gazes swing to me, clearly reading the Forest's punch of emotion. Flora locks eyes with Pine, her lips trembling as she says something impassioned to him in their leafy tongue. Pine knifes a murderous glare at me, his green face twisting with a look of outrage. "III is going to destroy you, demon witch," he seethes, "before you can make one move toward our Forest."

Before I can wonder who this Three is who is about to end me, the woods open up and I'm carried into a starlit clearing. A frisson of awe races down my spine.

An Ironwood tree stands in the middle of the clearing, towering above all the others.

It's taller than the Valgard Cathedral and shrouded in gauzy green mist, its mammoth branches rising to hold up the predawn sky. I can feel the tree's focus turning with planetary force as it fixes its attention on me.

A great, magical tide breaks from the tree and crashes forward, my eyes blown wide-open as its cataclysmal power sweeps into me, rushing around my lines with what feels like an incoming tidal wave of all the elemental magic in the world.

Vogel rears up with heightened ferocity.

His gray magic blasts around my lines with unbearable force, clawing in. I throw my head back and cry out, afraid I'll be torn clear apart, as my lines stretch toward the tree's incredible pull and Vogel pulls in turn. The realization hits me—

Three is III of myth. Descendant of the Sacred Source Tree from all the religions I read about in Jules Kristian's books. The Mages' Source Tree. *Everyone's* Source Tree. The heartbeat of the Forest, holding the power of all the elements combined.

Set against me.

III's power is like a storm with no end as it slams into me with wave after wave of typhoon-force magic. Vogel's power flattens against it like a sapling bent to the wind, granting me some slim agency over my besieged body as Vogel bucks against the elemental onslaught.

The Dryads drop my netted form and I cough out a pained huff, trembling against the fight for my lines. Pine and Vicious hoist me free of the net and force me to my feet, my broken ankle screaming. Grabbing one of the branches sheathed at his side, Pine murmurs what must be a spell, and my leg-bindings turn to ash. They begin to drag me toward the Great Tree, my ankle buckling as both Vogel's and III's power battles through me with bone-shuddering lashes of force.

Strengthening his control over my will, Vogel scrabbles my feet painfully against roots and uneven ground in a desperate effort to halt my advance. *"Heathen tree!"* he forces from my mouth as his control slips.

The beat of wings sounds on the air behind me, a rush of golden Wyvernfire aura blasting down from the heavens above.

Vogel whips my head around, explosive shock igniting in us both as Yvan swoops into the clearing, dark wings outstretched, an avenging blaze in his eyes.

My heart bursts wide-open as surprise shudders through the Dryads' combined elemental power and Vogel's manic hatred detonates with the force of a thousand runic explosives.

Winged demon!

My emotions seared through by the full rush of Yvan's fire power, I take him in with one astonished sweep of my gaze, seeing golden streaks of fire where the tears in his wings once were. *He's healing himself,* I realize, stunned to the core. So much stronger than he was in Verpacia.

Icaral of Prophecy strong.

"Elloren!" He steps forward, his fire aura surging through me.

"Get back, Wyvernkin," Pine commands. Both he and Vicious tighten their hold on my arms as the Great Tree grapples with Vogel's clenching grip on my lines.

Yvan holds up a gold-glowing palm, his eyes like burning stars. "Let her go or I will *take* her from you," he warns, the threat of violence clear in both his tone and coiled posture.

Vogel forces a hiss from my mouth, a harsh sting overtaking

my fingernails. Before I can register what's happening, my hands jerk out with brutal force and slice through my bindings with new razor-sharp claws. Then Vogel whips my body around and lashes my arms out at the Dryads, catching Pine in the shoulder and Vicious in the arm.

Their faces are masks of shock as they leap back, my demonic claws trailing Shadow.

My gaze pivots to Yvan as the Great Tree battles against Vogel's hold and Vicious readies her staff. Pine draws a branch that ignites with a green glow, the tang of elemental power crackling through the air. Yvan leaps toward me, alarm burning in his eyes as he knocks the weapons from the Dryads' hands.

Incredibly, Vogel's hold on my will drops away in that second, my control over my body abruptly restored even as Vogel battles III's power back. The reason for it swoops down in a terrible rush.

It's a trap.

Vogel *wants* me to move toward Yvan.

He *wants* me to get a fraction away from the Great Tree.

Because the second I do, he'll regain enough power over me to clamp fully down on my will and magic, then grab a Dryad weapon and decimate them all.

I meet Yvan's gaze for a heartbeat, the familiar heat flashing through the air between us, the split second stretching out as I remember it all—that time in the university kitchens when I first saw him smile at little Fern. How I started to love him in that moment, both of us fighting the tide of that love for months to no avail. How he challenged me over the next year, fiercely prodding me to change my mind about practically everything. How we worked together to free Naga and struggled to free Ariel. And then…that night in the North Tower—how he said no to our coupling, even though we were so hungry for each other, even though his body betrayed his powerful want. He put me first. He's always putting me first.

And that first Wyvern kiss—the feel of his fire bond spiraling through me as we embraced. He jumped in with his whole heart. He's always jumping in with his whole heart and fire.

I realize in that second, in a powerful sweep, that in both his love and Lukas's, I've found one inextinguishable thing that's true—

The force of good might be no match for the terrible might of Vogel's Shadow. All we have is a weak green Wand that flees and Watchers who just watch. But this love in our hearts—it's stronger than all the Shadow in the world.

And I want love to prevail.

The whole world arcs down as the split second passes, the entire story of me distilled to this one, last, free-will chance as tears sheen my Shadow-grayed eyes and a deeper understanding of Lukas's loving, courageous sacrifice enfolds me.

"I love you," I tell Yvan as my heart shatters around the giving up of him.

Around the giving up of *everything*.

And then, as Yvan lunges toward me, fervently calling my name, I turn toward the Great Tree and hurl myself at it.

CHAPTER
THREE

THE INFINITE DARK

Elloren

Northern Forest

I crash against the wall of trunk, and then, inexplicably, straight through its hard bark as if it's as insubstantial as vapor, my heart shattering over the loss of Yvan and Lukas and all my loved ones...over the loss of my life. And over the destruction of Voloi and the devastation of its people. Consumed by the rush of sorrow, I sail into the Great Tree's darkness, Vogel's scream tearing from my throat, his rage ratcheting up to a nightmarish level.

And then I'm falling into the Tree's darkness in a body I can't control, limbs splayed out, lines consumed by Shadow. I can sense the Great Tree's awareness of the corruption inside me as I'm enveloped in III's fury and I realize that this is truly the end.

You've won, I hurl out to the Great Tree as its fury stabs into me. *You're killing the Black Witch! It's too late for me now, but know that I never wanted to be this Shadow thing! So, go ahead! Kill me! Or Vogel will use me to destroy* everyone *and* everything!

Vogel lets loose a great, snarling cry, his claws of power raking at my lines with desperate, covetous force. A knifing pain stings through my magic. And then, a wrenching sensation of release as his magic is swept away in a spiraling vortex.

I struggle to catch my breath as confusion spikes through me and I regain control of my body, my limbs flailing then stilling in the infinite dark. And I wonder—*Is this what it is to die?*—before I'm swallowed up by grief, and the whole world goes silent.

I'm suspended in a great nothing, not knowing up from down. Completely alone as the tree's thick cloud of fury thins…

…then slowly withdraws.

The sting along my fastlines dissipates then disperses into the great darkness along with the last tendrils of Vogel's Shadow magic. Vogel's stolen Wyvernfire bond snaps away from my lines, the sensation of claws on my fingertips fading. My limbs splay out, freed from every last binding.

Suspended in the infinite dark.

And then…

…the sudden, burgeoning sense of branches lifting me, winding under and around my form like a great cocoon, but not confining.

Cradling. Waiting.

Listening.

My heart breaks open within me.

I wanted to help them, I whisper to III, too weak to move, my cheek pressed to what feels like a broad branch as I begin to sob. *I wanted to use the power to help my loved ones and fight the cruelty. But… I couldn't control the power…*

I'm dancing on the edge of consciousness as I cling to III and pour my heart out. I cry and rage and mourn as I tell the Great Tree the entire story of my life, my struggle, my grief.

My failure.

After a long time, I grow silent, completely spent. III's limbs wrap around me, and I begin a slow slide into unconsciousness.

And then, like the darkness surrounding me, I, too, fade to black.

CHAPTER FOUR

FOREST GUARDIAN

Elloren

Northern Forest

I awaken to a different darkness.

Filled with the sense of being cradled at the very center of the world, the very center of magic, as my heart breaks open and images of everyone I love and care about scroll through my mind. My brothers. My beloved friends and newfound family. Olilly and Nym'ellia and all of the people at risk in both Realms.

Lukas and Yvan.

The aching desire to have one more chance to be with them all and fight with them tightens my emotions. Along with the anguished yearning to work for a different future for Erthia. A future without division and oppression.

Free of the demon tide.

As if prompted by my surge of love and yearning, life is suddenly pouring back into my body. An invigorating warmth flows into my veins that has the feel of warm sap in a thawing trunk.

It prompts a deep, wavering intake of air as what feel like tendrils of branches wind around my legs, my arms.

Every last part of me.

Knitting my Shadow-ravaged self and broken ankle back together.

I gasp as the breath of the Great Tree blows through me and begins to flow magic into my affinity lines, element by element, my battered lines mending as I become startlingly aware of what these lines have been all along.

Not veins in the island of my body.

They're *roots*.

I'm not an island at all. I'm connected to something much bigger than myself.

My breath gathers strength in my lungs, my mouth strange to me as I test my jaw, grind teeth that feel unfamiliar, run my tongue over sharp molar edges that have never been sharp before. My ears stretch upward as if pulled by threads and the pain of my broken ankle is soothed by the gentle brush of leaves.

Dryad.

Dryad Guardian.

III's voice is as gentle as spring rain and as powerful as a fierce storm. And I can sense, all at once, the great span of III, how far its roots stretch out—throughout the whole Northern Realm and beyond. Throughout the whole world.

And into me.

A series of hazy visions of trees and forests begins to form in my mind, a mind once again completely my own as my affinity roots gather strength within me—

Fire, Earth, Air, Wind.

And Green Light.

The visions gain clarity, images that follow the Western Realm's network of forests down through leagues of ocean plant life and onto the shore of a realm that lies across a great sea. The vision swoops up from the ground into the sky, the landmass now viewed from high above, as if seen through the minds of birds, this unknown continent seeming bigger than both the Eastern and Western Realms put together.

Tree-memories light.

Cities and towns teeming with Kelts and surrounded by verdant forest and abundant life. The visions shift, and a knotty Sea Pine beside a seashore unfurls in my mind, the unfamiliar tree's needles gleaming gold instead of Western Realm green. The golden tree looks over a deserted seashore, its sand a burnished brass in the prestorm light, a foamy, steel tide rushing in.

A chill wind blows as a gray, spiraling wand washes up onto the shore and a young man strides into view. The lanky, brown-haired Kelt spots the wand, lowers himself, and grasps it, lifting it from the pulsing surf. A helix of dark smoke curls from its tip.

Revulsion rips through me as a sense of foreboding builds, the young man's eyes riveted to the Wand. I want to leap from the golden tree, run to him, and wrest the Wand from his hand. To warn him that he's not picking up some harmless branch.

He's picking up an invading force.

Lightning flashes across the ocean and the scene blinks out of sight to be replaced by scene after horrifying scene. The Wand in the hand of a Keltish king with glowing gray eyes astride a multi-eyed horse. An army of gray-eyed Keltish Shadow soldiers massing around the king as they advance on a city.

Death everywhere.

Screaming children and families. Slaughtered animals. Visions of the fall of the forests and the mutilation of the wilds as the Shadow's demon tide rolls in like a toxic fog and collapses the living world. Destroys the farms. Poisons the water. Corrupts the air.

I'm accosted by images of famine as food runs out and every element turns to Shadow. Great floods of Void water. Great storms of Void wind, dark lightning pulsing through it. Void fire consuming everything in its path and tunneling down to cause great rifts in Erthia, only a few Kelts managing to escape in ships, bound for the Western Realm.

Finally, as the last of the ships depart, the great Nothing descends.

A charred landscape cools to gray. Blackened trees hold up smoking branches, as if in supplication, toward an ashen sky.

Horror bears down on my mind.

Because I know, deep within me, that this is not just a vision of what happened in some distant realm beyond the sea—it's a foreshadowing of what is coming for the Western and Eastern Realms.

The vision fades, and I'm in the quiet dark once again, caught up in overwhelming despair over what has happened…and what could so easily happen again. Only this time, there are no more Realms to flee to.

But then…an invitation touches down.

Unspoken, but I can feel it hanging in the air around me, coursing gently through the branches that cradle my body. A spiraling green form shimmers into view in the back of my mind where the vision of horror once was.

The Wand of Myth.

The Wand present in all the stories of all the Realms' religions, suspended and shining as if lit from within. A darker, more vibrant green springs to life through its spiraling handle, and I watch as the deeply verdant hue circles up to the Wand's tip.

Branches burst forth from the spirals, leaves breaking out and multicolored flowers blooming on them as a living, breathing tree takes over my field of vision and I realize that the Wand of Myth was merely dormant all this time.

Verdyllion.

The Forest Wand.

Its true name sings in my mind, in my rootlines.

The vision telescopes backward, the Wand morphing into the shape of III surrounded by countless people from every group on Erthia, each of them holding up a palm imprinted with III's own image. And then I'm swooping up and up until I'm above

III's huge canopy, over the Ironwood forest, as my gaze sweeps out and I'm engulfed by a stinging rush of horror.

A wall of Shadow encircles the Forest, leagues of dead trees behind the Shadow tide's advancing corruption, the Void trees' charred branches twining poisonous smoke into a gray sky. I'm filled with the overpowering sense that the collective power of the people encircling III is the only thing that can keep this great Shadow at bay.

Crystalline clarity descends, bright and shining, as the invitation hovering in the air gains potency. I can feel its world-shifting power inside my very soul.

It's an invitation to join with the power of life. With the fragile and whole and complex magic that runs through III and the Forest and every living thing. And it's a call to welcome others into the fold. To link the Forest to more than just the Dryads.

To link the Forest to us all.

Birds made of starlight shudder to life, perching in the Wand-tree's hollows. They turn, as one, toward me. Watching. Waiting. As Ironflowers open their blossoms all over III and my heart fills with an inexplicable joy.

And hope.

Slender as a thread. But it's there, even as the threat of the Shadow presses in and the certainty gains ground that it holds no guarantee but one—

The story is not yet over.

The silent invitation shimmers in the air, like a hand held palm up, outstretched to me in gentle offering.

A lifeline.

A chance.

Wordlessly, I accept.

CHAPTER
FIVE

REBORN

Elloren

Northern Forest

I hang in the darkness at the center of the Great Tree as a tingling energy suffuses my wand hand. A rush of consolidated power flies through my rootlines, filling them with a breathtaking wholeness, my five elemental affinities not only balanced now but rooted to III. I draw in a long breath, my lungs filling with sweet air and sheer power.

The Power of III.

Invigorated, I close my eyes as a dazzling light flashes through my eyelids. I'm abruptly aware of a hard, rough surface behind my back, of ground beneath my hands and body, thrumming with the energy of life. I open my eyes and blink into the golden light of dawn, my vision no longer grayed but resplendently clear. Clearer and sharper than it's ever been before.

"Elloren."

Yvan's rough, deep voice prompts the rise of passionate emotion through my breast as I meet his stare, a flash of heat blazing between us. I push myself into a sitting position as he rises to his feet across the clearing, muscles flexing, wings fanning. I realize, in the space of a breath, that his wings are healed, the fiery scars gone.

The Dryads are gaping at me, wide-eyed and motionless, from where they stand in an arc at the clearing's edge, the dawn-lit Forest surrounding us washed in glorious, vivid color.

My heartbeat quickens as I'm flooded with a heart-wrenching ecstasy. The green of the rustling, sun-dappled leaves is so intense. Scarlet birds dart through branches. The jade grass of the clearing flecked with sky blue and cloud-white flowers.

The life-pulse of the Great Tree sounds through me.

I reach behind me to touch my palms against III, pulling in a fulsome, stunned breath as the rooted lines within me thicken, my magic strengthening and branching down and out, the shimmering sap of Forest magic running warm through it. A residual tingle along the edge of my ears has me reaching up to find them curved higher with subtle points.

Thrown, I glance around, blinking into the nourishing sunlight, then meet Yvan's eyes with ardent intensity. Eyes I thought I'd never see again.

My heart expands with emotion. I can sense the shock of the Forest, the rustle of its leaves stilling as the Dryads continue to stare at me, moon-eyed and uncomprehending. A branch falls from III's canopy and lands on my lap.

Surprised, I clamp my wand hand around the wood and read the reassuring, controlled power of the Great Tree coursing through it.

A living wand.

I hug the branch to my chest as bittersweet euphoria and heartache swell within me and III's power pulses toward the Forest in all directions. A great pause engulfs the Ironwood trees and the Forest beyond, as if all of Erthia has momentarily halted on its axis.

And then…an answering rush of power. Flowing from the entire Forest toward me.

I gasp as I'm engulfed by it, the Forest's aura no longer suffused with hatred...

...but with kindred, bolstering power, flowing into my rootlines. I close my eyes and arch back against III as I open myself to the Forest's magic, reflexively binding my lines to it.

"No! This can't be!"

My eyes flick open to find Vicious pointing her oak staff at me, the shoulder I slashed through miraculously healed, only a tear in her leafy garb remaining. Her fern-hued face is twisted with urgency as the wolverine by her side emits a low growl. Yvan darts toward me in a blur, his fire aura rearing as he sets himself between me and the Dryads.

"She's enthralled the Forest!" Vicious snarls to the other Dryad soldiers. "We need to slay her! Before she can wield the branch!"

Yvan's fire silently coils, readying itself to strike. I stare at Vicious in amazement, able to perfectly comprehend the language of the Dryads.

"No," Pine counters, his intense gaze fixed on me. "III has accepted her."

Overwhelmed, I rise, bracing myself against III, my transformed magic pulsing through me. I press my feet into the loamy ground, quickly gaining my footing, and find my limbs sturdier than ever before.

Rooted.

"Elloren, your fastlines..." Yvan says, clearly astonished. I meet his intent gaze and my fire aura leaps between us. Whole fire. Uncorrupted fire. Luminous green with a trace of crimson sparking through it. *Raz'zor's fire. Our horde-bond restored.*

I glance down at my hands and draw in a stunned breath. My fastlines are gone. And my skin's formerly faint green hue is now a deeper, shimmering forest green.

I'm free.

Grief cuts through my airy elation as I take in my wrists, the Sealing lines stripped from my skin, as well. Yes, I'm desperately glad to be free of my Shadow fasting to Vogel, but the loss of my Sealing bond to Lukas sends a shearing pain through my chest, my heart constricting with a lancing grief. More tears well in my eyes as I imagine Lukas's look of vast triumph if he could see me rising here, my rooted affinity lines untethered and whole. My whole self transformed because of his sacrifices, again and again. Because of his sacrifice for the entire East.

"I'm free," I force out to Yvan in a ragged voice, then stop and gasp.

Their language. Tripping off my lips. Dry and leafy.

Yvan's ruddy face and the Dryads' green forms blur. It's like coming home, being rooted to III. Rooted to the Forest. Rooted to the Dryad I always was.

The grief tightening my heart gains potency as the impossible wish rises for Lukas to be here with me, rooted to III, as well. Rooted to the Dryad he always was.

Vicious jabs a finger toward Yvan. "You're under some type of thrall, just like the Forest!" she snarls in the Common Tongue, and I'm surprised by her use of my language. She sweeps her glare over the other Dryads. "She is the *Black Witch* of the trees' foretelling! Her people...they're *destroying* ours!" She knifes her gaze at Pine. "Sylvan, we need to slay her *now!*"

"I'm on your side," I insist as the Great Tree's acceptance flows out in an embracing wave. Vicious looks to III in astonishment, as if she, too, sensed it.

Sylvan points at the Great Tree's black trunk, his gaze fixing on Vicious. "III has rooted her." He pivots to me, eyes blazing. "Show her your palm."

Confused, I slide the branch in my wand hand through my tunic's belt and splay out my palm, my breath catching as I take in the image now fused to my forest green skin.

It's an image of III. Identical to the image marked on all their palms.

Stunned, I look back at Sylvan.

"We will not kill you, Black Witch," he says, his voice deepening with finality. "Like us, you are part of the Forest now. III has named you Guardian.

THE EXPANDING CIRCLE

Elloren

Northern Forest

I glance down at the image of III on my palm, my skin's verdant shimmer gleaming in the bright dawn sunlight. Yvan draws nearer, his molten aura sweeping around us.

"I feel like I'm meeting you for the first time," he says.

Tears mist my eyes as III's strengthening power flows into me. "I feel like I'm meeting myself for the first time." I pause, choked up to be *here*, alive, with him. Alive with the Forest. "I thought..." I manage as the tears slide down my cheeks. "I thought it was over for me."

"No, not over," Yvan says roughly as he pulls me into a close embrace and I embrace him in turn, breaking into sobs against the hot skin of his shoulder.

"Lukas is dead," I rasp out, clutching Yvan as his wings arc inward to enfold us both.

"I know," he says against my hair in a shattered voice. "I'm sorry, Elloren."

And I can feel it in his fire's discordant flare, that he was able to sense Lukas's full sacrifice that moment on the river. That he knows that Lukas gave his life not just for me, but for the entire Realm. And for Yvan too.

I draw back, clutching his muscular arms. He's so incredibly *alive* beneath my palms, his fire shivering around me with ardent force. "How did you find me?"

He pulls in a breath and lets it out, streaming a pulse of his fire aura toward me, the edge streaked with vermilion flame.

"Raz'zor," I murmur in a flash of understanding.

"He and Or'myr were freed when we blasted back Vogel's magic," Yvan tells me. "Raz'zor horded himself to me, giving me access to his tracking bond to you. He stayed behind to fight the Mages and attempt to gather Naga's horde to your side."

My lips part in astonishment. "So...you and Raz'zor and I... we're all a horde now?"

He nods as his fire whips passionately around me.

But Sparrow...he gave no mention of Sparrow. I wince, remembering how Vogel ordered her brought back West. Is she being brought back to Gardneria? Or was she destroyed in the explosion? A host of other anguished worries rise. "My brothers and family..."

"I saw Trystan before I left for you," Yvan assures me. "The battle had turned—Naga's horde and the Vu Trin were taking out Vogel's remaining forces. It's likely the Lupines survived, as well."

I cling to the hope he's offering. Yvan has never been one to turn away from painful realities. He reaches up to caress my shoulder, his fire aura blazing through mine, but it's no longer anchored in my lines. The bittersweet pang cuts deep.

"Our bond..." I say. "It's gone." I search his eyes, freed not just from all fasting and Sealing bonds, but from him, as well.

"I know," he says, a flaring pain in his fire aura that my own flame rushes out to echo. A more liquid heat enters his gaze. "What I can sense of your fire...it's different now. Like *green sunlight.*" He reaches up to gently brush his fingertip along the edge of my ear. "And your ears..." His lips lift in a pained, affectionate smile. "They're pointed. Like mine."

I reach up to touch a point, marveling. "I feel...*reborn.*" I look to Sylvan, the fierce-eyed Dryad, to find him and the other Tree Fae watching Yvan and me with expressions of pure incredulity and, for a moment, I see Yvan and myself through their eyes.

The dread Black Witch and the revered Icaral of Prophecy, improbably both alive.

Embracing as staunch allies.

"I... I don't understand what's happened to me," I say to Sylvan, the Dryadin language rolling off my tongue. It feels more natural on my lips than the Common Tongue ever did, an effortless breeze, the words the truer names for things. "Why am I so altered?" I ask. "And why can I suddenly speak your language?"

"Do you not know your own history, Mageling?" a resonant male voice sounds out, its odd vibration seeming to tug my lines straight down toward Erthia's core.

I turn to find the pale, lime-hued Dryad I've named Darkness staring at me, his hood-shadowed dark eyes locked on to mine, all the colors of the world seeming to dim around him. I notice that he is the only one here who has black eyes instead of green, and that he lacks the others' tree-imprinted armor.

I brush away my reflexive wariness of this Fae, desperate for answers. "I know Gardnerians have Dryad blood." I reach up to touch my ear. "But...why am I so transformed?"

A slight smile forms on his lips, but it does nothing to dampen his aura of danger. On the contrary, it heightens it. Along with the way his black-clad form remains shadowed, even in dawn's bright light.

"You were dormant," he says, a hard edge to his words. "Like all Gardnerian Mages. Kept unrooted from the Forest."

His biting words trigger a disturbance through the Dryads' collective elemental power and I can tell from Yvan's shuddering flame that he senses it too.

Vicious's green glare turns incendiary. "You're twisting things, Hazel!"

I tense my brow at Darkness—Hazel—in confusion. "What do you mean when you say 'kept unrooted'?"

He narrows his midnight gaze and pins me in what feels like a thrall, everything around us fading and darkening, the sunlit world dimming. "Hundreds of years ago," he seethes, "the Dryads shunned your people. They set their elemental power against the Mages to keep you dormant and cut off from the source of your lentulym."

Lentulym. I instinctively understand this Dryad word—our affinity roots. The elemental lines inside me that I finally sense, now that I'm connected to the trees. And to III.

"Why would the Dryads cut us off from the Forest?" I ask, thrown as Yvan's fingers thread reassuringly through mine.

"For the same reason the Kelts despised you," Hazel rejoins. A jaded scowl twists his mouth. "Your blood isn't 'pure.'"

"That's *not* the reason!" Vicious growls.

Hazel bares sharp teeth at her, a bloodthirsty look entering his eyes that sends a chill racing down my back. "It *is* the reason," he snarls. "The Kelts hated the Fae and the Fae hated the Kelts. So, when a few Kelts and Dryad Fae paired to create the Mages, those Mages were cast out by *everyone*. Like the Death Fae were cast out." His dark eyes remain fixed on Vicious, glinting with outrage. "Isn't that true, Oaklyyn?"

Vicious's name falls into place in my mind, her acorn-festooned hair and River Oak staff signifying a kinship with oak trees.

Oaklyyn's look of sweltering ire turns scathing. "Our people were almost *wiped out* by the Kelts. Or has that escaped your halfling memory?"

Hazel lurches toward her, his movement so fast it's a blur, his eyes wild as he snaps suddenly elongated teeth at Oaklyyn and Sylvan thrusts his powerful frame between the two of them. Sylvan glares at Oaklyyn. "You overstep," he says, voice shot through with warning.

I'm stunned by the exchange and the obvious fracture in their group.

Division. Yet again.

Hazel swings his penetrating black eyes back toward me, ferocity in them. "My mother was a primordial Fae. And primordials live a *very long* time. She witnessed the casting out of the Mages. She was at the forest's edge when the Mages massed there and begged the Dryads—*begged them*—for protection when the Kelts were slaughtering them and enslaving them."

I look to half-Kelt Yvan and we share a brief look of surprise.

Hazel's damning gaze sweeps back to Oaklyyn, and I sense this is a long-standing source of resentment between them. "But instead of helping the Mages, the Dryads used their combined magic to leech away the Mages' connection to the Forest." He levels his stare back at me, his words loaded with import when they come. "The Dryadin cut your people off from the trees just when you needed them the most."

"What would you have had us do?" Oaklyyn rages, her green face tight with fury. "We were being *decimated* by the Kelts!" She sweeps her arm toward me in a wide, angry arc. "If we had accepted all of the Kelts' bastard offspring, our magic would have been *destroyed* within a few generations. Our branch magic watered down to the point where we'd need to layer dead wood in Mage *wands*—"

"And where has the quest for magical purity gotten you?" Hazel snaps, the air vibrating with a sudden darkness that further dims the light. "*Where?* Where has it gotten *anyone?*"

"You'd have us die!" Oaklyyn shoots back.

The fog of darkness intensifies, a pained look slashing through Hazel's eyes. "No, Oaklyyn. I'd have you *live!*"

"Oh." Oaklyyn coughs out a scornful laugh. "The primordial *Death Fae* is going to help the Dryads to live?"

I look to Hazel in surprise. "You're a Death Fae?" I remember Trystan telling me of his friendship with some of these mysterious Fae—Fae who had the highest of bounties placed on their heads during the first Realm War.

Hazel turns slowly toward me, another mirthless smile forming on his lips. "I've forbidden ancestry like you, Mageling." His words seem to drip acid. He looks to Yvan. "And you as well, Icaral. My mother was a Death Fae. My father, Dryadin." He grows quiet, loses his cold grin, and looks at the ground. Pulling in a deep breath, he pushes his shoulders back, as if drawing on the earth at his feet. Snakes suddenly slither out of the ground and coil around his legs, then up around his body, his neck and shoulders.

Hazel's voice is becalmed when it comes, almost mournful. "Death is the seed that enables the Forest to live." He raises his head and looks at Oaklyyn, his voice low and final when it comes. "The Circle is expanding. The Forest has deemed it so. Whether you want it to or not."

"But the witch Mage has no kindred," Flora puts in, splaying her dark green hand out toward me, a conflicted look on her delicate visage. A fog-hued heron hugs her side. "How can she be Guardian," she presses, "with no kindred called to her?"

"Ill has *warded* her," Sylvan counters. "Which means a kindred *will* manifest within moments." His tone is rock-solid sure, but when he looks to me, I see conflict in his pine eyes.

"What of the Prophecy, Sylvan?" the lightning-bolt-marked soldier cuts in as she slices a hand toward Yvan and me, her silver-furred panther slinking around her legs. "The trees have foretold of the Black Witch's war with the Great Icaral." She gives Yvan a hard look. "She is prophesied to bring you down."

"Do they look ready to cut each other down, Lyptus?" Sylvan bites out.

Yvan's wings stiffen. "I don't believe in your prophecy," he says, his flame surging around me with rebellious heat. "I love Elloren."

His fiery declaration sears through my battered heart, the

yearning running through his fire so deep it prompts a pained flare of my emotion and affinity power.

Oaklyyn is gaping at Yvan, like he's uttered the most heinous of blasphemies. Her wolverine bristles and bares its teeth. "This is impossible!" she insists, pointing her staff at me. "She's ensorcelled both the Icaral and III in some way!" She swings her staff toward Sylvan, leveling it like an accusatory finger. "It will be the death of our Forest if we *let her live*!"

"Dryad," Yvan says as he raises a gold-glowing palm. I pull in a shivering breath in response to the potent gathering of his power. "We are not your enemies," he emphatically states, warning shot through his level tone. "Don't force me to move against you."

Oaklyyn steps toward Yvan, smiling viciously at him as two more wolverines emerge from the forest edging the clearing, dark fur bristling, and her staff takes on a pulsing green glow. "Take care, winged," she warns in turn. "We don't worship you as some savior."

"Yet you've cast Elloren as the Prophecy's demon?" Yvan sharply rejoins, his hot hand rigid around mine.

"Oaklyyn," Sylvan puts down harshly, "III has *marked* her."

"A kindred *must* come," Lyptus insists, fixing me with a predatory look.

I reach for my wand branch, both my power and Yvan's flaring defensively just as a powerful *caw* splits the sky. We all look up, the breath wrenched from my throat as ravens bigger than horses burst through the canopy of leaves. I raise a hand to shield myself, branches crackling and raining down as the enormous flock lands around us with great, earth-jostling *thumps*.

And on the back of one of these impossibly huge ravens sits Tierney Calix, her blue-tressed head peeking over the shoulder of a black-clad, pale Fae male with midnight-dark eyes, lips, and hair. Gleaming obsidian horns rise from his head, and a small raven is perched on his shoulder.

"Tierney…" I manage. The giant ravens all set their gleaming, coal-dark eyes on me.

"Elloren…you're Fae," Tierney marvels as images from the Gardnerian holy book flood my mind—stories of the giant raven the prophetess Galliana rode to war against demons.

"The Errilor have returned," Sylvan says, his voice low with awe.

A resonant *caw* sounds, and I turn as the largest of the ravens struts toward me. The dark bird leans its massive head down as if in offering. The other ravens still, a momentous tension gathering on the air.

"Touch the Errilor'kin, Guardian," Flora murmurs, and I'm amazed by the acceptance in her tone. Feeling as if I've been thrust into mythical territory, I step forward, reach out and touch the raven's silken head.

The moment I make contact, I sense the flock's collective exhale through my rootlines, a connection clicking into place, like a lock fastening.

My Errilor flock.

III's sense of triumph emanates from behind me, further rooting my affinity power to the ground. The raven lifts his head, bright sunlight glinting off his black beak and gleaming eyes.

Errilith.

His name sounds in my mind as wonder blooms in my breast. "Where did these ravens come from?" I ask.

Tierney's companion fixes his inky stare on me. "There is a Reckoning at hand," he says, his voice eerily deep, a dark mist rising throughout the clearing. "So the Errilor have returned. Their enemy, the Shadow Death, is coming for the natural world. Can you feel it?"

Anxious recognition shivers through my lines. "III showed me a vision of a great Shadow," I tell him. "It was surrounding the last of the Forest." I look at Yvan. "Vogel's built an army in the Spine. Much bigger than the one he hid in the Vo Mountains. And his Shadow power keeps *growing*." I falter, struggling to describe III's foresight.

Yvan's fire catches me in a closer embrace as he takes hold of my hand once more. "What did you see, Elloren?"

"People from every group on Erthia...standing with the Forest. They all had this on their palm." I open my palm, revealing the imprint of III. "III wants us all to join with the Forest—"

"Only Dryads are Guardians!" Oaklyyn cries out, my gaze sliding from Yvan's to find her glaring at me. I'm caught up short by the pain shining in her eyes, her voice breaking when it comes. "You've cared for the Forest for one *minute*," she grits out, motioning sharply toward the other Dryads. "We've cared for it for *thousands of years*. And we'll still care for it well after you've all killed each other off and finished trying to destroy us, as well!" Her lips twist into a trembling sneer. "It will be just like all the times before. We'll be left to nurture the remnants of life you leave behind after your *senseless destruction*."

"There won't be any remnants left this time," Tierney cuts in. "I've seen the Shadow Void in the water. I've *felt* it." She pauses, as if struggling to convey something too hellish for words. "What this Tree told Elloren—it's true. There's a bigger fight underneath the obvious one. And we need to join together to face it. *All* of us. Allies and enemies alike."

The outrage in Oaklyyn's eyes intensifies. "You don't know what it means to join with our Forest!"

"Then *teach* us," I implore.

"It can't be taught!" Oaklyyn lashes back.

I take hold of the branch sheathed behind my belt and hold it up, magic flowing through my feet toward it in a low rumble. "I have Black Witch power. And I'm no longer bound by *anything* save the connection I've made to the Forest and my horde-bond. Show me how to use my Dryad power so I can fight with you to save Erthia." I look to them all. "I *need* you. We need each other."

I feel Sylvan's gaze on me and meet his formidable stare. "What do you seek, Black Witch?" he asks.

"To learn the Forest's spells and how to wield them." I tighten my grip on the branch as the image of a very different branch bears down on my mind. "And there's a Wand. A green Wand. III showed it to me in the vision. I used to possess it, and it left me. But... III wants me to find it. I think it's the Great Wand from all the religious myths."

Keen interest sparks in his gaze. "What did your Wand look like?"

I describe the Wand and his piercing look intensifies. "Where did you last see it?"

"On a mountaintop balcony overlooking Voloi. When Vogel took hold of my power, it fled and fell. A kestrel caught it and flew away."

"Even wands know to flee from her," Oaklyyn snipes witheringly.

Sylvan pays her hostile comment no heed. "What did III show you?"

I describe the III's vision of branches, leaves, and flowers springing forth from the Wand.

"Could it be the Verdyllion?" Flora asks Sylvan, her lilting voice shot through with astonishment. Surprise ripples through the Dryads' collective power at her voicing of the Wand's true name and I draw in a reflexive breath, the word like a balm to my soul.

The Forest's Heart.

Hazel shoots Oaklyyn a poignant look. "Do you accept her *now*, Oaklyyn?"

Oaklyyn's features twist with vitriol. "*Never*, Sylvan. I accept her *never*."

Her words cut, but there's no time to be thrown by her hostility. "What is the Wand, truly?" I press Sylvan, sensing an opening with him.

"That Wand," he replies, "is a central line accessing all the power of the Forest."

"Well, it sounds like we need to find that Wand," Tierney announces, casting everyone a significant look. "And get ready for Vogel's Shadow. *Together.*"

"There are a few things Vogel's power can't break through," Yvan says to Sylvan, suddenly confiding in him like they're long-time compatriots, his steady energy sparking a pained admiration in me. "Smaragdalfar varg runes, Wyvernfire, and your magic can beat back the Shadow," he says.

"And since Vogel will come after his Black Witch," Tierney adds, challenge in her tone, "we'd best link Elloren to the things that defend against Shadow, and *fast.* Along with everyone else."

Yvan turns to me, eyes suddenly burning. "I know of one way," he says, arcing his wings around us, a line of tension running through his fire. "Elloren," he says, voice low, "our Wyvernfire bond—I think we should restore it."

My own fire rears hot in response to the passion firing in his eyes and his flame. Conflict shudders through me. I shake my head. "Your fire bond...it's not just some defensive ward. I know what it means to you—"

"It means I *love* you," he insists, voice rough with feeling, his grip on my hand firming. "I've *never* stopped loving you. And I'm allied with you. *Forever.*"

Tears sheen my vision, grief rising as fierce love for both Yvan and Lukas blazes through my rootlines, shattering my heart and reforging it at the same time.

I can barely make sense of the turmoil storming through me. But I'm heart-wrenchingly certain of one thing that I know Lukas was certain of too—there's no more time for *anything* but this fight and the fierce, unbreakable love in all our hearts.

I give Yvan a small kindred smile as our fires whip around each other with the full force of our emotions, the two of us having been through hell and back, over and over. And yet, here he still is, this Icaral I'm only just starting to know and understand, his love and friendship as blazingly fixed as a guiding star.

"Ariel told me we should subvert the Prophecy," I confide, voice ragged.

His hand comes up to caress my cheek and I shiver from the warm contact, my breath quavering as I lean into his palm. "I don't just want to subvert it," he says, a rebellious glint flaring in his eyes. "I want to burn it to *ash*."

I nod, my warrior resolve rising hot around his own. I'm certain, too, that Lukas would want this for me. He would want me to rise as a warrior, as strong as possible, with every advantage possible.

In defiance of all the prophecies of all the lands.

"All right," I say as I open my power and my heart to it all. "Let's burn the Prophecy to ash."

A collective sense of the momentous ripples through our magic as Yvan draws me closer, his wings arcing tighter around us. He leans down, eyes molten, and brings his lips to mine.

We ignite like wildfire and I gasp against his kiss as his fire bond bolts through me, the intensity overtaking us both. My body arches against his, our powers fusing and blasting into a conflagration of Dryadfire and Wyvernfire combined, his hard body shivering against mine from the sheer strength of the heated rush.

I tremble against him as we send a spiraling inferno of flame through each other, my Dryad and hordefire heightening his blaze as the defiant heat of our rebellious, unquenchable alliance strengthens the conflagration, the two of us once more linked, bound.

Wyvernbonded.

But in a whole new way.

Icaral and Dryad Witch.

Ready to set the whole damned Prophecy on fire.

EPILOGUE

MIGRATION

THE KESTREL

Voloi, over the Vo River
Xishlon night, twenty-first hour

Verdyllion.

The name of the Forest Wand sounds like a beacon in the indigo kestrel's mind. It veers west over the Vo River, the Wand gripped in its talons—the Wand dropped by the green woman with gray-glowing eyes who was all *wrong*, the Shadow Thing twisting inside her.

But the bonding with this Wand was immediate, enough to override the bird's fear of the Shadow Thing, its migratory draw suffusing the kestrel's senses in a constant, satisfying rush.

Sweet migration. Sweet current of direction.

The kestrel swoops upward, led over the Vo Forest and Vo Mountain Range, flying unharmed through the storm band atop it, the Wyvern-crafted band magicked to allow nature's children through.

The bird soars over the Zonor River and Dyoi Mountain Range, an expansive plain opening up below, Vu Trin soldiers and their military base spread across it. Swooping low over lines of rune-marked tents, the kestrel flies toward a central building hewn from purple wood.

Four portals are positioned in the building's expansive center with frames of blue-sparking runes, their interiors rippling gold. Vu Trin soldiers, some on horseback, are moving toward the four portals, crone sorceresses bracketing the archways, glowing blue styluses raised.

One of the crones cries out in surprise as the kestrel dives toward the central portal and is consumed in a sea of gold.

The kestrel zooms out of the portal's golden shimmer and into another Vu Trin base located in a cavern cut into pale white stone. One of the soldiers yelps, startled, as the kestrel darts through a tunnel and out into the balmy dampness of an overcast dawn, the forest no longer purple but a rich, inviting green. Following the Wand's pull, the bird flies away from the hidden base, setting a long course under the clouds.

After a time, the skies clear and the parallel Spine mountain ranges come into view, their pale ridges bracketed by thick forest. The kestrel wings due west, following the Northern Spine. As the sun dips low in the sky, the bird notices a dark fog massed over its central peaks, tendriling up to the heavens. The kestrel startles, instinctively registering what this is.

The Shadow Thing.

The bird veers north, giving the fog a wide berth as it follows the Wand's pull northwest then due north, leaving the Spines and the fog far behind.

After a few days, the bird wings low through a rosy twilight. Darting through silver-tipped Alfsigr Pine trees, the kestral eventually dives down, following the path of a woodland stream. A painful spark of energy flashes through the kestrel's feet. Its talons splay open and it drops the Wand from its grip.

The Wand hits the stream's water and is drawn into its current as the kestrel arcs up and soars back East.

The Verdyllion draws its power down.

Surrendering to the pull of the current, its spiraling form is carried through the forest. Rocks halt its trajectory, and it lodges between two river–slick stones.

Summoning stored runic power, the Verdyllion lights up bright green, then blue, then silver, the power it drew from the Black Witch's rune markings coursing through it as it sends out a blast of air from its tip, forcing itself free of the rocks. Pulling momentarily against the current, it glides toward the center of the stream.

Its runic power spent, the Wand drifts downstream before reaching a spiraling whirlpool. It begins to rotate, the surrounding forest spinning faster and faster then disappearing as the Forest Wand is sucked down and down.

Into the sublands below.

THE ABYSS

Wynter Eirllyn

Maeloria, capital city of Alfsigroth
One week post-Xishlon

Wynter Eirllyn rasps out a cry as the silver rope around her neck gives a merciless tug. She stumbles forward, almost falling face-first onto the opalescent tiles, her Amaz garb filthy and torn, bloody welts oozing across her tattered wings. Veins of Shadow burrow under her skin.

Filthy Icaral, filthy Icaral rings in her devastated mind along with the horrific image of the Mages and Marfoir killing noble Queen Alkaia, driving insectile legs through her body again and again…

Thirteen Alfsigr Marfoir assassins surround Wynter, marching her through the Alfsigr capital city, the bizarrely stretched-out Elves gliding forward with disturbing uniformity. They clutch sharp, spiraling blades in long-fingered hands, their gray, insectile eyes pinned on the road ahead leading straight to the Alfsigr Monarchall.

Crowds of Alfsigr Elves line the road, their jeers spiking through Wynter, but not quite covering the sound of her boot heels scuffing against stone. Shamefacedly, she takes in the outraged throngs, their faces uncharacteristically animated as they snarl out invectives at the cursed Icaral in their midst.

A sword tip jabs into Wynter's side, and she lets out a sharp cry. Her enraged bird-kindreds caw and screech in a chaotic cloud above her, diving down in an attempt to attack the Marfoir again and again, only to be heartbreakingly burned up in flashes of steely lightning as they collide with the translucent runic shield the Marfoir have cast around their party. But the Shadowfire-shield doesn't stop the stones.

A large rock slams into the side of Wynter's temple and she bleats out another cry of distress, flinching and almost losing her footing.

"Demon creature!" an Alfsigr woman cries out.

"Deargdul!" yells another.

"Cut off her wings!"

Wynter can't hold back the choking tears as more stones batter her shoulders and head. She hunches and struggles to protect herself with her wings, the stones painfully raining down on her delicate, sensitive feathers. She is stunned by how worked up the normally placid Alfsigr crowd is. It's like something communal has been unleashed.

Something seeping in from the Zalyn'ors.

Wynter can feel Shadow twisting into her mind through her Zalyn'or imprint. Intensifying her revulsion for her winged body. Part of her wants to cry out along with the crowd, *Strip off her wings!* The yearning to take a knife to her feathers and atone for her grotesque form rises to new heights, her very existence a vile stain on Erthia.

The Monarchall comes into view, its whorling lines of granite resembling a giant seashell. Wynter takes it in with gathering dread as she's dragged forward, warm rivulets of blood trickling down her face. Dizzy and disoriented, she's tugged up gleaming stairs, through a vaulted, bone-white entry, then back outside again into a white marble courtyard. Neck chafed raw, she's forced toward a circle of runes marked in its center, a ring of Alfsigr soldiers surrounding it. And arcing around them, in a solemn semicircle, are the Monarch Iolrath Talonir, the Alfsigr high priestess, the Royal Council of Elves...

...and her parents.

Misery slashes through Wynter as she takes in the obvious shame in her mother's face. How her narrow-faced father won't even look at her. The monarch, priestess and Elfin Council eye Wynter with cold silver eyes, their gazes raking over her demonic wings. She pulls her wings more tightly around her trembling form, wishing she could blot out her existence as the crowds' words ring in her mind. *Winged refuse! Demonic filth!*

The Marfoir drag her toward the circle of runes then jerk her onto her knees. She lets out a squeak of pain as her kneecaps collide with the white marble.

Bereft and shattered, she glances up to find the high priestess taking her in with pitiless eyes, a gleaming crown on the holy woman's long, snowy hair, its silver wrought into the shapes of the Shining Ones' sacred flock of starlight birds flying in a transcendent swirl. Sacred silver runes mark the high priestess's flowing alabaster garments.

"Your child, I believe," a Council member intones, glancing condemningly at Wynter's father, who is peering down his long, pale nose at Wynter with an expression of revulsion.

Her father grimaces and points at Wynter as she trembles, crumpled on the ground. "That *thing* is not my child," he bites out, sharp as glass through Wynter's heart. "She is an *abomination*. We have repented for forming her and performed a Sacred Erasure of her stain."

The high priestess nods approvingly. "You have honored the Shining Ones' holy edicts, and now we will erase her, as well." The priestess strides toward Wynter, silver rune stylus in hand, then gracefully lowers herself while Wynter cowers, trembling on the ground. The priestess gestures in the air with a flick of her graceful finger.

Two Marfoir glide forward and take rough hold of Wynter's

wings. The second they touch her, a gray mist shrouds Wynter's empathic vision. She cries out in terror as the Shadow opens multiple eyes in the swirling gray and smiles.

Horror leaping, Wynter stages a futile protest as her wounded wings are forced open and she gasps, the pain of it sending sparks through her eyes. The high priestess grabs hold of Wynter's ragged tunic collar and wrenches it down.

"No, please!" Wynter cries out as her tunic's front is torn partially open to reveal the Zalyn'or imprint fused to her skin.

"We have brought the Deargdul creature here," the high priestess intones to those assembled, "to purge her from our midst in this life and the next." She levels her zealous gaze at Wynter. "The Holy Zalyn'or will *never* again be worn by a cursed Deargdul." Then she raises her stylus, presses its tip against Wynter's Zalyn'or imprint and murmurs a runic spell.

Sobs wrack Wynter's body as her Zalyn'or shimmers then morphs to a three-dimensional necklace, a sting racing along her bruised skin.

The priestess grips the Zalyn'or and yanks it outward, breaking the chain.

A violent vertigo assaults Wynter the moment the Zalyn'or breaks, the world seeming to tilt hard on its axis as the Marfoir release her wings. The multi-eyed Shadow snaps out of sight and she falls hard to her side, slamming against stone as her vision painfully brightens.

"Wynter Eirllyn," Monarch Talonir booms out as the world spins around her. "You are a cursed Deargdul, reviled by the Blessed Shining Ones. A stain on the blessed, sunlit soil of High Elkin—the unblemished Elfdom. You are evil and corrupted beyond redemption and a mortal danger to Alfsigroth's existence and to its very soul." He straightens, his prismatic eyes flashing sunlight. "I sentence you, Deargdul demon, to banishment in the sublands. The Realm of the Demonic. Where you belong."

Before Wynter can draw in her wings, the high priestess takes hold of her sleeve-covered arm and forces Wynter to her feet, a sick dizziness overtaking her.

"You seek to consort with heathens?" the high priestess sneers. "Then so be it. We will send you into the depths with the vilest of them. They will tear you apart, limb from limb." The priestess points her stylus at the circle of runes before Wynter and a hole appears in its center, dark as the depths of Erthia.

Wynter steps back, fright rising, as the Marfoir grab her arms, drag her forward...and hurl her in.

Wynter screams as she hurtles down through the darkness, her wound-riddled wings desperately flapping. She collides with hard stone, the air punched from her lungs as she crumples, one hip and leg wrenched sideways. The hole far above closes and all light snuffs out.

Terror swooping through her, she struggles to find her bearings, vertigo making it difficult to discern up from down in the all-encompassing dark. Slowly, she pulls her bruised body into an unsteady sitting position, the sound of water trickling beside her, but otherwise...

Silence.

A faint puff of green light pierces the abyss.

Wynter turns toward its source to find a small stream flowing through a high-ceilinged cave, something near the stream's bank suffusing the water with a luminescent green glow.

Desperate to not be left in the frightening darkness, Wynter crawls toward the light.

Surprise stirs. There, caught on some rocks, is something long and spiraling. A shape she's seen before, glowing as if lit from within by verdant starlight. Her heartbeat quickening, Wynter reaches into the ice-cold water and wraps her hand around the Wand.

She gasps as a sizzling energy flies up her arm, through her body, and into her wings, silver runes lighting in her vision, the veins of Shadow gone from her alabaster skin. A translucent flock of Watchers appear, white-glowing and perched on the stone ridges of the cave.

Wynter's eyes widen as she takes them in.

The Wand brightens, the bottom of its hilt blazing with a deeper flush of green that circles up its spiraling form as Wynter senses a starlight tree greening in the back of her mind, new leaves unfurling. She realizes, as runic shapes pulse once more in her vision, that it's not just a Wand but a rune stylus too.

Wynter quietly considers the green-lit Wand-stylus as the serene birds look on, Wynter's whole self expanding and opening as her vertigo begins to lift and she adjusts to the abrupt freeing of her mind from the Zalyn'or thrall.

"I am not a Deargdul demon," she murmurs softly to the Wand, as her shame and self-hatred slip away, an exhilarating love for her wings rushing in that makes her breathless. "I am Wynter Eirllyn," she whispers. "Elliontora of Alfsigroth."

More green light suffuses the cave behind her, multiple boot heels sounding.

Wynter glances over her shoulder and meets the gazes of several large Smaragdalfar men. They halt before her, curved varg swords made entirely of luminous emerald runes in their fists.

Just behind them, her brother, Cael, and his Second, Rhys Thorim, come into view, both of them dressed in green Subland Elf attire like the Smaragdalfar men, a fierce light in their eyes that Wynter has not seen for a very long time.

Love for the two of them swells in her heart.

"My sister," Cael breathes out, a stunned, impassioned energy blazing in his silver eyes.

Slowly, Wynter turns back toward the stream, her gaze flicking over the Watchers. And then she draws herself up to her full height and fans out her wounded wings to their full breadth, a spark of sterling Wyvernfire lighting in her breast.

My wings, she thinks, as her fledgling power kindles to flame and a healing warmth suffuses every feather. *My beautiful, Elliontoran wings.*

Gripping the Wand-stylus tightly in her hand, Wynter smiles, Icaral power rising, and turns to face them.

The
Zhilon'ile Prophecy

(Read from the storm elements of Air, Fire, Water, and Light)

**The Shadow Rises
Poisoning the Air
Corrupting Fire
Polluting the Water
Veiling the Light
Arise, oh Daughters and Sons of Wyvernkind
Fight the Demon Tide!**

* * * * *